HistoriCity

OR

FRAGMENTS OF BERLIN

HistoriCity

OR

FRAGMENTS OF BERLIN

Bryan Van Sweringen

First Edition 2022

ISBN: 978-1-950843-60-2

Parafine Press
5322 Fleet Avenue, Cleveland, Ohio 44105
www.parafinepress.com
Cover design by Meredith Pangrace, photo by Bryan Van Sweringen
Book design by Meredith Pangrace

For Dad/Ted

Theodore Curtis(s) Van Sweringen

July 20, 1922, Greensburg, Ohio
October 13, 1986, Akron, Ohio

The ways of my own life have led me elsewhere.
But I hope that some young foreigner has fallen
in love with this later city, and is writing what
happened or might have happened to him there.

—Christopher Isherwood,
The Berlin Stories

FOREWORD

THE STORY OF Thomas Vonaechron, which we will allow him to recount here—not so much for his sake (the reader will encounter an engaging though transparent young man) but rather for the sake of his story, which appears to us to be worth recounting. To Thomas Vonaechron's credit, however, it should be noted that it is indeed his story, and his story does not happen to everyone. History, on the other hand, does, in a sense, happen to everyone, although everyone is not, or perhaps chooses not to be, conscious of it. After all, we do have it on the very best of authority that, "One can very easily be in a story without understanding it."

Ιστορία, *historia*, history, is a product of human consciousness. Clio, the muse of history, like her half-sister Pallas Athena, springs from the head. A product of perception, imagination, invention, and even intention, history cannot exist apart from Thomas or anyone else. History might therefore be seen as the all-too-human attempt to give meaning to events among which causal or casual relationships may or may not actually exist. This attempt, ennobled by academe, has become the *raison d'être* of archivists and historians who, as we shall see, play no small part in helping Thomas lay the foundation for his story. Reincarnated in Germany in the early nineteenth century at Göttingen and Berlin, tightly laced into the corselet of historicism—*wie es eigentlich gewesen*—and repeatedly impressed into service of the state, Clio returned home mid-twentieth century to spare Göttingen and lay Berlin to waste in true Roman fashion (*wastare*). History ultimately remains the product of individual perception, imagination and intent, be it that of the historian, the politician, or, in this case, the storyteller.

This story might therefore be seen as an attempt by Thomas Vonaechron to fit his story into history, history thereby becoming the process through which Thomas attempts to discover both self and *Selbstbewußtsein*. As his story takes place in the past, covered with decades of accumulated dust and decomposition, it will be told within the historic mold appropriate to its setting. This should not prove disadvantageous to his story but perhaps just the opposite. Whether "the more past the better," however, remains to be seen. His story is set in the recent past, which may finally prove less valuable than the distant past for both story and storyteller, as historical significance often seems to decrease in relation to the present. Yet "the past" is not necessarily the function of the passage of time alone. The twentieth century, in a four-part lecture series given at Berlin in 1915, taught both time and space are relative. The past is rather cordoned off from the present by a recurring series of catastrophic, if not "world-historical," events creating historical rupture, chasms in continuity.

No need here, however, for the unnecessary, intentional complication commonly characterizing intellectual endeavor. The story takes place, and to make certain it begins rooted firmly in the past tense, took place, in the not-so-long-ago, in the days of the Cold War, before the Global War on Terror (GWOT), the beginning of which began so much of what is still beginning and ending. GWOT was the intentional, operational outcome of yet another false prophesy of the "End of History," erroneously heralding a transition to a posthistorical era of worldwide prosperity and peace. The very proclamation of an end of history was, of course, in itself folly, as history, as noted above, is artifice and does not exist outside human consciousness of it. Yet, some of the events recounted here by Thomas were nonetheless taken by some in positions of power and influence as heralding the global triumph of a particular *abendländische*, a particularly Western way of life. Here, rodomontade is not out of place. Choosing *kratos* over *ethos*, these individuals sought to influence and shape events according to their own unenlightened self-interest, attempting to manage Clio as if she were a *Vogue* model, though truth be told, she does tend to go in and out of fashion. Her fashion turns the flavor of the days. As a consequence, history became a cherry orchard harvested by hired thinkers and cherry pickers, and GWOT waged as a jihad against the perceived enemies of the end of history with the predictable, tragic results continuing to unfold. In lockstep with folly, history marches on.

Thomas's story, which predates GWOT, might likewise be read as a personal, unpolitical attempt to impose his self-concept, his story, upon history, in particular upon the history of Berlin, the city referred to by Thomas as the "HistoriCity," a city which, as noted above, has served as both the cradle and the target of history. He based his attempt upon the nineteenth-century notion that history is to be painstakingly distilled and reconstructed from archival records and architectural ruins, present forms of the past. Although Thomas diligently and deliberately lays his foundation in the past, Clio quickly catches up. After allowing him the precious, precarious privilege of standing with her at the edge of history for a very short time—a time when his story and history do indeed appear to be coincidental—she ultimately overtakes him, leaving him with only the reflections of an unhistorical man, his story. Although it has been said the owl of Minerva, previously the pet of Pallas Athena, only spreads her wings and flies at dusk, at the end of the night, the storyteller seeks to address the question posed at daybreak to another pilgrim by birds talking in the trees of the Dresden suburbs. So it went in the spring of '45. We return now to the summer of '82 and, given the magical, if potentially histrionic *Mannung* that only the exhausting can be interesting, we begin.

CONTENTS

SECTIONS
Layers of the *HistoriCity:*
Historische (Ge-)Schichten

(Thomas Vonaechron after Wilhem Dörpfeld)

BERLIN VII 1990 – ? : The Sublime City, *Bundeshauptstadt,* Capital of the Federal Republic of Germany

BERLIN VI 1945 – 1990: *West Berlin, West-Berlin, Berlin (West), Westberlin,* the combined American, British and French Sectors of "Greater Berlin" including the districts of: Charlottenburg, Kreuzberg, Neukölln, Reinickendorf, Schöneberg, Spandau, Steglitz, Tempelhof, Tiergarten, Wedding, Wilmersdorf and Zehlendorf

BERLIN V 1945 – 1990: East Berlin, *Ost-Berlin, Berlin (Ost)*, the Soviet Sector of "Greater Berlin," after 1949 Capital of the German Democratic Republic (GDR) including the districts of: Friedrichshain, Hellersdorf, Hohenschönhausen, Köpenick, Lichtenberg, Marzahn, Mitte, Pankow, Prenzlauerberg, Schönhausen, Treptow, Weissensee

BERLIN IV 1933 – 1945: *Reichshauptstadt*, Capital of the Third Reich *(Germania)*

BERLIN III 1918 – 1933: *Reichshauptstadt*, Capital of the "Weimar Republic"

BERLIN II 1871 –1918: *Reichshauptstadt*, Capital of the Kingdom of Prussia and the German Empire

BERLIN I 1701 – 1918: Capital of the Kingdom of Prussia
1709: Capital and Royal Residence, following mergers with: Friedrichswerder (1670), Dorotheenstadt (1674) and Friedrichstadt (1688)
1244: Berlin
1237: Cölln

CHAPTER I:
ARCHIVAL FOUNDATIONS OF THE HISTORICITY

Listen close my scholars dear,
Doctrines, politics and civilizations exurge from you,
Sculpture and monuments and anything inscribed anywhere are
tallied in you,
The gist of histories and statistics as far back as the
records reach is in you this hour, and myths and tales
the same,
If you were not breathing and walking here, where would they
all be?
The most renown'd poems would be ashes,
orations and plays would be vacuums.

All architecture is what you do when you look upon it,
(Did you think it was in the white or gray stone?
or the lines of the arches and cornices?)

—Walt Whitman, *Leaves of Grass*

The Republic
August 1982

WE WALKED down from Washington, the District of Columbia, Neal and I,
to celebrate the opening of The Republic, a new tavern in the old port city
of Alexandria, Virginia. The late-August heat and humidity were stifling.
We kept as close as possible to the Potomac. Mirroring the late-morning
sun through a haze of heavy air, the broad river seemed sluggish, unmoving,
offering no relief. Only green groves of trees lining the path at irregular
intervals along the riverbank offered sporadic sanctuary, *nemos*. As we skirted
the runways of Washington National Airport, takeoffs and landings shattered
the sky at regular intervals. Once we'd left the airport behind, we resumed
our conversation. As we walked, the recurrent droning of the aircraft became
ambient and enoesque, almost agreeable, suggesting the Chesapeake Bay to
the southeast and the surf of the unseen sea not green beyond.

Neal had played varsity baseball in high school and kept himself in good shape, even after his turn to the life of disillusion and poetry inspired his premature departure from Exeter. He now worked for a landscaping company in the District, tending the gardens of others. Our walk along the Potomac inspired him to wear his "boating costume," a well-worn, white Palm Beach suit over a collarless cotton work shirt. Curls of brown hair, moistened with sweat, hung beneath the black band of his battered panama. In his left hand, he carried an open beer bottle, sipping as we walked down the path, talking about the way ahead. Neal chose his words carefully, addressing me with an expression dark and difficult to read. I could sense the intensity informing his poetry. Once we reached the outskirts of Alexandria, raising his beer bottle for me to see, he called out, "Ho ho, Thomas! I do hope we get there soon, I'm almost out of beer!"

By the time we arrived at The Republic, celebrants were flowing in and out, around and through the heavy, dark, wooden revolving door, up and down the staircase, spilling out onto the South Union Street sidewalk. Unlit torches in black cast-iron sconces lined the two-story redbrick facade of the building, meticulously designed and constructed to resemble the eighteenth-century dockside warehouse it had displaced. Neal and I had come to drink Virginia Native, a locally brewed beer which, thanks to the art of an imported Bavarian *Braumeister,* promised visions of cool vaulted cloisters on this stifling summer afternoon. Unlike Neal, I hadn't come dressed for the occasion, but once inside, no one seemed to take notice of my worn-out pink polo shirt and cutoff camo pants. We apologetically made our way to the bar through the smartly dressed lunchtime crowd. Meeting the critical glance of an attractive young woman in a light cotton khaki suit, Neal confessed to her outright, "I want to wear my hair just like yours." She stepped aside, making room for us at the bar rail. We went *native.*

The Republic and its trendy lunchtime crowd were symptomatic of a shift gradually taking place in what was currently being marketed as "Olde Towne." The Grand Café, the Lee Street Café, the Biarritz, and The Wayfarers had closed their doors or been renovated beyond recognition. Our lanky, late-night Warehouse waitress fled to Florida. Small lunch counters with stainless steel and white porcelain ambiance were being eclipsed by smarter, upscale establishments. Late one night in drunken, disquiet desperation, Neal and I trained the two World War II Japanese naval guns mounted in front of the Potomac Intrarms waterfront warehouse on one of the establishments affronting the Potomac. The mild amusement of the fashionable clientele decisively defeated our attack, forcing our withdrawal and the surrender of our position. Once a busy port predating the District, Alexandria's markets had once offered human capital as well as produce. History brought Civil War, Federal occupation, freedmen, and the First and Second World Wars to this southern city on the Potomac. The Potomac brought sediment downstream, silting in the harbor, relegating Alexandria to the backwater. Another kind of sediment now seemed to be building up; the time seemed right to kedge off.

The *contiguous* District of Columbia—the Federal compound established as the artificial, compromise capital of the republic—posed different kinds of questions, both environmental and architectural. I frequently *flâner*-ed down Constitution Avenue from Capitol Hill, past the great representational buildings, a series of white or gray monumental variations upon Parthenon and Pantheon themes, exalting the power of this later-day republic: the US Courthouse, the National Gallery of Art, the National Archives and Records Service (my former employer), the Justice Department, the National Museum of Natural History, the Department of Internal Revenue, the National Museum of American History, and the Commerce Department. Upon closer inspection, the white or gray stone facades, the lines of the arches and cornices conceived and executed as concrete political statements, seemed more the elaborate *tromp l'oeil*. The lack of depth became more apparent in the evening when civil servants and servile citizens fled the District for their homes in neighboring Maryland and Virginia, while out-of-town tourists sought out the safe hotels and motels across the District line.

Not only two-dimensional and empty, but sinking. The *Washington Post* reported the Jefferson Memorial was slipping slowly into the mud of the Tidal Basin just forty years after its dedication, while its prototype, the Pantheon in Rome, stood essentially unchanged after two thousand. Shortly after site preparation began in 1938, a prescient *Post* reader drew capitol consequences: "Rome was built upon hills. Why do we in Washington ignore history and good judgment and select swamps or the lowest places we can find on which to erect some of our gems of architecture and engineering?" Although the nearby Lincoln Memorial, also built on pilings atop fill, had not yet begun to slip, the National Park Service had carefully installed tilt meter boxes just out of the line of sight of visitors just in case.

Walking out down by the Jefferson Memorial one evening, I was a chance witness to an hour-long harangue on the coming demise of the United States of America. As I later learned from the *Washington Star*, the speaker was the soon-to-be former president of the College of Mary & William, Professor Kens L. Suisse. Driving by the illuminated white marble pantheon on his way back to Marysburg, Virginia, President Suisse was apparently overcome by a sense of mission. Parking his beige Borgward in the center lane of US Interstate 395 South, he was nearly run down as he sprang from his car. Successfully dodging the drunken taxicabs of absolute reality, he slipped over the side of the bridge. Running 'round the rotunda, Rocky-ing up the white marble stairs, President Suisse joined Mr. Jefferson on his marble pedestal. Assuming a presidential pose, he presented a stream-of-consciousness assessment of the damage being done to the republic by the current administration, buttressing his argument with Jefferson's handwriting on the walls. Midnight cruisers alerted the United States Park Police who, after listening to President Suisse for a few minutes, politely persuaded him to descend from the presidential podium to the scattered applause of the few spectators and the approving yarks of their dogs. Before being escorted back down the white marble stairs to a waiting patrol car, President Suisse turned with open arms to those of us assembled, sweat and tears flowing freely down his face, and said, "Peace and friendship with all mankind is our wisest policy, and I wish we may be permitted to pursue it."

A frequent companion on my walks through Washington was *Doktor der Philosophie* Georg Friedrich *Freiherr* von Garlitz, an archivist from West Berlin I'd had the good fortune to meet while working at the National Archives and Records Service, or "NARS" to the initiated. He was one of a group of German archivists and historians involved in filming documents of the Office of Military Government (United States)—OMGUS, which occupied a Zone of Germany (by the sword) and a Sector of Berlin (by the pen) following the Second World War. In his late thirties, George was ten years my senior, and had completed his academic and archival training in Germany. Shorter, he was slender and trim, stylish while conservative in dress. His large, horn-rimmed glasses and longish brown hair rounded out the portrait of the European intellectual as a young man. Unfettered, either by German academic and aristocratic traditions or the anti-American sentiment fashionable among many Europeans, George enthusiastically embraced his work and his new life in the nation's capital. He'd written his doctoral dissertation on the occupation of Berlin by French troops under Napoleon in 1806, and was interested in reading the reports of the entry of American troops under Eisenhower into his city 139 years later.

After work, I would often give George a lift in my battered blue Chevrolet Malibu convertible to *Die Kleine Krone,* his home away from *Heim* on Capitol Hill. Along with The Old Heidelberg and The Bavarian, *Die Kleine Krone* was one of the few traditional German establishments in Washington, DC, to survive the cultural and culinary purges of the First and Second World Wars. Historically, the United States of America has not limited the search for enemies to the battlefield, but seeks them out in the kitchen and dining room as well. Our choice for dinner however, was Mr. Henry's on Pennsylvania Avenue at Washington Circle where, nestled in the dark wood wainscot of a Presbyterian Church predestined to be demolished, we would color our informal Washington-Berlin symposium with alternating red and green glasses of the Berlin specialty wheat beer, *Berliner Weiße*. Drawing upon his encyclopedic knowledge of the history of Berlin, George drew parallels between the two capitals. "In a way, Thomas, Berlin and Washington are sister cities, children of the nineteenth century. Although Berlin's origins date back to the thirteenth century, it really did not achieve prominence until the unification of Germany in 1871 following the Franco-Prussian War. Berlin's architectural development is actually a *Nebenproduckt*, a by-product, of its political development. Up until the reunification of the United States following your Civil War six years earlier, Washington was, like Berlin, largely a collection of villages."

"Yes, but perhaps in Washington," I replied, trying to keep up with George and practice my German, "the development was actually the other way around, *umgekehrt*. While your description of Washington in the late nineteenth century is accurate, the plan Pierre . . . I mean of course 'Peter,' L'Enfant originally presented to George Washington was for a baroque capitol on a European scale. To the best of my knowledge, there was nothing comparable in Europe at that time—urban design as musical composition with intricate variations within a repeating structure of circles, avenues, and streets. L'Enfant may have modeled Washington on Versailles, where his father worked as a painter. As punishment for his architectural vision, a complex of buildings on a concrete plaza in southwest Washington, rivaling the best of Berlin's postwar *Plattenbau*, was named in his honor!"

"*Ach ja*, the French influence," replied George, smiling with his eyes. "We find it in Berlin as well, East and West. Berlin's *Unter den Linden* and *Kurfürstendamm* were both modeled on the *Champs Élyssés*." *Trotz* sisterhood and shared French architectural heritage, the first half of the twentieth century would find Berlin and Washington aligned against each other twice, from 1917 until 1918 and then again from 1941 until 1945. From our work at the National Archives, we were both intimately acquainted with the devastating, dividing consequences of the second of these two World Wars for Berlin.

Following dinner, we would drive up the *menschenleere* Pennsylvania Avenue, which George compared favorably with the broad *Alleen* and *Dämme* of Berlin, the once-and-future capital where he lived, past the White House to Capitol Hill. Over time and *Berliner Weiße*, a Berlin constructed out of conversation began to conflate with Washington,

DC. Our Mr. Henry's symposia, coupled with the unusual work I had been given to do at the National Archives, finally persuaded me to leave Washington for Berlin. Both George and Clio, the muse of history, would be waiting for me there when I arrived.

When I first moved to the Greater Washington, DC, Metropolitan Area, as it was described in the US Civil Service Commission job announcement, it was to work in the Federal Records Center located at the corner of King and Union Streets in Alexandria. The Records Center was housed in a former torpedo factory built of cinderblock and steel situated directly on the Potomac. Neal and I walked along the facade of the white four-story building with its frosted chicken-wire windows as we made our way down Union Street to The Republic. The factory opened in 1919, too late to reply in kind to Germany's resumption of unrestricted submarine warfare. Twenty-two years later, Clio gave the frustrated factory a second chance. During the Second World War, over 9,000 MK-14 torpedoes were assembled in Alexandria and shipped to all Theaters of Operations. Once the Gates of Janus were closed in 1945, the torpedo factory became a repository for enemy documents captured by the victorious American armies, housing the German Military Document Section (GMDS). These records were in the custody of the Departmental Records Branch, the Office of the Adjutant General, Department of the Army (TAGO). With the passage of time, both GMDS and the former torpedo factory passed from TAGO to the General Services Administration (GSA) and its daughter service, NARS. Behind the building, a broad loading pier constructed of rough-hewn railroad ties extended out into the Potomac. On hot, sultry summer days, I left the Federal Records Center through the loading dock and walked out to the end of the pier, looking across the broad river to the antenna array of the US Naval Research Laboratory (NRL) and the stainless steel sheen of the Defense Intelligence Agency (DIA). Hidden off to the left in the woods, on the hill rising behind the riverbank, was our American Bedlam, St. Elizabeth's Hospital. The scent of creosote-soaked wood thickened the air, and in the haze, I imagined the ghostly silhouettes of battle-gray Victory ships, loaded with torpedoes, steaming down the Potomac to the Chesapeake Bay, the submarine dangers of an Atlantic convoy crossing, and the war laying waste to Europe beyond.

Nine months after I'd moved into a gracefully decaying white wooden-frame house just south of the torpedo factory on Booth Street, constructed after the Civil War to house freedmen, archival operations were relocated to the newly built Washington National Records Center in Suitland, Maryland. The WNRC was constructed on a federal compound just over the District line where, in addition to NARS, other Tenet agencies included the National Census Bureau (NCB) and the Office of Naval Intelligence (ONI). The WNRC was a vast, underground tomb of American history, a kind of archival Arlington, disrespectfully referred to by disgruntled NARSians as "the wastebasket of the nation." Although the main entrance, administrative offices, research room, and snack bar were aboveground, where sunlight was filtered through thick, tinted, plate-glass security windows, the records were kept underground on miles of gray metal shelving in cavernous subterranean concrete vaults numbered one through six. Shelving divided the vast, high-ceilinged concrete vaults into hundreds of dark, narrow corridors. But was it not actually the dust, coming from hundreds of cardboard Archives and Records Center boxes stacked to the ceiling on the high walls of shelving, which occasioned my uneasiness? It took twenty minutes to walk from the guarded entrance aboveground, past the "open storage" Vaults One, Two, Three, Four, and Five to the heavy metal doors of Vault Six, where I was reassigned following relocation from Alexandria to Suitland. Access to Vault Six depended not only upon possession of a top secret security clearance, but also upon the more elusive "need to know." A terminal in the WNRC director's office aboveground recorded the number of every employee ID slipped into the Vault Six key card slot for admission underground.

My job was to review security-classified US and foreign government documents held in secrecy behind the heavy metal doors of Vault Six. These documents, generated during the decade between 1944 and 1954, came from all agencies of the US government, retaining their original hot-and-cold wartime classifications of RESTRICTED, CONFIDENTIAL, SECRET, and TOP SECRET. There were other documents distinguished by code-word or special access programs, pertaining to operational planning and/or sensitive sources and methods of intelligence collection. Documents pertaining to Operation OVERLORD, the June 1944 landing of combined Allied forces on the Normandy coast, carried the special access code word BIGOT, a virtual compartment into which only "BIGOTed" individuals were admitted. Documents carrying code-word markings were segregated from other classified material and locked in wire cages within the vault.

The original intent was no doubt to hold all these classified documents in perpetual secrecy. The Executive Branch of the US government, the ultimate classification authority, temporarily yielding to both the demands of the demos and the charms of Clio, decided the vast majority of these millions of records no longer required protection. After careful declassification review and redaction by properly trained NARsians, they could be released to the general public with no damage done to national security. My underground initiation consisted not only of training provided by journeyman NARSians but also by representatives of those US government agencies that had originally classified the documents. In addition to the US Air Force, the US Army, and the US Navy, our mentors included representatives of civilian agencies, the Department of State, and the Department of Energy. Of particular sensitivity were the wartime and postwar intelligence alphabet agencies, the Office of Strategic Services (OSS) and its successor agencies: the Strategic Services Unit (SSU), the Central Intelligence Group (CIG), and the Central Intelligence Agency (CIA). We were carefully instructed in the organization, operations, and sensitivities of each institutional incarnation by Agency mentors, and only allowed to review documents after one year of closely supervised apprenticeship.

In addition to U.S. records, there were hundreds of thousands of documents provided by our wartime Allies, as well as the hundreds of thousands of documents taken from our wartime adversaries, including the German records stored in Alexandria. These documents carried administrative security classifications similar to our own. I once discovered a British document with a hand-written "TIPPY" inserted before TOP SECRET, no-doubt intended for Winston's eyes only. With a reading knowledge of German painfully acquired from *Herrn Dr.* Hans Schmidt during a Junior-Year-Abroad in Basel, Switzerland, I was given captured German documents to review for sensitive "sources and methods of intelligence." Of particular interest were the names of Allied intelligence operatives captured by wartime German security agencies, as well as all information pertaining to codes and cyphers. The latter was the responsibility of the enigmatic National Security Agency (NSA), an ENIGMA unto itself. German documents were classified as *VERTRAULICH, GEHEIM*, and *STRENG GEHEIM.* Certain documents generated by agencies of the National Socialist government such as the *Sicherheitsdienst (SD)* of the *Schutzstaffel (SS)* were often labeled with the more intimidating *GEHEIME REICHSSACHE.* It was fascinating and frequently heartbreaking work, deconstructing the "us" and "them" of the Second World War and the Cold War into thousands of reports, messages and letters written by as many human beings in situations ranging from the privileged to the desperate. As I became more intimate with Clio's secrets, I began to take her story, history, very personally.

One afternoon, not too long after I'd completed my training, a US Air Force Reserve officer brought a folder to my desk, requesting declassification review of the German documents it contained. As the infamous SS lightning runes were prominently displayed on the letterhead, he was concerned information contained in the records might compromise Allied intelligence operations. Noting there were also English-language documents in the file, he said, "I think you'll find this file of great interest," turned, and returned to his workstation. The documents were arranged in reverse chronological order. I carefully opened the legal-size manila file folder contained in the file, the edges brown and brittle with age, and began reviewing from the back. The original document had been prepared at SS Headquarters in Berlin—I made a note of the street address in a small notebook for future reference—and been taken by courier to the headquarters of the World Jewish Congress (WJC) in Geneva. As a consequence of the destruction sustained from the Allied bombing campaign, the National Socialist government was willing to consider trading the lives of one million detainees for ten thousand trucks. To establish their bona fides by showing "good will," the SS authorized immediate release of one thousand detainees. I had heard about this offer, but I now held it in my hands. Reading on, I learned the WJC translated the SS offer into English, forwarding it to the British government under a cover letter requesting immediate assistance. After determining they had neither the lorries on hand nor the industrial capacity to produce them, His Majesty's government added yet another cover letter and, turning westward toward the arsenal of democracy, respectfully requested the government of the United States consider both the original SS offer and the urgent request for assistance by the WJC. The final document in the file contained a long list of reasons why the US government was obliged to consider the offer unfavorably. Although I found it difficult to comprehend the carefully enumerated bureaucratic arguments, two caught my attention—the receipt of ten thousand trucks would undoubtedly prolong the National Socialist war effort, and among the one million detainees, there would likely be a number of clandestine intelligence agents, posing an immediate danger to the Allied war effort. I carefully placed the documents back into the envelope, then the envelope into the folder, and remained seated at my desk. Although sources and methods of intelligence had not been compromised, the folder contained evidence of a much greater compromise, with tragic consequences for thousands, perhaps a million people. The opportunity was lost to history. Declassification review in reverse chronological order could not bring it back.

The bulk of documents slated for review was enormous. Reviewers were strongly encouraged to work overtime on Saturdays and were rewarded with either time-and-a-half pay or compensatory time off. Empty of all researchers and most aboveground NARSians on the weekends, the Records Center became deathly still, more closely resembling a tomb than a wastebasket. Isolation and incandescent lighting gave a kind of *Huis Clos*-ness to weekend work, the passage of time marked only by the large, government-issue Lighthouse of the Blind clock mounted on the cinderblock wall over the metal frame inside the massive doors of Vault Six, the great doors of secret history. The work was not always disheartening, and occasional discoveries relieved the tedium. Reviewing Department of State post files from the US Embassy at Havana late one Saturday afternoon, I discovered a letter written in 1940 by a twelve-year-old Fidel Castro to his "good friend," the president of the United States, Franklin D. Roosevelt. In a polite but unfortunately unsuccessful attempt to acquire "a ten dollars bill green American," young Fidel offered to show Franklin the location of the iron mines in Mayarí, Oriente Province, "to make your ships." Before turning the page of the rotting, red, leather-bound correspondence file to read the reply, I wondered whether a ten-dollar investment in 1940 might have paid itself back with interest just nineteen years later.

These decomposing post files documented other lost opportunities now covered in historic mold. Six years after Fidel Castro wrote to President Roosevelt, President Ho Chi Minh wrote to President Harry Truman, "to congratulate you for the continuous and successful efforts your government has been making to maintain Peace and Security all over the World." He concluded his moving three-page summary of the struggle of the Vietnamese people to win their independence from the Japanese occupation forces and the French colonial administration by respectfully requesting President Truman "to interfere for an immediate solution of the Vietnamese issue. The people of Vietnam earnestly hopes that the great American Republic would help us conquer full independence and support us in our reconstruction work."

Saturday afternoons occasionally provided more fortunate NARSians with opportunities not possible during the workweek. The storage areas within the vaults were cavernous and inadequately lit by incandescent light tubes suspended from thirty-foot ceilings. Occasionally, a novice NARSian would go MIA, "missing in archives," in the underground labyrinth, causing the supervisory archivist on duty to send out a search party made up of experienced archives technicians. As dust and decaying leather from bound dispatches filled the air, covering all horizontal surfaces, we were authorized to wear jeans and sweatshirts to work. At least two reviewers were required to pull the boxes of documents down from the racks of metal shelving, carefully stacking them on wheeled dollies for transport to the work area. Not unlike the gurneys used in hospitals and morgues, the dollies were six feet long, slung low to the ground, and made of metal plate covered with thick, black rubber padding to prevent the boxes from slipping in transit. There were removable metal railings at both ends of the dolly, which served both to hold the boxes in place and allow NARSians to maneuver the dollies through the narrow, dark aisles to and from the lighted workspace at the front of the vault.

One Saturday morning, a colleague asked me to help her pull boxes from the back of the vault. Although we worked on different declassification teams, we'd spoken several times during aboveground coffee breaks in the snack bar. The aroma of frying scrapple in a white-tiled room peopled by neurotic NARSians, German archivists, historians, and other serious researchers gave the small, standard-issue government cafeteria a sensual, vaguely Central European café atmosphere. Although our conversations remained perfunctory, I learned she lived across the Potomac in the Commonwealth of Virginia. She'd apparently been out very late the Friday night before this particular Saturday morning, and after we'd left the lighted area at the front of the vault and the eye of the supervisory archivist, she asked if I would mind pushing her through the aisles on the dolly. As she was a lovely young woman with luxuriant red hair and electric green eyes, I readily agreed. She lay down on the dolly on her back, cushioning her head with her left hand, gently placing her right hand on her stomach. As I pushed the dolly deeper into the darkness of Vault Six, I looked repeatedly from the numbered shelves on both sides of the main aisle to the figurehead plowing through the darkness at my feet. Eyes closed, she sighed and slipped her right hand beneath the waistband of her jeans. In the time it took to us reach the back of the vault, far from our work area, she appeared to be fast asleep, breathing regularly. When I gently called her name to wake her, she stirred and rolled over on her side. I knelt next to her, and placing my hand on her shoulder, gently shook her. As she rolled back onto her back, my hand accidentally passed lightly over her breasts. Before I could remove my hand and apologize, she placed her left hand on top of mine and smiled with her eyes closed.

"Umm," she murmured, "That was very nice, please kiss me." Through her sweatshirt, I could feel her nipple growing erect in the palm of my hand as we kissed. Opening her eyes, she looked directly into mine and said, "Let's make love." The tone of her voice was as perfunctory as if we had been sitting in the snack bar, oddly appropriate to an erotic experiment deep in the recesses of Vault Six.

"Here, in the wastebasket of the nation?" I answered, feigning nonchalance, resisting nervousness, sensing passion.

"What better place?" she replied, turning her head toward me as she stood up on the dolly, facing the metal shelving. Smiling at me over her shoulder through her long red hair, she unbuckled her belt, unzipped her jeans and pulled them, together with her panties, down to her thighs. Her white skin shown like translucent marble under the light of the florescent tubes suspended from the ceiling above us. Vault Six stood transformed into the Villa Borghese, the archives of Cythera. As we were now of equal height, I followed her lead, then placed my arms around her waist, slipped my hands under her sweatshirt and bra, gently cupping her breasts in my hands. Bracing herself with one hand on the metal shelving, she leaned forward and took my penis into her other hand, easing it gently into her vagina. Moving her hand, she began to stimulate herself. I lowered my hand from her breast and placed it over hers. She allowed me to relieve her and, firmly grasping the metal shelving with both hands, pushed back against the dolly. Wheels designed to navigate the labyrinth of the past swiveled to accommodate the pleasure of the present and did not loudly protest. We came slowly apart and remained standing for a few seconds. I stepped back and, after carefully pulling up her panties and her jeans, pulled my clothes back into place. She turned, put her arms around my neck, kissed me, and said, "Now, let's pull those boxes."

Declassification review was arduous work, pitting intense concentration against ennui. An otherwise tedious text of great length could contain sensitive information requiring continued protection and consequently had to be read carefully. With experience, reviewers learned to recognize abbreviations and recurring set phrases, and scanned rather than read the documents. In order to relieve the tension, we would listen to recorded music or film soundtracks on headphones. One of Vault Six's greatest hits was a recording of *Casablanca*. A few of us listened to it so often we were able to recite entire scenes from memory. One day, while reviewing an unending number of multicolored State Department cross-reference sheets, I chanced upon a document referring to a "Fighting French Headquarters Report" from Casablanca. In order to lighten the heavy historical burden of one of my fellow reviewers, I photocopied the document, redacted the summary statement and over-typed: "INTERVIEW WITH RICK BLAINE (AMERICAN) CONCERNING THE DEATH OF MAJOR HEINRICH STRASSER (SS) IN CASABLANCA." I photocopied my forgery onto a blank piece of WWII-era pastel pink paper, cut it to the appropriate size and, placing it carefully on the floor, stepped on it several times for authentication. I lingered behind when he left Vault Six that evening, placing the document toward the back of the file he was reviewing, and promptly forgot about it. Two days later, he discovered my forgery. Jumping up from his desk, still wearing headphones and waving the cross-reference sheet wildly in the air, he shouted, "I knew it had to be a true story! It's simply too good. I knew it all along, and here's the proof!" Before the proper authorities could be alerted and appropriate action taken, which would no doubt have proven detrimental to my civil service career, I drew him aside and quietly explained. This amounted to a declaration of war, and before long, interesting documents on authentic letterheads began to appear in my files. Not wanting to catalyze a crisis of historicity at the National Archives, we agreed to keep a list of all bogus documents so we could extract them before the files were released to the public. Unfortunately, he transferred to the Department of Justice and we never had the opportunity to either consolidate our lists or extract the documents. At his going-away luncheon at the nearby Italian restaurant, Santa Maria de Suitland, we vowed over ice-cold beer in frosted plastic mugs that, in the finest tradition of US government service, following retirement from our respective agencies, we would coauthor an exposé titled *We Changed History.*

History. From the Greek *historia,* "learning or knowing by inquiry." The millions of documents in the National Archives, together with the millions of documents held by public and private archives throughout the world, comprise the raw material, the sources of what had come to be understood as "history." Largely a European construct, the modern discipline of source-based history was developed in Germany at Göttingen and Berlin during the nineteenth century. Superficially scientific, with historical hypotheses constructed upon *Quellen,* the questionable foundation of original sources, history was armed and impressed into the service of the Prussian, Imperial German, and then the National Socialist state. Classified reports of the US Strategic Bombing Survey (USBS) in Vault Six recorded the physical destruction of Berlin, one of the birthplaces of history. Released from active duty in the ruins of Berlin in May 1945, Clio chose to remain in the city for the next war, the Cold War. She would be waiting for me there, together with George, when I arrived.

As a declassification reviewer, I quickly learned intelligence sources may or may not contain "the truth," let alone liberation. Reporting included ratings for the reliability of the informant and the quality of the information, allowing the reader to establish the limits of historicity. Reviewing documents generated between 1944 and 1954, my attention was repeatedly drawn to the city of Berlin, one of the principal coordinates of wartime and postwar history. During my junior year abroad in Basel, Switzerland, I had visited Berlin, West and East, seven years earlier on a seven-day study trip. What survived the war stood in stark contrast to all the European and, for that matter, all the American cities I had visited to date. The storied *Berliner Luft, Luft, Luft,* the air of Berlin, tainted with destruction and loss, proved melancholy and inviting. When assigned a new declassification project, I would carefully examine the lists of boxes from the Departments of War and State shipped back to Washington, DC, from Berlin. In many instances, I discovered the boxes had not been opened since being shipped decades before. The documents they contained were often browned and brittle, covered with dust and historic mold. As I carefully reviewed the documents for sources and methods of intelligence, fragments of the history of Berlin between 1944 and 1954 passed before me in review. This decade, arbitrarily excised from the history of the city by an Executive Order of the president, was my introduction to the historicity of Berlin, the HistoriCity.

Opening boxes from Berlin proved to be less hazardous, however, than opening boxes shipped back to the United States from Saigon. Records Center personnel charged with "reboxing" records often discovered the administrative Non-Commissioned Officers originally charged with boxing the records in Vietnam literally shat upon them, no doubt in a gesture of defiant defecation, before sealing them for shipment. Records of the Vietnam War posed other, more subtle dangers as well. On one occasion, the archivist of the US Army, by coincidence a veteran of the Berlin Airlift, asked me to verify records contained in a particular box as copies of records already accessioned into the archives. The box contained exhibits used to prepare the "Report of the Department of the Army Review of the Preliminary Investigations into the My Lai Incident." Carefully opening a sealed envelope inside the box, I discovered eight-inch-by-twelve-inch prints of the authorized and unauthorized photographs taken by the combat photographer assigned to Charlie Company, First Battalion, Twentieth Infantry Regiment, during a four-hour operation in Son My Village, Quang Ngai Province, Republic of Vietnam on March 16, 1968. The images were immediate, horrifying, and unforgettable. I wished I hadn't opened the box.

The Berlin documents also contained evidence of human excretions and excesses of a happier kind. Letters written by American soldiers stationed in Germany during and after the war were subject to examination by the US Office of Censorship, under the watchful eye of Mr. Byron Price. Rather than sow their seed on site, some lovesick soldiers harvested it by hand and sent it back in letters to the girls' behinds they left—in one instance, carefully circled and annotated in ink with, "This is for you, Honey." Others fraternized with friendly local "Frawleins." One lonely GI in the American Sector developed an intimate relationship with a German girl, extending it to both her war-widowed mother and pet dachshund. He carefully recorded the adventures of the *menage a quatre* in black-and-white photographs for the viewing pleasure of the home front. Needless to say, neither the semen spots nor the porked pooch found favor with Mr. Price's office. The offending letters and their contents were officially pulled from the military mail, annotated and carefully filed away in the boxes, where I found them thirty years later.

There were also Allied agencies indigenous to Berlin, created in situ to deal with the unanticipated complexities of postwar four-power control. In an effort to preserve the spirit of wartime cooperation among the Allied powers occupying Germany, military liaison missions were created. The British Commanders'-in-Chief Mission to the Soviet Forces in Germany (BRIXMIS) was established in 1946, followed by *La Mission Militaire Française de Liaison* (MMFL) and the US Military Liaison Mission (USMLM) the following year. Soviet forces also maintained military liaison missions to the Western Allies (SOXMIS/SMLM) in the western Zones of Germany and western Sectors of Berlin. As these missions permitted freedom of movement throughout occupied Germany, they quickly became involved in intelligence-collection activities. NARS accession lists allowed me to identify and request those USMLM records slated for declassification review. These records were particularly fascinating as, in addition to the routine situation reports (SITREPS), Intelligence Information Reports (IIRs), and the annual "Unit History of the United States Military Liaison Mission to Commander in Chief, Group of Soviet Forces in Germany," they contained black-and-white photographs taken "on tour" in the Soviet Zone and, from 1949 on, in the German Democratic Republic (GDR). Although many years had passed, Berlin still remained an occupied city, the City of the Armed Camp, and I assumed USMLM was still on tour in the GDR and East Berlin.

Opening a Berlin box on the top of my gunmetal gray, US government-issue desk, I usually found the documents arranged in reverse chronological order. Working my way box-by-box backward, and then year-by-year forward in time from 1944 to 1954, I was able to identify the archival remains of two Berlins, the former *Reichshauptstadt* and then the occupied city, a city divided into four sectors of occupation, operationally bisected into East and West. In the late postwar diplomatic and intelligence traffic, Berlin was often referred to as the "Capital of the Cold War."

George was right. In comparison with other European capitals—Paris, Rome, or Athens—Berlin was a modern city. There were, however, other Berlins existing prior to the two I unearthed in Vault Six. In addition to classified records, the National Archives also held unclassified records in the "open storage areas," as well as even older records at the appropriately neoclassical Main Archives building on Constitution Avenue in the District, designed by American architect John Russell Pope. The Pennsylvania Avenue entrance to the Main Archives building, reserved for NARsians and serious researchers, was flanked by two massive limestone guardians, the *Past* and the *Future*. The former, a bald Socratic, leaned forward, solemnly urging passersby to "Study the Past," while the latter, a much younger woman sporting all Clio's traditional trappings, quoted William Shakespeare, "Past is Prologue." Numerous training rotations took me downtown to the Main Archives. Each time I entered the building, I stopped to pay my respects to the two guardians, taking the *Past* as an engraved invitation (in limestone) while unfortunately failing to understand the *Future* as a warning. If only I had stopped by the nearby Folger Shakespeare Library to look up the complete quotation from *The Tempest*: "Whereof what's past is prologue; what to come, in your and my discharge."

As my interest in Berlin expanded beyond the classified decade between 1944 and 1954, I began to seek out older records whenever opportunity permitted. At the Main Archives, I uncovered archival evidence of earlier Berlins. Counting West Berlin and Ost Berlin as two cities, and continuing to work out of habit in reverse chronological order, I was able to identify six Berlins. In the spirit of Wilhelm Dörpfeld, the assistant of and successor to that wacky Homeric Heinrich Schliemann, I arbitrarily assigned Roman numerals to each. In reverse chronological order, founded in 1945, West Berlin (Berlin VI) and Ost Berlin (Berlin V) were built upon the ruins of the *Reichshauptstadt* (Berlin IV), which in turn had inherited the remains of Berlin III, a short-lived, externally enforced experiment in parliamentary democracy, in 1933. Berlin III followed the demise of the *Kasierreich* in 1918. Imperial Berlin (Berlin II) was the capital of the German Empire from the Versailles Proclamation of 1871 until the abdication of Kaiser Wilhelm II, "*Kaiser* Bill" as he was referred to by my grandfather, a veteran of the First World War. His stories brought back to the farm from "Parisfrance" originally brought Berlin to my attention. Berlin I, the *Königliche Haupt-und Residenzstadt Berlin*, created in 1710 through the merger of the old trading towns of Cölln and Berlin with Dorotheenstadt, Friedrichswerder, and Friedrichstadt, was the residence of the Hohenzollern, serving as capital of the "Kingdom in" and later "of" Prussia prior to 1871. The periodicity of Berlin—I through VI, the HistoriCity as PeriodiCity.

My next step was to flesh out the records of Berlins I through VI found in NARS with additional reading ex archives. As a tell, Berlin had much to tell me. To my delight, I found myself in intriguing company. In October 1858, American academic-*im-werden* Henry Adams arrived in Berlin to prepare for the study of civil law at the university. Adams describes his city (Berlin I) as follows: "In 1858 Berlin was a poor, keen-witted, provincial town, simple, dirty, uncivilized, and in most respects disgusting. Life was primitive beyond what an American boy could have imagined." As George had observed during one of our Mr. Henry's symposia, the Franco-Prussian War of 1870–71, and the period of rapid industrialization and growth, the *Gründerzeit*, that followed, transformed Adams's "keen-witted provincial" Berlin I into Berlin II, the imperial capital.

Berlin II was apparently considered by some to be more the imperial city *im werden*. Sitting in his office at the US Embassy, the neoclassical *Blücher Palais* on *Pariser Platz* at the Brandenburg Gate, an American diplomat scanning the September 15, 1904, edition of the *International Herald Tribune* might have chanced upon the following architectural analysis of his city, Berlin II:

> There are few fields of the Emperor's activity in which he has scored as great a success as in his efforts to beautify Berlin. He has one great point in his favor, and that is that in the German capital he was not troubled much by historical landmarks and monuments of past ages, the doing away with which would have roused opposition. Nine-tenths of Berlin have as few historical associations as Chicago. A century ago Berlin contained a couple hundred thousand inhabitants; to-day it has reached the two million mark. Under these circumstances, the greater part of the city is modern and constructed on modern and sharp lines. The only historical part of Berlin is Unter Den Linden and the part lying within a half-mile radius of that avenue to the north and east.

German art critic and publicist Karl Scheffler was not convinced by Kaiser Wilhelm II's architectural activities, which he described as an imperial sanctioning of "degenerate urban eclecticism" through the use of modern industrial design for representational purposes. In his historical-cultural review of Berlins I and II, published six years after the *International Herald Tribune* article, he also compared Berlin with Chicago—to the detriment of both. From its pre-Berlin I origins as a fishing village, Scheffler saw Berlin as damned to becoming, never to be.

What architectural legacies of Berlins I and II there were were inherited by the reluctant Weimar Republic (Berlin III) and severely damaged by the *Reichshauptstadt* (Berlin IV) through the combined work of Adolf Hitler's "Haussmann" Berthold Konrad Hermann Albert Speer and, with Albert Speer's initial approval, the main offensive of the Royal Air Force Bomber Command under Air Marshal Arthur Travers Harris. The near-simultaneous postwar cities of Berlin V (East Berlin) and Berlin VI

(West Berlin), incorporating the four sectors of the occupied city, were constructed upon the ruins of Berlins I through IV. Just over one hundred years had passed between the proclamation of the new German Empire and my first visit to Berlin, but those years were characterized by an intensity and extremity extending far beyond the city limits into Europe, the world, and into history herself. Not only the "Capital of the Cold War," even more so than London, Paris, or Washington, Berlin—the HistoriCity— was capital of the twentieth century.

During my seven-day stay in the city seven years earlier, I had discovered ruins of the *Reichshauptstadt* still standing in the occupied city. The three Berlins thoroughly documented in the records reviewed in Vault Six—Berlin IV, Berlin V, and Berlin VI—converged architecturally at a number of points in the city—for example, at an observation platform on *Niederkirchnerstraße* in West Berlin. This Cold War coign of vantage was situated just off *Friedrichstraße*, not far from Allied Checkpoint Charlie, one of my two points of entry as an American citizen into *Ost-Berlin*, the former Soviet Sector. Looking out over *Potsdamer Platz*, once a major traffic hub and vibrant center of Berlin nightlife, the platform was originally constructed for use by Allied military personnel and the West Berlin police force. From this elevated perspective, the observer could see "the Berlin Wall" was actually composed of two parallel concrete walls, with a patrol road linking the watchtowers erected at intervals in the *intervallum*. Since the construction of the wall, nature had been steadily reclaiming the ground stripped of all prewar construction by war and deconstruction, creating a quiet green space separating Berlin V from Berlin VI. Wild rabbits, too nimble to set off trip wires intended for intruders, moved freely throughout this no-man's- land, giving the grassy *intervallum* a natural, peaceful appearance in spite of, or perhaps because of, the wall. The former *Reichsluftfahrtministerium*, a foreboding and, in spite of "Bomber" Harris's Main Offensive, largely undamaged massive, five-story residuum of Berlin IV, curiously reminiscent of the Rayburn House Office Building in Washington, DC, could clearly be seen in East Berlin (Berlin V) from the observation platform in West Berlin (Berlin VI). At the time, I approached East Berlin and West Berlin as a single architectural problem, *id est* the remainder of the *Reichshauptstadt* as quadrisected by the Second World War, then bisected by the Cold War. Later, while combing through the intelligence summaries (INTSUMS) and situation reports (SITREPS) for sources and methods of wartime and postwar intelligence, I began to understand Berlin as a repository of invisible, perishable architectures as well. The remains of these architectures, visible and invisible, divisible and indivisible, inspired and informed my decision to continue my investigation on-site.

Archivists working with classified documents were encouraged to take graduate courses on the Second World War, the Cold War, and US and foreign intelligence agencies to improve their subject matter expertise. The Government Department of Georgetown University offered an evening seminar on "Espionage, Counterespionage, Paranoia, and Xenophobia: Oversight of the US Intelligence Community." Once a week, I would drive in from the Washington National Records Center in Suitland, Maryland, to Washington, DC, along the George Washington Memorial Parkway, past the Pentagon and the early evening panorama of the District of Columbia, crossing over Key Bridge into Georgetown. One evening after class, while walking through the university library, an electric blue catalog with *Freie Universität Berlin* emblazoned on the spine caught my archival eye. Taking it from the shelf of university catalogs, I walked over to the reading chairs near the tall windows that looked out across the Potomac River to Rosslyn on the far side and sat down. Imprinted on the cover in black under *FU BERLIN* was the university seal, a Norman shield depicting a defiant, flaming torch bearing Berlin bear, illuminating three leather-bound books bearing the university motto, "*Veritas, Justitia, Libertas*"—Truth, Justice, Liberty. Flipping through the pages, looking up occasionally to look down at the Potomac below, I found a bewildering but inviting list of departments and institutes, each with its own list of seminars, colloquia, exercises, and faculty members. Records reviewed in Vault Six and conversations with George had kindled my interest in Berlin and contemporary history, *Zeitgeschichte*. Under the entry for the Department of Historical Sciences, *Geschichtswissenshaften*, I was astonished to find the *Hajo-Holborn-Insitut (HHI)*. From 1943 until 1945, Professor Holborn, an émigré from Berlin, had served as a special assistant to Harvard historian William L. Langer, Director of Research and Analysis in the Office of Strategic Services, the OSS, which was the predecessor of the Central Intelligence Agency. In Vault Six, I had reviewed the *Civil Affairs Handbooks* and *Guidebooks* prepared under his direction during the war for the occupation of Germany. After the war, Professor Holborn returned to Yale University while continuing to advise the State Department on occupation policy for Germany.

Among the list of institutes in the *FU* catalog, I found another familiar name, the *Lucius-D.-Clay-Insitut für Nordamerikastudien (LDCI)*. General Lucius DuBignon Clay, US Army, was the former Military Governor (United States) of Germany, Commander-in-Chief of European Command and, as I knew from my work, one of the founding fathers of the Free University Berlin. The records of his office, the Office of Military Government-United States, were the very records under review by George and his colleagues from West Germany. The *LDCI* offered interesting courses in North American literature, politics, culture, economics, sociology, and history, but then why leave the United States to study it in Berlin? Neither the importance of critical distance nor the significance of the role the United States continued to play in Berlin occurred to me at the time. Convinced by this happy coincidence, looking down at the Potomac from the Georgetown bluffs with the blue *FU* catalog in hand, I decided to leave Washington, DC, and Georgetown for West Berlin and the Free University. The history of Berlin, the HistoriCity, would serve as my dissertation topic. The *HHI* and perhaps even the *LDCI* would provide me with scholarly sanctuary within the university.

Graduate study required matriculation through the *FU*'s International Studies Office. Once admitted, I would have to submit a dissertation proposal to the *HHI*. Carefully following the instructions outlined for the admission of foreigners under *Zulassung von Ausländern* in the *FU* catalog—it was disconcerting to think of myself as a foreigner—I sent a letter with copies of my university transcripts to the *Akademisches Auslandsamt* at the address provided, *Bolzmannstraße 3*. Several weeks later, I received a letter of tentative acceptance, along with an invitation to attend a two-day German language proficiency test, which would determine my eligibility for matriculation. Archival research and after-work symposia with George provided the *Theorie*; I was now ready for the follow-on *Praxis*, a shift from the archival to the archeological and the academic. On-site exploration of the ruins of Berlins I through VI promised concreteness, if only shattered and fragmentary, not found in the records. Working under the operational assumption Clio might be in residence among the ruins of the HistoriCity, I was anxious to discover what she might reveal to me there.

Architecture of all sorts was the subject of conversation in The Republic on the afternoon of my departure. My discussion with Neal deliberately, if drunkenly, devolved into a personal plan for taking the city. The drone of the crowd, like the jets from National Airport, had receded into the background. In just a few hours, I would depart, inspired by initial undergraduate impressions, archival excavations, and an ill-defined sense of mission. Neal, poet by and against nature, worked directly from experience, distilling and editing as necessary. Bound by the prosaic dictates of history and archival science, I preferred operating from a base, with a research design. The ruins of Berlin offered common, if broken, ground for the poetic and the prosaic.

"Emulate the great European tradition and contemplate the ruins!" Neal suggested, "See if you discover something of value for yourself. Ruins are really a present form of the past, you know. Use what you find to build your own Berlin, Thomas, but be careful over there! You'll need inspiration, so I've prepared this poem honoring your departure. Dig this, Heinrich Schliemann Jr." Plato warns against the presence of poets in the *polis*, but it was much too late for me to build a watchtower as the Virginia Native had begun to affect my concentration. Neal read "Munich 1934" aloud, painting vignettes of viciousness and cruelty, of hate and history—words of warning. Only the last lines were intelligible above the white noise:

and the beer flowed
like Marlene's tiny blonde hairs
in the wind all down the autobahn
in the back of my *Amerikanischer* car,
and we laughed
with actual teeth shining in our heads. . .

Laughing with actual teeth shining in his head, Neal handed me the poem, which I laid on the wooden table, unintentionally mopping up libations poured, folded it carefully, and placed it into the side pocket of my shoulder bag. Doing my best to sound sincere, I replied, "Thank you, Neal, thank you so much for this. I didn't get it all, but will read it carefully after I arrive in Berlin."

The supple brown leather shoulder bag, a farewell gift from my father, contained another missive marking my departure, a letter from his friend Lorelei Rhine, an oddly appropriate name for this beautiful woman. When he first introduced me to her, she was running a Yoga lodge in the Amish country of Central Ohio. Dad told me she'd recently been invited by the Central Intelligence Agency to offer seminars at "the Farm" on the Virginia coast. He told Lorelei about my decision to leave Washington and study history in Berlin. Shortly before I left Suitland, I received a call in Vault Six from the security desk upstairs, took the twenty-minute walk up to the front entrance, and was handed a sealed envelope by an Agency courier. I took the letter out of my bag and handed it to Neal, wondering how he would react. Written in a beautiful longhand, Lorelei's heartfelt wishes for my studies concluded with a warning. She was concerned by the negative constellations found in various combinations of the six letters of B-E-R-L-I-N. Observing it would require a great deal of strength to keep these discordant forces in check, Lorelei warned they could prove destructive. Smiling sympathetically, Dean handed the letter back to me. Despite their common origins, there's a border between poetry and prophecy. Although not overly concerned by Lorelei's admonitions, the fact that her current employer sought her out in the rural Amish country of Central Ohio and brought her to a remote location on the Virginia coast to instruct the chosen merited some consideration.

Neal and I awoke from our beery dreaming at The Republic when it came time to leave for John-Allen-Eleanor-Dulles International Airport. As we rose from the bar, the attractive professional woman who'd blocked our path when we'd first entered stood before us again, blocking our path to the revolving door and Union Street. "Hello," she said, extending her hand. "My name is Bendis." She spoke English with a light Southern European accent. Her short dark hair so admired by Neal and her smooth, tanned skin set off her flashing eyes. With her single golden earring and the glass of white wine in her hand, she could have been the goddess descended for the *Bendideia*.

"Hello, Bendis," Neal replied, taking her hand in his. "I'm Neal, and if you've been listening in, which it seems you might have been, you know we must leave for Dulles now. My friend Thomas is flying to Berlin in a few hours."

"Hello, Thomas," she said, turning toward me and extending her hand. Turning back to Neal, she continued, "Then I can't make you stay? The celebration will continue all afternoon on into the evening. After sunset, there will be a torchlight parade down King Street to Union Street. Did you see the iron sconces on the front of the building? I'm told the torches will be lit by a rider dressed as George Washington!"

"On horseback!" Neal exclaimed, "That is indeed something new. Isn't there another alternative? You cannot force us to stay now, but you could persuade me to return."

Tossing her bangs, Bendis smiled, stepped aside, and said, "Please do return, Neal. I will wait for you here. Thomas, I wish you a safe flight and an interesting stay in Berlin. Perhaps we'll meet again. I studied classical mythology in Tübingen and spent several weekends in West Berlin with friends. We also visited East Berlin. I found Berlin quite different from any other city and would be very interested in your impressions." We took our leave, slowly but deliberately, making our way once more through the maddening crowd. Once caught in the vortex, we flowed with the other celebrants through the revolving door out onto Union Street, now oblivious to heat and humidity. Before turning left onto King Street, I stopped to look back at the former torpedo factory and Federal Records Center on the opposite corner. "Let's go, Thomas," Neal implored, "*Mon frère* will be waiting for us." Turning our backs on the yacht club occupying the site of the silted-in harbor, we followed the redbrick sidewalk, crowded with celebrants on their way down to The Republic, up King Street. In spite of its most recent reincarnation, Alexandria still looked much the old port city it once had been. Across the street, the windows of the Napoleon House were wide open. We could hear John Malachi gently jazzing the big Steinway. Neal and I had spent many evenings in the upstairs lounge in the company of bartender Tom Collins, listening to John play, sometimes accompanying Pam Bricker. Unlike The Republic, the Napoleon House didn't need sconces because Pam carried the torch all by herself. As we walked by, notes seemed to hang visible in the humid air, in perfect harmony with the architecture and the afternoon. Recognizing the reprise, the shuffling rhythm of Donald Fagan's "Home at Last" in Pam's voice, I suddenly felt a strong sense of longing—to stay or go I did not know. From King Street, we turned left onto South Fairfax Street, where Neal's brother Mark lived in a small one-bedroom apartment on the ground floor of a white wooden frame house. He had volunteered to give me a ride to the airport and was now waiting for us on his front porch with a can of beer in one hand, loudly encouraging tourists to "Go back to Bethesda!" indicating the general direction of Bethesda, Maryland with the other. After quickly changing into the clothes I'd brought along for the trip, we each took one last beer for the road and climbed into Mark's battered bronze Maverick. Pre-positioned in the trunk the night before to simplify today's departure was the burnt orange Westpak backpack my fellow NARSians presented me with for my new life as an itinerant archivist abroad. Several confided they had once contemplated a similar move but were prevented from doing so by obligations familial and financial. My colleague with the luxuriant red hair and green eyes gave me a brief kiss on the mouth and a look which carried me as far as the back seat of Mark's Maverick. For good luck, Mark backed into the telephone pole directly across the street from his driveway, heading for Washington Street and the George Washington Memorial Parkway.

Feeling as if I had already departed, I found it difficult to talk with Neal and Mark, who seemed to be sitting on the far side of a glass partition, as if I were a passenger in a DC cab. I was reminded of the old RCA Victor tube television I grew up in front of. Sometimes, I would turn it off and on again repeatedly just to watch the programs collapse into a horizontal white line, contract into a point, then disappear. It took a great deal of concentration and effort to keep turning the conversation back on. This sense of being apart heightened a sense of longing. Although I had been preparing for months, immanent departure triggered tangible anxiety. Over time, I had established myself in Washington, and would now have to start over again in a city that was largely documentary, constructed out of a week of impressions, weeks of conversation, and weak archival evidence.

Running north from Alexandria, the George Washington Memorial Parkway skirts the runways of Washington National Airport, paralleling the Potomac, retracing in reverse the route Neal and I had taken earlier in the day. Seen from under the glass of the Maverick's rectangular rear window, the District of Columbia passed in review along the far side of the river, the slowly sinking Jefferson Memorial, the Capitol, the clandestinely monitored Lincoln Memorial, Memorial Bridge, and somewhere behind it, Main Archives and all the other monumental buildings lining Constitution Avenue. The magnificent white or gray marble facades radiated the reddish light and warmth of the late-afternoon sun. On the horizon, the outline of the Washington National Cathedral and the slender towers of Georgetown University; below, houseboats on the Potomac and the Three Sisters Island. The river abruptly vanished into the trees lining the parkway. We passed the exit for the Federal Highway Administration (FHA), which also led to CIA headquarters in nearby Langley, Virginia. Hidden among the trees like St. Elizabeth's, the presence of the invisible Agency brought Lorelei's letter back to mind, along with the hundreds of OSS, SSU, CIG, and CIA documents reviewed in Vault Six. Did they really contain intelligence? Would Berlin, the subject line of so many INTSUMS and SITREPS, prove only a source of invisible, perishable intelligence, or was something more to be found? Was my decision to move there a mistake? After circumnavigation of the Capital Beltway isolating Washington from the rest of the unknown world, we exited onto the Dulles access road. Sunken back into the back seat, I kept shifting back and forth, looking out ahead through the Maverick's cracked windshield. Suddenly, I caught sight of a great sweeping wing, rising magnificently into the bright blue sky from the rolling countryside, an architectural invitation to flight, the John-Allen-Eleanor-Dulles International Airport, JAEDIA. Mark's standard operating procedure was to arrive as close to departure time as possible to prevent "long goodbyes." We were very close, too close, and our goodbyes very short. Suddenly, I found myself alone on the sidewalk among hundreds of other passengers in front of the glass facade of the terminal building, waving to a bronze Maverick with a battered rear bumper quickly consumed in the traffic of arrivals and departures. Running to the Pan American ticket counter, I checked my backpack through to Berlin and boarded the London flight for the first leg of my journey back to the HistoriCity.

City of Berlin

August 1982

Once on board, I learned why I'd been able to board so close to departure time—our flight had been delayed. During the routine preflight check, the captain discovered a crack in the windscreen of the aging Boeing

747. We were obliged to wait while it was replaced. Grateful for Pan Am's precautions, I was anxious to follow our progress up the Eastern Seaboard of North America during daylight. As our aircraft finally rose into the darkening sky, I could make out hundreds of slow-moving points of light on the highways below. Closing my eyes, I placed myself back in the back seat of Mark's Maverick on the way back to Alexandria, the Potomac, The Republic, and Bendis, falling into an uneasy sleep irregularly interrupted by perfunctory offers of food and drink.

Fortunately, landing allowed a glimpse of London from the air, as there was no time to see it from the ground. Late due to the Dulles delay, I ran to catch Pan Am's "Round-the-World" flight, taking me as far as Frankfurt am Main. Following Frankfurt, the flight continued on to New Delhi. Much to my delight, I found myself in the company of hundreds of Sikhs returning to India. The only pilgrim on board, I took my assigned seat next to a handsome Indian with short, graying hair and a broad engaging smile who, turning to me, nodded and politely introduced himself as Govinda. He was dressed in a dark green corduroy suit with a navy blue turtleneck sweater. Although he did not wear earrings, I noticed both his earlobes had been pierced. I introduced myself, telling him how relieved I was to have made the Frankfurt flight, and asked him how long the trip was from London to New Delhi.

"No, no," he smiled understandingly, "you do not correctly understand. You see, I'm flying to Frankfurt and then on to West Berlin to visit my dissertation advisor and friend Richard W. Schneider, an exchange professor at the Free University of Berlin." My embarrassment was immediately eclipsed by Govinda's mention of the Free University, and without hesitation, I told him about my plans to study at the *Hajo-Holborn-Institut* as if he were a fellow graduate student. "Ah then, you must call on Professor Schneider at the *Lucius-D.-Clay-Institut* for American Studies. He is a political theorist like myself and will be offering courses on lobbying and ombudsman in the United States and Germany." He paused for a moment and added, "If memory serves, he recently wrote he also plans to offer a seminar dealing with Berlin and *The Republic* of Plato, which, given your interest in Berlin, you might find useful. 'West Berlin: an Accidental *Polis*?' is the title, I believe. Let me write it down for you, along with his address and telephone number. Unfortunately, he is unable to meet me at the airport in Berlin or I would introduce you to him personally." On the back of his *carte de visite*, Govinda carefully printed the seminar title, along with the address and phone number of the *Lucius-D.-Clay-Institut* for American Studies. Accepting it gratefully, I turned it over and read, "Dr. Govinda

M. Nayaka, Professor of Political Science, University of Hawaii," before placing the card carefully into the side pocket of my shoulder bag with Neal's poem and Lorelei's letter.

Looking out my window as the 747 left the runway, I tried to catch another glimpse of London, but The City was obscured by clouds. Time varies with the intensity of conversation. An American citizen, Govinda was born in India, where he attended the Wardha school of Mahatma Gandhi, a friend of his father, also a London-educated barrister. The "M" in Govinda's name stood for Mahatma. Rather than law in London, Govinda chose to study political science at the University of California, Berkeley, and rather than return to India as originally planned, he remained in the United States to teach and raise a family. After many years of teaching, he returned to graduate school to complete his doctorate with Dr. Schneider. As a dissertation topic, Govinda chose his former teacher Gandhi as a "nation builder," a curious expression that immediately caught my interest. If a nation could be built deliberately, then, by definition, it was artifice, a kind of architecture. Working in this medium, the nation builder becomes a kind of architect. Govinda patiently explained how Gandhi and other nation builders, including Mustafa Kemal Atatürk and Vladimir Lenin, incorporated all available raw material, living and inert, cultural and historical, into the creation of a nation-state. Our common destination, Germany, was another case study, illustrating both thesis and antithesis. If a nation or empire could be intentionally constructed, then it could be intentionally deconstructed as well, from without as well as from within. The once-and-future German capital, Berlin, stood as concrete, if broken and divided, hypothetical proof.

I briefed Govinda on the architectural and archival inspiration for my decision to study in Berlin. "Fascinating," he exclaimed. "What an interesting coincidence! Our interests are very similar indeed. I can assure you, Thomas, Professor Schneider would also be very interested in assisting with your research work. You will not regret a decision to invest him as your Virgil!" The title of Dr. Schneider's seminar, "West Berlin: An Accidental *Polis?*" seemed almost too appropriate to be accidental.

Upon arrival in Frankfurt, Govinda and I deplaned and made our way to the gate for the connecting flight to Berlin. Tired, hungover, and oddly indifferent to this final, most important leg of the trip, I found myself once again in the role of the observer, watching Govinda and myself as we joined a small group of people waiting at the gate. They were, or at least seemed to be, quite different from the Washington-to-London passengers, even more exotic than the Sikhs flying from London to Frankfurt. It was difficult to determine exactly why. There was an eccentricity in dress and behavior. An air of unconventionality, inviting and unsettling, hung over the waiting lounge.

We sat down next to a slender, almost emaciated man wearing a dark felt hat with a black band, and a sleeveless vest covered with patch pockets. Glancing casually in his direction, I noticed that he was also wearing a white cotton shirt, jeans, and heavy black construction boots. My attention was immediately drawn to his face, which had an angularity highlighting the skull beneath. When he returned my gaze, I noticed that his eyebrows swept upward over his deep-set eyes, giving what otherwise might seem to be a vision of death, a pleading, angelic quality. There was a sense of immediacy and intensity about him, reminding me of Neal, the ex-poet of Exeter. Caught, too tired to look away, I smiled, greeting him with the textbook "*Guten Morgen.*"

He looked at me intensely for a moment, unsmiling, then replied: "*Jeder Mensch ein Künstler.*"

"*Bitte?*" I asked, not prepared for anything more than "*Morgen.*" He leaned forward, reached into his pocket, and, taking out a key ring, unlocked, then unzipped the large leather carry-on bag on the floor next to his feet, carefully removing a large object swathed in cloth. As he gently unwound the protective shroud, I could see the object was a white rabbit, mounted as a kind of hunting trophy. I was too tired to be surprised. His remarks, gestures, and the rabbit seemed oddly appropriate to the setting. He offered the rabbit to me, and after holding it for what I felt to be the proper length of time, I passed it on to a serenely smiling Govinda, who regarded it with great interest and polite amusement, graciously returning it to our fellow traveler with his thanks. As he began to carefully rewrap the rabbit, he spoke in English, "We are all artists, called upon collectively to create and reify the invisible architecture necessary for a new social order."

It had been quite a morning. An airborne seminar on nation building with a student of Gandhi followed by an artistic analysis of society as invisible architecture. Nations and societies were very visible kind of architecture. Perhaps invisible architecture was a kind of perishable architecture, similar to that detailed in intelligence reports. I required of the angelic artist more of what was referred to in those reports as Essential Elements of Information (EEI). Before I could formulate my question, we were called to board our flight to Berlin. I nodded and stood up. He nodded politely in return as Govinda and I walked through the gate onto the enclosed boarding ramp.

Through the windows, I could see we were about to board an old Pan Am trijet Boeing 727 with "City of Berlin" painted in blue script on the fuselage under the cockpit. With some concern, I noticed the letters were faded and chipped. The entire aircraft was in need of a new paint job, and I hoped there was no crack in the windscreen. After the initial impressions of my fellow travelers and the unexpected exchange in the waiting area, the trip increasingly took on an air of unreality, not unpleasant but somewhat disorienting. An attractive stewardess welcomed us on board. She radiated sensuality through her sky blue Pan Am uniform. Through the half-open cockpit door, I could see the flight crew involved in the preflight check, and caught sound bites of what sounded like a very serious conversation. A voice from behind the door, which I took to be that of our pilot, said, "To tell you the truth, I think I'm going crazy." Although neither of the Pan Am aircraft that had brought me this far were in the best of condition, the *City of Berlin* and her crew had seen better, and hopefully happier, days. The seats were threadbare, and the overhead baggage compartments wouldn't close properly. My seatbelt wouldn't lock, so I tied myself into my seat when the "Fasten Seatbelt" sign flashed on. On her walk down the aisle, the stewardess smiled warmly, nodding her approval of my improvisation. When the door wouldn't close properly, a member of the ground crew kicked it shut. We were now ready for takeoff. The aircraft protested loudly with a cacophony of metallic machine music as we left the gate and taxied to the runway. Having come this far, I resolved the *City of Berlin* would fly, and as we sped down the runway, I did my best to will her into the air one more time.

This final leg of my journey was flown in the late morning. From my well-worn seat, I could see neither Govinda nor our fellow traveler with the rabbit. Although I enjoyed talking to Govinda about nation building, and would have liked to have gleaned additional EEI on invisible architecture from the talented taxidermist, I was pleased to take the chance to relax and to prepare myself for arrival. From my window seat, I could survey the German countryside below. Fortunately, there were few clouds. I retrieved my shoulder bag from under the seat in front of me and, taking out my notebook, turned to the notes taken in anticipation of this flight back at my desk in Vault Six while reviewing reconnaissance photographs taken during the mission of March 6, 1944, the largest air attack conducted by the US Strategic Air Forces in Europe on the *Reichshauptstadt* (Berlin IV).

Looking out the RCA-Victor-screen-sized window of the Boeing 727, I saw a black-and-white sky punctuated by black flak bursts. It was filled with B-17 Flying Fortress and B-24 Liberator bombers escorted by P-47 Thunderbolt, P-38 Lightning, and P-51 Mustang fighters engaged in aerial combat with *Messerschmitt Bf 109* and *Focke-Wulf Fw 190* interceptors. Sequential photographs taken over the target captured strings of bombs falling on and exploding throughout Berlin. Once again, declassification review in reverse chronological order could not return those strings to the bomb bay for the flight to England, where they could be off-loaded and, as an American witness to the bombing of Dresden has suggested, carefully disassembled into components and buried safely in the ground. The mission of March 6 proved the most costly of the war. The US Eighth Air Force lost sixty-nine bombers and eleven fighters. Of the 701 airmen on board those aircraft, 229 were killed or missing. Reports compiled by the civil defense office in Berlin, the *Hauptluftschutzstelle*, used by the US Air Force to prepare strategic bombing surveys after the war, recorded the death of eighty-six Berliners and the destruction of buildings in the Berlin boroughs of Spandau, Zehlendorf, and Steglitz. Fifty-seven people were injured and 2,245 people left homeless. None of the assigned targets were hit. Nothing was accomplished.

As we began our descent into Berlin, I ordered the bombers and fighters back to base and, returning to 1982, changed the sky back from black to blue, watching closely for the vast Red Army training areas surrounding the city, and then for the Wall itself. From the US Military Liaison Mission reports, I knew the Wall ran for 161 "klicks," the circumference of the British, French, and US Sectors of Berlin (Berlin VI) combined, creating what was often referred to by the Western theologians of the Cold War as an "island in the Red Sea." As we began our final approach into the Berlin-Tempelhof Central Airport, I could clearly discern two distinct Berlin Walls with a patrol road running through the *intervallum*. These walls described the circumference of West Berlin, my Berlin VI and Dr. Schneider's "accidental *polis*."

Among the Berlin files found in Vault Six was also the after action report (AAR) of the Berlin Airlift, officially the Combined Air Lift Task Force (CALTF), prepared by Dr. Harry F. Danington, chief of the Historical Office of the US Air Forces in Europe (USAFE). USAFE succeeded the US Strategic Army Air Forces in Europe (USSAFE), which, in concert with the Royal Air Force (RAF), conducted the strategic bombing of Germany and Berlin during the Second World War. As a result of UK-US combined operations over the city, over one-third of the *Reichshauptstadt* (Berlin IV) had been laid to waste. Among the British records stored in Vault Six was an onionskin copy of the letter from the Commander of Bomber command, Sir Arthur Harris, to Winston Churchill, concluding, "We can wreck Berlin from end to end if the USAAF will come in on it." Yet, in one of those remarkable operational ironies of history, within three years, some of the British and American aircrews intent upon wrecking Berlin IV from end to end were repeatedly risking their lives to supply West Berlin by air. As the *City of Berlin* descended, I recalled how the dangerous approach into

Tempelhof Airport, skimming over the rooftops of apartment buildings, repeatedly tested the skills of the aircrews. An unfortunate few had failed the test. From a report attached as an appendix to the AAR, I copied the location of one crash site into my notebook, planning to recce it once in West Berlin. Tied securely into my seat, I looked out the window as rooftops and a graveyard flashed by. We were on the ground; the *City of Berlin* had returned home safely again. The broad wings of architect Ernst Sagebiel's gigantic stone eagle spread out to embrace the tired Boeing 727 as we taxied toward the terminal bay, our arrival heralded by the same metallic machine-music that had accompanied our departure. As we walked down the movable stairway to the tarmac, I was confronted with the sheer mass of the *Flughafen* Berlin-Tempelhof. The architectural antithesis of John-Allen-Eleanor-Dulles International Airport, Tempelhof seemed a summons, an order, to return to earth. A massive edifice of heavy gray and brown stone blocks of solid construction, it was anchored firmly into the ground. Although the building was in the intimidating, *Albert Speer-lich*-style of Berlin IV, "US ARMY AVIATION" stenciled in large white letters on the hangar doors reassured me the *Reichshauptstadt* had fallen and we had entered Berlin VI, the occupied city, the City of the Armed Camp. At the foot of the stairway, I brazenly took both hands of the Pan Am stewardess. I could feel the warmth flow from her hands into mine. She didn't seem to mind that I held them too long. Smiling, Govinda waited for me, and together, we walked up another flight of stairs into the arrival hall to collect our luggage.

The final leg of the flight to West Berlin, Berlin VI, had been a flight out of time. Time, history herself, seemed to stand still in this vast hall of stone and glass. I wasn't certain how to make it architecture as I looked upon it. There were so many impressions it was difficult to focus, scanning the vast interior and the few faces for George, my German colleague who had kindly offered to pick me up, or perhaps a fleeting glimpse of Johnny Vulcan and Edmund Dorf. Although Tempelhof posited the architectural antithesis of Dulles, the latter's namesakes, temporarily dutiful, grim American tourists had no doubt arrived here by air, just as I had. Two stories in height, the huge rectangular hall dwarfed passengers, families and friends, and employees. As the name *Tempel-hof* seemed to suggest, the great hall was a kind of cathedral of stripped classicism, flooded with light natural and artificial. Massive rectangular stone-block pillars supported a terra-cotta ceiling, highlighted by rectangular, artificially lighted recesses. While open areas were tiled or covered with terrazzo, the niches behind the pillars had inlaid marble floors. Each of the three Western airlines serving West Berlin—Air France, British Airways, and Pan American—had offices on the ground floor. Framed by floor-to-ceiling plate glass windows set into burnished brass frames, they invited the privileged to travel to Paris, London, and New York, though curiously not to my point of departure, Washington, DC. The baggage claim carousel ran like an oblong greyhound track in the center of the hall. Although anxious to retrieve my orange backpack and find George, I was held captive by the interior of the great hall. A balcony ran all the way around the second floor. At the far end, there was a restaurant overlooking the airfield and additional offices. Our luggage emerged from underground, and after retrieving my backpack, I saw George hurrying toward me with outstretched arms. "Welcome back to Berlin, Thomas, to the American Sector," he said warmly, grasping my shoulders. "Now we can—how do you say it?—'Pick up where we left off.'" George turned to Govinda, who joined us with his luggage, and, politely offering his hand, said, "Georg von Garlitz."

Smiling and shaking George's hand warmly, Govinda introduced himself, giving George his card. Turning to me, he said, "If I may, I will tell Professor Schneider you intend to call him once you are settled in, no hurry, please. When you do call, please mention my name. I'm certain he will be very pleased to help you in any way he can. Now, I must take a taxicab out to Dahlem. I wish you every success and much happiness with your studies, Thomas, and good health, too. If you have the chance, please do drop me a line and let me know how you are coming along. It is highly unlikely I will have the opportunity to return to Berlin in the near future. I enjoyed our conversation very much and am personally very interested in the progress of your work. If you are busy and don't have time to write to me however, please don't worry, I'll be watching from across the street."

"From across the street, you mean from across the sea," I thought to myself, but waving and smiling, radiating peace and *joie de vivre* as he walked, Govinda had already taken his leave. As I turned back to George, I caught sight of our fellow traveler carrying the leather bag containing the rabbit. He was met by a tall man wrapped in a long, black cloak, who, raising both arms in greeting, embraced him and kissed him firmly on the mouth. For a moment, both men were cloaked in black, then, turning toward the exit, they walked arm in arm down the stone staircase and out through the doors. They were gone before I could draw George's attention to them.

George and I likewise made our way, arm in arm, down the staircase, through the massive metal doorframes out onto the sidewalk in front of the airport. When we reached its edge, I turned around to face the facade towering over us. The frontispiece was as imposing as the bay. There seemed to be an individual door for each arriving and departing passenger. In the center, over the doors, were huge neon letters spelling out ZENTRALFLUGHAFEN. Stern stone eagles, wings folded, guarded the entrance to and exit from the semicircular driveway separating the terminal building from the parking lot. The ruins of Berlin IV in Berlin VI. There was considerably less traffic than at John-Allen-Eleanor-Dulles International Airport. The panorama of arrivals and departures at Tempelhof was dominated by principles of statics rather than of movement.

George stopped, turned around, and walked back to join me: "Look closely at the claws of the eagles. Something's missing." I looked closely and could see that something had indeed been chiseled from the marble eagles' claws in broad, rough strokes. "The *Hakenkreuze* of course, military government regulations!"

As we crossed over the drive and walked into the parking lot, I sensed the difference in and through the air. Like the August air of Washington, the Berlin air, the famous "*Berliner Luft, Luft, Luft*" was heavy. Yet it was a different kind of heaviness, gritty rather than humid, weary. It seemed to filter out, to drain the color from the buildings across the street, giving them a gray, grainy quality. Neither white nor gray, it was again difficult to decide what to do when I looked upon the buildings as architecture. Between the parking lot and the broad street, a huge concrete claw rising from a circular base spread three webbed, blunted talons westward into the sky.

Noting my interest, George remarked, "That is what we call the 'hunger claw' or the 'hunger rake.' You'll soon discover we *Berliner* have our own names for many of our monuments. It's West Berlin's memorial to those who lost their lives during the Berlin Airlift. Thirty-one Americans died. Their names are listed at the base of the memorial, together with the names of forty-one Britons and six Germans. See the bouquets of fresh flowers around the base? *Berliner* who lived through the winter of '48 and '49 have not forgotten." I mentioned the address of the C-47 crash site copied from the After Action Report in my notebook. "Oh yes, that would be *Handjerystraße* in Friedenau," he said. "Friedenau's just where we're headed now Thomas, *deine 'Kleine Krone'* is nearby!"

"One elegant Empire room"
August 1982

Before I could begin my on-site archival and architectural activities and enroll in the Free University, I needed to establish a base of operations in the HistoriCity. I considered renting an apartment in the *Studentendorf,* the Free University's student village. From my review of the post files of the Department of State, I knew the *Studentendorf*, the *Ost-Europa Institut* (Eastern Europe) and the *Werner-Finck-Institut* (political science) had been built by the *Freie Universität Berlin* with funds made available by the departing US Political Advisor (POLAD) to General Clay. Yet living in a student dormitory was not living in Berlin, and I wanted to be *eis tan polis*.

George had a colleague at the *Geheimes Staatsarchiv Preussischer Kulturbesitz*, the *Secret State Archives of the Prussian Cultural Heritage Foundation*, the Prussian Privy Archives, with a room for rent in an apartment building in Friedenau, a district of Schöneberg, one of the boroughs, the *Bezirke* of Berlin. During one of our Mr. Henry's symposia, George painstakingly described Berlin's various divisions and subdivisions to me. He laughed approvingly when I countered with the artificial archeological layers I'd developed based upon Wilhelm's Dörpfeld's excavations in Troy. In 1920, the composite of districts, cities, and towns surrounding Berlin III were incorporated into *Groß-Berlin*. The quadrisecting of *Groß-Berlin* in 1945 effectively created *Ost-Berlin* (Berlin V)—the Soviet Sector—and *West-Berlin* (Berlin VI), comprised of the three Western Allied sectors of occupation. My Berlin, West Berlin, Berlin VI, incorporated the twelve *Bezirke* of Reinickendorf, Spandau, Wedding, Charlottenburg, , Kreuzberg, Schöneberg, Neukölln, Wilmersdorf, Tempelhof, Zehlendorf, and Steglitz. During my seven-day stay in Berlin, I had lived in a *Studentenhotel* near *Rathaus Schöneberg*, where President John F. Kennedy had passionately proclaimed his solidarity with the citizens of West Berlin in 1963. Friedenau was administratively a part of Schöneberg. Recalling the broad avenues and side streets lined with leafy linden trees, I thought Friedenau might just offer the necessary sanctuary, *nemos*. Schöneberg, together with Steglitz, Kreuzberg, Neukölln, Tempelhof, and Zehlendorf, made up the American Sector within West Berlin. I was home away from home at last.

We set out for Friedenau directly from Tempelhof, turning left into the broad *Dudenstraße*. "It doesn't remind you much of Pennsylvania Avenue, does it?" asked George, smiling. Although the street was monumental in size, the buildings lining it were uniformly gray. The morning sun filtering through the haze shone through gaps illuminating wartime destruction, as well as illuminating the postwar attempts to bridge those gaps with prefabricated concrete buildings. "No, no," he continued, answering his own question, "we'll have to look for our Pennsylvania Avenue elsewhere in Berlin. Tempelhof was heavily damaged by wartime bombing raids. Many of the buildings here were erected in great haste to provide housing in the early 1950s." As we crossed over a bridge, I could see the *Stadt-Bahn—*

the *S-Bahn*—the city train tracks stretching back toward the original city center on my right, now East Berlin. In the other direction, the tracks ran out to the station at Wannsee, ending abruptly at the Wall. While staying at the student hotel in Schöneberg, we had taken the *S-Bahn* to *Bahnhof Friedrichstraße*, our point of entry into East Berlin, Berlin V. Directly ahead of us, in the distance, I could see the Berlin flag flying atop the tower of *Rathaus Schöneberg*, the city statehouse of West Berlin.

Dudenstraße became *Kolonnen Straße*. Looking out the window to the right as George turned left on to *Hauptstraße*, I saw a once elegant turn-of-the-century apartment building in a sorry state of disrepair. Large, hand-lettered, red banners hung from the balconies overlooking the intersection proclaiming, "*Lieber Instand-Besetzen als Kaputt Besitzen.*"[1] A street sign identified the intersection as *Kaiser-Wilhelm-Platz*, an architectural reference to Berlin II in Berlin VI. Anticipating my question, George said, "This apartment building has been taken over by *Instandbesetzer*, by 'squatters.' '*Instandbesetzen*' is from the word '*instandsetzen*,' to restore. Let me explain. Rather than restore the old, historic buildings, some owners intentionally allow them to run down until they are no longer legally habitable. The renters are expelled, and with the blessing and backing of the Berlin city government, the old buildings are torn down and new ones constructed—what you Americans call 'urban renewal.' Quite a few people, not just the homeless but young people, students, decided this didn't make sense and with the intent of renovating, '*instandsetzen*,' the apartment buildings, moved in. The first houses were occupied in the early seventies. Over the past decade, it's become quite a problem for the city government. In the meantime, about 200 buildings have been occupied in West Berlin. You'll see more *instandbesetzten Häuser* in Kreuzberg, also in the American Sector. Curiously, the *Instandbesetzer*, most of whom belong to Berlin's *Alternative Szene*, are supported by many *Berliner* who don't, but who still don't approve of the landlords' tactics."

As we headed down the *Hauptstraße*, I noticed a few modern facades amid the gray building fronts. The names "Pipeline" and, further along, "La Belle" on unlit neon signs caught my eye. They appeared to be bars or nightclubs. Standing adjacent to the modern two-story building housing La Belle was a massive gray building with a tower. George continued to unearth the historical and architectural foundations of my new home. "The building on the right is the *Roxy-Palast* built in the *Neue Sachlichkeit*, the New Objectivity style of the late twenties. Next door is the city hall of Friedenau. Friedenau was originally built as a *Landhauskolonie* for *Berliner*

---

1 "Better occupation and renovation than ruination through possession." Diary of Thomas Vonaechron, Diary Extract, 1982, trans. TV.

fleeing the growing *Großstadt* during the last quarter of the last century. It was, however, quickly swallowed up by Berlin, which," he smiled as he paused for effect, "as you hopefully remember, grew very rapidly following the Franco-Prussian War."

Exhausted, I was exhilarated to be back in West Berlin and tried to recall what George had told me about the growth of Berlin following the Franco-Prussian War: "If I remember correctly, French reparation payments provided funds for large building projects, ushering in *die . . . Gründerzeit.*"

George laughed, replying, "*Richtig!* You do indeed remember correctly, Thomas, and although three- and four-story brick apartment buildings were eventually built next to the smaller garden houses, if you look ver-r-ry car-r-refully, you can still see the original houses." We turned left onto *Hedwigstraße* and then left again into *Lothringerstrasse*, a street apparently untouched by either the Second World War or the Cold War, a remarkable remnant of Berlin II in Berlin VI. With branches of tall, lithe linden trees interlacing over the street, *Lothringerstrasse* retained much of the original garden-house character of Friedenau. I was pleased when George parked the car. Later, I learned from our *Hausmeister* that the apartment building had indeed been touched by the Second World War, by an incendiary bomb. Trained by the *Berliner Feuerwehr* to act in its stead, determined to save both the building and their possessions, the residents left the uncertain shelter of the *Luftschutzkeller* beneath the apartment building to smother the flaming white phosphorous fire with buckets of sand.

The room for rent was located on the second floor of a four-story apartment building. The handsome red brick, not unlike the majestic town houses on Capitol Hill, was set back from the street by a small front yard enclosed by a black, ornamental iron fence. A stone set into the facade above the entrance door proudly announced, "*Erbaut 1893.*" I looked at George, said "*Gründerzeit,*" and laughed.

"Just to be accurate, and as historians, Thomas, we must at least try to be accurate, the '*Gründerzeit*' only covers the period between 1871 and 1873, ending with the stock market crash of 1873, the so-called *Gründerkriese*, crisis. Technically, this apartment building was built during the period of '*Historicism,*' which lasted until the outbreak of the war in 1914." George opened the gate and we walked up to the stately entrance. The doorway and lintels, cast in neo-Gothic style, were creamy white, giving the building a solid, pleasant appearance. George found his colleague's name, "Dr. Karl Kahler," on the *Klingelschild* and rang the bell. After a few moments, an electronic buzzer replied. Leaning into the heavy wooden door, George shouldered it open. We entered a dark, high-ceilinged hallway. As the door slowly swung shut, he pushed an illuminated red button just inside the entrance on the right, turning on an overhead light. Although the *Treppenhaus* remained dark in spite of the natural light filtering in through the stained glass window four stories above us, the artificial light revealed a door-lined hallway leading to a wooden staircase at the far end. As we walked to the foot of the stairs, I could smell sandalwood incense, and heard faint sounds of a sitar and drum coming from a door on the right. There was a name on the brass plate over the doorbell, illegible in the semidarkness.

The wooden stairs were covered by a well-worn heavy red carpet, held in place by tarnished brass rods. As we climbed the stairway, I slid my right hand lightly over the smooth hardwood balustrade, cool to the touch. The entrance to the apartment was from the landing at the top of the first flight of stairs. Before George could ring the doorbell, the door opened, and Dr. Kahler stepped out onto the landing to welcome us, inviting us into the spacious, dark hallway of his apartment. He was middle-aged, of medium height, wiry, almost too thin. Clean-shaven, his closely cropped hair showed streaks of gray. Like George, he was fashionably but conservatively dressed. When he leaned forward, stretching out his right hand to take mine, he suddenly seemed quite familiar. Without the round wire-rimmed glasses, he bore a striking resemblance to the *Past* statue guarding the employees' entrance to the National Archives on Pennsylvania Avenue, "Whereof what's past is prologue; what to come, in your and my discharge." "Kahler," he said, with a tight, sincere smile, shaking my hand. The room for rent was just inside, to the right of the front door, facing *Lothringerstrasse.* Light was coming through two tall French doors that opened into a large, high-ceilinged room, which, according to George, was typical of fin de siècle Berlin apartments. The cream-colored walls were topped by a white ceiling, highlighted with stucco. Dr. Kahler explained, "This room originally served as the parlor, where callers could be entertained without revealing any further intimacies of the apartment." Large wood-framed windows at the far end of the room opened out onto the street below. With the exception of a large, Japanese-style futon bed, low to the floor, a red lamp suspended from the ceiling, a white-tiled *Kachelofen,* and next to it on the floor, a large, abnormally heavy brass dolphin clock, the room was empty. Nodding at the *Kachelofen,* Dr. Kahler smiled apologetically, explaining that throughout the coming winter, the *Kachelofen* would have to be fed at regular intervals with coal briquettes stored in the basement. "My colleague *Herr* von Garlitz tells me you will be a graduate student at the Free University and might require, if not too much has changed since the sixties, a desk," he said, offering to provide a smooth wooden door and two sawhorses. The deal was done quickly, sealed with another handshake.

George and I returned to his car for my shoulder bag and backpack.

"You've had quite a long journey today, Thomas, from Washington to West Berlin, from the American present to the German past," quipped George. "As you can see, we're not only on an island, we're somehow suspended in time as well, as if you'd taken a flight back in, or even out of history. But we can talk more about that tomorrow if you'd like. You should try to rest now. I remember very well how I felt when I first arrived at *Die Kleine Krone* after making the same trip in the opposite direction! If you do feel up to it tomorrow, however, please do come by the *Stadtstaatsarchiv*. Come anytime you like, I'll be there all day, and have some surprises waiting for you. Did you bring the Berlin map I gave you?" From the side pocket of my shoulder bag, I took out the folding *Falkplan* George had given me as an invitation when he'd returned to West Berlin from Washington. Placing it on the hood of his car, I unfolded it to the white cardboard declassification tab marking the location of the *Stadtstaatsarchiv Berlin*. George opened up the map like a paper accordion. Tracing the route from *Lothringerstrasse* to the archives with his finger, George said, "Take the underground train from *Friedrich-Wilhelm-Platz* to *Scharnweberstraße*. You only have to change trains once, from the 'U9' to the 'U6' at *Leopoldplatz*. Riding on the *U-Bahn*, you'll travel from the American Sector, through the British Sector to the French Sector, all part of West Berlin!" I refolded the map and put it carefully back in my shoulder bag.

"Once again, heartfelt thanks for picking me up today from Tempelhof and making all the arrangements for the room with Dr. Kahler and for the job at the *Stadtstaatsarchiv*."

George smiled and, taking my hand, said, "Welcome back to West Berlin, Thomas. You're officially a *Wahlberliner* now, so you must make the city your own." George got into his car and drove off down the linden-lined *Lothringerstrasse*. As he had so often done on Capitol Hill, I stood on the curb waving until his car was out of sight, then retraced my steps to the apartment building. This time, after turning on the light in the entrance hall, I stopped to look more closely at the brass nameplate next to the apartment door where I'd smelled sandalwood and heard the sitar and drum: "Govinda Hemd." Govinda—a name I'd never heard before, then twice within twenty-four hours! But Hemd didn't sound Indian, and I decided I would introduce myself to my new downstairs neighbor as soon as I had a chance.

When I returned to the apartment, Dr. Kahler continued the tour. Just past my room on the left, there was a large kitchen. A door at the back of the kitchen led to a small stairway, leading down to the shared *Hof* out behind the building and then to the basement and former

Luftschutzkeller, the air-raid shelter, where the soft coal *Briketts* were stored for the winter. We returned to the hallway from the kitchen, following it into the dark, high-ceilinged *Berliner Zimmer* facing the *Hof.* "This, *Herr* Vonaechron, is the so-called '*Berliner Zimmer,*' characteristic of many nineteenth- and early twentieth- century apartments built, as the name suggests, here in Berlin. Connecting the rooms in the front of the apartment, with those in back or in a wing, it typically has only one window, opening out onto the *Hof.* That's why it's darker than the other rooms. It was often used to entertain those privileged persons permitted to pass beyond the parlor," he said with a wolfish smile on his face. "Karl Marx's friend Friedrich Engels didn't care much for the *Berliner Zimmer.* Let me see now, how did he describe them, as 'shelters of darkness and suffocating air, . . . as refuges for self-satisfied Berlin philistines, unknown in the rest of the world. No thanks!' The telephone is here, on the wooden stand in the corner beneath the window. Please feel free to use it for your local calls."

"Thank you very much, Dr. Kahler! If I do have make a long-distance call, I'll of course make it from the post office."

There was a second bedroom off the *Berliner Zimmer,* the guest bedroom, connected by another set of French doors to my room. The hallway continued on the far side of the *Berliner Zimmer,* past a bathroom on the left, another large bedroom on the left, which I assumed to be Dr. Kahler's, and ended in a glass-covered *Wintergarten.* Dr. Kahler had had the *Wintergarten* furnished as his library and study. Built-in bookshelves lined the brick back wall from floor to ceiling, and a large, carved, dark wooden desk faced out over the *Hof.* On top of the desk was an old Smith Premier 1 typewriter, pushed back against the window. The stainless steel rings casing the round black keys shone brightly in the sunlight. In the corner of the *Wintergarten* stood a Victorian daybed covered by a colorful Iraqi rug and several threadbare, silk-covered cushions. Observing my interest, Dr. Kahler laughed and said, "That is my sofa for self-analysis!" Walking over to the windows of the *Wintergarten,* I could see the *Hofgarten* was walled in by apartment buildings on all sides. Joining me, Dr. Kahler said, "I'm very grateful the birds seem to enjoy my little walled *pairidaeza* just as much as I do. They come here early every morning to sing." Returning to my room, I noted with thanks that, with the exception of the *Wintergarten,* it received more light than any other room in the apartment. Remembering the poem Neal prepared for my departure and attempted to read aloud yesterday at *The Republic,* I picked up my shoulder bag and, sitting down on the bed, carefully took it from the side pocket. The dried Virginia Native gave it the color and texture of the parchment reproductions of the Declaration of Independence and Constitution for sale in the gift shop at George Washington's estate, Mount Vernon, south of Alexandria. Unfolding it carefully, I read aloud,

> One elegant Empire room was mine
> and an overcoat.
> The walls were high, eternal.
> I walked everywhere, and the *buildings*!

I also took Lorelei's letter from the side pocket and reread it carefully. Poetry or prophecy, Neal or Lorelei, I now had a base of operations, one high-ceilinged, "elegant Empire room" in the *Lothringerstrasse* was mine, my initial point of reference in the HistoriCity.

CHAPTER II:
Archival and Architectural Evidence of Berlin I, Berlin II, Berlin III, and Berlin IV in West Berlin (Berlin VI) and East Berlin (Berlin V)

Das ist auch so ein Unsinn, entweder sind alle Städte fremd, oder keine ist es.[2]

—Bernward Vesper, *Die Reise*

Die "historischen Schichten" der Architektur sind weniger Hypothek als Mahnung und zugleich Verpflichtung für die Zukunft.[3]

—Joschka Fischer

Stadtstaatsarchiv Berlin
August 1982

EXHAUSTED, EXALTED, exhilarated by my Washington-to-West Berlin odyssey, I took off my sport coat and shoes and stretched out on the bartered bed. The late morning light coming in through the large windows illuminated the intricate *fin de siècle* plaster of paris ceiling three meters over my head. Unable to sleep, I rewound the events of the past twenty-four hours, playing them back in chronological and reverse chronological order. Recalling George's recommendation and kind invitation, I decided to rest and report for duty at the *Stadtstaatsarchiv Berlin* in the French Sector the next morning.

During my seven-day sojourn in West Berlin, I was literally taken with and by the public transportation system, a nonstop network of light rail and buses integrating and incorporating all three Western sectors, passing underneath the former Soviet Sector, now capital of the German Democratic Republic. After returning to the United States, I was surprised to learn many American cities, including my own, had enjoyed comparable light rail networks but chose to sacrifice them on the altar of

2 "That is complete nonsense, either all cities are foreign, or none are." Diary of Thomas Vonaechron, Diary Extract, 1982, trans. TV.
3 "The historical layers of architecture are less a mortgage on the past than a warning and, at the same time, an obligation for the future." Diary of Thomas Vonaechron, Diary Extract, 1982, trans. TV.

the automobile. Fortunately, in spite of, or perhaps because of the war, this had not happened in Berlin. From the side pocket of my shoulder bag, I retrieved the folding *Falkplan* in a movement soon to become a reflex through regular repetition. Opening like a multicolored paper accordian, the plan placed a unified lettered and numbered grid over both Berlin (West) and Berlin (Ost), horizontally, left to right, A to Z, and vertically, top to bottom, eighteen to one. Over the coming months, I would carefully plot an ever-increasing number of points of reference on this grid, and through constant movement establish my own personal "lines of communication," to use the designation found in the military planning documents in Vault Six. My LOC would form an invisible architecture to be fleshed out with experience. I unfolded the map, carefully spreading it out on the bed. When completely unfolded, the map gave the impression of a unified city, though the street directory, like the city, was divided into Berlin (West) and Berlin (Ost). A jagged red line following the dictates of Cold War theology cut torturously through the city, not only separating Berlin (West) from Berlin (Ost), but isolating Berlin (West) from the German Democratic Republic (*Bezirk Potsdam*). Unified, if only on paper, the city was vast. The closest subway station to my one elegant Empire room in Friedenau (coordinates N6) was *Friedrich-Wilhelm-Platz* (coordinates M6). At *Friedrich-Wilhelm-Platz*, I could take the U9 north to *Leopoldplatz* (coordinates O13) and change there to the U6, the train to Reinickendorf, northeastern most of the *Westberliner Bezirke*, and the *Stadtstaatsarchiv* (coordinates M16). Carefully refolding the *Falkplan*, I slipped it back into my shoulder bag, took off my clothes, and stretched out on the bed, sleeping intermittently through the afternoon, evening, and night until first light, when I was awakened by a cacophony of birdsong coming from the linden trees lining *Lotheringerstrasse*: "Poo-tee-weet?"

Unzipping my backpack, I took out my blue and white light cotton yukata with kanji characters identifying me as a "great fireman," black Chinese slippers, Turkish towel, and kit bag. After slipping on the yukata and slippers, I quietly opened the tall French doors and crossed the hallway into the kitchen. Sunlight was coming in through the window looking out over the *Hof.* Dr. Kahler had already left for the Prussian Privy Archives. A note on a round wooden breadboard on the kitchen table invited me to help myself to freshly baked *Brötchen*, marmalade from the Black Forest, cheese, and tea, and afterwards, "to emulate the great Zen masters, and contemplate in a warm bath." After eating and washing up the dishes, I returned to my room for my towel and kit bag and walked into the cavernous *Berliner Zimmer*. Light coming in through the small window on the far wall allowed me to navigate my way around the chairs, a straight-backed settee, and plant stands to the hallway on the other side. With the exception of the entrance to the *Wintergarten* at the end of the hallway, all the doors were closed. The bathroom was the first door on the left. Taking the horizontally mounted bronze handle in hand, I pressed down and pushed the wooden door open. Much to my delight, in the center of the white-paneled room stood a ceramic bathtub with the draught of a dinghy. Anchored firmly on four cast-iron claws, it was bathed in the morning light filtering in through the large, leaded, stained glass window behind it. There was a white ceramic tank toilet with matching bidet, a tall pedestal sink with chrome handles, and a large rectangular mirror mounted above it. It looked like a stage set for *Cabaret*. Placing my towel and kit bag on a white bentwood chair next to the window, I inserted the hard rubber stopper into the drain. Taking off yukata and slippers, I slipped gently into the tub, filling it with warm water from the ceramic and steel handheld shower. Later, after discovering the inner workings of the apartment, I realized Dr. Kahler had not only recommended the bath but thoughtfully heated the water in advance. Relaxing in sunlit comfort, I contemplated my next steps as an itinerant archivist, amateur archaeologist, and future student of history.

Thanks to George, the professional training received at the National Archives now provided me with a source of income, as well as inspiration. Armed in advance with my credentials and soon student-to-be-status, he had arranged for me to work part-time in the *Stadtstaatsarchiv* as a *Magazinarbeiter*, placing me back into a familiar setting. Berlin, the HistoriCity, was by definition a city of archives. The *Stadtstaatsarchiv Berlin* where George worked was one of over 130 located throughout Berlin (West) and Berlin (Ost). The Prussian Privy Archives, where his colleague and my landlord, Dr. Kahler, worked, was another. Together, these repositories contained archived remnants of Berlins I through VI, subdivided thereunder by human activities ranging from the artistic to the nihilistic. The *Stadtstaatsarchiv*, soon to become my next reference point in Berlin VI, was housed in another building with a history—military history—a former munitions factory in Reinickendorf. Although now on the far side of the Atlantic and the "wrong side" of history, the historical fact that the redbrick, neo-Gothic building housed munitions production during both World Wars, a Prussian pendent on the Spree to the torpedo factory on the Potomac, provided an oddly comforting, if coincidental, sense of historical symmetry. Even the militaristic M16 coordinates seemed appropriate. That the *Kugellagerfabrik* and the torpedo factory were no longer used for their intended destructive purpose but, in one of those *eirönïa* Clio occasionally offers her initiates, to archive and preserve the records of destruction, offered purpose, the possibility of reparation, and perhaps redemption.

George told me the former factory complex, of which the *Stadtstaatsarchiv Berlin* occupied a relatively small part, was originally built between 1906 and 1918 (Berlin II) in Wittenau, part of Reinickendorf, by the German Weapons and Munition Factory, *Deutschen Waffen-und Munitionsfabrik (DWM)*. Enlarged between 1934 and 1942 (Berlin IV), it was composed of long, rectangular two-story buildings, each with a uniform neo-Gothic facade. A redbrick wall, interrupted at regular intervals by tall, black, cast-iron gates, ran the entire perimeter. In addition to the *Stadtstaatsarchiv*, the former munitions factory also housed the *Wehrmachtsauskunftstelle für Kriegsverluste und Kriegsgefangene (WASt)*, millions of records compiled on members of the German *Wehrmacht* killed in action, missing, or taken prisoner between 1939 and 1945. Moved out of Berlin in 1943, the records were discovered by US Army units entering the designated Soviet Zone of Germany in April 1945. Instead of handing them over with *Thüringen* or sending them to Alexandria, Virginia, they were returned to Berlin in 1946, where they were used by the "German Agency for Notification of War-Deaths of Former German Armed Forces to the Next of Kin." Once all next of kin had been notified, a quick-thinking American Army officer facilitated their transfer to the French Sector to prevent their destruction.

Wittenau, originally called Dalldorf, was also home to the *Städtische Irrenanstalt zu Dalldorf*, constructed in Berlin II between 1877 and 1879. When Berliners began using "Dalldorf" as a synonym for the madhouse, just as Londoners used "Bedlam," the nickname for the Bethlehem Royal Hospital, Dalldorf was renamed. The *eirönïa* that the Imperial War Museum, created in 1917 to capture the Great War in progress, moved to the former site of Bedlam in South London one year before the Gates of Janus reopened in 1937 certainly merits scholarly consideration.

Refreshed and relaxed after bathing, I dressed and set out for the *Stadtstaatsarchiv Berlin*. August on the Spree was much cooler than August on the Potomac, and I was happy I'd brought my well-worn tweed sport coat along. The sun, lower in the sky, was shining brightly but unable to dispel the light haze shrouding the streets. I walked back up *Lothringerstrasse*, turning right onto *Hedwigstraße*, which, according to the *Falkplan*, would lead me directly to *U-Bahnhof Friedrich-Wilhelm-Platz*. Standing on the corner under the street sign was a siren with shoulder-length, bleached-blonde hair, dressed in a short, sequined denim jacket, short shorts, and fishnet hose. She looked up at me through an attractive but hardened, heavily made-up face, demanding, "And just who are you?" in accent-free American English.

Startled, I muttered, "I'm ah, Thomas, and who are you?"

"Well, isn't that 'ah' obvious 'ah, Thomas,'" she replied, nodding at the street sign mounted on the gray metal pole above our heads. Inching her way past me angrily, she said, "I'm Hedwig, and this is my street." Turning abruptly on her open-toed high heels, she strutted off down *Hedwigstraße*.

"Of course, of course, I'm sorry, I should have known," I said to myself as she sashayed away, sequins flashing in the late morning light, not certain if I'd been insulted or propositioned. Watching her walk that way, I realized Hedwig was not a woman. Life in Berlin not unfrequently imitates the Broadway musicals. Continuing on toward the underground station, I walked slowly, scrutinizing passing pedestrians, comparing them with midmorning Washingtonians. West Berliners didn't seem to be as busy, as purposeful, moving slowly with a touch of resignation. Although late summer, with the exception of Hedwig's *haute couture*, there was little color in their clothing; dark gray, brown, or black prevailed. Apart from the small children, few were smiling, rather staring, grimacing. Waiting for the traffic light at the intersection with *Rheinstraße*, I could see the redbrick spire of the church on *Friedrich-Wilhelm-Platz* directly in front of me. Looking up and down what George had described the previous day as one of the main traffic arteries of West Berlin, I noted the midmorning traffic flow was light in comparison with Washington, DC. Once again, I reminded myself Berlin, West Berlin (Berlin VI), was not a capital city, though the former Soviet Sector, East Berlin (Berlin V) was officially the capital of the German Democratic Republic. The capital of the Federal Republic of Germany had been temporarily established in Bonn pending reunification. This was confirmed, George told, me by the "BN" on the license plates issued to residents of Bonn, an acronym for *Berlin Nebenstelle*, Berlin Branch Office. To my right, at coordinates N6, stood the massive gray *Rathaus Friedenau* we'd passed on our way to *Lothringerstrasse*. Just in front of the *Rathaus* was an outdoor market that hadn't been there yesterday. I decided to take a closer look. It had apparently been set up earlier that morning, as vendors were now busily dismantling the wooden frame and canvas booths, while Berliners bargained for the remaining fresh vegetables and flowers. Over the lively market ambiance towered the gray neo-baroque tower of the *Rathaus*. Although the once white, now gray stone building itself was massive, stripped of all ornamentation, the tower retained its faux columns and even a balustrade. The curved red-tiled roof was crowned with a bronze pedestal, a perch for a tall, slender angel robed in silver and sunlight. Hair haloed in red, golden wings arched gently behind as if about to take flight, the angel gracefully extended the green palm leaf of peace to the post- and preoccupied citizens of Berlin VI gathered at the market below.

Rather than retrace my steps, I rechecked the plan and decided to follow *Niedstraße* in the direction of *Friedrich-Wilhelm-Platz*. Trees and tall hedges lined the street, framing tiled garden houses and late nineteenth-century apartment buildings, a street from Berlin II in Berlin VI. Looking down at me through an opening in the tall hedge from the redbrick facade of a four-story apartment building was a crouching dragon, bat-ribbed wings widely spread, flanked on both sides by screaming gargoyles with large pendulous breasts and lions' claws. There were harpies in the HistoriCity. Above this unholy trilogy, a hooded monk lifted his eyes and the stump of his broken left hand to heaven. On his left, a raven, on his right, an owl holding up the mirror of vanity—*der Eulenspiegel.* Above his hooded head, a smiling satyr pointed to the hourglass held tightly between his goat legs. At the very top of the building, the cherubic face of yet another angel peeked out from Persian wings. I continued on in the direction of the *U-Bahnhof,* crossing over *Handjerystraße.*

Handjerystraße. George had referred to the street yesterday at Tempelhof. Stopping, I took the notebook out of my shoulder bag, flipping the pages back to the notes copied out in Vault Six. "Basic Ltr: Hq, Tempelhof Air Force Base, subj: History of the Command Sec for the period 1 to 31 July 48, dtd 13 Aug 48. At 0115 hours on 25 July 1948, this base experienced its first casualty under 'Operation Vittles.' A C-47 carrying food from Wiesbaden Air Force Base crashed two miles from Tempelhof, killing both pilots, 1st Lt Robert W. Stuber and 1st Lt Charles H. King stationed at Headquarters, US Air Forces in Europe." Although the crew members of the C-47 *Skytrain* were killed, miraculously no one on the ground was injured. I had examined the black-and-white photographs of the crash site while reviewing the investigation report, noting the street address, *Handjerystraße* 2, and the names of the crew in my notebook, names now inscribed on the base of the concrete *Hunger Claw* at Tempelhof Central Airport, reaching out to the west from this "island in the Red sea." Putting the notebook back in my shoulder bag, I continued along *Niedstraße* to the subway.

Shuffling toward me on the sidewalk, carrying what appeared to be a picture wrapped in heavy brown paper, was a large man wearing a beret. His eyes were cast down, and as he came closer, I could hear him speaking to himself in an agitated tone, repeating: *"Die Anna will es nicht! Sie will es einfach nicht haben!"*[4] He wore a well-worn, light-brown camel hair sport coat over a V-neck sweater with an open Schiller-collared shirt. Stopping in front of me, he looked up, directly into my eyes, his dark eyebrows *accents circonflexe* over the lenses of his wire-rimmed glasses, complementing the thick brown moustache covering his upper lip. Disheveled and somewhat distraught, he shrugged his shoulders and told me quite matter-of-factly,

---

4 "Anna doesn't want it! She simply doesn't want it!" Diary of Thomas Vonaechron, Diary Extract, 1982, trans. TV.

as if I'd asked for an explanation, "*Die Anna will es nicht. Sie will es einfach nicht haben! Bitteschön!*" holding the wrapped package out for me to take. Recalling the rite of the white rabbit in the waiting lounge of the Frankfurt Airport the previous day, I carefully took the package from his outstretched hands, nodding as graciously as Govinda had. As I began to unwrap it, he walked on past me, repeating "*Die Anna will es nicht! Sie will es einfach nicht haben!*" Too surprised to follow, I watched him disappear into the disappearing market crowd at the foot of the *Rathaus* tower. Rather than follow him, I decided to take the package to the *Stadtstaatsarchiv*. Placing it under my right arm, I continued on to the end of the *Niedstraße*.

In the center of a traffic circle stood the graceful neo-Gothic church *Zum Guten Hirten*, the Church of the Good Shepherd, a redbrick memorial to Berlin II in Berlin VI. Thanks to Providence and the lesser laws of physics, the tall, graceful static construction proved resilient, resistant to the bombs and shock waves of the Allied bombing campaign. I would discover many similar *Backsteinkirchen* scattered throughout Berlin V and VI, as testaments both to tectonics and the Teutonic *Kaiserreich*. A rectangular black metal frame, with "*U Friedrich-Wilhelm-Platz*" framed in electric blue, called my attention to the subway. Walking down the stairs, I followed the narrow, dark, low-ceilinged, white-tiled corridor that opened up onto a yellow and white-tiled platform lined with gray metal pillars holding the *Friedrich-Wilhelm-Platz* in place just above my head. The low, long underground station built to accommodate underground trains was very much in the style of West Berlin, Berlin VI. There was a large, freestanding metal and glass-framed map of the *U-u. S-BAHNNETZ* identical to the one in my *Falkplan*. I found *Friedrich-Wilhelm-Platz* and followed the *U9* north with my index finger as George had done yesterday when he dropped me off. I found the last station in the direction of *Leopoldplatz, Senftenberger Ring*. I bought a ticket from the yellow vending machine and as I canceled it, heard the train coming, emerging from the tunnel on the right, the dull yellow coaches familiar from my first visit. After the train stopped, I pushed grooved metal handles down, and the doors slid open.

Doors located on both sides at each end and in the center of the coach were connected by a center aisle, with *U-Bahn* passengers seated facing each other on vinyl-covered benches in eight open compartments. The walls were covered with brown plastic veneer. There wasn't much legroom for the four passengers forced to face each other, creating a kind of enforced *huis* closeness. When passengers sitting next to the windows stood up to exit, those sitting on the aisle would swing their knees outward in unison, like a gate, to let them pass. Fortunately, the train was almost empty and I shared my compartment with only one fellow traveler, an elegantly dressed elderly woman. She seemed to be as interested in me as I was in her, and although we nodded politely to one another, we did not speak.

Acceleration and deceleration marked the stations of our journey across *Westberlin, Bundesplatz,* with the exception of the beige tiles identical to *Friedrich-Wilhelm-Platz, Berlinerstraße,* tiled in white and green, *Güntzelstraße,* orange-tiled, *Spichernstraße,* white-tiled with yellow, blue, black, and green mosaics, *Kurfürstendamm*, the spiritual and material center of Berlin VI tiled in a sea of snot-green, the drear light of *Zoologischer Garten,* with large black silhouettes of antelopes and elephants, postwar cave paintings on the low, long yellow-tiled walls, *Hansaplatz,* white-tiled, *Turmstraße,* turquoise-tiled walls with flesh-colored tiles covering the supports, *Birkenstraße*, green-tiled accentuated with mosaics, *Pulitzstraße, Amrumer Straße,* and *Leopoldplatz.* Taken together, these identical stations composed the circulatory system of the HistoriCity. Changing trains at *Leopoldplatz,* I stepped out into another long, low green-tiled tunnel, broken up by patches of brown marble veneer. An illuminated sign pointed to the *U6* in the direction of Tegel. Climbing the stairs, I walked out onto an identical platform, distinguished only by the yellow and green tiles, with blue and gold insets. Soon, I was moving to the familiar rhythm of acceleration and deceleration. *Seestraße, Rehberge,* with supports depicting doe among the green tile forest foliage, *Afrikanische Straße, Kurt-Schumacher-Platz.* The tunnel came to an end when the *Untergrundbahn* defied its name and emerged into the sunlight, just before *Scharnwerberstraße.* I stepped out of the train onto an aboveground platform, open on both sides, surrounded by trees and shrubs. Signs directed me down the stairs, past a postmodern mosaic in the glass entrance hall to the *Eichborndamm* exit and bus stop. Although Bus Lines 15 and 21 would have taken me to the *Stadtstaatsarchiv,* I decided to walk *per pedes Pilgrimorum.* While some of the buildings along *Eichborndamm* were prewar, many were postwar construction, interrupted at arbitrary intervals by vacant lots where buildings once stood. The lots were not occupied by automobiles, either in parking lots or offered for sale. Although the facades of the prewar buildings had been stripped of decoration, there were occasional architectural hints of earlier Berlins, Venetian windows looking down over a paved-over canal. Pre- and postwar buildings alike were mottled, gray, and weather-stained, their drabness mitigated somewhat by the overarching big blue sky. Though granulated, it lent a welcome lightness to the Berlin cityscape I passed through on my way to the archives. Hung beneath a yellow-brick bridge displaying a white "S" on a green circle, a metal sign marked the border to Wittenau, the rechristened Dalldorf. Once in Wittenau, the apartment buildings fell away, and just ahead, I could make out the tall redbrick towers flanking the massive hall of the neo-Gothic *Kugelagerfabrik*, wondering if the bombs that apparently demolished the buildings on the far side of the bridge had been intended for this side. Across the street, an ornamental iron gate heralded the entrance to the *Stadtstaatsarchiv Berlin*. I carefully crossed over the broad *Eichborndamm*, walking through the open gate to the entrance doors on the left. Although there were no statues to admonish employees and researchers as at Main Archives in Washington, DC, carved in *Fraktur* on the lintel, running the entire length of the double doorway, was a foretaste of the immortality within, "*Nichts ist unsterblicher als ein Archiv.*"[5]

Just inside the large doors in the vestibule stood a small windowed office, where a gray-uniformed *Pfortner* patiently awaited visitors. "*Guten Morgen! Vonaechron meiner Name.*" I said, attempting to sound as professional as possible. "*Ah, unser Ami, Herr Dr.* von Garlitz ist expecting you," he said in English, smiling while reaching for the phone. George came to meet me, and as we walked together through the brightly lit hallways, he introduced me to his colleagues. Unlike the torpedo factory, which had retained its wartime battleship gray interior, the refitted munitions factory reflected its new function. Unlike the subterranean Washington National Records Center, records were stored in vaults in the center of the building, aboveground, accessible to the authorized from bright white corridors running along the outer perimeter. The ground floor housed the central reading room as well as offices for archivists and technicians. A corridor running along the back of the building led to laboratories for the restoration of documents, pictures, and films. As I had learned at the National Archives, immortality has its price. Archival sources, the essence of history, were constantly threatened by inherent and external vice. One of George's colleagues recently left the *Stadtstaatsarchiv* to take a position with the *Generaldirektion* of the *Bayrisches Hauptstaatsarchiv* in Munich, allowing George to temporarily assign me his former office, a bright, high-ceilinged room on the first floor. In the center stood a large blonde wooden worktable and chair. There was also a metal cabinet for filing microfiche and, much to my delight, a large window looking out onto the grounds bordered by the redbrick wall and the *Eichborndamm* beyond, a welcome change from Vault Six in Suitland. It was no ordinary window, but a large Palladian window. A research room with a view. George smiled and said, "After working underground, I thought you might like *mehr Licht*. My colleague Reinhard took all his pictures to Munich, leaving you with white walls but," looking at the

---

5 "Nothing is more immortal than an archives."—Günter Grass, Diary of Thomas Vonaechron, Diary Extract, 1982, trans. TV.

package under my arm, "I see you might have brought a picture along with you. That's odd, I don't remember seeing it yesterday at Tempelhof. How did you manage to fit a picture into your backpack?"

"I didn't!" Laying the package and my shoulder bag gently down on the wooden worktable, I recounted my morning encounter in the *Niedstraße*.

Smiling thoughtfully, George said, "Well, perhaps we should unwrap it. Although Anna didn't want it, you could certainly use it to decorate your new office." After untying the string, I carefully removed the heavy brown wrapping paper. It was indeed a print, a black-and-white etching of a fish, a *Bothidae* flounder, and a human ear. The flounder's open mouth was uncomfortably close to the severed ear, crowned by a small tuft of unruly dark hair, with a fishy facial expression implying it was about to impart some fearful secret.

"Where did you meet the giver of this unusual, unwanted gift again— did you say *Niedstraße*?" asked George, scanning the print for a signature. Although my predecessor Reinhard had removed his pictures, he'd thoughtfully left the picture hangers on the wall. I picked up the etching and hung it on the wall to the left of the worktable. Instead of reminding Anna of an artist rebutted, the fish reminded me of Lorelei Rhine's admonition, the negative "constellations of power" found in combinations of the six letters B-E-R-L-I-N. What were her words of warning? "Personal strength and discipline would be required to keep those discordant forces in check. Failure to do so might prove destructive"? Was that what the flounder was whispering?

"Yes, the *Niedstraße* just down from *Rathaus Friedenau*. Perhaps it was intended for me, not Anna, after all," I replied. "It just might have been," nodded George, smiling thoughtfully in agreement, "and it certainly belongs right where you hung it!"

My job at the *Stadtstaatsarchiv* was to arrange microfiche copies of documents created by the Office of the Military Government Berlin Sector (OMGBS) between 1945 and 1949. Back in the research room at the Washington National Records Center, George had carefully reviewed, selected, and tabbed the historically significant documents he wanted copied from the declassified files. They were then sent to the photographic lab for filming, and now packages of microfiche mailed from Suitland had begun to arrive in West Berlin, retracing in reverse the route across the Atlantic taken by the original documents decades before. Duplicate copies had to be separated from the originals and filed. The remaining fiche had to be arranged and described in a subject index for use by researchers at the *Stadtstaatsarchiv*, a *Findmittel*—a "finding aid." At the Washington National Records Center, I had spent much of my time reviewing captured

German documents underground. In the *Stadtstaatsarchiv*, I would spend my time aboveground reviewing photographic images of American documents. There was a kind of archival continuity in both subject matter and procedure, reinforced by the architectural continuity between the Federal Records Center and the *Stadtstaatsarchiv*.

Several weeks later, after hanging out my fish and beginning to arrange the fiche, I arrived to find the door to my office closed. I opened it to discover an elderly gentleman, elegantly dressed in a conservative brown suit and tie, examining large architectural blueprints carefully laid out upon my wooden worktable while speaking slowly and deliberately into a handheld dictation machine. I could read the model name—"Portable Dictator." He looked up at me unsmilingly while speaking, fixed me in his dark eyes for a moment, and, arching his eyebrows, returned to the blueprints. His face, his eyes, were familiar. Not unlike the dark eyes of the fellow traveler with the stuffed white rabbit in the Frankfurt waiting lounge, but without the depth, compassion, and sorrow. I glanced at the flounder on the wall, and though obviously alarmed, the fish had nothing more to confide. George did, however, smiling knowingly behind his desk when I entered his office, waiting for me to arrive. "We have a visitor this morning," he said, "I'm very sorry that I couldn't tell you in advance, but the director didn't want his presence to disturb the other researchers. "*Herr 'R-r-reichsminister,'*" George rolled "*Reich*" with *Casablanca*-like artificial American articulation, "Albert Speer has consented to review and comment on his plans for Berlin, or should I say for *Germania*, for the historical record."

"Albert Speer," I echoed in amazement, belatedly recognizing the somebody sitting in my chair, "of course." Dark eyes that shared an architectural vision for Berlin IV with Adolf Hitler looking up at me. "Is he going to stop by Spandau Prison for old times' sake when he's finished, George?"

George laughed, "Who knows? When he's finished, and for the sake of the historical record, I think we should indeed wait until he's finished, we just might ask him. I do believe former Prisoner Number Five has, however, exhausted his interest in that particular example of redbrick neo-Gothic; after all, he did have twenty years to study it. You might not know the prison was originally built in 1876 as a military prison, one of those *eirönïa* we are privileged to as historians. The subject of today's dictation is, however, not the neo-Gothic, but rather the neoclassical. This is the kind of architecture he is, or should I say he was, very interested in. He discusses it at some length in his book *Erinnerungen*, which was published in 1969. Here's a copy from our library." After handing me the book, George continued, "You and I have often talked about *Ruinen betrachten*—'contemplation of the ruins.' With this very concept in mind, Albert Speer developed a theory of intentional 'ruin value' as an element of construction. As an *Archivar und Archeologe-im-werden*, I think that you might find his theory—how did your Wolfgang say it?—'ver-r-ry inter-r-r-resting.'"

During one of our Mr. Henry's symposia, George and I had discussed German and American stereotypes. He particularly enjoyed my impression of Arte Johnson's *Laugh-In* impersonation of Wolfgang the helmeted German soldier observing from behind the bushes. "Ver-r-ry inter-r-resting," pronounced with an over-articulated American-German accent, became one of our Berlin bywords.

"Anticipating the eventual demise of the 'Thousand Year Reich,' Hitler directed Speer to develop construction techniques for modern buildings that, once they were in ruins, would continue to stand as a 'bridge of tradition' to the future, just as the ruins of ancient Rome inspire us to this very day. To the best of my knowledge, Hitler never discussed the end of the Reich with anyone but Speer. Among members of the National Socialist elite, it would have been considered heresy. In his *Erinnerungen*, Speer explains how he, at Hitler's request, developed his concrete concept of 'ruin value' by combining material with principles of statics to insure the ruins of the Third Reich would stand in the future as monuments to its past greatness. I don't have any declassification tabs here at the archives, so I marked the pages in Speer's book for you with a paperclip." Ruins as a present form of the past was one of the subjects Neal and I touched upon during our drunken, predeparture seminar at The Republic in Alexandria. The concept of a built-in ruin value, replacing chance with intent, offers a different perspective on the classic "contemplation of the ruins." Neal, the ex-poet of Exeter. I hadn't heard from him since my departure and often wondered if he'd returned to The Republic and Bendis after dropping me off at the airport.

"Adolf Hitler considered himself to be an artist, an architect. He set down his architectural aspirations in *Mein Kampf*: '*Ich hoffte, dereinst als Baumeister mir einen Namen zu machen und so, in kleinem oder großem Rahmen, den mir das Schicksal dann eben schon zuweisen würde, der Nation meinen redlichen Dienst zu weihen.*' Let me try to translate that for you, Thomas: 'I hoped to make a name for myself as an architect someday, and thereby, in the small or large space assigned to me by destiny, dedicate my honest service to the nation.' Tragically, Hitler's architectural medium turned out to be Europe itself, not only mortar and stone but flesh and blood." George's words brought to mind the airborne *City of Berlin* seminar with Govinda on nation building back in August. Seven weeks had passed, and I still hadn't contacted Professor Schneider. Again, I reminded myself to do so. "Adolf Hitler defined architecture as '*steingewordene*

Weltanschauung', a 'world-view turned to stone,' a means of acquiring and maintaining political power. Architecture as political statement. Remember our walks along Constitution Avenue down from Capitol Hill?"

Albert Speer's theory of ruin value was the invitation to begin my on-site excavation in Berlin IV. As my office was now occupied by its proponent, I decided to leave the *Stadtstaatsarchiv* for the ruins of the *Reichshauptstadt*. In addition to *Erinnerungen*, there was another guidebook available. Cornelius Ryan's chronicle of the battle of Berlin had maps of the city in 1945 reprinted on the flyleaves, pinpointing the loci of power inside the Third Reich. "Do you also have a copy of *The Last Battle* in your library?" I asked.

"*Aber natürlich*," answered George. "We like to believe we have a copy of every book ever written on Berlin, as well as the *Quellen*—the sources— for all those yet to be written. By the way, we do expect two complementary copies of your book, when it's finished of course! Wait here, I'll be right back." I read the passage George had tabbed for me, deciding to enter the HistoriCity aboveground where I'd left off underground at the Washington National Records Center, at the *Reichshauptstadt*. Sampling Schliemann on his home turf, I would be able to fix Berlin IV at the moment of its destruction, deconstruction, and division in 1945, then move forward to Berlin V and VI or backward to Berlin III, II, or I, as my on-site explorations progressed.

George returned with two books in hand, the requested hardback copy of Ryan's *The Last Battle* and another hardback, *Von Berlin Nach Germania: Über die Zerstörung der "Reichshauptstadt" durch Albert Speers Neugestaltungsplannung*. "I thought you might be interested in this book as well." he said. "It was prepared by my *Chef*, the director of the *Stadtstaatsarchiv* from the very plans *Herr* Speer is commenting upon today."

The book was bound in bright red, with white lettering on the front cover. An aerial reconnaissance photograph of Berlin in ruins taken by a US Strategic Bombing Survey mission was superimposed over a black-and-white drawing of Hitler's "Great Hall," Berlin IV in *Theorie und Praxis*. Taking both books from George, I recognized the black-and-white photograph of Soviet war poet Jevgeny Dolmatsky speaking to victorious Red Army soldiers in front of the Brandenburg Gate on the dust cover of *The Last Battle* and opened the book. The maps were printed on the flyleaves. Although the antebellum *vallum* had not been superimposed over the wartime map of "the Center," I could see most of the government buildings identified were now in East Berlin (Berlin V).

Reaching for my shoulder bag, I took out the *Falkplan* and, spreading it out upon George's desk, began to transfer locations from *The Last Battle* maps to coordinates on the folding map with my black *Skillcraft*, US government-issue, retractable ball point pen, a souvenir from Vault Six. "Do you know which of these buildings are Speer's, George?"

Smiling, shaking his head, George sat down on the edge of the table. "This is exactly why I thought the *Germania* book might help you, Thomas. Fortunately for Berlin, Albert Speer was not able to realize his plans. Adolf Hitler designated him as the architect responsible for the redesign of Berlin in 1936, presenting him with two sketches he, Hitler, had drawn a decade before. An organization was created under Albert Speer in 1937 to execute Adolf Hitler's plans. As the designated *Generalbauinspektor für die Reichshauptstadt*, or *GBI*, he was given almost unlimited administrative power, to the point of removing the mayor of Berlin, who mistakenly believed he had a voice in city planning. The two sketches given to Albert Speer by Adolf Hitler were of an immense domed—perhaps doomed would be the better word—hall—*die Große Halle*, the Great Hall, and a triumphal arch, which incidentally would have been over twice the size of the *Arc de Triomphe*. Ah, the French influence once again! We have the original model of the Great Hall here in the *Stadtstaatsarchiv*. The hall and the arch, the original two points of reference from which the *GBI* started, were integrated into two axes—one running north-south and the other east-west, crisscrossing the entire city. Berlin would then be enclosed by a 'beltway,' not unlike the one around Washington! A series of concentric circles inside the beltway were to be joined by roads radiating from the city center with the road network complemented by a rail network. The intersection of the axes near the *Brandenburger Tor* was to have been the *Schwerpunkt*—how do you say it? The center of gravity for the *Neugestaltung* . . . for the redesign of Berlin. Upon completion of the hall and arch, projected for 1950, Berlin was to be renamed *Germania*."

"The realization of *Germania* would have been the destruction of Berlin."

"In reality," answered George, "it amounted to the same thing. Although only a few of the construction projects were actually undertaken, much of the required demolition was completed. When deliberate deconstruction, preserving the original material for reuse, proved to be both costly and time-consuming, the *GBI* directed the use of explosives. Once the war started and the Allied Strategic Air Campaign began to inflict heavy damage upon Berlin, Speer initially welcomed the destruction as an expedient!

"His first project was the renovation of the *Reichskanzlei*, the chancellery. Another, which was not completed, was construction of the *Haus des Fremdenverkehrs*, the 'House of Tourism.' Both buildings, located in Ost Berlin and West Berlin, respectively, were deliberately deconstructed following the Second World War. By the way, I recommend you visit the site of the *Haus des Fremdenverkehrs*, here," pinpointing the location on the plan with his finger, "at the intersection of *Potsdamer Straße* and *Reichpietschufer*. There's a postwar architectural surprise waiting for you there." Circling the point on the map, I noted the coordinates (O9). "To the best of my knowledge, all that remains of Albert Speer's work is the *Ost-West Achse* and Embassy Row in the Tiergarten. Construction on the western section of the east-west axis began in 1937. Running west through the Tiergarten from the Brandenburg Gate, the *Charlottenburger Chausse* connected the *Großer Stern* with *Adolf-Hitler-Platz*, formerly *Reichskanzlerplatz* and now *Theodor-Heuss-Platz*. The streetlamps designed by Albert Speer to provide an unobstructed view of the east-west axis still illuminate the *Straße des 17. Juni, Bismarckstraße*, and *Kaiserdamm* between the *Großer Stern* and *Theodor-Heuss-Platz*. The *Siegesaüle*, the 'Victory Column' referred to by your countrymen as 'the Chick-on-the-Stick,' and the statues of Bismarck, Roon, and Moltke now on the *Großer Stern*, originally stood on *Königsplatz* in front of the *Reichstag*. The *GBI* had them moved in preparation for the construction of the Great Hall. Hitler ordered the *Siegesaüle* increased in height. Speer redesigned and increased the size of the foundation.

"You might also look for the ruins of *Germania* in the *Tiergarten Viertel*. Although neither the Italian nor Japanese Embassies were designed by the *GBI*, he ordered the enlargement of the Tiergarten to place the embassies of Germany's wartime allies on a kind of local Rome-Berlin-Tokyo axis. As the buildings incorporate many of the same principles and are, particularly in ruins, quite '*Speer-lich*,' you might be able to test the validity of his hypothesis. The former *GBI* will no doubt have need of your office for the rest of the day, so why don't you begin your on-site examination this morning? Should he still be here when you return tomorrow, you'll be able to compare notes and, when he has finished, perhaps ask him about a *Betriebsausflug* to Spandau.

"You might begin with the east-west Axis. Instead of taking the *U-Bahn*, take the *S-Bahn* from the *S-Bahnhof Eichborndamm* to the *Tiergarten S-Bahnhof*. The *S-Bahn, Stadtbahn*, was designed to cover larger distances in shorter periods of time than the *U-bahn*, streetcars, or buses. The *S-Bahn* will take you to Tiergarten more quickly and even allow you to pass underneath East Berlin!" Once again, George mapped out the route on my *Falkplan* with his index finger. There was no direct connection between Berlin VI and Berlin IV. In order to get to *S-Bahnhof Tiergartern*, just north of Speer's east-west axis at coordinates M10, I would have to change trains at *S-Bahnhof Friedrichstraße* in *Ostberlin*, Berlin V (coordinates P10). The *S-Bahn* linking Berlin V with Berlin VI, East Berlin with West Berlin, belongs to the *Deutsche Reichsbahn*, which in turn belongs to the German Democratic Republic. As a consequence of Clio's handwork, I would be able to ride with her on the *S-Bahn* through history, from Berlin VI back through Berlin V to what remained of Berlin IV.

"When you leave the *Stadtstaatsarchiv*, Thomas, turn right on *Eichborndamm* and follow it to *S-Bahnhof Eichborndamm*." Take the train heading east toward Schönholz. The station after Schönholz, *S-Bahnhof Wolankstraße* is actually located in Pankow, a *Bezirk* of East Berlin," noticing my expression, which much have resembled the flounder's, he continued, "please don't be concerned, Thomas. The station is part of the West Berliner *S-Bahn* network, and all passengers are able to pass through without control." Anticipating my question, he added: "All exits from the *S-Bahnhof* into East Berlin have been bricked-up." I carefully folded the map and put it, along with the two library books, in my shoulder bag. Leaving Albert Speer's *Memories* on George's desk, and Albert Speer at my worktable recording his commentary on *Germania* into the *Portable Dictator* under the watchful eyes of the flounder, I set out from Berlin VI, the occupied city, the City of the Armed Camp, for the ruins of the *Reichshauptstadt*, Berlin IV.

West Berlin (Berlin IV)
October 1982

Waving to the friendly *Pförtner*, exiting the *Stadtstaatsarchiv* through the iron gate, I turned in the direction of *S-Bahnhof Eichbornstraße*. The neo-Gothic buildings of the former *Kugelagerfabrik* were indeed impressive. Unlike the buildings formerly lining the lower end of Eichborndamm, the red brick complex housing the munitions factory survived the Allied strategic bombing campaign apparently unscathed, like the church *Zum Guten Hirten* on *Freidrich-Wilhelm-Platz*. Ahead, a white "S" on an electrified green background heralded the above ground entrance to the *S-Bahnhof Eichbornstraße*. Inside the arched entrance of yellow brick, a staircase led up to a platform surrounded by trees and bushes. The wooden trestlework supporting the roof had been painted green, the yellow brick stationmaster's office decorated to resemble a small cottage in the forest. I checked the overhead signs for trains heading east, in the direction of Schönholz. Aboveground, I could see the two-tone ochre and red color train arriving before I heard it. After coming to a halt, the pressure was released from the air brakes in a mechanical sigh of relief. Opening the door, I found my coach completely empty. Seating was similar to the *U-Bahn*, though the windows were larger, allowing for *mehr Licht*. The seats were made of light wood, varnished slats screwed to a bent metal frame—not unlike a park bench—with burnished aluminum hand railings on the backs. A claxon horn heralded the closing of the doors, and after departing the station, the train sped through a green tunnel of trees and bushes that had overgrown the edge of the roadbed on both sides of the tracks. As the train gained speed, the pleasant sensation of traveling through a forest was periodically interrupted by brief vignettes of cars and pedestrians on the streets below. With the rhythm of acceleration and deceleration now punctuated by the air brakes, the *S-Bahn* passed thorough stations built during Berlin II: Wittenau, with the *Karl-Bonhoeffer-Nervenklinik*—successor to the *Städtische Irrenanstalt zu Dalldorf*, Alt-Reinickendorf, and Schönholz. At Schönholz, metal trestles replaced the wooden trestlework. An old engine house covered in illegible graffiti stood off to the side in the brush. The train approached the Wall separating Berlin VI from Berlin V and, turning south, passed through the *S-Bahn* station at *Wollankstraße* (Berlin V), set in the midst of an ensemble of prewar apartment buildings, and then turned west at Gesundbrunnen (Berlin VI). Tracing the tracks with my index finger on the *Falkplan*, I noted they bordered along Humboldthain Park (coordinates P13). Humboldthain! In Vault Six, I had reviewed a series of intelligence summaries (ISUMs) prepared by the US Strategic and Tactical Air Forces in Europe in 1944. At Adolf Hitler's request, six massive concrete antiaircraft bunkers were designed and constructed by the *GBI*. One of the bunkers was located at Humboldthain. I quickly unzipped my shoulder bag and pulled out Cornelius Ryan's book, scanning the index for Humboldthain, I looked up as the train emerged from a tunnel, catching a glimpse of the two remaining concrete flak towers just before the train entered the *S-Bahnhof Humboldthain*. After the war, French occupation authorities demolished the southern half of the bunker, covered it with debris and earth, and incorporated it into the adjacent Humboldthain Park begun during Berlin I and completed in Berlin II. Due to its close proximity to the rail lines, the northern half of the bunker and the two towers were left standing. Like the famous hill at Hiscirlik, another place of the fortresses and site of Heinrich Schliemann's amateur adventures in archaeology, Humboldthain exposed the layers of Berlin I through VI. At least in its operational wartime variant, Albert Speer's theory of ruin value had stood the coincident tests of time and strategic bombing. In the course of this extraordinary morning, I had seen and been seen by the architect, and seen his architecture. A "bridge of tradition" to the future was standing in the present, spanning the chasm of continuity to the past.

Departing *Humboldthain* station, the *S-Bahn* passed by a cemetery on the left and a rusting railroad bridge on the right. Then, temporarily metamorphosing into a *U-Bahn,* it continued on under the Wall from Berlin VI back to Berlin V. The train slowed but did not halt, passing through the "ghost stations," *Geisterbahnhöfe,* along the line leading to *S-Bahnhof Friedrichstraße.* Through the large windows, I could see armed guards partially hidden in the shadows of the dimly lit, yellow and red-tiled station platform. On a sign near an empty staircase, I could make out "*Nordbahnhof*" in *Fraktur.* As we passed through *Oranienburgerstraße,* the red and orange-tiled stationmaster's office was visible in the yellow light. Although I didn't see any guards, I knew they were there. These trains were closely watched. These eerie apparitions heightened my growing sense of uneasiness as the train approached the *Friedrichstraße* station. Although the *S-Bahnhof Friedrichstraße* was located in Berlin V, passengers coming from and changing trains for travel back to Berlin VI were not controlled. Recalling the Daedalic labyrinth of laminated passageways and shuttered windows from my first visit to East Berlin, I carefully followed the "In-Transit" signs leading to the platform for trains in the direction of Wannsee, taking me to the *S-Bahnhof Tiergarten* and Albert Speer's east-west axis. Several of us waited in uneasy silence on the platform. I was much relieved to hear the familiar sound of the train approaching. From the darkness of *Ost-Berlin,* the train emerged into Berlin West and the light of day at the *Lehrter Stadtbahnhof.* Although I had had no reason to be concerned, the uneasiness experienced being "over there" faded, and I joined the *S-Bahn* brakes in a mechanical sigh of relief. With the familiar rhythm of acceleration and deceleration punctuated by the brakes restored, we continued on through the aboveground yellow brick, barrel-vaulted station at Bellevue to *S-Bahnhof Tiergarten.*

As the train slowed and pulled into the station, I could see the broad *Straße des 17. Juni,* the western section of Albert Speer's *Ost-West-Achse,* extending in both directions directly beneath the platform. It was longer, broader, and even more sylvan than Pennsylvania Avenue in Washington, DC. Clio had played her part in the naming conventions as well as in the de- and reconstruction of the HistoriCity. Following the war, Albert Speer's *Achse* once again became *Charlottenbuger Chausee.* Following Soviet suppression of the 1953 workers' uprising in the German Democratic Republic, it was rechristened *Straße des 17. Juni.* To the east, it crossed over the *Grosser Stern* and the *Siegesäule,* continuing on through the Tiergarten to the *Brandenburger Tor,* ending abruptly at the Wall. On the far side, in Berlin V at *Pariser Platz,* it metamorphosed into the legendary, literary *Unter den Linden,* continuing through *Mitte,* the historic heart of Berlins I through V. Running west, in the opposite direction, it connected Berlin VI with Berlin II, becoming *Bismarkstraße, Kaiserdamm,* and finally, *Heerstraße*, continuing west to Spandau and the military prison on *Wilhelmstraße*, where Albert Speer's planning had taken him. Of the original seven prisoners sentenced by the Nuremberg International Miltary Tribunal to imprisonment in Spandau Allied Prison, only Rudolf Hess remained incarcerated.

The imposing black, cast-iron streetlights designed by Albert Speer to illuminate the *Achse* running along both sides of the broad avenue in both directions were clearly visible from the *S-Bahnhof Tiergarten* platform. Each stanchion held two lanterns, upright so as not to obstruct the view, dramatic even in defeat. With the coming of autumn, the *Berliner Luft* had become increasingly grainy, giving an indefinite quality to the vanishing points east and west. In spite of the naming and renaming, the *Achse* remained a bridge of tradition to both present and past, connecting Berlin VI not only with Berlin IV, but also with Berlins V, III and II, if only in name. Looking to the west, I could see the monumental columns of the Neo-Baroque *Charlottenburger Tor*, counterpoint to the *Brandenburger Tor*, marking the *Charlottenburger Brücke* over the *Landwehrkanal*. Intending to walk along the *Achse* east to the Wall, I noticed a vast flea market of hundreds of wood-and-canvas booths, similar to those at the foot of the tower of *Rathaus* Friedenau, running parallel to the *Straße des 17. Juni* between the *S-Bahn* station and the gate. Deciding to put the *GBI* and the ruins of Berlin IV on hold for a while, I decided to Go West, walking down the stairs to take a closer look.

At the bottom of the staircase, after waiting for the light to change, I crossed over *Stygian Straße* and entered the flea market. Although midmorning, it was as lively as the market in Friedenau. Strolling slowly down the center path between the booths, I was surprised to find artifacts from Berlin II through Berlin VI offered for sale. Among the mismatched plates, silverware, dolls, a model of *Junkers Ju-52 "Immelmann II"* missing the rudder, pictures, pitchers, and other lost-and-found objects, there was an accidental still life with *Zylinder* and *Stahlhelm*. Next to the top hat and helmet, a folding metal magazine rack displayed colored engravings of Adolf Hitler. Further along the path, in front of a stand displaying canceled postage stamps from the *Kaiserreich,* Weimar Republic, *Drittes Reich,* and the ongoing Occupation, there was a wooden wine barrel brimming over with the astronomically inflated, worthless currency of the Weimar Republic. The brightly colored bills with denominations running into the millions of *Reichsmark* were decorated with engravings of maps and major architectural monuments of Berlin III. At the deflated price of ten *Pfennig* a piece, I bought as many different *Scheine* as I could find, planning, with George's expert assistance, to note their coordinates on the *Falkplan* when

I began to work backward from Berlin IV to Berlin III. Another stand, set somewhat off the beaten the path, displayed European and American military regalia and helmets, covering and coloring the history of Berlin with military flags and guidons. Among the pile of *Pickelhauben* and *Stahlhelme*, those of WWII vintage with swastikas carefully covered to reveal what was underneath, I was very surprised to see a mint condition Russian *Ssh 68* helmet with "*ВЕРДИН VII*" stenciled in white letters on flat green. An authority on Russian helmets once told me the *Ssh 68* was unavailable outside of the Warsaw Pact countries. Registering my interest, the vendor stood up from her folding chair and walked over, momentarily blocking my view, and politely asked me if she could be of assistance. She was a lithe young woman with short dark hair, bright eyes, and smooth, tanned skin. She could have been Bendis from The Republic in Alexandria. She wore a single golden earring and spoke German with a light Southern European accent. When I inquired about the *Ssh 68*, she looked at me with a sympathetic smile and said apologetically, "*Es tut mir leid. Zur Zeit führen wir keine russische Waren.*" When I politely insisted I had indeed seen a Russian helmet, she stepped aside so I could show her, but the *Ssh 68* with "*ВЕРДИН VII*" stenciled on the side was no longer there. Smiling sympathetically, she suggested, "*Kommen Sie später wieder, vielleicht in sieben Jahren oder so, dann bekommen Sie ganz bestimmt den Helm, den Sie brauchen werden!*"[6]

Embarrassed, confused, and somewhat disoriented by our exchange, I apologized, thanked her, and retraced my steps back through the flea market. Passing beneath the *S-Bahnhof Tiergarten*, I walked east on the *Ost-West-Achse,* bordered on both sides by trees of the Tiergarten, edged in the bright, dry colors of October. Directly ahead, rising majestically over the *Großer Stern* was the *Siegessäule* (coordinates 10N). During my first stay in Berlin, I had climbed it to take in the panoramic, unifying view of the city from the top of the Victory Column. In Washington, George later provided me with essential elements of information (EEI) on the *Siegessäule* as we walked passed the Washington Monument on our way down the Mall to the Tidal Basin.

A monument to both the militant birth of Berlin II and the architectural ambitions of Berlin IV now standing in Berlin VI, the Victory Column was originally commissioned to commemorate the 1864 victory of Prussia over Denmark. By the time it was completed in 1873, Prussia had also defeated Austria and, with the assistance of other German states, France, unifying

---

6 "I'm so sorry, at present we don't have any Russian goods. . . . Come back again later, perhaps in seven years or so, then you will certainly find the helmet you will need." Diary of Thomas Vonaechron, Diary Extract, 1982, trans. TV.

Germany under an imperial capital, Berlin II. A bronze statue of Victoria was set atop the sandstone column to commemorate all three "Wars of German Unification." Known among Berliner as *Goldelse*, the "Golden Girl," Russian troops entering Berlin in May 1945 rechristened her the "Tall Woman." Two months later, American occupation forces, in the postwar parlance George had picked up on, tagged her "the-Chick-on-a-Stick."

A relief running around the base and the captured cannon adorning the column itself commemorated the three Wars of German Unification. Clio, out on the firing line with Prussian Chief of Staff Helmuth Karl Bernhard Count von Moltke when his fifty-ton Krupp steel siege guns forced Paris to her knees in January 1871, returned with French occupation forces to Berlin in 1945 to observe as the relief was dismantled and shipped back to Paris. In 1987, Clio again accompanied the relief as it traveled back from Paris to Berlin, watching while it was remounted in celebration of the 750th birthday of the HistoriCity. The base, designed by Albert Speer at Adolf Hitler's request, still held both the stick and the chick firmly in place.

I reached the *Großer Stern*, an intersection of five broad avenues clearly intended by Albert Speer to be a major traffic hub on the *Ost-West-Achse*. The members of the French work detail dismantling the relief at the base of the column in 1945 must have been reminded of the *Place de l'Étoile*, another star in the center of another city, but George-Eugène Hausmann's, not Albert Speer's. The latter's monumental infrastructure easily swallowed the modest numbers of cars, military vehicles, and buses circling the *Großer Stern,* halting occasionally to discharge or pick up passengers.

Walking around the *Großer Stern* to the north, I happened across the monumental marble statue of Count von Moltke, together with the no-less monumental weathered bronze statue of Albrecht Theodor Emil Count von Roon. When I first saw them nine years ago from under the glass of a tour bus circling *Goldelse,* the "Golden Girl," I had taken them for granite. The former seemed at ease, leaning against a podium with his military missions accomplished, while the Prussian Minister of War seemed more martial in his uniform, with *Pickelhaube* in hand, than his famous field marshal. In an act of premeditated revisionism, a later-day activist, armed with a can of red spray paint, had sprayed *"Blutsau," "Blood Sow,"* at close range beneath the engraved "ROON," the dried droplets running like frozen blood down the marble pedestal. Almost hidden in the trees of the Tiergarten, guarded by his marble marshal and bleeding bronze minister, stood the *Schwerpunkt,* Otto Eduard Leopold, Prince of Bismarck, Duke of Lauenburg. Several smaller bronzes gathered at his feet. On the left was a seated woman, possibly the Prussian cousin of Clio guarding the Pennsylvania Avenue entrance to the National Archives in Washington.

She was hooded and, although apparently studying the book opened upon her lap, had neither admonition nor quotation to offer me. Rather than sitting in a neoclassical chair, she was draped over an Egyptian sphinx. She appeared unimpressed, either by Atlas struggling at Bismarck's feet to keep the heavens balanced upon his shoulders or Germania triumphant, with her outstretched, oversized sandal firmly planted on the lion's neck. Along with the *Siegesäule*, these three architects of Imperial Germany, and indirectly of Berlin II, together with their attendants, had been banished from their place of honor on *Königsplatz* in front of the Reichstag to make room for the *Ost-West-Achse* by the later-day architects of Berlin IV.

Safely past this Prussian Cerberus without throwing a sop, I continued east on the *Ost-West-Acshe*. Once I'd left the *Großer Stern* and the *Siegessäule* behind, pedestrians and automobiles seemed to vanish from the *Straße des 17. Juni*. This last segment of Albert Speer's *Achse* was as empty as Pennsylvania Avenue in the evening. Darkness was descending upon the Tiergarten as I made my way toward the Brandenburg Gate, heightening the indefinite quality of the autumn air, melancholy, impressionistic. Albert Speer's streetlights had been replaced by the tall, slender, metal streetlights of West Berlin, forming a florescent "V" leading to the illuminated *Brandenburger Tor*. Shortly after crossing *Moltkestraße*, I noticed the barrel, boogie wheels, treads, and turret of a Russian *T-34* tank protruding from the foliage on my left. As I walked toward the gate, the panorama opened to reveal the Soviet War Memorial flanked by two *T-34s* with two *ML-20 152*mm gun-howitzers in support. A monumental Red Army soldier, wearing a helmet, predecessor to the one I thought I'd seen earlier at the Tiergarten Flea Market, bayonet fixed on the rifle slung over his right shoulder, extended his left arm in a Soviet *saluto romano*. Impressed by the monument, purportedly built with red marble and granite taken from the ruins of Albert Speer's *Reichskanzlei*, I was also relieved to see the Soviet honor guard. I wasn't alone in the Tiergarten after all. The memorial was the grave of approximately 2,200 Red Army soldiers killed during the last battle for the nearby Reichstag. From my reading of the annual "Unit History of the United States Military Liaison Mission to Commander in Chief, Group of Soviet Forces in Germany" back in Vault Six, I knew the Soviet War Memorial, the Spandau Allied Prison—former residence of Albert Speer—and the Berlin Air Safety Center (BASC)—colocated with the Allied Control Council at Kleist Park—were the last three remaining outposts of the Red Army in the Western sectors of the city it had taken at such great cost in blood and treasure in the spring of 1945. Of the three, "BASC" was unique. In the operations center, American, British, French and Soviet military personnel had worked together daily since 1945, monitoring the three designated twenty-mile-wide air corridors to West Berlin and the twenty-mile-radius air traffic control zone over East and West Berlin, clearing individual flights to and from the city.

As part of the study trip to Berlin, we had taken a bus trip out to Potsdam to see the Hohenzollern palaces of *Sans,Souci.* and *Cecilienhof,* the former the refuge of Frederick the Great, the latter site of the 1945 Potsdam Conference. In accordance with Frederick's wishes, *Sans,Souci.* had been constructed atop a terraced vineyard, a *Weinberg.* On a terrace leading down from the palace, we met a group of Soviet soldiers, also touring the grounds. Soon we were walking together, and although we had no common language, we were able to communicate through facial and hand gestures. One of the soldiers politely indicated he would like to have his picture taken with one of the young women in our group. She agreed, and as I took the picture with his camera, after first putting his hand lightly on her shoulder, he dropped his arm and came to attention. The approximately forty soldiers, the same size as our group, followed us back to our bus, waiting as we boarded, then waved as we departed for the long road trip from Potsdam around East Berlin to back West Berlin. Sitting in the back of the bus, I flashed the then-popular peace sign through the rear window. The soldier who'd asked for the photograph stopped waving, took a step forward, and after looking cautiously to the right and then to the left, flashed the peace sign in return. The other soldiers joined him as they all disappeared in the dust kicked up by our bus leaving the parking lot. After my day in Potsdam, I understood the soldiers were much like we were, and realized it would be very difficult for me to ever lift a weapon against a soldier of the Red Army.

Recalling my discussion with George at the *Stadtstaatsarchiv* that morning, it occurred to me the Soviet War Memorial marked and coincidentally blocked the proposed intersection of the *Ost-West* and the *Nord-Süd-Achsen.* I checked the coordinates on the *Falkplan,* 10P, under the streetlight. From my standpoint within West Berlin, within the HistoriCity, this seemed historically appropriate. Now quite close to the *Brandenburger Tor,* I decided to have a closer look before continuing on to the *Reichstag* and the former *Königsplatz,* where Motlke, Roon, and Bismarck had held court under Victoria until 1939.

Approaching the *Brandenburger Tor,* glowing pale green in the growing darkness, I could see more statues spaced at intervals along the edges of the Tiergarten, lining both sides of *Straße des 17. Juni.* Statuesque but not statues. Hearing my footsteps, those closest to me gracefully turned their heads. The soldiers of the Red Army Honor Guard were not the only ones keeping watch in the darkness. They were beautiful young women, uniformly dressed in short white leather coats, white stockings, and calf-length white leather boots, priestesses at the columns of the *Brandenburger Tor* instead of the columns of the *Aedes Vestae* in Rome. One of the votaries approached and, after politely wishing me "*Guten Abend*," whispered, "*Es wird kälter. Bei mir zu Hause ist es schön warm. Ich könnte es für uns beide sehr gemütlich machen. Möchtest Du nicht mitkommen?*"[7] She spoke slowly and warmly, with sensuality radiating from each of her words.

"*Nein, aber vielen Dank*," I whispered in reply, already under her influence.

"*Schade*," she said, softly drawing-out the "*sch*." Looking into my eyes and smiling, she returned to her pedestal at the edge of the park, just across the *Straße des 17. Juni* from the Basin of Venus.

I walked up to the Wall running round the *Brandenburger Tor*, running my right hand over the rough, cold, concrete surface, then stepped back and to look up at the Brandenburg Gate. Modeled upon the Propylaea entrance to the Athenian Acropolis, the neoclassical gate was originally constructed as the "Gate of Peace," the *Friedenstor*, designating the customs boundary of Berlin I. The intent of architect Carl Gotthard Langhans was that Berlin become "Athens on the Spree." Riding high over the center of the Brandenburg Gate, her back up against the Wall and West Berlin, Eirēnē, goddess of peace, was borne by her quadriga. Abducted into Parisian captivity, upon her return to Berlin II following the defeat of Napoleon, Eirēnē was militarized by sculptor Gottfried Schadow, metamorphosing into an earlier incarnation of nearby Viktoria, bearing an Iron Cross in a laurel wreath, crowned with the Prussian eagle. Together with Clio, Viktoria observed the foundation and fall of Berlin II and was even pressed into military service as a machine gun position in 1919. During Berlin III, she watched cocaine dealers, artists, and American diplomats linger with intent on Pariser Platz. Pressed once again into service as a stage prop for the *Reichshauptstadt*, she was damaged, then demilitarized during Berlin V, stripped of her Iron Cross and Prussian eagle. Just behind her flew the flag of the German Democratic Republic. Although the gate retained its architectural affiliation with the Athenian polis, it had lost its function. It was no longer a point of entry into the accidental *polis*, Berlin VI, and for the time being, was no longer a Gate of Peace. Although the Wall made it impossible, a large red-bordered white metal sign, held in place by four-by-fours sunk in concrete pylons number 117 and 118, warned passers-by in bold black and red lettering, "*ACHTUNG Sie verlassen jetzt West-Berlin*." I stopped, taking out the copy of *The Last Battle* I'd borrowed from the

---

7 "It's getting colder. At my house it's very cozy. I could make it very comfortable for both of us. Don't you want to come with me?" Diary of Thomas Vonaechron, Diary Extract, 1982, trans. TV.

Stadtstaatsarchiv. Although the cover photo of the victorious Red Army soldiers had been taken on the other side in Berlin V, I was very close. I put the book back into my shoulder bag and, with the security lights illuminating the way, followed the Wall north, weaving around to the left, right, and then left again, along the jagged edge of the British Sector to the *Reichstag* building (coordinates 11P). Stopping under a security light and leaning against the Wall for support, I pulled out the other book George had lent me from my shoulder bag, flipping through the pages for a copy of Albert Speer's plan for Berlin IV. Perhaps at that very moment, still sitting at my worktable under the *Bothidae* eyes of the frightened flounder, the architect might be commenting on the original. Albert Speer had proposed that the *Reichstag*, like many other older buildings, be deconstructed. Adolf Hitler objected, directing it be incorporated as an annex into the *Große Halle,* his "Great Hall." The Allied Air Campaign concurred. The *Reichstag* remained standing in Berlin VI as a bridge of tradition to both the past and the future.

The Wall ran directly behind the *Reichstag*, but rather than continuing, I made my way around to the left, to the *Platz der Republik*, the former *Königsplatz*, where Bismarck, Moltke, Roon, and the golden "Chick-on-a-Stick" once bathed in the imperial splendor of Berlin II and were then forced to become the backdrop for the demise of Berlin III. In spite of my research in the National Archives, I wasn't quite prepared for the small "r" revelation Clio had prepared for me. Looking up at the lines of the arches and cornices of the *Reichstag* bathed in artificial light, I walked up the broad entrance ramp to the *Porticus*. Stopping under the portico of the monumental main entrance, I stepped back to read the inscription overhead: "*Dem Deutschen Volk,*" "To the German People." As the last battle approached Berlin from the east along *Reichstraße 1*, the burnt-out *Reichstag* building was incorporated into the CITADEL planning for defending HistoriCity center. The *Porticus* metamorphosed into a portcullis, with doors and windows bricked up and fitted out with gun ports. Continuing down the ramp on the far side of the entrance, while all the time looking up at the lines of arches and cornices, I stopped under the second window. From this window, Philipp Scheidemann proclaimed the death of Berlin II, "the old and rotten, the monarchy," and announced the birth of Berlin III, "the German Republic." Turning to look out over the dark, empty field, the *Platz der Republik*, the former *Königsplatz*, I saw the black-and-white panorama photograph of the expectant crowd of workers and sailors taken on November 9, 1918. The window of opportunity above my head described the fault line between Berlin II and Berlin III, between *Kaiserreich* and *Republik*. While spooning his potato soup in the *Reichstag* deputies' dining room, Scheidemann was interrupted with the unpleasant news that his former colleague Karl Liebknecht was about to proclaim a Free Socialist Republic from the *Berliner Stadtschloß* at the far end of *Unter den Linden*. Wanting to be the first one on the boulevard with the news, *Herr* Scheidemann, a gifted orator, stood up, walked to the window, improvised the proclamation of the German Republic, and returned to the dining room to finish his soup.

Walking back up the entrance ramp to the *Porticus*, I set out over the vast, open field in front of the *Reichstag*, the *Platz der Republik*, repeatedly turning around to look back at the building. Built in 1895, a by-product of the birth of Berlin II, it had also been the *Tatort* of its death. The burning of the Reichstag on February 27, 1933, heralded the coincident death of Berlin III and the birth of Berlin IV. Away from the security lighting, it was too dark to scan *The Last Battle* for the obituary, though I knew Berlin IV had also died here in May 1945. One of the major obstacles preventing the capture of the *Reichstag* by the Red Army was the deep ditch dug for the underground entrance to Adolf Hitler's Great Hall. The war, which initially willingly assisted the *GBI's* execution of his plans for *Germania*, brought all construction to a halt. Flooded and fortified, the excavation site served as a defensive barrier, shaping the architecture of the last battle.

The *Reichstag* Fire Decree, enacted by the National Socialist government as a "defense against Communist state-endangering acts of violence," inspired *Generalissimus* of the Soviet Union, Iosif Vissarionovich Stalin, to order the commanders of the Red Army to capture the Reichstag Building by May Day 1945. In another one of the *eirönïa* Clio shares with initiates, as the *Reichstag* building had been heavily damaged by fire in February 1933, the decree had actually been passed in the Kroll Opera House on the far side of the *Königsplatz*, across from the *Reichstag*. Soviet assault groups assigned to take the *Reichstag* would have to first deal with determined defenders holed up in the Kroll Opera House. After assembling on *Washingtonplatz*, Red Army units fought their way across the Moltke Bridge, continuing across the now empty field on my left, wheeling left to storm the *Reichstag*. Taking decimating fire on their right flank, they realized there were hostile forces in the Kroll Opera House, and were forced to delay the final attack upon the *Reichstag* long enough to dislodge and destroy them. The Red Army troops then turned again to the *Reichstag*. Fighting was intense. All soldiers involved knew the capture of the *Reichstag* would end the war in Europe. Only a fanatical minority was determined to die with peace so close at hand. While hand-to-hand combat continued within the *Reichstag* itself, two Soviet sergeants raised "Red Army Banner No.

5" on the roof at the back of the building shortly before May Day, 1945.

Streets surrounding *Königsplatz* had been built up as a diplomatic quarter and fashionable residential area. The war had laid it, together with the aggregate architecture of Berlins I, II, III, and IV, to waste, wiping it clean, at least aboveground. Between the *Reichstag* and the *Moltkebrücke*, only one building still stood on the last battlefield. All windows were dark, but a floodlight on the roof illuminated the flag of the Swiss Legation fluttering in the night wind. Switzerland. Basel. The ancient city on the Rhine, an Archimedean Point that had provided me with a *Weltanschaung*, a perspective not only on Berlin but on Washington, DC, as well. Looking out over the *Platz der Republik*, I thought of Jacob Burckhardt, the preeminent, prejudiced, prescient Basel historian, deeply skeptical of the rise of a new German *Reich* and an intentionally ahistorical United States of America. Once a battlefield, now an empty field, the *Platz der Republik* remained a *champ de Mars*. Its vastness and emptiness were overwhelming. *Öde und Leer*, the West Berlin air. Surrounded by darkness and a penetrating silence, I tried to comprehend the chaos, violence, and loss of life. Off to the left, the fixed bayonet and top of the helmet, visible through the trees of the Tiergarten, marked the graves of the 2,200 Red Army soldiers who bought the *Reichstag* with their lives.

In keeping with both architectural and historical traditions of the HistoriCity, the death of Berlin IV coincidentally heralded the near-simultaneous births of Berlin V and Berlin VI. Feeling temporarily like Schliemann at *Troija*, high on Hisarlik, it occurred to me I'd found the location and moment of destruction of Berlin II, III, and IV in Berlin VI, just over the Wall from Berlin V. This was the *Schwerpunkt*, the center of gravity of the HistoriCity. Stratigraphy as spent strategy, with *Platz der Republik* providing the necessary lateral continuity. Not just the fault line between Berlin II and Berlin III, Berlin III and Berlin IV, Berlin IV and Berlin V, the *Reichstag* described the fault zone of the HistoriCity.

But there was still more of Berlin IV to be discovered in Berlin VI. My next objective would be the ruins of the Italian and Japanese Embassies found in the enlargement of the Tiergarten developed in accordance with Albert Speer's instructions, and the postwar architectural surprise George referred to that was waiting for me on the site of his deconstructed *Haus des Fremdenverkehrs*. In order to more effectively evaluate any remaining ruin value, I decided to continue my on-site excavations by daylight. With the gravity of the HistoriCity weighing me down, I felt like Atlas before Bismarck; it was time to return to Friedenau for rest and relaxation. I shifted my *Blick* back to the *Reichstag*, back-lit by security lighting, glowing green under the all-consuming emptiness of the night sky overhead and the vast field before it. Violently deprived of architect Paul Wallot's illuminating cupola of glass and steel by British Occupation Forces in 1956, the *Reichstag* could indeed have passed for a giant, headless ape, ein *Königlicher* or even a *Kaiserlicher* Kong defecating in the darkness at the edge of the Tiergarten. Someday, Great Britain might make amends, providing an architect to reconstruct Wallot's vision of transparency for a reunified German Parliament.

Though sorely tempted, I was too tired to retrace my steps back to the *S-Bahnhof Tiergarten*. Deciding to bus back from the Reichstag to *Bahnhof Zoo*, then take the U9 to *Freidrich-Wilhelm-Platz* and Friedenau, I walked out across the dark, deserted *Platz der Republik* to a lighted bus stop on *Scheidemannstraße*, which in the distance looked much like an Edward Hopper painting. Just after I'd reached it, Bus 69, a double-decker, appeared out of the darkness. The lone passenger under glass on the upper deck, I was given a windshield tour of Berlin VI in reverse chronological order. Back through the Tiergarten, down *Eleanor-Dulles-Allee*, past the postwar ruins of Hugh Stubbins's thin-shelled *Kongresshalle*, the fragile architectural antithesis to the massive postwar apartment buildings lining the *Stalin-Allee*, to the *Spree Weg*, returning to the *Großer Stern*, Moltke, Roon, Bismarck, and high above it all, Viktoria, the golden "Chick-on-a- Stick" radiant in her spotlights. As Bus 69 careened around the *Grosser Stern*, crossing over the *17. Juni Straße*, I caught a glimpse of the *Brandenburger Tor* in the distance and thought about the proposition I'd received earlier. The bus turned into *Hofjägerallee* and then *Klingelhoferufer*, crossing over the *Landwehrkanal* and turning into *Kurfürstenstraße*. Just before reaching the *Refugium* of postwar pop, *Bahnhof Zoo*, we passed by the Kaiser Wilhelm Memorial Church, the center and spiritual *Schwerpunkt* of West Berlin.

As a student in Basel, I had taken a seminar on European religious architecture, embellished with complementary study trips to Austria, Germany, France, and the indispensable Italy. While many of the celebrated cathedrals and cloisters we visited also stood in ruins, the *Kasier-Wilhelm-Gedächtnis-Kirche* stood alone. An example of late European emperor worship, it served to sanctify the German Empire established under Kaiser Wilhelm I. Having met Moltke, Roon, and Bismarck on the *Großer Stern* during our bus tour of Berlin, I was surprised to find them again on a relief in the solitary surviving tower of the Memorial Church, the bell tower, grouped around their *Kaiser* seated at the map table. Just above their heads was another, smaller relief of Jesus, tormented by doubt in the Garden of Gethsemane. As his disciples slept, an angel offered him the chalice. Just below, a citation that, given the destruction of the empire in 1918 and the church sanctifying it twenty-five years later, seemed oddly appropriate: "DOCH NICHT MEIN SONDERN DEIN WILLE GESCHEHE."

Accidentally like the centuries-older churches of Northern Italy, the bell tower, as a consequence of wartime destruction, stood apart from the sanctuary. The interior of the octagonal sanctuary was lined with thick panes of stained glass from Chartres, predominately blue, set into concrete frames, forming a peace-filled honeycomb, sheltering and soothing the tired tourist and willing worshiper alike. Although constructed and consecrated during Berlin II as a national monument, during Berlin III, the area around the *Gedächtnis-Kirche* became a magnet for the fashionable. Destroyed during the Second World War through the combination of Allied bombing, the Red Army advance, and ironically, the German *Luftwaffe* firing on a suspected Soviet sniper site in the bell tower from the flak towers at Humboldthain, the church was intentionally reconstructed as a ruin. Through the human agencies of architecture and armed force, the monumental metamorphosed into the memorial, though not in accordance with the theory proposed by the *GBI*. More than just a bridge of tradition, the broken tower of the *Kasier-Wilhelm-Gedächtnis-Kirche* rose above the national, the fashionable, and finally, the operational, to proclaim the possible.

Thanking the driver, I stepped out of Bus 69 at the *Bahnhof Zoologischer Garten*, stopping for a moment to look at the illuminated broken bell tower of the Memorial Church. Across the street from the church, a neon sign running across the roof of a functional, postwar office building proclaimed, "*Berlin bleibt doch Berlin.*" But which Berlin—Berlin I, II, III, IV, V, or VI? "*Bahnhof Zoo*" served as the primary passenger train station for West Berlin, as well as a subway station and bus stop. In addition to receiving all those passengers just passing through, it had become a *Refugium* for many who had fallen through the postwar decades, *Halbstarke*, hippies, and now, in the post-punk era, punks, sharing a communal life of alcohol and drugs. "*Ey Alter, haste 'ne Mark für mich?*"[8] was their mantra, a chorus they shared with those just passing through. *Bahnhof Zoo* was also a meeting place for expatriate Africans and Asians, who were involved in other kinds of transactions taking place at the edges. There was another kind of refuge within *Bahnhof Zoo*, the *Heinrich Heine Buchhandlung*, a small bookstore with a large, thoughtful selection of German literature. Solace in the midst of sadness and loss.

Walking quickly through the station, head down to avoid eye contact, I

---

8 "Hey, old man, do you have a Mark for me?" Diary of Thomas Vonaechron, Diary Extract, 1982, trans. TV.

took the escalator to the underground platform and the U9, returning me to *Friedrich-Wilhelm-Platz*. Walking across *Renée-Sintenis-Platz*, a small circular park framed in the sylvan *Schönheit* of *Gründerzeit* Berlin II, I began to relax. Crossing over the *Hauptstraße* onto *Hedwigstraße*, I was hoping to meet Hedwig again but didn't. I did, however, meet my landlord, Dr. Kahler, in front our apartment building, returning home with a liter of wine under his arm.

"Ah, *Herr* Vonaechron, good evening! Well met! Might I invite you for a glass, perhaps even two, glasses of wine?" he asked with his tight, wolfish grin. Although we'd exchanged pleasantries *pro forma* in passing over the past weeks, we had not yet had the opportunity for a longer conversation. During the workweek, he rose early, and often went out in the evenings. There had been visitors and late night conversation in the Berliner Zimmer, and even the occasional houseguest, but he seemed very much the lone wolf. "Much to my delight, I just discovered a dry *Trollinger*, a red wine from *Württemberg* where I come from. Unfortunately, I developed a liking for it while working at a used bookstore in Tübingen many years ago. There was, still is, a hotel, *der Helm*, "the Helmet," just across the *Holzmarkt*, where I would stop in after work for a *Viertele*. Do you know this Swabian expression for a quarter-liter of wine? Perhaps I associate the lightness of the wine with the lightness of the life I enjoyed there." Although tired from my foray into history, I couldn't resist his kind invitation. We climbed the stairs together and, after dropping off my shoulder bag, I joined him at the large wooden table in the kitchen. He had opened the bottle and poured it into two large glasses. "You see the twist-off top, it's really just a *Tafelwein, un vin ordinaire*—what's the English word?—a 'table-wine,' but nonetheless, I let it rest, just for a moment, more to savor the color than to allow it to aerate."

"I'm very grateful to you," I said sitting down at the solid wooden table, "I've had quite a day and a *Viertele*, or two, of *Trollinger* might just be what I need. In the kitchen light, the wine radiated warmth, a kind of mystic heat. There was something extraordinary about the color, and I was pleased when he reached out his hand to take his glass so I could join him. "*Sehr zum Wohl*," I said, raising my glass.

"Cheers," he replied. Though genuine, his smile seemed strained; there was a wolfishness about it, highlighted by his closely cropped hair and pointed ears. I was thirsty, so rather than sip the wine, I drank it, immediately sensing the warmth as it spread from my heart into my arms and legs. Dr. Kahler laughed and said, "Ah, I see you, too, are a follower of Michel de Montaigne, *Herr* Vonaechron. Although French, he recommends drinking wine in the German fashion—let's see, how would it be in English?" Leaning back in his chair, Dr. Kahler looked up at the high ceiling and said, "'The Germans drink almost indifferently of all wines with delight; their business is to pour down and not to taste; and it's so much the better for them: their pleasure is so much the more plentiful and nearer at hand.' Cheers!" he repeated, drinking deeply from his *Rotweinglas*. "Over the years, I have found certain essayists and poets to be reliable drinking companions." I thought again of Neal, and our symposium in The Republic. "Not just the French mind you, but the Chinese, too. Perhaps you have heard of Li Po and Tu Fu? No? Well, we'll save their drunken poetry for another symposium. Tonight, I'm interested in your impressions of Berlin. You've been a *Wahlberliner* for now, how long? Could it be seven weeks?"

I nodded, but before I could answer, the telephone rang in the *Berliner Zimmer*. Excusing himself, Dr. Kahler left the kitchen, giving me the opportunity to take another drink and take stock of my impressions. There were so many impressions from this day alone. Someday, all these impressions, like documents in an archives, would have to be arranged, arranged and described, or, like exposures, fixed, fixed and developed, but seven weeks wasn't enough time.

He was gone for some time and returned with an apologetic expression on his face. "Please do forgive me, *Herr* Vonaechron, a close friend urgently needs my assistance, and I must go to her at once." Noting my glass was empty, he smiled and refilled it. He then returned briefly to the *Berliner Zimmer*, and when he came back, he handed me a Penguin Classics edition of Li Po and Tu Fu in English translation. "I do apologize, *Herr* Vonaechron, I really am interested in your impressions of Berlin, but know from personal experience, in my absence, Li Po and Tu Fu will keep you in good company. I might be quite late, so please do not wait up for me. But do help yourself to *Trollinger*. Red wine spoils quickly once it's been opened!" I stood up to shake his hand and, after he left, concerned about too many as well as Tu Fu, screwed the top back on the bottle, placed it on the wooden countertop, and carried my wineglass and the slender volume of poetry to my room. Although I would have made the attempt to catalog my seven-week old impressions, I was grateful I didn't have to do so, preferring to enjoy the intoxicating effect of the *Trollinger* while keeping company with Li Po.

When I awoke early the next morning to the inquiry of the birds outside my window, "Poo-tee-weet?" Dr. Kahler had already come and gone. Refreshed, I took a short handheld shower in the bathtub, dressed, and decided to continue my exploration of Berlin IV in Berlin VI rather than return to the *Stadtstaatsarchiv*. Carefully moving the empty wineglass aside, I unfolded the *Falkplan* to the page where I'd circled the intersection of *Potsdamer Straße* and *Reichpietschufer*. From my shoulder bag, I took out the copy of *Von Berlin Nach Germania* George'd lent me, flipping through it until I found the reproduction of Albert Speer's plans for *das Haus des Fremdenverkehrs*, part of an ensemble of buildings to be constructed on *Runder Platz* on the north-south Axis. I outlined the ensemble on the map George had given me at the coordinates O9. Opening *The Last Battle*, I found the intersection on "the Center" map on the flyleaf. Just beyond it, I noted the locations of the wartime navy and army headquarters, also within the same coordinates, sketching their locations on the map. Refolding the *Falkplan*, I flipped through the pages of the index to check public transportation connections. The *S1* ran directly from Friedenau to *Anhalter Bahnhof*, where I could either catch Bus 29 or walk back along the *Landwehrkanal* to the intersection of *Reichpietschufer* and *Potsdamer Straße*, site of Speer's *Runder Platz* and the *Haus des Fremdenverkehrs*. Afterward, I could walk along the *Reichpietschufer* to the former *Oberkommando der Marine*. From the former naval headquarters, I could continue *per pedes Pilgrimorum* to *Stauffenbergstraße* and the *Bendlerblock*, former *Oberkommando der Wehrmacht*, and then to *Tiergartenstraße*, site of the former embassies. It would be another long day, giving *Herr* Speer ample opportunity to complete his commentaries.

S-Bahnhof Friedenau was just around the corner from the *Lothringerstrasse*. I was tempted to turn left onto the *Hedwigstraße* to see if Hedwig was out on patrol today but decided to stay on mission. Turning left on the next street, *Bahnhofstraße*, I saw the half-timbered, painted brick *S-Bahnhof Friedenau* just ahead. Although *heruntergekommen*, like many architectural remains of earlier Berlins in West Berlin, it still retained the suburban character of the Berlin II *Landhauskolonie* George had described. Just before the *Bahnhof*, on my left, stood a more functional modern building, with a large, inviting, outdoor beer garden. I had to look twice at the sign—"*Mazi Biergarten*"— to make certain it was not a set from the film *Cabaret*, which provided part of the soundtrack for my decision to move to Berlin. No, no, it was indeed "*Mazi*," and there was only one customer, an attractive young man or woman—I wasn't quite certain—comfortably dressed in white linen clothing with short, white-blonde hair and radiant blue eyes, who smiled as graciously as Govinda, nodding pleasantly as I passed. Nodding in return, I saw the S1 approaching the station and walked quickly past the *Biergarten*, down the stairs, and then back up onto the platform marked *RICHTUNG FROHNAU,* boarding the train just before the doors closed to the sound of the claxon horn. Although the S1 would also pass under East Berlin on the way to Frohnau, I would leave the train prior to that at *Anhalter Bahnhof.*

After stopping at the aboveground stations *Schöneberg* and

Yorckstraße, just before reaching *Anhalter Bahnhof*, the *S-Bahn* once again metamorphosed into an *U-Bahn*. Alighting from the train to the squeal of the air brakes, I once again stepped back in time. Although largely deserted, the four parallel tracks, and the largest platform I had seen in Berlin, evidenced the once-busy train station above. Dimly lit, dirty, white-tiled walls and aquamarine support columns gave the station an underwater ambiance. I followed the illuminated signs marked *"AUSGANG"* and, surfacing, was surprised to discover only the front facade of what must have been a magnificent station. Back at the *Stadtstaatsarchiv*, I learned Albert Speer's *Germania* would have deprived *Anhalter Bahnhof* of its tracks, as he intended to convert it into a public bath. In November 1943, it was severely damaged by the same Royal Air Force mission that destroyed the *Kaiser-Wilhelm-Gedächtnis-Kirche* and then intentionally deconstructed in 1960. As one of the three Berlin rail stations used for the deportation of Berlin's Jews between 1941 and 1945, it was a station with a history. Beginning in 1942, extra cars were attached to the early train departing on track one for Dresden, where they were then routed on to the Theresienstadt Ghetto.

Only the entrance, a portico composed of three ornately decorated arches, remained. Seated on top of the portico, on either side of an empty *Oculus*, were two seated, robed figures, as different as night and day, *Tag und Nacht*. While the figure on the left seemed to seek shelter under her billowing robe, the figure on the right looked skyward, lifting the hand of his outstretched right arm above his forehead, heavenward, as if he had anticipated the approach of the British bombers. At the base of the portico, a few pale yellow taxis of indefinite reality waited patiently on the circular driveway, *ante portas*, for passengers. A young man with unruly brown hair and aviator sunglasses, dressed in a black T-shirt and the light cotton drawstring Bhagwan pants popular with university students, his right arm draped through the open sunroof of his cab, took the cigarette from the corner of his mouth, smiled pleasantly, and asked, "Taxi?" With no hat on, he was still about six inches taller than his taxicab.

Smiling in return, doing my best to emulate Govinda, I shook my head and said, *"Nein, aber vielen Dank,"* coincidentally noting the light on the roof of his Mercedes sedan. Underneath the ubiquitous "TAXI" that was stenciled in yellow letters on a black background, the light also advertised "(American Literature)." For a moment, I seriously considered taking him up on his invitation as far as the nearby intersection of *Potsdamer Straße* and the *Reichpietsch Ufer*, the location of architectural surprise promised by George, just to ask him about "(American Literature)," but once again, I decided to resist temptation, save money, and continue on *per pedes Pilgrimorum*.

Walking under the center arch, still held firmly in place by massive redbrick columns pockmarked with bullet and shell holes, stepping carefully through and around the unhinged wooden entrance doors, I continued out across the parking lot and overgrown field that used to be the *Anhalter Bahnhof.* Many of the tracks had been torn up, the platforms demolished. Truck trailers stood stationary where trains once arrived from and departed for Dresden, Prague, Vienna, Rome, Naples, and Athens. Turning to take a look at a trailer on my left, I realized it wasn't a trailer at all but a wooden boxcar. Carefully making my way across the field littered with trash, I discovered the boxcar was standing on a short spur, the tracks overgrown, the four *Güterwagon* wheels rusted to the rails. Although the red paint was faded and flaking from the wooden slats, "DR," *Deutsche Reichsbahn,* was still legible. The door had been pushed open, so after testing the rusted iron stepladder, I climbed up, looked inside, and asked, "Hallo?" The boxcar now provided temporary shelter for those West Berlin hoboes with no rails left to ride. There were empty wine and beer bottles and a pile of blankets at one end of the boxcar. Scattered over the wooden floor were hundreds of slips of white paper. Just inside the door opening where I stood looking in was a weathered *Zettel* with something written on it. I took it in my hand and read: "*Thos=Mann=Tick.*" Thinking about the poem from Neal, the letter from Lorelei, and the flounder rejected by Anna, I decided this *Tick*-et was a *tessera* unclearly intended for me. Climbing down from the boxcar, I opened my shoulder bag, carefully placed the slip of paper into the inside pocket, and resumed my walk.

As I followed the dirt path through the field to the *Schöneberger Straße*, I passed a massive gray concrete *Hochbunker*—no arches and cornices here—with aboveground iron-grilled air vents, likely built to provide protection for hundreds if not thousands of passengers during air raids. My walking hypothesis was supported by block handwriting on the concrete wall over the entrance, "*WER BUNKER BAUT WIRFT BOMBEN.*"[9] *Schöneberger Straße* led me to *Reichpietschufer* bordering the *Landwehrkanal,* dug during Berlin II under direction of Prussian landscape architect Peter Joseph Lenné to lighten water traffic on the Spree. Architects certainly had had it in for the HistoriCity over the years, Carl Gotthard Langhans's "Athens on the Spree" and Albert Speer's *Germania.* I imagined the latter sitting at my worktable under the horrified eyes of the flounder, commenting on his plans for the *Haus des Fremdenverkehrs.* It was a short walk along Lenné's tree-lined canal to coordinates Q9, the intersection with *Potsdamer Straße.*

Just before reaching the intersection, I took the annotated map from

---

9 "Whoever builds bunkers drops bombs." Diary of Thomas Vonaechron, Diary Extract, 1982, trans. TV.

my shoulder bag. To my right stood the *Staatsbibliothek*. Directly in front of me, on the far side of the broad, six-lane street, stood Ludwig Mies van der Rohe's *Neue Nationalgalerie*, the buildings and street now occupying the site of Albert Speer's uncompleted *Haus des Fremdenverkehr*. When I returned to the archives, George explained that these buildings, together with the *Philharmonie*, were elements of a postwar *Kulturforum* purposefully designed and executed to eradicate any remaining ruin value. Although I hadn't realized it when he pointed out the intersection on the *Falkplan* yesterday, I had visited the *Kulturforum* during my first trip to the HistoriCity. Walking over *Potsdamer Brücke*, my attention was drawn to graffiti in large black letters written on the white bank of a stairwell leading down to the *Landwehrkanal*: "*Warum (nicht) Kunst?*" The red (*nicht*) appeared to have been sprayed in later as an antithesis to the larger concrete thesis posited by the three elements of the *Kulturform: die Philharmone, die Neue Nationalgalerie*, and *die Staatsbibliothek*. Through a combination of wartime destruction and intentional postwar deconstruction, the ensemble effectively eliminated any ruin value inherent in the three uncompleted elements of *Germania, das Haus des Fremdenverkehr, Runder Platz*, and *die Nord-Süd Achse*. At this intersection in space and time, Albert Speer's bridge to tradition had been broken. Berlin VI stood triumphant over Berlin IV.

The collection of the New National Gallery was as remarkable as its architecture. As time went by in West Berlin, I would often stop in the museum café to drink *Milchkaffee* or, weather permitting, sit outdoors in the sculpture garden to drink cold, dry Riesling and listen to "Jazz in the Garden." Afterward, I would look at those few paintings which, over time, I came to regard as two-dimensional friends, as I had done at the National Gallery of Art in downtown Washington, DC. The lifelike presence of Edvard Munch's life-size portrait of Harry *Graf* Kessler hanging in West Berlin's New National Gallery seemed more than just pigment in my imagination.

Ahead of me, on the right bank of the *Landwehrkanal*, stood the *Shell-Haus*, rising, rippling like vertical white waves above the autumn foliage. Standing in front of the building, which housed BEWAG, the "Berlin State Electrical Joint-Stock Company," I looked up at the seemingly unscathed, magnificent facade, composed of six identical, regularly spaced waves, rising in height from six to ten stories. *Stadtstaatsarchiv* sources informed me the building had been designed by Emil Fahrenkamp for a subsidiary of Shell Oil. The map on the flyleaf of *The Last Battle* identified it as the former Supreme Naval Headquarters.

Uneasy about visiting the *Bendlerblock*, the former Supreme Military

Headquarters and site of Klaus von Stauffenberg's execution, I crossed over *Stauffenbergstraße* and continued along *Reichpietschufer*. From captured German documents in the former torpedo factory on the Potomac, I knew *Reichpietschufer* had once been *Tirpitzufer*. Clio had once again played her part in the naming conventions of the HistoriCity. Headquarters of the *Abwehr*, the German Military Intelligence Service under Admiral Wilhelm Franz Canaris, was located at *Tirpitzufer 76/78*. Here, the white marble waves receded, replaced by a more traditional gray stone grandeur; even the lines of the arches and cornices underlined the building's military function. Indirectly implicated in the attempt to assassinate Adolf Hitler, Wilhelm Canaris was hung, together with Dietrich Bonhoeffer and other prisoners, at Flossenbürg Concentration Camp in April 1945, two weeks before US Army units arrived. In Vault Six, I held the testimony of an eyewitness to the execution in my hand. It was time to walk back to *Bendlerblock*. Retracing my steps along the *Reichpietschufer*, I turned left into the *Stauffenbergstraße*.

The facade of the former *Oberkommando der Wehrmacht* stood apart from the two other former military headquarters buildings. As I approached the entrance to the foreboding, five-story, weathered gray building, I could see a large rectangular opening leading into an interior courtyard. My heart began to race. One of the heavy black-barred iron gates stood open and, as there was no one to ask, I walked through, into the inner courtyard. My eyes were immediately drawn to the larger-than-life-size bronze of a lone prisoner, naked and bound at the wrists. Mounted on the wall of the courtyard, directly behind the statute, was a black metal plaque indicating where Ludwig Beck, Friederich Olbricht, Claus Graf Schenk von Stauffenberg, Albrect Ritter Mertz von Qurinheim, and Werner von Haeften died for a Germany different than Adolf Hitler's. In school, I had been deeply moved reading about the events of July 20, 1944. Those same schoolboy sentiments now surfaced through the dry discipline of history and factual reporting found in Vault Six.

Returning to the center of the courtyard, I turned around slowly, following the relief depicting the history of German military headgear from 1756 until 1918 running between the first and second floors of the buildings. When my eyes returned to the rectangular entrance, I looked up at the grainy blue sky, framed by the gray walls of the former supreme headquarters of the *Wehrmacht*. After a few more minutes, having met or seen no one else, I looked again at the weathered bronze, thoughtful in expression, resolute in stance, and then left through the rectangular gate, turning left on *Stauffenbergstraße* toward the Tiergarten and the ruins of the *GBI's Tiergartenviertel*.

I didn't have far to go. When I turned into *Tiergartenstraße*, a spectacular panorama of ruins and foliage began to unfold before me. The former embassies lay in ruins, outwardly untouched since May 1945. Nature had, however, been quite busy with under- and overgrowth, providing a pleasant, if unusual and unexpected, sense of harmony. There was a kind of ruin value—not so much a bridge of tradition to the past but rather a gradual, natural reclamation, to a time further back, back beyond Berlin IV, III, II, and I, back to a natural state, back to the state of nature. Focused on the former Italian and Japanese Embassies, I was surprised to find ruins of other buildings as well, all built in the same *Speer*-lich style. The Japanese Embassy was of particular interest to me, not only for on-site evaluation of its ruin value but as an example of perishable architecture.

From the US Army Signals Intelligence Service (SIS) intelligence records in Vault Six, I knew the garden of the Japanese Embassy in Berlin yielded the only known surviving pieces of the PURPLE cipher machine, used by the Japanese Foreign Office throughout the war to encrypt and decrypt classified information. The "System 97 Printing Machine for European Characters" had been duplicated by SIS before the war, allowing American cryptanalysts to read sensitive communications between Berlin and Tokyo, which were distributed to the vetted under the code name MAGIC. While quite certain SIS had left no stone in the Japanese Embassy garden unturned after the war, I couldn't resist looking for myself.

Continuing along *Tiergartenstraße*, I crossed over *Hofjägerallee*. On my right, I could see the Chick-on-a-Stick, golden in the sunlight, high above the *Großer Stern* on her sandstone column, and thought again about the woman in white on the sidewalk nearby. I crossed the street, following the edge of the Tiergarten. Looking up at a street sign, I was surprised to discover I was no longer on *Tiergartenstraße*, but *Thomas-Dehler-Straße*. Confused, I sat down on a concrete staircase leading to the portico of a massive building at the corner of *Drakestraße* to orient myself. The first-floor windows had been bricked up, as had the ceremonial entrance, into which an uninviting, windowless, gray metal door had been set. Setting my shoulder bag down on the step beside me, I took out *The Last Battle* and *Von Berlin Nach Germania*, unfolding my *Falkplan* to coordinate N9. Ryan's book identified only the Swedish Embassy, which I'd already passed. As I was flipping through *Germania*, looking for the *GBI*'s plan for the *Tiergartenviertel*, the metal door in the former ceremonial entrance behind me opened. Jumping up, I quickly turned around, meeting the face of a large man not wearing a beret but otherwise closely resembling the frustrated artist from Friedenau. Seizing the element of surprise, he demanded, "*Was machst Du hier, vor meiner Haustür? Bist Du etwa von TUWAT?*" Noting my surprise, he modified his harsh tone somewhat and continued, "*Dürfte ich mich vorstellen? Gabriel Kielerförde. Wie heisst Du?*"[10]

My surprise modulated to confusion, I fell back upon the first virtue, politeness: "*Guten Tag, ich heisse Thomas, Thomas Vonaecheron. Ich wollte eigentlich die ehemalige italienische und japanische Botschaften sehen, und habe mich dabei leider verlaufen.*"[11] Curious, instead of apologizing, I asked him, with a bit of Berlin slang thrown in for good measure, "*Wat bitte ist TUWAT, so 'wat wie BEWAG?*"

He laughed out loud. "Ah, are you English or an American? You have an accent. No, no, *TUWAT* is something quite different from *BEWAG*, not— ah, how should I say it—as illuminating? Ha! Ha! In fact, *TUWAT* is rather destructive. I know this area very well and would be pleased to take the time to escort you to the two embassies you are looking for. This is one of the few areas of West Berlin left untouched after the war—well, almost untouched anyway. The embassies, you see, remain the property of their respective countries. Although they're no longer used for diplomatic representation, they are used for a variety of undiplomatic, even illegal activities, so you must be careful. Gabriel raised his right hand, pointing to graffiti on the wall between the bricked-up first-floor windows of his building: "'*HIER WARTET DER TOD*. But do not be afraid, Thomas, I am not 'Death waiting here,' I am an artist working here. You might even say I am working against Death. Look here," he closed the metal door behind him and pointed to a hand-drawn *Klingelschild*. "I am living here while working on my project, an arrangement of found objects with which I hope to illuminate the past."

Relieved and happy to find an artist-archeologist among the ruins, I told Gabriel about my archival work in Washington and Berlin, beginning with Berlin IV and the theory of ruin value. "Albert Speer's in your office, Heinrich Schiemann and Wilhelm Dörpfeld have inspired your on-site research—well, I see you understand at least something about German history," he mused. "In a way, we're working on similar projects, Thomas. I find and arrange objects, you find and arrange words. I too, try to make history visible, as a present form of the past. These ruins do have something to tell us, if we're willing to listen. Listen!"

"West Berlin is, like Troy, after all, a 'tell!'"

"*Ach, auch das noch!* What literature do you have there?"

I picked up the books from the *Stadtstaatsarchiv* and, together with my annotated map, handed them to Gabriel.

"Perhaps because I was looking only for the former Japanese and Italian

---

10 "What are you doing here in front of my door? Are you with *TUWAT*? Who are you? Might I introduce myself? Gabriel Kielerförde. Who are you?" Diary of Thomas Vonaechron, Diary Extract, 1982, trans. TV.

11 "Actually, I'm looking for the former Italian and Japanese Embassies and seem to have lost my way." Diary of Thomas Vonaechron, Diary Extract, 1982, trans. TV.

Embassies, I was surprised to find more buildings here. Were they all part of Albert Speer's plan?" I asked as he looked through *Germania*.

"Oh, yes. Here, you'll find ruins of the Spanish, Norwegian, Greek, and Danish Embassies and Legations. Even Krupp A. G. had an embassy. Do you know William Manchester's book *The Arms of Krupp*? The Krupp building now houses the *Canisius-Kolleg*, a Jesuit school. I live here in the former Danish Legation. Hmmm, one moment please. I have a more detailed map of the plans for the *Tiergartenviertel* inside, let me grab it and lock up, just in case the *TUWAT* do show up again." Handing the books and the map back to me, he smiled warmly and said, "I'll be back in just a moment, Thomas. In the meantime, please do make yourself comfortable on my front porch!"

When Gabriel returned, he handed me an oversize xerox copy of a map, including the location of the *Oberkommando des Heeres,* as well as *Runder Platz* and *Haus des Fremdenverkehrs* on the *Nord-Süd-Achse*. At the bottom I read: "*DIE NEUGESTALTUNG BERLINS UNTER DER LEITUNG DES GENERALBAUINSPEKTORS FÜR DIE REICHSHAUPTSTADT NEU- UND ALTBAUTEN DER AUSLÄNDISCHEN MISSIONEN IM TIERGARTENVIERTEL.*"[12] This will show you how the Japanese and Italian Embassies fit into Albert Speer's overall plan for an enlarged Tiergarten. It's an extra copy, so please keep it with my complements. I'm planning to use it as an illustration in my book on the archaeology of the war. We'll walk first to the former Japanese Embassy, here," pointing to its location on the map, "just off *Tiergartenstraße* on *Graf-Spee-Straße*. Given Japan's great interest in the German Navy, it's an interesting coincidence, though given the tragic end of the war, I think *Hiroshimastraße* would be much more appropriate" he said, "and then on to the former Italian Embassy, here. The Italian Embassy is perhaps the most imposing of all the embassies and, you might be surprised to learn, the only one still 'in business,' not as an embassy, of course, but as the *Consulato Generale d'Italia a Berlino*!

"You also asked me about *TUWAT*. Here's an invitation to one of their events." Taking the handbill in my hand, I read: "*Kraaker, Anti-AKWer, Intandbesetzer, AJZ-Kämpfer, Anti-Imperialisten, Feministen, Chaoten, Punks, Hippies und Gammler, Schwarze und Indianer, Schwule und Lesben, Alternative und Grüne Radler, Anti-Militaristen, Sozialisten, . . . die Menschen die für die Freiheit kampfen.*"[13]

---

12 The Redevelopment of Berlin under Direction of the General Inspector for the *Reichshauptstadt*: New and Existing Foreign Mission Buildings in the Tiergarten Quarter, from the exhibition catalog for "Embassies: Archaeology of a War," Gabriel Kielerförde, Berlin Museum, 1986.

13 "Rowdies, Anti-Nuclear Activists, Occupiers, Autonomous Youth Center Activists, Anti-Imperialists, Feminists, Chaotics, Punks, Hippies and Drifters, Blacks and Indians, Male and Female

"What you don't find listed here are '*Archiluten*,' those who needlessly, thoughtlessly, destroy fragmentary evidence of the past, as they did when they occupied this building last year."

"Now I understand your challenge to my occupation of your porch, Gabriel!"

"I do apologize for my lack of manners, Thomas. I'll try to make it up to you!"

We crossed back over the *Hofjägerallee*, walking along *Tiergartenstraße*, turning right at *Graf-Spee-Straße*. Rising over the top of the massive building on the corner was not the sun but a faded golden chrysanthemum. "Here," said Gabriel, "is the former Japanese Embassy." Although the combination of stripped classicism with the six rectangular columns reaching to the roof certainly seemed *Speer-lich*, there was still something Japanese about this huge building, perhaps the half-story attica bearing the symbol of the Japanese royal family, the decorative touches. Attica, Athens-on-the-Spree. "The building was actually designed by Ludwig Moshammer under the direction of Albert Speer. The original Japanese Embassy, like so many other buildings, fell victim to Albert Speer's plans for the *Nord-Süd-Achse*." As we approached the ceremonial entrance, I noted oriental ornamental design on the bars over the widows, the heavy iron doors, and the oriental lamps. The lamps reminded me of the *GBI*'s streetlights on *Charlottenbuger Chausee*, a kind of light-*motif*. Large iron urns flanked the stairway leading to the entrance. "Let's walk around the side of the building," Gabriel suggested. We worked our way carefully through the undergrowth and broken glass. Debris and litter were scattered everywhere. Pieces of the white marble facade had fallen from the corner of the building, heavy marble balcony supports had collapsed onto one another like giant dominoes. We continued around behind the building to what must have been a parking lot. The marble facade gave way to brick. The chain link fence topped with barbed wire, set up to discourage the curious, had long been breached, whole sections pulled away from the metal fence posts. Someone had used one section of the fence to build a chicken pen. Chickens ran in and out of wooden coops. The backside of the embassy was riddled with shell and bullet holes. "Do you know where the garden was located?" I asked, and told Gabriel about the MAGIC surrounding the Japanese PURPLE machine.

"I don't know for certain, but it must have been over there. Let's take a look. Even if we don't find a piece of the PURPLE machine, there might be some other object of interest." As we carefully picked our way through the rubble field, I noticed several aboveground entrances to underground bunkers. Footpaths through the rubble field led to heavy, metal, airtight,

Homosexuals, Alternatives, Green Cyclists, Anti-Militarists, Socialists, . . . all those who fight for freedom." Diary of Thomas Vonaechron, Diary Extract, 1982, trans. TV.

bombproof doors now standing wide open, with metal levers in the "*AUF*" position. Standing next to a bunker, Gabriel said, "In 1982, you might not find love in the ruins, but if you look hard enough, you can most certainly find a fuck. For a price of course!" His loud laughter echoed throughout the empty bunker. "Here, you'll find not only *Berliner*, but many *Pariser* as well. You know two can play at your word games, Thomas! The garden must have been here somewhere." Although there were parts and pieces scattered everywhere, none of them resembled the pictures of the pieces of the PURPLE machine I'd seen in Vault Six. With our eyes on the ground before us, we continued on around the building, making our way back to the front. Pointing to the right, Gabriel invited me to "Look up, over there." Beyond the chain link and barbed wire fence, across an open field, stood another massive building, a complementary pendant to the Japanese Embassy. "That is the former Italian Embassy, the current *Consulato Generale d'Italia a Berlino*, the other defining point on Berlin's Tokyo-Rome axis. Shall we have a closer look?"

Gabriel was certainly right, the *Consulato Generale d'Italia a Berlino* was the most monumental of all the Tiergarten embassies, even in ruins. "Although the buildings appear similar from a distance, as we get closer, you'll notice some differences. Hitler rejected the Italian government's original design—interesting, *nicht wahr*, that Hitler should have a say? Under the direction of Albert Speer, Friedrich Hetzeit designed the embassy in a more traditional, neoclassical style." The arched internal balconies, colonnade, and weathered pink color, crowned with a white attica, mitigated the pompous political statement, making the building less *Speer-lich*. With a white or gray stone or marble veneer, it would have fit in seamlessly into the panorama of great representational buildings on Constitution Avenue in Washington, DC. As we made our way through rubble, piles of stacked tiles, rocks, and sand, Gabriel mused, "Perhaps more than anything else, the *Travertin* sets the Italian Embassy apart from the other embassies in the *Tiergartenviertel*." As at the Japanese Embassy, an effort had been made to wall out the curious with wooden and wire fencing. These too had been breached. We made our way around behind the building, following the path of those who'd come before us. Two wings, one of which was burned out and bricked up, were connected by an attractive colonnade at the rear of the building. Continuing on, we passed another bricked-up entrance, with marble stairs leading up to a marble-framed mosaic of glazed brick and concrete. The majestic front entrance to the building and the Italian Consulate appeared untouched and unused, an outpost of civilization in the ruins of the *Tiergartenviertel*.

The war, an instrument of politics, had demoted the Italian Embassy to a consulate general and destroyed or deprived the other embassies and legations in the *Tiergartenviertel* of their purpose, political significance, their "*steingewordene Weltanschauung*"—only the stones remained. These stones formed a bridge, not of tradition to the past as Albert Speer had originally conceived but to something else, to a dialectic of construction and deconstruction with disastrous consequences for Europe and the world. They also served as a warning to what has been and might come again. But there was something else here to, something unintended, something biophilic. Here in the *Tiergartenviertel*, artifice had been enhanced by neglect. Trees, bushes, and grass grew uncultivated around and in the ruins, in unique and not unpleasant harmony. "Truly remarkable," I muttered to myself.

Noting my interest, Gabriel said, "Those are . . . how do you call them in English, a British botanist cataloging plants here in the Tiergarten told me, ah . . . 'Black Locusts!' He said before the war, Black Locust had largely disappeared from Berlin but afterward began to come back in those parts of the city that had been most heavily bombed. Interesting, isn't it?"

"Very interesting!" I replied, without feigning the German accent.

From the half-circle drive leading to the consulate, Gabriel and I made our way back to *Tiergartenstraße*. On the far side of the street, I saw a seated sculpture, resolutely looking out over the ruins of Albert Speer's *Tiergartenviertel*. "That's Richard Wagner," said Gabriel, "still up on his pedestal, though somewhat worse for the war and the wear. Gathered at his feet, you'll find Wolfram von Eschenbach accompanied by Wagner's 'Fantastic Five:' Tannhäuser, Brünnhilde, Siegfried, Albrecht, and even a Rhinemaiden."

"Richard Wagner," I replied. "He certainly had a grand-*Tier-Garten* seat for Adolf Hitler's *Götterdämerung*, didn't he? You know, it occurs to me as I look at his 'heroic' statute surrounded by the ruins of the *Tiergartenviertel*, that war is a kind of opera, a kind of 'reality opera,' structuring space and time to achieve political purpose."

Laughing loudly once again, Gabriel said, "Have you ever thought about becoming a *Kabarettist*, Thomas? Please do forgive me, but I've got to go now," he said. I must get back to work, and I'm also afraid *TUWAT* might try to *tu* something to-day. I'd like to try and prevent it. I've enjoyed our conversation very much. You now know where I live. When you're back in the Tiergarten, please stop by, knock loudly, and if I'm not in, you're always welcome to sit on my stairs. If you'll give me your address, I'll send you an invitation to my *vernissage* at the Berlin Museum." I took the NARS notebook out of my shoulder bag, wrote my name, address, and Dr. Kahler's telephone number on the last page and, tearing it off, handed it to Gabriel.

"Thanks very much for taking the time to show me the embassies and also for the map, Gabriel. I think I've had enough of *Germania* and ruins for the present *bzw.* past, and would now like to look for more of Berlin I, II, and III in Berlin V, in East Berlin. And then there's more of Berlin VI, West Berlin to be recce-d too. It seems to me something very important's going on here in West Berlin. Your project is part of it. What luck to sit down on your steps when I'd lost my way. I could have found no better guide. Thank you, again!

"An American, *unterwegs in Berlin mit Albert Speer und Heinrich Schliemann,* I wish you every success, Thomas! Who knows? Maybe one day you'll even write a book about me, the artist Gabriel Kielerförde!" He took my hand in his, shook it once, turned, and walked back down the *Tiergartenstraße* toward his temporary lodgings in the former Danish Legation.

There was a solitary yellow telephone booth standing in *Tiergartenstraße,* not far from the Italian Consulate. George might still be at the *Stadtstaatsarchiv.* I decided to call. From *Anhalter Bahnhof,* I could take the *S-Bahn* up to Wittenau or back to Friedenau. Opening the door, I quickly discovered it had not only been used to make phone calls but as a *Pißort,* too. Blocking the door open with my foot to let in the fresh air, I carefully set my shoulder bag down on the metal rack where the telephone books used to be. On the thick glass behind the phone, just above what appeared to be a bullet hole, someone had written "KLJ was here!" in blood red lipstick. There was no answer at the *Stadtstaatsarchiv.* Maybe George was in my office, talking with Albert Speer about *Germania.* It was late in the afternoon, another day filled with architecture visible and invisible. There was much for me to think about, almost too much. I decided to return to home base in Friedenau and, hopefully, a *Viertele* of *Trollinger.*

Turning my back on the Chick-on-a-Stick, I walked down *Klingelhöferstraße,* crossing the *Herkules Brücke* over the *Landwehrkanal.* Walking along *Lützow Ufer* across from *Reichpietschufer,* I passed by both the former *Oberkommando des Heeres* and *Oberkommando der Marine* buildings and could see the entrance to *Staufenbergstraße.* Crossing over *Potsdamer Straße,* I stopped to look again at the *Neue Nationalgalerie,* intending to return. The *Schöneberger Ufer* led on to the *Schöneberger Brücke* and *Schöneberger Straße,* back to the bunker and the portico of the *Anhalter Bahnhof.* There were no taxis out front. Although the *S-Bahn* would take me directly to Freidenau, I thought again about the taxi with the "(American Literature)" sign, but now there was neither taxi nor taxi driver. I was the only one here, and no one was talking to me. Perhaps I would meet up with him again on the streets of West Berlin. Back on the *S-Bahn,* I let myself fall back into the comfortable start-stop rhythm punctuated by the air brakes. Opening his ivory box, Morpheus closed my eyes. I wandered through postwar Washington, DC, walking down Constitution Avenue in ruins, the monumental buildings broken and burned out, deprived by the war of the political power they were built to express. The air brakes awoke me. Looking out from under glass, I read "Lichterfelde-West." I'd missed my stop in Friedenau and would have to take the *S-Bahn* back.

After the train departed, I walked to the other side of the platform to wait for the next *S1* back to Friedenau. On the far side, a passenger train of olive drab coaches, with "US Army Transportation Corps" lettered in white, was being made up by a small red switch engine. At the end of the train, there was a caboose that could have been the Little Golden Book's "Little Red Caboose" in olive drab. A red *Deutsche Bundesbahn* V 200 diesel locomotive coupled to the head of the train. Behind the passenger train, adjacent to *S-Bahnhof Lichterfelde-West*, was a single-story white and brown *Fachwerk* building that might have been more appropriate in Bavaria or Switzerland. A rectangular metal sign identified the building as the US ARMY BERLIN RAIL TRANSPORTATION OFFICE (RTO). A circular sign below it carried the Transportation Corps's insignia, the four modes of military transport superimposed on a US highway shield. West Berlin, last stop east on the Dwight D. Eisenhower National System of Interstate and Defense Highways. This was the very US Army duty train I'd read about in Vault Six being made up for its overnight run to Frankfurt. The US Army Berlin Command Historical Reports contained not only compilations of statistics but interesting reports of incidents occurring en route as the sealed trains made their way back and forth across the Federal Republic of Germany and the German Democratic Republic, from the Frankfurt RTO to the Berlin RTO and back. Carrying military and civilian personnel, their dependents, and other authorized travelers, the trains departed coincidentally every evening from Berlin and Frankfurt, an agreeable way to cross sector and zonal borders. I envied the privileged passengers. My *S-Bahn* arrived, taking me back through the stations I'd slept through—*Botanischer Garten, Rathaus Steglitz, Feuerbachstraße*, and finally, Friedenau. After my follow-on foray into the *Reichshauptstadt*, Berlin IV, I was pleased to be back in my one elegant Empire room. Taking off my shoes, setting my shoulder bag down on the desk, I stretched out on the bed and closed my eyes to replay the events of the day, sleeping through until first light, when the birds outside my window, harmonizing with those on the *Hof*, once again inquired, "Poo-tee-weet?"

Returning to the *Stadtstaatsarchiv* on the following day, I replied to the friendly greeting of the *Pförtner* and walked directly to George's office to provide my after-action report. "No Thomas, *Herr* Speer is no longer our guest. He was called back to Heidelberg before finishing his dictation. I'm afraid we won't be able to ask him about a trip out to Spandau after all! In any event, I'm quite certain the information he provided will be very useful to researchers trying to understand what was planned for *Germania* and what happened here between 1936 and 1945. If I understood correctly, he's expected in London and won't be returning to West Berlin anytime soon, if at all, so please feel free to return to your office." Holding up the copy of Albert Speer's book still lying on his desk, George smiled and asked, "How did his theory of ruin value, dare I say it, hold up?"

Taking the books from my shoulder bag, I related the events surrounding my excavation of *Germania* over the past two days. "You certainly do meet some interesting people, Thomas. Living alone in the former Danish Legation, he'll no doubt be quite the melancholy Dane by the time he's finished. I would indeed very much like to accompany you to his *vernissage*! Perhaps the artist Gabriel Kielerförde would be interested in the architect Albert Speer's comments on his plans for the *Tiergartenviertel*. Please keep the books as long as you need them. I know where they are, and if you need more, please help yourself. Just remember, we're expecting two copies of yours!"

"By the way, I received a call from my counterpart at the *Archiv der Hauptstadt der DDR* in East Berlin. You know, Thomas, here in Berlin we have at least two of everything—governments, universities, operas, galleries, even city archives! We're both trained archivists and should, like Clio herself, be able *darüber zu stehen*. He would like to talk about a project for a *Findmittel*, what do you call it? A finding aid, a finding aid combining all our archival holdings, at least on paper, giving researchers an overview of what is available in both East and West, in your *Schliemann'sche bzw. Dörpfeld'sche Schema* Berlin V and VI. Berlin reunified at last, at least on paper! Archivists rush in where politicians fear to tread."

"Well, George, only the letter 'r' separates 'archival' from 'archrival!'"

"To be quite honest, that hadn't occurred to me, Thomas, but in any case, I think it's an excellent idea both professionally and personally. We made a tentative appointment for the first week in December. Hopefully the application will be approved by then. This would be our first meeting, an informal discussion over lunch. You are welcome to ride along. Not as a participant of course. I shudder to think how the East German authorities would react to an American passport, let alone an American archivist! I could drop you off at Checkpoint Charlie, and after you walk through, I could pick you up on *Unter den Linden*. While I'm at lunch, you could look around *Ost-Berlin*, and afterward, we could explore it together. The *Archiv der Hauptstadt der DDR* is housed in the *Marstall*, the former stables of the *Stadtschloß*, the City Palace. I'm afraid the stables are about all that's left of the palace. Although the *Stadtschloß* survived the war with severe but repairable damage, the German Democratic Republic, in the person of Walter Ulbricht, decided to have it deconstructed in 1950. Even in ruins, feudalism apparently had no place in modern socialist society! Although not an architect, Ulbricht certainly sponsored a number of building projects of historical significance, tearing down the *Stadtschloß,* building up the Wall. You know, it occurs to me there's a kind of 'inverse theory of ruin value' at work here—no ruins, no contemplation of the ruins, no bridge of tradition to the past. The *Palast der Republik,* or *Ballast der Republik* as some *Berliner* call it, has replaced the *Stadtschloß* with one exception—the entrance to the palace that framed Karl Liebknecht as he called out a free socialist republic shortly after his former colleague Philipp Scheidemann called out a republic at the far end of *Unter den Linden.* Even if Karl Liebknecht was second on the street with the news, his proclamation provided the *sozialistischer Staat der Arbeiter und Bauern*[14] with its historical legitimacy. *Schloßportal Nummer* IV, was, therefore, carefully excised from the *Stadtschloß* prior to demolition and transplanted onto the facade of the State Council Building, the seat of the East German government. I'll show it to you when we're in East Berlin."

"Ver-r-ry inter-r-resting, George! I like it very much. 'The Von Garlitz Inverse Theory of Ruin Value.' You might be able to apply it here in West Berlin, too! The construction of the *Kulturforum* was likewise a deliberate attempt to eradicate architectural remnants, not of the monarchy but of *Germania.*"

"You're right, Thomas, though certainly the *Stadtschloß* should be placed in its larger and, from our standpoint here in West Berlin, more positive historical perspective, First World War aside, of course. Berlin publicist Wolf Jobst Siedler went so far as to say '*Berlin war das Schloß.*' I'm not so sure Berlin was the City Palace, but there's something to it. Let's take a look around Berlin V together to see what we can find of Berlin I, II, and III!"

Back in my office, I decided to take back the books on Berlin IV and look for additional sources complementing the reading and research I'd done at the Main Archives Building in Washington, DC. Just before leaving for the library, I looked over at the flounder, who seemed even more terrified than when I'd left him alone with Albert Speer. I wondered what he might have overheard the former *GBI* confiding to the *Portable Dictator.* "Please don't be afraid, friend Flounder," I said, "I've returned from the ruins of *Germania* to tell you there are other forces, counterforces, even positive forces, out there at work in the fields of West Berlin. His expression

---

14 "The Socialist State of Workers and Farmers," Diary of Thomas Vonaechron, Diary Extract, 1982, of trans. TV.

remained unchanged. Opening the door, leaving it intentionally open as an "all clear" signal, I walked down the brightly lit white hallway to the library, thinking about what Henry Adams might have meant by "primitive life" when describing Berlin I back in 1858.

On November 11, I was seated at my worktable under the eyes of the flounder, perusing documents and black-and-white photographs taken from *Stadtstaatsarchiv* holdings. To commemorate Armistice Day, I took a break from preparing the finding aid for the Office of Military Government—Berlin Sector, Berlin VI, to review primary and secondary source materials documenting the demise of Berlin II and the birth of Berlin III. In the library, I even found a book of photographs depicting these events taken by Heinrich Hoffmann and edited by a young German researcher I met in Washington, Ueli Heartfeld. While downtown at the Main Archives, I had translated the German captions on Heinrich Hoffmann's glass plate negatives, seized by the F1F3 US Military Government Detachment in April 1945. Heinrich Hoffmann had been Adolf Hitler's court photographer, and his glass plate negatives became part of the captured German records collection. When Ueli came to Washington to look through the negatives at the Still Picture Branch of the National Archives, my colleagues once again asked for my assistance. I was pleased to find Ueli's book now in print. Among the pictures he'd selected was a flamethrower detachment deployed on *Alexanderplatz*, the machine gun emplacement and rifle detachment positioned under the chariot wheels of *Eirēnē*-Viktoria, guarding the entrance to the HistoriCity from the Brandenburg Gate, and the crowds assembled on the *Königsplatz* to hear Philipp Scheideman proclaim the death of the monarchy and the birth of the republic. There was even a photograph of him, standing erect in his window of opportunity with paper in hand, perhaps the notes for his improvised address hastily jotted on the back of a potato soup-stained menu.

Leaving Ueli's coffee-table-sized book open on my worktable, I picked up a folder of documents labeled "US Army—Berlin: 1918–1919," which contained copies of a series of fascinating reports compiled by Colonel Arthur L. Conger Jr., a military intelligence officer on the staff of General John Joseph "Blackjack" Pershing. Due to his prewar connections and postwar position, Colonel Conger enjoyed unrestricted access to the highest levels of the German government, not only to the military but to civilian leadership and academe as well. Having spent hours in Vault Six reviewing intelligence reporting compiled during and following the Second World War, I was particularly pleased to have the opportunity to read intelligence reports prepared during and following the First World

War in Berlin. They offered engrossing vignettes of the HistoriCity in the grip of revolution, as observed from the balcony of Colonel Conger's comfortable temporary duty quarters, the Hotel Adlon in Berlin-Mitte.

George walked into my office with a letter in his hand. When he saw Ueli's open book and the reports spread out upon my worktable, he said, "Let me guess, Thomas, if I recall your *Schemata* correctly, you must be working on Berlin II and III today."

"Right you are, George! Today is Armistice Day, and to commemorate it, I took a break from OMGUS-BD and am working my way back, in reverse chronological order of course, from the Weimar Republic to the revolution and the end of the monarchy."

"Armistice Day, November 11, 1918, *ja, ja,* of course. In Germany, we don't celebrate the Armistice, but we do commemorate the fallen soldiers on *Volkstrauertag*—later on this month."

"Apropos Armistice, have you seen these fascinating reports from Colonel Conger, George? The US Army was active here in Berlin long before July 1945."

"Yes, yes, of course I've read Colonel Conger's reports, and I meant to tell you about them. Please forgive me, Thomas! A student from the Free University used them to write her dissertation a few years ago. She was quite an attractive young lady with an enchanting name. What was it? Ah yes, Viki—Viktoria Luise von der Linde. She told me Colonel Conger was from Akron, Ohio. Have you ever been there?"

The Free University! Adrift in the archives, I hadn't given much thought to my next move! Professor Schneider had been in Leipzig when I called the number Professor Nayaka had given me to set up an appointment. The helpful secretary at the *Lucius-D.-Clay-Institut* told me his seminar on Berlin as an "accidental *polis*" would be offered during the upcoming summer semester, but to be able to join it, I would have to apply to the university soon.

Before I could answer the question about Colonel Conger's birthplace, George continued, "I just received the official invitation from my colleague at the *Archiv der Hauptstadt der DDR* to a meeting over lunch at the *Marstall* just before Christmas. I hope one month will be sufficient to have the request approved by my bosses as well. I'm afraid my request will have to go up to the *Senatskanzlei*. Government to government contact— you know what that means, Thomas. On the other hand, it concerns the future only insofar as it concerns the past, so hopefully it won't pose too much of a politcal problem. In any case, it is only an informal, preliminary meeting. If it were to produce a project proposal, it would have to be vetted by both sides, as if just one bureaucracy weren't bad enough! Whether or not anything comes of it, we'll have our trip to East Berlin, your Berlin V, Thomas, and I'll be able to show you *Fragmente* of Berlins I, II, and III!" George's request was granted, and the date was set for the December meeting. As the day approached, I became increasingly uneasy. Memories of the day-long study trip to East Berlin during my first visit to West Berlin were not as pleasant as those of the day in Potsdam. I intensely disliked the intentionally intrusive procedures for crossing the sector border practiced at *Bahnhof Friedrichstraße* and, once finally in East Berlin, the penetrating, bleak atmosphere of industrialized grayness.

East Berlin (Berlin V)
December 1982

The days became darker with sunrise around 7:30 and sunset at 4:30 in the afternoon. It never seemed to become light—gray-light rather than daylight. The birds had fled the bare linden trees and the *Hof* behind the *Lothringerstrasse* apartment building. December in Berlin was damp and cold, *naßkalt*. The night before my foray into East Berlin with George, Dr. Kahler fortified my courage with another bottle of *Trollinger*. This time, there was no phone call from a friend in distress In the interim, I had been able to develop, distill, and fix some initial impressions of West Berlin into words. My thoughts, however, kept returning to the following day and the trip to *Ost-Berlin* with George.

"I can well imagine why it might feel strange for you, as an American, to travel to East Berlin. Here in West Berlin, you are one of 'us,' but 'over there,'" he sang, "please forgive my musical attempt at humor, you suddenly become one of 'them.' Although there are similarities, actually more than one might think, there are also pronounced differences, many of them architectural. Although the German Democratic Republic also tries to use *Ost-Berlin* as a display window, the 'Schaufenster des Sozialismus,' they simply don't have the resources available here in West Berlin, heavily subsidized of course by the Federal Republic. Who knows, this may prove to be an advantage in the long run. The journalist who lives upstairs told me more architectural damage has been done in West Germany by developers following the war than by the Allies during the war. I must say, I find that very hard to believe, and it certainly was not the case here in Berlin. In East Berlin you'll find more ruins, excluding of course those buildings like the *Stadtschloß* intentionally ruined after the war. Yet do take a good look! Ask *Herr* von Garlitz to drive you down *Frankfurter Allee*, the former *Stalinallee*. An architect I know tells me the apartment buildings there are among the best built in Berlin after the war, East or West, solid and spacious. On and near the Museum Island you will find what remains of the former imperial capital. I understand your uneasiness, but use it to sharpen your senses, like a wolf," unintentionally emphasizing his point with his tight-lipped, lupine smile. Rising from the kitchen table, he emptied the bottle of *Trollinger* into my glass and said, "*Gute Nacht Herr Vonaechron, und schlafen Sie gut. I'll look forward to your impressions of East Berlin over our next bottle of *Trollinger*!"

George picked me up early the next morning. Although there were no longer any birds to pose the question, "Poo-tee-weet?" was on my mind. After last night's conversation with Dr. Haller, I found myself almost looking forward to *Ost-Berlin*. *Wahnsinn*, if only I could somehow dispense with the unpleasant sector-crossing formalities. George opened the passenger-side door with a smile: "Although cold and gray, it's not supposed to rain today. I brought my umbrella along, just to make certain it stays that way!" Early morning rush hour traffic was unusually heavy, flowing slowly up *Hauptstraße* from Friedenau through Schöneberg, toward Kreuzberg and Allied Checkpoint Charlie. Retracing the route he'd taken the day he picked me up from the airport, George turned right at *Kaiser-Wilhelm-Platz*. December darkness gave the morning a pointillistic quality. Silhouettes of buildings, illuminated by interior lighting, blended into the gray sky. Ahead of us, *Flughafen Tempelhof* rose out of the gray *Berliner Luft, Luft, Luft*. Just before the airport, George turned left onto *Mehringdamm*. The outline of the *Hungerkralle* reached up into the overcast sky. Crossing over *Merhingbrücke*, *Mehringdamm* metamorphosed into *Wilhelmstraße*, a name synonymous with political power during Berlin I, II, III, and IV, the return address on the letterheads of many of the letters I'd reviewed in the State Department post files. We then turned right onto *Kochstraße*.

Stopping just before the corner of *Kochstraße* and *Friedrichstraße*, George pointed out the legendary Checkpoint Charlie, an unassuming, white, functional single-storied structure. "Here you are, Thomas. As a West Berliner with a vehicle, I'll take *Invalidenstraße* over the bridge, not a bridge of tradition mind you, but a bridge of transit into East Berlin. Once you pass through the *Grenzübergangstelle* on the other side," noting my facial expression, which once again must have resembled the flounder's, he paused and said reassuringly, "and you will pass through, Thomas, I'll pick you up at the corner of *Friedrichstraße* and *Unter den Linden*, at one time a very fashionable place for a pickup! We would have been in the very best of company there. Just walk up *Friedrichstraße*. You can't possibly miss *Unter den Linden*, and besides, you have your *Falkplan* with you, valid in both

Ost- and *West-Berlin!* Even though I have an official invitation, it might take some time until we meet up again, so please don't worry. Use the time to explore East Berlin on your own! When you reach *Unter den Linden*, turn left and walk west toward the *Brandenburger Tor.* You can't quite get to it, but close enough. Perhaps if you think about Berlin II and III, you'll forget all about Berlin V!"

Thanking George, I waved until his car disappeared, hoping I would see it again soon. Running along the entire width of the long, narrow building was an illuminated white metal sign displaying the American, British, and French Flags. The American flag also flew from a flagpole at the far end of the checkpoint, directly across from the border crossing point. Checkpoint Charlie was in Kreuzberg, in the American Sector. When I opened the metal door and walked inside, a friendly young military policeman dressed in his immaculate Class A uniform said, "Good Morning, Sir, you're certainly up bright and early today! Off to the old Soviet Sector for a bit of Christmas shopping and sightseeing?" Over the left sleeve of his dark green sweater, he wore the black Military Police brassard, and above the brassard, the shoulder sleeve insignia of the United States Army Berlin. I recognized the double-handled flaming sword on the dark blue Norman shield from the cover of reports reviewed in Vault Six. I also noted his nameplate and rank insignia, Sergeant First Class Keith.

Heartened by his polite, easygoing manner, I handed him my passport and replied, "More sightseeing than shopping today, Sergeant Keith. The last time I visited East Berlin, I didn't have too much luck with the shopping part."

"Well, you'll have to think of something to spend your money on, sir, you know you're required to exchange twenty-five West marks for twenty-five East marks, and not allowed to bring back the change."

"Twenty-five marks? The price of admission has gone up! Nine years ago at *Bahnhof Friedrichstraße*, I only had to exchange twenty marks. I tried to buy East German and Russian flags with the money, but couldn't find any for sale. Considering they were flying everywhere, it seemed odd to me at the time."

Laughing, SFC Keith handed me my passport. "No doubt a question of demand and supply, sir. I don't know about Russian flags, but if you find a Russian soldier willing to sell you military insignia, belt buckles, or even a uniform, please remember me!"

"Military insignia, belt buckles, and uniforms! Isn't that illegal?"

SFC Keith laughed again, "Welcome to Berlin, sir! Have a good time and remember to be back before midnight. If you aren't, you'll turn into a pumpkin and have problems with the *Volkspolizei.* In any event," he turned and, nodding to a large poster hanging on the wall directly behind him, said "we're always here to help you!"

The poster depicted an American infantryman holding an M1 Garand Rifle at the ready position, the bold heading simultaneously posing the question and providing the answer: "Soldier: Why are You in Berlin? . . . to fight like hell, if necessary for US rights and a free Berlin."

Buoyed by our brief exchange and the propaganda poster, I thanked SFC Keith, left Checkpoint Charlie, and walked toward the entrance to the concrete labyrinth, just across the sector border separating *Kreuzberg* from *Mitte*, under observation from a massive concrete watchtower, just behind the Wall. Jimi Hendrix's cover of Bob Dylan's "All Along the Watchtower" ran through my mind on a loop track. On my left stood the last building in Kreuzberg, an architectural remnant of Berlin II. The facade of the four-storied apartment house was intact, as was the crown molding. Although the first floor had been painted in the same light-reflecting white as Allied Checkpoint Charlie, the upper floors were off-white, cream color. An eagle spread its wings over what once was likely the entrance to a pharmacy but was now the Café Adler. The large bay windows, in particular those on the third floor framed by four caryatids, a kind of *Gründerzeit* porch of the maidens, would have provided David Cornwell with the perfect observation point.

When I crossed over at *Bahnhof Friedrichstraße,* I was one of forty students. Today, I was on my own. Following the pedestrian traffic signs, I entered a single-story structure on the right, not unlike the Allied checkpoint. In spite of all the *Angst* I'd carefully invested ahead of time, the border-crossing procedures proved perfunctory. Although my passport disappeared for a few minutes behind a curtained window, it was returned promptly, still warm from the copier, stamped with an entry visa for *Grenzübergang Friedrichstraße*. I was firmly but politely directed to proceed to the exchange window. This task too, was accomplished efficiently, accompanied by perfunctory best wishes for a pleasant *Besuch in der Hauptstadt der DDR*. The guard pushed a button under the counter, and a buzzer indicated the metal door to Berlin V now stood open. I walked back out onto the *Friederichstraße*, but in *Berlin Mitte*, East Berlin. In Dr. Haller's words and in my own mind, I was now one of "them."

The architectural differences between Berlin VI and Berlin V began to emerge through the gray, granulated air, the smoky-sweet aroma of burning *Braunkohl* unifying *Ost-* and *West-Berlin*. The former Soviet Sector of the city was now capital of the German Democratic Republic and, as in Berlin VI, the political powers chose to showcase progress through postwar construction. Although the rubble had been cleared away, most all the prewar buildings bore the pockmarked facade of the war. Walking north in the direction of *Unter den Linden*, I crossed *Leipziger Straße*. In the center of *Friedrichstraße* was the entrance to *U-Bahnhof Stadtmitte*, the "City Center." Citizens of East Berlin, dressed in dark winter coats, scarves, and hats, were flowing up and down the stairs, hurrying past each other with their collars turned up and their eyes turned down. There was little conversation. It was impossible to make eye contact. Crossing over *Johannes-Dieckmann-Straße*, I could see the silhouette of another large building at the far end of the street. When I stopped for a moment to take a look, a shorter, portly young man with unkempt brown hair, wire-rimmed glasses, and an upturned collar stopped beside me for a brief moment, and whispered, *"Fischersinsel,"* moving on before I could reply. As he walked away, I noticed he was wearing a pair of white sneakers. An odd choice for December. Curious, but hesitant to follow, I continued on to the next intersection, hoping it would be *Unter den Linden*. It was *Französische Straße*. In order to reassure myself, I stopped for a moment and took the *Falkplan* from my shoulder bag. Using the Wall, the jagged red line bisecting the map, to orient myself, I quickly found Allied Checkpoint Charlie at coordinates Q9 and then the intersection of *Friedrichstraße* and *Unter den Linden* at Q10, just two streets ahead. During a two-*Berliner Weiße* Mr. Henry's symposium, George explained how both *Unter den Linden* and the *Kurfürstendamm* had been upgraded from bridle paths to boulevards in the grand style of the *Champs-Élysées*. The intersection was, as George had said earlier, unmistakable. But there was no traffic moving between *Friederichstraße* and the Brandenburg Gate on my left. The broad, six-lane *Unter den Linden* had been rendered a Cold War cul-de-sac by Clio and the Wall. The cycle of construction and destruction of Berlin IV had even taken the "linden" out of *Unter den Linden* for a while. Cut down and replanted in Berlin IV, then replanted again after the war in Berlin V, they resembled the spherical rendering of trees, adding the obligatory touch of nature to an architect's conception of a modern boulevard. Through and beyond the trees stood the Brandenburg Gate, Architect Carl Gotthard Langhans's classical entrance to Athens on the Spree. I walked toward it, hoping to get as close as possible to the point where I'd left off in West Berlin back in October. In spite of destruction, deconstruction, and reconstruction, *Unter den Linden* was still impressive, if not imposing in the midmorning light. At first, there seemed to be no white stone here, only gray stone concrete, but after crossing *Glinkastraße*, the embassy compound of the Union of Soviet Socialist Republics opened up on my left. Bright white in the gray daylight, it was an artificially illuminated *Musterbeispiel* of the Stalinist neoclassical architecture scattered throughout Berlin V. The main entrance was set back from the street in a forecourt formed by two wings reaching out to *Unter den Linden*. In the center, mounted on a red marble pedestal, stood a white, larger-than-life-size marble bust of Vladimir Ilyich Ulyanov, another "nation builder." If not for the curious attica crowning the main entrance, together with the former Italian Embassy in the *Tiergatrten*, the building could have stood on Constitution Avenue in Washington, DC. *"(Did you think it was in the white or gray stone? or the lines of the arches and cornices?)"*

Continuing on past the embassy compound toward the *Brandenburger Tor*, I came to *Otto-Grotewohl-Straße*. Referring to the *Falkplan*, I discovered it was the other end of *Wilhelmstraße*, the same street George and I had taken earlier en route to Checkpoint Charlie. Clio had a hand in the naming conventions of East Berlin as well as in West Berlin. Chastised by the war and rechristened, *Wilhelmstraße* was no longer the *Regierungsviertel* it had been during Berlin I, II, III, and IV—an *Empörer* had dethroned the Emperor. Hotel Adlon, one of the loci of high society during Berlin II, III, and IV, once stood across the street. Although Colonel Conger's post-WWI quarters survived the last battle in May 1945, a fire in the wine cellar following the surrender of the HistoriCity spread, gutting the main building. The surviving rear wing was eventually demolished, together with the ruins of the Academy of the Arts, the Embassy of the United States of America, and the other representative buildings that once stood on the once fashionable *Pariser Platz*. An older colleague of George's recounted her last meal in the Hotel Adlon over lunch in the less-fashionable *Stadtstaatsarchiv* cafeteria. She and her husband were dining there when the air raid alarms sounded. Together with the other guests, they took refuge in the bomb shelter beneath the wine cellar. Although the Adlon remained standing, shock waves from the high-explosive bombs shattered the bottles stored overhead. Ankle-deep in champagne, she and her husband patiently waited with the other guests for the all-clear signal to sound.

A patrolled metal security fence, broken up at regular intervals by red-and-white-striped barriers, prevented me from *flâner*-ing out on what had been *Pariser Platz*, now a high-security area on the border between East and West Berlin. I crossed over *Unter den Linden*, stopping in the center to look west through the Brandenburg Gate. The panoramic view through to the *Strasse des 17. Juni* and the Tiergarten beyond was obscured by the Wall on the far side of the gate. A song from a Berlin-based New Wave band lamenting the loss of the view, came to mind, "Shit . . . something's standing in front of it!" In the distance, beyond the Wall in the British Sector, the golden Chick-on-a-Stick rose into the western sky. Directly in front of me, atop the Brandenburg Gate *Brandenburger Tor*, Eirēnē-cum-Viktoria bore down *Unter den Linden* at the reins of her quadriga, bearing high the flag of the German Democratic Republic and the demilitarized laurel wreath *sans* Iron Cross. Continuing across to the far side of the street, I turned to look at the gate, then began walking back toward *Friedrichstraße*.

Nervously preparing myself for loitering without intent in East Berlin, I was surprised and very relieved to see George walking toward me, waving. "As a consequence of being expected, I was expedited! This gives us some time before my appointment. The *Marstall* is at the far end of *Unter den Linden*. I parked on the *Chauseestraße* just up from *Bahnhof Friederichstraße* and have everything I need right here," he said, patting his black leather briefcase. "So let us go then, you and I, with East Berlin spread out before us against the morning sky. Hopefully, you had enough time to walk over to the Brandenburg Gate. Did you see the Soviet Embassy on the site of the former Tsarist Embassy, political if not architectural continuity? Unfortunately, the British, American, and French Embassies have not yet been rebuilt. Perhaps someday, when our island in the Red Sea again becomes a piece of the continent, a part of the mainland!"

"At this intersection, Thomas, we would have had to choose among the Café Kranzler, the Café Bauer in the Hotel Bauer, and the Café Viktoria. Although hard to believe, this intersection was once quite fashionable, the downtown pendant to the *Künstler* cafés *an der Gedächtnis-Kirche*. Please remind me to show you photographs *von damals* at the *Stadtsarchiv tomorrow*." Although greatly relieved to meet up again with George so soon, and, as a consequence, much more comfortable in East Berlin, I was already looking forward to discussing *Ost-Berlin* with him safely back in West Berlin, where I would once again be one of "us."

With George as my Virgil, our walk down *Unter den Linden* turned into a historical review, told in the obligatory reverse chronological order, of the HistoriCity from Berlin V back through Berlin IV, III, II, and I. Though the damage inflicted by the *General Bauinspektor*—together with his strange bedfellows, the Air Officer Commanding-in-Chief Royal Air Force Bomber Command, Commander of the United States Strategic Air Forces, and the General Secretary of the Central Committee of the Communist Party of the Soviet Union—had indeed been great, ruins and reconstructions remained standing for our consideration and contemplation.

After crossing *Charlottenstraße*, George stopped in front of the great gray pillars of the *Staatsbibliothek* at *Unter den Linden* 8, an enormous edifice occupying an entire HistoriCity block. "This is the State Library, originally founded in Cölln—you remember, Thomas, Berlin's sister city, in 1661. It was originally housed in the building across *Unter den Linden* on *Bebelplatz*, formerly the *Forum Fridericianum*." Pointing to the building,

George said, "Humboldt University now occupies the building. The library became one of the largest in the world, moving into this neoclassical building in 1914, just before the First World War. This same building also housed the *Königlich-Preußische Akademie der Wissenschaft*. Here, in the *Kuppelsaal*, the domed lecture hall of the *Staatsbibliothek*, Albert Einstein presented his four-lecture series on *Relativitätstheorie* in 1915."

"Einstein's Theory of Relativity, proclaimed here in the HistoriCity? Somehow that seems historically appropriate. But a question please, George. *Bebelplatz*. Wasn't that the site of the infamous book burning in March 1933?"

"Yes, it was. Most of the *ungefähr* 20,000 books were taken by students from the University Library, not the State Library though. The *Universitäsbibliothek* is the next building up on this side of *Unter den Linden* at number 6. Not that it matters from which library they were taken. Books are books, and as Heinrich Heine wrote "*Dort wo man Bücher verbrennt, verbrennt man am Ende auch Menschen.*'[15] When this building was damaged by the same air raid which destroyed the domed lecture hall in 1941, the collection was distributed throughout Germany. Many of the books stored in what became the Soviet Zone were returned here in 1946. Those stored in the American and French Zones were also returned, but to West Berlin. Another *Staatsbibliothek* was built to house them, right where you found it on the *Kulturform*, site of Albert Speer's *Haus der Fremdenverkehrs* on the *Runder Platz*, less than two kilometers from here. But as you now know, Thomas, *hier* in Berlin, we have two of everything, two State Libraries, two State Archives, two Berlin State governments, even two governing mayors!"

In the center of *Unter den Linden* stood a commanding equestrian statue, a comrade-in-arms of the mounted American Civil War-era general officers guarding Pierre L'Enfant's composition of circles and avenues in Washington, DC. "As this isn't Washington, it's highly unlikely that's a statue of General George D. McKiernan mounted on 'Kentuck.'"

Shaking his head, George laughed and said, "As you well know, Thomas, that is King Frederick II of Prussia, 'Frederick the Great.' What you probably don't know is the name of his horse, 'Condé,' sculpted along with Frederick by Christian Daniel Rauch."

"Of course, George, the three-cornered hat and the cape should have been a Fred giveaway."

"Should have been a what giveaway? To tell the truth, which we historians must continually strive to do, Thomas, Frederick hasn't been back in Berlin for all that long. Dedicated a decade before General

---

15 "There where books are burned, people will eventually be burned as well" (*Almansor, Vers* 243f., 1823). Excerpt from the diary of Thomas Vonaechron, trans. TV.

McKiernan rode to fame in the American Civil War, the statue survived the Second World War encased in concrete, only to be sent into exile at *Sans, Souci.* in Potsdam, which Friedrich would have approved of. He reappeared here only two years ago, supported by seventy-four of his contemporaries, among them Immanuel Kant. There you see Plato's ideal, the philosopher in the service of the state. But perhaps the musical monument behind the statue, the *Staatsoper Unter den Linden*, is as appropriate as this marital one." From our Mr. Henry's symposia, I knew George to be an *aficionado* of the opera, attending performances here in East Berlin as well as at the *Deutsche Oper* in West Berlin. Having two of everything does have certain advantages. "Shortly after becoming King of Prussia in 1740, Friedrich commissioned it as his court opera. Over the years it has, just like the *Staatsbibliothek*, been destroyed by fire, reconstructed, and remodeled. Yet, as you can see, Thomas," pointing to the tympanum inside the triangular pediment, "it has retained its original neoclassical appearance, a monument to Friedrich's love of arts other than war. '*Fridericus Rex Apollini et Musis.*'" Although the bullet and shell holes in the six columns supporting the pediment had been expertly filled and smoothed over, and the statutes guarding the heavy entrance doors placed back upon their pedestals, like so many other buildings in East Berlin, the *Staatsoper Unter den Linden* still retained the pockmarked facade of war.

"You know, George, *Fridericus's* interest in war and opera do not seem, to use the local parlance, dialectically opposed. While walking through the Tiergarten, Gabriel Kielerförde and I discussed war as a kind of opera, a reality opera structuring space and time for political purpose. But apropos arts other than war, George, I understand Frederick was greatly interested in viticulture, as well as in culture. Did you know grapes cultivated under his supervision at *Sans, Souci.* were used to make wines celebrated throughout the courts of Europe, in Austria, France, and even in Italy? Frederick actually used wine as a tool of diplomacy. He was so successful, he became known throughout Europe as . . . 'Frederick the Grape.'"

"'Frederick the Grape?'" echoed George, shaking his head in disbelief. "I think you better have a coffee, Thomas! We can try to get a table at the *Operncafé* across the street and sit for a few minutes. You seem to be *etwas überfordert* . . . what's your American expression? A little 'stressed out' this morning!"

"No, no, George, please forgive my attempt at humor. It was retro-comedy, and neo-comedy is called for these days—you know, 'neocom.' Let's continue on, I'll have time enough for a cup of coffee while I'm waiting for . . ." My words were abruptly scattered by the unmistakable sound of leather jackboots smacking on the pavement. A squad of *National Volksarmee* soldiers goose-stepped out from behind another, smaller neoclassical building ahead of us, just beyond the university.

"Don't be alarmed, Thomas, they're not going to arrest you for your wordplay, though it does border on *lèse-majesté*! It's just the changing of the guard at the *Neue Wache*, the East Berlin equivalent to Arlington Cemetery's Tomb of the Unknown Soldier. To be correct, although originally known as the *Neue Wache* when it was dedicated in 1816, it is now officially the Memorial to the Victims of Fascism and Militarism. Yet prewar, or should I say 'prewars,' Berlin still resonates through Karl Friedrich Schinkel's timeless design. Built originally as a guardhouse, history has made it a guarded house, complete with Prussian *Stechschritt*.

"Another one of Clio's *eirönïa*, almost a double entendre. They seem to be scattered throughout Berlin at all levels—I, II, III, IV, V, and VI. Alternative ways of looking at architecture over time, through history"— *"All architecture is what you do when you look upon it, (Did you think it was in the white or gray stone? or the lines of the arches and cornices?)"*

"I wonder if these all these fragments can somehow be reassembled. There are so many things to think about, to examine and consider! Are they leading me somewhere?"

"Of course they are, Thomas, they're leading you to your own Berlin, your own HistoriCity." Looking at his watch, George said, "Ah, I'm afraid I must slowly leave you now to make my way to the *Marstall* for the meeting. You might look here for a few more fragments of history, in the *Museum für Deutsche Geschichte*. The building, *das Zeughaus*, is the oldest on *Unter den Linden*, built in the baroque style by Frederick III. Just like your former torpedo factory and my former *Waffen- und Munitionsfabrik*, this elegant building used to be an arsenal. Since 1875, however, it's been a repository for military artifacts marshaled to defend changing interpretations of history, *wechselende Weltanschaungen*. All national museums do this really, retell the myth of the state; your excellent National Museum of American History on Constitution Avenue is no exception. Competition among England, France, and Germany in the nineteenth century for museum supremacy was almost as intense as for military supremacy! Perhaps I *übertreiben* . . . ah, exaggerate a bit, but there's some truth behind it.

"Directly across *Unter den Linden* is another part of the neoclassical ensemble making up Berlin, the reconstructed *Kronprinzenpalais*. The original building, which actually predates occupancy by the Prussian crown prince, was built during the mid-seventeenth century as a private residence. With baroque and neoclassical facade lifts, it stood here until March 1945. Although the rear section survived, it too was eventually demolished. The original *Kronprinzenpalais* was the birthplace of both *Kaiser Wilhelm I* and your grandfather's old adversary, *Kaiser Wilhelm II.*"

"*Kaiser* Bill was born here?"

"Yes, well, in the original palace that once stood here. During the Weimar Years, the palace became an annex of the *Nationalgalerie* on Museum Island, with a *Galerie der Lebenden* for contemporary art, which, according to some knowledgeable people, was the inspiration for the Museum of Modern Art in New York City. How wonderful it would be if one day, 'MoMa' would come to grace our gray Berlin with an exhibition! The 'Berlin Museum War' between partisans of Impressionism and Expressionism was fought here, all swept away as *Entartete Kunst*, 'Degenerate Art,' by the National Socialists in 1936. Although a reconstruction, the *Kronprinzenpalais* does retain Johann Heinrich Strack's neoclassical design, very much in harmony with the *Staatsbibliothek, Staatsoper Unter den Linden, Neue Wache*, and the *Museum für Deutsche Geschichte*. Unfortunately, the harmony ends next door, with the Foreign Ministry of the German Democratic Republic. Ironically, and here's another of Clio's *eirönïa*, it was built on the site of Karl Friedrich Schinkel's *Bauakademie*. Although badly damaged, the Academy of Architecture was also initially slated for postwar reconstruction, but unfortunately fell victim to financial constraints and postwar planning for a more representative socialist city center.

Looking up at the ten-story, windowed rectangular box housing the *Ministerium für Auswärtige Angelegenheiten der DDR,* I added, "It would fit in perfectly with the buildings on L'Enfant Plaza in Washington, DC."

Laughing and nodding his head in agreement, George continued, "Here, at the eastern end of *Unter den Linden,* the *Ministerium* signals a shift from the traditional to the socialist. I believe I told you the *Stadtschloß,* which once upon a time stood on the far side of the *Kupfergraben,* an arm of the Spree, survived the war severely damaged but repairable. It was torn down in 1950 to make room for the *Palast der Republik,* irreverently called '*Der Ballast der Republik*' by *Berliner* East and West alike. Fortunately, our sense of humor cannot be separated by sectors! Yes, even in ruins, feudalism simply had no place in a modern socialist society. It occurs to me the Palace of the Republic is just across *Marx-Engels-Platz* from the *Marstall.* It would be a good place for us to meet, a good '*Treff*—isn't that the operative word?—for us to meet after my meeting. Let's meet in the espresso bar on the first floor. Prices are quite reasonable, so you'll find a few fellow travelers—I meant fellow tourists of course—there, along with the locals, a good place to spend your *Ostmark.*

As we crossed over the *Kupfergraben* on the *Marx-Engels-Brücke,* George asked, "Do you remember your proposed 'inverse theory of ruin value?' No ruins, no contemplation of the ruins, no bridges of tradition to the past? I've wondered if one of the reasons for renaming the *Schloßbrücke* is that there is no longer a *Schloß* on the other side. People just might become curious and ask, 'What happened to it?' As *Schloßbrücke* once led to the *Stadtschloß,* the *Marx-Engels-Brücke* now leads to *Marx-Engels-Platz.* By the way, when we crossed over the *Marx-Engels-Brücke,* we crossed onto *die Spreeinsel,* the actual birthplace of Berlin or, once again to be historically correct, of Cölln, which was first documented in 1237. Although the *Haupt- und Residenzenstadt Berlin* didn't officially swallow up Cölln, along with Friedrichswerder, Friedrichstadt, and Dorotheenstadt until 1709, according to the Vonaechron-Dörpfeld'sche schemata, it clearly belongs to Berlin I!

"Before I walk over to the *Archiv der Hauptstadt der DDR,* I'd like to show you one last thing of interest. As if at Clio's command, *Unter den Linden* suddenly metamorphosed into *Karl-Liebknecht-Straße,* honoring the former *Reichstag* deputy who, shortly after Scheidemann shoved his soup aside to proclaim the republic from a window of the *Reichstag,* proclaimed a free socialist republic from *Portal IV* of the *Stadtschloß.* Liebknecht *ante portas!*"

"George, will there still be time following your meeting in the *Marstall* to see *Schloßportal IV?*"

"Yes, yes, of course, Thomas. After we meet up again, we'll walk across the *Schloßplatz* to the *Staatsratsgebäude,* take a look, then continue on to *Werderscher Markt,* and walk down *Französische Straße* and around the nearby *Gedarmenmarkt* on the way back to *Friedrichstraße.* As I told you, *Schloßportal IV* was carefully removed from the *Stadtschloß* prior to demolition and grafted onto the facade of the *Staatsratsgebäude.* Its political significance lies in the fact that Liebknecht's proclamation provided the Socialist State of Workers and Farmers with necessary historical legitimacy."

"So, once an entrance into a palace, *Schloßportal IV* is now an entrance into a modern socialist state, an entrance into history, a kind of a doorway to the dialectic."

"I don't know if I'd go that far, Thomas, but it's certainly better than 'Frederick the Grape!'" As George and I continued up *Karl-Liebknecht-Straße,* a magnificent, lime tree-lined park opened on our left. "That is the *Lustgarten,* though it doesn't look as *lustig* as it used to," George commented. "Originally, it was the garden of the palace kitchen. In the middle of the seventeenth century, during the reign of the Great Elector, it became a formal garden. True to his nickname, *der Soldatenkönig,* the 'Soldier-King,' Frederich the Great's father, later uprooted the garden in favor of a sand-covered parade ground for his soldiers. Although the *Lustgarten* once again became a garden under Friedrich Wilhelm II, after occupying Berlin in 1806, Napoleon used it as a parade ground for his troops. The *Altes Museum*, the Athenian temple you see at the far end, was designed by Karl Friedrich Schinkel, the *Lustgarten* itself redesigned by Peter Joseph Lenné. The 'Old Museum' was one of the elements of a larger architectural ensemble surrounding the *Lustgarten*, including the *Zeughaus,* the *Stadtschloß,* and the *Berliner Dom.* It had a political as well as a military function. Mass demonstrations were repeatedly held here during the early twentieth century, including one in February 1933 opposing the National Socialist government. The following year, the *Lustgarten* was paved over as an arena for National Socialist spectacles. The paving stones you see here date to that time. After Berlin fell to Soviet forces in May 1945, the *Lustgarten* again served as a parade ground for the victorious Red Army. We have a copy of the black-and-white Russian film documenting the victory parade, which took place here at the *Stadtstaatsarchiv.* But it's not the *Lustgarten* I want to show you, Thomas, but this, the *Berliner Dom.*" George pointed to a mammoth, war- and weather-blackened, neo-Renaissance church weighing down the far side of the *Lustgarten.* The gravity of its four towers and massive dome threatened to pull the entire architectural ensemble into the Spree.

As we approached the battery of staircases facing the *Lustgarten*, I could see that although the walls were still standing, the *Dom* was an unrestored ruin, fire-blackened and pockmarked with bullet and shell holes, souvenirs of the war in the HistoriCity. One of two enormous bronze entrance doors stood open, tourists and school classes ascended and descended the staircase. George and I joined them. Entering into the sanctuary from a high-ceilinged hallway, I noticed certain sections had been roped off. The marble floor was covered by water and, looking up, I saw an off-center oculus in the large dome, not a monument to Hadrian as in Rome but apparently a monument to Harris, Air Marshal Sir Arthur Harris. A hand-lettered sign in German and English informed visitors that destroyed on May 24, 1944, by the Royal Air Force and US Eighth Air Force, the *Berliner Dom* was slowly being restored with pennies saved by the schoolchildren of the German Democratic Republic.

"Once again, to be historically accurate," George continued, the "Supreme Parish and Collegiate Church was destroyed at least three times: once by the British and the Americans—some of the damage was no doubt caused by the Red Army as well—but also twice by the Hohenzollern. According to Schinkel's plans, the buildings surrounding the *Lustgarten* were to compose an ensemble. Did you notice how out of proportion the *Dom* is to the other structures? Originally built in the Baroque style by Johann Boumann, Schinkel remodeled the church in the neoclassical style.

Your grandfather's old adversary, *Kaiser Wilhelm II.*"

"*Ach du Lieber,* '*Kaiser* Bill' once again!"

"Yes, '*Kaiser* Bill' decided the Boumann-Schinkel church simply wasn't grand enough to capture the grandeur of the Hohenzollern. So as *summus episcopus,* he had it demolished, destroying the architectural harmony of the *Lustgarten* along with it. What you see standing here was built by Julius Carl Raschdorff in the late nineteenth century as a Prussian pendant to St. Peter's Basilica in Vatican City. Personally, I wish the *Pfennige* of the schoolchildren of the German Democratic Republic would be used to deconstruct this *Dom* and rebuild the Boumann-Schinkel church, restoring architectural harmony to the Museum Island!"

"So, the construction-deconstruction dialectic did not begin in Berlin IV with the the *General Bauinspektor* and the air marshal after all?"

"No, no, Thomas, not at all, it's much older than that, it's the *Handwerk* of history, and Berlin is, after all, according to you, the 'HistoriCity.' Now, I really must leave you. Nodding in the direction of the mammoth, rectangular, white marble building on the other side of the street, George said, "Let's meet at, say 3:00 in the *Espressobar* on the first floor. The *Ballast der Republik* has thirteen restaurants, a discothèque, and even a state-sanctioned *Kabarett,* but only one *Espressobar.* You can't miss it! If it's closed for some reason, we'll meet in front of the entrance. Although I do not anticipate any delays, if something comes up, remember you can always just walk out the way you walked in, down *Friedrichstraße* and back out through Checkpoint Charlie."

The self-confidence I'd begun to enjoy left with George, replaced by the sense of again being one of "them." Perhaps it also had to do with the written reference to the Eighth US Air Force. I'd reviewed records of the Eighth Air Force and the US Strategic Bombing Survey in Vault Six. Although the Strategic Air Campaign had been directed at National Socialist Germany, not the German Democratic Republic, the wording of the hand-lettered sign under the burnt-out dome seemed more contemporary, more Cold War. The *Berliner Dom* was cold and wet, *naßkalt.* Rather than descend into the crypt, I decided to explore Museum Island for other surviving elements of Schinkel's architectural ensemble. As George had suggested, perhaps by focusing on Berlin I, I could dissipate the damp, gray December gloom of Berlin V.

Leaving the *Dom* by the *Karl-Liebknecht-Straße* exit, I walked over to the Spree embankment, stopping on the western side of the *Liebknecht-Brücke,* another bridge of tradition. Ahead stood the towering *Fernsehturm* near *Alexanderplatz.* Although obscured by clouds, late-morning sunlight reflected off the stainless steel spherical dome of the revolving restaurant on the top of the concrete shaft, forming "the Cross of Light." During the study tour of East Berlin, our guide had referred to the *Fernsehturm* as "*Sankt Walter*," noting Walter Ulbricht had directed the erection of the tower in the historic center of Berlin. Repeated efforts had been made to mitigate the metallic reflection, but the *Lichtkreuz* remained. Rather than continue on to the *Fernsehturm*, the *Marienkirche* with its medieval dance of death in the entrance hall, and the *Rathaus Schöneberg* of East Berlin, the *Rotes Rathaus*, I retraced my steps, turning right onto *Am Lustgarten*, the street running between the *Lustgarten* and the *Berliner Dom*. Walking past the *Altes Museum*, I came to a colonnade and climbed the stairs into an elegant peristyle. In the center stood the neoclassical *Alte Nationalgalerie*. Here was Athens on the Spree, at the far end of *Unter den Linden* from the Propylaea entrance at *Brandenburger Tor*. Without George's reassuring presence, I hesitated to enter and decided to continue my exploration outdoors *per pedes Pilgrimorum*. The colonnade led to the ruins of the *Neues Museum*. Although large sections of the neoclassical facade were still intact, the roof was gone, exposing the interior walls to the elements—Parthenon on the Spree with a British air marshal playing the part of Venetian Admiral Francesco Morosini. As in the ruined embassies of the *Tiergartenviertel*, nature had begun to reassert herself, creating that curious, pleasant harmony between natural growth and ruined artifice. Walking over to more closely contemplate the ruins, I was startled by an armed soldier standing guard over them. Momentarily forgetting my "them" status, I asked if I could take a photograph of him in front of the ruins of the *Neues Museum*. With his sharp "*Nein*," Athens on the Spree and Berlin I fell simultaneously, and, once again, I became one of "them" in Berlin V. Quickly lowering my camera in compliance, I walked to the *Kupfergraben*, turning to follow the embankment. The full extent of the wartime destruction of *Neues Museum* was laid open before me. Statues and pieces of masonry stood arranged in an open courtyard where the corner of the *Neues Museum* once stood. A provisional dam held back the Spree. Ahead, I could see the massive right wing of the *Pergamonmuseum*, housing the Pergamon Altar and other architectural ensembles imported from ancient cities, the Market Gate of Miletus, the Ishtar Gate of Babylon. Berlin, which once empowered its agents to acquire ancient architecture to embellish its own, now stood in ruins itself, ruins within and without. As a member of the Basel study group, I'd spent several engrossing hours in the museum. The ancient historical sites had been meticulously reconstructed, recreated *in situ*, allowing visitors to struggle with the Greek gods for the supremacy of order over chaos, stroll across the marketplace in Miletus, or process into ancient Babylon through the Ishtar Gate. Standing in the massive courtyard of the entrance to this remarkable museum, recalling those impressions years later, comparing them with what I'd seen today, I suddenly felt tired and incapable of contemplating any more ruins, ancient or contemporary.

Turning my back on the *Pergamonmuseum*, I walked to the small pedestrian bridge across from the courtyard and crossed over the *Kupfergraben*. Following the Spree, I returned to the *Zeughaus* and *Unter den Linden*, which, thanks to George's tutoring, were now reassuringly familiar landmarks. Retracing the route we'd taken together earlier, I walked over the *Lustgarten* back to the *Berliner Dom*, directly across the street from the Palace of the Republic. Metal beams running horizontally and vertically across the rectangular white marble facade held large, sun-reflecting, thermopane windows in place. The windows broke up the reflection of the *Dom* into pieces of a giant puzzle. Here stood yet another concrete exercise in architectural displacement in the HistoriCity, with the Palace of the Republic replacing the *Stadtschloß* of the Hohenzollern. Crossing *Karl-Liebknecht-Straße*, I walked up the ramp leading to the sidewalk running along the front of the building to the main entrance. Before entering, I walked down the staircase, out into the vast parking lot, and looked up. Over the bank of entrance doors, crowning the staircase, was the national emblem of the German Democratic Republic, a hammer and compass encircled in a wreath of rye. Climbing back up the stairs, I walked through the doors and, much to my delight, into a spacious open foyer, brightly lit on this drab December day by hundreds of glass globes suspended on chrome cables from the high ceiling above.

"*Da oben sind die bekannten gläsernen Blume* . . . excuse me, the 'glass flowers.' It is actually a sculpture from Reginald Richter and Richard Wilhelm. The real name is *The Glass Tree*, but most people think it looks more like flowers. What do you think, more like flowers or a tree? Please excuse me, but I believe you might be a visitor to the Palace of the Republic, may I be helpful to you?"

Looking up at the ceiling, I hadn't seen the young woman walk over to meet me as I passed through the entrance doors. Dressed in a zippered, mustard yellow jumper worn over a black-and-white polka-dot blouse with a Schiller collar, she smiled warmly. Although the cut of her abundant dark brown hair reminded me somewhat of a helmet, it was not unattractive. Over her left breast, she wore a golden name plate: *Frl. Asta Otto, Hostess*. "Yes, yes, please, *Fräulein* Otto, *vielen Dank*! I'm looking for the *Espressobar*, it is supposed to be somewhere here on the first floor." Once again, curiosity triumphed over caution. "May I ask how you know I'm a visitor?"

She laughed, tossing her hair, "*Ja, ich weiß nicht aber,* I shouldn't say so but . . . your jeans. We have jeans too you know, but they're, well, they're different. Just look around you." There were quite a few other visitors to the *Palast der Republik*, retirees, school classes, and tourists, many of them also obviously enchanted by the glass flowers overhead. Many of the younger people were also wearing jeans, but they were different. This seemed to be a place for people, if not for "the people." "Please forgive me, but this isn't the first floor, it is the ground floor, *das Erdgeschoß*. The first floor is upstairs, just take any one of the escalators." There were several escalators to choose from in the spacious foyer, bringing to mind the John-Allen-Eleanor-Dulles International Airport and my departure, which now seemed years ago. In her tailored hostess uniform, *Fräulein Otto* reminded me of the sensuous Pan Am stewardess on the *City of Berlin*. "The *Espressobar* is on the first floor, there's a *Milch- and Mokkabar*, too. I'd be happy to show you where they are. Do you have a reservation?"

"Is a reservation required for a cup of coffee?"

"No, no, not for a *Kaffee* but for a table." She laughed. "It can be quite crowded around lunchtime you know, but let's go take a look. Perhaps I might be helpful to you." At the top of the escalator was an information desk womaned by uniformly dressed hostesses. They looked up at us, smiling at *Fräulein* Otto. "*Ich komme gleich wieder, will nur unserem Gast die Espressobar zeigen,*"[16] she said over her shoulder, while escorting me to the escalator.

"Might I ask where you learned English?"

Turning back to me she said, "I used to work as a travel guide for the state travel agency in Berlin, but I simply couldn't resist the opportunity to work here. There's the *Espressobar*, just ahead." She led me through the door, greeting the maître d', who was dressed in a complementary dark brown suit and bow tie. He was standing next to a large, white metal sign, displaying the written instructions, "*BITTE WARTEN Sie werden plaziert!*"[17] in red and black letters, quite similar to the "ATTENTION You are leaving the American Sector" signs on the far side of the Wall. I was glad *Fräulein* Otto had graciously offered to escort me. As she chatted with the maître d', I looked around the *Espressobar*. In spite of the intimidating instructions spelled-out on the sign, it radiated an agreeable ambiance, decorated in brownish tones with a cream-colored ceiling. Bauhaus-style leather and chrome chairs were grouped in twos, threes, and fours around round café tables. Most of the tables were taken; those still open had cards in the center with "*Reserviert*"

---

16 "I'll be right back, I just want to show our guest to the *Espressobar.*" Diary of Thomas Vonaechron, Diary Extract, 1982, trans. TV.
17 "Please wait, you will be placed/seated!" Diary of Thomas Vonaechron, Diary Extract, 1982, trans. TV.

printed on both sides. My hostess turned back to me and asked, "Would you mind sitting at the bar, or are you meeting someone?"

"I am indeed meeting a friend, but he won't be coming for an hour or so. A seat at the bar would be just fine, thank you very much, *Fräulein Otto*." Walking over to the bar, I chose a barstool at the end of the counter where I would have room to spread out the *Falkplan*. Setting my shoulder bag gently down on the marble-tiled floor, I tried to pull the barstool back from the bar.

Fräulein Otto laughed, then smiled apologetically, "I'm sorry, but it's bolted to the floor."

We laughed together. "You have been very kind *Fräulein Otto*, may I invite you for an espresso?" She shook her head.

"Unfortunately, no espresso is available in the *Espressobar*, only Mokka! No, but I thank you for your invitation. You are most kind. Under other circumstances, I would be pleased to join you, but now I must go back to the foyer, back to work. You never know, maybe someone else is looking for the *Espressobar* down on the *Erdgeschoß*. Before I leave you, might I draw your attention to the mosaic on the back wall, behind the bar? It is made of *Meissener Porzellan*—do you know Meissen? It is very famous throughout Europe." I was tempted to tell her the story of a Meissen figurine found in the ruins of Dresden in February 1945 by an American prisoner of war, but given the story's tragic end, decided against it. Instead, I studied the porcelain mosaic running the entire length of the long bar. In complementary brown, yellow, and blue tones, it depicted a couple reclining in a garden of flowers. Sensuality was possible in a socialist state. A line from Heiner Müller's *Germania Tod in Berlin* also came to mind, but once again, I thought better of it.

"How lovely, it does have a kind of, and you'll forgive me please, socialist sensuality about it," I said, hoping *Fräulein* Otto wouldn't take offense, as my impression of the mosaic began to merge with my impression of her. She didn't seem to, she knew. Tossing her thick brown hair and laughing, she shook my hand and politely took her leave to return to her duty station at the entrance to the foyer. "Under other circumstances, I'd be pleased to join you . . ."

The maître d' took my overcoat, signaling the bartender to wait on me. Thanks to *Fräulein* Otto, I felt like an insider. I knew better than to ask for an espresso, ordering a Mokka instead. From my shoulder bag, I took out the *Falkplan* and my notebook, unfolding the map to pages three and four, working my way from West to East, and the grid over Berlin V, intending to plot the morning's coordinates and make a few notes. I looked up at the mosaic again, then out over the tables, listening to the white noise of conversation accented by sounds of silverware, coffee cups, and plates.

George was right, there were quite a few fellow tourists today, looking at maps and writing postcards, but there also appeared to be a fair number of East Berliners enjoying themselves as well. As the *Espressorbar* filled, others began to take seats at the bar. No longer feeling like one of "them," I felt like one of them, enjoying the restorative powers of simply sitting in a café with strangers. The *Naßkälte* in my bones from the *Dom* across the street began to recede. The sudden sound of the Mokka service set down on the surface of the countertop returned my attention to the bar.

"*Bitteschön, der Herr!*" As the uniformed waiter turned to serve another customer, the maître d' walked over and politely asked if I needed anything else.

"No, thank you, it really is quite nice here in the *Espressobar!*" I said.

"Thank you, sir! We do *Asbest* as we can under the circumstances" he replied, smiling as he walked back to the entrance.

I returned to the *Falkplan* lying open to Berlin V on the countertop and my notebook. Although I had intended to concentrate on Berlin I and III, my thoughts were filled with architectural and archival impressions of all levels of the HistoriCity, the encounters I had had since arriving in Berlin, *Fräulein* Otto, the Pan Am stewardess. Sex and the HistoriCity. In only a few hours, thanks to George's expertise, I had been able to walk back through Berlin I, II, and III and then, on my own, jump ahead to the present, to Berlin V, East Berlin. Together with my previous explorations in Berlin VI, in West Berlin, I was slowly beginning to piece together fragments of the HistoriCity, uniting archives with architecture, fascinating but oddly tiring work. When I first visited West Berlin, I felt an immediate attraction, though I wasn't sure why. My study of German history, Ryan's book *The Last Battle*, or perhaps simply the possibility of a human encounter as I made my way through the sparsely lit streets at night, searching for the artificial light and warmth, marked and marketed by the bars, cafés, and yes, old chum, the cabarets. This indefinite attraction had been heightened by my work at the National Archives. Now that I was on-site, it occurred to me I might be searching for something else, something more personal in the HistoriCity. Suddenly, George was standing beside me at the bar. An hour had passed. Although I'd ordered a second Mokka and had pen in hand, I had not yet begun to write. "*Hallo, mein lieber* Thomas, I see you found the *Espressobar!*"

"Hello, George, yes, yes, I did, but not without the help of a very kind, state-sponsored hostess, *Fräulein* Asta Otto. You know, a proletarian palace might not have been such a bad idea after all! But how did your meeting at the *Archiv der Hauptstadt der DDR* go?"

"Ha ha, whether or not the *Palast* was a bad idea still remains to be seen! Although the meeting was more *anstrengend* than I anticipated, it seemed to go quite well under the unusual circumstances. For one thing, there were two more participants. My colleague was there, but so was his supervisor and one other person, who did not appear to be an archivist." George smiled. "In any case, we discussed the project proposal in some detail. My colleagues were very interested to learn about the OMGUS documents you are working on!" Patting his briefcase he said, "My preparations were not in vain. For both personal and professional reasons, I find the possibility of reunifying Berlin, if only in a finding aid, exciting. The meeting was not too long and the lunch surprisingly good, but I must say, Thomas, I'm quite tired now. Perhaps it was the excitement. What did you do after we parted? Did you find any more fragments of Berlin's history?"

"Yes, I did, so many, maybe too many to catalog. I had intended to write some down but have been sitting here just enjoying the mosaic and the Mokka instead. *Mensch*, no wonder you're tired! You gave me an in-depth tour of *Unter den Linden* before your meeting even started, for which I'm very grateful to you! But for some reason, I'm tired, too." All the barstools were now taken. I surveyed the room to see if a table had opened up. "Would you like a Mokka, George?"

"No, no, but thank you, Thomas, we had coffee with lunch. Perhaps we should walk back to *Friedrichstraße*. Soon it will begin to get dark." Taking the last sip from my cold Mokka, I folded the *Falkplan*, placing it, along with my notebook, back into my shoulder bag. I paid the bill of 1.90 DM, 23.10 DM to go from the 25 DM, and, reclaiming my overcoat from the rack, nodded my thanks to the maître d'. As we walked over to the escalator, I looked over at the hostesses standing behind the information desk. Unfortunately, *Fräulein* Otto was not among them, though one of them smiled in recognition and waved. I waved back. We walked through the brightly-lit foyer to the main entrance (*Fräulein* Otto wasn't there either: "Under other circumstances, I'd be pleased to join you . . ."), through the doors, down the stairs, and back out into the dark December day I'd left behind for an hour in the *Palast der Republik*.

Getting dark. The gray, granulated *Berliner Luft* increased in darkness and density in winter, a heaviness which had to be born outdoors. Walking across the former *Schloßplatz*, George pointed out the historic *Schloßportal IV*, now a *Spolie* in the facade of the *Staatsratsgebäude*, the State Council Building. "There's your 'doorway into history,' Thomas!" We crossed over the *Kupfergraben*. "This is the *Werderscher Markt*, the church, the *Friedrichswerdersche Kirche*, is also from Schinkel." I expected George to remark on the shift from the neoclassical to the neo-Gothic, but he didn't. He was tired.

I couldn't resist one more question, a clarification. "How about that large building to the left?"

Before George could answer, a short, portly young man with unruly brown hair and wire-rimmed glasses, the collar of his wrinkled knee-length raincoat turned up against the cold, stopped beside us and whispered, "That is *Fischersinsel*, Fischer's Island." He seemed familiar. Yes, it was the very same young man with the white sneakers who'd said the very same thing to me that morning, when I stopped briefly at the corner of *Friedrichstaße* and *Johannes-Dieckmann-Straße*. So this was the large building I'd seen from the other end of the street.

"No, no," said George, "I'm very sorry, but you are mistaken. This is the former *Reichsbank* building, which currently houses the headquarters of the Socialist Unity Party of Germany, *die Zentrale des SED. Die Fischerinsel* is across the bridge behind us, over there," pointing back over the bridge to the *Spreeinsel*.

Turning to George, he said, "I'm not convinced," then turning back to me said, "*Die 'historischen Schichten' der Architektur sind weniger Hypothek als Mahnung und zugleich Verpflichtung für die Zukunft.*" Lowering his head, he walked away quickly, just as he had earlier in the day.

"What did he say?" George asked. "Was he American or German? He seemed somewhat disoriented!"

"Or perhaps he was talking about something else, George. I'm not certain, I thought I heard him say, '*Fischers Insel*' not '*Fischerinsel.*' Anyway, I think he said, 'The historical layers of architecture are less a mortgage on the past than a warning and, at the same time, an obligation for the future.'"

"Well, he certainly picked just the right person in all of East Berlin to pass that insight along to, didn't he now? I've never heard of '*Fischers Insel*' before. Perhaps he is unstuck in history too, like you! You certainly do seem to have an uncanny ability to attract interesting people in East as well as West Berlin! Come along now, we'll follow *Französische Straße*, walk over to the *Gendarmenmarkt*, then return to *Friedrichstraße*. When we came to a large church, George turned left onto *Dr.-Wilhelm-Külz-Straße*. Once we passed the church, a large square opened up majestically on our right. A broad set of stairs led up to the entrance of a neoclassical building, and there was another, apparently identical church to the one we'd just passed at the far end of the square. This was the most magnificent architectural ensemble I'd seen so far in Berlin, East or West.

"Is this the *Gendarmenmarkt*, George?"

"Yes, it is, Thomas, although the Huguenot *gens d'armes* have long departed. Friedrich Schiller, who used to stand there in the center of the *Gendarmenmarkt*, has departed too, for West Berlin. Maybe he'll return one day, like *Friedrich der Große* did to *Unter den Linden*—after all, '*Ein guter Abgang ziert die Übung.*'[18] The neoclassical building in front of us is the *Konzerthaus,* and as you might have guessed by now, also built by Schinkel. On the right is the *Französicher Dom,* on the left the *Deutscher Dom.* The French church was built by the Huguenots invited to take refuge in Berlin in the early eighteenth century. The German church was built in a complementary style a few years later by Lutherans." I was waiting for George to expand on the architects and architecture of the two churches, but he didn't. He was tired! In a way I was glad, as I was tired too, full, perhaps too full of impressions of Berlin. He did have something else in mind, however. "Before we return to *Friedrichstraße,* there's one other building I'd like to show you, Thomas,' George smiled, "not as beautiful as these, but 'ver-r-ry inter-r-resting!'" Continuing along *Dr.-Wilhelm-Külz-Straße,* we came to a large, prewar building at *Otto-Nuschke-Straße.* "This is the former Prussian State Bank, one of the few buildings on the *Gendarmenmarkt* with relatively little war damage. It was built just after the turn of the century. The building I want to show you, however, is just up the street, built as an extension to the bank in the thirties." As we followed along the facade, Historicism abruptly yielded to stripped Classicism. The four-story extension would have complemented the Tiergarten embassies, the buildings of the Bendlerblock compound, or the Rayburn House Office Building on Capitol Hill in Washington, DC. Even the iron light fixtures flanking the twin entrance doors at 22–23 played heavily on Albert Speer's light-motive. Pausing for a moment in front of the entrance, George continued, "a series of underground vaults were constructed beneath this building, just like at the Washington National Records Center! According to some sources, *der Schatz des Priamos,* the 'Treasure of King Priam,' which had been carefully crated up in 1939 and stored in the basement of the Royal Museum for Ethnologie, where it had been on display since 1885, was moved here in January 1941 and stored in . . . Vault Six! Yes, Thomas, in Vault Six! At the end of 1941, it was moved to the *Flakturm Tiergarten,* the 'Zoo Tower.' During the chaos of the Battle of Berlin in May 1945, the golden treasure of King Priam disappeared."

"The treasure of Priam, King of Troy, stored here in Vault Six, and then in one of Albert Speer's massive concrete *Flak* towers? Somehow, that all seems not only appropriate here in the HistoriCity, George, but ironic as well—*Eirönïa*! According to the more critical accounts of Heinrich Schliemann's excavations, he had Priam's treasure boxed up and shipped

---

18 "A proper departure embellishes the exercise" (Schiller), Diary of Thomas Vonaechron, Diary Extract, 1982, trans. TV.

to Berlin via Athens and London, without the permission of the Ottoman authorities, smuggling it out of Anatolia. He 'looted' it! Maybe the Red Army did the same in 1945."

"That's very likely, Thomas. Hopefully the thousands of artifacts which make up the collection are still together, safely stored in the basement of a Moscow museum. But now that's more than enough history for today. We can take *Jägerstraße,* I mean of course *Otto-Nuschke-Straße,* back over to *Friedrichstraße.*" We retraced our steps along the facade. George guided us expertly through the backstreets of East Berlin, where Clio had been busy naming and renaming. As we walked back across the *Gendarmenmarkt,* I simply let the architectural harmony work on me without trying to understand or analyze it. *"All architecture is what you do when you look upon it, (Did you think it was in the white or gray stone? or the lines of the arches and cornices?)"*

George stopped when we reached *Friedrichstraße.* "Well, Thomas, once again, it's time for us to part. You turn left here and walk back through Checkpoint Charlie. It wasn't so bad after all this morning was it? I'll turn right, pick up the car in the *Chauseestraße,* and drive back into West Berlin at *Invalidenstraße.* We'll *rendezvous* where I dropped you off this morning, at the corner of *Friedrichstraße* and *Kochstraße.* If it goes like it did this morning, it shouldn't take too long but, once again, you can never know for sure. *Tschüß!*" While waving goodbye to George, my attention was drawn to the old prints and books attractively displayed in the large windows of a shop on the corner. As I still had over twenty marks to spend, I overcame my hesitation and walked inside, greeted by a bell. A portly, older gentleman wearing a thick sweater came out from behind the velvet curtain at the back of the store. Although bald, he wore his white hair long, with enormous sideburns. He eyes were deep set and kindly, highlighted by bushy eyebrows and an aquiline nose. *"Guten Tag! Dürfte ich Ihnen vielleicht behilflich sein?"*

"Guten Tag! Haben Sie vielleicht einen Bilderband über Ost-Berlin, ah . . . ich meine natürlich über die Hauptstadt der DDR?"[19]

"Ah, I understand, you are an American and still have some money to spend before you return to West Berlin. Please don't be nervous my young friend. Given the location of the store, it happens quite frequently, believe me." He spoke American English with a light German inflection. Looking at me over the top of his wire-rimmed glasses, he said, "Believe it or not, I used to be in the US Army. I was a sergeant during the last war, in France, Normandy, and then here in Germany. Psychological Warfare Division,

---

19 "Good Day! Do you have a picture book of East Berlin, ah . . . I mean of course the Capital of the German Democratic Republic?" Diary of Thomas Vonaechron, Diary Extract, 1982, trans. TV.

PWD." He smiled broadly, registering my puzzled expression. "Books are quite inexpensive here in the German Democratic Republic you know, and quite a good investment. I've even written some myself." Before I could ask for titles, he continued, "Let me see." He walked over the floor-to-ceiling wooden shelving that ran around the room, running his fingers gently over the spines of the books. "Here is a particularly nice picture book, with high quality black-and-white and color prints. It's new, printed in Leipzig, and only costs ten *Mark*." He took the book from the shelf and handed it to me. I flipped through the large format, heavyweight pages. It neatly covered my day in Berlin V. I was especially pleased with the pictures of the *Palast der Republik*. There was even an interior shot of the *Espressobar* and the mosaic.

Handing the book back to him, I said, "This is perfect, just what I had in mind! Why, thank you very much for your recommendation, *vielen Dank!* We walked over to the cash register together, where I noticed a wooden bin of prints labeled "*Alt-Berlin.*"

As he held the book in his hands, he shook his head and muttered aloud to himself in English, "Someday there won't be a German Democratic Republic. It will be nothing but a footnote in world history."

"Excuse me, just a moment please, before you ring up the book. May I look through these prints? Perhaps I'll find a picture of one of the buildings I saw today as I walked through Berlin."

"Why yes, of course, please do help yourself, though most of the prints here are of buildings destroyed during or after the war . . . *deswegen* 'Alt-Berlin.'"

"Oh yes, I understand, thank you." After looking through a number of different views of the deconstructed *Stadtschloß* and *Sperlingsgasse*, I found a wood engraving of a handsome, four-story brick building. The entrance, set off by five archways, was flanked on both sides by Palladian windows, just like the one in my office at the *Stadtstaatsarchiv*. Pedestrians had gathered on the street corner to talk, and a horse-drawn tram was just about to pass by. The caption underneath read, "*Die neue Kriegsakademie.*" I handed it to the friendly bookseller. "How much is this print please?"

"Ah yes, the 'New War Academy,' an annex to the old Prussian Academy of War in the *Dorotheenstraße*. It was designed by Franz Schwechten, the same architect who designed the Anhalter *Bahnhof* and the Kaiser Wilhelm Memorial Church. I'm afraid that true to its name, the *Neue Kriegsakademie* was a casualty of the last war. What did we used to say back in the States? 'The chickens came home to roost!' I wonder if they still say that?"

"They still say it in Ohio."

He laughed heartily. "That's good to know! Do you know what is now on the site of the *Neue Kriegsakademie?* The Embassy of the Democratic Republic of Afghanistan. Afghanistan, the 'graveyard of empires,' playing field of the 'great game.' It is ironic, one of the many ironies of history. You're an American, you may not be familiar with Theodor Fontane's '*Das Trauerspiel von Afghanistan*,' "The Tragedy of Afghanistan." He stopped smiling, focused his eyes upon me, and began to recite from memory.

Die hören sollen, sie hören nicht mehr,
Vernichtet ist das ganze Heer,
Mit dreizehntausend der Zug begann,
Einer kam heim aus Afghanistan.

Let's see, how would that go in English? 'Those that should hear, don't hear anymore, the entire army was destroyed by war, with thirteen thousand soldiers the operation began, only one came home from Afghanistan.'" His smile returned. "Americans should read more history, there's some things to be learned. It's difficult to imagine why empires, great- and superpowers, continue to be interested in this small, not-so-great country. All the way back to Alexander the Great. Not just the British. You know, of course, five years ago the Soviet Union sent over 100,000 troops into Afghanistan. Could you imagine the United States ever sending troops into Afghanistan?" Holding the engraving in both hands so he could study it more closely under the artificial light, he said, "In spite of the sobering subject, it is indeed a very nice print." Turning it over, he said, "Also ten *Mark*. That should just about use up your money. Hopefully, you have enough left for a cup of coffee."

Laughing, I replied, "I had two Mokka already, in the *Espressobar* of the *Palast der Republik*."

"I see, I see. Well then, in that case, you'll have some small change left for the Red Cross." He wrapped the book and the print carefully in heavy paper, placing them gently into a large paper bag. "Here you are young man, I hope the book and the print will remind you of a pleasant day here in 'East Berlin,' ah . . . I mean, of course, the capital of the German Democratic Republic." We laughed together.

Handing him two ten-*Mark Scheine*, I replied, "Thank you! They will also remind me of time spent in pleasant conversation with you, and the ambiance of your store."

Smiling in reply, he said, "Oh no, no, it's not my store, though I guess in a sense it is. I don't work here, just minding the store for a friend. In any case, it belongs to the German Democratic Republic, it belongs to the people. But thank you for your kind words nonetheless. I'll pass them up, ah, I mean, along! Ah, that idiomatic American language!"

Leaving the store to the ringing of the bell, I walked back down *Friedrichstraße* to the *Grenzübergangstelle*. It seemed as if I had been in East Berlin much longer than only a few hours. It was dark, and the enhanced security lighting illuminated the postwar ensemble of blockhouse, tower, and the Wall. In spite of the forbidding picture presented, my departure from Berlin V was pretty much the same as my entrance that morning, in reverse chronological order. My passport was returned promptly, still warm from the copy machine. Although I placed both the paper bag containing my purchases and my shoulder bag on the table for inspection, I was waved on through. After slipping 3.10 *DM* in coins through the slot of the metal collection box for the *Deutsches Rotes Kreuz*, the buzz saw buzzer sounded, announcing the door back to the West was now open for me. I walked through the Wall from *Mitte* back into *Kreuzberg*, from the Soviet Sector back into the American Sector, from Berlin V back into Berlin VI. Passing by the Café Adler, I looked up at the bay window on the third floor. There was no control officer to acknowledge my safe return. Directly ahead, a floodlight illuminated the American flag hoisted on the flagpole adjacent to Allied Checkpoint Charlie. I stopped inside, hoping to find SFC Keith, the friendly MP I'd spoken with that morning. His watch was over, and another military policeman now stood behind the counter. I took my passport from the inside pocket of my sport coat and handed it to him. "Good Afternoon, sir, welcome back to the 'frontier of freedom.' Anything unusual happen? I see you've done a bit of shopping."

"Yes, Sergeant, I have. I bought a souvenir picture book of East Berlin and a print of the old Prussian War College. Unusual maybe, but not unpleasant. It was only my second trip to East Berlin, but much more pleasant than the first." This was no doubt due to George's presence but also to the opportunities I had had to talk, if only briefly, with *Fräulein Otto* and the former US Army psychological warfare sergeant-turned-writer.

"Thank you, sir," he said handing me back my passport. Once again, my attention was drawn to the double-handled flaming sword patch on the MP brassard worn on his left sleeve, "United States Army Berlin." Although blue in 1982, the Norman shield had been black in 1944, when US forces under the command of General Dwight D. Eisenhower fought in the European Theater of Operations. I witnessed the change from black to blue back long after the fact in Vault Six, turning back the cover sheets of countless documents created by the US Army between 1944 and 1954. But I was no longer sitting underground in Vault Six; I was standing aboveground at Allied Checkpoint Charlie on *Friedrichstraße*, on the border between East and West Berlin, conscious of the past but very much in the present. With the color change from black to blue, from night to day, the shoulder-sleeve insignia, a symbol of America's wartime involvement in Europe, became a symbol of America's commitment to Western Europe, West Germany, and West Berlin during the Cold War. "Soldier: Why are You in Berlin? . . . to fight like hell, if necessary for US rights and a free Berlin."

"Thank you," I said, placing my passport securely back into the inside pocket of my coat, "Thank you very much, Sergeant." I walked back out through the door, down *Friederichstraße* to *Kochstraße*. Although the street was dark and, apart from the security lights behind me, ill-lit, I felt a sense of relief. Once again, I was one of us, though my sense of "us and them" had been blurred by the day's foray into Berlin V. Walking over to the far side of the street, I found a place to lean against the wall of a building to wait for George, hoping the formalities wouldn't last too long. I was very tired, and once again longing for the rented comforts of my one elegant Empire room in Friedenau.

CHAPTER III:
THE PURIFIED CITY (THE ARMED CAMP)

We are convinced that our remaining in Berlin is essential to our prestige in Germany and in Europe. Whether for good or bad, it has become a symbol of the American intent.

> —Lucius DuBignon Clay, General,
> US Army, Military Governor
> (United States) and
> Commander-in-Chief,
> European Command

> TOP SECRET Memorandum 13 June 1948
> DECLASSIFIED NND775-119 13 Aug 1981, TV

He Practices His German
March 1983

The one elegant Empire room in Friedenau, a temporary office in the *Stadtstaatsarchiv Berlin* in Reinickendorf, and the Free University Berlin in Dahlem became my primary points of reference in West Berlin, Berlin VI. The electric blue *FU* catalog in the Georgetown University Library suggested the *Hajo-Holborn-Institut*, the Department of History, and the *Lucius-D.-Clay Institut* for North American Studies might provide platforms for my on-site research into the HistoriCity. Following the chance meeting with Govinda Nayaka on board the *City of Berlin* back in August, I began to think about West Berlin, Berlin VI, as an accident of history, as an "accidental *polis*." This interest *im werden* was circumscribed, refined, by my experience to date out on the "frontier of freedom" in West Berlin, Berlin VI, and the one-day foray with George into East Berlin, Berlin V. An undergraduate course in Western Political Thought under the tutelage of a gifted Hungarian professor had introduced me to the Greek notion of the *polis* and Plato's *Republic*. Plato and Professor Schneider just might help me to discover the additional essential elements of information about the HistoriCity, and myself, I was looking for.

Preparation of the finding aid for the documents of the Office of Military Government Berlin Sector (OMG-BS) for *Stadtstaatsarchiv Berlin* researchers provided a welcome opportunity to reread documents reviewed in and released from Vault Six and to think about the handful retained due to "sources and methods of intelligence." The brief, pleasant encounters with the US Army military policemen at Allied Checkpoint Charlie infused my underground, archival HistoriCity with a sense of reality and vitality. Now that my contract assignment at the *Stadtstaatsarchiv* was almost finished, I began to shift my focus to the university, *die Freie Universität.* The OMGUS-fiche had been arranged, described, and fixed in a *Findmittel.* I now looked to the *FU* as the follow-on, a place where I could hang up *bzw.* out my frightened fish and flesh out the HistoriCity.

Once again, happy coincidence arrived at the archives in the form of a person. The last researcher I assisted before completing my contract was Dr. Johannes Festzelt, a historian contracted by the *FU* to prepare a history of the university. He was particularly interested in the reports of the "Education and Cultural Relations Branch" found in the microfiche copies of the records of the Office of Military Government—Berlin Sector I had declassified in Vault Six, then carefully arranged and described at the *Stadtstaatsarchiv.* Although George had originally selected the documents for filming back at the Washington National Records Center, he had not yet had the opportunity to review the fiche in the *Stadtstaatsarchiv,* and asked if I could help Dr. Festzelt. It was a pleasure, for personal as well as professional reasons. A jovial, jocular scholar in the Goliard tradition, Johannes regularly joined George and me for lunch in the *Kantine,* the *Stadtstaatsarchiv* equivalent of the snack bar at the Washington National Records Center. He was an imposing figure, tall and broad, robust, with curly red hair and beard. Unfailingly dressed in the dark suit, white shirt, and the thin black tie obligatory for serious academics and jazz musicians, his bright green eyes, sonorous laughter, and animated gestures betrayed the bacchant beneath. The informal Mr. Henry's seminar series George and I had initiated in Washington, DC, continued at the *Stadtstaatsarchiv* in West Berlin, enhanced and informed by the expertise provided by chance and visiting scholars. *O Fortuna,* Johannes offered essential elements of information on history, Hegel, higher education, and the Free University, which proved useful, if not essential, for my on-site education.

George's "*hier* in Berlin we have two of everything" hypothesis applied equally well to universities as well as to other public institutions in *Ost-* and *West-Berlin.* Records rereviewed for the second time in the *Stadtstaatsarchiv* revealed the *FU Berlin* to be, like me, a child of the Cold War. Conceived by Berlin students and faculty, together with their new American friends in the Office of Military Government, it was established as an American Sector alternative to the *Humboldt Universität zu Berlin* located in the

Soviet Sector at *Unter den Linden 6*, adjacent to the *Staatsbibliothek*. George and I had walked by the palatial forecourt of the Humboldt University during our stroll down *Unter den Linden* last December. Over lunch in the *Kantine*, Johannes painted a verbal vignette of the main building, the former palace of Heinrich von Preussen, brother of Frederick the Great, highlighting the historical significance of the red marble staircase in the magnificent entrance hall. The handwriting on the wall, in golden letters above the grand staircase, was taken from Karl Marx's "Eleventh Thesis on Feuerbach," "*Die Philosophen haben die Welt nur verschieden interpretiert, es kommt aber darauf an sie zu verändern.*"[20] Marx himself may have labored up this very staircase as a student in Berlin II, several years before Henry Adams arrived to study in that "poor, keen-witted, provincial town, simple, dirty, uncivilized, and in most respects disgusting."

For our benefit and lunchtime entertainment, Johannes continued his virtual tour of the university, "On the ground floor, there are doors on each side of the grand staircase leading out onto a large courtyard," opening his arms in an angular, Egyptian gesture, "enclosed by the two wings of the building. It's really quite elegant, still retaining all the *ambiance* of a palace of a Prussian Prince. Students sit outside on the *Hof* between classes next to memorials to members of the *AntiFa* executed by the Nazis. If you leave the courtyard through the back gate and cross over *Clara-Zeltkin-Straße*, you come to *Hegelplatz*. Poor G. W. F. Hegel, exiled across the street from the university where he labored for thirty-three years. Historian Theodor Mommsen has a marble seat out in front on *Unter den Linden*, together with the Brothers Humboldt."

George commented, "Maybe it's *ein Beispiel*, an example, of what Hegel referred to as 'the universal irony of the world?'"

Johannes laughed, "At least of the local irony of Berlin. If you look carefully among the trees on *Hegelplatz*, you'll find his weathered bronze bust, looking much like a middle-aged Roman citizen. While still alive and occupying the chair of philosophy across the street, Hegel impressed his concept of universal history not just as irony, but revealed reason upon his impressionable students. Although Marx only transferred to Berlin from Bonn in 1836, five years after Hegel's death, he fell in with the 'Young Hegelians.' *Der Staat* was not only to be history's final revelation, but the End of History itself. Marx was to later famously stand Hegel on his head, though shortly before he died, Hegel reportedly uttered what may have proven to be prophetic: 'And he didn't understand me.' Perhaps these last words should be added, in gold leaf of course, as a pre-Marxian postscript to the *Marxzitat* above the red marble staircase!"

20 "Philosophers have only interpreted the world differently, the point is to change it" (Marx, 1845). Diary of Thomas Vonaechron, Diary Extract 1983, trans. TV.

"By the way, according to a former student, historian Felix Gilbert, the historical seminar occupied the second floor of the left wing of the palace. He recalled when looking up from the long wooden library table, he was eye-to-eye with Christian Rauch's equestrian statue of Fredrick the Great on *Unter den Linden*, 'riding steadily forward on his horse.' It just occurred to me, in spite of their pronounced political differences, the *HU* and the *FU* do have something historical, something fundamental in common. Both universities are actually the fruit of foreign military occupation. The *Universität zu Berlin* was established after *Fridericiana* University at Halle on the Saale was closed on order of the victorious Napoleon Bonaparte. Hmmm. One could say, French bayonets were the starting 'points' of the Prussian *Renaissance*."

Looking at me and laughing, George interrupted, "'Could say' but doesn't have to! 'Starting points?' Auaaa! Thomas, if you haven't yet told Johannes your 'Frederick the Grape' story yet, please don't."

"Now I don't get the 'point,' gentlemen. You do mean 'Frederick the Great,' don't you, George?"

George smiled. Shaking his head, he said, "No, no, unfortunately not Johannes, but you do have a 'point.' You might remember, I wrote my dissertation on the French occupation of Berlin from 1806 to 1808. Coupled with the defeat of the Prussian Army at Jena and at Auerstadt, the occupation catalyzed great change in Prussia, particularly here in Berlin. But please do continue."

"Enlarged and rechristened *Friedrich-Wilhelms-Universität* in 1828, it would become the *Universität zu Berlin* once again when reopened under the Soviet Military Administration in Germany. In 1949, it was renamed in honor of the brothers Wilhelm and Alexander Humboldt, not the Grimm fate it might have had."

"*Et tu*, Johannes, *ach*, there's two of you!" exclaimed George.

Laughing, I said, "Clio has been active in the naming conventions of higher education as well as city planning in the HistoriCity."

"Indeed she has!" exclaimed Johannes. "Just listen! After three student editors of the US Military Government-licensed student publication, *Colloquium*, were forcibly ex-matriculated from the *Universität Berlin*, they called for the creation of a 'Free University' at a public demonstration. Guess where that demonstration was held? In the *Kaisersaal* of the *Hotel Esplanade* on *Potsdamer Platz* in the American Sector, just across the Soviet Sector border. Interesting isn't it, OMG-BS licensing a Soviet Sector student publication? Ironically, the *Kasiersaal* where the student demonstration was held is where *Kaiser Wilhelm II* used to hold court!"

In unison, George and I exclaimed, "*Kasier* Bill! Ver-r-ry inter-r-resting!"

"*Ja, ja, Kasier* Bill," replied Johannes. "'*Donnerwetter, Donnerwetter sind wir Kerle!* [21] OMG-BS, in the person of a Sorbonne-art student-turned-colonel, with great hair by the way, presciently anticipated this turn of events, making buildings of the former *Kaiser-Wilhelm-Gesellschaft* in Zehlendorf available in advance for the new Free University. Buildings occupied by US Military Government agencies were also made available at the silver-haired colonel's command. The *FU* was established in 1948 at a ceremony in the *Puck Palast*, an undamaged film theater in nearby Steglitz. It's still there, on *Hauptstraße*. Architecturally the building is quite interesting, from the late twenties, *Neue Sachlichkeit*. 'Free' was not understood in the sense of freedom from all political ideology and orientation, but operationalized in the service of a particular understanding of freedom, more of a mission statement. Allow me if you will, gentlemen, to read to you from the remarks of the first Rector, Friedrich Meinecke—please take note a professor of history—let me see, I have them somewhere here in my notes, yes, yes, here's a translation of his speech. 'And our attempt to establish a new, free university is only a single point on the great battlefield of the world, in the great struggle between spirit and real power.' End quote. The Free University Berlin as 'a single point on the great battlefield of the world.' So christened at the beginning of the Cold War, 'free' took on an equally ironic tone during the Vietnam War. Many *FU* faculties became parochial schools for all possible variants of Marxism, though no doubt quite different from the Marxism presented above the staircase and in the lecture halls of the *Humboldt Universität*, only twelve kilometers and a *Weltanschauung* away." Once again in unison, George and I responded with *"Eirönïa!"* Johannes shook his head, smiling. Wrapping up his historical review of the *FU*, he noted student activism in West Berlin seemed to diminish at the end of the Vietnam War that had fueled it. Resignation reigned on campus until it was resuscitated and revitalized by the 1979 NATO-*Doppelbeschluss* decision and the election of Ronald Wilson Reagan as President of the United States in 1980.

Now, in the early eighties, more anarchistic, unfocused political undercurrents like *TUWAT* ran close to the surface of the political, artistic, and linguistic ferment that was West Berlin. Concerned about social unrest, the government of West Berlin continued to evict *Instandbesetzer* from occupied houses. In January, the elegant turn-of-the-century apartment building on *Kaiser-Wilhelm-Platz* George and I passed by on our way from Tempelhof to Friedenau was *geräumt*, the city government's reply to the hand-lettered banner that hung from the balcony overlooking the

21 "Lightning and thunder, lightning and thunder—aren't we a wonder!" Diary of Thomas Vonaechron, Diary Extract, 1982, trans. TV.

intersection of *Kolonnen Straße* and *Hauptstraße*, "*Lieber Instand-Besetzen als Kaputt Besitzen*."[22]

Early one morning in mid-March, equipped with my letter of tentative acceptance and the additional essential elements of information provided by Johannes, I set out for the *Akademisches Auslandsamt* of Free University. Winter had begun to loosen its *naßkalten*, gray grip on the HistoriCity. Greater resolution became possible. With the coming of spring, I anticipated the return of the questioning birds to the Linden trees in front of the apartment building and Hedwig in his sequined hot pants to *Hedwigstraße*. The reports of the "Education and Cultural Relations Branch" used by Johannes disclosed the Foreign Studies Office of the Free University was housed in the former Military Government Finance Office, another building with a past. Constructed during the First World War as the *Kaiser-Wilhelm-Institut für Biologie*, following the Second World War, it served the US Army before becoming the main building of the nascent Free University Berlin. In accordance with (IAW), my established standard operating procedure (SOP), I mapped out the route to the *Auslandsamt* on the *Falkplan*: walk from *Lothringerstrasse* through Friedenau to the underground train station at *Rüdesheimerplatz* (coordinates L6), take the U-Bahn to *Thielplatz* only four stops away. *Boltzmannstraße* (coordinates J4) was only a short walk from the *U-Bahnhof*. Over the past seven months, the *U-Bahn*, *S-Bahn*, and *Bus* networks had become my primary lines of communication (LOC), linking an ever-increasing number of points of reference scattered throughout West Berlin.

The former *Kaiser-Wilhelm-Institut für Biologie*-turned-OMGUS Finance Office-turned-*Akademisches Auslandsamt* proved elusive. Residential streets seemed to lead with insidious intent through Dahlem, *Faradayweg*, *Hittdorfstraße*, *Van't-Hoff-Straße*, and at long last, *Boltzmannstraße*, bringing me face-to-facade with the *Henry Ford Bau*, a large white neo-Bauhaus building occupying the entire intersection of *Boltzmannstraße* and *Garystraße*. Once again, the building standing before me was a concrete reification of the archives behind me. Reviewing the Department of State post files in Vault Six, I found the message traffic between Washington and Berlin on the Ford Foundation financing and construction of the Henry Ford Building. Noting my disorientation, a friendly *Student* asked if I needed assistance and then kindly walked me down *Boltzmannstraße*, pointing to a gray, weathered, but still elegant three-story villa. Walking up to the double-doors beneath the balustrade, I was relieved to read "*Akademisches Auslandsamt*." Just above my head,

22 "Better occupation and renovation than ruination through possession." Diary of Thomas Vonaechron, Diary Extract, 1982, trans. TV.

below the balustrade, was a bronze bust of Pallas Athena, Corinthian helmet pushed back upon her forehead revealing a thoughtful, almost sorrowful expression. Her gray eyes were downcast, neither looking at nor singing to me. What might she, goddess of wisdom and prudent warfare, have seen passing in and out of these doors over the past seventy years—a parade of scientists, soldiers, and students? Entering the poorly lit hallway, I found all doors with the exception of one, marked by an *Anmeldung* sign hanging from the ceiling, shut. Taking the letter from my shoulder bag and holding it firmly in my right hand as a talisman, I walked down the hallway and entered the office. "*Guten Morgen, dürfte ich Ihnen behilflich sein?*"[23]

Greeting the slender, silver-haired receptionist politely in return, practicing the Govinda smile, I handed her my letter of acceptance with, "*Bitteschön.*" Smiling, she nodded and took it from my hand. After reading it, she pulled out a drawer of the green metal US government-issue file cabinet next to her desk, taking out a folder labeled "Vonaechron, Thomas." *O Wunder, I vas exspechted.*

"*Ach ja, Herr* Vonaechron," pronouncing my surname as "von Aechron." "You still must take the German language examination to complete your matriculation to the university, *die Sprachprüfung, Sie verstehen schon.*" I assured her I did understand, and registered to take the two-day examination the following week. Fortunately, I'd been well prepared in the required German language reading comprehension and composition by both Dr. Schmidt in Basel and my old-school instructor at the Goethe Institute in Washington, DC, a distinguished daughter of the *Freistaat Bayern, Frau Dr.* Bretzl. On the first day of class, held in a restored redbrick townhouse in the former "Little Germany" section of Washington, DC, on Seventh Street, just off Pennsylvania Avenue, she informed us, the only time she ever spoke English during the entire seven weeks, "I will not make it easy or fun for you, you will just learn it!" And so it went.

The day after the two-day test, I returned to the former biology-turned-finance-turned-university building, passing under the gray-eyed goddess, to pick up the results. Thanks to the good Drs. Bretzl and Schmidt and the hours spent reviewing "Captured German Records" in Vault Six, I'd been evaluated with "*sehr gut*" and matriculated into the Free University, regaining my identity as a *Student.* The next step was to review requirements for the *Doktor der Philosophie* in history; select the relevant exercises, lectures, and seminars; find a *Doktorvater*, or a *Doktormutter*; submit a dissertation proposal; and upgrade my simple *Student* status to that of *Doktorand.* German student life in the

---

23 "Good Morning! May I help you?" Diary of Thomas Vonaechron, Diary Extract, 1983, trans. TV.

early eighties was wonderfully unstructured in comparison to the rigid, repetitive requirements and sequentially numbered courses of American undergraduate and graduate life. *Studenten* and *Studentinnen* had social status and a comfortable, state-subsidized lifestyle. My only expenses were for room, board, and health insurance. True to its name, the Free University was free, the cost of living in West Berlin low. As I would learn over the next few years, this posed an inherent danger, if not vice. The *Studentleben* lotus was tempting and delicious to eat, with the acute danger of becoming an addict, possibly even a casualty, *eine Karteileiche*. An anchor was required to avoid becoming an anchorite.

In the small *Schreibwarengeschäft* situated at the back of the *Auslandsamt*, filled with colorful pencils, pens, and notebooks, all arranged according to *Deutsches Institut für Normung* standards, I bought the obligatory ("been there, done that") white *FU* sweatshirt (the only color available), *FU* notebooks, and, much to my delight, my own personal copy of the famous electric blue paperbound *FU* "*Namens- und Vorlesungsverzeichnis*," with its wonderfully bewildering array of *Fachbereiche, Zentral Institute*, and *Zentral Einrichtungen*. It was the latest edition of the very same catalog I'd held in my hands in another life, looking down from the Georgetown bluffs on the Potomac below! Employing my practiced "sources and methods of intelligence" scan on the list of *Fachbereiche* and *Zentralinstitute*, I quickly found the address of the *Lucius-D.-Clay-Institut für Amerikastudien* at *Boxerstraße 5–9*. Although it had been seven months since my airborne discussion with Govinda on the *City of Berlin*, I had not yet reached Professor Schneider by phone. I decided to stop by the *LDCI* on my way back to Friedenau. Govinda had strongly recommended investing him as my Virgil; hopefully, he'd spoken to Dr. Schneider about me. Now that I was officially a *Student*, perhaps Dr. Schneider could help me successfully navigate the maize of *FU* faculties, central institutes, seminars, lectures, and exercises, finding the *diritta via* to my doctorate.

Professor Schneider in the Accidental *Polis*
March 1983

At coordinates K5, the *Falkplan* placed the *LDCI* directly behind *U-Bahnhof Dahlem-Dorf*, just one stop from *Thielplatz*. Still wary of Dahlem's winding streets, I fell back upon my established LOC, the *U-Bahn*. Climbing the stairs from platform to street level, I found myself surrounded by fellow students in a small, half-timbered, thatched-roof train station. Although Dahlem, like Friedenau, had been swallowed by the *Großstadt*, it still retained an undigested bucolic ambiance. Once again, thanks to George, I'd known what to expect. The essential elements of information were drawn this time not from the Washington National Records Center or the *Stadtstaatsarchiv Berlin* but from his own past. After fleeing the family farm in the German Democratic Republic for West Berlin, his father administered the *Domäne Dahlem*, a large farm owned by West Berlin, directly across the street from the *U-Bahnhof*. George had grown up there. Orienting the *Falkplan* on the elegant two-story, gray, gabled *Herrnhaus*, I turned two consecutive corners to find the three-story redbrick former elementary school at *Boxerstraße 5–9*. A staircase led from the sidewalk up to the entrance. Just inside, a uniformed woman sat in a glass enclosure, just like the *Pförtner* at the *Stadtstaatsarchiv*. Each of the *FU* faculties and institutes published *Kommentierte Vorlesungsverzeichnisse*, detailed descriptions of courses offered each semester. After purchasing a copy from the friendly *Pförtnerin*, I went back outside to join my *Kommilitonen* on the stairs in front of the *LDCI* and peruse it, savoring my newly reacquired *Student* status.

There were seminars, lectures, and exercises on familiar topics and personalities in American history, literature, and politics. In addition to "WestBerlin: An Accidental *Polis?*" offered by visiting Professor of Political Science Dr. Richard W. Schneider, I also found a seminar on "The Marilyn Monroe Doctrine: American Popular Culture as a Transnational Threat" offered by former American Ambassador Hubert Spero. There was also an "Independent Study Course" for graduate students organized by Professor Henri Paul Adams. A later-day Henri Adams in Berlin! I took the coincidence as a good omen. Although office hours, *Sprechstunden*, had not yet been posted for *Sommer Semester*, I decided to see if Professor Schneider was in his office. Walking back up the stairs, nodding politely to the *Pförtnerin* in passing, I reached the ground floor, *das Erdgeschoß*—thank you *Fräulein* Otto ("Under other circumstances I'd be pleased to join you . . ."). The *LDCI*, like the *Auslandsamt*, was dimly lit. *Mehr Licht!* There was sufficient light, however, to recognize a bronze bust of General Lucius DuBignon Clay, US Army, which, in the fashion of *Preussischer Kriegsminister* Roon's pedestal on the *Großer Stern*, had been drip-painted à la Paul Jackson Pollock. Mounted behind General Clay's bust, forming a stainless steel and glass rectangular halo, was the *LDCI* directory. Professor Schneider's office was on the first floor. Nodding very respectfully to the bespattered general, walking past the wooden US government-issue library card catalogs lining the hallway, I climbed the second set of stairs to the first floor. An aluminum-framed, frosted-glass doorway opened up onto another long, dark hallway.

All doors on both sides of the hallway were shut, with the exception of one standing wide open halfway down on the left, the light coming from inside forming a "V" on the hallway floor. As I walked toward the light, student shapes began to appear out of the darkness, silent, sitting motionlessly on benches outside the other office doors. Turning into the open door, I came face-to-face with a tall man in his early sixties with thick, wavy white hair, eyes the color of the Aegean Sea and an engaging smile— Govinda's smile. "Excuse me, Professor Schneider? I'm Thomas Vonaechron. Professor Nayaka recommended I contact you. I tried calling some time ago, I believe you were in Leipzig. This morning, I was over at the *Akademisches Auslandsamt* to complete my matriculation and thought I would come by to see if you were in. Am I disturbing you?"

"No, no, not at all! I'm delighted to meet you at last, Mr. Vonaechron. Please do come in. That is precisely the reason my door is standing open. My American colleague Hubert Spero and I are trying to introduce the American 'open-door' policy to the Clay Institute. As you can see, we haven't enjoyed much success among our German colleagues yet. Govinda told me about your conversation. If memory serves, you have quite an interesting background at the National Archives in Washington. It seems we might share some common academic interests. Extending his hand, he said warmly, "Richard Schneider, pleased to meet you." Gesturing to a chair next to a gunmetal gray US government-issue desk awash in books, academic journals, and articles, he said, "Please make yourself comfortable, Mr. Vonaechron, and excuse me for just a moment." Thanking him, I sat down and looked around. The shelves behind his desk, which to my surprise was identical to my former desk in Vault Six, were crammed with books, journals, and papers. Stacks of books stood on the green carpeted floor like the broken pillars of a Greek temple. Returning my gaze to his desktop, I saw a white, weathered bust in the right-hand corner, partially concealed by a pile of academic journals, returning my gaze. I stood up and moved the pile aside. The bust was of a bearded, balding individual with a satyr-ical expression on his face, wearing a cloak over an undershirt. Looking closely, I could make out the Greek letters "Σψκράτής." Joining a fraternity as an undergraduate proved useful after all. At that moment, Professor Schneider returned to his office.

"Ah, I see Socrates has been keeping you company in my absence. He's actually half of a double herm, back to back, head to head as it were, with Seneca. It's a twentieth- century copy of a third-century copy of a first-century Roman original, found in 1813 during excavation of the *Villa Mattei* in Rome. Socrates is the souvenir of my academic year in Berlin. I ordered the copy from the *Gipsformerei* of the *Stiftung Preußischer Kulturbesitz.*" Turning his desk chair to face me, he sat down. Dressed in a well-worn tweed sport coat and dark tie, the top button of his wrinkled white dress shirt was open, one collar point bent upward. Leaning forward, placing his open hands palm down upon his knees, he said, "Well, before I tell you how I came to be here, Govinda asked me to give you his very best regards. He found your conversation quite stimulating. Although 'up in the air' apparently you weren't, and he was quite certain you would eventually contact me."

"I apologize for not doing so sooner, Dr Schneider. For the past seven months, I've been working as a contract employee at the *Stadtstaatsarchiv Berlin*. It's hard to believe I've already been in West Berlin for seven months! Somehow, time spent in an archives reading thirty-year-old documents is out of joint. I had a similar sensation working at the National Archives, reviewing old documents all day long in an underground vault."

"No apologies necessary, Mr. Vonaechron, I understand completely. Half of my year here at the Clay Institute is already *vorbei*! I'm only here for a total of two semesters. Kent State University set up a faculty-exchange program with the *Freie Universität Berlin* way back in 1953. Every year, a professor from a different faculty at Kent teaches here at the Free University, while a colleague from the Free University teaches in the Western Reserve. Last year, it was Political Science's turn, so while I'm here in West Berlin, Professor Alfred Albrecht from the Werner Finck Institute is teaching at Kent. The relationship between the two universities became even closer following the shootings of June 2, 1967, and May 4, 1970, the latter sometimes referred to as the 'Kent State Massacre.'" Dr. Schneider paused for a moment. "When one thinks about it, massacres have played an interesting part in history, Mr. Vonaechron. Thomas Jefferson wrote from France, 'the tree of liberty must be refreshed from time to time with the blood of patriots and tyrants. It is its natural manure.' Did you know a young woman of German parentage, Sandra Lee Scheuer, was among the four students shot and killed on the Kent Campus by members of the Ohio National Guard? Her parents had immigrated to the United States from Germany to ensure their children—how did her mother phrase it?—'live in a country with freedom.' Sandra wasn't involved in the protest, just returning from a class that had been canceled due to the demonstration. A colleague of mine from the Department of History had Allison Krause, the other young woman killed on May 4, in her Introduction to History course. During an impassioned classroom discussion of the meaning and the uses of history, Ms. Krause stated—just a moment please, Mr. Vonaechron, I wrote it down on an index card, here it is—'Dates and facts are not enough to show what happened in the past. It is necessary to delve into the human side of history to come up with the truth. History must be made relevant to the present to make it useful.'" He leaned back in his chair, cupping his face in his hands. "As a member of the Kent Friends Meeting, I was on campus at the time, trying to promote peaceful protest of the invasion of Cambodia . . . but I digress. We can save that discussion for another time. Let me tell you about my interest in Germany and, perhaps more importantly for you, about the Accidental *Polis* Seminar, so you can decide if it might be of interest."

"I first came to Germany, to the Palatinate, *die Saarpfalz* as it was then called, to be exact, as a teenager with my mother in 1937. She was gathering sources for her dissertation on the 1832 *Hambacher Fest*. In those days, it was quite unusual for a woman to pursue a doctorate. She and my father met here in Germany following the First World War while working for the American Friends Service Committee. You might have read about the '*Kinder-*' or '*Quäkerspeisung*,' the AFSC's effort to mitigate the starvation among German children caused by the continuation of the wartime blockade. While she worked in the archives, I went to school, to the *Gymnasium* where I received an introduction to . . . an introduction, no, no, an indoctrination into I should say, National Socialism. We even had the opportunity to see Adolf Hitler perform before returning to the United States, just prior to the invasion of Poland. It was both fascinating and frightening to observe him, in particular the effect his presence had on an immense audience. While his message was crude, inconceivable, his methods were well honed and very effective, exhibiting a mastery of mass psychology. Speaking for hours, he used a deluge of words to put his listeners into what might best be described as an emotional trance. In the final analysis, however, it wasn't as much what he said as how he said it, building to a frenzied crescendo through a theatrical use of climax and motif in a manner reminiscent of Wagnerian opera. Afterward, my mother told me his performance, for that's exactly what it was, reminded her of the film *Das Cabinet des Dr. Caligari*, which she and my father had seen together after the First World War in Germany.

"When the United States entered the Second World War, as a Friend, I filed for conscientious objector, 'CO,' status and volunteered for alternative service. I was assigned to Eastern State, an asylum on the outskirts of Marysburg, Virginia. When I first arrived, I asked for a map of the grounds to orient myself. The only one available was for the *Maison de fou* dated 1778! Have you seen the film *King of Hearts*? My wife and I saw it at the Kent International Film Festival at the KIVA not too long before coming to Berlin. A tragicomic commentary on the First World War, it brought back memories of Eastern State during the Second. One member of our Kent Friends Meeting did join the US Army and served as a medic during the Battle of the Bulge, but forgive me, I digress once again.

"I'm a political theorist by training and still find the Socratic dialogue best suited for teaching, though I understand it can be confusing for students, undergraduates in particular, who are oftentimes unfamiliar with it. Although I've often returned to Germany over the years, all of my research work has been done in the Federal Republic proper. The opportunity to spend an entire academic year in West Berlin was consequently most welcome, allowing me to expand on my previous work in the Federal Republic and the United States on lobbying at the state or *Land* level, and the role of the ombudsman. West Berlin adopted the executive ombudsman model three years ago. Are you familiar with the term?"

"No, Professor Schneider, I'm sorry, I'm not. The first time I heard it was when Professor Nayaka told me about you and your Accidental *Polis* Seminar on board the *City of Berlin*."

"Once again, no apologies please, Mr. Vonaechron! There's another topic for a future discussion, I'm certain we'll find a few more! You're of course here today to talk about the Accidental *Polis* Seminar. The Clay Institute was open to suggestions for other topics, in addition to lobbying and the ombudsman. While considering offering a graduate course in American Political Thought, it occurred to me, placed within the context of postwar international relations, and as an 'accident' of history, West Berlin approaches the classical Greek definition of the *polis*. Not only from the standpoint of governance but also other concerns addressed by Greek thinkers—warfare, education, literature, poetry, and music. Unlike my other courses, I understand this seminar more as an experiment, an examination of West Berlin as a political community in the broadest possible sense. At the outset, we'll briefly review writings on the *polis* by a number of Greek thinkers: Homer and Herodotus, Aeschylus, Aristophanes, and Aristotle. Our primary guide to the *polis*, however, will be Plato, who may have recorded what Socrates had to say on the subject in *The Republic*. We'll consider the issues raised in *The Republic* and in *The Laws*—in *The Laws*, Socrates's place is taken by the 'Athenean Stranger'— and attempt to determine if there is any relevance, any resonance for West Berlin. I'm hopeful there will be student interest in topics such as literature, poetry, music, and law, as well as in politics, allowing us to work both forward from Athens and backward from West Berlin, weaving the various strands together during the course of the upcoming *Sommersemester*.

"Given the significance of West Berlin in postwar American Foreign Policy, I thought such a seminar might be particularly appropriate for the Clay Institute. Fortunately, my German colleagues graciously agreed. After all, West Berlin has been considered by some as an American city. Upon arrival in 1963, President Kennedy described West Berlin as 'a city we consider to be part of us,' both a sign of solidarity and an unmistakable warning to the Soviet Union. As Govinda described it to me, your academic interest in Berlin, complemented by your work at the National Archives, would constitute an invaluable resource for the seminar 'West Berlin: An Accidental *Polis*?' The *polis* is by nature interdisciplinary, so although you are planning to pursue your doctorate in History, please don't be concerned about taking a Political Science seminar. Someone much more insightful and witty than I once observed, "History is the despair of Political Theory." I might also mention, there will be at least one other American graduate student taking part, also a historian by training—a military historian, Dwight Durchschouer. A graduate of West Point, he holds the rank of Major in the US Army. Given his subject matter knowledge and his enthusiasm, he should be able to make a 'major' contribution to our seminar!"

"I was struck by the concept of an 'accidental *polis*' when Govinda first mentioned it to me last August and have been thinking about it ever since. I'm very glad you decided to offer the seminar during summer semester, Professor Schneider! While working at the National Archives, my attention was repeatedly drawn to Berlin by the documents I reviewed for declassification, initially to the National Socialist *Reichshauptstadt*, then to West Berlin, and finally back to the earlier Berlins, the capital of the Weimar Republic and the imperial capital." For a moment I considered sharing my Schliemann'sche strategy with Professor Schneider but decided to wait. "While working at the archives, I had the good fortune to meet an archivist from the *Stadtstaatsarchiv Berlin*, Georg-Friedrich *Freiherr* von Garlitz. George selected documents for filming from those we'd reviewed and declassified as part of the 'Office of Military Government US,' 'OMGUS Project.' We would meet at lunch and after work to discuss Berlin and Washington, DC. Our after work 'symposia' were usually fueled by alternating red and green glasses of *Berliner Weiße*." Nodding his approval, Dr. Schneider smiled. "The more I reviewed, the more George and I talked, the more I came to think of Berlin as a kind of crossroads of micro- and macro-history, as the 'HistoriCity.' With George's encouragement and assistance—he kindly set up the contract job for me at the *Stadtstaatsarchiv*—I decided to leave Washington for Berlin, at that point in time a city constructed largely of decaying documents, conversations, and memories. I'd been here once before years ago, but only for seven days. As a *Historiker-im-Werden*, West Berlin seemed to me the only place to be. What I had considered, but not really appreciated until I moved to Berlin from Washington, was the significance of the part played by the United States, not just in the de facto establishment of West Berlin in 1945 but from 1945 until 1954, the last year we could review for declassification under the standing Executive Order, and particularly from 1954 until the present. The foundation, the fundament of West Berlin is the military presence of the three Western Allies. As an undergraduate, I took a course in Western Political Thought with a gifted Hungarian professor. We expended considerable effort on Plato's *Republic*. If I remember correctly, at some point in its decline, the *polis* becomes an 'Armed Camp.' Well, West Berlin certainly is an armed camp. Coming back to your notion of West Berlin as an 'accidental *polis*,' the *LDCI* . . . the Clay Institute becomes an accidental academy in the American Sector. I'm interested not only in the postwar politics surrounding West Berlin but in its history, literature, and music as well. As you well know, there's a lot going on here."

"To be quite honest, Mr. Vonaechron, I'm also hoping to use this seminar to better inform myself about what is going on here culturally and politically, and I am counting upon my students to educate me. Siegfried Kracauer argues the number of places where improvisation is allowed determines the status of the city. There seems to be quite a lot of improvisation going on in West Berlin. I'm hopeful German students will also take part, sharing their interests and bringing me up to date!"

"On a practical level, I have to narrow down my interest in the history of Berlin to a doable dissertation topic. Now that I'm *immatrikuliert*, I must prepare a dissertation proposal for the *Hajo-Holborn-Institut*. I have copies of the *FU Namens- und Vorlesungsverzeichnis* and the *Komentiertes Vorlesungsverzeichnis* of the Clay Institute, and I plan to stop by the *HHI* to pick up one for the History Department, along with the *Promotionsordnungen*, on my way home. Once I work my way through the requirements, I should have a better idea of how to proceed."

"Ah, just a moment Mr. Vonaechron, I just might have a copy of the summer semester annotated list of courses for the *Hajo-Holborn-Institut* somewhere here on my desk, which you'd be welcome to. Here it is! I've already perused it, so please keep it. It was given to me by a colleague I met at a conference on student dissent last semester, an American, who teaches at the Holborn Institute. Perhaps she might be able to help you with your proposal. I'd be pleased to contact her on your behalf. Her name is Duana Jordan. She's American but holds a doctorate from the Sorbonne. She wrote her dissertation on city planning in Paris under Napoleon III. Maybe she'd be willing to take on Berlin under Ronald Reagan with you!" Dr. Schneider made a note on his desk calendar. "Have you been over to the *Holborn-Institut* yet?"

"Not yet, but I'm headed there now."

"It's located in a charming Italianate villa with yellowish stucco walls, a columned porch and a red tile roof at *Hittorfstraße* 2–4, just across the street from the *Rostlaube*, not far from here at all, a ten-minute walk at most. Turn right as you leave the *Clay-Institut*, take the first left onto *Fabeckstraße*, then the first right onto *Kiebitzweg*. It will lead you directly to the Holborn Institute. Here's a copy of the Accidental *Polis* Seminar syllabus and reading list, too, if you'd like to look over them prior to our first meeting. Once you've had the opportunity to do so, if you have any questions about the seminar, the Clay Institute, or the *FU*, I'd be pleased to help to the best of my ability. How does that old song from *One Touch of Venus* go? 'I'm a stranger here myself.' But no doubt one of my Clay Institute colleagues, or maybe even Professor Jourdan at the *Holborn-Institut* could help you with the peculiarities of the *Promotion*. Our first meeting is scheduled for next week on Friday, April 1, April Fools' Day. What does Pope, Alexander Pope that is, say? 'Fools rush in where Angels fear to tread.' Who knows? Maybe Pope John Paul II says that in the meantime too! I do hope to see you then, Mr. Vonaechron. Last semester, I discovered German students are oftentimes reluctant to initiate and participate in discussion. As you know from studying Plato, discussion is essential to the Socratic dialogue. I would therefore be very grateful to you, and by the way, I asked the same of Mr. Durchschouer, if you would please help me facilitate it, to help get the seminar started. And please don't forget the 'open-door policy.' By the way, there's something I'd like to show you one day, which you might find of interest, just across the street in the *Museum für Indische Kunst*."

Placing the *HHI* course list, the "Accidental *Polis*" syllabus, and reading list carefully into my shoulder bag along with the *FU* catalog and the Clay Institute course list, I replied, "Thank you very much for your time today, Professor Schneider, for the *HHI* list, and for your offer to contact Professor Jordan at the Holborn Institute. I'd be very grateful to you if you would. I'll pick up a copy of the *Promotionsordnungen* at the *HHI* and head back to Friedenau and begin working my way through it. See you on April Fools' Day, and thank you again!" Following the 'V' back out into the dark corridor, I walked past the students in limbo, through the frosted-glass doors, down the first set of stairs, past the Pollocked general officer and the friendly *Pförtnerin,* down the second set of stairs, out through the front door into scattered spring sunlight, and took a seat on the stairs. Directly across the street from the Clay Institute was the white, Bauhaus-y entrance to *Museum für Indische Kunst*. What did Dr. Schneider want to show me? Govinda's words came to mind, "If you are busy and don't have time to write to me, please don't worry, I'll be watching from across the street."

Spring was reluctantly returning to West Berlin. Retrieving the *Falkplan* from the side pocket of my shoulder bag, I decided to take my fate into my feet and *flâner* to the *Hajo-Holborn-Institut* according to Dr.

Schneider's directions, return to the *Clay-Insitut*, and then walk back to the *Lothringerstrasse*. By following *Königin-Luise-Straße* and *Grunewaldstraße* to *Rathhaus Steglitz*, I could avoid the labyrinthine residential streets, follow *Schlossstraße* to *Rheinstraße*, *Hedwigstraße*, and home. Perhaps Hedwig would be out patrolling the perimeter on this spring day. I set out from the Clay Institute for the Holborn Institute, replaying my conversation with Professor Schneider. What did he say? "History is the despair of Political Theory?" Govinda was right, he would be a most able and amicable guide. In seven months, with the help of friends, strangers, and the incomparable Berlin public transportation system, I had begun to construct my own personal Berlin to replace the District of Columbia left behind on the Potomac. Shelter, work, study—all bases of operations. As I unlocked the heavy wooden front door of my apartment building, pushing it open with my left shoulder, a single bird called out from a tree on the far side of the *Lothringerstrasse*: "Poo-tee-weet?" Inside the *Treppenhaus*, the aroma of sandalwood incense and sitar music filled the *Erdgeschoß*.

Professor Schneider's seminar met in Rooms 3–4 on the ground floor of "the Villa," a gray, two-story stucco house adjacent to the Clay Institute. After the expiration of *sine tempore* and *cum tempore*, five students had taken their seats for the first meeting. Unlike American students, German students did not register for courses in advance, preferring to shop the *Colloquia, Forschungsseminare, Hauptseminare, Seminare, Übungen*, and *Vorlesungen* at the beginning of each semester, checking out the instructor, the requirements, and the participants before committing to take part, to write a paper, or to make a presentation. "*Guten Tag*, a good day to you all and welcome to the initial meeting of *Hauptseminar* 'West Berlin: An Accidental *Polis*?' I am Richard W. Schneider, Professor of Political Science at Kent State University in Ohio, and I sincerely hope you all are not here accidentally but intentionally! I understand from my colleagues, it's unusual for a seminar to meet on the first day of the semester: *April! April!* But I assure you, it's not an April Fools' joke! There's much for us to do together, and the sooner we begin, the better. As I might have mentioned to those of you I've already met . . ." The front door of the villa suddenly slammed shut, rattling the windowpanes in our seminar room, announcing the arrival of two more prospective seminarians.

Two striking young women in their early twenties stood, arm in arm, in the doorway. Tall, lanky, similar yet dissimilar, complementary, fashionably dressed in early eighties *Berliner chic*, cheap fur from Kreuzberg secondhand stores, plastic raincoats, and shoes. One wore her long, uncombed blonde hair loose over her shoulders, the other her jet black hair cut short à la Ziggy Stardust, emphasizing hazel eyes highlighted by delicately drawn facial features. Startled to find the seminar already in session, they froze arm in arm, framed by the doorway, Schadow Sisters immediately drawing our attention and interest away from Dr. Schneider.

"Welcome, welcome to the first meeting of the seminar 'West Berlin: An Accidental *Polis*?' Please do come in and join us if you'd like to. Your timing's perfect. Now that we have a quorum of seven, we can begin. I'm Dr. Richard Schneider, visiting Professor of Political Science from Kent State University in Ohio."

"Thank you, Professor," they replied in unison, smiling, scanning the room, and taking adjacent seats at one of the white conference tables forming a rectangle in the center of the room. The blonde woman sat down directly across from me. As she leaned back to pull her raincoat off her shoulders, I saw an enameled black star pinned just below the bateau neckline of her red sweater. White skin. She caught my glance. Smiling broadly, her large mouth highlighted with bright red lipstick, she stretched her legs out underneath the conference table, leaned back in her chair, and turned toward Dr. Schneider.

Dr. Schneider skillfully drew our attention back to the seminar. "Last semester, here at the Clay Institute, I began a two-part series on lobbying at the State and *Land* level, and on the role of the ombudsman in the United States and the *Ombudsmann und Ombudsfrau* in the Federal Republic. With the concurrence of my colleagues, I decided to add another course this semester. At Kent, I teach an undergraduate introductory course on 'Western Political Thought' and a graduate seminar on 'American Political Thought.' While preparing for my senior year abroad here at the *FU*, it occurred to me that West Berlin appears to meet some of the criteria understood under the Greek notion of πόλις, the '*polis*.' Whether it is by accident or intention, it is something I would like to examine with you through this seminar, which is more of an interdisciplinary experiment.

"In the *Politics*, Aristotle observes, 'it is evident that the state is a creation of nature, and that man is by nature a political animal.' The Greek *polis* defined and provided the necessary context for personal growth through social interaction. Think of the *polis* as a petri dish. Men and women were not just animals living in the *polis, politikon zoon*, but actually became men and women through the *polis*, a transformation catalyzed by the creative combination of community and architecture. Some thinkers even see the city as an attempt to rise above human limitations through the imposition of artificial, external limitations. As an aside, I should mention other thinkers argue life in the *polis* effeminized the male inhabitants. For our purposes, however, it is important to recall the *polis* influenced all human activities, not just government, or should I, out of respect to

Socrates, say not just 'just' government, but war, economics, education, ethics, law, metaphysics, music, and poetry as well, aesthetics. I agree with Lewis Mumford's argument that, "it is art, culture, and political purpose, not numbers that define a city." At Dr. Schneider's mention of music, the Schadow Sisters turned to each other, smiling and nodding, signaling their approval and interest. "Together with you, I would like to examine the notion of West Berlin as a *polis*, an accidental *polis* at that, though to be quite honest, I'm not at all certain where our efforts might take us. I know two of you, Mr. Durchschouer and Mr. Vonaechron, are historians by training and," turning to the Schadow Sisters said, "it appears you ladies both have an interest in music." Surveying the seven students sitting around the rectangle formed by the conference tables, he continued, "I would be very interested to learn from each of you what brought you here today and what your particular areas of academic interest might be. As you know, the Clay Institute is interdisciplinary by design. Perhaps some of you are from other institutes, perhaps even other universities. Although listed in the institute's catalog under 'Political Science,' the *polis* is by definition interdisciplinary. I therefore most heartily endorse and encourage an interdisciplinary approach.

"The first challenge facing us will be to determine whether or not West Berlin constitutes a *polis*, either in the classical sense of the word, or perhaps in a more contemporary, postwar sense. *Polis* is often translated into English as 'city-state,' into German, I believe, as '*Stadtstaat*.' As you are all well aware, West Berlin is closely affiliated with, but not part of the Federal Republic of Germany. It is nevertheless considered, coincidentally, a city, *eine Stadt*, and a state, *ein Land*, once again, *ein Stadtstaat*. Bremen and Hamburg are the other two. The other states or *Länder* of the Federal Republic are considered '*Flächenländer*,' not to be confused with the '*Flachland*.' Unlike the rest of the Federal Republic, which I've often heard referred to here in West Berlin as '*Restdeutschland*,' West Berlin remains *de jure* under foreign military occupation. Although the state government, *Land Berlin*, governs day to day, the three Western military commandants retain ultimate political authority, even exercising it upon occasion. As a consequence, West Berlin might also be considered to be, once again in the words of Lewis Mumford, 'a kind of political fossil of the military state, dear to Plato.' 'Dear to Plato!' Because of the continuing presence of the three Western Allies, the Soviet Union considers West Berlin a *selbständige politische Einheit*, an independent political entity, unintentionally lending support to a *polis* hypothesis. Ironically, for those of us living in West Berlin, some thinkers, ancient and contemporary, argue a *polis* is primarily defined architecturally, by a wall."

"Professor Schneider, please excuse the interruption, but I would like to submit to you that Sparta did not have a wall. In terms of territory, Sparta was the largest *polis*, though it could be argued Sparta was not a *polis* per se but a network of villages. In either case, the Spartans' reputation as consummate soldiers made a wall, a defensive wall superfluous. In *The Laws*, Megillus the Spartan boasts 'O best of men, we have only to take arms into our hands, and we send all these nations flying before us.'"

Professor Schneider laughed, nodding his head in agreement. "Yes, that is indeed correct, Mr. Durchschouer. Thank you for your observation, an important exception to the rule, which we must consider in our deliberations. West Berlin is, after all, as Mr. Vonaechron suggested to me when we met last week, an armed camp.' Is *Urbs in rure*, urbanity without walls, possible? Perhaps widespread popular perception of Spartan military prowess served as a 'wall' in the minds of their adversaries, something which would have appealed to their Chinese contemporary Sun Tzu, 'a wall of no wall.'" Mr. Durchschouer was *sans doute* Major Durchschouer, the West Point military historian Professor Schneider had told me about. Instead of regulation student attire, he wore pressed khaki slacks and Lord Raglan's own sweater over a button-down collared shirt, his thick, peppery hair cut short but stylish. Instead of the standard issue GI black, plastic-framed, "anti-baby" eyeglasses, he wore gold-framed aviator glasses with clear lenses. His rugged facial features were etched by lines of deep expression, giving added weight to his words when he spoke. Like me, he was a few years older than the other students. Dr. Schneider's reference to Sun Tzu found his enthusiastic concurrence. "Aristotle shares your skepticism, Mr. Durchschouer. In Book III of the *Politics* he writes," looking down at his notes, '… for it does not depend upon the walls; for I can suppose Peloponnesus itself surrounded with a wall, as Babylon was, and every other place, which rather encircles many nations than one city, and that they say was taken three days when some of the inhabitants knew nothing of it.' This also appears to have been the case here in Berlin in late April and early May 1945.

"Berlin has been referred to as 'Athens on the Spree.' Let's now turn our attention to Sparta's sometime ally and adversary. The circuit wall, *teikhos*, of Athens, though incomplete until late in Athenian history, defined the limits of civic order, separating the *polis* from natural, as well as from external, political threats. The wall stood as a border between peace and war though, as Herodotus informs us, the Athenians were once forced by the Persians to abandon their city for the safety of the 'wooden walls' of their ships. Seen superficially, the description of the Athenian circuit wall might also apply to 'well-walled' West Berlin after August 1961. There is, of course, one significant difference. What might that be?"

True to his professional calling, the good Major had led the way. It was now my turn to jump in the gap. I raised my hand. Dr. Schneider smiled at me and said, "Mr. Vonaechron."

"The wall around West Berlin was not built as a defensive wall by its citizens or its occupiers, but by its adversaries. The Council of State of the German Democratic Republic, East Germany, evaluated the West Berlin enclave as a threat to its national stability, so they had it walled in!"

"Very good, Mr. Vonaechron, thank you for joining the discussion. Perhaps that very act, the building of the Berlin Wall, might just provide us with the 'accident' we're looking for, an accident of history. If memory serves, prior to its construction, the council chairman, Walter Ulbricht, told German journalist Annamarie Doherr, '*Niemand hat die Absicht eine Mauer zu errichten!*'[24]

"As Plato does in *The Republic* and in *The Laws* as well, we might want to consider the origins, development, and decline of the *polis*. In this context, it is important for us to recall that for Plato, the *polis* was the individual writ large. *The Republic* is as much about the individual as it is about society and social harmony. In addition to the circuit wall, the harbor, as a means of egress and communication, and the agora also help to define the *polis*. The market was a place for the interchange of both products and ideas. Socrates supposedly taught in the marketplace. His student Plato places great emphasis on education, in both *The Republic* and *The Laws*. As the Clay Institute is part of the *Freie Universität Berlin*, we might want to look at education in West Berlin, too. Mr. Vonaechron, at our first meeting, you mentioned an interest in the teaching of history in Berlin. We have an *FU* and a *TU*, the *Technische Universität*. The *FU* is not as old as the *TU*, or for that matter, the *HU, Humboldt Universität* in East Berlin, but it has a fascinating history nonetheless." Thanks to the lunchtime symposia in the *Stadtstaatsarchiv Kantine* with Johannes Festzelt and George, many essential elements of information on higher education in the HistoriCity were already at hand. Perhaps I could focus on the teaching of history in West Berlin to get started. Limited to West Berlin, it would not only make a good topic for my Accidental *Polis* seminar paper but could be expanded into a dissertation as well.

Professor Schneider continued, "You all have heard President Kennedy's historic speech at *Rathaus Schöneberg*, but did you know he also spoke afterward, here at the Free University on June 26, 1963? The role of higher education in West Berlin was precisely what he spoke about. After being made an 'honorary citizen' of the *FU*, he charged faculty members and

24 "No one has the intention of building a wall" (Ulbricht, 1961). Diary of Thomas Vonaechron, Diary Extract, 1983, trans. TV.

students alike to reify the university's motto, '*Veritas, Justitia, Libertas,*' 'Truth, Justice, and Freedom,' here in West Berlin. I'd like to read an excerpt from his speech to you, as it might point out a direction one or more of you might be interested in taking."

> The shield of the military commitment with which we, in association with two other great powers, guard the freedom of West Berlin will not be lowered or put aside as long as its presence is needed. But behind that shield it is not enough to mark time, to adhere to a status quo, while awaiting a change for the better. In a situation fraught with challenge . . . in an era of this kind, every resident of West Berlin has a duty to consider where he is, where his city is going, and how best it can get there. The scholar, the teacher, the intellectual, have a higher duty than any of the others, for society has trained you to think as well as do. This community has committed itself to that objective, and you have a special obligation to think and to help forge the future of this city in terms of truth and justice and liberty.

Looking up from his notes, Professor Schneider looked at us over the rims of his glasses and continued, "The question of justice is perhaps the central question posed by Plato in *The Republic*. In a legal sense, it's central to the existence of West Berlin, as is the question of freedom. Truth is *sine qua non* for both justice and freedom. As understood by President Kennedy, '*ein Berleener,*'" Professor Schneider emphasized President Kennedy's unique pronunciation, "education seems to be just as important in the accidental *polis* as it was in Plato's intentional *polis*." He laughed, looked at us, and said, "In Athens, Plato taught in a garden adjacent to the Lyceum, not in the Lyceum itself. Instead of meeting here in Seminar Rooms 3–4, perhaps we should meet in the parking out lot behind the Villa?" Seeing our startled faces, he said, "*April! April!*"

"But that's more than enough for now, I've given you some of my thoughts concerning this seminar, and hopefully have thereby raised a few questions and even topics of possible interest. Might I ask each of you to please introduce yourselves? If you already have a topic in mind, and you don't have to commit to it today, please do mention it. Mr. Durchschouer, our Lacedaemonian defender, might I ask you to please begin? We'll just work our way around the table."

"Yes, certainly Dr. Schneider! Good afternoon, I'm David Durchschouer, and as you probably all have guessed by looking at my haircut, I'm an American soldier." Several of my *Komilitonen* exchanged guarded glances at the words "American soldier." "I have a bachelor's degree in history from the United

States Military Academy and have just completed the one-year course at the *Führungsakademie* in Hamburg in preparation for my assignment here. I'm interested in the history of the US military presence in West Berlin personally as well as professionally. At West Point, I had several opportunities to meet with army veterans who served in Berlin immediately after World War II, and others who were stationed here during the First and Second Berlin Crises. Those discussions, together with a long-standing interest in European military history, inspired me to request an assignment in Berlin. In keeping with the interdisciplinary spirit of the seminar, I would like to add that although I'm a soldier, I'm not just interested in the military *an sich* but also in activities associated with the US military in Berlin, like the American Forces Network, 'The Great 88,' which seems to enjoy a large audience here in West Berlin."

"And not just in West Berlin, in East Berlin too! 'The Great 88' is preset on the radio in my taxi," replied the *Komilitone* sitting next to David. Although about the same age as David, like me a few years older than the other students, he sat in superficial contrast to him. With his "old-timer" nickel-rimmed glasses, long unruly brown hair, black T-shirt, and cotton drawstring pants, he might have been more at home in the late sixties than in the early eighties. He had a very friendly, open, easygoing manner and seemed somehow familiar to me. "You might also be interested in taking a look at the West Berlin club scene. Much of the soundtrack is driven by what AFN Berlin is playing. I have many GIs and 'Frawleins,'" overemphasizing the American pronunciation, "as fares and would be happy to take you to some of the clubs around town." Turning from David back to Dr. Schneider, he said, "My name is Rainer Wallfahrt, Professor Schneider. For a long time, too long, I've been working on a *Magister*, master's degree in American Studies and Russian Language, a 'dual-major' I believe it's called in the States, while driving taxi in West Berlin. I've been trying to bridge the two subjects with American literature of the early Cold War, for example Thomas Berger's *Crazy in Berlin* and Thomas Pynchon's *Gravity's Rainbow*, which has just appeared in German translation as *Die Enden der Parabel*. In any case, I'm very interested in postwar Berlin in American literature, particularly as it pertains to the Soviet Union. Perhaps I could look at literature in the *polis*."

"You'll find quite a bit on that subject in both *The Republic* and *The Laws*," replied Dr. Schneider. "I remember reading *Crazy in Berlin* when it first came out in 1958, riding the *Capitol Limited* from Cleveland to a Friends Committee on National Legislation meeting in Washington, DC. Having survived *Gymnasium* in the *Saarpfalz* in the late thirties, I found Berger's examination of anti-Semitism through the person of the former German diplomat Bach quite thought-provoking."

Turning to Rainer, David said, "Thank you for your invitation, Rainer. If you're serious, I'd be very happy to take you up on it, as a paying passenger of course! Outside of the Checkpoint Club on *Clayallee* and the WACS Wings Club at Tempelhof, I've been to the Riverboat and the *Eierschalle*, but that's about it."

"What is the meaning of 'WACS Wings,' Mr. Durchschouer, a reference to Icarus?"

"No, no, but that's an interesting thought, Professor Schneider, I hadn't thought of that before. It stands for 'Washington Air Corridor Service,' the Berlin-Washington connection."

"*Quelle suprise!* AFN Berlin and the Berlin club scene, Laura, this just might be the seminar for us after all! To be 'onest, we weren't certain at first, that's why we 'esitated." The Schadow Sisters were up next. Lady Stardust spoke first, "My name is Nadja d'Oment, I'm a *échange étudiante* from the Sorbonne. This year, my friend Laura," Nadja turned briefly to the blonde *Studentin* sitting across the conference table from me, "and I 'ave been writing about trends in Black American music for 'Dreams and Dollars.' I also cover the Berlin club scene and write reviews for local and Parisian magazines. This is all very interesting; there are parallels with Paris. Black American music came to Paris with the American Army during the First World War." Turning to David, she smiled and asked, "'Ave you ever 'eard of Lieutenant James Reese Europe and the 369th Infantry 'ellfighters' Band, Mr. Durchschouer?"

"No, I haven't, but I'd certainly like to. Please drive on *Madamoiselle* d'Oment!"

"'Drive on,' *Monsieur* Durchschouer?"

"*Pardonez moi, Madamoiselle*, I meant please continue!"

"Oh, I like that *expression* very much, 'drive on!' Jazz was quickly adopted, integrated into the Paris music scene. Following World War II, the same thing 'appened 'ere in Berlin, though jazz 'ad already established itself 'ere after the First World War. *Même les Nazis* were unsuccessful in their attempts to exorcise 'degenerate' jazz from Germany's capital. *Avec les Américains* came AFN in 1945. Rainer's right, broadcasting to soldiers, AFN Berlin rapidly gained a 'shadow audience' in both West and East. Music *est très important* for life in West Berlin today, but I must say in a different way than in Paris. It 'as a somewhat different *fonction*— entertainment, yes, of course—but something else. Perhaps more a political *fonction*, as you suggested, Dr. Schneider. I would be interested in reading what Plato 'ad to say about the political significance of music. At the *lycée* in Paris, I learned Greek and Latin, and I am even familiar with some of Plato's writings, though I must admit to you more as an unpleasant exercise in *traduction*, in translation. I do recall something else though from translation, something from Ovid. Didn't Apollo 'elp Posiedon build the walls of Troy by playing his lyre?"

"Yes, yes, very good indeed *Madamoiselle* d'Oment, from *The Heroides*. Of course, when the subjects are music and masonry," replied Dr. Schneider smiling, "we should also keep the Book of Joshua in mind. After marching around the walls of Jericho seven times, 'So the people shouted, and [the priests] blew the trumpets, and it came to pass, when the people heard the sound of the trumpet, that the people shouted with a great shout, and the wall fell down flat, so that the people went up into the city, every man straight before him, and they took the city.' Or in the text of the old African American spiritual, 'Joshua Fit de Battle of Jericho,' probably composed by slaves in the mid-nineteenth century, 'And the walls came a-tumbling down.' Apparently music can be destructive as well as constructive. I wonder what effect the contemporary music scene in West Berlin might have, if any at all, on the Wall? I'd be very interested in your thoughts on the 'political function' of music. Thank you very much, Ms. d'Oment, for your informative comments!"

It was now 'my friend' Laura's turn. I found myself very interested in what she had to say. "I'm Laura Anders, working on a degree in American Studies focusing on American popular culture, specifically music and film. I also work part time in the Clay Institute Library. Like Nadja, I write about contemporary Black American music, but I also find postwar film fascinating." Turning to Rainer, she continued, "I'm particularly interested in the relationship between men and women depicted in the Cold War feature films featuring Berlin as a backdrop. Many are *Literaturverfilmungen. The Spy Who Came in from the Cold* is, for example, well known, but there are others, perhaps even better ones. Billy Wilder's films, *A Foreign Affair* and *One, Two, Three*, for example. George Seaton's 1950 film, *The Big Lift*, features poignant portrayals of two German women intimately involved with American airmen during the Berlin Blockade. One of my favorites is *The Quiller Memorandum*. The *Drehbuch*, screenplay is by British playwright Harold Pinter. Professor Schneider, I found your remarks about the *polis* as the place where men and women actually become men and women very stimulating. What are we, for example, 'becoming' in West Berlin? In many of the films I've watched, West Berlin is used largely as a set, a *karge Kulisse*, a barren background against which human, oftentimes male-female relationships, are played out. Is West Berlin only a set, or is it something more? Does it have a role to play, too?"

The young woman sitting on Laura's left listened attentively. Spreading the fingers of her right hand, she gently combed back her long, thick black hair back over her shoulder in a practiced gesture. Unlike Laura's unruly blonde hair, it had been carefully cut and brushed. The angular severity of the thin black metal frames of her glasses was softened by her dark eyes, eyebrows, and eyelashes and her fine Eurasian facial features. Dressed casually, but more traditionally than Laura and Tanya, she briefly surveyed the students sitting around the table, smiled briefly, and, turning to Dr. Schneider, said, "Ah, I'm afraid my interest is much more mundane than film, music, or literature, perhaps more along the lines of Mr. Durchschouer's." She hesitated for a moment and flustered, "Oh, please forgive me, Mr. Durchschouer, I didn't mean to suggest . . ." Laughing, David waived his hand in a gesture indicating no offense taken. A smile broke through her serious, all-business expression as she spoke, "My name is Sophia Sweelin Werner. I'm studying *Jura*, law at the *FU*. The legal framework surrounding the presence of the Allies in West Berlin interests me, a topic Dr. Carstens, my advisor at the *Juristische Fakultät* refers to sarcastically as the 'Theology of Berlin.' I've already done some research work on it and would like to use this seminar to do more. From my studies, I'm also familiar with Plato but more so with *The Laws* than with *The Republic*.

"I'm not surprised," replied Dr. Schneider. "While both *The Republic* and *The Laws* construct 'cities in speech,' the former focuses on the ideal state, the latter on what might be possible, drawing upon the experience of Crete, Athens, and Sparta. Written law is not mentioned in *The Republic*, only in *The Laws*. As an accidental *polis*, West Berlin would apparently fall into the realm of the possible rather than the ideal, but closer examination might lead us to another conclusion."

"Like Nadja, I'm also interested in comparative study. Perhaps I'll even discover a relationship between law and music!"

"According to Plato, that relationship does indeed exist," exclaimed Dr. Schneider. "My wife and I often drive up from Kent to Severance Hall to attend concerts of the Cleveland Orchestra. There's a citation from Plato engraved on the wall in the entrance hall. I've committed it to memory, let me see: 'Music is a moral law. It gives a soul to the universe, wings to the mind, flight to the imagination, a charm to gaiety and life to everything. It is the essence of order and leads to all that is good, just and beautiful.' Your knowledge of *The Laws* would make a valuable contribution to our seminar, *Frau* Werner. As in *The Republic*, music is also a topic of discussion.

"Well, well, we already have a fascinating variety of interests, and we're only halfway around the table!" Looking at me, he continued, "I met Mr. Vonaechron when he dropped by the office to see me last week. By the way, I encourage all of you to follow his good example. If I can be of help to you, do come by my office when you are in the Clay Institute. Mr. Vonaechron is an historian and archivist by training, *ein Archivar*. He's worked at the National Archives in Washington, DC, and at the *Stadtstaatsarchiv* here in West Berlin. I learned of his interest in Berlin and his intent to study at the Free University from a former student and colleague of mine, Govinda Nayaka, Professor of Political Science at the University of Hawaii."

"Thank you, Professor Schneider. I'm Thomas Vonaechron. Seven months ago, I moved to West Berlin from Washington, DC, where, as Professor Schneider mentioned, I worked for the National Archives. While in Washington, I studied at both George Washington and Georgetown Universities. When I first visited Berlin during a junior year abroad in Basel, Switzerland, nine, now ten years ago, I found it fascinating, in so many different ways, on so many different levels. After returning to the United States and finishing up my BA in history, I decided upon a career in the civil service and applied for a position at the National Archives and Records Service, "NARS." I was offered a job as an archives technician and, because I already had a BA in history, was enrolled in a two-year professional training program leading to a master's degree in archival science from George Washington University. After receiving my MA, I became an 'archivist' and was assigned a team of archives technicians reviewing classified US and foreign government documents created between 1944 and 1954 for declassification. It was at the Archives—not downtown Washington, DC, where the Declaration of Independence, Constitution, and Bill of Rights are displayed, but off-site, underground, at the Washington National Records Center in Suitland, Maryland—where I picked up the historic paper and photographic trail that led me here."

Smiling at me, Rainer laughed and said, "We can't understand why anyone would want to come to West Berlin to study. We're all trying to get to America to study, *trotz Star Wars* and your President Reagan! It's too bad you missed his visit to West Berlin last year, Thomas. There was quite a bit of excitement, demonstrations, barricades, *Strassenschlachten* on *Nollendorfplatz* and *Winterfeldplatz*, burning cars and police vans, *Wasserwerfer*. The Berlin police tore down *Transperente*, banners, critical of Reagan, '*Wein' nicht wenn der Reagan fällt*'[25] and so on. After all the bad publicity given his visit in advance, I wanted to see him for myself and hear what he had to say. So I applied for a ticket to the big garden party at *Schloß Charlottenburg*, out 'on freedom's edge' as he put it."

"I followed President Reagan's trip to Bonn and Berlin very closely while preparing for my year here at the Free University," said Dr. Schneider. I read the speech he gave at *Schloß Charlottenburg* and remember that curious

---

25 "Don't cry when Reagan [*der Regen*—the rain] falls." Diary of Thomas Vonaechron, Diary Extract, 1983, trans. TV.

phrase, 'on freedom's edge,' *Herr* Wallfahrt. He also said to be a Berliner is to 'live in the great historic struggle of this age.'

Major Durchschouer added, "You know, I've heard of the 'frontier of freedom,' and the 'outpost of freedom,' but I must admit, 'on freedom's edge' is new to me too."

Rainer nodded and continued his after action report, "Reagan was helicoptered in, just like his fellow actor Robert Duvall in *Apocalypse Now*! Although it was probably written for him, I found his speech interesting. In spite of the obligatory finger-pointing and standard American anti-Soviet propaganda, I had the impression he was sincerely trying to reach out to Brezhnev. Most of the thousands of invited guests left the garden party shortly after he took off. I decided to loaf for a while and invited my soul to sit in Reagan's chair on the speaker's podium and read the *Tagespiegel*. It was the day after Rainer Werner Fassbinder died. Hmmm, classified documents, underground, Thomas, are you sure you don't work for the CIA? Sent by President Reagan to the Free University Berlin to find out what those radical German students are up to?" Everyone laughed.

I laughed too. I didn't work for the CIA, but I did know something about their activities in postwar Berlin, at least up to 1954. "Through my work, which I admit, Rainer, was somewhat unusual, but very interesting," I didn't hold and roll the r's this time, "I became interested in Berlin, and Berlin is not Washington, though there are some similarities. I would like to use this seminar to develop my dissertation topic. Writing a comprehensive history of Berlin is too ambitious. West Berlin offers an interesting historical subset of the whole. A friend and colleague, a German archivist at the *Stadtstaatsarchiv Berlin*, set up a contract for me to arrange microfiche copies of the American 'Office of Military Government—Berlin Sector' documents. This was particularly interesting as I had reviewed some of them for declassification. I also had the chance to meet and help Dr. Johannes Festzelt, a historian who's writing a history of the *FU*. For my seminar paper, I'm thinking about looking at how capital "H" History has been taught here in West Berlin after the war." Turning to Dr. Schneider, I said, "I found the excerpt you read from President Kennedy's speech inspiring. What is the 'special obligation' of the scholar to, let me check my notes, 'think and to help forge the future of this city in terms of truth and justice and liberty?' Can knowledge of the past be used to 'forge the future?' What's the line from *The Tempest*? 'Whereof what's past is prologue; what to come, in your and my discharge.' Perhaps I could look at how history's been taught at the universities in the accidental *polis* from 1945 until the present. What purpose or purposes has it served? For a dissertation topic, I could extend this examination into the past and look how history's been taught in Berlin over the *longue durée*." Turning to Rainer, I added, "But I'd also be very interested in riding along with you and David to take in the AFN-powered West Berlin music scene!"

"That tour would interest me too. If only Elvis Presley had been stationed in Berlin instead of Friedberg," exclaimed the handsome young man sitting on my left, who wore his long blonde hair combed back over his ears in a "duck's ass," à la Elvis. "My name is Eddie Strabler," he said, smiling at Nadja and Laura, who smiled in return. They knew each other. Turning to Dr. Schneider, he said, "I will leave history, movies, music, literature, and law to the others. Although I still need more time to think about it, like Thomas, I was interested by the excerpt you read from John F. Kennedy's speech, which, to be honest, I hadn't heard before. Together with the speech he gave at *Rathhaus Schöneberg,* it suggests the larger significance of JFK for West Berlin as a possible topic. Perhaps more the Kennedy persona than the person, more the Kennedy myth than the man. Yes, the significance, the political significance of the Kennedy myth for West Berlin. Something like that, though, I'm not quite certain how it fits into the seminar."

"Actually quite well," replied Dr. Schneider. "John F. Kennedy had much to say about West Berlin, although in his famous *Rathhaus Schöneberg* speech, his point of reference appears to have been Rome, not Athens: '*civis Romanus sum.*' Plato has much to say about the importance of leadership in the *polis.*" Picking up a well-worn, brown buckram copy of *The Republic of Plato* from the conference table, Dr Schneider flipped through several pages and read aloud, "'Let us note among the guardians those who in their whole life show the greatest eagerness to do what is for the good of their country, and the greatest repugnance to do what is against her interests.' From the speech he gave here at the *FU*, President Kennedy might be seen as a 'guardian' of West Berlin in the platonic sense, a man demonstrating 'the greatest eagerness,' 'of a spirited temper,' or—what was the word he often used himself?—'vigor.'

"Thank you very much! Thank you all for your comments. I believe we have all the ingredients necessary for a stimulating and very productive seminar assembled at this table. Your insights encourage me to conclude there is some sense, some purpose in pursuing the experiment. I do hope each of you will consider joining me as we take a closer look at West Berlin over the summer semester. In preparation for our meeting next Friday, please refine and develop your interests into topics. In addition to the assigned readings, you might also skim over the books of *The Republic* and note the topics under consideration, for example, 'justice, social organization, education, literature, poetry, music,' *und soweiter.* Develop a research topic corresponding to your interests. Here are copies of the syllabus for you. I have placed the readings in the *Handapparat* in the library, although it just occurred to me I forgot to include *The Laws. Frau* Anders, if I bring my copy down to the library, could you please place it in the *Handapparat?*" Laura smiled and nodded her head. "Please do read the assigned material carefully, and come to class prepared to participate. Informed discussion is the essence of the dialectic. As we consider these topics during the course of the semester, I hope we'll be able to draw some conclusions about West Berlin as an 'accidental *polis*,' and, who knows, perhaps even publish our essays as a book! Once again, my sincere thanks to each of you for coming today. I'm looking forward to working with you and would be pleased to meet with you during and outside of the *Sprechstunde.*" Turning to look at me he said, "My colleague Ambassador Hubert Spero and I are doing our best to encourage an 'open-door policy' here at the Clay Institute so, once again, if my door is open, please do come in."

As soon as Dr. Schneider had finished, the German students rapped their knuckles enthusiastically on the tabletop. David Durchschouer and I followed suit. Eddie slipped his notebook into a large stressed-leather saddlebag and walked over to talk with Nadja and Laura, leaning down between their chairs, blonde on blonde and black, black star, white skin. They turned to face him and began talking. I overheard "*Dschungel*" and assumed they were planning to meet somewhere uptown that evening. Sophia quickly and efficiently gathered up her notes, stood up, and asked Dr. Schneider if she could meet with him following the seminar. Smiling, he said, "Of course!" Rainer turned to David and asked, "So, when would you have time to 'drive on' around West Berlin, David? The later in the evening, the better."

Placing my shoulder bag on the table, I stood up and walked around the table and asked Rainer and David, "May I join you?"

"Please do, Thomas!" David stood up from the table, extending his hand to me, and then to Rainer, "Thomas, Rainer, please call me 'D3.'" He and I were about the same height, well over six feet. During the discussion, he'd impressed me with his knowledge and his genuine, midwestern manner.

"D3?" Rainer and I asked in unison.

"Nickname. My full name is Dwight David Durchschouer. Needless to say, my parents, citizens of the great Commonwealth of Pennsylvania, are great admirers of General Dwight David Eisenhower, US Army (retired). He and his wife, Mamie, were still living on the farm in Gettysburg when we first visited the Civil War battlefield. Both the battlefield and the farm made a lasting impression on me. I guess that's one of the reasons why I ended up at West Point. On the other hand, like the Free University, there's no tuition!

"D3 and Thomas, if you have some time now, there's an interesting restaurant in an old *Landhaus* just around the corner from the Villa, across the street from *U-Bahnhof Dahlem Dorf*. Why don't we have a beer together and plan our tour around town?"

"Approved! You don't by any chance mean *Luise,* do you, Rainer? I'm a great admirer of *Königin* Luise von Preußen, described by Napoleon Bonaparte as 'the only man in Prussia.' There's even RUMINT of a possible liaison between the two! Whenever I can escape from my office for lunch, I try to dine under her portrait in the side room off the bar."

"RUMINT? I've reviewed documents stamped HUMINT, human intelligence, and COMINT, communications intelligence, at the Archives, but I've never seen or heard of RUMINT, D3."

"Rumors intelligence, yuck, yuck, yuck!"

"Ach, you Americans and your acronyms! That's the place, D3! Unfortunately, it's still too cold to sit outside under the trees in the *Biergarten*, but perhaps the table under Luise's portrait's free today. It shouldn't be too crowded—on Friday afternoons the *FU* empties out very quickly."

As we gathered up our notebooks and put on our jackets, Nadja and Laura stood up and walked toward the door with Eddie. Just before leaving, they turned in the doorway and said in unison, "*Tchüß!*" I unsuccessfully tried to catch Laura's eye. It seemed today's shopping expedition had been successful, and I hoped they were planning to return the following Friday. Sophia and Dr. Taylor were already involved in an animated, informed discussion on the legal framework of West Berlin. Standing next to Dr. Schneider, I could admire Sophia's long, beautiful dark hair more closely. She tossed it as she spoke, once again in graceful, practiced gestures. Although still a *Studentin*, she already had the demeanor of her chosen profession.

"*Auf Wiedersehen, Frau* Werner *und Herr Dr.* Schneider"—somehow "*Tchüß*" did not seem appropriate. "We've decided to continue the seminar as a symposium off-site."

"A very good idea, gentlemen. Socrates would no doubt approve. Perhaps the rest of us might be able to join you next week."

Leaving the Villa, we turned left onto *Boxerstraße*, and then left again onto *Takustraße*. Parked on the curb was a big yellow taxi, a Mercedes 200D W 123 limousine. Underneath the "TAXI" sign stenciled in yellow letters onto a black background, the roof light also advertised "(American Literature)." "*Ein Moment* please, Thomas and D3, I have to get my cigarettes and wallet from my taxi and let CityFunk know I'll be off duty for a few minutes," said Rainer, opening the passenger door of the late-model Mercedes sedan.

Of course I had seen Rainer before, leaning on his cab on the circular driveway in front of *Anhalter Bahnhof*! He'd even offered me a ride. "Ah, I thought so!" I said out loud.

"Say again, Thomas?" said D3.

"I thought I'd seen Rainer before today, and the "(American Literature)" sign just brought back where—at the taxi stand in front of *Anhalter Bahnhof*."

"Roger that, Thomas! Many university students drive taxis in Berlin to earn their livelihood, I know because I've ridden with a few myself, but I must admit Rainer's is the first taxi I've seen offering *en route* instruction!" Rainer rejoined us, cigarette dangling from the corner of his mouth, just as I first saw him. D3 said, "Rainer, please give us a background briefing on your '(American Literature)' light."

"*Ja, bitte Rainer*! You probably don't remember, but last autumn, you offered me a ride as I walked past the portico of the *Anhalter Bahnhof* on my way to the intersection of *Potsdamer Straße* and *Reichpietsch Ufer*. Although determined to walk, I almost took you up on the offer just to find out about your sign."

Rainer laughed. "Unfortunately, *meine Herren*, as it turns out, I have to go back to work now. I apologize. *Ein Bier bei, bezieungsweise unter* Luise was my idea. One of my regular fares called CityFunk while we were in the Villa. Normally, someone else could cover for me, but it was a by-name request. Could we postpone until next Friday? Perhaps Dr. Schneider and some of the others will join us?"

"Yes, yes, of course, but only if you tell us about your sign before you drive on."

"*Einverstanden!* While I was traveling across the United States by Greyhound Bus in the mid-seventies, 'ridin' them dogs,' I found an old *Newsweek* magazine in the waiting room of the bus terminal in Akron, Ohio. There was an interesting article on the 'Intellectual Taxi Company.' The author, I can't remember his name but I still have the article back at my *WG*, suggested out-of-work academics could earn money by driving taxis with their major subject area displayed prominently on top of the cab. Although I'm not an out-of-work academic but a working *Akademiker-im-werden*, the idea's still a good one. I had the sign custom made at an *Autowerkstatt* in Kreuzberg. Believe it or not, it actually works! Over the past few weeks, I've been *unterwegs* with readers of Thomas Wolfe, Thomas Berger, Thomas Pynchon, Herbert Huncke, Henry Miller, Charles Bukowski, and Jack Kerouac. American literature is not only a subject at the Clay Institute but also good for business on the streets of West Berlin."

"'On the road' in West Berlin, back and forth across town instead of the North American continent, well, why not?"

Rainer laughed, replying, "Perhaps our peculiar paradox here in the American Sector, here in West Berlin—is that we are fixed and certain only when we're moving."

"That's pretty good, Rainer, but please do be careful about decrying Wolfe! We'll hopefully see you next Friday in and after class, and we'll do our best to carry on without you this afternoon. Cheers!" Driving off in the direction of Steglitz, Rainer opened the Mercedes's sunroof and waved.

D3 and I continued down *Takustraße*, turning left onto *Königin-Luise-Straße*. Through the tall iron fence, we could see the elegant *Landhaus* framed by budding trees in the *Biergarten*. Arriving at the iron gate in front of the house, we walked up the stairs into the restaurant. The portrait of *Königin* Luise hung in a high-ceilinged, comfortable room off to the left of the entrance. On the far wall, hung just above the dark wooden wainscoting running around the room, was a portrait of her nemesis as a young man, Otto von Bismarck, with his clear eyes focused on the queen. The only other painting in the room was of the first German emperor, Wilhelm I, in the field on horseback. Rainer was right—the room, with its massive wooden table in the center, was deserted. With cream-colored walls above the wainscoting, the former parlor retained the elegance of Imperial Berlin, Berlin II. Against the front wall, between the windows facing *Königin-Luise-Straße*, there was a smaller dark wooden table with two chairs, directly under the portrait of the queen, "the only man in Prussia." We sat down, ordering two half-liter *Königin Pilsener* from our waitress, a pleasant young woman in black jeans wrapped professionally in a long, white apron, who appeared to be a *Studentin*.

"It's good to meet you, D3. Dr. Schneider told me about you when I stopped by the Clay Institute last week. He also asked me to help you get the discussion rolling. I hope we were successful this afternoon! As he mentioned in class, I met his former student Govinda Nayaka by chance on the Pan Am flight from London to Frankfurt last August on my way here. Since then, I've been working on contract at the *Berlin Stadtstaatsarchiv*, arranging and describing microfiche copies of records of the Office of Military Government—Berlin Sector. A friend and colleague I met at the National Archives, George von Garlitz, set up the job for me. He belonged to a group of German archivists and historians filming the records of the Office of Military Government (US), which administered the US Zone of Germany up until 1949. As part of my contract work, I prepared a finding-aid to the 'Office of Military Government—Berlin Sector' records, which might be useful for your research. I'd be happy to make a copy for you."

"Thank you, Thomas, I'm sure it would be very useful. I'm happy to meet you, too. We must have arrived in Berlin just about the same time, I 'PCS'd'—excuse me, Permanent Change of Station, Rainer's missing out on more American acronyms—from Hamburg last summer, though I took some home leave to visit my family in Pennsylvania before reporting for duty."

"Please forgive my curiosity, D3, but because I've reviewed so many US Army reports dealing with Berlin at the *Stadtstaatsarchiv* and at the National Archives, may I ask to which unit you're assigned? Are you with the Headquarters, US Command Berlin, or Berlin Brigade Headquarters?"

"Well," D3 paused for a moment, "although we do have an office here in West Berlin, actually just a few blocks away from here on *Föhrenweg*, I'm actually stationed in Potsdam, home of *Friedrich der Große*."

"Potsdam! Ah, you must be assigned to the US Military Liaison Mission to the Commander, Soviet Ground Forces Germany!"

Startled, D3 replied, "Well now, that was a pretty good guess, Thomas! May I now ask you how you know about USMLM?"

"Sure, D3, from my work in the Declassification Division! After I'd finished my training and went to work, I requested all declassification projects containing documents created by US and foreign government civilian and military agencies in Berlin. I reviewed all the USMLM annual unit histories submitted between 1947 and 1954, and I even found some British BRIXMIS and French *MMFL* reports in the files. While some of the information was pretty routine, if you know what I mean, much of it made for fascinating reading. I particularly enjoyed the attached black-and-white photos of Soviet military equipment and installations taken during the USMLM tours in East Germany. After I'd finished reviewing one of those US Military Liaison Mission unit histories, I felt like I'd been along for the ride!"

"Could this really be a coincidence? You probably know more about USMLM than I do, Thomas! With your permission, of course, I'll arrange for a follow-on seminar in the *Föhrenweg*. I know our Chief of Mission, Colonel Riley Patrick, would be very interested in hearing about the early history of USMLM. We don't keep copies of the unit histories at the Mission—they're forwarded to Heidelberg after the Chief signs off on them. You probably know USMLM reports directly to the Commander-in-Chief, US Army, Europe, 'CINCUSAREUR.' I've stopped by the History Office in Heidelberg several times to look for answers to 'historical questions' affecting current operations. With your professional background, you'd likely be interested in the Mission here in West Berlin too, a building with a past, a brown past, built according to plans drawn up by Albert Speer . . ."

"Albert Speer again, oh no! He occupied my desk in the *Stadtstaatsarchiv* last year while recording comments on his plans for *Germania*. I'll check with George to find out whether he also commented on the *Föhrenweg* building. George told me all of the buildings Albert Speer designed for Berlin had either been destroyed during, or deconstructed after, the war. Together with the *Flak* tower at Humboldthain, apparently another span in his 'bridge of tradition' has apparently survived intact."

"You saw Albert Speer here in West Berlin last year, just before he died in London! I wonder if he visited Spandau while he was in town?"

"That's just what I asked George, though he recommend I not ask him until he was finished with his commentary."

"Probably a good idea! That's very interesting, Thomas, yet another reason for you to come to the Mission. We know the building was completed in 1936 and used as an alternate headquarters by the Supreme Commander of the Armed Forces, *Feldmarschal* Wilhelm Bodewin Johann Gustav Keitel, during the war. A command and control center was set up for him underground in a two-story, steel-reinforced bunker. That's where the USMLM operations center and classified conference room is now. With your 'underground' background, yuck, yuck, yuck, I'm quite certain we could arrange for you to see it!"

"Thank you, D3. I'd be very grateful. I've spent a fair amount of time looking for the remains of Berlin IV, excuse me, Adolf Hitler's *Germania*, in West Berlin." Although I didn't know Albert Speer had designed it as an alternate headquarters for Field Marshal Keitel, I am familiar with the building at *Föhrenweg 21* from my work in Vault Six. Allen Dulles personally selected it for the headquarters of the Office of Strategic Services when the OSS team first arrived in Berlin on July 4, 1945. That October, it became the Berlin Operational Base (BOB) of the Strategic Services Unit. The SSU became the Central Intelligence Group (CIG) and in 1947, the Central Intelligence Agency. The building at *Föhrenweg 21* remained CIA headquarters until the mid-fifties when it relocated to building . . . a building on the Kennedy headquarters Compound, and USMLM was assigned the building on *Föhrenweg*. Drinking *KöPi* in the pleasant late-Friday afternoon ambiance of *Lusie,* the Mr. Henry's symposia with George on Washington Circle came to mind, inspiring my decision to back-brief D3 on the *Schliemann'ische* schemata I'd developed for my excursions and excavations in the HistoriCity.

"Berlin I through VI. Thomas, the history of Berlin, the history of Germany for that matter, is *ein weites Feld* for the historian, the military historian as well as the civilian historian. As I said in class this afternoon, history also brought me here to West Berlin. After receiving my commission as a second lieutenant, I volunteered for duty in Vietnam. Although direct US involvement was rapidly winding down, I was anxious to observe up close what I had been studying from a distance for four years, the war. Attached to a special operations team, I discovered a number of the operations I participated in weren't so 'special' after all, forcing me to either go beyond what I'd been taught at West Point or go insane. It was not a pleasant experience. I seriously considered leaving active duty after my five-year commitment was up. As you can see, I decided to stay in, but my experiences in Vietnam caused me to begin a serious study of war as an instrument of politics. Promoted to captain after returning to CONUS—acronym alert, 'Continental United States'—I was also selected to attend Command and General Staff College at Fort Leavenworth, Kansas. Have you heard of 'CGSC?'"

"Yes D3, I have, and I've even heard the expression 'CONUS' before. Have you heard the story about Captain Dwight David Eisenhower catching Second Lieutenant F. Scott Fitzgerald working on his novel, cleverly concealed in a copy of *Small Problems for Infantry* at Leavenworth?"

D3 laughed, "I don't recall reading that story in *At Ease*, but to tell ya the truth, it doesn't surprise me! In retrospect, Leavenworth was the ideal place for me to work my way back into the army. Although the American frontier had moved on—why, if you buy the dream, Thomas, it's been running through Germany and Berlin since the end of the Second World War—you can still feel the frontier in Leavenworth. It's the oldest army post in continuous operation west of the Missouri River. It's so real it's unreal, like an abandoned set for a spaghetti western, hot, humid, empty, a bluff looking down on the Missouri River. If the United States Army had a soul, it would be inscribed on a commemorative plaque hanging on the wall of Memorial Chapel at Fort Leavenworth. It's all there at Leavenworth, the sacrifice and the sacrilege. At CGSC, I found a like-minded group of captains and instructors, civilian and military, reeling in the aftermath of Vietnam, trying to understand what had happened to the United States Army. And not only to the US Army. There was also a *Bundeswehr Hauptmann*, Winfried Wolf. At the end of the Second World War, the US Army began a love affair with the *Wehrmacht* that continues to the present day. Fortunately, we had Winfried, "W2" as we called him, to keep us honest. We christened ourselves 'the Dead Carl Club,' meeting outside of the classroom to study and discuss the writings of Carl von Clausewitz, Hans Delbrück, and other European strategic thinkers. Differences of opinion were occasionally resolved by translation, kindling my interest in

German. Needless to say, in all things German, Winfried always had the last *Wort, auf Deutsch natürlich*! Well, I'd survived the mandatory French courses at the Academy in pretty good shape, so I thought I might as well add *Deutsch* to my toolbox."

"Ah, *deswegen Madamoiselle d'Oment*!"

"*Bien sur*! Fortunately, both Winfried and I were selected to remain at Leavenworth for a second year in the SAMS program—sorry, Thomas, 'School of Advanced Military Studies'—allowing me to also complete basic German language training at the same time—with Winfried's help of course. I wrote my monograph *On Clausewitz Now: Deconstructing the Art of War*, a direct reference to the film *Apocalypse Now*, which didn't play as well with some of the faculty members as it did at the movie theaters. By the time I completed SAMS, I had arrived at a few important conclusions about war and the use of the military as instruments of politics. Briefly, the military is only one of the tools in the toolbox used by policy makers. Diplomacy is another, as is foreign aid, both military and economic. If in 1944, it is in the interest of the United States government to bomb Berlin, then the US Strategic Air Forces in Europe bomb Berlin. If, four years later, it is in the interest of the United States government to supply Berlin by air, then US Air Forces in Europe supply Berlin by air. Back at West Point, I talked with an Army Air Corps veteran who told me how, during the early days of the blockade, he'd flown supplies into West Berlin in a B-17 bomber. Now if that isn't an irony of history! It's a policy decision, Thomas. It's the policy makers who decide how to invest the nation's blood and treasure. Policy makers were the problem in Vietnam, not the airmen, sailors, soldiers, and marines who tried to execute the mission they were given. The Independent Services will always do their best when called upon, but despite their best efforts, they cannot succeed if put into a no-win situation by the policy makers. By "no-win," I mean a situation in which the military instrument is inappropriate, in which it cannot be used to solve the problem. Professor Schneider referred to the Chinese thinker Sun Tzu during our seminar today. Sun Tzu sez there are 'commands of the sovereign which must not be obeyed.' For this reason, I find the interrelationship among policy, strategy, and warfare outlined by Clausewitz not only intellectually stimulating but professionally useful as well."

"So, D3, you followed Carl von Clausewitz from Fort Leavenworth to Hamburg, and then 'on to Berlin.' Although your namesake wouldn't allow General Simpson's Ninth US Army to take Berlin in 1945, you took it on your own thirty-seven years later!"

"Roger that, Thomas! In addition to the assigned duties and responsibilities, my current assignment allows me to tour battlefields, not only around Berlin but throughout East Germany, Jena-Auerstadt, Großgörschen, Leipzig, following Clausewitz and his two 'case studies,' Napoleon," he paused for a moment to look up and raise his glass to *Königen* Luise, I followed suit, "and Frederick the Great. I've been out to the Seelow Heights, too. You might say I'm lookin' for 'ground truth.' By studying individual engagements, it's possible to gain insight into the larger operational architecture, as well as into the strategy and the grand strategy behind them."

"Operational architecture?"

"A structuring of space and time to dominate the battlefield and achieve the strategic goals established by the political leadership, '*Der Krieg ist eine bloße Fortsetzung der Politik mit anderen Mitteln.*'"[26]

"That sounds a lot like Clausewitz, D3. So, war can also be considered a kind of architecture, or rather a kind of counter-architecture, an antithesis in the never-ending human dialectic of creation and destruction."

"Why, Thomas, that statement qualifies you for honorary membership in the Dead Carl Club! Seriously, I wish I had some ready answers for you. Maybe Dr. Schneider will join us next week. I've already worked my way through *The Republic*. I have the same translation as Dr. Schneider does, right here. It seems to me, in Plato's 'just city,' the professional military—those skilled in the art of war play the critical role in the preservation of its freedom. This invites comparison with the situation here in West Berlin. In any case, I look forward to getting together with you and Rainer for a recce 'round West Berlin—what an interesting piece of work he is!" D3 checked his military-issue Elgin wristwatch. "Uh oh, gotta go now, Thomas, excuse me, please. I'm 'on tour' tomorrow and need to stop by the Mission before I head for home tonight. Die *Rechnung, bitte!* The beers are on me today. I'll let you pick up the tab next time, when Rainer, Dr. Schneider, and the others join us—yuck, yuck, yuck!"

"Thanks, D3! I'm convinced Clio, the muse of history herself, not just pure coincidence, must have seduced us individually and brought us together here in West Berlin, out on 'freedom's edge,' for some obscure reason known only to her."

"Now, that's funny you should take it upon yourself to reference the muse of history, Thomas. I once came upon Clio during a terrain walk of the Gettysburg battlefield, up on Lower Culp's Hill, also known as 'Spangler's Hill.' She was apparently recording the small unit actions taking place there between July 1 and July 4, 1863, on a stone tablet from her

---

26 "War is only the continuation of politics by other means." trans. Captain Dwight D. Durchschouer, US Army, School for Advanced Military Studies, Fort Leavenworth, Kansas, *On War*, p. 16.

coign of vantage atop the monument of the 123rd New York Infantry Regiment—First Brigade, First Division, Twelfth Corps, just in case you're interested." D3 smiled. "Apparently, it's the only monument on the battlefield depicting a woman! Hmmm. Well, Clio didn't look up from her tablet, and to be honest, Thomas, I just wasn't motivated enough to climb up on her granite pedestal to read what she had written down. I did notice, however, she'd lost her stylus. Maybe it was for the best. Her tablet was probably a *tabula rasa*."

"You made the right decision, D3. One should never take history for granite!"

"Did you actually just say, 'take history for granite, Thomas?' I'll pretend you didn't and, on that note, take my leave. *Tschüß!* See you next week!"

The following Friday, all seven students returned to Seminar Rooms 3–4, taking the same seats as on the previous Friday. As other seminars had now begun to meet in the Villa, the hallway was crowded with *Studenten, Studentinnen*, and *Professoren* on their way to and from classrooms, slamming the outside door at irregular intervals. Just before expiration of CT, a man in his early forties, who appeared to be a faculty member, entered the room, walked over to Dr. Schneider, and introduced himself. Although he wore jeans, his tailored sport coat, open white shirt, and horn-rimmed glasses seemed more appropriate to the *Juristische Fakultät* than the Clay Institute. Nadja and Laura were dressed in variations on the previous week's *Berliner Chic*. Sophia wore a navy blue sport coat over a white blouse with a navy skirt, well suited for a court appearance.

"Well, I must say I'm very pleased to see you all have returned, truly delighted to see each one of you again. In all honesty, I was afraid I might have frightened you away with my experimental, accidental seminar! Hopefully, you've been able to give additional thought to your topics. Perhaps we can finalize them today, but before we do, we have a presentation! Following our meeting last week, *Frau* Werner and I met to discuss her topic. As she told us, she has already done a considerable amount of research on the legal framework of West Berlin. As we spoke, it occurred to me that West Berlin's legal status offers a useful starting point for our seminar, a framework and foundation for our examination of the 'accidental *polis*.' I asked her if she would be willing to share her work-in-progress with us this afternoon in an informal presentation, and she kindly agreed to do so. Her faculty advisor from the Law Department, my colleague, Dr. Uwe Carstens—Dr. Carstens, welcome to you once again—joins us today for *Frau* Werner's presentation. Thank you very much *Frau* Werner for your willingness to initiate our investigation of the 'accidental *polis*.' Unless there are any questions for me, the floor is yours." We shook our heads.

"Thank you, Professor Schneider, I've been working on this subject for some time now out of personal as well as professional interest. Please let me explain briefly. My father is an *Urberliner*. After the war, he studied international law in Bonn and afterward entered the German Foreign Service. He first overseas posting was to the embassy in Bangkok, Thailand, where he met my mother. Although my family has been stationed throughout Asia and the Middle East in the meantime, with a tour in Bonn in between overseas postings, my father remains deeply committed to Berlin. He passed along his commitment and his interest to me through countless conversations and visits to West Berlin, where his parents, my grandparents, still live. This is the reason I chose to return to Berlin following my *Abitur*, to study international law at the *Freie Universität*.

"When one more closely examines the agreements comprising the legal framework supporting the presence of the three Western Allies in the three Western sectors, in West Berlin, there appears to be quite a bit that is provisional, even 'accidental,' and, as a consequence, oftentimes quite controversial. It is important to note the military occupation of Berlin is without legal precedence. According to the London Protocol of September 12, 1944, and I quote," as Sophia looked down to read aloud from her notes, her hair swept forward over her right shoulder in a shining black wave, "'[t]he Berlin area, (by which expression is understood the territory of "Greater Berlin" as defined by the Law of the 27th April, 1920) will be jointly occupied by armed forces of the USA, UK, and USSR, assigned by the respective Commanders-in-Chief.' End of quotation. The 'Greater Berlin area' was to be jointly administered by '[a]n Inter-Allied Governing Authority,' the *Kommandatura*, made up of the three Commandants." Looking up from her notes, she said, "By the way, the Allied *Kommandatura* is located just a few blocks away from the Clay Institute, at *Kaiserwerther Strasse 16–18*. The creation of a French Sector from the assigned American and British Sectors was the consequence of a decision taken by the European Advisory Council. Once again, all these actions were without international legal precedence, inviting ongoing debate as to their original intent and implementation. In short, military occupation is the *sine qua non* of the Allied presence in West Berlin and, consequently, the existence of West Berlin. Had West Berlin become a *Land* at some point in time following the creation of the Federal Republic of Germany in 1949, the legal basis for the presence of the three Western Allies, the Occupation Statute, would have been terminated. In one sense, the 1958 Berlin Crisis was a crisis of legality. Soviet Premier Nikita S. Khrushchev challenged the right of the Western Allies to remain in their sectors, in West Berlin, once the Soviet Union relinquished all occupation powers to the government of the German Democratic Republic through conclusion of a bilateral peace treaty. Although the deadline passed without incident, tensions among the four former Allies, aggravated primarily by immigration from the German Democratic Republic to the Federal Republic of Germany through West Berlin, lessened only with the construction of the Wall in 1961."

Dr. Schneider leaned back in his chair, "So, in a sense *Frau* Werner, one might say the physical wall served, albeit in a very brutal manner, to both recognize and reinforce the paper wall, the existing legal framework. It's almost the inverse of what the Ephesian philosopher Heraclitus proposed—citizens of a city should fight for their laws as they would fight for their city walls. *Eirönïa.*"

"Yes, Professor Schneider, it's certainly ironic. Furthermore, by halting the population exodus destabilizing the German Democratic Republic, the Wall decreased political tensions, as Thomas suggested last week. Normalization came only twelve years ago, with the 'Quadripartite Agreement.' To add yet another interesting dimension to the 'accidental *polis*,' the Quadripartite Agreement refers to West Berlin as 'the relevant area.'"

Leaning "forward in the foxhole," D3 was eager to join in, "Well, the relevant area is certainly relevant to our seminar! Now if I understood correctly, *Frau* Werner, what we know as West Berlin, composed of the three individual Western sectors—American, British, and French—is framed by the individual occupation rights of each of the Western Allies. I submit to you that the presence of Allied military forces in 'the relevant area' guarantees the preservation of those rights, and coincidentally the freedom of the West *Berliner.*"

"Yes, Mr. Durchschouer, that is correct. Oftentimes to the dismay of the West *Berliner* but perhaps to the greater good of the international relations, the primary objective of the Western Allies has consistently remained the preservation of their occupation rights, access to their sectors, and freedom of movement throughout all sectors." Listening to Sophia, I thought about the "Soldier: Why are You in Berlin?" poster hanging on the wall behind the counter in the Checkpoint Charlie guard shack, " . . . to fight like hell, if necessary for US rights and a free Berlin." Sophia continued, "In this context, it is important to recall American, British, and French forces did not occupy their sectors of Berlin at the conclusion of hostilities but only two months later, in exchange for territory occupied by their forces in the designated Soviet Zone of Germany. Based upon the precedent established when the French Zone of Germany was created out of the designated American Zone, the French Sector of Berlin was created out of the American and British Sectors. The Western Allies took West Berlin by the pen, not by the sword."

D3 joined in, "Concur, *Frau* Werner. I've spoken with several army veterans involved in that operation. They referred to it as 'Rolling the Carpet.' A retired lieutenant colonel told me how German mothers standing along the roadside begged him to take their children, their babies, with him as his convoy passed through Halle on the way to the American Sector in July 1945. The inhabitants knew the Russians would follow the Americans and were afraid of what might happen to them."

"That must have been an exceedingly difficult emotional experience for all concerned, Mr. Durchschouer."

"This concludes my short précis on the legal framework of West Berlin. Before I conclude my presentation, I would also like to address two relevant issues raised by Plato in *The Laws*, legislation as accident in Book IV, and the 'Nocturnal Council' in Book XII. These references seem particularly relevant to our consideration of West Berlin as a *polis*, accidental and occupied. On a summer day in Crete, an Athenian, known as the 'Stranger,' the Spartan Megillus," Sophia glanced up briefly from her notes and smiled at D3, "and the Cretan Cleinias made a pilgrimage from Knossos to the cave of Zeus on Mount Ida. As they walked, the Athenian Stranger who," Sophia glanced up again, this time at Dr. Schneider, and continued, "may or may not be Plato, offers the following observation on the accidental nature of legislation.

> I was going to say that man never legislates, but accidents of all sorts, which legislate for us in all sorts of ways. The violence of war and the hard necessity of poverty are constantly overturning governments and changing laws. And the power of disease has often caused innovations in the state, when there have been pestilences, or when there has been a succession of bad seasons continuing during many years. Anyone who sees all this, naturally rushes to the conclusion of which I was speaking, that no mortal legislates in anything, but that in human affairs chance is almost everything.

It seems to me then, the notion of West Berlin as an 'accidental *polis*,' the result of war, poverty, and chance, at least from a legislative standpoint, is indeed supported by Plato.

"When I read the dialogue describing the origin and function of the 'Nocturnal Council,' it brought to mind the residual *Kommandatura*, composed of the three Western commandants. The Nocturnal Council anchors the state, just as the *Kommandatura* anchors West Berlin. Although Berlin is considered a *Land* by the West German government, and though American Major General Timothy O'Cracy, British Major General

Anthony J. Maude, and French Major General Jean-Luc Le Tissier rely upon the *Berliner Senat* to govern West Berlin, they retain final approval authority over all the decisions it makes." In Book XII, just prior to the closing remarks, the Athenian Stranger summarizes this responsibility, 'And that means, Clenias and Megillus, that we now have to consider whether we are going to add yet another law to the code we've already expounded, to the effect that the Nocturnal Council of the Authorities, duly primed by the course of the studies we've described, shall be constituted the legal protector of the safety of the state.'"

Turning to D3, I said, "If I remember correctly from the documents I reviewed in the National Archives, the US Commander Berlin, 'USCOB,' reports to both the US Ambassador to the Federal Republic of Germany in Bonn, and to the Commander-in-Chief, U.S. Army Europe in Heidelberg."

"That is correct, Thomas." confirmed D3.

"I would like to conclude my presentation with the observation while walls protect the *polis* from external threats, laws protect the citizens of the *polis* from internal threats, from themselves. Thank you all for your *Aufmerksamkeit*, I'd be pleased to address any questions you might have to the best of my ability, though I must admit I still have quite a few questions myself, which I hope to be able to answer in the course of the semester. As I mentioned at the beginning of my presentation, given the fact there is no legal precedent, West Berlin's framework remains open to a variety of interpretations. Perhaps this provides the flexibility necessary to adapt to the changing international security environment. 'Accidental' does indeed seem to apply to West Berlin from the legal standpoint. The occupation of West Berlin by the Western Allies will only come to an end when all four former Allies agree upon German reunification. At that point in time, whether in seven years or seventy, the 'accidental *polis*' will cease to exist."

Dr. Schneider rapped his knuckles enthusiastically on the tabletop. We joined in, grateful to Sophia for volunteering to make the first presentation. "Excellent, excellent! We are all very grateful to you for your truly thought-provoking presentation, *Frau* Werner. It certainly was anything but mundane." Smiling, turning to D3, he said, "Mr. Durchschouer was no doubt greatly relieved! As I suspected when we spoke after class last week, you have provided us with a legal frame of reference which we can now use to further examine West Berlin as an accidental *polis*, together with its Greek *Vorbild*, during the coming semester. The other seminar topics can now be considered within and integrated into this broader framework. Once again, thank you very much for your fine presentation, *Frau* Werner."

Dr. Schneider then asked each of us for our topics. True to his profession, D3 decided to examine the discussion of warfare, warriors and the security of the *polis* in *The Republic*. Turning to D3, brushing her hair back with her fingers and smiling, Sophia said, "You might want to take a look at *The Laws* too, Mr. Durchschouer. I made a note here. In Book I, Clenias, the Cretan, says of the legislator, 'He seems to me to have thought the world foolish in not understanding that all are always at war with one another; . . . For what men in general term peace would said by him to be only a name; in reality every city is in a natural state of war with every other, not indeed proclaimed by heralds, but everlasting.'"

"Now that's quite interesting *Frau* Werner. Clenias sounds a lot like Thomas Hobbes! Thank you very much for your recommendation, I'll do just that. Perhaps you could provide me with the reference?"

"Yes, of course, I wrote it down for you when I first came across it." Sophiahanded D3 a slip of paper.

Rainer had been busy taxiing around West Berlin, and had not given too much additional thought to his topic since last Friday. Leafing through *The Republic* while waiting for a fare, he found a discussion of the relationship between art and truth in Book X. "I'm thinking about literature in Plato's *polis* and the literature of the early Cold War. I mean, do the Berlin-based novels of Berger and Pynchon reveal any truths about the struggle between East and West, or is Berlin just an interesting setting for a story? Book X seems to support the storyline." Picking up his copy of *The Republic*, Rainer read aloud, "'Thus far then we are pretty well agreed that the imitator has no knowledge worth mentioning of what he imitates. Imitation is only a kind of play or sport…'" Rainer reminded us *Veritas* was one of the three magic words in the motto of the Free University handed back to West Berlin's scholars, teachers, and intellectuals as a mission statement by John F. Kennedy. Was truth to be found in the literature depicting West Berlin, or in the flux of Thomas Pynchon's postwar Zone?

Inspired by the previous week's introductory session, Nadja visited the library of the Institute for Greek and Latin Philology, where she not only found copies of Πολιτεία and Νόμοι but Professor Dr. Diotima, a friendly female philologist offering a seminar on Plato this semester. "Perhaps you should invite her to join us," suggested Dr. Schneider.

"I did, but she offers a seminar at the same time. Listen to what we found about music in *The Republic* in Book IV, 'for any musical innovation is full of danger to the whole State, and ought to be prohibited.' Political stability as a *fonction* of music in the *polis*. This is what we touched upon last week, *n'est pas?* I would like to look at music in West Berlin from this perspective, both its stabilizing and destabilizing influences."

Laura had also been encouraged by last week's meeting. Though the effects of "musical innovations" were also of interest, she found Plato's

"Allegory of the Cave" more inviting. Instead of going to the *Institut für Griechische und Lateinische Philologie* with her friend Nadja, she went to the movies instead. "Reading about Plato's Cave, I was reminded of an underground cinema, and thought about the films made after the war in Berlin from this underground perspective. Do film directors try to encourage their audience to break out of the *Alltag* and see the realities behind the shadows, to discover 'truth,' '*Veritas,*' or as Rainer said, simply try to tell or to 'sell' a good story? In my opinion, Billy Wilder's *A Foreign Affair,* filmed in Berlin in 1947, attempts to do both. I'd like to examine it, and perhaps other films made after the war in Berlin, in Plato's Cave."

"To be honest, I hadn't thought of Plato's Cave in that way *Frau* Anders, but it does makes sense. The shadows of the artificial objects projected on the Wall, the forms, do constitute 'moving pictures!' I agree with you, the question of truth and representation in art addressed by *Herr* Wallfahrt would seem to apply here as well."

Laura continued, "It occurred to me, the Wall—I like the term you used, 'circuit wall'—running around and defining West Berlin, the Wall *als eine Art* ideogram for West Berlin. The Wall is also a *Kulisse,* a screen— *Leinwand* might be the better word—onto which films can be projected. In some of the films, West Berlin becomes even more than just a stage prop, the city itself becomes a character in the film."

Overeager to enter into conversation with Laura, I decided to offer an observation, even though it was outside her area of interest, "A few years ago, the American Film Institute at the Kennedy Center in Washington, DC, sponsored a 'Festival of New German Cinema.' As a kind of preparation for moving from Washington to Berlin, I went as often as I could, two or three times a week. Some of the films, for example Werner Herzog's *Stroszek: A Ballad* and Lothar Lambert's *Die Alptraum Frau,* also use West Berlin as a *Kulisse.* Perhaps you might also look at how the 'shadows' of West Berlin projected on the Wall have changed from the postwar period to the present."

Laura laughed and smiled at me, "*Die Alptraum Frau* in Washington, I can just imagine how that was received!"

"I particularly like the scene where Beate Meitner walks by the shattered roof of the *Kongresshalle* and says something along the lines of, 'Shit! That could only happen in Berlin!'"

"I've been looking exclusively at films made in Berlin just after the war, but a comparison might be interesting, Thomas, thank you for your suggestion. In any case, I would very much like to talk to you about the American Film Institute and about Washington."

Following last week's seminar and some preliminary research work, I called Johannes Festzelt for his recommendations on how to proceed with both seminar paper and dissertation. Our informal lunchtime seminars at the *Stadtstaatsarchiv* fed my interest in the history of Berlin's universities, in particular in the teaching of history at the universities. For the purpose of Dr. Schneider's seminar, Johannes suggested focusing on the study of history in West Berlin, in the accidental *polis*. It would not be only a "doable" topic for a seminar paper but could then be extended into the past for a dissertation topic. He kindly offered to share the results of his research on the history of the Free University with me. At Johannes's suggestion, and with Dr. Schneider's concurrence, I decided to work through G. W. F. Hegel's *Vorlesungen über die Philosophie der Geschchte*, in addition to *The Republic* and *The Laws* of Plato. Johannes had studied Hegel in depth. His insights would help me to develop a working hypothesis. If this approach worked for the accidental *polis* (Berlin VI), it just might work for the HistoriCity writ large (Berlin I through VI) for a dissertation proposal. In 'archival-retentive' fashion, I could start with the "accidental *polis*" and then work backward. Dr. Schneider had underlined the significance of education for the *polis* in his introductory remarks. The excerpt he read aloud from John F. Kennedy's 1963 address to the *FU* faculty and students seemed Taylor-made for my topic. Curiously, the President's words did not seem as politicized as the "single point of the great battlefield of the world" bedside broadcast made by Founding Rector Friedrich Meinecke, a historian, at the foundation of the *FU* five years earlier. In any case, I had my topic.

Following up on remarks made by Dr. Schneider the previous week on the Guardian as a "man of zeal," Eddie found the "man of zeal," along with "Timocratic Man" and "Oligarchic Man," waiting for him in the pages of *The Republic*. "I have given my topic more thought since last Friday and would like to examine the 'Myth of John F. Kennedy in the Mythology of West Berlin,' using the speeches he made in and about West Berlin, in terms of the characteristics provided by Plato. Listening to Rainer talk about Ronald Reagan's visit to Berlin, it occurred to me President Reagan might also be a candidate for demythologizing, but he's still in office. Maybe he'll come back to West Berlin one day and make a more mythological speech! As I thought about the significance of the Kennedy myth, it occurred to me that West Berlin had also acquired mythological status during the Cold War. The Kennedy myth became part of the larger myth of West Berlin. I'm still not certain exactly how to organize my research and would very much like to meet with you, Professor Schneider to discuss it."

"Yes, of course, by all means. Let's try to do so early next week, before our next meeting. I have some primary and secondary source materials in my office, which might be useful for you. I must say, I too continue to find President Kennedy's speech to the faculty and students of the Free University uniquely inspiring. As I said last week, I consider myself to be very much a part of this experimental seminar, and for my part, I have decided to pursue the notion of justice, *Justicia*, looking at justice in *The Republic* and *The Laws* and then in West Berlin. To be quite honest with you, there's some overlap with the research I did on the executive ombudsman during *Wintersemester*, but thinking about it in the context of our seminar has put it in a new light. Why don't I address Plato's concept of justice next Friday? It would follow nicely from *Frau* Werner's presentation, and it will allow all of you additional time to develop and prepare your presentations. Next week, we'll also schedule the presentation dates for the *Sommersemester*. I would also like to build in one or two excursions—there's a German word I like very much, '*Betriebsausflüge*'—into our seminar. *Frau* Werner mentioned the *Kommandatura* is nearby. I've only seen it from the outside. Mr. Durchschouer, do you think it might be possible for you to arrange a visit and possibly a short briefing for our seminar?"

"I'd certainly be pleased to give it a try, Dr. Schneider. As you might know, during and following the Vietnam War, the relationship between US forces stationed in Berlin and the Free University . . .," pausing to smile at the members of the seminar, he continued, "the students in particular, has been strained, though it never degenerated into open hostility as it did in the Federal Republic. Perhaps this has something to do with the unique relationship between the Allied Forces and the West *Berliner*. The PAO—sorry, Rainer, the Public Affairs Officer—might see the request as an opportunity to improve the relationship—I'll send it forward." Turning to Laura, D3 said, "While you were talking *Frau* Anders, it occurred to me that given enough advance notice, the 'Outpost,' the American cinema on *Clay-Allee*, might be willing to screen *A Foreign Affair*. Although Billy Wilder's very well known as a director in the States, I'm quite certain most of the Americans stationed here, myself included, have never heard about this particular Wilder film, much less seen it, and would be very interested in his take on American military life in Berlin in 1947. Perhaps you could be persuaded to introduce the film?"

D3's suggestion was immediately embraced by Laura, who responded through her broad, bright, red-lipped smile with, "That would be just great!"

Afterward, we turned to our assigned readings on the Greek *polis*. True to his mentor, the Kent State Stranger taught using the Socratic method, confusing and challenging to students who were used to listening passively and occasionally taking notes, to enter into what proved to be an initially frustrating but finally rewarding exercise. Socrates and Plato were not the only Athenians Dr. Schneider summoned to Seminar Rooms 3–4. He also cited Plato's predecessor Solon of Athens, whose words of warning seemed more suited to the United States than to the walled object of its postwar foreign policy: "But the citizens themselves, persuaded by wealth, are willing to destroy a mighty *polis* by their follies, and the mind of the leaders of the people is unjust. For the leaders it is prepared that they should suffer many griefs as a result of their great hubris."

When our seminar came to an end, D3 suggested anyone interested was welcome to continue it as a symposium around the corner at *Luise.* "While working my way through Book I of *The Laws*, I discovered a discussion of drinking parties as an educational device! Dr. Schneider laughed, nodding his head in agreement. Everyone seemed amenable, and, gathering up notes and coats, we left Rooms 3–4. I walked out of the front door of the Villa just behind Sophia and Dr. Carstens. As we reached the end of the driveway, a jeep with four US Army soldiers drove down *Boxerstraße.* Turning back to me, Dr. Carstens said, "Nothing against you personally, of course, *Herr* Vonaechron, but I imagine your countrymen must feel somewhat uncomfortable, riding in a military vehicle through the middle of a university campus."

"Oh, I don't know Dr. Carstens. The soldiers in the jeep probably don't even know it themselves, but several of the buildings now housing the *FU* were originally occupied by the US Army in 1945. In fact, the very first building occupied by the *FU* at *Boltzmannstraße 3*, the former *Kaiser-Wilhelm-Institut für Biologie*, housed the Military Government Finance Office. General Clay, the colorful army officer on the ground floor of the building next door and namesake of our institute, directed the building be vacated and turned over to the Free University. The *Akademisches Auslandsamt* is located there now. Besides, the four men in the jeep seemed quite pleased to see Sophia." Stopping as the other members of the seminar walked on ahead, I gave an amused Sophia and her faculty advisor an oral *précis* of the essential elements of information on the founding of the Free University gleaned from Johannes Festzelt over lunch in the *Stadtstaatsarchiv Kantine.*

"Please, no offense intended, Mr. Vonaechron. I knew, of course, there was a historical connection between the US Army and the *Freie Universität* but didn't realize it was so close. Although it complements your presentation, Sophia, it still seems like an oxymoron, the involvement of the US Army in the foundation of a university."

"What do you mean 'oxymoron,' what about West Point? Would you care to join us for a beer at *Luise*, Dr. Carstens? Now that Thomas has briefed you on the *FU*, I'd be very happy to provide you with a short history of the U.S. Military Academy over a *KöPi*, though it might take two! Here in the American Sector, out on the 'edge of freedom,' 'Duty, Honor, Country' and '*Veritas, Justitia, Libertas*' seem almost complementary to me!" D3 had come up behind us as we stood facing *Boxerstraße*, my attention momentarily drawn to the *Museum für Indische Kunst* across the street, as if someone had called out my name in greeting. What did Dr. Schneider want to show me?

"No, no, but thank you very much just the same, perhaps another time, Mr. Durchschouer. I'm actually supposed to be teaching right now but asked a colleague to stand in so I could hear Sophia's presentation. I often joke with her about her academic interest in the 'Theology of Berlin,' but I must admit there does seem to be something to it, Sophia. Your presentation was very well done. Perhaps we could meet later at the Law Library and discuss it further? In the meantime, let me wish you all a productive *Symposium bei 'Luise.' Tschüß!*"

So involved in my harangue on higher education in West Berlin, I didn't notice if the Schadow Sisters had turned the corner in the direction of *Luise*. D3 had walked back to the Villa, looking for us. Together with Sophia, we retraced our steps of the previous Friday. An enormous green Ford four-door sedan with distinctive military plates stood where Rainer had parked his taxi on *Takustraße* the week before. Entering the Luise room, we found our four *Komilitonen* and Dr. Schneider seated around the massive wooden table in the center. *Königin* Luise's portrait presided over the meeting from the back wall, hanging over the empty wooden table where D3 and I sat the week before. There was no one else in the room. Fortune smiled again—I was able to sit next to D3, directly across from Laura.

"We thought perhaps you weren't coming along with us," she said, taking me pleasantly by surprise.

"Thomas felt obliged to give poor Sophia and Dr. Carstens, who did ask for it I must say, a short lecture on the history of the Free University Berlin." Turning to me, he said, "I didn't realize you had also volunteered to make a presentation today, too. As I found out here after class last week, Thomas seems to know a lot about Berlin."

"Nadja and I hope he also knows a lot about Washington, DC, too—let me tell you why. The *FU* has a *Direktaustausch* program, a 'direct exchange' program with American University," turning to me she asked, "Do you know American University, Thomas? What can you tell us about it?"

"Yes, Laura, I do." I answered, pleased to be able to pronounce her name, intentionally slowing my tongue to taste the "L" as I did so. Laura. *l'aura.* "It's in Northwest Washington, up on Nebraska Avenue at Ward Circle—quite a nice campus, sylvan, much like Dahlem. The neighborhood is also largely residential, but once again like Dahlem has a few interesting stories to tell. Across the street from the university is the US Naval Security Station, home of naval code-breaking activity since World War II. Just down Nebraska Avenue is the house where Kim Philby lived while he was stationed in Washington as liaison between the British Secret Intelligence Service, MI6, and the Central Intelligence Agency. Further down, Nebraska Avenue will take you to Connecticut Avenue, where you'll find restaurants, cafés, bakeries, and bookstores. Thanks to former Washington mayor Walter Washington, there's a Metro Station, a *U-Bahnhof*, close to the AU campus at Tenleytown, taking you downtown DC on the 'red line' in just a few minutes."

"Sounds great! Not long ago, I learned my application for *Direktaustausch*, for the direct exchange program, has been accepted. I'm planning to spend two semesters at American University. Like Rainer said," Rainer turned toward us and smiled, "it is kind of funny you know, Thomas, you coming to Berlin from Washington, and me trying to get to Washington from Berlin. Nadja hopes to be able to join me for a while. We plan to write a series of articles on the contemporary Black music scene in the United States for *Dreams and Dollars*. 'Chocolate City' seems like a good place to start! There also seems to be an interesting café and club scene downtown. Have you heard of DC Space and the 9:30 Club?"

"Yes . . . ," I was just about to taste the "L" in her name again but fortunately caught myself, "I've been to both." At Laura's mention of Parliament's funky tribute to the nation's capital, "Chocolate City," Nadja turned to me. Looking out from under her Bowie bangs, she smiled, shook her head and said, "doesn't it seem somehow ironic to you, Thomas, that the nickname for the capital of the United States is 'Chocolate City?'

As a former resident of the Greater Washington, DC, Metropolitan Area, I just couldn't resist picking up the gauntlet and replied, "Not at all, Nadja! After all, the United States of America is 'One Nation Under a Groove!'"

Laughing and clapping their hands in surprise, the Schadow Sisters turned to each other, exclaiming in unison, "Funkadelic!" Our waiter came into the room and took our order for five "*KöPis*," two glasses of *Riesling* for Laura and Nadja, and a *Milchkaffee* for Sophia, who was headed back to the Law Library afterward. We continued our conversations until our waiter returned and distributed the drinks. Dr. Schneider rose to propose a toast, "With the change of the premises from the Clay Institute to *Luise*, and as a distinguished Polish colleague of mine at Kent State, a graduate of Harvard University I might add, often reminds me, 'it's never too late to change the premises,' we have moved on from *The Republic* to the *Symposium*. No one is required to give an *encomium* this afternoon, but hopefully we'll be able to continue our discussion in these delightful surroundings. *Frau* Werner has already given us much food for thought, for which we thank you once again, and we've just received refreshment. *Frau* Anders, *Mademoiselle* d'Oment, and Mr. Vonaechron have placed Washington, DC, and music on the table, the latter a subject of great joy but, as we learned from *Mademoiselle* d'Oment today, also of great concern for Plato. And on that note, or 'on those notes' I should say, I wish you all—what do they say on television?—*gute Unterhaltung!*" We raised our glasses. After Dr. Schneider once again took his seat, he turned to Sophia, returning to the subject of her *Referat*.

Eddie and Nadja joined Rainer and D3 for a discussion of the West Berlin Club scene. D3 took out his notepad and began to plot out an itinerary. Although also interested in the itinerary, I wanted to continue talking with Laura about Washington, DC, or any other place she might want to talk about. Love, after all, was the subject of the *Symposium*. As time went by, less light came in through the windows. The portraits of Luise, Bismarck, and his emperor began to dim. Sophia departed for the law library. Dr. Schneider generously paid for all our drinks with the explanation, "I was a student once myself," and returned to the Clay Institute. Rainer resumed taxiing around West Berlin. When Nadja and Eddie stood up to go, Laura excused herself, joined them, and then turned back to me. "We're going to meet later tonight at the '*Dschungel*' on *Nürnberger Straße* if you'd like to join us there, Thomas. You'll have the chance to dance! *Tschüß!*"

The Shield of Achilles
April 1983

"Are you doing anything right now, Thomas? It appears you might have plans for this evening!" Leaning back in his chair, D3 smiled and said, "I'd like to show you something, something pertaining to the conversation we had last week." Walking out the front door, we turned right and then right again, back to *Takustraße*. The spring sun, already low in the big Berlin sky in the afternoon, had set. The large, green four-door sedan was still parked where Rainer's yellow cab had been the week before, now illuminated by a single streetlight overhead. "Look at this old Ford, D3, it's in great shape. I saw it when we walked over to *Luise*. Back in DC, it would be nondescript, but here, on the streets of Berlin-Dahlem, it screams, 'America!'"

D3 laughed. "That's just what it's supposed to do, Thomas! This is no longer the standard USMLM mission vehicle. For the past few years, we've been using the Mercedes *Geländewagen* 2.81 V-6 'Four-by-Four,' much better suited for off-road forays. This particular vehicle is unique, however, and I think you'll appreciate why I've fought to keep it on 'property book.' It's a modified Ford Galaxy 500, bought back in 1970, when the US government was under direction to 'Buy American.' You're right, Thomas, it 'screams America.' Built as a 'Custom Police Interceptor,' it is equipped with a 370-horsepower, 429-cubic inch, P-code ThunderJet V8 engine with a 4-barrel carburetor, dual exhaust, and a C6 heavy-duty automatic transmission with a 3:1 ratio *traction-lok* rear limited slip differential, generating about 480 pounds of torque. Now, I know that's a lot of car talk for a historian, but it all adds up to an ideal vehicle for paved road pursuit and evasion while on tour in the German Democratic Republic. But that's not the reason we keep the vehicle; on tour *drüben* in the *DDR*, we're usually more off the road than on. Please take a close look at the hood, Thomas." It occurred to me, D3 had parked the Ford under one of the few streetlights on *Takustraße* for this very purpose.

As I walked around the side of the car, the hood appeared painted the same government-issue green as the rest of the Ford. Now standing in front of the car, I noticed silver pin-striping shining in the artificial light, three fine lines running around the edge of the hood, setting it off from the fenders. Leaning forward, I looked more closely. Under the deep, many-layered clear-coat finish, there was something else, a picture or series of pictures, grouped into five folds by the contours of the huge sheet metal hood covering the ThunderJet V8. The earth, the heavens, and the ocean, the radiant sun and the full moon, the constellations, the Pleiades, the Hyades, the Hunter Orion, and Ursus the Bear, had all been delicately depicted. There were two cities, or perhaps two halves of the same city, one the image of peace, the other of war. A festive marriage procession, accompanied by torch bearers and musicians, made its way through the city streets to the forum, where the elders solemnly deliberated upon a murder, with a prize of two golden coins set aside for the better argument. An army lay siege to the other city, while apprehensive citizens stood watch on the Wall. The god of war, Ares, and the goddess of prudent warfare, Pallas Athena, arrayed in all their terrible beauty and golden armor, led the defenders outside the Wall to prepare a place of deadly ambush for the unsuspecting attackers. Innocent shepherds and their flocks were caught in the middle of the ensuing carnage, depicted with grim realism. The metal contour of the big Ford's hood separated peace from the ambush. Plowmen were refreshed with goblets of wine as they plowed their furrowed fields. Mowers cut the wheat, then bound in sheaves by gatherers, with children carrying in the brown sheaves of corn. A banquet for all the laborers, prepared by women, had been laid out on the ground in the shadow of a spreading oak. In a yellow-golden vineyard, young men and women carrying woven baskets on their heads, sang and danced while harvesting the ripe grapes. Herdsmen watched horned oxen plodding on toward a meadow on a rushing river. Their watch dogs could not prevent two lions from goring the herd bull. In the meadow, young men and women surrounded by onlookers, danced hand-in-hand. Dressed in soft linen simars, the girls wore flowers in the hair; the young men sported golden knives on their silver belts. Around the hood rim ran the Ocean River.

Amazed by the vision beneath the clear-coat lacquer, I looked at D3, now standing next to me, haloed in the solitary streetlight, and said, "The Shield of Achilles."

"I knew you'd recognize it, Thomas, taken directly from the *Iliad*. A former USMLM chief of mission, Colonel John Dabrowski, had it custom-painted at an auto-body shop in Chicago. From my colleagues who knew him, I understand the good colonel was rather eccentric, reciting Greek poetry along with lines from the film *Casablanca* whenever the situation seemed appropriate, which was apparently quite often."

"*Casablanca*, what a coincidence! The soundtrack also was quite popular in Vault Six at the Washington National Records Center."

"Hmmm, zat so? In any case, it turns out the hood was painted by an apprentice, Judith l'Angelos, a name you might recognize from her later work, after leaving the body shop. It is beautiful isn't it, Thomas? Truly a work of art! Subdued, subtle, somehow it captures what we're trying to defend here in West Berlin and, for that matter, in the United States as well."

"I agree, D3, it is beautiful, breathtakingly beautiful, but remember your *Iliad*. The second shield of Achilles was forged by the lame god Hephaistos to replace the first, taken as booty by Hector from the lifeless body of Achilles's friend Patroclus outside the walls of Troy. Infuriated by Patroclus's death, Achilles rejoined the war, slaughtering Trojans and killing Hector in revenge while carrying the shield. As Achilles knew, his victory would be short-lived. His own death at the hands of Apollo followed shortly thereafter. 'Drive on' D3, but please do so with the prudence of Pallas Athena, while carrying the 'Shield' or should I say 'Hood of Achilles' around the circuit wall of West Berlin!"

D3 laughed and smiled thoughtfully. The overhead streetlight illuminated his face, highlighting the depth of the expression lines tracing his facial features. "Well spoken, Thomas! How would you like to accompany me on a tour, a kind of private 'staff ride' in the DDR? I can make arrangements for you to ride along in the Shield 'off pass.'" Noting my puzzled expression, he explained. "Without Soviet diplomatic credentials, but still under

USMLM protection. In the Shield, as I call the car, sector and zonal borders become invisible. USMLM can travel unrestricted throughout the German Democratic Republic, with the exception of those 'places of disposition of military units.' One of my Russian colleagues, a member of the Russian equivalent of the Dead Carl Club, informed me Carl von Clausewitz was exhumed from a military cemetery in Breslau in 1971 and reburied with his wife in a civilian cemetery near a Soviet military installation in Burg, his birthplace. He gave me a map of both the cemetery and of Burg, where Clausewitz's childhood home still stands. After all the hours I spent reading and discussing Marie Sophia and Carl von Clausewitz at Fort Leavenworth, I'd very much like to visit their graves. Wanna come along, Thomas?"

"I wouldn't miss it, D3, and visit the Mission, too! Please tell the good colonel I'd be very happy to tell him everything I know about the history of the US Military Liaison Mission, the architecture of Albert Speer, and even quote at length from *Casablanca* if that would help."

"I'm on my way back to the *Föhrenweg* now and will talk to the colonel about it this evening. Please give me a good phone number and I'll call you on the weekend." Taking my notebook out of my shoulder bag, I opened it to the last page, wrote my address and Dr. Kahler's home number on it, carefully tore it out, and handed it to D3. "Thanks, Thomas. Have a good time at, or should in say 'in,' the *Dschungel* tonight. I haven't been there, but I've heard a lot about it. Maybe Rainer will include it on our tour. One of our older LNs—excuse me, 'local nationals'—told me there used to be a nightclub in the same building on the *Nürnberger Straße* in the late forties, the *Femina-Bar*, where intelligence operatives of all services and nations used to gather to prey on each other. He mentioned an American operative by name, most likely a cover, and a rather curious one at that—Tyrone Slothrop. There was also a cabaret in the building with the suggestive name of *Die Badewanne*. 'The Bathtub,' yes that was it, '*Die Badewanne*.'"

"The '*Femina-Bar*,' *Nürnberger Straße*, that sounds familiar. Let me take a look in my notebook. Here it is, *Nürnberger Straße* 50–56. The address kept turning up in the INTSUMS of several different agencies, so I noted it down. I wanted to check it out, see what's there now, for history's sake. Now I know what's there—the '*Dschungel*'!"

In the *Dschungel*
April 1983

Feeling heady from *KöPi* and conversation, I decided to once again take my fate in my feet and walk back to the *Lothringerstrasse*, following the route I'd taken in March. After returning to my one elegant Empire room, I took off my coat and shoes and took the *Falkplan* and notebook from the shoulder bag. Opening the cast-iron door of the *Kackelofen*, I decided to burn another soft coal brick, keeping the room warm until departure time for the *Dschungel*.

Stretching out on the bed, I opened up the map beside me to reconnoiter my route. The *U9* would take me directly from *Friedrich-Wilhelm-Platz* to the *Kurfürstendamm*. Walking past the *Kaiser-Wilhelm-Gedächnis-Kirche*, I could follow *Tauenzientraße*, turn right into *Nürnberger Straße*, and follow the numbers to 50–56. Laying my head back on my pillow to study the stucco on the ceiling, I promptly fell into a deep sleep. The sound of the apartment door opening woke me, Dr. Kahler returning. "Late, late, it must be late," I thought, sitting up on the edge of the bed. Dr. Kahler turned on the radio in the *Berliner Zimmer*, and as I refolded the *Falkplan*, placing it and my notebook back into my shoulder bag for my foray into Berlin VI, I heard the AFN-Berlin announcer solemnly say, "It's midnight in Central Europe." I looked at the abnormally heavy brass dolphin clock for confirmation—it was midnight in Central Europe. Quickly putting on my coat and shoes, I left the apartment without stopping in the *Berliner Zimmer*, slipping down the stairway and out the front door. Not yet accustomed to West Berlin nightlife, I thought I might be too late, when I was actually much too early. The *U9* arrived just as I reached the platform. When we reached *Walter-Schreiber-Platz*, I realized I was headed in the wrong direction, away from the *Dschungel,* away from Laura. Unfortunately, the train headed uptown departed just as we arrived, so I waited twenty minutes for the next one. When the *U9* finally did arrive, it was full of *Berliner* and *Berlin Besucher*. With the exception of a few unpleasantly intoxicated older punks who kept to themselves while addressing everyone in the car in loud voices, most were *gut gelaunt*. I tried to relax by looking at my fellow travelers, always an effective diversion in Berlin. Walking up the exit stairs at *U-Bahnhof Kurfürstendamm*, a West Berlin travel poster suddenly appeared before me. Cars and buses circumscribed the *Kaiser-Wilhelm-Gedächnis-Kirche*, trails of their headlights hanging in the air in time lapse after they'd passed by. The *Chartres* blue of the octagonal sanctuary, illuminated from inside, and the new bell tower, topped with a golden globe crowned by the Cross. In between the sanctuary and the new bell tower stood the old, the broken bell tower, '*der Hohle Zahn,*' a hollow tooth in the mouth of West Berlin. A monument to the dialectic of construction and destruction dating back to 1870, it was beautiful in its HistoriCity way—all the blue peace and salvation one could see and hope for in an accidental *polis*. This aura of peace and salvation was cast into stained glass by Gabriel Loire, who mused "*Berlin est la paix—le bleu—et la joie—les notes de coleur sur le bleu.*"

Walking quickly past the lighted storefronts lining *Tauenzienstraße*, I turned into the darkness of *Nürnberger Straße*. On my left, I could discern the outline of what appeared to be another large building in the "New Objectivity" style running the length of the block. Following the sidewalk past darkened office- and shopwindows, I saw small groups of people loitering out front of an illuminated entrance. Over two chrome doors, a neon sign lit the night: *Dschungel*. Hoping Laura, Nadja, and Eddie were still there, I made my way to the door. "*Ey Alter, da kommste nicht mehr rein!*"[27] said a voice from the darkness.

Entrance to the *Dschungel* was guarded by a single-headed Cerberus, an imposing older punk with a spiked Iroquois haircut, wearing sunglasses and a long, dark green leather coat, worn openly to display heavy silver chain mail underneath. "*Tut mir leid*," he said, blocking my path through the silver doors.

"But I'm supposed to meet some friends, from the *FU*, here tonight," I stammered out in English.

"I'm sorry, it's full. You can't go in now."

Disappointed, I turned around and found myself face-to-face with Nadja. "*Tiens* Thomas, you're early! Laura, André, and Eddie are coming later. I came early, to sit at the bar and work on an article, before it gets too full."

"Early? We're both too late, Nadja! It's full, he's not letting anyone else in."

"Full, *quatsch*, it's empty at this 'our! You will follow me please." When the bouncer saw Nadja, he stepped to the side and said "*Hallo, Nadja!*" Turning to me, he said, "I'm sorry, I didn't realize you were with Nadja," and opened the chrome doors for us. Behind the second set there was a cashier, who also waved us on through into the *Dschungel* with a "*Hallo, Nadja!*"

"It costs ten *Mark* Thomas, but they all know I write for the scene magazines 'ere in Berlin and Paris. When I write about the *Dschungel*, people come 'ere to see 'what's goin' on,' and you're with me!"

"Ah, I see, I'm now a special friend of Rick's."

"*Comment?*"

"It's a line from *Casablanca*."

"But of course, I know it! Shall we ask the DJ to play *La Marseillaise*? Yes, Thomas, you are a special friend of Nadja's. Let's 'drive on' to the bar and 'ave a drink, shall we? Laura, André, and Eddie went to a *vernissage*, they will join us later. *Die neuen Wilden*, neo-Expressionists on *Lützowplatz*, friends of André. We checked our coats at the *Garderobe* and took seats at the bar. "Would you like a champagne cocktail, Thomas? Victor Lazlo would insist!" Nadja was right, there were only a few people sitting on the red leather love seats lining the walls, standing on the dance floor talking.

---

27 "Hey old man, you can't get in there!" Diary of Thomas Vonaechron, Diary Extract, 1983, trans. TV.

No one was dancing. The industrial intensity of the neon lights defied any attempt at intimacy. Chrome accents throughout the room were set off by the mirrors behind the bar. There was a circular staircase leading to a second level. Nadja watched me survey the room.

"You won't believe it, Thomas, but the *Dschungel* used to be a Chinese restaurant! Upstairs is the *Aquarium*, where the all the local veeps meet, musicians from out of town, too, when they come to West Berlin to perform." Tanya noticed my puzzled expression. "The veeps, the Germans say *fips*, you know, Thomas, the 'very important persons,' or so they think! The *Türsteher* out front stands there to increase interest in getting in. Those who pass through feel as if they've passed through a kind of *processus de sélection* and now belong to the select. Please don't take being turned away seriously, Thomas, it's actually all quite arbitrary. We should 'ave mentioned it to you this afternoon at *Luise.*"

"Thank you for coming to my rescue all the same, Nadja, I'm very glad you decided to come early, but please don't let me disturb your writing. I'm content to sit here as a *voyeur* and might take some notes, too. But one question please, you mentioned Laura, Eddie, and one more person will join us later?"

"André. He is Laura's *amoureux*, her lover. They live together not too far from here. He's a painter, one of the new *Fauve.* 'Is father is French, from Paris like me, 'is mother American. They live where you used to live, in Washington, DC. That's another reason Laura applied for *Direktaustausch* with American University. André 'as 'is *atelier* on Fourteenth Street."

"Fourteenth Street? That's quite an interesting part of DC, Nadja!" I remembered driving up Fourteenth Street in my Malibu convertible with George after watching *Madam Kitty,* the X-rated story of a Berlin bordello at RKO Keith's Theater on Fifteenth Street. The theater marquee announced, "It's so dark in here you can do anything you want!" The records of *Salon Kitty,* run by the *Sicherheitsdienst* to record compromising information on clients during Berlin IV, were stored in the *Stadtstaatsarchiv Berlin* where George works. Top down, we cruised up Fourteenth Street, past the Vegas-lit The Butterfly and This is It? Nocturnal sirens sang out, "Hey, Sugar, you need a date?" as we cruised Peter L'Enfant's traffic circle with its splendid equestrian statue of Major General George Henry Thomas, the "Rock of Chickamauga," cast from captured bronze Confederate cannon, and drove on, down Massachusetts Avenue, back to *Die Kleine Krone.*

"Yes, he's told us a lot about the DC art and music scenes. He's a very nice guy. You'll like 'im, Thomas. But you look a little sad, ah, *je comprends*, because of Laura? Don't worry. Soon they'll turn up the music, and you'll 'ave your chance to dance your way out of your afflictions!

"But tell me, Thomas, what do you think about our seminar? I like Dr. Schneider very much. He's ah, quite different than most of the German professors at the Clay Institute, more open and friendly, if *parfois* 'ard to follow. Although I studied classical languages as a *lycéenne*, I never thought about connecting Plato with what I'm doing now, you know, with music. It's actually fun to read through the *dialogues* from a different perspective. David's quite an interesting guy, too—'Drive on *Mademoiselle* d'Oment,' I liked that very much, like a line from a military movie! I've met American soldiers in the clubs here in Berlin and in Paris too, on USO tours, but never really 'ad a serious conversation with one. I hope Rainer will put his taxi tour of the Berlin club scene together for David. Although I know the clubs pretty well, I'd like to ride along too. 'E may have to borrow a *Kombi*!"

"Rainer, Eddie, and D3 already started working on the tour at *Luise* this afternoon. D3, David, who asked us to call him by his nickname, an acronym for Dwight David Durchschouer, took notes. He is an interesting guy. We had a beer at *Luise* last week after class. Rainer was going to come along too, it was actually his idea, but had to pick up a customer. We ended up talking about what brought us to West Berlin. I'm convinced we were both brought here by Clio, the muse of history."

As if in response to the mention of the muse's name, synthesized music filled the room, the percussion track, a xylophone made of bones punctuated with sharp, single rifle shots. In a monotone chant, a male voice ordered us out onto the dance floor. Nadja set her champagne cocktail gently down on the bar. Taking my hand she said, "Come on, Thomas, let's 'ead out on the dance floor. This is your chance to dance your way out of your … 'eartbreak, you poor Thomas!" While we talked, the *Dschungel* had been filling up, and now everyone headed out on the dance floor in droves, from the bar, the leather love seats, and down the circular staircase from the *Aquarium*. I hadn't danced since leaving Washington. The first song was unfamiliar, and as Nadja and I danced, I tried to catch the lyrics, something about history repeating itself and the approaching crisis. 'We've got to beat it or we'll have to repeat it!' Europe had succumbed to fascism in the past and, according to the lead singer, was still sulking.

The fragments of lyrics I could follow were oddly political, bringing to mind Rainer's account of President Reagan's visit to Berlin, the defeat of the Democratic Party and the rise of fascism in the United States. The beat remained steady as our DJ worked her way through the playlist, one song fading into the next, there was no reason to stop. Clio sat in on the next few tracks, driving home the point that nothing's really new, just the noise of history repeating itself. She stayed on message with another historical track, this time around in German with Fehlfarben's "*ein jahr (es geht voran)*," and, once again,

Ronald Reagan's rise from B-movies to global domination. The title of the next track, "The Western World (Is Going Down)," had ominous Spenglerian overtones. Then a shift from the historical and the political to the personal and the prophetic with Iggy Pop's "The Passenger." When a female vocalist began to mourn in a sonorous monotone that all is lost, or maybe it was all is love, Nadja said, "I'll be back *tout de suite*, Thomas. I think I know the DJ." I walked back over to the bar and finished off my champagne cocktail.

"*Noch eins?*" shouted the bartender over the music.

Looking at Nadja's empty glass, I shouted back, "*Noch zwei, Bitte!*" I'd just taken a sip when I heard the introduction to "One Nation Under a Groove." Nadja was back, standing beside me, smiling. "I thought I recognized the DJ from *Weg Werk*. This chance is for you, Thomas." I took Nadja's hand and we returned to the dance floor. *Funkadelic* went down well with the crowd. Requests for more funky hymns from the power *Stadt* for the *Mauerstadt* followed. We danced our way into a trance. Nadja seemed to change. Although her hairstyle remained the same, she grew smaller, more delicate and *petite*; her clothes were different. Then she was the same again. "Sorry to leave you so long. I saw Laura and the others and wanted to let them know we were out on the dance floor."

"But you were here all the time dancing, Nadja, weren't you, different somehow? Shorter and dressed a bit differently, did you change clothes? But your hairstyle is unmistakable."

Nadja laughed, her hazel eyes gleamed, "No, Thomas. *Je pense* that was someone else . . . but 'ere are Laura, Eddie, and André!" Laura put her arms around my neck. I kissed her on the cheek and she turned the other. I shook hands with Eddie and André, a striking young man, wiry with short hair, dark eyes, and an engaging smile, but before we could talk, Laura took my hand and we began to dance. My heart felt like the target of ABC's "Poison Arrow," a sensation heightened by the distinctive two-note synthesizer introduction to Soft Cell's cover of "Tainted Love." Nadja was right, "poor Thomas." Laura, Nadja, Nadja's *Doppelgänger*, Laura, Nadja—I danced until I could dance no more, then made my way through the crowd back to the bar. Nadja's glass was empty. I leaned back against the barstool, surveying the room while I finished mine. Nadja was sitting with her back propped up against the wall on the floor next to the dance floor. I walked over and sat down next to her. "*Je suis fatigué*," she said. "I 'aven't danced so much in years and just can't dance anymore. My feet failed me. 'Ow about you poor Thomas, your afflictions, your 'eartbreak?"

"All gone, Nadja, all gone, *merci beaucoup*, dance therapy, just what the doctor ordered. I'm exhausted too, *trés fatigué*. As soon as the feeling returns to my legs, I'm going to get my coat and walk home."

"Walk home? *Tu es fou*, Thomas!"

"Yes, yes, I know. The *U-bahn's* stopped running, but it's a straight shot for me. I like to walk. I mix my labor with the city and it's mine. I take a walk and see what's mine!"

"Why don't you treat yourself to a taxi tonight, we all do it once in a while." Laura, André, and Eddie joined us on the floor laughing. "Thomas wants to walk home, I told him he should take a taxi."

"Where do you live?" asked Laura.

"In Friedenau, *Lothringerstrasse*, just off *Hauptstraße*."

"Then I've got a better idea," said Eddie. "How about one last *Flens*, a *Flensburger Pilsener* at *Slumberland*—it used to be the *Dschungel*—before bedtime, Thomas, it's just a short walk from here on *Winterfeldplatz*. Laura and André live nearby. We can relax at *Slumberland*. There's no dance floor anymore and the music's not so loud. Afterwards, you can walk if you want to or take the *Nachtbus* down *Potsdamerstraße* to *Hauptstraße* to Friedenau. I'll walk you to the bus stop. Besides, you've been dancing all night long with Nadja and Laura, and I haven't had the chance to talk with you."

"Sounds good, Eddie." I stood up slowly and walked back over to the bar to pay for our drinks and pick up my shoulder bag. Shaking his head, the bartender smiled and waved off my *D-Markschein* with a friendly "*schon gut*." When Nadja walked over to retrieve her purse, I asked, "Special friend of Rick's?"

"No, Thomas, special friend of Nadja's, remember? But you can leave 'im a nice *pourboire, Trinkgeld,* a nice tip, if you like. If you do, perhaps 'e'll remember you next time, just in case I'm not with you!"

"If you're not with me, I won't even be able to get in the door!" Nadja laughed. After retrieving our coats from the *Garderobe*, we walked out through the chrome double doors, back out into the darkness of *Nürnberger Straße*. Small groups still gathered outside the *Dschungel* door.

Walking back up to *Tauenzienstraße*, we turned right, past the monumental *Kaufhaus des Westens*. George told me it was the largest department store in Continental Europe. Built during Berlin II, expanded during Berlin III, destroyed during Berlin IV, '*KadeWe*' was reopened and completely rebuilt during Berlin VI, becoming something more than just a department store. In West Berlin and throughout West Germany, *KadeWe* was a concrete political and economic statement, a flagship, the "*Schaufenster des Westens*." Just across the street stood a reminder of Berlin's past, *U-Bahnhof Wittenbergplatz*. The art nouveau entrance hall had been carefully restored during Berlin VI to evoke the ambiance of prewar Berlin III. Berlin IV had not, however, been forgotten. In front of the underground train station, directly across *Tauenzienstraße* from

KadeWe, stood a large frame, bent from black metal tubing. Yellow letters on individual black metal plaques riveted to the frame, documented, "*Orte des Schreckens, die wir nie vergessen dürfen.*"[28] Auschwitz. Stutthof. Maidenek. Treblinka. Theresianstadt. Struthoff. Buchenwald. Dachau. Sachsenhausen. Ravensbrück. Bergen-Belsen. Trostenez. Flossenbürg. As they crossed back and forth between Berlin VI and Berlin III, pedestrians were confronted with the architectural horrors of Berlin IV.

Over fifty thousand Berliners were among the murdered. During one of our Mr. Henry's seminars on Washington Circle, George recounted how, beginning in 1941, Berlin's Jews had been deported to ghettos in Riga and Warsaw, then from 1942 until 1945, directly to the concentration camps Auschwitz-Birkenau and Theresianstadt from the freight station adjacent to *S-Bahnhof Grunewald*. Located at the edge of the Grunewald Forest on the western outskirts of Berlin, the *Reichsicherheithauptamt* and *Staatspolizei* employed the forest's natural cover for unnatural acts.

Although I'd been inside both *KadeWe* and *U-Bahnhof Wittenbergplatz*, closed, with minimal security lighting, they looked like giant *mausolea*. Another monumental mausoleum stood directly ahead of us in the darkness on *Nollendorfplatz*, the *Metropol*, the former *Neues Schauspielhaus*. Turning to Laura I asked, "Wasn't the demonstration against President Reagan last June here on *Nollendorfplatz*?" Rainer mentioned two locations, both *Plätze*, last week in class.

"Yes, *Nollendorfplatz* and *Winterfeldplatz*, just behind *Slumberland* where we're going for a beer. *Die 'Schlacht am Noli'* was something to see, Thomas, just like Rainer said, barricaded streets, burning cars and police vans. Nadja and I took part in the *Frauen-Trauer-Demonstration*, which had been sanctioned and was peaceful, but unfortunately, we got caught up in the confrontation on our way back to *Winterfeldplatz*. Although West Berlin has more than its share of *Anarchos* and *Autonommen*, many of the hardcore crazies came from West Germany. Some members of the local alternative scene were afraid the imported violence might turn the largely sympathetic West Berlin against the *Instandbesetzer*."

On the corner, just across the street from the *Metropol*, the bright neon lighting inside Café Swing threw a beacon on the pavement out front. "We could have a drink there," Laura suggested.

"I don't know. It's another *Musikclub*, Laura. Don't you think we've had enough music for tonight?" asked Eddie. "I'm still for a *Flens* at Slumberland."

"Forgive me, Laura, but I agree with Eddie. I've had enough music and neon too, for tonight. Perhaps we could all go together to the Café Swing

---

28 "Places of horror we must never forget." Diary of Thomas Vonaechron, Diary Extract, 1983, trans. TV.

another time. I'd like to go there with you . . . with you all, sometime."

From *Nollendorfplatz*, we turned right into the *Maaßmanstraße*, crossing over the *Nollendorfstraße. Nollendorfplatz, Nollendorfstraße,* "Just a minute please, I want to check something in my notebook." Walking over to the streetlight, I took my notebook out of my shoulder bag and flipped through the pages. "Here it is, *Nollendorfstraße 17,* that's where Christopher Isherwood lived in Berlin; you know Christopher Isherwood, *The Berlin Stories,* basis for the play *I Am a Camera* and the film *Cabaret.*

"Are you certain, Thomas, how do you know?"

"Isherwood wrote about his time in Berlin in his autobiography, *Christopher and His Kind.* I wrote down the address, along with the other addresses I found in documents at the National Archives. He came back to Berlin after the war to visit his former landlady, so the apartment building must still be standing. Let's take quick a look." We found it right where Christopher Isherwood had left it, two blocks down the street. Although there were plaques on many buildings throughout West Berlin memorializing famous occupants, nothing indicated Christopher Isherwood had lived here. The play, the musical, and the films based on his short stories had inspired me and countless others to come to Berlin, even though the cabaret was over, or was it?

"David was right, you do know a lot about Berlin, Thomas. You should write a letter to the *Senator für Kultur.* Perhaps he'd put up a plaque." Retracing our steps to *Maßenmannstraße,* we continued on to *Winterfeldplatz.*

Slumberland was impossible to miss. An oasis of azure in a sea of darkness lit by neon buoys. Warm yellow light came under the window blinds, through the line of dust-covered plants. The illuminated white and blue etiquette of *Flensburger Pilsener* beckoned, the red lighthouse that guided the sailing ship into port guided us to the entrance door. There was no *Türsteher* to select the select. All were welcome here. A few former inhabitants of the *Dschung*el and the post-punk bar *Stonz* on *Winterfledplatz* sat on stools scattered around small circular tables, on corner benches, and at the bar running the length of the room. There were also hippies, and construction workers having a beer for breakfast before work. The floor was covered with sand, giving this traditional Berlin *Eckkneipe* a casual beach bar ambiance. A cloud of yellow smoke rubbed its muzzle on the windowpanes inside. Eddy was right. Slumberland was the ideal place for that last beer before bed.

We hung our coats and bags on wall hooks, pushed two of the round tables together, and ordered five beers. The walk from the *Dschungel* to Slumberland had cleared my mind of music, my eyes of the bright sting of the neon. Pleasantly tired from dancing, I wanted to hear about the *vernissage* and asked if Gabriel Kielerförde had been there. Surprised, André turned to me and said, "Yes, Thomas, he was."

"How do you know, Gabriel?" asked André. I recounted my walk through the Tiergarten looking for the ruins of *Germania*. "He told me he would invite me to his *vernissage*. I hope he hasn't forgotten."

"No, I'm certain he hasn't, but I don't think his exhibition will be ready before next year," said André. Although he's doesn't belong to the new *Fauve, die neue Wilden*, I find his 'found objects' exhibitions very interesting. He also did one on the *Anhalter Bahnhof*. Laura told me you're from Washington, DC. That's where my parents live. I still have a small studio in a loft on Fourteenth Street, NW. Two, almost three years ago now, I came to Berlin for the summer. I'd heard about the *Neue Wilden* in Washington and Paris and wanted to see for myself. Although I intended to return to Washington at the end of the summer, I met Laura and decided to stay longer in West Berlin. If you're interested, some of us plan to exhibit at the Pictures of Chairman Mao Gallery on *Lützowplatz*. Once the date's been set, I'll have Laura give you the information. It's very likely Gabriel will be there, so you'll have the chance to see him again, too."

"Thanks very much, André, I'd enjoy that very much, I'll touch . . . I mean, of course, I'll keep in touch with Laura at the Clay Institute."

"Clay Institute, that's my cue," said Eddie. "I wanted to ask you about John F. Kennedy and Berlin, Thomas. Would there be any information for me available at the National Archives?"

"I'm sure there is, Eddie, but you'll want to direct your questions to the John F. Kennedy Presidential Library in Boston, Massachusetts. While I was working on my master's in archival science at George Washington University, I had two archivists from the JFK Presidential Library, Brenda Thompson and Alan Reger, as instructors. They're good people, kind, knowledgeable, and very helpful. I'd be happy to give you their address. You might also ask them about other references to West Berlin in JFK's papers, not just his Berlin speeches." Our beers were served and with each sip, I slipped further into the arms of Morpheus.

"Hey, Ginger Rogers and the Fred Astaire are falling asleep on their stools. Time to head home to bed."

"As a special friend of Nadja's, I insist on paying for the beer. I've been drinking and dancing on her good name all night long."

"Many thanks, Thomas! I'll make certain you get drunk on *Blanc de Blancs* at our *vernissage!*"

I kissed Nadja and Laura, who once again put her arms around my neck, on the cheek, and shook hands with André. "I'm looking forward to your *vernissage*, and not just for the *Blanc de Blancs!*" Eddie and I walked out across *Winterfeldplatz*. There were small groups of punks, more refugees from *Stonz*, abandoned outside on the cold sidewalk of time by fashion and music. At the sound of our footsteps, their voices rose as one in supplication, a chant I would often hear throughout West Berlin, Berlin VI, *"Ey Alter, haste 'ne Mark für mich?"*[29] Our indifference was met with a chorus of curses, *"Ihr Arschlöcher!"* I was too tired to reply.

Waiting for the *Nachtbus* at the bus stop, I saw Nadja without Laura and André on the far side of the *Potsdamer Straße*, walking down toward *Hauptstraße*. "Hey, Eddie, there's Nadja! What's she doing walking? Hey, Nadja!"

"No, no, Thomas wait, that's not Nadja! It's someone who looks a lot like Nadja for sure, same hairstyle. But look closely, that person is shorter, thinner, and dressed differently. Actually, I think it's a guy." Our view was suddenly blocked by the 48 Bus, my ride back to Friedenau. I thanked Eddie, waving goodbye through the glass door as the bus drove away. Sitting down on the other side of the bus, I looked out the window and saw Nadja's *Doppelgänger* waving at me while he walked down *Potsdamer Straße* toward *Hauptstraße*. I waved in return and he was gone, a queen of oblivion.

Orestes and the Origins of Justice
April 1983

I returned to my one elegant Empire room just before dawn. The birds on the *Hof* were already up talking, asking me, "Poo-tee-weet?" as I opened the heavy front door. After I hung my coat in the hallway and set my shoulder bag on my desk, I walked into the *Berliner Zimmer*, hoping to meet Dr. Kahler and apologize for my sudden midnight in Central Europe departure. He didn't seem to be home, so after visiting the WC, I returned to my room, once again stretching out on the bed to study the stucco, now illuminated by the morning light. It was early afternoon when I awoke. Sitting up on the edge of the bed, I heard footsteps in the adjacent bedroom room and the *Berliner Zimmer*.

When I walked in, Dr. Kahler looked up and smiled at me. "Ah, *Herr* Vonaechron. Good morning, I mean, of course, good afternoon! Without waking you, and I sincerely hope I did not, I was hoping you might wake up."

"Good Afternoon, Dr. Kahler. I'm sorry I left so abruptly last night shortly after you returned home. I'd planned to meet some new friends from the *FU* at the *Dschungel* and thought I was running late. As it turns

29 "Hey old man, do you have a Mark for me?" Diary of Thomas Vonaechron, Diary Extract, 1983, trans. TV.

out, I was running early! Things begin much later in Berlin than they do in Washington."

Dr. Kahler smiled, "Please, no apologies necessary, *Herr* Vonaechron, you're free to come and go whenever you please without taking leave. You remind me of myself as a young man in Tübingen, always on the prowl. Apropos 'new friends,' one of them called for you this morning, a Mr. Durchschouer. He asked that you please give him a call at this number sometime tomorrow afternoon. For an American, he speaks excellent German. In fact, sounded a little bit like a *Bundeswehroffizier*, his intonation I mean."

Laughing, I said, "Well, he did have a *Bundeswehr Hauptmann* for an instructor in Kansas."

"A *Bundewwwehr Hauptmann* in Kansas? You'll have to tell me that story over our next bottle of *Trollinger*. Perhaps you might even invite Mr. Durchschouer to join us and let him tell it to me! But now, I have another proposition for you. I also received a phone call from a friend this morning. We had planned to see the *Orestie* this afternoon at the *Schaubühne am Halleschen Ufer*. Unfortunately, something unexpected came up, and she is unable to join me. As a consequence, I have an extra ticket and would be very pleased to invite you, if you, of course, don't have anything planned, and you can take two late evenings in a row, the play is nine hours long."

"Nine hours long!"

"Yes, but that includes two one-hour intermissions, so actually it's only seven hours long. Refreshments are included in the tickets. Perhaps they'll offer a Greek red wine. *Xinomavro* would be excellent. If you don't already know the director, Peter Stein, I can highly recommend him to you, and Aeschylus is, after all, Aeschylus! But a word of caution, one must be very careful in West Berlin *Herr* Vonaechron, there's simply too much going on. One could easily enjoy oneself into a state of exhaustion! If you would like to accompany me, however, we'll have to leave quite soon if we want to be on time. The *Schaubühne* is in Kreuzberg, not far from Checkpoint Charlie."

"Thank you, Dr. Kahler, I'd be very happy to join you! Give me just a few minutes to freshen up and dress. Perhaps the *Schaubühne* will offer *Dolmades* to go with the red wine."

West Berlin metamorphosed into Mycenae as we walked through the doors into the darkened auditorium of the *Schaubühne*, taking our seats on the floor. A musician, sitting cross-legged on the city walls above, unsettled the audience with mournful notes played on the syrinx. Voices came from the darkness surrounding us, words, sounds, some unintelligible. A chorus of old men mumbled. Brought from Troy by King Agamemnon as a concubine, Cassandra recounts the tragic history and future of the royal house before being murdered by Clytemnestra, who had already killed Agamemnon, her husband, in his bath. Food and drink was to be had before and during the hour-long intermissions, dry Greek red wine and pita bread. But it was blood and milk, not red wine, that would run down from Clytemnestra's bared breasts. Her son, Orestes, returns from Phocis accompanied by his cousin Pylades. Wearing a slouch hat with a sword concealed under his trench coat, he meets his sister Electra at the grave of their murdered father. He avenges his father's death, killing his usurper Aegisthus and his mother Clytemnestra, her breasts bared, begging for mercy. The matricide infuriates the Furies, who pursue Orestes first to Delphi, then on to Athens, where Pallas Athena intervenes and successfully defends him before the court of Areiopagus. As a consequence of the court's decision, the rule of law supersedes revenge, and Orestes is able to live at peace in the *polis*. A fascinating, physically exhausting production, coincidentally touching upon many of the same issues raised by the Accidental *Polis* Seminar. Dr. Kahler and I departed Mycenae for West Berlin.

After returning to *Lothringerstrasse*, Dr. Kahler opened the promised bottle of *Trollinger*. We sat together at the wooden kitchen table, talking into the early morning hours, when the birds on the *Hof* asked, "Poo-tee-weet?" I awoke Sunday in the early evening. "Did you sleep well?" he asked, looking up from his newspaper, *Die Neue Züricher Zeitung*, smiling his tight, wolfish smile, when I walked through the *Berliner Zimmer* on my way to the WC. Wrapped in my yukata, I felt like a lost member of the chorus of Argive elders from the previous day's play, in spite of the *kanji* print.

"Yes, I did, and thank you again for a fascinating evening. I hope you slept well, too. I must agree with you, however, there's so much going on in West Berlin, one could easily continue moving from event to event until reaching the point of collapse." Unfortunately, though alerted to this danger by Dr. Kahler, it was precisely the path I followed in the months ahead.

Dr. Kahler smiled, "My warning comes from personal experience, *Herr* Vonaechron. Remember, you're always free to decline. In fact, you must learn to decline, to say 'no.' Otherwise, West Berlin will exhaust you. Please don't forget to call *Herr* Durchschouer and pass along my compliments on his excellent command of the German language! Relaxing in the lion-footed ceramic tub, I played the events of the past forty-eight hours backward and forward. After drying off and returning to the *Berliner Zimmer*, I called D3. The phone number connected me with USMLM.

"Hi, Thomas, I understand you had a late night at *Die Femina,* how did it go?

"I met Nadja at the door and we danced until we could dance no more, but alas the lovely Laura is living with an American artist."

"*Quel dommage, mon ami*, but I have some news about our other girlfriend, Clio, which just might cheer you up. The chief has approved your visit to the Mission, to include a house tour, and an "off pass" tour in the Shield to Burg *bei* Magdeburg! Your work with USMLM documents at the Archives and the fact you held a top secret clearance—you're still in the system by the way—did the trick. If you could put together a short brief on the history of the unit, he'd be very grateful. We'll even wine and dine you afterward. As there's no current mission requirement for a tour to Burg, we'll pass it off, get it 'off pass,' pass it off, yuck, yuck, yuck, as a flag tour."

"Flag tour?"

"Show the flag of the United States of America in the German Democratic Republic. As you 'observed,' to use Dr. Schneider's word, the Shield does scream 'America!' We'll set a date for your presentation during the first week in May, following the festivities in East Berlin—what's your terminology, 'Berlin V?'" Hopefully that will give you enough time to get with your buddy George at the *Stadtstaatsarchiv* and find out if Albert Speer had anything to say about *19/21 Föhrenweg*. I've set our flag tour/staff ride date for Monday, June 6, D-Day—I just couldn't resist! My namesake, General Eisenhower, would approve! We'll pick you up in the morning at 'zero-dark-thirty,' head south for the *Brücke der Einheit*, our crossing point into the DDR, and drive on to Burg *bei* Magdeburg. See ya Friday, Thomas, out here!"

"Out here, D3?"

"Haven't you heard that expression before, Thomas? I'm surprised, though it's used more on air than on paper. It means 'end of transmission,' so the party you're speaking with knows you've finished speaking. 'Over,' on the other hand, means 'over to you.'"

"I get it, and I like it. See you Friday, D3. Out here!"

When the Accidental *Polis* Seminar reconvened the following Friday, I recounted my nine-hour excursion to Mycenae at the *Schaubüne* the previous Sunday. Dr. Schneider was surprised and quite pleased, "As you all might recall, the topic for today's session is 'Justice.' What a useful coincidence, Mr. Vonaechron, I was even planning to refer to the *Oresteia* in my introductory remarks! To the best of my knowledge, the trial of Orestes on the Acropolis in Athens, presided over by Pallas Athena, is the initial introduction of law into the *polis* in Greek literature. I saw a production at Mount Union College in Ohio some ten years ago and, to be honest, did not know about the *Schaubühne* production. The timing could not have been more advantageous."

"I knew the *Schaubühne* was offering the *Oresteia* as part of its ongoing *Antikenprojekt* but, also to be honest, didn't realize its significance for our seminar." Sophia turned her head to face me, her dark hair cascading down over her shoulder. "Do you know if it will be presented again?"

"Just a moment please, Sophia, I brought the program with me, here it is. Yes, it will be offered again. Please take a look."

"Thank you, Thomas. I must see it while it's playing here. Could you please borrow me your program, I'll return it to you next week." Brushing her hair back behind her shoulder, she echoed Dr. Schneider's words, "'What an interesting coincidence!'"

"Perhaps those of us who have not yet seen the *Oresteia* might consider going together," suggested Dr. Schneider. At our previous session, we talked about the possibility of incorporating excursions into our seminar; this seems like a perfect opportunity. The *Oresteia* provides the perfect literary introduction to today's topic, justice. In this 'case,' the decision is made by a jury representative of the citizens of Athens, relying upon institutions established by the patron—or should I say matron—of the *polis*." After briefly summarizing the plot, Dr. Schneider underlined the significance of the concept of justice for the *polis*, the overcoming of revenge through legal proceedings, citing Aeschylus/Athena, "Thus I ordain it now, a council-court pure and unsullied by the lust of gain, sacred and swift to vengeance, wakeful ever to champion men who sleep, the country's guard." He then turned to the assigned readings, "Today, we're looking at what Plato has to say about justice in *The Republic* and *The Laws*. What does he mean by 'Justice?' Is it defined by law or by a legal system, by lawfulness? Is it a virtue?"

"Something more than that, Dr. Schneider, a principle of organization, of order in the individual as well as in the *polis*," answered Sophia. Other members of the seminar gradually became more willing, even eager to join in the discussion. Together, we concluded that in the *polis* of Socrates and Plato, the city in speech, justice was harmony, both within the individual and the state. Moderation opposed to acquisition and the right of the stronger. We then turned our attention from the ideal and best possible *polei*, to our accidental *polis*, West Berlin.

Perhaps due to the recent outbreak of violence in connection with President Reagan's visit to Berlin, the discussion of justice in West Berlin focused primarily on justice and political dissent. Referring to the anti-Vietnam demonstrations of the late sixties and early seventies, Rainer argued actions taken by Berlin authorities had been 'unjust.' More recently, Berlin's minister of the interior had taken a hard line against the *Instandbezeter*.

Nadja joined in, "The Swiss band Grauzone recently released a deconstructed, synthesized version of the old German children's song

'*Maikäfer flieg,*' substituting '*Lummerland*' for 'Pommerland!'"

"That's very interesting, Ms. d'Oment, I'm familiar with the text from *Des Knaben Wunderhorn.* Dr. Schneider sang to us, '*Maykäfer flieg! Der Vater ist im Krieg. Die Mutter ist im Pommerland. Pommerland ist abgebrandt.*'[30] So now it's '*Lummerland ist abgebrandt.*' Yes, yes, *Innensenator* Heinrich Lummer, a fellow political scientist, and graduate of the Free University's *Werner-Finck-Institut* I might add. If my sources are accurate, the postwar student protest movement may have begun here, at the Free University, as early as 1966, with a sit-down strike protesting a *Senat*-imposed *Hochschulereform* setting time limits on matriculation. The shooting of Benno Ohnesorg, an *FU* student, during the state visit of the Shah of Iran to West Berlin in June 1967, politicized the movement, culminating in 1968 with the attempted assassination of student leader Rudi Dutschke in April, and the anti-Vietnam protest march in May. For some students, the Free University wasn't free enough, so a new *Kritische Universität* was founded. This is of interest, as it suggests negative identification as an element of self-identification. I was involved with the peaceful protest of the American invasion of Cambodia, which tragically culminated in the killing and wounding of Kent State University students by members of the Ohio National Guard in May 1970. In the aftermath of the shooting, we tried to understand how it happened. One of my colleagues at Kent State, an authority in the field of political psychology, suggested an 'unconscious collusion' between protestors and authorities might have played a part. Collusion, in the sense that each needs the 'other' for a sense of self—negative identification, which in turn informs actions intended to reinforce it. But unfortunately, I see we've run out of time. We'll continue our discussion next week." Dr. Schneider asked for topics and assigned tentative dates for the remaining presentations. D3 reported he'd submitted the request for our visit to the *Kommandatura.* Slowly, our accidental *polis* began to rise from Seminar Rooms 3–4.

On Tour with Major Durchschouer

June 1983

In May, I was invited by the chief of mission to make a presentation on the history of the US Military Liaison Mission in the Mission at *Föhrenweg 19–21.* D3 told me Colonel Patrick had requested my security clearance be temporarily reinstated in advance so I could talk and respond to questions

---

30 "Fly, ladybug, fly! Father is in the war. Mother is in Pommerland. Pommerland is in ashes." Diary of Thomas Vonaechron, Diary Extract, 1983, trans. TV.

at whatever level deemed appropriate. Set back off from the *Clay-Allee* on a parallel street, the redbrick villa built under Albert Speer's direction in 1936 as an alternate command post for *Generalfeldmarschall* Keitel was surrounded by security fencing. Members of the German Guard Battalion, patrolling the perimeter with submachine guns, nodded and smiled as D3 escorted me up the stairs into the house and down into the underground briefing room, where we were cordially received by the Chief of Mission, Colonel Riley Patrick, and his staff. Colonel Patrick held a BA in history from Gettysburg College and was a graduate of the US Army War College at Carlisle Barracks, Pennsylvania, not far from Gettysburg. He was interested in the initial organization and early history of the USMLM, in particular the agreements reached with the Soviet authorities regarding liaison duties and responsibilities. Following my briefing, he asked several detailed questions about the 1947 Huebner-Malinin Agreement, which I was unable to answer without the USMLM records in hand. He was pleased to learn he could officially request and read the documents in Vault Six at the Washington National Records Center. Together, we drafted a request for submission through US Army channels to the National Archives so the documents would be available for his use during his upcoming temporary duty trip to Washington. Afterward, as D3 promised, I was treated to dinner, not at the Mission but at the Harnack House, the former guesthouse of the *Kaiser-Wilhelm-Gesellschaft* now serving US Army Berlin as the officers' club. Much to my surprise, the legacy of Albert Speer joined us there, too. D3 told me the architect-turned-armaments minister had presided over a meeting of German scientists in the ballroom of the Harnack House in 1942 to determine the priority to be given to the development of atomic weapons. Albert Speer again—West Berlin was certainly a kind of *Speer-gebiet*! I was surprised his picture wasn't hanging on the ballroom wall with those of the other illustrious guests.

After a dark, wet winter and a reluctant spring, AFN Berlin announced Monday, June 6, promised to be a summer's day. D3 and the US Military Liaison Mission driver, Sergeant Christian Miller, picked me up in the Shield at "zero six-hundred hours." Dressed in battle dress uniforms with the woodland camouflage pattern—"BDUs" as D3 called them—both wore the distinctive USMLM shoulder-sleeve insignia, a variation on the US Army, Europe shield, with the American flag flying above the flaming sword under the rainbow, identifying them as members of the "United States Military Liaison Mission. Potsdam." Sergeant Miller kindly opened the left rear door of the Shield for me. After I sat down and buckled myself into the four-point harness, a bird perched in the Linden tree directly above asked, "Poo-tee-wet?" Surprisingly, given the hour, Hedwig was standing on the corner, sashaying slowly, watching us as we drove by. Morning traffic was beginning to fill the street. On the adjoining sidewalks, Berliners were dressed in their fifty shades of black and gray. As we turned left onto *Hauptstraße*, I looked out through the vertical venetian blinds running the length of the Ford's back window. The golden angel on top of *Rathaus Friedenau* seemed to turn on the bronze pedestal in our direction, gracefully extending the green palm of peace to the green, government-issue Shield of Achilles. *Hauptstraße* became *Rheinstraße*, *Rheinstraße* became *Unter den Eichen.* When we stopped for the traffic light at *Plantanenplatz*, I looked out the window to see a tall, white-haired man wearing horn-rimmed glasses walking a smooth dachshund under the spreading sycamore trees. He looked back at me, waving as the light turned green. I returned his unexpected greeting. The stately German oaks lining *Unter den Eichen* escorted us past the US Army Hospital to *Berliner Straße.* We drove on through the center of *Zehlendorf,* unofficial capital of the American Sector. *Berliner Straße* became *Potsdamer Chausee,* the broad, tree-lined boulevard took us southwest through Wannsee, becoming *Königstraße* after crossing over the *Kleiner Wannsee.* Continuing on through the forest, we passed the American *Golf Klub* on our left and the *Jagdschloß Glienicke* on our right, Sergeant Miller slowed the Shield. Before us, was the *Brücke der Einheit,* the "Bridge of Unity" cum Unification, the bridge of sighs linking Berlin with Potsdam and East Germany.

Passing through the Allied checkpoint at the eastern end of *Glienicke Brücke,* we were waved through the Soviet checkpoint by a Russian officer who saluted D3, then smiled and waved as we passed by. Returning his salute, his smile, and his wave, D3 turned to me and said, "We're expected today, Thomas." D3 was right. In the Shield, the Wall was invisible. "Rather than take the *Autobahn,* Sergeant Miller and I thought we would *recce* Route 1, aka *Reichstraße 1,* with you, taking us back through Potsdam, our point of departure earlier this morning, and head west through Geltow, Werder *an der* Havel, Brandenburg *an der Havel,* Genthin, Hohenseeden, on to Burg, just northeast of Magdeburg. You'll have the chance to get a look at life in the German Democratic Republic close up and personal and take a tour through German history as well, from West Berlin back through the Third and Second *Reich* and Prussia, to an ancient east trade route connecting the North Sea with Novograd. The Soviet forces used *Reichstraße 1* in April and May 1945 when they drove west from the Seelow-Heights into Berlin."

The cities and towns we passed through along the way were uniformly gray, standing in stark contrast to the blue lakes and bright green fields of the former *Mark Brandenburg,* resplendent in the morning sunshine.

Under decades old residue of carbon and coal, many of the older structures, though dilapidated, were still intact, possessing the dormant promise of restoration. In West Germany, many buildings damaged but not destroyed during the war had been reduced to rubble afterward, then removed to make way for new, lucrative, artless construction. *"All architecture is what you do when you look upon it, (Did you think it was in the white or gray stone? or the lines of the arches and cornices?)"* Passing through Potsdam and Brandenburg *an der Havel*, we often shared the road with Russian military vehicles. "Those 'BMPs,'—ah, sorry Thomas, 'Infantry Combat Vehicles' and 'Armored Personnel Carriers,' 'BTRs'—are from regiments of the Thirty-Fifth Motorized Rifle Krasnograd Red Banner Division headquartered at Krampnitz in Fahrland, between Potsdam and Spandau."

"How many Soviet forces are currently stationed in the German Democratic Republic, D3?"

"Approximately 546,000 military personnel and civilians."

"546,000!"

"The Group of Soviet Forces, Germany, *'Gruppa Sovetskix Voisk Germani,' 'GSVG,'* our employer, is the largest, most powerful group of Soviet ground forces. It's made up of the First Guards Tank Red-Banner Army headquartered at Dresden, the Second Guards Tank Red-Banner Army at Fürstenberg, the Third Combined-Arms Red-Banner Shock Army at Magdeburg, the Eighth Guards Combined-Arms Order of Lenin Army at Weimar-Nohra, the Twentieth Guards Combined-Arms Red Banner Army at Eberswalde-Finow, and, last but not least, the Sixteenth Red-Banner Air Army at Wünsdorf. Depending upon how one classifies and counts them—which takes up much, too much, of our time, doesn't it Sergeant Miller?—there are seven tank, eight motorized rifle and five aviation divisions. In addition, there's a front artillery division, three army artillery brigades, five army ground attack helicopter regiments, and other ground force combat and support units. The *GSVG* is literally a 'front in being.'"

"How many Allied forces are stationed in West Berlin, the Armed Camp?"

"About 12,000, 5,000 of which are American." But don't forget, Thomas, there are also about 255,000 American forces stationed in the Federal Republic, British and French troops as well. We'd like to think they'd come help us in an emergency, but the V and VII Corps Commanders and the Commander-in-Chief, US Army, Europe and Seventh Army, our other boss, don't always get along that well!"

Most of the Red Army soldiers smiled and waved when they saw the Shield, and we returned their greetings. On the road, we also met a few

East German *Trabant* and *Wartburg* automobiles, cowed by the Shield screaming "America" as we passed. People on the sidewalk, farmers in the fields, stopped what they were doing, turning to watch us as we drove by. We arrived in Burg midmorning, greeted by an architectural fugue of church, castle, and water towers. "In addition to being the birth and final resting place of the Clausewitzes, Burg is also the location of the Headquarters, 933rd Surface-to-Air Missile Verkhnedneprovsk Red-Banner Order of A. Nevskiy Regiment, our hosts today."

D3 consulted the directions given to him by his Russian colleague, passing them on orally to Sergeant Miller. Instead of a *Heldenfriedhof*, we found the *Ostfriedhof*, a German civilian cemetery not far from a Soviet military installation. Sergeant Miller parked the Shield in the cemetery parking lot, remaining with the car. D3 and I walked through the trees, following the sketch, and found the Clausewitz grave behind a small chapel—a large, elegant, marble cross.

Hier ruht
in Gott
Carl Philipp Gottfried v. Clausewitz
Kongl. General Major u. Inspecteur der Artillerie
geb. d. 1. Juni
1780
gest. d. 16. Nov.
1831

D3 was pleased to see Carl von Clausewitz had been reburied with his wife, Marie Sophie von Clausewitz geb. *Grafin von* Bruehl, *Oberhofmeisterin Ihrer Königlichen Hoheit der Prinzessin Wilhelm.* "Frau von Clausewitz was instrumental in the publication of her husband's work after his death from cholera," he said, looking at the cross, "She wrote the 'Foreword' and, according to my Command and General Staff College classmate, Winfried, edited, compiled, and may have even written parts of *Vom Kriege* based upon her husband's notes. As we stood at the foot of the grave, D3 opened his well-worn, leather-bound copy of *Vom Kriege*, which closely resembled Dr. Schneider's well-worn copy of *The Republic of Plato*. "I'd like to read two passages aloud, Thomas. An excerpt from her 'Foreword' to *Vom Kriege*, then something from Clausewitz himself."

"Drive on, D3!"

"In her *Vorrede, Frau* von Clausewitz writes, '*Wer unsere glückselige Ehe gekannt hat und weiß, wie wir alles miteinander teilten, nicht allein*

Freude und Leid, sondern auch jede Beschäftigung, jedes Interesse, des täglichen Lebens: der wird begreifen, daß eine Arbeit dieser Art meinen geliebten Mann nicht beschäftigen konnte, ohne auch mir genau bekannt zu sein.'"[31]

"That says as much about love between a woman and a man as it does about *On War*, D3."

"Roger that, Thomas. Here are Clausewitz's thoughts on the relationship between reason and human behavior, something I find very useful as I try to make sense of my profession and myself, for that matter:

Obgleich sich unser Verstand immer zur Klarheit und Gewißheit hingedrängt fühlt, so fühlt sich doch unser Geist oft von der Ungewißheit angezogen. Statt sich mit dem Verstande auf dem engen Pfade philosophischer Untersuchung und logischer Schlußfolgen durchzuwinden, um, seiner selbst sich kaum bewußt, in Räumen anzukommen, wo er sich fremd fühlt, und wo ihn alle bekannten Gegenstände zu verlassen scheinen, weilt er lieber mit der Einbildungskraft im Reiche der Zufälle und des Glücks. Statt jener dürftigen Notwendigkeit schwelgt er hier im Reichtum von Möglichkeiten; begeistert davon, beflügelt sich der Mut, und so wird Wagnis und Gefahr das Element, in welches er sich wirft wie der mutige Schwimmer in den Strom.[32]

D3 closed the book and stood silently for a moment. "After all our discussions at Leavenworth, to think I'd one day be standing at their grave. The map provided by the Russian representative of the Dead Carl Club shows the location of Clausewitz's parents' house at *Schulstraße 12*. Let's do a drive by, and show the flag in Burg on our way back to Route 1. We found the house at the corner of *Brahmstraße*. Like many of the old houses, it was badly in need of repair but still standing. Returning to Route 1, we drove through the fields in the direction of Magdeburg. Through my window, in the middle of a field, I saw what appeared to be a mobile missile launcher with a tarp thrown over it, a white star visible under the edge of the tarp

---

31 "Anyone who experienced our joyful marriage, knew that we shared everything with each other, not just happiness and sorrow, but every activity, every interest of daily life; he or she will understand that a work of this kind could not occupy my beloved husband without being completely known to me." trans. Captain Dwight D. Durchschouer, US Army, School for Advanced Military Studies, Fort Leavenworth, Kansas, *On War*, p. VI.

32 "Even though our mind always strives for clarity and certainty, our spirit is often attracted by uncertainty. Instead of following the intellect along the narrow path of philosophical inquiry and turning to logical conclusions, in order to, unknown even to itself, arrive at places, where it feels unfamliar and everything familiar seems to be lost, spirit would rather spend time with fantasy in the realm of coincidence and chance. Instead of bare necessity, spirit revels in a richness of possibilities, inspiration giving wings to courage, so hazardous undertakings and danger become the element into which it dives, a brave swimmer in the current." trans. Captain Dwight D. Durchschouer, US Army, School for Advanced Military Studies, Fort Leavenworth, Kansas, *On War*, p. 14.

over the wheels—a mock-up of an American vehicle?

"D3, Sergeant Miller, did you see that? It looked like a mock-up of an American mobile missile launcher with a tarp thrown over it."

"No, I missed it, Thomas, good eye! Although today's tour was planned as a 'staff ride' to Burg, Magdeburg, and back, I guess we should go back, take a look, and possibly a few pictures for the Annual Unit History and, of course," smiling at me, "the Records Declassification Division of National Archives." Slowing down, Sergeant Miller braked and turned onto a stone field access apron, stopped, and carefully backed the Shield back out onto Route 1.

"There it is, in the field on the right."

"Got it, thank you! Thomas, please wait here in the Shield with Sergeant Miller. According to this morning's brief, this field is not a 'place of disposition of military units' so I'm going to take a quick look and a few pictures. Our Russian colleagues knew our route in advance today, not our usual SOP. They just might want us to see something. Sergeant Miller, please open the trunk." Sergeant Miller unlocked the trunk from inside and D3 got out of the Shield to retrieve the camera. Walking by my window on the way out into the field he said, "This should just take a minute or two, Thomas, then we'll be on our way."

Sergeant Miller met D3 outside the Shield when he returned fifteen minutes later, securing the camera in the trunk. D3 seemed preoccupied, and then, turning to me, said, "Sergeant Miller and I mapped out a real nice road trip back to Berlin. From Magdeburg, we planned to take Route 184 to Dessau, passing through Gommern, Leitzkau, and Zerbst."

"Dessau. Isn't that where Walter Gropius's *Bauhaus* is?"

"Yes, indeed, Dessau home of the *Bauhaus* and the Seventh Guards Tank Kiev-Berlin Order of Lenin Twice Red-Banner Order of Suvorov Division in Dessau-Rosslau. From Dessau, we would have taken Route 187 through Coswig to Lutherstadt-Wittenberg, home of the Fifty-Fifth Guards Tank Vasil'kov Order of Lenin Red-Banner Orders of Surov and B. Khmel'nitsky Regiment, and then northeast on Route 2 through Marzahna, Treuenbrietzen, site of the Battle of Halbe and the massacre of German civilians at the end of the war, Buchholz und Beelitz. Thirty klicks to the east of Beelitz is the headquarters of the *Gruppa Sovetskix Voisk Germani* at Zossen/Wünsdorf." Looking over at Sergeant Miller, who had returned to the driver's seat after stowing the camera in the trunk, D3 smiled and said, "Sergeant Miller and I also work for the *GZGV* Commander, General-Colonel Mikhail M. Zaytsev. The Sixteenth Air Red-Banner Army is headquartered there too. It's quite a fascinating complex, the former headquarters of the *Oberkommando der* Wehrmacht,

Feldmarschall Keitel's other headquarters! The orders for the invasion of Poland in 1939 and the invasion of Russia in 1941 were promulgated there. Now it's the headquarters for Russian forces in Germany!"

"*Eirönïa!*"

"Say again, Thomas?"

"*Eirönïa*, one of those ironies of history Clio offers her initiates."

"Roger that! Much of the complex was underground, in huge concrete bunkers. In accordance with the Potsdam Agreement, the Russians began demolition at the end of the war but stopped when the Cold War began to heat up. From Beelitz, it's just a few klicks to Potsdam, the *Brücke der Einheit*, and the American Sector. It would have been a very interesting trip, *ver-r-ry inter-r-resting*. Unfortunately, Thomas, you porked the pooch! You identified what appears to be a mock-up of a Pershing II M1003 Erector Launcher—a modified Pershing 1a M790 launcher, scheduled for deployment in the Federal Republic later this year. They're using an MAZ-543 tractor for the M983 HEMTT, but otherwise it's pretty accurate. We should get these pictures, and I just couldn't resist peeking under the tarp, reflex action I guess—back to the Mission as quickly as possible. Our Russian friends wanted us to see this today, and we should oblige them by sending the pictures on to Heidelberg ASAP." We entered the *Autobahn* just a few kilometers southwest of Burg, northwest of Magdeburg.

"It's too bad we didn't have the chance to drive through Magdeburg, perhaps we'll have another chance. Magdeburg was decimated by the Strategic Air Campaign of the Second World War and taken, not by the Red Army, but by the Thirtieth Infantry Division, "Old Hickory," in April 1945. Among the POWs taken was *Major* Werner Pluskat, perhaps the first German soldier to observe the OVERLORD armada from his command post on the Normandy coast in the early morning hours of June 6, 1944, thirty-nine years ago today! Have you seen the film *The Longest Day*, Thomas?"

"Yes, I have, D3, many years ago as a nine-year-old boy. Even so, that particular scene remains unforgettable. Who played *Major* Pluskat?"

"Hans Christian Blech. But for me, Thomas, Magdeburg is not World War II but the Thirty Years War. In 1631, the city was sacked and burned by Imperial troops under the command of Count Gottfried Henry von Pappenheim. Perhaps as many as 20,000 inhabitants were killed. Seventeen years later, when the Treaty of Westphalia ending the war was signed, only a few *Magdeburger* remained alive to celebrate. That was 'total war.' Last winter, I visited Magdeburg in search of its famous son, Baron Major General Freidrich Wilhelm August Heinrich von Steuben, chief of staff to General George Washington. In spite, or perhaps because of, postwar attempts at repair and reconstruction, an atmosphere of total destruction still remains."

"*Wastare*."

"*Wastare*."

"Well, I'm sorry I—what did you say?—'porked the pooch?' I would've liked to see Magdeburg today. I hope we'll have another chance."

"Yeah, this happens!"

"You mean 'shit happens,' don't you, D3?

"This happens, shit happens, it's all the same thing, just rearrange the letters!" The return trip went much more quickly over the *Autobahn*, though Sergeant Miller held to the 100-kilometer-per-hour speed limit. In spite of the Ford's heavy-duty suspension, we were jostled at regular intervals. "Those are the '*Hitlerrillen*,' the line where the concrete sections join. Because this *Autobahn* is a *Transitstraße*, the West German government pays for its maintenance. Unfortunately, they haven't been able to eliminate this particular legacy of the Third *Reich*." Not a "bridge," but an unintended "*Autobahn* of tradition." Once again, we were waved through the checkpoints at both ends of the *Brücke der Einheit* without having to stop.

"Would it be possible for you to drop me off at the Clay Institute? I'd like to pick up a few books from the library."

"*Null problemo*, Thomas, it's right on the way to the *Föhrenweg*. One other thing, as you know, we temporarily reinstated your clearance for your briefing at the Mission, not because there's anything secret to see there but so you could talk freely about the USMLM documents you reviewed at the National Archives. Today's tour was supposed to be our Clausewitz pilgrimage to Burg. Thanks to you, Sergeant Miller and I unfortunately have to go to work, so we and the chief would be very grateful if you would please file today's post-Burg activities in the National Archives of your mind under 'SECRET,' along with the other USMLM activities you read about requiring continued protection."

"Of course, D3. *Null problemo*. I was just thinking. As I sat there in Vault Six, reading through the USMLM reports, looking at the black-and-white photographs, I often wished I could have been on one of those tours. Today turned out to be both T- and D-Day!"

"You know what we say in the United States Army, Thomas? 'Be careful what you wish for, you just might get it!'"

It was late in the afternoon when D3 and Sergeant Miller dropped me off in front of the *U-Bahnhof* Dahlem Dorf. "Thank you, Sergeant Miller, for driving today, and thank you, D3, for making all the necessary arrangements for a fascinating tour to Burg. It was an honor and a pleasure for me to accompany you on your pilgrimage to the Clausewitz grave. Sorry I messed up the rest of it."

"You're certainly welcome, Thomas. Let's see whether you messed it up or maybe even made it. I have the feeling the chief of mission will be quite pleased with your discovery. See you Friday at the Clay Institute!"

Once again, there were so many, too many, impressions I needed to fix, develop, and arrange. Instead of walking directly to the Clay Institute, I decided to sit for a moment in the *Biergarten* under the trees at *Lusie* and have a *KöPi* . Although I wanted to pick up the books from the library before returning to Friedenau, it would be useless to try to read them this afternoon. I paid for my beer when served, and when I stood up a few minutes later, I felt comfortably disoriented, sensual from the beer and tired from the tour to Burg.

The Ladder in the Library
June 1983

In the lull between the afternoon and evening classes, the Clay Institute was deserted. It was hot and humid in the library. Although all the windows stood wide open, there was not the slightest breeze. There was no one at the desk. As I made my way back through the stacks, I saw Laura standing on the top step an old wooden ladder with metal hand railings, taking books from the platform on the top and putting them back on the shelves. Laura. *L'aura.* Wide, the width of the library aisle, the ladder was mounted on casters, allowing librarians to reshelve books on both sides. She was wearing an ankle-length, brown, loose-fitting, cotton, flower-print dress. I could see dark circles of sweat under her arms as she placed the books back on the shelves. As she turned to face me, I saw sweat had also darkened circles around her nipples. Although she had her hair pulled back, drops of sweat were running down her face. She smiled and began to carefully make her way down the ladder one step at a time, holding on to the railing with her left hand, books in her right. When she reached the last step, she turned around and said, "Hi, Thomas, what a nice surprise! I found these books while reshelving and thought you might be interested."

As I walked up to her to take the books from her hand, she dropped them and put her arms around my neck. Kissing her gently, I could taste the salt on her lips. I lowered my head and kissed her nipples through the wet cotton, taking them gently between my teeth. They were erect and salty, like her lips. Laura took her arms from around my neck and slowly dropped them to her sides. Taking a step backward, she cautiously extended her arms behind her, catching the metal rails running along both sides of the ladder. She then began to climb slowly up the ladder backward while smiling at me. As she raised her long legs, step by step, her dress fell away, revealing the inside of her thighs. When she was halfway up the ladder, she stopped and said, "That's enough for now, Thomas. Please pick up the books I dropped and give them back to me."

Instead, I took a step forward and ran my hands very slowly along the outside of her legs, up underneath her dress. Her thighs were warm and wet from her sweat. I could feel the tiny blonde hairs as the palms of my hands passed over them. When I reached her hips, I slipped my fingers in her panties and pulled them down slowly to her ankles. As I began to unbutton her dress from the bottom, she sighed, "Thomas," leaned back into the ladder, and closed her eyes. When I moved the palms of my hands tenderly to the inside of her thighs, she opened her legs slowly, spreading them until her knees touched the metal handrailing on both sides of the ladder. Gently moving my hands underneath and then around to the back of her thighs, I leaned forward, pressing my mouth against the inside, kissing, moving up slowly, until I had her pubic hair in my mouth. Gently separating her *labia majora* with my fingers, I found her clitoris, circling it with my tongue. After Laura died her *petite mort*, I slowly pulled up her panties, running my hands along her calves and thighs, buttoned up her brown dress from the bottom, and then carefully picked up the books she had dropped on the floor.

CHAPTER IV:
Motion and Music

Perhaps our peculiar paradox here in the American Sector, here in West Berlin—is that we are fixed and certain only when we're moving.

—Rainer Wallfahrt after
Thomas Wolfe, *You Can't Go Home Again*

Composition
June 1983

Rereviewing, reflecting in reverse chronological order, I should have paid closer attention to the warning first raised by Lorelei Rhine in her letter and then by Dr. Kahler in conversation. There was much to do, too much, and a price to be paid. Over time, my three primary points of reference, the *Stadtstaatsarchiv Berlin* in Wittenau, my one elegant Empire room in Friedenau, and the *Lucius-D.-Clay-Institut* in Dahlem-Dorf, were compounded by secondary, then tertiary points of reference throughout West Berlin— Berlin VI. These points, carefully plotted out on the folding *Falkplan*, became my personal operational architecture in the HistoriCity. Although conscious of East Berlin on the far side of the Wall, with the exception of my one-day foray with George, Berlin V was largely outside my area of operations (AO). My movement connected the points across established lines of communication (LOC) within West Berlin, establishing a communications zone (COMZ). A zone *politikon*, often *per pedes Pilgrimorum*, I was supported in my attempt to become fixed and certain by Berlin's incomparable public transportation system, *Bus*, *U-Bahn*, *S-Bahn*, and even the *Berliner Verkehrsbetriebe (BVG) vaporetto Michael Kohlhaas*, ferrying passengers across the Havel from *S-Bahnhof Wannsee* to Kladow. As a coincidental consequence of Dr. Schneider's Accidental *Polis* Seminar, these modes of transportation were now augmented by Rainer Wallfahrt's big yellow CityFunk taxi. Although the illuminated sign on the roof of his Mercedes 200D limousine advertised "(American Literature)", we quickly discovered a common *Freundeskreis* of European and American authors, providing us with both *Zünd- und Gesprächstoff*. Through the chatter on CityFunk, the radio communications network used to dispatch taxis throughout West Berlin, Rainer received regular updates on new points of interest. A means of transportation, his taxi also became the medium for synchronizing these points with music. In addition to Radio in the American Sector of Berlin (RIAS), Rainer had programmed, the British Force Broadcasting Service (BFBS), *Radio forces françaises de Berlin, Sender Freies* Berlin (*SFB*) and *Radio Wolga* into the Mercedes' built-in *Blaupunkt* push-button radio. Radio station playlists were augmented by Rainer's portable cassette library, custom-tailored for taxiing around Berlin VI, motion and music in West Berlin, *unterwegs in medias RIAS.*

During the empty hours of the early morning, when fares were few, Rainer would often taxi to Friedenau and pick me up. Together, we would cruise the brightly-lit main thoroughfares and the dark side streets of West Berlin to the soundtrack of late-night radio, until hailed on the street or dispatched by CityFunk. Not everyone who hailed a cab was looking for a ride. Late one *RIAS Rocknight* out on the *menschenlerre Munsterdamm* in Schöneberg, we were flagged down by an amateur astronomer who insisted we park and observe the rings of Saturn through the telescope he'd set up on the *Insulaner*, one of the artificial hills erected upon ruins of Berlin II–IV. Taxiing within West Berlin was circumscribed and defined by the Wall. When a fare found Rainer, I would bail out, falling back on public transportation, utilizing alternate lines of communication to return to Friedenau. With constant motion throughout a COMZ continually expanding within the circuit wall described by the accidental *polis*, came the coincident transfer and loss of energy. Paradoxically, the movement required to fix and make certain proved exhausting. Dr. Kahler was right, "A word of caution, Mr. Vonaechron, one must be very careful in West Berlin—there's simply too much going on. One can easily enjoy oneself into a state of exhaustion."

Grounded in an initial consideration of law and justice, the Accidental *Polis* Seminar began to focus upon the symbiotic relationship between the city and the individual citizen, Plato's intent in *The Republic*. Returning to the *Leitmotiven* of his introductory remarks, Dr. Schneider emphasized the transformation of the individual through architecture and community, and the attempt of the citizens to set themselves apart from nature, time, and space through artifice. The *polis* could be seen as a conscious, communal, and ultimately constitutional attempt to transcend the finite nature of existence through *praxis* within the *polis,* a localized striving for immortality. Referring to Aristotle's concept of *Bios politikos* refined and developed by Hannah Arendt, Dr. Schneider argued that while the end of the *polis* was to achieve the good life, to realize the human capabilities and capacities of its citizens, it could be life-taking as well as life-giving. The sense of immortality gained from living within its walls could ultimately prove artificial, illusory, and futile. "In his discussion of *The Laws*, Leo Strauss suggests, for Plato the city is '. . . tragedy par excellence.' At the same time Strauss argues, and I quote, 'The city has its origins in human needs: every human being, just or unjust, is in need of many things and is at least for this reason in need of other human beings.' This is why Pericles refers to the Athenians as *erastai*, 'lovers of the city.'"

One Friday afternoon in mid-June following the seminar, Dr. Schneider asked D3 and me to accompany him to his office. "This morning, a colleague gave me three tickets to the performance of Händel's *Giulio Cesare in Eggito* tomorrow afternoon at the *Deutsche Oper*. Although on extremely short notice, I wondered if you two might like to join me. As an army officer, I thought you might particularly enjoy Händel's musical treatment of Julius Caesar's Egyptian campaign, Mr. Durchschouer, and I know Mr. Vonaechron to be a friend of the Baroque opera. In any event, I did want to take this opportunity to express my gratitude to both of you for your active support of our seminar. I honestly don't believe we would have gotten off to such a good start, maybe we wouldn't have gotten off at all, without your enthusiasm and engagement." D3 and I gratefully accepted Dr. Schneider's kind invitation, deciding to *rendezvous* in the *foyer* of the *Deutsche Oper* at "eleven-hundred hours" for a glass of champagne prior to the noon performance. "You'll recall from our discussion of political dissent in West Berlin, how the shooting of the *FU* student Benno Ohnesorg just outside the *Deutsche Oper* on June 2, 1967, galvanized the Berlin student movement. I'd like to visit the site if I can locate it, perhaps because of my own experience on the Kent State campus on May 4, 1970, just three years later. I'll check the available sources. Perhaps *Frau* Anders could be of assistance in the library." Laura in the library. "But just in case something else comes up, let me give each of you your tickets now."

The *Deutsche Oper* occupied the same space as the *Deutsches Opernhaus*, destroyed by the same Royal Air Force Bomber Command *sortie* of November 23, 1943, which laid waste to the *Kasier-Wilhelm-Gedächtnis-Kirche*. Regardless of the markedly different original intentions of the two Wilhelmine architects, the intent of the Churchillian mission planners had the same leveling effect. In Charlottenburg at Bismarckstraße 35, on the former *Ost-West-Achse*, the *Deutsche Oper* had been designed by a former designer of operatic scenery, the ideal theater for military operations set to music. The *U-Bahn* took me to the opera with only one change at *Bahnhof Zoo*, from *Linie 9* to *Linie 1*. At *Bahnhof Zoo*, I once again deliberately made my way through the preterite, *Halbstarken*, hippies and punks passed over by the postwar decades of Berlin VI, now sharing their communal life of alcohol and drugs. *"Ey Alter, haste 'ne Mark für mich?"* echoed through the underground passageway as I made my way to the *Linie 1* platform. Two stations later, from my vantage point atop of the stairs at *U-Bahnhof Deutsche Oper*, I saw D3 on point outside the broad bank of glass entrance doors. As I carefully crossed over the eight-lane *Bismarckstraße* and walked toward him, Dr. Schneider came around the far corner of the building.

"Good morning to you both. I hope I haven't kept you waiting. I was indeed able to find the location where Benno Ohnesorg was shot by police detective Karl-Heinz Kurras," pointing back in the direction from which he came, he said, "it's on the other side, around the next corner in the *Hof* at *Krumme Strasse 66*. If you'd like, we can stop by there afterward." The great gray slab, prefab walls of the *Deutsche Oper* were austere and rough, radiating a concrete *Kälte* on this warm June morning. The interior, however, had an agreeable early sixties ambiance. Black metal staircases and landings suspended in open space reminded me of the *Palast der Republik* down *Bismarckstraße* on the far side of the Wall in East Berlin, and *Fräulein* Otto, "Under other circumstances, I'd be pleased to join you . . ." D3 guided us up the stairs to the small, round, standing-height bistro table he'd reserved for us in the *foyer*. Three glasses of champagne pearled on the white linen tablecloth. D3 lifted his glass, proposing a toast "to the accidental *polis*!" I raised my glass in reply, "Hear, hear!" Dr. Schneider added, "Well, since we're actually here in the accidental *polis*, perhaps I should add 'Here, here!'"

Conversation returned to the shootings in *Krumme Strasse* and at Kent State, the radicalization of the student movement in the Federal Republic and the United States, and the war in Vietnam. The ambient noise level increased as the *foyer* filled around us, drawing my attention away from D3 and Dr. Schneider to our fellow operagoers. Dress for *Guilio Cesare* ranged from afternoon formal to evening outré. I could not imagine the costumes for Händel's *dramma per musica* could be any more dramatic. Imitation punks in well-worn leather with multicolored spiked mohawks—I hoped we were not seated behind them—stood patiently in line with serious citizens, retirees, students, and the ubiquitous tourists, bused and flown into West Berlin from the four corners of the world, for preperformance refreshments at the foyer bar. A festival of humanity, gathered together for four hours and forty-five minutes for Georg Friedrich Händel's celebration of music and military history in well-walled West Berlin. By the time the third bell urgently summoned us to our seats, I was already anticipating intermission, another opportunity to see, and perhaps even to be seen.

The victory of Julius Caesar over Pompey at Pharsalus during the Great Roman Civil War set the stage for the first act, transforming the HistoriCity, former capital of Germany, into Alexandria, former capital of Egypt *waybac* in 48 BC. Although he had decided to spare Pompey's life at the request of his wife, Cornelia, and son, Sextus, Caesar is unexpectedly presented with Pompey's severed head by the commander of the Egyptian Forces, Achillas—a gift from Tolomeo, coruler of Egypt. As Caesar movingly countertenored the cruelty with "*Empio, dirò, tu sei,*" D3 leaned over and whispered in my ear, "That's one way to get a head in the army!" Achillas returns to Tolomeo, who, informed of Caesar's outrage, now commissions Achillas to kill him, promising the hand, together with the rest, of Pompey's comely wife. Laying down his arms for those of Cleopatra in act II, Caesar becomes a pawn in her strategy to depose her brother, Tolomeo, and secure the throne of Egypt for herself. Targeted by Tolomeo and Achillas, Caesar leaps from Cleopatra's palace window into the Mediterranean, apparently drowning in the attempt to escape.

Intermission provided an opportunity to compare costumes on- and offstage. Many members of the audience were not only at but in the opera, with operatics extending from the stage into the auditorium, continuing out into the foyer, where we returned to our bistro table for wine and warm pretzels. Dressed in a tightly tailored black jacket and skirt-suit with matching heels, Cleopatra stood at the table adjacent to ours, flirting with a bearded Marco Antonio. Although I didn't recognize or wasn't recognized by anyone other than D3 and Dr. Schneider, I felt that same strange sense of community with the other members of the audience as I had at *Die Orestie*. Summoned by the bell back to our seats for act III, we found Caesar washed up, looking for troops, while the forces of Cleopatra and Tolomeo battled for the throne of Egypt. Victorious over his sister—as she was brought before him in chains, I couldn't resist whispering, "Seize her!" in D3's ear—Tolomeo is assassinated by Sextus, son of Pompey. Deprived of the promised Cornelia by Tolomeo, Achillas passes his command to Caesar, who triumphantly enters Alexandria at the head of the Egyptian Army. He proclaims Cleopatra queen, the liberation of Egypt from tyranny, and his intent to spread the glory of Rome. Although Niccolò Francesco Haym's libretto provided an entertaining, highly personal retelling of the history surrounding *Guilio Caesare in Eggto*, Händel's music gave structure to Caesar's campaign. The power of his musical score radiated out from the *Deutsche Oper* into West Berlin, giving structure and meaning to the afternoon, the day, to the HistoriCity itself.

Following the performance, we stopped into the *Restaurant Deutsche Oper* for a follow-on glass of wine at Dr. Schneider's invitation, "One glass of wine for each act—*Eggito est omnia divisa in partes tres!*" Once we'd been served and raised our glasses to the health of our host, D3 leaned back in his chair and said, "I wonder what storyline Haym would have taken had Pompey pursued Caesar after decisively defeating him at Dyrrachium, the battle preceding Pharsalus. Pompey might have been able to end the Great Roman Civil War without involving himself in Egyptian . . . let's see, would 'affairs' be the right word? Yuck, yuck, yuck! How does '*Gnaeus Pompeius Magnus en Illyrium*' sound as a title?"

Dr. Schneider laughed, replying, "Händel would have nonetheless risen to the occasion and composed an aria for Pompey, something along the lines of 'And what should I do in Illyrium?' It would have no doubt gone down well at King's Theater on Haymarket in London."

Laughing, D3 continued, "Roger that, Professor Schneider, but on the other hand, the campaign just wouldn't be the same without Cleopatra's '*V'adoro, pupille.*' It occurs to me, thinking about Händel's *dramma per musica* and the campaign on which it is based, and a discussion Thomas and I had following our first Accidental *Polis* Seminar, a campaign can be seen as a 'reality opera,' an attempt to structure space and time for political purpose."

"An interesting thought, Mr. Durchschouer, in what sense? Please elaborate, or should I say 'Drive on!'"

D3 laughed and said, "Roger that!" Well, a campaign—for example, the Soviet 'Berlin Strategic Offensive Operation' that took this city in April 1945—is the attempt to structure, to orchestrate space and time to achieve a specific political objective, to impose the will of one side upon the other. Looking at me, D3 said, "Remember Carl von Clausewitz, '*Der Krieg ist eine bloße Fortsetzung der Politik mit anderen Mitteln.*' From our seminar, we know the *polis*, the state, is artifice. War is an instrument for the execution of state policy, the military a tool employed by the state to create and to destroy as deemed necessary. Opera also structures space and time, in this case for four hours and thirty-five minutes. The objective is, however, more immediate and far less destructive . . . unless, of course, the composer was Richard Wagner," he replied, smiling. D3's reference to our conversation under the eyes of *Königin Luise* also brought to mind my discussion with Gabriel Kielerförde while looking at the statue of Richard Wagner in the *Tiergartenviertel*, and George's thoughts on the *Staatsoper Unter den Linden* as a monument to Frederick the Great. Frederick's interest in war and opera did not seem dialectically opposed, rather complementary. Was the military campaign as a work of art justification for the profession of arms, a rationalization of human destructiveness? Could Julius Caesar and King Frederick II of Prussia be considered artists? Perhaps not in the same sense as Georg Friedrich Händel, but there was something to the argument nonetheless. Military campaigns and opera, history for that matter, were all products of human invention, artifice, all architectures designed and executed for purposes political, artistic, and/or academic.

I thought out loud, not certain where my thoughts were leading: "In a sense, all organized human activity creates artifice or architecture, whether opera, operational planning, or architecture itself. What was the term you used at *Luise*, D3, 'operational architecture?' Although in the case of *Giulio Cesare in Eggito*, perhaps 'opera-rational architecture' would be more accurate! But following your argument, D3, war could be considered both architecture and coincidentally anti-architecture, an antithesis in the never-ending human dialectic of creation and destruction."

"'Opera-rational architecture?' That's pretty good, Thomas! The 'human dialectic of creation and destruction'—in music and in military operations, the mastery and coincident destruction of an existing architecture, dare I use the word 'paradigm,' might be considered 'genius,' *zum Beispiel* Julius Caesar and Frederick the Great. Fascinating, isn't it? Our accidental *polis* has been and continues to be the stage for all of the above, architecture, art, opera, and, of course, ongoing contingency planning."

Draining the dregs of our wineglasses, we joined the last few fellow operagoers departing the *Deutsche Oper,* following Professor Schneider to the *Hof* at *Krumme Strasse* 66. Standing under a security light, Dr. Schneider said, "I brought along two photographs which you might find interesting." From his inside sport coat pocket, he took out Bernard Larsson's picture of Friederike Haumann comforting the mortally wounded Benno Ohnesorg lying on the pavement where we were now standing, and John Filo's photograph of Mary Ann Vecchio screaming in anguish over the body of Jeffrey Miller on the pavement of the Kent State University campus. Powerful images individually, the similarity in subject matter and composition was striking—*Pietà* with political consequence. "With *Frau* Anders's help, I was able to find additional information on the shootings and the origins of the student protest movements in both the United States and Germany. I hadn't know, for example, there was a major violent demonstration in front of the *Amerika Haus* on May 9, 1970, to protest the shooting of the students at Kent State and the invasion of Cambodia." Leaving the *Hof,* we walked back to *Bismarckstraße*. Although Albert Speer's streetlights had been removed from the sidewalk in front of the *Deutsche Oper,* they illuminated the blocks on both sides of the former *Ost-West Achse*, on the left forming a "V" pointing toward the the Wall, the Brandenburg Gate, and Berlin V.

D3 had driven, and kindly offered to take Dr. Schneider and me home. "As the Berliners say, '*Null problemo!*' Friedenau is on the way to Dahlem, and I do need to stop by my office this evening." The

Shield was parked in one of the diagonal parking spaces in the center of the broad, eight-lane *Bismarckstraße* just across from the *Deutsche Oper*. Fortunately, the ambient lighting provided by Albert Speer's streetlights from the far side was adequate for Dr. Schneider to admire the Shield of Achilles on the hood. "Remarkable, truly remarkable, Mr. Durchschouer! I didn't bring my copy of the *Iliad* along, but if memory serves, everything's here!" D3 had alluded to, but not mentioned our tour to Burg in search of the Clausewitz grave and innocuously referred to the Mission as "my office." I wasn't certain how much he had told Dr. Schneider about his current assignment and wanted him to be the one to do so. Sitting in the back seat during the Dead Carl Club tour to Burg, I hadn't noticed the Shield was equipped with the same *Blaupunkt* radio and tape deck as Rainer's taxi. After firing up the ThunderJet engine, D3 inserted a prerecorded *Deutsche Grammaphone* cassette into the dashboard. To the opening strains of *Giulio Cesare in Eggito*, he carefully eased the Shield of Achilles out onto the *Bismarckstraße* in the direction of *Ernst Reuter Platz*.

"I wondered about your reference to '*V'adoro, pupille*,' D3, as if you'd heard it before."

"Of course I had Thomas, twice—last night! After Dr. Schneider kindly invited us to accompany him yesterday, I stopped by the post library on *Clay-Allee* to see if they had a recording of the opera, and, much to my surprise, they did." Shaking his helmet-haired head, he said, "Those librarians are simply the best! I played the tape last night in the office while working as classical sound cover. Cleopatra's seductive siren song drew my attention from the paperwork, so I just had to hit rewind and play it again, Sam."

"Bravo, Major Durchschouer!"

"I'm impressed, D3. I knew you were a 'FAO,' but I thought it stood for 'Foreign Area Officer,' not 'Foreign Aria Officer!'"

Händel accompanied us down *Hardenbergstraße*, turning right onto *Joachimsthalerstraße*, passing by the *Kaiser-Wilhelm-Gedächnis-Kirche*, a symphony in Chartres blue, upholding the Cross over West Berlin. It would have been much faster for D3 to drive directly back to Dahlem on the *Automobil-Verkehrs- und Übungsstraße*, the *AVUS*, a racetrack built during Berlin III and now serving Berlin VI as a section of the *Stadtautobahn*. No speed limit, it would have been ideal for the Shield, but I was grateful to D3 for making the detour through Friedenau. When he dropped me off in the *Lothringerstrasse*, I thanked him for the ride home and the champagne reception at the *Deutsche Oper*. "Dr. Schneider, thank you very much for inviting me to accompany you, it was an unforgettable experience, enhanced of course by your good company."

D3 laughed, "See ya next Friday, Thomas. *Dormi bene!*" The Shield slipped around the corner into *Hedwigstraße*. I climbed the staircase to sitar music coming from Gowinda Hemd's apartment, soothing, also structured but differently so than *Giulio Cesare*. I kept meaning to introduce myself to him but hadn't yet found the right opportunity to do so.

Syncopation
June 1983

D3 and I were on the road again the following Friday with Rainer at the wheel of the big yellow taxi. As Laura, Nadja, and Eddie were unable to join us, he suggested we visit one of the oldest West Berlin bars catering to Allied service personnel, not just to Americans but their British and French brothers-in-arms. The *Leierkasten*, advertised as the "hottest jazz club on the continent," "on the island" might have been more accurate, was on *Zossener Straße* in Kreuzberg, one of the six Berlin boroughs making up the American Sector. Although the *Hurdy-Gurdy* featured music from across the jazz spectrum, Dixieland was the house favorite, bringing artists, students, citizens, and soldiers alike in from the capital of the Cold War on Friday nights to hear the Alpha Jazz Band. With a straight face, D3 asked Rainer if there were also Bravo and Charlie Jazz Bands. "No, only Allied Check Point Alpha has its own band," he replied, shaking his head. Following the Accidental *Polis* Seminar, we drove directly to Kreuzberg, stopping for *Kebabs* and cold, half-liter cans of *Berliner Kindl* at a Turkish restaurant near *Görlitzer U-Bahnhof*.

The *Leierkasten*, like so many of the neighborhood bars in West Berlin, was an *Eckkneipe*, a corner bar. A concrete facade replaced the *Stuckwerk* over and on both sides of the entrance to the four-story Berlin-II apartment building. A single circular vent fan blew blue smoke from inside over the heads of customers passing in and out through the metal door. Although no Cerberus stood guard over the entrance outside, just inside the door we were met by a woman in her early forties with bleached blonde hair, dressed in a sleeveless cotton blouse and jean skirt. Although youthful beauty had faded from her face, she was very attractive in a hard way well-suited to her tasks. Tonight, she was clearly in charge, collecting the cover charge for the music. Next to the cash register on the hardwood bar beside her was a sign offering a reduction for invalids, retirees, and students. When my turn came, I said, with as much confidence as I could muster, "*bin Student!*"

"Äääh, a student! You look a little old to be a student to me! Do you have an *Ausweis?*" she asked in accent-free American English. Hedwig? No, but there were certain seductive similarities . . .

"Yes, I do!"

"Can I please see it?"

"Yes, of course!" I took the red laminated *Freie Universität Berlin Studentenausweis* from the blue plastic wallet holding my *BVG* monthly ticket and handed it to her. She looked at the photo, looked at me, and then, with her left hand, gracefully lifted her skirt and wiped my *Ausweis*, face up, on her ass. Fortunately, she was wearing panties. The look on my face must have somehow registered with the woman behind the Friday night facade.

Laughing, she handed my ID back to me, "I'm sorry, Thomas, that wasn't very nice of me now was it? Please let me make it up to you. You are my guest for as long as you'd like to stay at the *Leierkasten* tonight." After D3, Rainer, and I found a small table at the back of the club, next to three uniformed French soldiers sitting on a worn-out SOFA, she brought us three *Faßbier*. "The first round is on me. He," she said pointing at me, "is my guest and drinks for free all evening."

It took a while for D3 and Rainer to stop laughing. "You should have seen the look on your face, Thomas, when she took your ID card and wiped it on her ass. I wish I'd had a camera!" The French soldiers heard us speaking English and, turning to face us, raised their glasses in a friendly toast, "*Aux États Unis!*" Much to their threefold delight, D3 diplomatically returned the courtesy in fluent French, but before they could enter into conversation, the Alpha Jazz Band took the stage. And what a stage it was, black walls covered with a larger-than-life-size painting of a jazz funeral. The ceiling was lost in a cloud of dark blue cigarette smoke, stirred by the vent fan over the entrance door, dark blue rain clouds moving across the night sky. Instead of *Canal, Decatur, Basin* and the streets of the *Vieux Carré*, the street signs depicted in the painting displayed Kreuzberg street names: *Zossener Straße, Gneisenau Straße, Bergmann Straße*. Although still early, the Alpha Jazz Band knew why their Friday afternoon regulars were here. Leading off with "Basin Street Blues," they went directly into the unofficial anthem of New Orleans, "When the Saints Go Marching In." They would play it again and again during the course of the evening, with an ever-increasing number of spirited saints, inspired by *Bier*, shots of *Schnapps*, and *Persico* joining the conga line stumbling through the *Leierkasten*, knocking over chairs and tables. Throughout the *mêlé*, the band members held to their Dixieland roots, improvisation among the front line instruments with the trumpet carrying the melody.

D3 leaned over the table, lowering his head to talk under the music, "It's really too bad Nadja couldn't join us, she would have enjoyed the music and the club. Remember her reference to Lieutenant James Reese

Europe and the 369th Infantry 'Hellfighters' Band at our first seminar session? I listened to 'Memphis Blues' at the AFN Berlin music library afterward and would like to learn more about Black American military musicians. Apparently, I don't know as much about the United States Army as I thought I did!" Nodding in the direction of the French soldiers, he continued, "She might also have enjoyed talking with her *compatriotes*."

When the band took a break, D3 and the French soldiers immediately entered into animated conversation. From what I could observe through the cigarette smoke, and overhear from the cacophony of coincident conversations, there seemed to be American and British soldiers, as well as a room full of regulars, artists, and *Berliner Typen*. Everyone seemed to be talking with everyone, regardless of rank, nationality, or sexual orientation—no sense of hostility in West Berlin's Big Easy tonight, *vat a vundervoll Vorld!* Another round of beer appeared. Rainer leaned over to me and said, "After we finish this one, unless you'd like to stay here longer, I suggest we visit another music club, something quite different, a discotheque popular with Black American GIs. It's actually quite close to where you live, in Friedenau."

"What's it called? Where in Friedenau?"

"*LaBelle*, on *Hauptstraße*."

"I've seen it, Rainer, right next to *Rathaus Friedenau*, in that modern *Neue Sachlichkeit*-style building."

"That's it, Thomas! I thought we might listen to the music for a while, hopefully dance with some American girls, and afterward, maybe I can pick up a fare." D3 was agreeable, so when the Alpha Jazz Band took its next break, we finished our beer and, taking leave of our French Allies with a three part "*au revoir,*" walked toward the front door. As we walked past our blonde *maître d'hôtel*, she looked at me and smiled. "Please come back later if you'd like to my sad little student. Your friends, too, of course. My offer's good until we close. *Tschüßi!*"

Much to D3's delight, the drive from Kreuzberg to Friedenau turned into a round of *Jeopardy* for German military strategists, crossing *Waterloo Ufer*, *Blücherstraße*, and *Gneisenaustraße*. The category turned to German literature when we turned onto *Mehringdamm*, following the route back to Friedenau George and I had taken, when I returned to West Berlin last August, almost a year ago. When we passed Tempelhof Central Airport, Rainer said, "You know, I wouldn't mind going back to the WACS Wings Club again, I haven't been there in a while. Perhaps we could suggest it to the others, a final symposium celebrating the end of the semester and our seminar."

"That's not a bad idea, Rainer," I replied. "I still haven't been there yet. I bet Laura, Nadja, and Eddie would come."

"Approved! I have been there, and it might be fun for those who haven't. Maybe Sophia would join us, too. We could even extend the invitation to Dr. Schneider. After all, what could be more 'West Berlin' than Tempelhof Central Airport, home of the 'Big Lift?'"

Although now evening, it was still early for *LaBelle*. We found a parking place just around the corner from *Hauptstraße* on *Stierstraße*. Like the *Dschungel*, the building housing *LaBelle*, the *Roxy-Palast*, had been built during the *Weimar Republik* in the post-World War I spirit of the New Objectivity. Intentionally devoid of ornamentation, it occupied much of the block, its rectangular lines illuminated by long, rectangular glass block windows, reminding me of the cinder and glass block torpedo factory. Unlike the *Dschungel*, there was no *Türsteher* to intimidate and select. After paying the cover charge, we were admitted *problemlos*. I wondered if Nadja was known here, too. I should have guessed. Many of the tables surrounding the dance floor were already occupied, and much to our surprise, we saw Nadja in the company of a fashionably dressed man sitting with his back to us. They were engaged in conversation, looking through what appeared to be notes and clippings lying on the café table. She looked up and, recognizing us, stood up, calling out, "*Allô!* Thomas, Gerhard, *et* D3, *Quelle supris!* Won't you come join us? This is my American friend, Clarence, from New York, a musician who covers Afro-American music for *Thumpasorus People* magazine. 'E's writing an article on the popularity of Black American music among Germans in those areas where large numbers of American soldiers are stationed. GI's as overseas ambassadors of American popular culture, carrying on in the tradition of Louis Armstrong's "Real Ambassadors." Clarence, these are my friends, Thomas, Rainer, and D3, who also 'appens to be an American soldier. 'E might 'ave some suggestions for you. All three are from the seminar I told you about. What a coincidence to meet you three 'ere tonight!

"*Enchantez*, Clarence," said D3, extending his hand. "We've just come from the *Leierkasten*, where Thomas here had his *Ausweis* polished. Pure Dixieland! 'Memphis Street Blues' and, of course, 'When the Saints Go Marching In.'" Turning to Nadja, he said, "There were three French soldiers sitting next to us on an old SOFA, so I took the opportunity to ask about life in the French Sector. Two of them were from Bayeux in Normandy and seemed genuinely pleased to meet a French-speaking American soldier. With Dixieland in the background and French in the foreground, it seemed more like the French Quarter than the French, I mean the American Sector! There was even a New Orleans jazz funeral painted on the stage. We were just talking about you, Lt. James Reese Europe and 'Memphis Blues.' You would have enjoyed the company of your *compatriots*—and now here you are!"

"Lt. James Europe and the 369th Infantry 'Hellfighters' Band, I must say I'm quite impressed with your knowledge of Black American Music, D3. May I call you D3? In New York and then Paris, throughout France for that matter, their specialty was syncopation, 'ragtime.' When they first arrived in Paris as part of General Pershing's forces in 1918, they played a syncopated arrangement of *la Marseillaise*, which, at first, their French hosts did not recognize as their own national anthem! I was stationed in Germany at Baumholder a decade ago, toward the end of the Vietnam War, and remember the enormous popularity of American music, not just Jazz and Soul, but country and western and rock, much of it no doubt due to AFN. It was a very difficult time for the United States Army, and music provided many of us with a release of sorts. I played trumpet in a small jazz combo, still do. Wherever we went in West Germany, we were warmly received by our German hosts. To be quite honest, as a Black American, I often felt more comfortable in Germany than I did in parts of the United States. I've been thinking about writing a story about the scene ever since and was finally able to convince my editor at *Thumpasorus People* to send me back, at his expense of course. I arrived in Frankfurt two weeks ago, visited clubs there, in Kaiserslautern, Stuttgart, and Munich. From Kaiserslautern, I drove back down to Baumholder for old-times' sake. Berlin is the last stop on the tour before returning to New York next week. Nadja kindly agreed to show me around town. She seems to know just about everybody connected with the Berlin music scene."

"That's for sure! I must confess, Clarence, it was actually Nadja who first brought the 'Hellfighters' Band to my attention. Rainer here kindly offered to introduce me to the West Berlin music scene, and Thomas is along for the ride. On our way here, we passed by the WACS Wings Club, one of the few clubs I've visited. As you no doubt recall from your time at Baumholder, the officers and NCO clubs also offer music on the weekends."

"Oh, yes, we played a number of those clubs, D3. My favorite was the Gettysburg Club at Grafenwöhr, although we were often upstaged, perhaps off-staged would be the better word, by the topless dancers. This time around, the PAOs in Frankfurt and Stuttgart made arrangements for me to visit clubs on post, so I've been able to get a pretty good idea of what's going down on- and off-post. Pointing to the clippings and notes on the table, he said, "This is my take so far, once I've taken a look at Berlin, I'll be good to go."

While D3, Clarence, and Nadja discussed music and the American military presence in Germany, I took the opportunity to look around *LaBelle*. Rainer was right. Many of the customers were Black American women and men. Although fashionably dressed in casual, off-duty civilian clothes, regulation haircuts disclosed their profession. There were also quite a few young German and Turkish women sitting at the tables. *LaBelle* seemed to be a place to meet Americans, a musical interface between the civilian and military populations of West Berlin—Berlin VI, just around the corner from my one elegant Empire room. Rainer walked over to the bar to order drinks, promptly engaging himself in conversation with two attractive young Black women, who appeared to be American soldiers. The DJ pumped up the volume.

"That's Defunkt's 'Thermonuclear Sweat,'" said Nadja, "now we just can't "Avoid the Funk" Thomas, can we?" Before I could answer, she took my hand. "Let's let Clarence and D3 talk shop for a little while—that's the correct expression, 'talk shop,' isn't it?" Rainer and one of the female soldiers he'd met at the bar joined us on the dance floor. The syncopated, repetitive bass beat and the rhythm guitar got almost everybody up to dance—but Defunkt also had something to say.

As we danced, Nadja leaned forward to talk under the music, putting her mouth close to my ear, "Laura and Eddie are 'elping André prepare for a *vernissage* next Tueday. 'E won't be exhibiting any of 'is paintings but some other kind of artwork, something 'e made out of a jacket 'e found in a Kreuzberg *Trödelladen*. Why don't you come, Thomas? I know 'e'd like to see you again, perhaps your artist friend might be there too." After we returned to the table, Nadja took a small green envelope from her purse and handed it to me. "See you Tuesday, Thomas?" Drinks had been served. Rainer returned to our table without the soldier, Melissa, but with her telephone number. "She's here with a girlfriend tonight. Probably a good thing for me because, unfortunately, I should get to work."

"Null problemo, Rainer," said D3. "Clarence and Nadja have work to do here. I'll catch the bus back to the office and drive home from there. I have to be at work early tomorrow morning. Before I go, Nadja, what do you call the kind of music you and Thomas were just dancing to?"

"Ask Clarence, he's the expert, D3!"

Clarence answered, "Why thank you, Nadja, that's quite a compliment coming from you. That's 'funk,' D3, a fusion of rhythm and blues, jazz, and rock. Although the term funk actually dates back to 1910 and Buddy Bolden's tune 'Funky Butt,' the music began to take hold in the late sixties. It's been very influential, not only in Black American music but across the board, rock as well. Joe Bowie's band is, by the way, from my hometown, New York."

"Over the bass line, I can hear trombone, trumpet, and from what little I understand of music, syncopation, but it's quite different from 'Memphis Blues.' I like it too! Wasn't Lt. James Reese Europe also from New York?" Clarence nodded and smiled. "Rainer, thanks very much for the American musical mystery tour, from Dixieland to funk, all right here in West Berlin! Clarence, it was a pleasure to meet you. Have a safe trip back to New York. I'd be very interested in your article, so please send me a copy. Nadja, my special thanks to you for making me look smart in front of Clarence. Take care, Thomas, I'll see you three next Friday."

It was a short walk home for me. I was tired. Once again, there was almost too much to think about, to work through, to fix and develop. Leaving *LaBelle,* I walked down *Hauptstraße,* past *Rathaus Friedenau* to *Breslauer Platz.* Once I'd crossed over *Hauptstraße,* I turned back to look at the tower. The angel on top now seemed to be looking in my direction, holding out her green palm of peace. I turned and walked down *Hedwigstraße.* Laughing out loud, I thought again about the *Wirtin* at the *Leierkasten* and made a mental note never to wash my *Ausweis.* Hedwig wasn't out on patrol. Once again, I climbed the wooden staircase leading up to my one elegant Empire room to the soothing sound of the sitar and the scent of sandalwood. Dropping off my shoulder bag and sport coat in my room, I walked through the *Berliner Zimmer* to the WC. Dr. Kahler was out for the evening.

Although I tried to restrict my nocturnal activity to the weekend, it proved to be impossible. Rainer often came by at night during the week. The event calendar in back of the Berlin biweekly Nadja wrote for ID'd something of interest going on every day, at all hours in West Berlin—Berlin VI: exhibitions, festivals, music, museums, theater, film, lectures, cafés, clubs, and yes, even cabaret. The names of the venues, some familiar, some new, invited and exhausted: *Neue Nationalgalerie, Akademie der Künste, Gemäldegalerie, Im Haus am Lützowplatz, Galerie Rampoldt, Weekend Gallery, galerie no name, Galerie Freiraum, Berlin Philharmonie, Deutsche Oper, Hochschule der Künste, Quartier Latin, Quasimodo,* Flöz, *Jazzkeller, Leierkasten, Musik-Hall, Metropol, Deutschlandhalle, Waldbühne, Hebbeltheater, Komödie, Brücke-Museum, Berlinische Galerie, Haus am Waldsee, Martin-Gropius-Bau, Lot Quartier, Theater des Westens, Renaissance-Theater, Schiller-Theater, Schloßpark-Theater, Freie Volksbühne, Schaubühne, Vaganten-Bühne, Berlin Museum, Bauhaus Archiv , AKI, Filmbühne am Steinplatz, Bali-Kino, filmkunst 66, Kant-Kino, Die Kurbel, Astor-Filmtheater, Arsenal, Lupe 1, Lupe 2, Thalia 1, Thalia 2, Kid, Klick, Cinema, Capitol Dahlem, Broadway, Studio, Ufa-Palast, Delphi-Filmpalast, Gloria-Palast, Cinema Paris, Cinema Bundesallee, Amerika Haus, Off-Kino, Notausgang, Zoo-Palast, Urania, Go-In, SO36, Café Wellenstein , Harlequin, Blue Boy, Fugger Eck, Anderes Ufer, Schöneberger Weltlanterne, Chez Romy Haag, Chez Nous, Die Stachelschwein, Reichskabarett*—exhausting but still not exhaustive.

The threefold purpose of my move from Washington, DC, to Berlin had been archival, archaeological, and academic, "A3." With the assistance of Professor Schneider, I'd mapped out the requirements for *Promotion* to *Doktor der Philosophie* and, with the assistance of Johannes Festzelt, outlined a dissertation proposal built upon the presentation I made to the Accidental *Polis* Seminar. Unfortunately, Professor Schneider was returning to Kent State at the end of the semester in late July and, in any case, would not be able to be my "Doctor Father" as he was a political theorist. He had, however, contacted his colleague Dr. Duana Jourdan at the *Hajo-Holborn-Institut* and given her a copy of the draft of my proposal. I was hoping for a positive response from her and to be able to submit the proposal to the *HHI* at the beginning of *Wintersemester*. There was still much work to be done!

Eddie had just begun his presentation on "John F. Kennedy and West Berlin: A Study in Cold War Mythology" when the door to Seminar Rooms 3–4 suddenly burst open and a motley crew dressed in the regulation *Anarcho* style, carrying a red banner and posters depicting Berlin Senator of the Interior Heinrich Lummer, noisily made their way to the front. Before any of us could react, one of them shouted out, *"Großdemo am Leuschnerdamm! Der Turm wird geräumt!"* They were working their way, room by room through the Villa, looking for students and faculty to help prevent eviction of an apartment building occupied by squatters. Although I hadn't been inside, I'd walked by "the Tower," the surviving wing of a five-story apartment building crowned with parapet and crenels, on one of my walks along the Wall. In addition to spraying red stars and slogans such as, *"WIR SIND DIE ALLERSCHÄRFSTEN!"* and *"Der Turm hat immer Recht!"*[33] on the exposed gray walls, the occupants had also modified the sign mounted on an adjacent wooden pole designating the sector border.

YOU ARE LEAVING
THE fucking
AMERICAN SECTOR
SIE VERLASSEN DEN
AMERIKANISCHEN
KILLER SEKTOR

As we had learned from Sophia, though the *Eirönïa* would likely have been lost on the *Instandbesetzer*, the American Sector, together with the British and French Sectors provided the foundation, the freedom, necessary for their alternative lifestyle. Dr. Schneider welcomed them, introduced himself, and turning to us, asked if any of us would like to participate in

---

33 "We are the hottest!" and "The Tower is Always Right!" Diary of Thomas Vonaechron, Diary Extract, 1983, trans. TV.

the demonstration. None of us did, so in righteous indignation, the group moved on to the next room, slamming the door as they left. Afterward, Eddie continued his presentation with renewed vigor.

After the lascivious late afternoon with Laura in the library on D3-Day, I hadn't seen her outside of Seminar Room 3–4. Outside of Dr. Schneider's Friday afternoon seminar, I spent much of the *Sommersemester* as a researcher back at the *Stadtstaatsarchiv Berlin*, working my way carefully forward and backward through files I'd declassified in Vault Six and arranged at the *Stadtstaatarchiv*, distilling essential elements of information (EEI) on higher education and the study of history in West Berlin. As I didn't want to spend too much of my decreasing resources on photocopies, I took extensive notes from the fiche on five-by-eight notecards. No longer a contract *Stadtstaatsarchiv* employee with a fearful flounder hanging on the wall of a borrowed office, I sat at one of the long wooden library tables in the *Lesesaal* with my fellow researchers. Johannes Festzelt had completed his research and returned to *Restdeutschhland,* the West German mainland. He continued to be very helpful, generously sharing with me the results of his research and writing.

Mannerism
June 1983

There was nothing inside the green envelope Tamara passed to me at *LaBelle.* The envelope was the invitation, the date and time of the *vernissage* stamped on the underside of the flap, "*Galerie Buraq, Dienstag 28. Juni 19 Uhr.*" Nadja's description of André's work made me curious, and I was longing to see Laura outside of the Clay Institute. Perhaps Gabriel Kielerförde would also be there and I could remind him about the promised invitation to his *vernissage* of found objects from the former Danish Legation.

Galerie Buraq, like many of the West Berlin art galleries, had been set up in a former retail store. It was located in Wilmersdorf, in the British Sector. I took the *U-Bahn* to *Adenauer Platz,* then proceeded *per pedes Pilgrimorum* down *Ku'damm* to *Olivaer Platz.* In the distance, I could see the Cross rising above the *Kaiser-Wilhelm-Gedächnis-Kirche.* Turning right, I walked down *Pariser Straße* to *Ludwigskirch Platz.* In the center stood *Sankt Ludwig,* another neo-Gothic redbrick memorial to Berlin II and survivor of the Strategic Air Campaign. Stopping for a moment to read the plaque next to the entrance, I was surprised to discover the patron saint was King Louis IX of France, St. Louis. Turning onto *Emser Straße,* I could see people walking in and out of an open door, *Galerie Buraq.* Walking in, I was once again taken in with the diversity in dress and lifestyle. While many of the younger gallery-goers affected the Berliner chic *beliebt* by Laura and Nadja, jeans, sport coats, open collars, and cocktail dresses were worn by others. As at the *Leierkasten* and in the *foyer* of the *Deutsche Oper*, everyone mixed freely with everyone else in the colorful, animated ambiance of West Berlin. The white walls in the front room were covered with oversized paintings radiating the bright colors of the "New Expressionists," *die Neue Wilden*. Raw, primitive brushstrokes, primary colors, yet familiar—somehow "new" did not seem to apply. The style appeared more manneristic, revisiting themes and techniques from Weimar Berlin—Berlin III. Resurrected and repackaged as a tried and tired art form for the tried and tired inhabitants of West Berlin, it was decorative nonetheless. But I hadn't come for the paintings but for André's work, though I didn't know what or where it was, and for Laura.

"Hi, Thomas, how nice to see you here! Nadja told me you might come. Would you like a glass of *Blanc de Blancs*? It will take the taste out of your mouth, from the paintings I mean!" Laura laughed. Tossing back her unruly blonde hair, she handed me a glass of white wine. She was wearing her signature bright red lipstick, a color complemented by her shoes and the painting on the wall behind her.

"*Hallo*, Laura!" She'd taken me by surprise as I was thinking about her. Unfortunately, I was thirsty from the walk and drank the wine too quickly. Neither mystic nor heated, it was cold, dry, and very refreshing. She took the glass from my hand, turned, and, looking back over her shoulder, walked over to the wooden worktable set up as a bar to refill it. As she walked that way, I noticed she was wearing the same brown, loose-fitting cotton flower-print dress she'd worn in the library and wondered whether it was by intent or coincidence. Better not to wonder, not to think in reverse chronological order, better to observe. André joined me.

"Hello, Thomas, good to see you again! I'm grateful to Nadja for inviting you—she's coming later with Clarence. This is not the exhibition I told you about when we first met at the *Dschungel*. That will be later, unfortunately much later, at the Pictures of Chairman Mao Gallery on *Lützowplatz*. You'll receive an invitation. I'm exhibiting just one object here tonight, though I'm not certain if it's as a favor to or from the owner. What do you think of it? Have you seen or heard my *Audiocoat* yet?"

"Hello, André, it's good to see you too! I haven't yet, in fact I was looking for your work when Laura surprised me with a glass of wine."

"*Bien*, Thomas! When we first met, I promised to get you drunk on *Blanc de Blancs* and am happy to hear Laura's already taking care of you. May I show you my work? It's in the next room. Honestly, I'd be very interested in your reaction. Whether or not they've ever told you, Laura and Nadja seem to value your opinion. Take it as a compliment, Thomas, believe me!" André led me to a farther room, where there were fewer paintings and more exposed white walls reflecting the bright interior ceiling lighting. We were beneath the light and the music of the farther room, familiar music. A white rectangular box stood on end in the center of the room, supporting a chrome valet stand. A tweed sport coat with patched elbows almost identical to the one I was wearing hung on the stand. Four small speakers had been carefully sewn on the front of the jacket, one on each lapel and pocket flap. They were connected inside the sport coat with wiring running down and out the left sleeve, plugged into to a *Sternrecorder R 4100* cassette tape player, also sitting on top of the white box. Next to the cassette deck, there was a jumble of prerecorded cassettes, "Heaven 17," "Funkadelic," the "Preservation Hall Jazz Band," "Lily Berlin," "Paula Lead," "*Fehlfarben*," "*Deutsch- Amerikanische Freundschaft*," "*Bandsalat,*" "*Mahler. Zemlinsky. Lieder,*" even the very same *Deutsche Grammaphone* tape-recording of *Giulio Cesare* D3 had inserted into the *Blaupunkt*. There were also a few self-recorded cassettes. One was playing. I recognized both the pianist and the female vocalist singing the refrain of Steely Dan's "Home at Last."

"André, is that Pam Bricker with John Malachi accompanying her on piano?"

"Why, yes it is! Thomas, you continually surprise me. She's a friend from Washington. I recorded her live when I went back to Washington for a week last August, singing in the Napoleon House on King Street in Alexandria. It was early afternoon and still empty. Do you know her, too? We seem to have a lot of friends in common. Apropos 'friends in common,' here's Gabriel!"

"Hallo, André! *Ach*, together with my fellow *Tiergartenviertel* archaeologist, how nice to see you again, Thomas, isn't it? Your name is on the invitation list I sent to the Danish Embassy for my *vernissage*. I didn't realize you two know each other."

"And I didn't realize you two knew each other either, Gabriel! Laura introduced us." She joined us as we talked, glasses of wine in her hands, one of which she placed gently into mine.

"Hi, Gabriel! Thomas told us about your meeting in the Tiergarten. *Berlin ist doch ein Dorf, nicht wahr?* How nice we could all meet here tonight. Nadja's coming too, later with Clarence, a journalist friend from New York. Do you have a date for your exhibition yet?"

"Sometime this fall, after the summer holidays. The date is up to the Danish Embassy and, of course, the *Berliner Galerie*. I'd like to reach as many people as possible, not just artists but educators, historians, and particularly politicians. The objects have been selected and arranged.

The draft of the catalog is almost finished, I hope to send it off to the printer's by the end of this month. Once the funds for the reception have been approved by the Danish Embassy in Bonn and coordinated with the *Berliner Galerie*, they'll set the date and send out the invitations."

"What about your group exhibition, André?" Gabriel asked. "Your *Audiocoat* is interesting, very much in the pataphysical spirit of Alfred Jarry. What did he say? 'Each hero brings his décor with him,' but I hope it hasn't taken you away from painting."

"No, no, Gabriel, my paintings for the exhibition are finished, have been for some time. Unfortunately, several of my colleagues are not yet ready, and regretfully, we're not as far along with the organization as you are. It probably won't be ready until next spring. Laura will be leaving for a year in Washington, DC, in August, and I'm returning with her. As you know, I hadn't intended to stay so long in West Berlin but," André turned to look at Laura and smiled, "I'm very glad I did. If my *compatriotes* are ready by spring, I'll return for the exhibition. In the meantime, I want to work on some new paintings in Washington. Perhaps Franz Bader would be interested in mounting a show of Berlin-inspired work."

Laura was relocating to Washington, DC, from West Berlin to study American music and cinema, exactly one year after I moved from Washington, DC, to West Berlin to study the HistoriCity on-site. As André and Gabriel discussed the West Berlin art scene, I finished my second glass of *Blanc de Blancs*, which was having the desired effect. My eyes kept returning from the faces around me to the bottom button of Laura's brown, loose-fitting, flower-print dress. I caught myself, and when I looked up, Laura was smiling a Tom Wesselmann smile at me. Taking the empty glass from my hand, she said, "*Ich komm' gleich wieder*" and walked back to the front room. Other artists joined us, drawing André and Gabriel into conversation. I decided to take the opportunity to look at the paintings. As I excused myself, Laura returned, handing me another glass of cold *Blanc de Blancs*.

Walking back into the front room from the farther room, I sat down on a white wooden workbench set back from the wall. The large paintings were hung closely together. Although Expressionist antecedents were clearly evident in subject matter and color, the carelessness with which the paintings had been executed gave them a lightness, a playfulness, redeeming them from the calculated intent of the originals hanging in the *Neue Nationalgalerie*. The paintings were fresh, *frech*, and fun. I liked them.

"Are you from Washington? Are you also a painter? I overheard your conversation with André." There was a middle-aged man seated next to me on the bench, unshaven, short, dark hair with a receding hairline. He wore a white-collared dress shirt with a black, plastic bow tie, blue bib overalls, and worn out tennis shoes. Had it not been for the bib overalls and tennis shoes, he might have been a tired West German businessman out to see *Berlin bei Nacht*. He looked directly at me, his dark brown eyes and facial expression sincere, waiting for my answer.

"I am from Washington, but I'm not a painter. I'm a kind of historian, a student at the *FU*, a friend of Laura's, André's girlfriend. Thomas Vonaechron." I extended my hand. "Are these your paintings?"

He shook my hand. "François Fontane. Ah, I see, a friend of Laura's, but not of André's. Very interesting! No, no, I'm not a painter either, I'm an actor." He shook my hand. "Although my first name is also French, I come from an old Berlin Huguenot family. I'm not exactly a friend of André's either. Let's say rather, I'm an acquaintance of André's, *ein Bekannter*. He sometimes paints scenery for our productions. Though I've seen her several times at the theater and recognized her here tonight, I haven't met Laura. She's a very attractive young woman. Maybe it's better you're not a friend of André's. A 'kind of historian,' that sounds kind of interesting. We are staging a kind of historical trilogy at the *Saubühne* that just might interest you."

I wanted to correct his impression about my relationship to Laura—or was his impression correct?—but the *Blanc de Blancs* and the name of the theater held my attention. "The *Schaubühne*. I your production of 'Orestie.' It was so thought-provoking I'm still thinking about it! I'm sorry I didn't recognize you. Did you play Orestes?"

"No, No, not the *Schaubühne*, the *Saubühne, the 'Sow-Stage'* on *Klausner Platz*. No, I did not play Orestes at the *Schaubühne*, but I do play a king, King Ubu at the *Saubühne*. Do you know Alfred Jarry's *Ubu Roi?*" He continued before I could answer, "It should be obligatory viewing for all kinds of historians, political scientists, and for that matter, politicians too. What is your name again please?"

"Thomas, Thomas Vonaechron." Taking a notepad from the bib pocket of his overalls, he wrote down my name as I spelled it out for him.

"Was it originally 'Von Aechron?'"

"Funny you should ask, the secretary at the *Akademisches Auslandsamt* of the university pronounced it just that way."

"Hmmm. In any case, there will be complementary tickets for you at the box office. Here's my card. *Teil* 0 is this Thursday evening, the day after tomorrow, at 8:30, *Teil* 00 Friday at 8:30, and *Teil* 000 on Saturday, also at 8:30."

I'd planned on working through the rest of the week to make up for the time spent at the *vernissage* but found myself unable to decline his kind invitation. "Thank you very much, François, I'll be there!"

"Then I'll leave you alone with your beautiful blonde, Thomas von

Aechron. *Tschüßi!*" He stood up and walked out the door onto *Emser Straße*. The *Blanc de Blancs* gave our brief conversation a distant, dreamlike quality. I had just returned my attention to the large painting hanging on the wall in front of me when I heard Nadja's voice.

"'*Allo*, Thomas, my special friend! I'm so glad you 'ave decided to come after all, I was afraid you wouldn't! 'Aave you seen Laura and André?

"Hi, Nadja. Hello, Clarence, good to see you again! Laura and André are in the next room looking at, or should I say listening to, his *Audiocoat*, which you two might enjoy too, a kind of wearable West Berlin boom box. There's even a jazz tape from Washington, DC. Clarence, do you know the jazz pianist John Malachi?"

"Yes, I do, Thomas, truly one of our great jazz pianists!"

"I decided to sit here for a while, digest the paintings, and drink the *Blanc de Blancs* Laura keeps bringing me."

"Ah, *pauvre* Thomas, wine is a poor substitute for love! It must be very difficult for you to be in love with someone who likes you but does not love you. Well, maybe we'll 'ave the chance to dance out your afflictions again later tonight. Although it's not really a GI 'angout, Clarence wants to see the *Dschungel.* We'll say 'ello to the others, listen to André's work, and see you later." After they left, I emptied my glass and turned my attention back to the nude portrait of a blonde woman in red heels before me, suddenly eclipsed by a brown flower print dress. Leaning forward, I kissed the button in front of me. Laura laughed, took a step backward, and, taking my glass from my hand, handed me another.

"Thank you very much, *Liebe* Laura, but this will have to be my last glass tonight. Please tell André you have fulfilled his promise. I'm drunk!"

"I wondered where you'd gone, Thomas. Nadja told me you were in here. Too much gallery talk? We're planning to eat nearby afterward, then go to the *Dschungel* or the Café Swing on *Nollendorfplatz*, you remember. Wouldn't you like to join us?"

"I would Laura, but I must return home and get some sleep. I'm tired and still have quite a bit of work to do yet on my dissertation proposal. To be honest, I'm not certain I'd survive another night of dancing in the *Dschungel.* Hopefully, we'll have another chance to dance at the Café Swing before you leave for Washington."

"*Schade*, well, goodnight then, Thomas. Sleep well!" Laura bent down and, placing her hands on my shoulders, kissed me briefly on the mouth. Before she stood up, she bent forward and unbuttoned the bottom button on her dress, smiling at me as she did so. "It's hot in here, just like it was in the library," she said as she turned and walked back into the farther room.

After she disappeared, I set my glass down and took the *Falkplan* from my shoulder bag. Hoping to walk off the *Blanc de Blancs* along the way, I charted my route back to *Lothringerstrasse*. Rather than follow the busy *Bundesallee* to *Friedrich-Wilhelm-Platz*, I decided to walk along *Prinzregentenstraße*, which became *Handjerystraße*, sad site of the airlift accident in Friedenau. A left turn at *René-Sintenis-Platz* would take me to *Hauptstraße*, *Hedwigstraße*, and home at last to my one elegant Empire room.

I slept through the night and much of the following day. There was no time left to work on the dissertation proposal. A personal operational architecture for West Berlin, Berlin VI, a zone composed of points and lines, was becoming my work-in-progress. Less than forty-eight hours after receiving the royal summons from King Ubu, I found myself back in the British Sector, in a residential neighborhood in Charlottenburg, looking up at a five-story *Gründerzeit* apartment building. As was sadly the case with many prewar Berlin buildings, all stucco on the facade that might have survived the fall of Berlin IV had been stripped away on orders of West Berlin's director of city planning. Although the modernized, Schwedler-ized exterior was now covered with neutral gray plaster ("*Did you think it was in the white or gray stone? or the lines of the arches and cornices?*"), the arched doorway, balconies, and step gable still recalled Berlin II in Berlin VI. I double-checked the address on the *carte de visite* François Fontane had given me at the *Gallerie Buraq*. It was correct. Then I noticed a sign directing me through the arched entrance onto the *Hof.* There I found a second sign, directing me through a rectangular doorway onto the second *Hinterhof,* where I discovered what appeared to be a former factory building. Later, I learned timely *Instandbesetzung* by activist actors, assisted by a sculptor, had saved the building from demolition. Fellow theatergoers were standing in front of the entrance door, over which hung a large black-and-white triptych depicting François as King Ubu suspended on bicycle tire tubes, the center of adoration. When I gave my name, I received an envelope marked "Thomas von Aechron" containing tickets for all three performances and joined the audience. Making our way slowly up the staircase to the fourth floor, we entered a large, darkened room lined with white wooden benches, just like the one I'd unknowingly joined King Ubu on two days previously at the *Galerie Buraq*. The former factory hall was filled, the last few theatergoers still looking for *place* when *Mère* and *Père* Ubu seized the stage with the legendary "*Pscheisse,*" translated into German from the French "*Merdre,*" which brought the audience in the *Salle du Nouveau Théâtre* in Paris to its feet on December 10, 1896.

As the *mêlée* unfolded before us, Thursday evening became Friday evening, which became Saturday evening, as *Teil 00* and *Teil 000* followed

Teil 0. With the exception of Friday's Accidenta*l Polis* Seminar, I had no clear recollection of the time spent in between. More murderous and brazen than Lady Macbeth, *Mère* Ubu inspired her husband to regicide. Ghosts far outnumbering the unfortunate Claudius and Banquo implored the wronged Prince Boggerlas to revenge the deaths of his father, King Wenceslas, and mother, Queen Rosamund. *Père* Ubu, as a consequence of his crimes now holding more titles than Macbeth, initially locked his conscience in a chest, then forced it down the toilet. He was nonetheless pursued by a bear, which enters rather than exits, but unlike Antigonus, *Père* Ubu emerged victorious. A winner's tale. A tempest took *Mère* and *Père* Ubu, together with their few surviving supporters, past the haunted ramparts of Castle Elsinore, along the coast of northern Germany to France, foreshadowing a future in which not just folly, but avarice and stupidity, might hold sway in a declining West.

After the applause died down following the conclusion of part 000 and the audience began to leave the theater, King Ubu, who had apparently seen me sitting on the white bench, jumped down from the stage and walked over. Standing up, I extended my hand, "Bravo, François."

"Thomas, thank you very much for coming, for all three nights no less! You no doubt had more important things to do, to study, write, or even to make history. But let me ask you, as a 'kind of a historian,' what did you think? Was there enough history for you? Rereading '*Ubu enchaîné*' in preparation for this performance, I came across a citation which the muse of history moved me to write down for you." Taking a piece of folded paper from the front pocket of his bib overalls, he handed it to me. "*Voila!*" Unfolding it carefully, I read, "*Cornegidouille! nous n'aurons point tout demoli si nous ne démolissons même les ruines! Or je n'y vois d'autre moyen que d'en équilibrer de beaux édifices bien ordonnés.*"

"Thank you very much, François, but I'm not certain if I understand …"

"Let me try to translate it for you, Thomas, '*Cornegidouille!*' Now that's untranslatable, something like 'silly horn.' 'We will not have demolished everything, if we don't demolish the ruins! But I see no other way to demolish the ruins than by using them to construct many beautiful, well-designed buildings!'"

Yes, this was definitely meant for me. Thank you, François, thank you very much, for the invitation, too. I enjoyed the production very much, as much as I did the *Orestie*, and believe me, I won't ever confuse the *Saubühne* with the *Schaubühne* again! I read some Shakespeares in high school, and Shattuck's book on Alfred Jarry as an undergraduate. Gabriel surprised me when he quoted Jarry in conversation with André at the *Galerie Buraq* Tuesday evening—was it only Tuesday evening? It seems so long ago! I enjoyed Jarry's wordplay. But beneath the playful obscenity, there seems to be something darker, some terrible truth about human nature revealed through politics and history. Yes, I'm convinced Clio staged the *Scheißtrilogie* and put these words into your hands for me."

"Gabriel, Gabriel Kielerförde the artist, quoted Alfred Jarry in conversation?"

"Yes, referring to André's *Audiocoat*. He said 'each hero brings his own décor with him.'"

"Now that's an interesting coincidence, isn't it, Thomas, considering we both chose the same bench to sit on Tuesday evening? It must have had something to do with that big blonde hanging on the wall dressed only in her bright red lipstick and shoes. Unfortunately, the lovely Laura is not here this evening. As a kind of consolation, I would be very pleased to introduce you to my stage wife *Mère* Ubu, Victorine, at the cast party downstairs. I told her about our meeting at *Galerie Buraq* last Tuesday. She is quite interested in meeting a 'kind of historian.' I had quite forgotten she studied *Geschichte* and *Theaterwissenschaft*. Carefully refolding the piece of paper, I placed it in my shoulder bag, following King Ubu to my audience with Queen Ubu one floor below.

The queen was costumed in a floor-length, fringed, white vest worn open over a long-sleeved, red velvet shirtwaist and extremely short, red satin running shorts. Black garters ran from under her satin shorts into the funnel tops of her thigh-high, soft leather boots. Her long, luxuriant red hair reminded me of my former fellow NARSian and the underground encounter in the wastebasket of the nation all those Saturdays ago. Although still in costume, Victorine the professional actress was already out of character. After spending the past three evenings with *Mère* Ubu, I had a more difficult time making the transition. Stammering out, "Your most obedient servant, madam," I managed to congratulate her on the performance and tried to regain composure when François introduced me to her.

Laughing, she replied "And I am yours, *Herr* von Aechron," she replied, unsettling me once again. Fortunately, she continued, "So you're the 'kind of historian' François told me about. Thank you very much for taking the time to spend the past three nights with us in this kind of theater. I hope we didn't take too much valuable time away from your studies. While at the university, I studied both contemporary history and *Theaterwissenschaft*— what would that be in English now, 'theater science?' No, 'drama' would probably be the better translation. Although many of my friends couldn't understand why, I found the two subjects complementary, ingrown. There's much theater in history—not just in the history of Poland, in German history as well. There's much history in theater, and not just in Shakespeare. Perhaps because of my interest, history demanded almost as much of my time as drama. What is your particular area of interest, *Herr* von Aechron?

"The history of Berlin. Unfortunately, or fortunately as the case may be, it seems to be too big of a topic. I have to break down . . . break it down, somehow. Although I came to West Berlin to work at the *Stadtstaatsarchiv Berlin* and study contemporary history at the *FU*, I seem to be following Clio, the muse of history, around town instead. I've come to think of Berlin as her city, as the HistoriCity. She has led me here to you, to the *Saubühne* I mean, of course, over the past three days for a purpose. François provided written evidence this evening, and you have just confirmed my suspicions."

"Why thank you, *Herr* von Aechron, it's quite a compliment to be taken as a messenger of the muses, Clio and hopefully Thalia too. I wonder what I might offer you in return, but unfortunately, I must leave you now." Extending her hand, she continued, "I am very pleased to have met you and sincerely hope to see you again here at the *Saubühne* or perhaps somewhere else in West Berlin. Maybe I'll be where Clio next leads you. *Berlin ist ein Dorf, nicht wahr?* So you won't forget me, and more importantly Alfred Jarry's *Ubu*, please allow me to take my leave from you as *Mère* Ubu. She suddenly turned her back to me, her long red hair brushing my face and taking a step in the opposite direction, placed her thumbs in the waistband of her running shorts and pulled them down, bending forward as she did so to thrust her bared buttocks at me. She was wearing a black lace garter belt under her red satin running shorts but no panties—apparently she hadn't been during *Teil 000*. She pulled her running shorts up quickly and, without looking back, disappeared into the cast party. Exclaiming "*aber* Victorine," François laughed, shook my hand warmly, shrugged his shoulders in a feigned gesture of helplessness, and followed her. Taking a glass of cold white wine from the nearby buffet table, I drained it and made my way down the staircase, through the remaining theatergoers, across the *Hinterhof* and the *Hof* to *Klausener Platz*.

Determined to be in bed by midnight, I walked back to *U*(bu)*-Bahnhof Sophie-Charlotte-Platz* for the short ride on the soon-to-be-legendary *Linie 1* to *Bahnhof Zoo*. Accompanied by the preterit chorus of "*Ey Alter, haste 'ne Mark für mich?*" I walked to the *Linie 9* platform and the trip back to *Friedrich-Wilhelm-Platz*, thinking about what I'd learned in the *Saubühne* theater about history. *Mère* Ubu's parting gesture had put me back in the play. The subway platform provided a gratuitous example of the *Ubumensch* in action in West Berlin. In a fit of senseless Luddite violence, someone had smashed one of the new *BVG* ticket machines, spraying "*Die Welt ist alles was der Abfall ist*" across the top in red paint, an aphorism that could have been lifted directly from the *Saubühne* production. In my contemplation of the sad ruins of this trashed technology, I was joined by a handsome man of about my age, impeccably dressed in a dark suit and white shirt, necktie, rich and modest, with dark brown hair and a thoughtful expression on his face. He looked very much like a diplomat. Turning to face me, he smiled, shook his head, and said, "*Die Leiden des jungen Entwerters!*" He was still standing there, smiling and shaking his head when *Linie 9* arrived to return me to my one elegant Empire room.

As I turned the corner from *Hedwigstraße* into *Lothringerstrasse*, Rainer pulled up in front of my apartment building. Turning off the "(American Literature)" sign on the top of his taxi, he rolled down the window. "Hi, Thomas, *was für ein* 'Rainer' *Zufall!* Reiner *Zufall*, get it? 'Yuck, yuck, yuck,' as D3 would say! It's been a long day *unterwegs*, I'm *fertig* and thought I might go for a midnight sauna at *Baan Vietnamienne* before going home. Would you like to join me?" Although too tired to taxi around West Berlin, mentally preparing a polite but firm refusal to do so, a midnight sauna did sound inviting. A midnight sauna would help me to distance myself from the *Scheißtrilogie* and sleep well. Although I'd once again lost a weekend of work, perhaps I'd learned something about history, about Clio's *Handwerk*. "We will not have demolished everything, if we don't demolish the ruins! But I see no other way to demolish the ruins than by using them to construct many beautiful, properly proportioned buildings!" I walked around the big yellow taxi, opened the door, and took my place in the passenger seat. The heavy curtains in Govinda Hemd's front window opened briefly as Rainer pulled away from the curb and drove down *Lothringerstrasse*, turning right onto *Hauptstraße*. Although I wanted to tell Rainer about the play and *Mère* Ubu's parting gesture, I was too tired to do so. So I listened.

"The *Baan Vietnamienne* is directly ahead on *Potsdamer Straße*, just before *Potsdamer Brücke*." As we approached the *Bülowstraße* intersection, pedestrian traffic on the sidewalk began to pick up. Less elegant coworkers of the collegiates standing before the columns of the Brandenburg Gate stood on the stairs leading up to the columned entrance of the decrepit prewar *Hotel Potsdam Spielcasino—ein Stundenhotel*, soliciting passersby. *Schräg gegenüber,* on the far side of the intersection, the door of the *Luna Günter* suddenly swung open as the bartender escorted a long-haired, wild-eyed patron dressed in a worn-out leather *Trachtenjanker* out to the sidewalk. Returning to the bar, the *Wirt* brought out a parrot in a large golden cage, which, in an abrupt change of manner, he gently handed to the expellee. When the light changed, Rainer turned into the *Pohlstraße*, parking the taxi in front of yet another *Schwedler*-ized prewar apartment building. We walked back to *Potsdamer Straße*, turning left in the direction of the bridge over the *Landwehrkanal*.

On the far side of the bridge over the canal, the *National Galerie* occupied the site of Albert Speer's *Haus des Fremdenvehrkers*. There were fewer people on the street here. Postwar poured-concrete construction dominated this side of *Potsdamer Straße*, a wall of faceless buildings, foreboding, *verlassen, verloren, vergänglich* in the sparse street lighting. A disheveled businessman walked toward us from the direction of the *Landwehrkanal*, carrying a pair of shoes in his right hand. His clothing was wet, as if he'd been swimming. He held his shoes up to the streetlight so we could see them, then spoke directly to Rainer in a hushed tone.

Rainer replied "*'tut mir Leid mein Herr, vielleicht am Bahnhof Zoo . . .*" Smiling in reply, the soaked seagull from the Spree continued *per pedes* up *Potsdamer Straße* in his wet stockinged feet.

"He's looking for a pair of shoes, Thomas, size 34. Maybe he'll find what he's looking for at *Bahnhof Zoo!* Rainer rang the bell of the *Baan Vietnamienne*. A buzzer responded immediately. Opening an aluminum door with frosted-glass panes, we crossed a dark hallway to the elevator on the far side. The stainless steel doors opened as we approached. After they closed behind us, Rainer pushed the button for the *Dachterrasse*. The *Baan Vietnamienne* was on the roof. When the stainless steel doors opened again, we walked out of the midnight darkness of Cold War West Berlin into the brightly lit, white lobby of the *Hôtel Continental* in colonial Saigon. The large reception room was structurally broken up through archways and columns, teakwood chairs carefully arranged around small circular tables providing a sense of intimacy. A few were centers of quiet, late-night conversation. In spite of the late *bzw.* early hour, we were cordially greeted by our graceful Vietnamese hostess, dressed in the traditional *áo dài*. Recognizing Rainer as a regular, she took his hand in hers and said, "*Ah Herr* Wallfahrt, *wie schön daß Sie wieder bei uns sind. Sie haben sogar einen Freund mitgebracht.*"[34] Extending her hand to me, she said "*Enchanté.*" She handed each of us a white plastic bracelet with a golden key attached, a heavy white cotton bath towel, and led us to the wood-paneled dressing room. "In addition to the sauna, there is also a Turkish bath, a steam room, and a remarkable swimming pool," Rainer said. After we'd undressed and taken the prescribed warm shower, we picked up our towels and walked through the dressing room to the sauna. We were followed by the *Saunameister* who, after closing the door, poured a pine-scented *Aufguß* out over the hot rocks. Steam rose to the wood-paneled ceiling. While most women and men sat silently on towels spread out upon the wooden benches with eyes closed, a few patrons were engaged in quiet conversation.

---

34 "Ah, Mr. Wallfahrt, how nice to have you with us again. You have even brought a friend along with you." Diary of Thomas Vonaechron, Diary Extract, 1983, trans. TV.

After sitting down on one of the lower benches, Rainer turned to me and said softly, "If you haven't been to the sauna in a while, you shouldn't stay in too long, Thomas, ten minutes at most. I'll probably stay somewhat longer, so let's meet in the pool for a drink. Yes, in the pool for a drink. You'll see what I mean."

Although the ten minutes seemed to pass quickly, light-headed and somewhat disoriented, I knew I'd had enough. Shutting the door carefully behind me, I decided against a cold shower, following the signs to the swimming pool instead. Rainer was right, it was remarkable! Instead of a courtyard, the Continental Shelf, the bar, opened out onto an Olympic-size pool illuminated by soothing, underwater blue lighting shimmering off the white ceiling. Patrons relaxing in the pool could walk or swim to the bar running the entire width of one end of the pool. Some were standing waist-high in water, drinking at the bar, others sitting on blue-tiled barstools just below its surface. Guests dressed in street clothes sat directly across from the nude guests on the far side, looking out over the pool. At the other end, bathers could swim under the plate glass window running the width of the pool to an outdoor terrace where ornamental iron chairs and chaise lounges were grouped around café tables. Folding my towel, I laid it down on a chair near the pool. Walking slowly down the stairs into the water, I slipped below the surface and swam out under the glass wall. Climbing the stairs leading up from the pool to the outdoor terrace, I found myself looking back down *Potsdamer Straße* toward Schöneberg and Friedenau, out over West Berlin. Once I reached the terrace, I turned around and looked up *Potsdamer Straße* toward *Potsdamer Platz* and East Berlin. I was alone. With steam rising from my body into the cool night air, I spread my legs to the width of my shoulders and raised my arms, parodying *le proporzioni del corpo umano secondo Vitruvio*. Although my intent was *Ubuesque*, I felt something different, a kind of corporal harmony with West Berlin—Berlin VI—a sense of being in time, proportional to the accidental *polis*. Suddenly, Rainer was standing next to me. I hadn't heard him disturb the surface of the water. "Are you alright, Thomas? You seem distant, distracted, tired." Lowering my arms, I turned to face him. "I'm fine Rainer, just fine. Magnificent, isn't it? Let's have a *Weizenbier* at the bar. I believe I might have seen Sir Hugh Carlton Greene sitting on the other side, drinking with his brother, Henry."

Departures
July 1983

Dr. Schneider agreed with Rainer's suggestion, strongly supported and "approved" by D3, that we hold the final meeting of the Accidental *Polis* Seminar at the WACS Wings Club in Tempelhof Central Airport. It was coincidentally a farewell party for Professor Schneider, who had completed his exchange year at the *Lucius-D.-Clay-Institut,* and was leaving West Berlin to return to the Western Reserve. Among many other things, I was very grateful to him for introducing me to Professor Duana Jourdan at the *Hajo-Holborn-Institut.* After reviewing the draft proposal I'd prepared, she agreed to accept me as a *Doktorand.* With her encouragement and the assistance of both professors, I'd been able to complete my dissertation proposal and submit it the *HHI* for approval.

A native of Nebraska, Dr. Duana Jourdan had come to the *Freie Universität Berlin* from the *Université de Paris* in the early seventies. Although she'd left Paris several years before Nadja began her studies, Nadja knew of her by reputation. In addition to writing a dissertation on the renovation of Paris under Emperor Napoleon III's prefect of the Seine, Georges-Eugène-Haussmann, she had personally tested Haussmann's architecture of crowd control in May 1968. By coincidence, she had also spent a year teaching at Georgetown University. Dr. Schneider met her shortly after, during an interdisciplinary conference on student revolt. She was a tall, lanky, broad-shouldered, pendulous-breasted woman in her early forties with an air of sovereignty and sensuality. I was very pleased to have her as my *Doktormutter.*

On the way back from our meeting with Professor Jourdan, Dr. Schneider and I had finally stopped by the *Museum für Indische Kunst,* directly across *Boxerstraße* from the *Lucius-D.-Clay-Institut.* "I've been meaning to show this truly remarkable figure to you since we first met. Now I'll leave it with you, here in the museum of course, as a parting gift." He led me through the dark rooms of the museum complex, which also housed the *Museum für Ostasiatische Kunst.* Spotlighted in a glass case, between the goddesses Ganga and Krishna, was a terra-cotta statue of a seated Buddha, right hand raised, palm outward, the left hand, with upturned palm, resting in the lap. It was Govinda, Govinda from the fifth century AD. Facial expression, his smile, the pierced ears—all very familiar to me from our meeting on the *City of Berlin* a year earlier!

"Why, it's Govinda, remarkable! When we parted at Tempelhof last August, he asked me to keep him informed of my progress and said, 'If you are busy and don't have time to write to me, please don't worry, I'll be watching from across the street.' I thought he meant to say 'from across the sea' or that perhaps I had misunderstood him. Maybe not."

Smiling in reply, Dr. Schneider said, "I've kept him up to date on your progress, even sent him a copy of your dissertation proposal. Perhaps he might be able to offer you something more than just subject matter expertise. In any case, or perhaps I should say in this glass case, you now know where to find him . . . in terra-cotta across the street from the Clay Institute! Almost appropriate, *nicht wahr?*" As we wound our way back through the museum to the *Boxerstraße* exit, I tried to make a mental map of the location of the glass case.

The party at the WACS Wings Club was also a farewell for Laura, who would shortly depart West Berlin with André for her direct exchange year in Washington, DC. D3 had arranged for early admission to the club and was even able to reserve a private room just off the dance floor for our use. He'd been equally successful in arranging for a briefing at the *Kommandatura* and for a screening of *A Foreign Affair* at the Outpost Cinema, attended by members of the American and Allied Military communities. Laura had had a full house for her insightful and entertaining examination of the female lead characters, Phoebe Frost and Erika von Schlütow. She and the other members of Accidental *Polis* Seminar, with the exception of D3, were surprised when asked to stand for "The Star Spangled Banner" before the screening of the film. Although the Outpost was full, Marlene Dietrich, who played Erika von Schlütow, seemed to be singing Friedrich Hollaender's "In the Ruins of Berlin" just for me.

D3, Rainer, Nadja, Laura, Sophia, Eddie, Dr. Schneider, and I now gathered around our makeshift conference table in the WACS Wings Club in the same seating order as in Seminar Rooms 3–4. The departures of Dr. Schneider and Laura and the end of the Accidental *Polis* Seminar made, at least at first, for a subdued atmosphere, as if a very long-running opera or play cycle in which we had all participated was now ending. In the WACS Wings Club, we concluded West Berlin, Berlin VI according to my *Dörpfeld'sche* divisions, did indeed meet the classical definition of *polis*, notwithstanding its accidental character. Through our weekly, four-month long consideration of "The Legal Status of the Allies in West Berlin"; "Justice in West Berlin"; "Warfare, the Warrior and the Security of the Polis in Plato's *Republic* and West Berlin"; "Crazy In and About Berlin: Literature of the Early Cold War"; "Music and Political Stability in West Berlin"; "Cinematic Shadows on the Wall in West Berlin"; "*Wie war es eigentlich Gewesen?* Teaching History in West Berlin's *Hochschulen*"; and "The Myth of John F. Kennedy in the Mythology of West Berlin," we also had, perhaps more significantly, become increasingly conscious of our personal relationships with the *polis* in which we'd chosen to live. This may have been, after all, Plato's intent—President Kennedy's too. Our seminar ended as a symposium, D3 once again reminding us that Book I of *The Laws* contains a discussion of drinking parties as an educational device!" "I've come to the conclusion," he said, "that West Berlin is a kind of magic island, with the magic supplied by the military!" Enlightened by academia and alcohol, we acknowledged we too were *erastai*, "lovers of the city," even though our *polis* was West Berlin, not Pericles's Athens, and thanked Professor Schneider for this opportunity to discover more about our city and ourselves with him.

My academic responsibilities did not end with the summer semester. On the contrary, once my proposal had been approved by the *Hajo-Holborn-Institut*, I could finally begin researching and writing my dissertation. Unfortunately, I was becoming increasingly entangled in my ever-expanding operational architecture for West Berlin—Berlin VI. Gabriel Kielerförde and André Keler had, perhaps unintentionally, provided me with entrée into the West Berlin art scene. With intent, Nadja provided entrée into the multicultural, multifaceted West Berlin music scene until she returned to Paris to prepare to join Laura and André in "Chocolate City."

Architecture and art were in the *West Berliner Luft*, and not just on Friedrich's radio program. Major exhibitions of contemporary and temporary art were mounted with intent. The *Martin-Gropius-Bau*, the former Berlin Museum of Applied Arts, attempted to distill the essence of the early eighties *ZEITGEIST. ZEITGEIST* instrumentalized Neo-Expressionism in its various incarnations—*Die Neue Wilden,* the new *Fauves*—and coupled them with historic Expressionism in a calculated attempt to shatter the dominance and sterility of Abstract Expressionism and redirect the attention of the art world from New York to West Berlin. The *Martin-Gropius-Bau* was itself an architectural work-in-progress, an alternative "bridge of tradition" back to Berlin II. George told me the *Kunst-Gewerbe-Museum zu Berlin* had been built in the neo-Renaissance style between 1877 and 1881. Until 1885, it had housed the "Treasure of King Priam," smuggled out of Troy to Athens-on-the-Spree via Athens by none other than that Homeric henchman Heinrich Schliemann. Named for architect Martin Gropius, the museum was located in Kreuzberg in the American Sector, just over the Wall from the former *Preussischer Landtag* in Berlin-Mitte, the former Soviet Sector. The building, which had been taken over by the *Geheime Staatspolizei*—the Gestapo—was severely damaged during the Second World War. Restoration and renovation begun in the late seventies and continued on into the early eighties. At the end of 1981, the *Martin-Gropius-Bau* served as the staging area for *Preussen-Versuch einer Bilanz,* an all-source retrospective on the Prussian State as a work of art and artifice. Forged by the House of Hohenzollern, democratized by the Weimar Republic, *gleichgeschaltet* by the National Socialists, and finally deconstructed by Allied Control Council Enactment No. 46 of February 27, 1947, *Preussen* posed a thought-provoking case study in nation building and deconstruction, one which Govinda would have greatly appreciated. *Suum cuique.*

Exiting the *S-Bahn* at *Anhalter Bahnhof,* turning to briefly contemplate the ruin of the portico and scan the circular drive for Rainer's taxi, I followed *Stresemann-Straße* to the Wall. A wilderness of construction sites and mountains of dirt surrounded the *Martin-Gropius Bau.* A discarded metal sign, one of the splintered wooden signposts still attached, was lying on the ground, white words of warning in bold black letters:

EINSTURZGEFAHR!
Betreten des Grundstücks verboten
Wegnahme von Gegenstände wird
Als Diebstahl verfolgt
Der Eigentümer
Stiftung Preussischer Kultur-
besitz[35]

Hopefully, the danger of collapse had been addressed by the Prussian Cultural Heritage Foundation before the opening of *ZEITGEIST.* I assumed all objects worth finding had already been found, perhaps even arranged into an exhibition of found objects. It was interesting to learn Prussia had not entirely passed from the scene. A foundation still existed to protect the remaining cultural inheritance. It occurred to me the Privy Archives, where my landlord Dr. Kahler worked, was also part of this *Stiftung Preussischer Kulturbesitz.* The culture of Prussia had survived the Prussian State, if only in ruins and archives. *Eirönïa!* Following the Wall toward ruins of that cultural inheritance now under reconstruction, I was shocked and awed to discover the severed wing of an Avro Lancaster bomber, the faded red and blue British roundel still visible, propped up against the side of the former *Kunst-Gewerbe-Museum zu Berlin*, an accidental memorial to one of the "between 400 and 500 aircraft" and their aircrews invested by Arthur Harris in the Battle of Berlin.

With my back to the Wall, I walked up the staircase, past the bullet-scarred, decapitated seated statues flanking the entrance to the *Martin-*

---

35 "DANGER OF COLLAPSE! Trespassing is illegal. Removal of objects will be prosecuted as theft. The Owner—Prussian Cultural Heritage Foundation," Diary of Thomas Vonaechron, Diary Extract, 1983, trans. TV.

Gropius-Bau. After purchasing a ticket, curious to see whether or not the uniformed saleswoman would also polish my *FU Studentenausweis*—she did not—I walked down another staircase into a sunken atrium flooded with light coming through the glass ceiling. Two-story arcades, composed of pillars and arches surrounded this remarkable interior court. Another mound of dirt and artifacts, not unlike those surrounding the building, rose from the center of the sunken atrium. I wondered if the written warning concerning "found objects" applied inside as well as out. Looking up at the glass ceiling, I saw a larger-than-life silhouette of a familiar figure carrying the leather bag containing the wrapped white rabbit. Looking down, I saw that very same familiar figure standing before me without the rabbit, my fellow traveler on the final leg of the Washington to Berlin flight. "Are you looking for the muse of history here, here among the *Hart Mounds?*" he asked. "This is SOCIETAL ARCHITECTURE, a temple dedicated to the modern muses mustered to overthrow the ancient muses." Before I could think about what he'd said and inquire about the fate of Clio and her sisters, he turned and walked across the courtyard.

In turn, I turned my attention to the paintings hung in the galleries surrounding the atrium. Although Peter Bömmels' *Sprung aus der Geschichte* seemed to depict the violent separation of Clio from the truncated remains of human history, she remained here on-site within these rebuilt walls, together with Argonauts, Agamemnon, Apollo, Athena, Hyperion, "Mars in the Air," Venus, and "Xanthus." The title, if not the subject matter, of Bruce McClean's *Contained (Historically, Politically, Physically)* seemed to speak directly to the postwar situation of the citizens of Berlin East and West, while Helmut Middendorf's *Flugzeugtraum* might have depicted the *Reichshauptstadt*, Berlin IV, at its Schliemannian moment of destruction. Bisecting the night sky above the burning city were the wings of the bomber, just like the one propped up against the outside wall—shock and awe resonated inside and outside the *Martin-Gropius-Bau.* Berlin was not the only target of history selected for illumination. Robert Morris's *Firestorm Series* I through VI graphically illustrated documentation of the death and destruction of Hiroshima.

My encounter with Albert Speer in the *Stadtstaatsarchiv*, and the follow-on attempt to evaluate the validity of his theory of "ruin-value" in Berlin VI, set me up to be shocked and awed for the second time that afternoon by Andy Warhol's *Zeitgeist* paintings. Silk-screen critiques of the monumental architecture conceived and executed under Albert Speer's direction for Berlin IV—*Monument for 16 Soldiers, Friedrich Monument, Reflected,* and *Stadion.* An anxious aesthetic of brutality ran throughout *ZEITGEIST*. Was this the spirt of the times? The playfulness of the large paintings hung in the *Gallerie Buraq,* the wearable music of Andre's *Audiocoat* was missing. Not only serious about art, *ZEITGEIST* was also serious about itself. Perhaps this seriousness was an integral part of the strategy behind the *ZEITGEIST International Art Exhibition*, creative instrumentalization of Neo-Expressionism and its Expressionist antecedents to unseat Abstract Expressionism and refocus attention from New York to West Berlin— Berlin VI. In any event, *ZEITGEIST* put at least half of Berlin back into the big picture.

ZEITGEIST was not only contemporary, but like the smaller exhibition of the *Neue Wilden* in the *Galerie Buraq*, temporary. This temporality encouraged me to seek out more fixed and developed points of reference in the HistoriCity. The *Neue Nationalgalerie* had been one of the many bus stops built into the seven-day study trip ten years earlier. In the limited time available, our guide had introduced us to a few highlights of the collection. Impressions of two paintings, Caspar David Friedrich's *Mondaufgang am Meer* (1823) and Paul Klee's *Abfahrt der Schiffe* (1927), accompanied me back to Basel. Separated by over one hundred years and the dictates of highly personalized styles, both paintings played masterfully upon the complementary themes of arrival and departure. Common natural elements of sea, night, and moonlight endowed each painting with a sense of undefined longing. Returning to the *Neue Nationalgalerie* years later as a *Zone politikon* with time to invest, I found solace and stability in these and other paintings and sculptures in the permanent collection. Clio sprang fully disarmed from the "coal-scuttle" helmet of Otto Dix, who deployed with her on both fronts during the First World War, painting *Flandern* as his after action report just four years before the outbreak of the Second. She likewise turned a critical eye to Georg Grosz's *Stützen der Gesellschaft* (1926), and a kinder eye to the Weimar Republic depicted by Ernst Ludwig Kirchner in *Brandenburger Tor* (1929*)*. Knowing Berlin III would not last, she prophesied the birth of Berlin IV in Erró's *Die Geburt Hitlers* (1966). Arnold Böcklin's *Selbstbildnis mit fiedelndem Tod* (1872) offered the viewer an answer to the question "Why (not) Art?" But it was in the intimate *Balcony Room, Balkonzimmer* (1845) of Adolf von Menzel, a painter known for his historical drawings, engravings, and paintings of Frederick the Great, where eye found the sought-after inner peace.

Regardless of what I was searching for on any particular day, I began each visit to the *Neue Nationalgalerie* standing before Edvard Munch's life-size portrait of Harry Graf Kessler—painted in three days over three-quarters of a century earlier, when the artist was a guest of the director of the *Großherzogischen Museum für Kunst und Kunstgewerbe* in Weimar. Of medium height, slender, right hand on his hip, the count was fashionably dressed in a dark suit and vest, blue-striped shirt worn with tie and stand-up collar, a fitting companion for J. Alfred Prufrock, ready to walk out into the world. A wide-brimmed white Panama hat framed his fine-featured face, confident, yet empathetic, very much the Beau-Brummel, hard on dandyism, all against an old supernatural gold ground. Over time, a two-dimensional relationship developed between us. I enjoyed a three-dimensional relationship with Ernst Barlach's sculpture *Lesende Mönche* (1932). Each time I crossed over the *Landwehrkanal* on the *Potsdamer Brücke*, the black and red dialectical graffiti on the white bank of the stairwell leading down to the canal would ask, "*Warum (nicht) Kunst?*" Each visit to the *Neue Nationalgalerie* brought me closer to an answer.

Designed by Ludwig Mies van der Rohe, the New National Gallery was an integral part of the larger *Kulturforum* initiative, conceived and executed to eradicate architectural traces of *Germania*—Berlin IV—in particular, the *Runden Platz* with Albert Speer's unfinished *Haus des Fremdenverkehr*. The three structures composing the *Kulturforum*—the *Neue Nationalgalerie,* the *Staatsbibliothek* and the *Philharmonie*—constituted a postwar antithesis not only to the plans for *Germania* but to Albert Speer's concept of "ruin value." In spite of, or perhaps because of, the ongoing dialectic of construction, deconstruction, destruction, and reconstruction, however, the *Kulturforum* was characterized less by architecture than by openness, an emptiness not unlike the *Bundesplatz*, the former *Königsplatz* in front of the *Reichstag. Öde und Leer,* the West Berlin air. This emptiness, the absence of all architecture, was at once a defining, unifying topographical and temporal feature of Berlin VI, of West Berlin.

Although the *Philharmonie* was visible on the far side of the *Kulturforum* and the *Staatsbibliothek* across the broad *Potsdamer Straße*, the only other structure standing in the immediate vicinity of the *Neue Nationalgalerie* was the towered *St.-Matthäus-Kirche*, a memorial to Berlin I in Berlin VI. Standing in the way of the planned *Nord-Süd-Achse*, one of the two primary traffic arteries planned for *Germania*, the neo-Romanesque Protestant church was slated by the *Generalbauinspektor für die Reichshauptstadt* to be deconstructed and reconstructed in Spandau, where the former *GBI* would later spend twenty years of his life. *Eirönïa!* In contrast to the fashionable quarter of artists, businessmen, and high-ranking civil servants it once served, the *Geheimratsviertel, St.-Matthäus-Kirche* had survived planning architectural and aerial. Both Paul Tillich and Dietrich Bonhoeffer had been ordained there, lending coincidental theological implications to the accident of survival. Two blocks west of the church stood the *Bendlerblock*, former headquarters building of the *Oberkommando der Wehrmacht*. Swept clean of all surrounding structures through collaborative efforts of the *GBI*, the Royal Air Force, the US Strategic Air Forces in Europe, and the Red Army, the *St.-Matthäus-Kirche-Platz* was now threatened with envelopment by the *Kulturforum*. The *St.-Matthäus-Kirche*, however, continued to stand alone.

Originally designed to be built on Cuba—another strategic island in the Cold War—as an office building for Bacardi, the redesigned, repurposed *Neue Nationalgalerie* now distilled major trends in modern art from the combined collections of the *Nationalgalerie* and the *Galerie des 20. Jahrhunderts*. Yet another (glass, steel, and) concrete example of George's "in Berlin we have two of everything" theory, the New National Gallery was built as a consequence of the 1948 administrative partition of the *Nationalgalerie* on Museum Island in East Berlin. Much of the collection that had survived the "degenerate art" purge of National Socialism and the destruction of the Second World War was returned to, and subsequently remained in, Berlin V—East Berlin. West Berlin, Berlin VI, required a representational modern art museum for a small occupied city. Redesigned by the architect Ludwig Mies van der Rohe, the former Bacardi building seemed ideal for the *Kulturforum*, eight cruciform columns supporting the flat steel roof even played upon the Parthenon theme, a modern contribution to the *Spree-Athen*. In Berlin VII, the same columns would invite sprucing up with tree trunks, sticks, and stones, creating a kind of pre-Parthenonian *nemos* within what was once a temple to the lesser gods of the Cold War.

The first-floor exhibition hall, high glass walls surrounded on all sides by the emptiness of the *Kulturforum*, was actually as, if not more, interesting than many of the temporary exhibits it housed. Although massive pieces of modern metal sculpture had been placed around the *Neue Nationalgalerie* to anchor it, my eyes were consistently drawn to the delicate silhouette of *St.-Matthäus-Kirche*. It was the museum's permanent collection, housed in an open underground labyrinth of white walls that invited me to keep returning to the *Neue Nationalgalerie*. Along with the entrance ticket, visitors received a *Führer durch die Neue Nationalgalerie* printed on heavy-grade white paper in red and black. Turning the *Führer* to orient myself, I was surprised to discover a death's head composed of right angles, with the twin staircases leading to the subterranean galleries for teeth and the museum café and restrooms for empty eye sockets. Descending the flat black metal staircases, nude and clothed visitors alike were serenaded in the center court by a cacophony of water and metal machine music emanating from a stainless steel fountain. Presiding over the court were the three post-primitive deities of Max Ernst's *Capricorn*. Walking quietly behind the two beautiful nymphets, *Barbara und Gaby* (1974), framed preening themselves in the circular mirror hanging on their bathroom wall, I walked over to see Harry Graf Kessler before entering the galleries.

Open space subdivided by walls, the permanent collection of the *Nationalgalerie* was a maze of modern art. A turn to the right took the visitor back to the nineteenth century and Romanticism, a turn to the left to the early twentieth century and Expressionism, antecedent of the *Neue Wilden*. The wall of French Expressionism spanned the divide, opening up onto a subterranean sculpture garden at the rear of the museum. On summer weekends, small jazz combos and local caterers would set up "Jazz in the Garden," a cultural oasis in the desert of the deserted *Kulturforum*. In addition to painting, sculpture, and music, the café of the *Neue Nationalgalerie,* located in the left eye socket, offered space for contemplation, croissants, and an excellent *Milchkaffe*.

The best *Milchkaffee* in West Berlin was found not too far from the New National Gallery at the *Café Wellenstein*, a Viennese café, back across the *Potsdamer Brücke*, down *Potsdamer Straße* on *Kurfürstenstraße*. Although the Accidental *Polis* Seminar had come to an end, and Dr. Schneider had returned to Kent State, I occasionally met with my former *Komillitone* remaining in Berlin. Sophia suggested meeting at the *Wellenstein*, a villa once the home of Henny Porten, star of the German silent screen. The *Wellenstein* would become yet another *Orientierunspunkt* in Berlin. As Fortuna would have it, Professor Duana Jordan, my *Doktormutter*, was a close friend of the owner, DDr. Anna Schmidt, who generously supplied us with food and drink on the house during our meetings to discuss my dissertation-in-progress. Sophia was considering expanding the paper she had written for the Accidental *Polis* Seminar on the legal status of the Allies into a dissertation proposal, and she wanted to discuss sources available at the National Archives. She also wanted to apply for a research grant for the coming academic year. Laura, Nadja, and now Sophia, drawn from West Berlin to Washington, DC, in pursuit of education and personal fulfillment, three out of the seven members of our seminar. Rainer was right, everyone seemed to be moving in the other direction. Had I made a movement in the wrong direction, *eine falsche Bewegung?*

Falkplan in hand, I took the *U-Bahn* to *Kurfürstenstraße* and walked down the street in the direction of *Nollendorfplatz*. Ahead on the right, I saw a red-orange brick neo-Renaissance villa. *Gründerzeit*, another memorial to Berlin II in Berlin VI. Small groups of young girls and a few boys, mostly teenagers, stood out on the street in front of what indeed turned out to be the *Café Wellenstein.* For a brief moment, I thought they were waiting to get in and I might have to once again undergo the critical glance of a *Türsteher*. They were waiting for something else. "Hallo, Thomas!" It was Sophia, coming from the other direction, from the aboveground subway station at *Nollendorfplatz*. She was casually dressed in a green *Trachtenjanker*, blue jeans, with matching pumps, her long dark hair brushed back over her shoulders. Only the stern, angular frames of her glasses gave her away. We shook hands and walked together up the driveway to the entrance stairs. "I'm sorry, Thomas. I didn't think to tell you in advance. This is the so-called '*Baby-Strich*,' where teenagers, mostly girls, sell themselves to finance their drug habit. It's very sad to see, and, of course, illegal. West Berlin authorities are trying to do something about it, but as you can see, so far they have been unsuccessful." In the elegant entrance hall at the top of the stairs, there was a wooden staircase leading to the upstairs gallery of the *Deutscher Akademischer Austausch Dienst (DAAD)*. "I would like to apply to the German Academic Exchange Service for a research grant and am very grateful for your help today, Thomas." We walked through swinging doors, down stairs into the café. Although they swung back together smoothly with a rubbery rush of air and didn't slam, many of the patrons looked up instinctively from their café tables. "This is one of those places to 'see and be seen' in West Berlin, a meeting place for literati and those who would like to become literati." Smiling, Sophia continued, "To tell you the truth, Thomas, I'm not certain many of the patrons actually have much more to say than Henny Porten did in her films, though we'll try this afternoon!" The café was quite full, and at first, we had difficulty finding a table. When a table for two finally did open up, it came with a view of the walled garden behind the villa, another *pairidaeza*. Playing the part of the midwestern-American-turned-continental-European, I made the mistake of ordering a *"café au lait."* The waiter who, along with the ambiance had been imported from Vienna, retorted *"Meinen Sie damit einen Kaffee mit Milch?"*[36] Like many American students of European history, I operated under the impression that much of twentieth century culture had originated in the cafés of Europe. European writer Hermann Kesten described the coffeehouse as "the waiting room of poetry." Many *coffeehaus* patrons, myself included, were still waiting.

It was dark by the time we finished reviewing Sophia's proposal and all the National Archives Record Groups of possible interest. Though visibly tired, Sophie seemed very pleased, even excited. Carefully gathering up her notes and placing them into her briefcase, she said, "You've given me just what I needed to complete both my dissertation proposal and the *DAAD* application, Thomas. If my application is successful and I do make it to Washington, DC, it will be thanks to you!"

36 "Do you mean by that coffee with milk?" Diary of Thomas Vonaechron, Diary Extract, 1983, trans. TV.

"If you do make it Sophia, please take the Metro to Mr. Henry's on Pennsylvania Avenue at Washington Circle and lift a *Berliner Weisse, Himbeersyrup,* or *Waldmeister,* your choice, to the success of my studies here in West Berlin. My research seems to be taking me out of the archives and libraries and into the streets." She told me she would do that and, as we parted in front of the *Wellenstein,* kissed me briefly on both cheeks and then turned back toward *Nollendorfplatz.* I walked back down the *Kurfürstenstraße* to the underground station, trying not to look at the lovely young girls looking at me.

Little America
August 1983

D3 and I met regularly at *Luise,* convenient to both the Clay Institute and the Mission, for lunch. Although we did not pick up the trail of our prematurely terminated tour of the German Democratic Republic, he kindly offered to give me a "windshield tour" of the US military installations making up "Little America" in West Berlin from the shotgun seat of the Shield. "Don't forget to bring your passport along, Thomas, you might need it to enter Little America!" We met at the Mission on a weekday morning in early August. The tree-lined residential neighborhood surrounding the compound provided natural cover. Only the gatehouse at the entrance to the large parking lot and the high-security perimeter fencing hinted at something other than the residential. D3 came out the front entrance of the large redbrick building, walking down the staircase to meet me at the gatehouse, and invited me inside for a cup of *Douve Egberts* coffee. He was wearing his woodland pattern battle dress uniform, "BDUs" with subdued insignia. As we walked back up the stairs together, I noticed a frieze above the doorway depicting a boar hunt I hadn't seen during my previous visit. Fortified for our foray into Berlin VI, we walked back out to the parking lot and climbed into the Shield. The ThunderJet engine caught on the first try. D3 punched in "the Great Eighty-Eight," AFN Berlin, into the *Blaupunkt* commenting, "the perfect soundtrack for Little America. Although headquarters is only a short drive, we'll need the Shield to visit the other installations." Turning right out of the parking lot, we drove down *Föhrenweg,* turning right again onto *Auf dem Grat,* taking us back out onto *Clay-Allee.* Directly across the street was the Outpost, where Laura had given her presentation on *A Foreign Affair.* Laura, a foreign affair. Our short trip to headquarters also took us past the post library on our right, and the Apartment Hotel Dahlem on our left. D3 pulled the Shield up in front of the large main gate flanked by twin gatehouses. A German guard checked D3's ID and my passport and opened the front gate. "That's Building One, directly ahead of us." Passing under the four eyes of two *Luftwaffe*-turned-US-Army-eagles, we drove up the boulevard, parking the Shield in one of the parking spaces directly in front of Building One. "As a student of architecture, I'm sure you can see most of these buildings were not constructed by the United States Army, they're too well built, obviously of air force construction. German Air Force that is! Yuck, yuck, yuck! I even did a little research in preparation for today's tour. Do they look familiar to you, Thomas? Well, they should. The architect, Ernst Sagebiel, also designed Tempelhof Central Airport. Built between '36 and '38 as headquarters for *Luftgaukommando III*, a regional air defense command, the compound composed of eight office buildings became *Luftgaukommando Mitte* 1943. Air defense for all of Germany was coordinated right here. You know the National Socialist leadership. Do you remember *Reichsminister* Hermann Meier?"

"Yes of course, D3, I even recall a memorable quotation from Minister Meier found in a report prepared by the American air attaché, let's see, how did it go? '*Wenn auch nur ein feindliches Flugzeug unserer Reichsgebiet überfliegt, will ich Meier heissen.*'"[37]

"You're good, Thomas, I just can't get one past you, can I? Let's stroll around the compound a bit." D3 took me into the ceremonial entrance hall in Building One. "The army occupied the compound on July 5, 1945. By the end of the year, this building housed General Clay's headquarters. He and Brigadier General Frank Howley, Commandant of the US Sector, both had their offices here during the blockade of the three Western sectors. USCOB, the US Commander, Berlin sits upstairs now." Red, rectangular oriental carpets covered the black marble floor. We walked through black marble columns to a staircase. At the top, illuminated by four floor lamps and light coming through the window behind, stood a larger-than-life bronze statue of an infantryman at parade rest, Mk 2 hand grenades attached to his battle harness. At his right, the American flag, at his left, the flag of the United States Army, with battle streamers. "Meet the 'Doughboy,' Thomas. His twin brother stands in front of the Infantry School at Ft. Johnnie E. Wilson in Georgia. I think of our Berlin Doughboy here as the 'Sun Tzu soldier,' personifying the successful, if unintentional strategy employed by US forces stationed in Europe since the end of the Second World War. Remember your Sun Tzu? 'Hence to fight and conquer in all your battles is not supreme excellence; supreme

---

37 "In the event even one enemy aircraft should overfly the territory of our *Reich*, you can call me Meier" (Hermann Goering, 1943).

excellence consists in breaking the enemy's resistance without fighting.' In other words, you're well-trained, well-equipped, and ready to fight—and you make certain your adversary knows it—but you don't attack, you remain on the defensive. And oh, by the way, Thomas, here's another 'fun fact' for you. The real-life model for the doughboy was a nineteen-year-old soldier actually stationed here in Berlin, Staff Sergeant Thomas Love. Ya gotta love it, Thomas! Get it? Love it, Thomas! Yuck, Yuck, Yuck!" Behind the doughboy, twin staircases ran around the white walls to the floor above. Walking to the top, we entered a large meeting room. "This room is used for receptions as well as briefings. Look at the handwriting on the wall." It was a quotation from President Kennedy highlighting the mission of the US Command Berlin,

> The world must know that we will fight for Berlin. We will never permit that city to fall under Communist influence. We are defending the freedom of Paris and New York when we stand up for freedom in Berlin.

"It's interesting President Kennedy mentions New York not Washington, DC." Scanning the vast conference room, D3 remarked, "This room would make a great film set." Leaving the conference room, he and I walked down the other staircase, past the doughboy and out the entrance hall. Leaving Building One, we walked between Buildings Two and Three, out through the front gate, crossing over the broad *Clayallee* to Truman Plaza. I hoped we might have the chance later to walk by Building Six. I knew from declassification review the Berlin CIA Station had relocated from *Föhrenweg* into that building in the mid-fifties. The German Labor Service guard at the gate leading to Truman Plaza examined D3's ID and my passport, nodded, and waved us through. "Back in the pre-RAF days, Truman Plaza was open to all. You had to have an ID to shop at the Commissary and PX, but everyone was free to walk around." If the Kennedy Headquarters complex across the *Clayallee* was the brain, Truman Plaza was certainly the heart of Little America. The commissary, post exchange, bank and travel agency, Foodland, Class VI store, laundry and dry cleaning, bookstore, beverage shop, army post, and *Bundespost* offices—even a Burger King and an *Eisdiele* were all here. The sidewalks lining the parking lot in the center of the plaza were alive with soldiers, civilians, and family members. Everything here was either built or brought in to make military members, civilian employees, and their dependents feel at home while stationed far out on the "frontier of freedom." From the review of General Lucius D. Clay's classified message traffic in Vault Six, I knew he considered the presence of American families to be a critical component of the US military commitment to West Berlin. Exiting by the *Marshallstraße* gate, on the far side of Truman Plaza, D3 pointed out the building housing Youth Activities. I laughed when I saw the *Tom-Sawyer-Weg* street sign.

"Tom Sawyer here in Berlin? That's got to be a US Army import!"

"Maybe so, but think of *Onkel-Toms-Hütte*, Thomas! Berlin imported Harriet Beecher Stowe without the army's help. Furthermore, in spite of what he wrote about that awful German language, Mark Twain was a great fan of Germany. He lived in Berlin for several months, even met with Kaiser Wilhelm II at the latter's request, but seems to have left his heart in Heidelberg. Some scholars argue a raft trip he took on the *Neckar* broke up his writer's block, some kind of literary logjam, inspiring Huck and Jim's adventures on the Mississippi."

"I'm impressed, D3! How do you know so much about Mark Twain in Germany? Did you study American literature at West Point too?"

"From a pamphlet I picked up at the Army and Air Force Exchange Service Bookstore in Heidelberg. I'm a quick study, Thomas! It is amazing what they have on the shelves down there. They even have an English translation of *Mein Kampf!*" Crossing *Hüttenweg*, we turned left, D3 gesturing toward the swimming pool and the Cole Sports Center as we walked by. "The facilities here in Berlin are the best of any US military installation in Germany. As a happy consequence of the occupation statute Sophia told us about in Dr. Schneider's seminar, all funding is provided by the German Federal Government. On the right we have a concrete example of 'stairwell' housing built for military families." At the next corner, D3 stopped, pointed to a modern church, and said, "It's not only All Saints but all-denominational as well. Turner Barracks, headquarters of Company 'F' 40th Armor, 'Guardian of the Outpost of Democracy,' is just up the street on the left. Directly across the street from Turner Barracks is the AAFES Garage and . . . excuse me, Thomas, the Army and Air Force Exchange Service Garage and New Car Sales." We turned around, walking back down *Hüttenweg* toward *Clayallee,* passing by the Thomas A. Roberts School. Instead of crossing the street and walking back down to headquarters, we turned left onto *Clayallee.* "When we met at the Outpost for Laura's presentation, I wasn't certain if I'd pointed out the library next door or not. It was closed in any case." We walked into the white, modern two-story building, set back off the street. "The head librarian, Nancy Small, is my hero, or should I say heroine? If what I'm looking for is not on the shelf, and oftentimes it's not, she orders it for me through interlibrary loan from Heidelberg, sometimes even from CONUS." Turning to look directly at me, D3 continued, "You know Thomas, you should think seriously about joining the US Army Reserve Europe—you'd be eligible for library privileges." He laughed, and we walked back out onto *Clayallee*. "Let's head back over to Building One and pick up the Shield. There's a few other American installations here in the Great Southwest I'd like to show you."

"Before we do, D3, could we please take another quick look at the Outpost from the outside? I saw it again when we drove by this morning. It's quite different from the functional architecture of Truman Plaza, not to mention *Herr Professor* Sagebiel's monumental *Luftgaukommando Mitte* across the street."

"Roger that, Thomas. I like it, too. From the little bit of background research I did here at the library in preparation for Laura's presentation, I know an American architect named Arnold Blauvelt received a commission from the US Army, Europe to design the Outpost. Built in the early fifties, he designed it to look like the movie theaters of the twenties and thirties. It looks a lot like the Columbia Theater, next to the *Columbiahalle* across the street from Tempelhof. I wonder if Mr. Blauvelt received a commission from the US Air Forces in Europe too? Never underestimate the intensity of the army/air force rivalry!" Standing out in front of the Outpost, I admired the smooth lines and rounded corners of the building. "*All architecture is what you do when you look upon it, (Did you think it was in the white or gray stone? or the lines of the arches and cornices?)*" Glass block and windows had been integrated into the design to suggest films, like the *Roxy Palast* housing the *LaBelle* disco. "On the other side of the Outpost is the childcare center."

We walked back down *Clayallee*, through the main gate of the headquarters compound to the Shield. The *Blaupunkt* came in right on cue with the ThunderJet engine, "The Best in the West, AFN's 88 FM!" D3 laughed and said, "Well, Thomas, you've seen the *Allied Kommandatura*, the Harnack House, Tempelhof Central Airport, and the Outpost. Perhaps we should now drive by the most important building in Little America, who knows, perhaps in all of West Berlin. According to Rainer, maybe in East Berlin too!" Driving out of the gate, he turned left onto *Clayallee* and again onto *Sargemünderstraße*. "The modern one-story redbrick building on the corner is the *Checkpoint* NCO Club, a great place for live music on the weekends, but the best is yet to come. And there it is, Thomas, AFN Berlin!" The studios of the American Forces Radio and Television stood in a modern complex set back from *Sargemünderstraße* behind a security gate on our right. "I was surprised to learn from Nadja, AFN has been broadcasting in Berlin since August 1945. Not from here, of course, but from a requisitioned villa on *Podbielskiallee*. They moved here in the late seventies. We'll head over in that direction shortly, I want to show you the USCOB Residence." Maneuvering the big Ford sedan agilely through the maze of Dahlem's winding residential streets, D3 turned left onto *Thielallee*, passing by buildings of the Free University and George's childhood home, the *Domäne Dahlem*. The "AFN Morning Show" set the houses on fire with Talking Heads' "Burning Down the House." D3 laughed, "That song always reminds me of the old army saying, 'Be careful what you ask for, you just might get it!'" *Thielallee* became *Pacellialle*. Through my window I saw a guard standing before the elegant residence of the commanding general at 14–16. "From the physical security standpoint, the USCOB Residence is much too close to the street. You might have heard about the shot RAF took at the Commander-in-Chief of the US Army, Europe and Seventh Army General Kroessen and his wife with an antitank rocket in Heidelberg two years ago. Yet, the residence has a beautiful garden out back, perfect for receptions, one of which I was fortunate enough to be invited to."

We drove once around the *Platz der Wilden Eber* "just for kicks," then drove down *Podbielski Allee* past the former home of *AFN Berlin,* crossing over the *Könige-Luise-Straße* and turning right into *Altensteinstraße*, which borders the *Botanischer Garten*. "I must say, D3, I'm simply amazed at your ability to navigate these insidious streets in the Shield, I often get lost walking. Until I saw the Botanical Gardens, I'd lost my orientation."

D3 laughed, "West Berlin is a piece of cake, Thomas. It's a little more difficult in East Berlin with my SMLM colleagues tailing me at a nonregulation distance!"

"Smell-em?"

"Soviet Military Liaison Mission!" Turning onto *Fabeckstraße*, we drove past the entrance to the modern MEDDAC, the army hospital at *Fabeckstraße* 60–62, parking on the street next to the security fence. D3 waved to the guard, who waved back. We sat in the Shield for a few minutes, waiting for the Clash to finish "Rock the Casbah." "The whole album, 'Combat Rock,' is good. Have you listened to it, Thomas? The aftermath of colonialism, the tragedy of the Vietnam War, the failure of the 'Great Society'—it's all in there somehow. I particularly like 'Sean Flynn,' about Errol Flynn's son, a freelance photojournalist who went missing in Cambodia." D3 sang over the fade out of "Rock the Casbah." As he reached to turn off the ignition, the "Phrase of the Day" came up on the AFN Berlin Morning Show.

"Today's German phrase means the cleaning woman will not harm you. "*Die Putzfrau wird Sie nicht stören.*"[38] That's "*Die Putzfrau wird Sie nicht stören.*" Learn to build your own phrases. Enroll in a German class at your education center. That's "the cleaning woman will not harm you." Today's

---

38 "The cleaning lady will not disturb you." Diary of Thomas Vonaechron, Diary Extract, 1983, trans. TV.

phrase of the day."

Once we'd stopped laughing, D3 shut down the ThunderJet, gestured out the window, and said, "The hospital used to be in this less functional but much more beautiful *Backstein* building, which has since been returned to the German government. It's a hospital with a history. Former patients include casualties of the First World War, and SS and Red Army casualties of the Second World War. The US Army took over in August 1945. As Rainer told us in class, Thomas Berger was stationed here in the fifties." When he turned the ignition key, we were back in the middle of the AFN Morning Show and David Bowie's "China Girl." Listening closely to the lyrics, D3 commented, "That's pretty heavy stuff for a pop song."

"You're right, D3, it is a 'Pop' song! I believe Bowie originally wrote the song for his friend Iggy Pop. I actually prefer Iggy's original version. His desperation comes through. Rainer has the tape. I'm sure he'd lend it to you!"

Once we crossed the tree-lined, six-lane *Unter den Eichen, Fabeckstraße* metamorphosed into *Tietzenweg,* crossing over the train tracks not far from the Rail Transportation Office at *Lichterfeld-West.* At the intersection with *Gardeschützenweg* stood Roosevelt Barracks. Red brick step gables rising from behind the redbrick walls suggested another American military installation with a German history. D3 turned down AFN. "The barracks is named for Brigadier General Theodore Roosevelt Jr., son of President Roosevelt and, by the way, the only general officer to land with the first wave on Utah Beach in Normandy on June 6, 1944. He died of a heart attack six days later in Cherbourg. This compound was built in the late nineteenth century for a Royal Prussian guards regiment, hence the original name, *Gardeschützenkaserne.* After the war, it was used by the police and later became the German Army Ordnance School. A German Labor Service unit, the 6941st Guard Battalion, responsible for the physical security of our installations in Berlin, the Mission, the headquarters, the USCOB Residence, and Truman Plaza—you saw them in action this morning—is billeted here now."

"When I'm not at *Luise* for lunch, I frequent the German *Kantine* here on post. You'll find one on almost every American military installation in Berlin, throughout the Federal Republic for that matter. When I'm TDY to Heidelberg and don't have the time to go downtown, I eat at the German *Kantine* on Campbell Barracks. Why don't we have a little lunch before we drive on, Thomas? On me today. I think you'll find the *Kantine* dining experience 'ver-r-ry inter-r-resting.'"

"Approved!" The guard waved us through the gate. D3 parked the Shield in front of a long redbrick building just inside. Although the facade of the *Kantine* was in keeping with the *Kaserne*, the interior served up an eclectic mixture of German and American popular culture, in large portions. Noisy and smoky, everyone seemed to be having a good time with background music provided by AFN Berlin. Half of the room was taken up with the heavy wooden tables and chairs found in any traditional Berlin *Gastätte*. The other half was an open kitchen of stainless steel and glass, set off from the tables by the cafeteria line. Lunch was prepared and served by local nationals in hairnets and heavy white cotton aprons. Their practiced routine indicated they'd been doing this for a very long time. Above the dark wood paneling, the walls of the *Kantine* were decorated with posters and traffic signs. Sixteen-wheelers with custom cabs and paint jobs crossed the American West. Airbrushed American Indians, arrayed in Bald Eagle-feathered war bonnets and buckskin leggings, looked out longingly over their sacred land now lost. Cowgirls in fringed leather hot pants sat astride motorcycles, brandishing their weapons. Expired license plates from every state in the Union filled the gaps between posters. A Wild West saloon, way out on the "frontier of freedom." Manifest destiny rides again. The lunchtime clientele was a mixture of Central Europeans in the faded olive drab fatigues of the German Labor Service and American soldiers in their well-worn woodland camouflage. Bottles of *Bier* and Coke stood side-by-side on every tabletop. Picking up standard-issue plastic trays, we fell in at the end of the line. The lunch menu was heavy, *deftig*, traditional Berlin fare. D3 and I both ordered the "special," *Currybouletten*, and grabbed a small *Berliner Kindl* from the stainless steel and glass cooler. Covered in curry ketchup, two *Bouletten* were served on an oversized white plate with generous portions of green peas and boiled potatoes. Somewhere between the Federal Republic of Germany and the United States, the *Kantine* occupied a middle ground composed of stereotypes and mutual misperceptions. Germans and Americans stopped by our table to greet D3, who politely introduced me as his classmate. D3 was a regular here. After we'd finished, he said, "Well, Thomas, there's a couple more installations I'd like to show you this afternoon before the Z-Monster attacks."

"The Z-Monster, D3?"

"Yeah, Thomas, you know—Z3, ZZZ!"

"Roger that, D3!" Putting our napkins in the trashcan, our silverware in the soap basin, and our trays on the rack, "Thanks, Pardner," we walked out through the swinging louvered doors to the Shield parked out front. Leaving Roosevelt Barracks, D3 followed *Gardeschützenstraße* to *Curtiusstraße*, turning left onto *Kadettenweg*, a beautiful, tree-lined street of brick villas and apartment houses set back and fenced off from the street. "Just as *Gardeschützenstraße* once led to the *Gardeschützenkaserne*, so *Kadettenweg* once led to the *Preussische Hauptkadettenanstalt*, the Prussian 'West Point.' By the way, there's an interesting novel about the *Hauptkadettenanstalt* written by Ernst von Salomon. Do you recognize that name, Thomas?"

"No, D3, I don't. You got me this time!"

"At last! Von Salomon provided the Mercedes touring car used in the assassination of German Foreign Minister Walter Rathenau in 1922. *Reichsminister* Herman Meier was also a graduate of the *HKA*. There were, however, a few other tenants in the years between 1873 and 1874, when it was built, and the arrival of the US Army in early July 1945. Shut down by the Treaty of Versailles, the *Hauptkadettenanstalt* became the *Staatliche Bildungsanstalt Hans-Richert-Schule*, but here in Berlin, once an *Anstalt* always an *Anstalt*. It later housed the police, and then units of the *Sturmabteilung*. After Adolf Hitler became chancellor and the *SA* leadership was decapitated and decimated by the SS with the support of the *Wehrmacht*, the compound was taken over by his bodyguard, *SS Leibstandarte Adolf Hitler*. But now, courtesy of the Red and US Armies, it's Andrews Barracks and here we are! D3 pulled up to the main gate on *Finkensteinallee*, handing his ID to the guard, who saluted and promptly opened the gate for us. I held my passport at the ready in my hand, but the guard didn't ask for it. Parking the Shield on the parade field in front of the main building, D3 suggested we get out and stretch our legs a bit. "Given the significant role this installation has played in the history of Berlin, the HistoriCity as you call it, it would be an ideal location for an archives someday. You know Thomas, FDR actually proposed the Pentagon, the 'War Department building' as he called it back then, be used as an archives after the Second World War to house 'dead records.' If only he'd been able to keep the French from moving back into Indochina as he originally intended. Who knows? You might have had the chance to work in Arlington instead of Suitland!"

"You're forgetting the 'police action' in Korea, D3."

"You're right, Thomas! It was, in fact, the Korean War that catalyzed the Cold War build-up of US forces in Europe. Although the North Atlantic Treaty was signed during the Berlin Airlift, it didn't have any teeth until the invasion of South Korea. French support was required in Germany. The short-term trade-off was tacit American support of French interests in Indochina. One of the long-term consequences for the United States was the War in Vietnam. No, unfortunately, I don't believe there's much chance President Roosevelt's proposal for the Pentagon will ever be executed." Grinning, D3 asked, "I wonder if he even believed it himself?"

"The combined ceremony marking the official occupation of the American Sector and the departure of the Red Army took place here on

July 4, 1945. If you examine Signal Corps photographs of the ceremony closely, you can see both American and Soviet flags flying from the frieze above the pillars on which *Leibstandarte Adolf Hitler* is plainly visible." As we walked around the compound, I noted a sign designating Building 904 as "Headquarters, US Army Field Station Berlin," a unit designation that put me back in Vault Six for a moment, but decided not to point it out to D3. He knew. "Andrews Barracks was named for Lieutenant General Frank Maxwell Andrews, West Point Class of 1906, killed in an aircraft accident in Iceland." We walked around the barracks and then back to the Shield. Leaving Andrews Barracks, D3 turned up AFN for the Police singing "Every Breath You Take" and turned to the right. On the corner stood a typical *Berliner Eckneipe* with the atypical name of "Home Bar." A sign in the window provided the explanation, "When your folks call from the States, just tell them you were 'at Home!'"

Driving around the well-walled Andrews Barracks, D3 turned right onto *Goerzallee*: "If we'd turned left Thomas, we'd be on *Hindenburgdamm*, *Hindbenburgdamm*, it's hard to believe—fortunately, there doesn't seem to be a *Ludendorf*-anything in Berlin West or East, though Damn-*Ludendorf* might be appropriate!" Clio and the naming conventions of the HistoriCity. Field marshal during the First World War and *Reichspräsident* during the Weimar Republic, not a bridge, but a "Damm of tradition" to the past. "*Goerzalle* parallels the *Teltowkanal*, which here in the great American Southwest forms part of the sector border. It's interesting when you think about it, Thomas, McNair Barracks, where all three combat battalions of the Berlin Brigade are headquartered, the Fourth, Fifth, and Sixth of the 502nd Infantry, is only a few hundred yards from the German Democratic Republic." Billboards popped up at the intersections as we drove down *Goerzalle*. The Marlboro Man had established himself as an icon of American pop culture in Europe long before my arrival. In a clever attempt to play off of his popularity, a new brand of German cigarettes suggested "Let's Go West." An American brewery jumped on the Conestoga wagon with imported beer as "Fresh as a Country Song." These slogans, superimposed over scenes of the American Southwest, much like those in the German *Kantine*, were ubiquitous, not only in the Southwest American Sector but throughout West Berlin, the Frontier of Freedom.

"I hope the Soviet Forces stationed on the other side of The Wall don't take "Let's Go West" too seriously, D3!"

He laughed. "Don't worry, Thomas! If they do, we're ready. Someone even suggested we position the Class 6 Stores out front, you know alcohol and tobacco sales, as our first line of defense." Turning right from *Goerzallee*, D3 drove out onto a vast, empty parking lot, the characteristic topograhy of Berlin VI. "Like BG Roosevelt, Lieutenant General Lesley J. McNair also died in Normandy, not of a heart attack but an air attack, victim of a 'friendly fire' incident, close air support provided by the U.S. Eighth Air Force. Legend has it, positive identification was made possible only by the West Point class ring, Class of 1904 by the way, on his severed finger -- the only part of his body to be recovered. Unlike the *John F. Kennedy Headquarters Building*, the *U.S. Army Hospital Berlin* and *Andrews Barracks, McNair Barracks* was not a former military installation, it was a *Telefunken-Werke*, a factory for the production of 'phones and communications equipment. As you know Thomas, parade fields and golf courses are *sine qua non* for U.S. Army headquarters, so the Army had to build its own, *der Platz der 4. Juli*. This is where the Fourth of July Festivities are held every year. Maybe you'd like to attend next year? I could have Protocol add your name to the invitation list, with your permission, of course."

"Approved!"

D3 laughed, "Well, that's probably enough of Little America for both of us today Thomas. I don't know about you, but after *Mittagessen* at the *Kantine* I'm ready for a short nap before returning to work. There's a cot with my name on it waiting for me at the Mission. AFN aside, my favorite installation is the U.S. Army *Wannsee* Recreation Center, the former *Villa* Openheim, a big gothic house with a checkered history. We'll save the house and the history for our next in-town tour. Next door to the *Hotel am Wannsee* by the way is the American Yacht Club. Maybe we could even take out a sailboat. The Commander's Guest Residence is out there too, *am Sandwerder*, quite an impressive hideaway on the *Wannsee*, built back in 1935 for the "zipper king" of Germany. Just like his product, his fortunes went up and down—yuck, yuck, yuck! I'm headed back to the Mission, can I drop you off somewhere along the way?"

"Thanks very much for the windshield tour, D3. Fascinating! Little America gives me a better understanding of the foundation on which the Accidental *Polis* is built. Could you drop me off at the *S-Bahn* station in *Zehlendorf*? I can catch the *S1* back to Friedenau. Turning the Shield around on the paved parade ground, D3 drove back to *Goerzallee*. "It's hard to believe we're actually driving along The Wall."

"Indeed it is Thomas, on your right is the main entrance to *Andrews*. We'll turn north here on *Teltower Damm* taking us back to Zehlendorf and Dahlem. Up ahead on the right, the white compound, is the John F. Kennedy School, a Berlin public school. Many of the military families stationed here send their children to JFKS instead of to the DoDDS schools, excuse me, Department of Defense Dependent Schools. It's a good thing to venture out of Little America and take advantage of the host nation, or should I say host sector, environment. D3 pulled up to the bus stop at *S-Bahnhof Zehlendorf.* Jumping out of the shotgun seat and shutting the door, I waved until he passed underneath the *S-Bahn* bridge over *Teltower Damm* and was out of sight.

The *S1* arrived just as I reached the platform at the top of the stairs. Opening the doors, I sat down on the wooden bench inside. Again, there was much to *verarbeiten*, to fix and to develop. D3 had not included one of the most architecturally interesting installations, the US Army Field Station Berlin, on our windshield tour. To be fair, it was in the British sector, on top of the *Teufelsberg*, another artificial *Brocken* of broken Berlin. Field Station Berlin was built over the unfinished ruins of Albert Speer's *Wehrtechnische Fakultät.* Albert Speer again. Was "ruin value" still valid if the ruins were buried under the ruins of the city? Was a "bridge of tradition" to the past still standing if underground? Heinrich Schliemann would no doubt say "*Jawohl!*" I was familiar with the mission and operations of Field Station Berlin from those records withdrawn from the files for review under "sources and methods of intelligence" by representatives of the National Security Agency in Vault Six. "T-Berg," as it was referred to in the documents, was the collection site for the US Army Intelligence and Security Command unit, Field Station Berlin, housed at the former *Preussische Hauptkadetenanstalt*-turned-*Staatliche Bildungsanstalt*-turned-*SS Leibstandarte Adolf Hitler*-turned Red Army Barracks-turned Andrews Barracks. Visible and invisible, perishable and nonperishable architectures remained in place and operational in Berlin VI—West Berlin.

Looking out the window when the *S-Bahn* came to a stop, I saw "*Schöneberg*" and realized I'd once again gone one station too far. Rather than wait for the next *S1* headed back in the direction of *Düppel*, station to station, I decided to walk back to my one elegant Empire room. The walk would do me good, maybe even keep the Z-Monster at bay for a while. *Dominicustraße* led from the *S-Bahnhof* directly to *Hauptstraße*, taking me from *Schöneberg* back down to *Friedenau* and *Lothringerstrasse*. Reaching the intersection, I remembered *Rathaus Schöneberg*, site of John F. Kennedy's speech of solidarity with West Berlin—". . . a city which we feel to be a part of us"—was nearby. Although I'd walked past the *Rathaus* numerous times, often stopping to reread the bronze memorial plaque next to the main entrance, Eddie's presentation on "The Myth of John F. Kennedy in the Mythology of West Berlin" inspired me to take another look. After admiring Kennedy's courageous profile and rereading the *Gedenktafel*, I decided to have another beer before returning home. No work today. Somewhere nearby was the *Studentenhotel* where I'd stayed with the study group from Basel. Perhaps the bar was still open. Continuing on past *Rathaus Schöneberg*, I came to *Warburgstraße*. In the distance, I saw a sign for what appeared to be a small neighborhood bar, *Arlecchino*—just what I was looking for.

The bar was dark, a traditional Berlin *Kneipe*, none of the neon-lit, emergency room ambiance which penetrated the scene bars like *Dschungel* and Mink. It seemed empty. There was an old ceiling-grid, two-tone Dodgem car from an amusement park, parked just inside the front door. I had always enjoyed crashing in these same bumper cars as a child, and I took its presence in the *Arlecchino* as a good omen. Walking over to the dark wooden bar, I saw another customer, a slender, somehow familiar figure, dressed in jeans and a red checked shirt, seated on a barstool. After I sat down and ordered a *Pils*, he looked up, closed the book he was reading, and smiled at me, nodding politely as he did so. "Hello," he said, extending his hand, "I'm Robert Jones"—he spoke the King's *bzw.* the Queen's English. His smile genuine and engaging, his face etiolated, another lost angel in the city tonight.

"Pleased to meet you, Robert, I'm Thomas, Thomas Vonaechron."

"Is that a German name, 'Von Aechron?'"

"It's funny you should ask. The name might be originally, but I'm an American, studying at the Free University."

"Yes, I do detect the American accent now. A student, now that's the life, Thomas, though I must say, and I do hope you will forgive me for saying so, but you do look a bit too old to be a student. You're no longer a young American!"

"I'm actually a graduate student, Robert. I should be sitting at my desk working on my dissertation, but I find myself sitting at yet another West Berlin bar, stalking Clio, the muse of history, around town." Robert laughed.

"That's a good one! I like that very much, 'stalking Clio, the muse of history, around town.' Maybe I can use it. In a way that's what I'm doing here too, stalking the muse, but Euterpe not Clio, around West Berlin. Are you studying German at the university?"

"German history actually." As I talked to Robert, I began to unintentionally affect an English accent. "I'm trying to focus on Berlin, which has proven to be rather difficult. There are actually several Berlins, not just West and East, but historical Berlins as well, the *Reichshauptstadt*, the capital of the Weimar Republic, Imperial Berlin. Ruins of these earlier cities, these historical cities, are still standing in West Berlin. Clio hides among the ruins ånd in the archives."

"That's quite interesting indeed. I'd like to take a look in those Berlin archives too one day. I once visited the Public Record Office at Kew

Gardens in London. I'm actually an actor, a performance artist by training, and am quite interested in how Berlin, how all of Germany for that matter, was staged by the National Socialists. I've just been reading in an English translation of *Mein Kampf*." He pushed the book across the bar so I could see the dust jacket. It was the original 1939 English-language translation made by the New School for Social Research in New York. "Among other things, Hitler was a composite media artist, one of the first rock stars. He staged the whole country, actually."

"Two of my friends, one German and the other American, make a similar case for Frederick the Great, another friend of the opera, though I can't guess what he might have said about Richard Wagner." Robert laughed again. "Please forgive me, Robert, but you seem very familiar, have we met before?"

"I've been thinking the same too, Thomas, and believe we might have seen each other at the *Dschungel,* though we didn't really meet, didn't talk much, if at all. I believe we might have even shared a dance; however, I can't dance. You kept calling me 'Nadja.'" Before I could respond, Robert raised his hand. "No, no, Thomas, no apologies necessary, I've often been mistaken for a woman and have been called much worse than 'Nadja!' But now I must ask you to please forgive me, as I have to return to work. Perhaps you should stop chasing Clio around town this evening, though truth be told, there might be something to be gained by doing so, and follow my good example. Get back to work!" Robert laughed again. "Actually, I've arranged to meet two musicians at a recording studio near the Wall. If I didn't have the appointment, I would enjoy sitting here and talking about German history. I don't meet many historians in my line of work. I come here occasionally, to the *Arlecchino* to read and relax. As an historian, you might know *Arlecchino,* the harlequin, was also a performance artist, a character in the Italian *Commedia dell'arte.* In England, where I studied, harlequinade comic theater is closely associated with mime. Harlequin wore a variety of masks, and his checkered costume played upon a possible evil origin, perhaps the devil himself. Dante describes the devil "Alichino" in Cantos XXI and XXII of *The Inferno.* But I've no sympathy for the devil. As I said, I come here to read and relax, 'Far from the madding crowd's ignoble strife.' Do you know your Gray, Thomas? I hope we might meet again here at the *Arlecchino,* or at the *Dschungel* again someday." Extending his hand he said, "Goodbye, Thomas, many thanks for the conversation, and for the dance. The very best of luck with your studies!" As he stood up to leave, the bartender served my *Pils.* Our conversation had lasted only seven minutes. Savoring both the conversation and the *Pils,* I ordered another. Afterwards, I walked back past the mythical *Rathaus Schöneberg* to *Hauptstraße* for the long walk back to my one elegant Empire room, and the Z-Monster lying in wait.

Far Out
August 1983

The doorbell rang just outside my room in the hallway, wrenching me from the clutches of the Z-Monster. Someone was at the door downstairs. It was dark outside, either very late at night or very early in the morning. Disoriented, I rolled over to look at the large, abnormally heavy dolphin clock on the floor of my room. I'd slept through the late afternoon and the early evening. It was just after 11:00, "twenty-three hundred hours," as D3 would say. Getting up from my bed, I swung open the French doors, walked out into the hallway, pushed the entry button on the wall, and opened the apartment door. Who could it be so late at night? Had Dr. Kahler forgotten his keys? The downstairs door opened, the light came on in the *Treppenhaus,* and Rainer walked up the stairs. "Howdy, Thomas! I just dropped off a fare in *Hedwigstraße.* She, though I'm not sure if it was a girl or a boy, gave me quite a large tip, so I thought I'd treat myself to a beer, burger, and fries at Mendelsohn's Burger Shop on Lehniner Platz. Wanna join me?"

"Howdy, Rainer, why yes, thank you . . . come in and sit down for a moment. I'll splash some water on my face and I'll be good to go." Although still full from the Roosevelt *Kantine* lunchtime "special" and the two follow-on beers at the *Arlecchino,* I'd read about Mendelsohn's, a popular West Berlin drive-in in the architectural ensemble designed by Erich Mendelsohn on Lehniner Platz, and wanted to see it for myself. Built in the New Objectivity style in the early thirties, the *Komplex* combined cultural activities with living and retail space, originally including a movie theater, a cabaret, a Café-Restaurant, a hotel, apartments, and even tennis courts of all sorts and a parking garage. Although the cultural and culinary establishments had changed out over the past half-century, Kurt Robitscheck's *Kabarett der Komiker* was no more. As tired as I was, I just couldn't pass up the opportunity for a late-night drive with Rainer back to Berlin III.

"Sorry, Thomas, did I wake you?"

"Yes, Rainer, but it's OK. I took a tour of Little America with D3 earlier today. We had an enormous lunch at the German-American *Kantine* on Roosevelt Barracks, and then on the way home, I stopped off at a *Kneipe* and drank two more beers. There was only one other customer there, a

British performance artist reading an English translation of *Mein Kampf!* We had a short but very interesting conversation about the staging of Germany by the National Socialists and Adolf Hitler as a rock star."

"*Naja*, there might be something to that, but why don't you get ready and tell me about it on the way. I've been on the road since early this morning and I'm hungry!"

Mendelsohn's on Lehniner Platz picked up German-American pop culture where the German-American *Kantine* on Roosevelt Barracks left off, as if a European interior design firm had reinterpreted the classic American drive-in in a kind of "German Graffiti" way, without the outdoor parking. Everything was outré. The waitresses, costumed in tightly-tailored black toreador pants with buttoned-down white blouses and coordinated overseas caps, skated round an oblong wooden track ringing the raised booths, carrying large trays of food and drink. Light came from neon tubes framing the American highway road signs and advertisements that were likewise running around the walls. Unlike the *Kantine*, no airbrush fantasies of "sixteen-wheelers" were displayed; there was no place here for dispossessed Native Americans and undressed cowgirls. Mounted on the black drop ceiling, video monitors offered customers *2001: A Space Odyssey* as a silent film. The soundtrack was provided by a vintage *Würlitzer 1015* jukebox, resplendent with revolving color columns, bubble tubes, and revealed record changer. We sat down in a red Naugahyde tuck-and-roll upholstered booth, where we were promptly greeted by our high-wheeled, low-cut waitress, Wanda. Still partial to President Reagan, Rainer ordered the "Cap Wein-Burger" with a side of "freedom fries." After the Roosevelt Barracks *Bouletten*, I couldn't eat a hamburger, so I ordered a large beer, which proved to be a wise decision when Wanda later wheeled back up to our booth with the largest hamburger I'd ever seen. Surprised by the size, Rainer offered me his "freedom fries," which somehow tasted differently way out on the "frontier of freedom." "You know, Thomas, there's a new disco next door, Far Out. According to the chatter on the net, it's owned by the Bhagwan sect and rumored to be a recruitment center for Poonah. Maybe we should check it out after we eat, which could take a while."

"'Approved!' In case of trouble, we can cover each other's ashram!"

There was no trouble. No sectarian Cerberus guarded the entrance to the new dance temple, just polite young women dressed in loose-fitting orange and red clothing. We paid the entrance fee, which also covered our first drink. Hoping for Poona, we found ourselves back out on a West Berlin dance floor, the largest one I'd seen yet. It was different than the *Dschungel*, though, enclosed in white marble walls with a small fountain in the center. The interior lighting was warm and welcoming, a soothing change from the cold, penetrating neon lighting of the West Berlin scene bars. A huge portrait of Bhagwan Shree Rajneesh hung over the dance floor. Although many of the celebrants also wore orange and red, there were also alternatives, hippies, punks, post-punks, students, and well-dressed patrons. A young woman dressed in a conservative style reminiscent of Sophia—matching silk dress jacket and skirt, low heels—smiled at us warmly and said, "Hallo," as we made our way slowly through the Far Out crowd. Medium height, with her silky blonde hair cut in pageboy style, she was slightly plump and very attractive. The indirect lighting gave a warm glow to her smooth white skin.

"Hallo," we answered in unison. Rainer spoke first, "*Ich bin Rainer, und das ist Thomas, mein amerikanischer Freund.*"

She extended her hand to both of us in turn: "Silka." Turning to face me, she said in accent-free English, "An American! I lived with an American family in Indiana last year. After finishing my *Abitur* in Hamburg, I spent a year at Shortridge High School in Indianapolis with the American Field Service, 'AFS.' It was a wonderful year, and I hope to be able to return to the United States while studying at the *FU*, maybe even spend a year at IU in Bloomington!"

"Rainer and I both study at the *FU*, too, at the Lucius D. Clay Institute for North American Studies."

"I'll start winter semester. I came to Berlin with a friend from Hamburg yesterday to look for an apartment or *WG*. We're staying with her friends who live near here. They recommended Far Out to unwind after a long day of reading classified ads and knocking on doors, only to find out we were too late. Someone just asked my friend to dance, so she left me on my own for a while. Would one of you like to dance with me?"

"Yes!" we answered, once again in unison.

"Well, why don't the three of us dance together, then? With everything one reads about Poonah in *Der Spiegel*, '*Orgie oder Offenbarung,*'[39] I think the Bhagwan would approve," she said nodding to the portrait of his benevolence presiding over the dance floor. After our first *danse a trois*, another cover from *Cabaret*, Rainer and I took turns dancing with Silka. After an hour or so, her friend from Hamburg returned with her dance partner to ask Silka if she wanted to accompany them to a party in Kreuzberg. "Could I stay here with you, Rainer and Thomas? I'm enjoying myself very much and I'd like to dance some more." We eagerly embraced her suggestion, assuring her friend we would make certain Silka returned to the apartment in Wilmersdorf where they were staying. Both women

---

39 "Orgy or Revelation," Diary of Thomas Vonaechron, Diary Extract, 1983, trans. TV.

were relieved when Rainer, with his encyclopedic knowledge of the streets of West Berlin, positively identified the location.

The music at the Far Out was not as far out as the name implied, rather a mix of modern, mainstream, oldies, and the occasional real oldie. Silka and Rainer waltzed gracefully across the floor when the crowd thinned out at the opening strings of Johann Strauss's *Wiener Blut.* The crowd surged back with the very next song, Ian Drury's "Sex & Drugs & Rock & Roll," an unintentional hymn to Poonah offering libertarian advice to the dance crowd. The huge dance floor was once again filled to capacity. Body temperature raised the room temperature. After another hour of dancing nonstop, we were soaked in sweat. When we took a break for drinks at the Bhagwan Bar, Silka took off her dress jacket. Her white blouse and bra were soaked through. Rainer suggested a late night-early morning swim in the nearby *Teufelsee,* the Devil's Lake.

"Let's Go!" said Silka. Leaving Far Out and Lehniner Platz, we walked to the big yellow Mercedes taxi Rainer had parked across *Ku'damm* on *Nestorstraße.* Silka laughed when she saw the sign on the roof advertising "(American Literature)." "How about driving us to 'Big Sur' instead of *Teufelsee,* Rainer?" she asked, taking her place in the shotgun seat next to him. I climbed into the back seat, thinking about the Parisian taxi scene in Henry Miller's *Tropic of Cancer,* triggered by Silka's mention of Big Sur.

"I'll see what I can do," he laughed, starting the Mercedes, simultaneously opening the sunroof and tuning the *Blaupunkt* to "RIAS Rock Night," already in progress. "Fade to Gray" faded out into "God Save the Queen," which seemed somehow sacrilegious in the British Sector. But in the early eighties, "No Future" vied with "*Justia, Veritas, Libertas*" as the motto of the *FU.* We drove north, passing under *S-Bahnhof Charlottenburg,* turning left onto the broad *Kaiserdamm,* the former *Ost-West-Achse.* At *S-Bahnhof Heerstraße,* Rainer took a left turn onto *Teufelseestraße,* which became *Teufelseechausse* when we entered the dark green Grunewald Forest. "Thomas, I wonder if your countrymen on duty up there in their white tower are also listening to RIAS Rock Night on their black headphones, or perhaps to something else? Looking up, I was startled to see US Army Field Station Berlin, towering directly over us, high atop the *Teufelsberg,* the Devil's Mountain, a coincidental continuation of the tour of Little America with D3. Backlit in cold, pale green security lighting, the domed white tower and twin radomes of the *T-berg* formed a giant phallus, a gleaming white temple to Pan in West Berlin. And at the foot of the Devil's Mountain, the Devil's Lake, the *Teufelsee,* a glacial lake deep in the Forest Grunewald. We parked the taxi and walked to the shore. When Silka reached the shoreline, she stopped and carefully took off her shoes, dress jacket, skirt, blouse, bra, and bikini panties, folded them neatly and placed them in a pile. Lunar light revealed her natural beauty as she undressed, highlighting the lines of her full breasts, hips, and thighs, magically morphing the *Teufelsberg* into the *Venusberg*, and Silka into Selene, Greek goddess of the moon. I wondered if this vision of divine beauty was also under close observation by Field Station Berlin. Turning to face Rainer and me, her blonde hair and marble skin radiant in the moonlight, she said, "Come, Rainer, come Thomas, let's jump in! Turning back to the lake, she ran into the water. We followed as soon as we had undressed. The water temperature immediately betrayed the lake's glacial origins. After a short swim, we walked together back to the shore. Silka, walking between Rainer and me, wrapped her arms around both our necks, pulling us closer to her, kissing us in turn deeply on the mouth. I could feel her firm, full breasts pressing against my upper arm as she kissed me. "Thank you both for this magical evening, it's wonderful!" We dressed quickly and briefly considered waiting for the sun on the shore. With the glacial chill still in our bones, we decided to return home. Back in the taxi, engine running, heater on full, we exchanged addresses and telephone numbers, promising to contact Silka if we heard about openings in a *WG*. We dropped her off at the Wilmersdorf address where she was staying. When I climbed out of the shotgun seat of the taxi in the *Lothringerstrasse*, thanking Rainer and wishing him a "good morning," the birds in the linden trees asked, "Poo-tee-weet?" The magical meeting with Silka at Far Out and our mythical trip to the *Teufelsee* provided a shot of exhilaration, temporarily masking my growing exhaustion.

Decomposition
August 1983

Of all my former Accidental Polis Seminar *Komillitonen*, I saw Rainer most often, at least once a week, sometimes more often depending upon his work schedule. My work schedule was becoming increasingly erratic, as my COMZ continued to expand throughout Berlin VI. There was always something to be done, seen, or heard in West Berlin, *eine neue Instandbesetzung*, a new club, a *vernissage*, a play, or a concert. One unusually warm evening in late August, Rainer and I taxied to the *Tempodrom*, a large circus tent pitched before the Wall on the western side of *Potsdamer Platz* in *Kreuzberg*, in the American Sector, for a jazz concert. The eastern side of *Potsdamer Platz* was in *Mitte*, in the Soviet Sector—East Berlin. The Wall runs through it. We parked at *Anhalter Bahnhof*, where I'd first seen Rainer and his "(American Literature)" light in the semicircular drive in front of the surviving portico the year before, and walked across the street. Entrance to the circus tent was through a large, freestanding mural. Against the background of an enormous black Prussian eagle, beak open, wings widespread, was the cloud-covered blue planet Earth, eclipsing the sun. Only its rays were still visible. Between the Earth and the viewer, a child, who'd let go of the empty trapeze swinging behind him, was falling forward like Icarus, arms and legs spread, past the viewer into space.

"Let's get our tickets now in case they sell out, and then get something to eat before the concert. There's a Greek restaurant, *Berlin Euteikheon,* just down *Stresemannstraße.* I haven't tried it yet, but I've heard good things about it on the net. It's owned by the same family that owns The Athenian Stranger in Neukölln. I've been there a few times. They serve excellent Greek food and smooth *Retsina*! By the way, the Paula Lead Band is not a mainstream jazz band, Thomas, not Dixieland like the Alpha Jazz Band we heard at the *Leierkasten* with D3 either. I listened to a few tracks from their latest album, *Societal Science,* late one night on SFB and bought a copy. I've haven't had a chance to tape it yet; once I do, I'll give it to you."

"Many thanks, Rainer. *Societal Science?*"

"Strange title, isn't it? But somehow appropriate. Some traditional jazz music, tango, for example, *aber gleichzeitig* repetitive, deconstructed. There's something kitsch and strange about it. I've been hoping they'd come to West Berlin so I could see and hear them perform on stage. I'm somewhat skeptical of studio album sound, if you know what I mean." As we left the *Tempdrom,* I turned around to look at the mural again. Although the expression on the child's face was more one of curiosity than of anxiety, it reminded me of the frightened fish hanging on my wall in the *Lothringerstrasse.* Was the Icarus-child, like the flounder, trying to communicate with me in my communications zone? Anticipating the evening performance, I began to feel uneasy, almost afraid. Rather than go Greek, we decided on the nearby *Café Stresemann,* where we'd eaten once before during a late night foray into Berlin VI. Although no doubt named for the street, as a follower of Clio, I had to think of former Foreign Minister Gustav Ernst Stresemann, statesman of the Weimar Republic, as I entered the café. For his successful diplomatic efforts helping Germany to reenter the community of nations following the First World War, he was awarded, together with his French colleague Aristide Briand, the Nobel Peace Prize. Clio consequently awarded him a street and a café in West Berlin. Although housed in a postwar building, gray and angular, broken up only by the large plate glass windows on the ground floor, the interior of the *Stresemann* had a dark wood Weimar Republic ambiance, complete with period wooden coat stands. The perfect place to wait for imaginary passenger trains arriving at or departing from *Anhalter Bahnhof.* *Außenminister* Stresemann would no doubt have been quite comfortable sitting at a wooden table by the window, annotating his draft copy of the Dawes Plan. As we crossed over *Stresemannstraße* to *Café Stresemann*, Rainer pointed out a prewar building standing alone on the empty field that was once the western side of *Potsdamer Platz*. "That's Hansa by the Wall Studio." I wondered if it might be the same studio Robert had referred to at *Arlecchino*.

After dinner, we returned to the *Tempdrom* for the Paula Lead Band, an eight-man ensemble led by pianist Paula Lead, a young woman wearing a white pantsuit with wild, red-running-to-blonde hair. In keeping with the across-the-street Weimar ambiance of the *Café Stresemann*, the concert began with music reminiscent of Berlin III. Kurt Weil came to mind. As Rainer had mentioned, I could hear hints of the tango and other familiar Latin American musical motifs. Unfamiliar motifs and instruments, human voices, a walkie-talkie, and electronic feedback soon began to intrude, sowing disharmony and discord. As in the more traditional Dixieland played by the Alpha Jazz Band, a single instrument often held the music together. Each foray into the unfamiliar was followed by a return to Weil and Weimar, to the familiar, with dissonance, dissonance resolved. But then, Paula began to determinedly deconstruct, to decompose the music. It became increasingly mechanical, moving slowly at first, like the metal machine music of Pan Am's *City of Berlin*, slowly gaining momentum while taxiing to the runway for the flight from Frankfurt am Main to West Berlin. As the momentum increased, the music became increasingly hectic, an effect heightened by Paula's masterful control of the cacophony. With any decrease in momentum, the music began to fall apart. An intentionally off-key male vocalist monotonically repeated a lyric seemingly set in the long dark hallway of *Herr* Kahler's *Lothringerstrasse* apartment outside my one elegant Empire room. An unfocused fear began to rise in my chest, as if we were witnessing the deconstruction, disintegration, and destruction of not only of the music but, by extension, the HistoriCity itself. Paula mistressfully reassembled her musicians and her music, now grown heavier, but the memory and anticipation of possible repetition remained, a fear momentarily heightened by a broken record effect which fortunately resolved itself into a final fanfare worthy of Kurt Weil. It had been an intellectually and emotionally fascinating, deeply disturbing, draining performance. I was relieved when we left the *Tempodrom*. I did not turn to look back at the Icarus-child after leaving the circus tent, fearful I might see myself falling into space.

"What do you say, Thomas, let's have a last beer before we head back home. There's an interesting place nearby, right over there." Rainer pointed across dark, empty space to a seventeen-story, modern apartment building standing in isolation. Rather than following *Anhalterstraße*, we walked across the rubble-strewn field, carefully making our way around piles of bricks and mounds of dirt, just like those found outside and inside the *Matin-Gropius-Bau—Westberliner Zeitgeist*. As we approached the building, I could see a brightly lit external elevator moving slowly up and down tracks on the outside of the building. Strobe lights flashed through large, two-story plate glass windows at the top. When we reached the parking lot at the base of the building, we joined the line for the elevator under the illuminated circular sign advertising the T-T Music Cafe. The ride up the side of the building in the glass elevator was spectacular, rising slowly over the field of ruins, looking northeast into both West and East Berlin, Tiergarten and Mitte, the vast darkness below divided by the Wall, punctuated by lights in the distance.

"This is Excelsior House, Thomas. There used to be a Canadian steakhouse on the top floor but it didn't make it. Too far away from the *Ku' damm*, from the tourists. Rumor has it the CIA once had an observation and listening post here, maybe they still do. Anyway, the Turn-Tower Music Café took over. There's a great view from the top." As the elevator approached the top floor, I could feel a beat resonating through the concrete. When the doors opened, the glass elevator was immediately flooded with music so loud we were unable to talk. The Turn-Tower was filled far beyond capacity. We made our way to the bar through the punks, post-punks, *Anarchos*, and *Instandbesetzer*, dancing, gesturing, and just hanging around. The smell of smoke, sweat, stale beer, and marijuana hung in the *West Berliner Luft, Luft, Luft*. The bartender was dressed in a white T-shit prominently displaying the Turn-Tower logo, a portrait of the artist with sunglasses with an uncircumcised penis for a proboscis and a hair-covered scrotum for a beard. Through hand and head gestures, Rainer was able to order two beers. He handed me one, smiling and saying something it was impossible to understand. Beer cans in hand, we made our way slowly back through the crowd to one of the glass walls running around the perimeter of the room. Through the reflections of the strobe lights, I could make out a few points of light in the distance. Security lights illuminating the death strip behind the Wall at regular intervals told me I was looking into East Berlin, Berlin V. Earlier in the evening or later in the morning, the Turn-Tower would have provided a unique coign of vantage over the HistoriCity, East and West, a new point of reference. Perhaps there was something to Rainer's CIA RUMINT. I'd have to come back. The volume and intensity of the music was unrelenting as one song hemorrhaged into the next. The fear I felt during the Paula Lead performance began to rise again, rapidly spreading from my chest out through my arms, into my hands and fingers.

I had to get out. Draining my beer, I signaled my intention to Rainer by pointing to the elevator, and he nodded in agreement. Fortunately, arrivals still outnumbered departures and we didn't have long to wait. The moment the stainless steel elevator doors walled off the music, still pounding as we began our descent into the darkness, the fear began to lessen its grip. I turned to look out from under glass onto the HistoriCity rising up through the darkness to meet us.

"*Mann, mann, mann,* Thomas, I'm sorry! That was much too loud! We'll come back another time earlier in the evening or later in the morning! Let's walk back to the *Stresemann* for a beer."

"Instead of another beer, could we just walk around for a bit, Rainer? I need to relax. Too much dissonance tonight." Much of the area on the western side of the Wall south of *Potsdamer Platz* bordered by *Körthener-* and *Wilhelmstraße* was barren, only a few isolated buildings survived the Strategic Air Campaign, Berlin Strategic Offensive Operation, and the deliberate *démontage* that followed the Second World War. The street signs had, however, been replaced, marking the intersections of the deserted streets. Streetcar tracks set into the brick streets testified the area had not always been a wasteland. Wasteland, yes, but not empty. After leaving the T-T Music Cafe, we followed *Anhalterstraße* to *Wilhelmstraße*, walking toward a prewar apartment building.

A mural covered the exposed brick side facing Excelsior House. Under the broken arrow of anarchy, three witches conjured bombs from a bubbling cauldron in the ruins of the city. A second mural on the exposed wall of the *Hinterhaus* played upon the first, prophesying a future transformation from bubbles to bombs to balloons, floating peacefully over a later city, a new city, in which Excelsior House, with its external elevator to the Turn-Tower, was visible. "This is the '*KuKuCK*' Thomas, the *Kunst und Kultur Zentrum Kreuzberg.*" *Instandbesetzt. Transparente* hung from the facade of the building. Posters and handbills covered the ground-floor walls and windows. The original facade above was still intact. Six rows of six windows framed vertically by seven faux columns. Before the war laid the adjoining buildings to waste, it must have been quite elegant. "*All architecture is what you do when you look upon it, (Did you think it was in the white or gray stone? or the lines of the arches and cornices?)*" Large black block, letters on a hand-painted banner on the ground floor, *Erdgeschoß* designated the *INFO-RAUM*. The doors had been barred shut from the inside to prevent *eine Räumung*, an eviction by the West Berlin police.

Continuing down *Anhalterstraße*, past the *KuKuCK* and the Marlboro Man keeping watch over the empty lot next door, we arrived at the

Suttgarter Hof. Although it had not always been a single-story hotel, the truncated facade had been recently renovated and painted white. Flower boxes underlined each of the four remaining ground-floor windows. Ornamental lamps on both sides of an ornate arched doorway invited guests into an inner courtyard, a bit of *Restdeutschland* in West Berlin. Looking across the street, Rainer said, "That's *Das Autodrom,* a dirt track raceway for old cars, like the demolition derbies you have at county fairs in the States. It's a *Verkehrsübungsplatz* where you can learn how to drive. You don't need a license to drive there, and because of all the curves, you can't drive very fast. It's a lot of fun and very popular."

"A demolition derby track next to the Wall?"

"Why not, Thomas? No one wants to build here because of the Wall, except of course Axel Springer. Can you believe it, I had him as a passenger in my taxi one night! The *Autodrom* runs along *Wilhelmstraße.* The building that stood here on the corner was the *SA* headquarters, later annexed by the *SS.*" Turning left on *Wilhelmstraße,* we walked along the perimeter of *Das Autodrom,* coming to King Charlie, a café-restaurant in a single-story, whitewashed building at the corner of *Wilhelm-* and *Kochstraße.* Light and music came through the dirty yellow windows. An old Cadillac sedan, not encased in concrete, with US forces plates was parked in the lot on the far side of the street. Street signs in front of King Charlie pointed right, down *Kochstraße,* to border crossing points on nearby *Friedrichstraße (für Ausländer),* Checkpoint Charlie, where George had dropped me off for our one-day foray into East Berlin and *Prinzenstraße (für Bundesbürger).* Another street sign depicted the once powerful *Wilhelmstraße* dead-ending dead ahead into the Wall, illuminated by the security lighting on the other side. Turning around, we walked back up to *Anhalterstraße,* following it back to *Askanischer Platz, Stresemann Straße,* and the now familiar, somehow reassuring ruins of *Anhalter Bahnhof.*

"Would you mind walking down *Stresemanstraße* as far as the Wall before heading back?"

"We certainly can't walk much farther than that now can we, Thomas? As D3 would say, 'Approved!'" Although there were no buildings, the streetcar tracks offered imaginary tram rides through the night, the emptiness, and the Wall itself back to the prewar Berlins. After reconnoitering the Wall at the intersection of *Stresemann-* and *Köthener Straße,* running my hands along its rough concrete surface, I turned around and looked back into West Berlin. In the distance, through the darkness, I could see the illuminated tower of the *Mathäiskirche* marking the middle of the *Kulturforum.* Again, that overwhelming sense of emptiness so characteristic of West Berlin, so much empty space in the city. But something was missing.

"Wait, wasn't there a large building still standing somewhere here a few years ago, Rainer? When I first came to West Berlin with the study group from Basel nine, ten years ago now, we drove by here in our bus after crossing back into West Berlin. It was partially in ruins, but largely intact. Unfortunately, we couldn't get out of the bus to take a closer look. There were arches running along the sides and a circular pavilion at one end."

"Yes, Thomas, that was *Haus Vaterland*, a restaurant, or should I say a *Haus*-full of restaurants run by *Kempinski*. Once, I had a passenger who asked me to bring him here before taking him to the *Hotel am Zoo*. He was writing a book about 'Berlin's Department Store of Pleasure.' He told me there was a cinema, a ballroom, the largest café in Berlin, several different German theme restaurants and beer halls, an Austrian restaurant, a Japanese teahouse, a Turkish café, an Italian bar, a Spanish wine cellar, and yes, Thomas, even a 'Wild West' bar in *Haus Vaterland*. He told me the bar was decorated as a blockhouse 'way out in the real prairie.' One could travel the Germanophilic world without leaving Berlin!"

"A 'Wild-West' bar! It's too bad it's not here anymore. What could be a better location than directly on the Wall, way out on the 'frontier of freedom?'"

Rainer laughed, "It must have been quite something before the war. Perhaps Thomas Wolfe stopped in for a drink. He came to Berlin twice you know, once in 1935 and then again for the Olympics in 1936. After the war, *Haus Vaterland* was partially renovated and reopened, but burned once again during the June 1953 uprising in East Berlin and closed permanently."

"Twice burned, once during the war and once during the revolution, Clio must have really had it in for the architect!"

"It's an interesting story. The building originally belonged to East Berlin. Following an exchange of properties about ten years ago, it became part of West Berlin. For four years, *Haus Vaterland* stood empty, an architectural middle ground between East and West. A friend of mine used to go there at night with others and walk through the rooms. They talked to and met with the *Vopos* posted at the far end of the building. There were rumors of romantic relations. The building was finally torn down in 1976."

"Fascinating!" Determined to return as soon as possible, camera and *Falkplan* in hand to recover and claim the terrain for my communications zone, I said, "Thanks pardner, are you ready to head back to the ranch?"

"Yes, I am! And unlike that other Thomas, you can go home again, I'll take you there!"

Once securely back in my one elegant Empire room, I opened the windows and lay down on the bed. I was extremely agitated, hyper, and had difficulty falling asleep. There were too many impressions, running coincidentally in chronological and reverse chronological order, too much to be fixed and developed. The intentionally off-key, repetitive *chanson* of the Paula Lead Band soloist seemed to haunt the hallway outside the French doors, or was it just Dr. Kahler returning? Uneasiness returned with the memory of the music in the *Tempodrom* and the T-T Music Café. I was tempted to get up and check the kitchen table for an open bottle of *Trolliger*. Alcohol seemed to mitigate the fear, at least temporarily. When the birds outside my window began to ask "Poo-tee-weet?" I opened my eyes and went back to sleep. It was midafternoon when I awoke. The fear was gone, leaving a residual emptiness in its place. After washing up and changing clothes, I decided to return to the Turn-Tower. I picked up my shoulder bag, checking to be certain I had both the *Falkplan* and my camera. Before leaving, I sat right down at my makeshift desk and reread both Lorelei's letter and Neal's poem. Looking up, I saw the flounder looking directly at me from the far wall with his fear-filled, fishy facial expression. I looked down at the heavy brass dolphin clock on the floor below. If I could arrive in the late afternoon, perhaps it would still be possible to get something to eat and take in the remarkable tower view, before the T-T Music Café refilled with people and music.

Handwriting on the Wall
August 1983

Walking up the stairs from the underground platform at *S-Bahnhof Anhalter Bahnhof*, I noticed a large hand-painted sign advertising *FLOHMARKT SAMSTAG SONNTAG* affixed to the railing. Another place to purchase artifacts from Berlins I through VI. Taking the notebook from my shoulder bag, I jotted down the times for future reference. Rather than walk across the rubble-strewn field as Rainer and I had done the night before, I followed *Stresemannstraße* from *S-Bahnhof Anhalterbahnhof* back to the Excelsior House. Even though the sun was shining, its rays were filtered through the grainy haze blanketing Berlin in the summertime, much like the day Neal and I walked along the banks of the Potomac just over a year ago, on the day of my departure from Washington, DC. Washington, District of Columbia. The artificial, compromise capital where Laura, Nadja, and, soon, Sophia were researching and writing. Laura. Once again, the threefold purpose of my relocation from Washington, DC, to Berlin passed before me in review, "A3"—archival, archaeological, and academic. Although my research continued on-site, it was into the HistoriCity itself rather than in the archives or at the university. I wasn't doing much writing at all, though I planned to have at least one, hopefully two, draft chapters ready to show Dr. Jourdan by the beginning of winter semester. There were still seven weeks, and although not ready, I was nonetheless looking forward to our meeting at the *Café Wellenstein*. In the gray light, the distances didn't appear as great as they had last night. By the time I reached the glass elevator at the foot of Excelsior House, I had resolved to abandon the ruins of the HistoriCity for the time being and return to the dissertation the following day.

No one was waiting in line for the elevator under the T-T Music Café sign. I pressed the call button. The stained steel door opened and a smiling young Charon extended his hand, charging one mark for his services, fifty *Pfennig* for the ride up, fifty *Pfennig* for the ride back down. As the doors closed, I turned to survey the HistoriCity as we rose above the ruins. Through the shimmering late summer haze, I could see the Wall separating Tiergarten in Berlin VI from Mitte in Berlin V and positively identify the landmarks of last night's walk that I wanted to document with my camera and map: the occupied *KuKuCK*; the stunted *Stuttgarter Hof*; the old cars, trails, and trees of the *Autodrom*; King Charlie on the corner—all bordered to the north by the Wall. On the far side, I could see the *Fernsehturm* and the *Berliner Dom*. Somewhere between the two stood *der Palast der Republik* and *Fräulein Otto,* "Under other circumstances, I'd be pleased to join you . . ." As the elevator car approached the top floor, I was greatly relieved not to feel a bass beat pounding through the stainless steel and concrete. When the doors opened, there was no music at all. Without music and the maddening crowd, the T-T Music Café stood exposed as an enormous empty (e.e.) room with a large rectangular bar in the center. All decoration had been stripped away, leaving a white, rough, concrete wall on one side and two-story plate glass windows on the other three. I hadn't had anything to eat since the *Stresemann* and decided upon a late lunch before working my way around the glass walls. Walking over to the bar, I sat down on a stool, taking the stained, sticky, laminated *Speisekarte* in my hand. There wasn't much, pizza, hamburger and the ubiquitous Berlin specialties, *Currywürst* and *Currybouletten*. I ordered two *Currybouletten mit Brötchen* and a bottled beer from the bartender, not the same one from earlier that morning but a young woman wearing the same signature T-T Music Café T-shirt, a provocative, hermaphroditic mix of male and female primary and secondary sexual characteristics. The only other person at the bar was an older, white-haired gentleman with horn-rimmed glasses, who appeared to have been sitting there for some time. He wore a worn-out, faded pink polo shirt with "Last Flight Out" embroidered over what appeared to be a Berlin Blockade-era C-47 Candy Bomber and cut-off shorts made from a US Army desert battle dress uniform. Looking over at me, he smiled pleasantly, nodding as if we knew each other, and then returned his attention to the notebook and the glass of Riesling in front of him on the counter. I hadn't noticed *Wein* on the menu. He, too, seemed familiar. I was curious but relieved when he showed no sign of wanting to converse. After mopping up the remaining *Curryketschup* with the last piece of *Brötchen*, I discovered I'd emptied my beer and ordered another for my walking windshield tour of the HistoriCity.

Rainer was right about the view. As Excelsior House stood just a dirt block away from the fortified sector border dividing the American from the Soviet Sector, West Berlin from *die Hauptstadt der DDR*, Berlin VI from Berlin V, the coign of vantage was spectacular, unifying. By decreasing the size of the Wall in proportion to its towering height of seventeen stories, the Turn-Tower allowed Berlin VI and Berlin V to be viewed as one city, the *Falkplan* effect, though the jagged white band of the Wall was clearly visible. Directly across from the dirt track, on the far side of the Wall, stood the former *Reichsluftfahrtministerium*, once headquarters of Hermann Goering, aka Hermann Meier, *Reichsluftfahrtminister* and graduate of the *Hauptkadettenanstallt* in Lichterfelde-West. My research into the construction of Tempelhof Airport and the John F. Kennedy Headquarters Building informed me Ernst Sagebiel was also the architect of this massive complex, constructed in the stripped classicism style propagated by Albert Speer. Given the intensity of the Strategic Bombing Campaign conducted by the Royal Air Force and the US Strategic Air Forces in Europe, together with the violence of Soviet ground operations supporting the Berlin Strategic Offensive Operation, the apparently undamaged state of the *RLM* qualified it as another of "bridge of tradition," regardless of its ruin value. It was yet another of the architectural *eirönïa* authored by Clio in Berlin.

Beer in hand, I made my way once slowly around the glass perimeter, noting the location of objects of interest. Returning the empty bottle to the bar, I took the SLR camera from my shoulder bag and walked the glass wall a second time. Although I usually took color slides, I'd loaded an East German *Orwo* black-and-white print film into my camera. It really didn't matter. Haze filtered out much of the color from the panorama below— Berlin IV and V were gray cities. "*All architecture is what you do when you look upon it, (Did you think it was in the white or gray stone? or the lines of the arches and cornices?).*" Looking through the lens at the objects below, I recalled the black and white prints attached to intelligence reports I'd reviewed in Vault Six. The Turn-Tower was indeed an excellent location for an observation and/or listening post, with visible architecture providing concrete cover for the invisible architectures of intelligence collection, sources, and methods. It was possible that some of the Berlin reporting I'd reviewed underground in Vault Six was based upon information collected here. Continuing my personal collection activities, I completed a third circuit of the glass walls, eye and a camera. Electronic feedback abruptly terminated all my collection activities. Technicians were setting up the sound stage. No music yet, but the unmistakable signal for my immediate departure. As I reached the elevator, the stained steel doors opened unexpectedly, releasing a band of post-punks onto the floor. White letters on the back of black leather motorcycle jackets, and black letters on white T-shirts, identified them as members and groupies of "the Fuckers." When I stepped aside to let them pass by, the Fucker closest to me looked up and said, "Oh, I beg your pardon, please excuse me!"

Surprised, I replied without thinking, "Why, you're the politest Fucker I've ever met." He laughed and walked on. Before rejoining Charon in his elevator, I turned and looked out over the room. The white-haired gentleman with the horn-rimmed glasses, pink polo shirt, and chocolate chip shorts was still sitting at the bar. He missed the "Last Flight Out." Just before the doors closed, he lifted his empty Riesling glass in my direction and called out, "No future!"

Back on the ground, I retraced the route Rainer and I had taken earlier that morning. Just ahead on *Anhalterstraße*, the three witches loomed up on the wall of the *KuKuCK*: "*Fair is foul, and foul is fair: Hover through the fog and filthy air.*" If the INFO-RAUM was now open, I could find out more about the *KuKuCK*. Unbarred, the metal door below the banner stood open, inviting me into a large, dark room, comfortably furnished with discarded sofas and chairs. There was music, but not so loud as to interfere with the conversations taking place. It might even have been AFN. Occupiers and occupied mixed in small groups or sat alone, reading by lamplight, as all ground-floor windows had been securely boarded up. Most were young men and women uniformly dressed in alternative lifestyle-style clothing. Cotton shirts, drawstring pants accented with color-coordinated *Palitücher*. A sawhorse café in the corner, reminding me of my waiting desk, offered coffee, tea, wine, and beer. Intending to order a cup of coffee instead of another beer, I changed my mind when I noticed the cups and glasses hadn't been washed. Sinking down into an overstuffed armchair, placing my shoulder bag at my feet, I leaned forward to set down my beer and pick up one of the flyers scattered on the large wooden packing crate serving as a coffee table. *Deutsch Amerikanische Freundschaft*. Sitting directly across from me on a complementary overstuffed sofa was a large, big-boned woman wearing a long, cotton print skirt, orange cotton blouse, and leather sandals. Fair-skinned, she wore her *rotblond* hair done up in dreadlocks. When I sat back in my chair, leaflet in hand, she looked up at me, pale blue eyes through gold, oval, wire-rimmed glasses, smiled, and said, "Hi, I'm Nicole."

"Hi, Nicole, I'm Thomas. I heard about the *KuKuCK* late last night, early this morning I should say, from a friend and thought I'd stop in the INFO-RAUM today. Do you live here?"

"No, I don't, but since moving to West Berlin last year, I often come here to meet friends who do and talk with visitors. The building has been occupied since January '81. Quite an interesting place really, part of an attempt to create an independent SO 36 within West Berlin. There are schools and childcare centers, too. Many people, not just young people, are coming to West Berlin, looking for an alternative way to live, like me. I come from West Germany. My parents are both medical doctors and would very much like me to become a medical doctor, too. So after a year of medical studies in Tübingen, I left and came to West Berlin. While still at the university, I'd heard about the *Instandbesetzer* trying to prevent the destruction of old apartment buildings here, so I decided to join them and am now living in an occupied house in Kreuzberg."

"An occupied house in the occupied American Sector."

Nicole laughed, "Yes, yes, in the occupied American Sector. I thought you might be American."

"Yes, I am. I'm a student, a graduate student at the Free University. I came here last year, too. I thought you might be American because you said 'hi,' but now I detect a British accent. Are you English?"

"No, no, I'm German. I picked up 'hi' from watching American television programs. Maybe that's why my parents decided to send me to school in England for a year, to Anglicize my English—just what a doctor's daughter should do, don't you think? Now that's quite a different story, an American studying in Berlin. Most of the students I know in Berlin would rather study in America."

"So I've been told. Three members of the seven members of the seminar I took last semester at the *FU* are now in or on their way to Washington, DC, where I came from. Sometimes I have the feeling I'm moving in the wrong direction."

"I have that same feeling sometimes, too. That's why I left Tübingen and came to West Berlin, to figure out what to do next. Although my parents don't approve of my lifestyle here, they continue to support me financially. I don't like it, but I don't have any other choice right now. To be quite honest with you, I'm not certain West Berlin is the alternative I'm looking for either. Although there are many different ideas about alternative lifestyles, they all seem to falter on who's turn it is to wash the dishes, the clothes, prepare the meals, and look after the children. Housework seems to fall on the women, while the men read, meet, and theorize about alternative lifestyles. Although they dress differently, many are as chauvinistic as their fathers. Some come to West Berlin to avoid serving in the *Bundeswehr*. It's compulsory in the *Bundesrepublik* you know."

I laughed, "Yes, I know, and in a way, it's ironic. At the last meeting of the seminar I mentioned, which was held not at the *FU* but in the WACS Wings Club at Tempelhof, we concluded West Berlin qualifies as an 'accidental *polis*' built upon the postwar military presence of the Western Allies, the Americans, the British, and the French. This military presence allows the majority of West Berlin's citizens to pursue relatively normal lives while coincidentally providing the opportunity for some, *Berliner* and *Wahlberliner* alike, to pursue alternative lifestyles, even to avoid the very military service that protects their alternative way of life in West Berlin."

"You know, to be quite honest, Thomas, I hadn't thought about it that way before, but I do tend to agree with you. Not to change the subject, but I noticed you picked up a flyer for tonight's *Rock für die Instandbesetzer* concert at *SO36*. Are you going?"

"A concert?"

"Yes, to raise money for the *Instandbesetzer*. Not only rock bands but theater groups as well. Even actors from the *Schaubüne* have performed here to help raise money. A group from *Restdeutschland, Deutsch Amerikanische Freundschaft* is playing at *SO36*, a club in Kreuzberg, tonight. *DAF* is very popular here, have you heard of them?"

"No, well, at least I don't think I have. I haven't been out dancing since my *Komilitonen* left for Washington. I did see *Deutsch Amerikanische Freundschaft* on the flyer but thought it might be a discussion on the relationship between the Federal Republic and the United States."

Nicole laughed again. Her teeth were small, her smile perfect. "Oh no, Thomas, *DAF* is *Neue Deutsche Welle*, part of the New German Wave! To be honest, I don't like their music very much. It's extremely loud, and their song lyrics refer to Mussolini and Hitler. Perhaps it's because I took classical piano for ten years—just what a doctor's daughter should do, don't you think? But I must confess I do love classical music, and I enjoy playing whenever I can find a piano to play. There aren't too many available in *besetzten Häuser!*"

"I've been listening to *Neue Deutsche Welle* but don't remember *DAF*. The music sounds interesting. A pianist! Have you heard of the jazz pianist Paula Lead?"

"Yes, I have. Her band played across the street at the *Tempdrom* last night. Although not New Wave, much more traditional and more intellectually stimulating, I also find her music destructive. I didn't go. Music can and should challenge our sensibilities, our *Weltanschauungen.* Now there's an untranslatable German word for you. Think of Erik Satie or even Karol Szymanowski. But at the same time, I strongly believe music should offer some kind of resolution, structure, or aesthetic order, particularly in those places and within those personalities where none is to be found. Does that make any sense? Deconstruction of music is 'de-composition,' potentially fertile but coincidentally an invitation to chaos and the emptiness."

"Well, I did go to the Paula Lead Band concert last night, Nicole. It was, as you say, 'intellectually stimulating' but emotionally disturbing, just for the reasons you mentioned. 'De-composition,' I like that. Decomposition amplified a sense of uneasiness and dread, even fear. I must say, I was very happy when the band had finished and we left the *Tempodrom.*"

"Well then, Thomas, I recommend you do not go to *SO 36* tonight to hear *DAF*, even though it's for a good cause. *DAF* is reductionist and destructive, much more so than The Paula Lead Band. Primitive. On the other hand, it's great dance music, especially if you're trying to dance your way through or out of something!"

Dance therapy! Another chance to dance my way out of my afflictions. I scanned the flyer quickly, folded it, and put it in my shoulder bag. "I would like to take a few more pictures today before it gets too dark. Would you like to join me for a short walk along the Wall, Nicole?"

"Yes, I would. One of the *Nachteile*, one of the disadvantages, about sitting in the INFO-RAUM, in addition to the dirty dishes, is the lack of natural light on the ground floor. All the windows have been boarded up to prevent the police from coming in and evicting everyone."

"*Räumung.*"

"Exactly!"

"More light!"

"Exactly, and that's why I'd like to come along with you. What would Eliot say, 'Let us go then, you and I . . .'? Believe it or not, American literature came along with my English language training!" We stood up and, picking up purse and shoulder bag, walked out through the unbarred metal door into the light of the early evening. Gray light turning powder blue. We *flâner*-ed past the lonesome Marlboro Man looking out over his empty lot, stopping to take pictures of *Stuttgarter Hof.* Reaching *Wilhelmstraße*, we turned left just as Rainer and I had done hours earlier, skirting the edge of *Das Autodrom* to King Charlie. The battered Cadillac with US forces plates was still parked across the street. Maybe King Charlie was American? Although I'd originally intended to go inside, now that Nicole had joined me, I decided to continue on *per pedes Pilgrimorum*. King Charlie would have to wait for another foray. We continued up *Wilhelmstraße* to the Wall, past the black-and-white sign informing us YOU ARE NOW LEAVING THE AMERICAN SECTOR, which was, of course, impossible. There was a wide path running parallel to the Wall leading back over toward the *Martin-Gropius-Bau*. We followed it, the fenced-in field behind the dirt track on our left, the Wall on our right. Although trees and brush had grown up between the path and the Wall, I could see it was particularly brutal at this point—massive, rough, horizontally laid concrete ties crowned with barbed wire strung from steel "Y" supports, repeatedly asking, "Why? Why? Why? Why?" as we walked. Walking up the stairs leading to the entrance of the *Martin-Gropius-Bau*, we turned around to see the former Prussian Parliament building on the far side of the Wall. We could, in turn, be seen from the two observation posts symmetrically placed over the prostyle, and from the watchtowers all along the *intervallum*. I wondered if our black-and-white portraits, captured on ORWO film, would be attached to a report and filed with others in an underground archives for government researchers with the proper clearance and "need to know" to review.

Beyond the *Martin-Gropius-Bau*, the facade of the Wall metamorphosed, becoming smoother as the horizontal concrete ties and barbed wire were relieved by massive identical sections of concrete topped with round pipe. The pipe prevented prospective wall jumpers, attempting to scale the Wall from West to East, from getting a grip. In West Berlin, it was possible to touch the Wall. In East Berlin, there were actually two walls with an *intervallum*, a mined death strip, running between. Both were untouchable. Perhaps in an effort to make the Wall less offensive to the citizens of West Berlin, the concrete had been painted flat white, providing a cold, hard canvas for graffiti and occasional artwork. There were many observations, political and personal, in handwriting on the western side of the Wall, directed to the governments of West, "*Brandt-Wehrner-Schmidt Volksverätter*," and of East Germany, "*Mauermörder*." Others commented on the absurdity of the Wall itself: "What a Boring Place to Build a Wall"; "ANTI-ARTIST ON HOLIDAY"; "This Ain't Pink Floyd's"; and its peculiar political implications, "*HALT—HIER ENDET DIE <u>FREIHEIT</u>*, JUMP OVER AND JOIN THE PARTY." An arrow indicated the direction to jump, providing the distance to the "SOCIALIST PARADISE 100 m." For those unwilling to jump over, a ladder had been painted on the surface of the Wall to facilitate climbing. One observation even introduced the question of *Wahrheit und Dichtung*: "This Is the Real Berlin Wall, This Wall is Not for the Movie 'Tunnel 28.'" In order to make "HILFE HELP AFGHANISTAN" visible in East Berlin, it had been painted backward on the Wall in West Berlin. "*Interzone*," painted on the Wall as background for the album cover shot of the band of the same name, had been modified to the more accurate "in a zone." "BOWIEHEROES" proclaimed the handwriting on the Wall, spray-painted lyrics on location. There were advertisements for Kreuzberger clubs as well, "TEENAGE JESUS *SO36*," with another arrow pointing back in the direction we'd just come from.

It was growing darker. Just ahead of us was the site of *Haus Vaterland*. I could almost see its massive silhouette through the dark blue haze. We had entered Tiergarten in the British Sector of Berlin. "Shall we continue on around to the *Philharmonie* and the *Brandenburger Tor* or walk back along the Wall to Kreuzberg?"

"Let's walk back, Thomas. I should be getting back home before too long." Retracing our path to King Charlie, rather than following the signs down *Kochstraße*, we took the path along the Wall. As we skirted the western edge of Potsdamer Platz, I noticed a piece of masonry partially buried in the path. Stopping, I worked it free from the earth and held it up so Nicole and I could examine it in the cold florescent light flowing over the Wall. A delicate, almost oriental pattern traced in blue onto a cream-colored tile, still firmly attached to a shattered piece of concrete.

"It's probably a piece of flooring from one of the buildings which used to stand here, perhaps from the *Potsdamer Bahnhof*, an artifact from an earlier Berlin." Although the surface aboveground had been swept clean by the war, underneath the grass and a thin layer of soil were, to the extent they remained untouched by the war and its aftermath, the remains of earlier Berlins: foundations, sewer systems, wiring conduits. I placed the broken tile carefully into the bottom of my shoulder bag so as not to damage the camera. Continuing along the Wall, we saw someone waking toward us rapidly, a short man wearing a slouch hat and a trench coat, carrying a stepladder. Reaching a graffiti-free stretch of the Wall, he walked over to it and set up his stepladder. Stepping back off the lighted path into the shadows, Nicole and I stopped to watch. He climbed the rungs to the top of the ladder. A wall jumper? Surely he wasn't going to attempt to jump over. Even with the ladder, he couldn't reach the round pipe running along the top of the Wall. Reaching into his trench coat, he pulled out a large cylinder. For a moment, I thought it might be a non-improvised explosive device of some kind, a grenade or a mine, but when he shook it, we heard the unmistakable sound of a mixing ball and realized it was a can of spray paint. We watched as he painted, in large black, block letters on the Wall, carefully moving his ladder as he wrote: "DURCH LERNEN LEIDEN."[40] Once he'd finished, he put the spray paint can back under his trench coat,

40 "Suffer through Leaning" (vice Learn through Suffering), Diary of Thomas Vonaechron, Diary Extract, 1983, trans. TV.

climbed down the ladder, folded it, and putting it securely under his arm, looked back over his shoulder and quickly continued on his way. There was no indication he had seen us. "I'm not certain Nicole, but I think that might have been Orestes."

"Orestes, Thomas?"

"Not Orestes, but the actor who played Orestes at the *Saubühne*."

"Don't you mean the *Schaubühne*, Thomas?"

"Yes, yes, of course Nicole, at the *Schaubühne*." We continued walking along the Wall. The dirt path ended just before Checkpoint Charlie, my point of entry into East Berlin—Berlin V. Florescent security lighting in East and West heightened the surrealism of a surreal scene, a crossing point between two empires of light. Through the window of the guard shack, I could see an American military policemen framed as if in an Edward Hopper painting, and I thought of SFC Keith, the friendly MP I'd talked to before leaving the American Sector for the capital of the German Democratic Republic last December. We continued down *Kochstraße*, which metamorphosed into *Oranienstraße* after we crossed *Lindenstraße*. Just down *Lindenstraße* was the Berlin Museum, one of the many stops built into our seven-day study trip. When Nicole and I reached *Moritzplatz*, I saw another checkpoint on our left, *Prinzenstraße*, for citizens of the Federal Republic. Nicole turned to me and said, "I'll leave you here, Thomas. Thanks so much for chatting me up and for the walk along the Wall. Do you have something to write on? I'll give you the phone number of my *WG*. Maybe we could meet again." Reaching into my shoulder bag, I pulled out the *Rock für die Instandbesetzer* flyer. Nicole wrote her name and number on the back. Turning the flyer over, she read it as she handed it back. "I know you're not interested in going to hear *DAF* tonight, but the *SO36* is straight ahead on *Oranienstraße*, in an old movie theater. During the fifties and sixties, Kreuzberg became a mecca for Turkish immigrants—yes, Thomas, Turkish immigrants in the American Sector! After the *Kino* closed, the owner rented it out for Turkish marriages and circumcision ceremonies, which still take place there. Perhaps there will be another *Rock für die Instandbesetzer* concert with a more 'composed' band we could attend together! I'll watch for flyers in the INFO-RAUM."

"Thank you very much, Nicole, I've enjoyed talking and walking with you, too. It would be nice if we could meet again. I'd like to hear more of your thoughts on music, perhaps even hear you play, if we could find a *besetztes Haus* with a piano." I wrote my name and *Herr* Kahler's telephone number on a corner of the flyer, tore it off, and gave it to her.

"Thank you, Thomas. By the way, did your surname used to be 'von Aechron?'" Before I could answer her, Nicole laughed, turned, waved, and walked down *Prinzenstraße* away from the Wall. I watched her walk that way, then turned back to look again at the crossing point. There was little activity. I thought about taking the *U-Bahn* to *Kottbusser Tor,* change to *Linie 1* to *Zoo,* where I could catch the *U-9* back to Friedenau and my one elegant Empire room. I had work to do tomorrow morning. In spite of my apprehension, Nicole had unintentionally sparked an interest in the music of *Deutsch Amerikanishe Freundschaft,* Mussolini, and Hitler? I thought about my conversation with Robert Jones at the *Arlecchino.* If *DAF* were too loud, too dissonant, too 'decomposed,' I could leave and catch *Linie 1* at *Görlitzer Bahnhof,* maybe even have a *Kebab* before returning home. Tomorrow, it was back to work on the dissertation. I reached into my shoulder bag for the flyer, *SO36* was at Oranienestraße 190. It was close by, I didn't need the *Falkplan* to find my way.

In the Ruins

August 1983

When I reached number 190, I joined a small group of people forming up on the sidewalk in front of the former film theater, a few meters back from a large, black metal scissors gate blocking the entrance doors. Between the group and the gate, there were thirty or forty human shapes, sitting or lying on the concrete in front of the theater. A member of our group knew what to do, signaling to the gatekeeper that we had money to pay for tickets. He slammed open the gate, clearing a path for us through the shades, who began to rise from the pavement and plead for money, *"Ey Alter, haste 'ne Mark für mich?"* After he slammed the gate shut behind us, I bought a ticket and followed the others down a long, dark, smoke-filled hallway, lined on both sides with more human shapes. The hallway opened up into the large room, which had once been the movie theater. All seating and carpeting had been ripped out, leaving only the concrete floor and a bare stage, visible through the smoke. Two large ventilator fans mounted directly over the stage swirled heavy blue smoke, a mixture of pot and tobacco, as it rose from the dance floor. There was no bar. Warm cans of beer were being sold for one *D-Mark* directly from the stacks of cardboard boxes they'd been delivered in. The bartender ripped the top off a box to hand me the beer I'd paid for. The music hadn't started yet, so I walked around the dance floor. The crowd was as diversely dressed as the operagoers at the *Deutsche Oper.* Many wore the alternative uniform of the *Instandbesetzer.* One young woman with dreadlocks saw me smiling at the white rat sitting on her shoulder and asked me if I would like to pet it.

Taking this as a sign of trust, I did so, speaking softly to the rat. She took me into her confidence. "*Mein Weinachtsgeschenk. Ick muss ja uffpassen. Die Skins...*" she nodded very discreetly in the direction of a group of skinheads standing apart from the rest drinking beer, "*. . . haben mal versucht sie zu töten, die Arschlöcher!*"[41] Although I'd often seen individual skinheads riding the *S-* and *U-Bahnen*, this was the first time I'd seen this many together. They too had their uniform—shaved heads, white T-shirts, blue jeans, and heavy work boots. Although they kept to themselves, crushing beer cans in their hands once they'd finished, occasionally surveying the room, they radiated brutality and violence. A woman surround by a small entourage of admirers walked by us. Heavily made-up, with her henna hair in an updo, she too wore a white T-shirt, cut away to reveal her small breasts. "*Kieck 'mal! Das ist ja Zazie de Paris, eigentlich ein Mann, ein Franzose, der sich zur Frau umwandlen leisst. Ick hab' ja voll Veständnis dafür. Männer sind olle Scheißkerle. Nur ficken wollen sie olle!*" Turning back to me she smiled and said, "*Dich hab' ik ja natürlich nischt damit gemeeint!*"[42]

Petting the rat as a furry farewell to the rat girl, I continued sailing around the room. Just as I reached the wall on the far side, carefully keeping the skins in my peripheral vision, what little light there was went down and *DAF* took the stage. Two brutally handsome young men dressed in black leather vests, pants, and boots—one, the drummer, was blonde; the other, the lead singer, dark. Both wore their hair cut very short and stylish. A woman, looking like Paula Lead's evil twin—dressed in black, sleeveless dress, leather boots, and stiff black hair blown out punk-style—carried out a small synthesizer, which she carefully positioned on top of an aluminum folding table and plugged into the sound system. Once the drummer was seated with drumsticks in hand, and the singer had taken the microphone from the stand, Paula's twin pushed a button. Five notes on a preprogrammed playback loop fed through the synthesizer electrifying the *SO36.* The drummer joined in as the vocalist began leaping across the stage, swinging his arms wildly, not so much dancing as convulsing. Many in the audience began to do the same. The music was deafening, decomposing. Smoke generators on the stage poured white smoke into the air, floating projection screens for colored lights flashing with the pounding beat. In his deep, monotonic *Sprechgesang*, the vocalist ordered the crowd to dance, clap and move their bodies to a beat even more penetrating than the one I'd felt the night before in the T-T Music Café. I heard "Mussolini." Sweating

41 "My Christmas present. I have to watch out, the skins tried to kill her once, the assholes!" Diary of Thomas Vonaechron, Diary Extract, 1983, trans. TV.
42 "Look there, that is *Zazie de Paris*, a man, a Frenchman, who decided to become a woman. I understand completely. Men are all shitheads. They only want to fuck . . . I didn't mean you, of course!" Diary of Thomas Vonaechron, Diary Extract, 1983, trans. TV.

heavily, he ordered the dancers to turn to the right, and began to rave about "Hitler." He then commanded them to move like "*Jesus Christus.*" Some dancers began to parody the crucifixion. After adding "*Kommunisnmus,*" he returned to Mussolini, repeating his previous instructions to the crowd. The fear rose rapidly—not from the music but from within me. From my chest, it spread out through my arms into my fingers. I had to get out. This proved to be more difficult than I had imagined. The space above the dance floor was filled with writhing limbs of ecstatic dancers. I tried to make my way to the exit through the shapes lining the walls. Before I was halfway to the exit, *DAF* transitioned to their next song. In the same dark, measured *Sprechgesang,* the vocalist sang about the darkness of their clothes, the beauty of their boots and the intensity of their screams. The skinheads had apparently been waiting for this line. One wearing hobnail boots leapt up onto the stage screaming "Oi, Oi, Oi!" The others joined in from the floor, raising their right fists as they did so. Two security guards came from behind and shoved him off the stage into their waiting arms. *DAF* didn't miss a synthesized beat.

As I continued to make my way along the wall, I heard the lead singer call out for a new dance, a wild and evil dance, the dance of everyone against everyone. This was anarchy—this was the end. Working against paralyzing panic and the maddening crowd, I found my way back to the hallway and the gated exit to *Oranienstraße.* The gate guard had just cleared a path through the shapes, which I used to make my escape, making my way through the preterit chorus chanting, "*Ey Alter, haste 'ne Mark für mich?*" as they rose from the concrete. I walked back the way I had come, hoping the fear would recede as I walked. It didn't. If I stopped moving, I knew I wouldn't be able to take another step, seized by *torpeur involontaire,* so I kept going. Walking back to *Moritzplatz,* I turned into *Prinzenstraße* with my back to the Wall, walking in the same direction Nicole had. On the far side of the *Landwehrkanal, Prinzenstraße* became *Baerwaldstraße.* I continued on, hoping by some unlikely chance I might meet Nicole on the street. I didn't. Reaching *Gneisenaustraße,* I turned to the right, trying to work my way back over to *Potsdamer Straße* and the familiar walk back to Friedenau. Although the *Falkplan* was in my shoulder bag, I couldn't risk stopping to look at it, I had to keep moving. *Gneisenaustraße* became *Yorckstraße.* An iron bridge from an earlier Berlin carried me safely over the S-Bahn tracks. I saw the sign for the *S-Bahnhof* but decided to continue on foot. People walked past me on their way to the *S-Bahnhof,* on their way to work. On the far side of the bridge was *Goebenstraße.* Crossing over a broad street, *Goebenstraße* became *Pallasstraße.* A park opened up on my right. At the end closest to me stood another red *Backsteinkirche* from Berlin II.

I walked toward the entrance, *Sankt Matthiaskirche. Winterfeldtplatz.* The broad street I'd crossed over must have been *Potsdamer Straße.* I'd missed my turn off, gone too far. It was no use to try and open the heavy wooden doors, I knew they were locked. "*Jesus Christus.*" I knocked. There was no answer, but I wasn't alone. Shades began to rise from the stairs on both sides of the entrance doors, "*Ey Alter, haste 'ne Mark für mich?*" Turning my back on them before they had the chance to stand, I hurried back down the stairs.

Walking back to *Potsdamer Straße*, I saw a familiar red and white beer advertisement illuminating the front of a *Gaststätte* on the far side of *Winterfeldtplatz.* Another beer would help me overcome the panic and make it back to my one elegant Empire room. Using the beer light as a guiding light, I walked toward the silhouette of what at first appeared to be an apartment building. When I reached the edge of *Winterfeldplatz*, I could see it was only the shell of a bombed-out apartment building, a ruin. But the red and white beer light, mounted on the shell facing the street, was on. The apartment building was in ruins, but the bar, *die Ruine*, was in the ruins. Taking a step up into what once was the front room, I saw a metal door on the far side, leading to a farther room. I made my way carefully across the floor, which appeared to be sound. The metal door was unlocked. Opening it, I found myself in *die Ruine*, in the Ruins. Empty and half-empty glasses, beer and wine bottles littered the floor. A few tables and chairs were scattered about the room. Three customers were sitting in chairs, three others lying on the floor. An impromptu exhibition of objects and individuals, their arrangement a function of accident, use, or abuse. There was no music, no conversation. Behind the old dark wooden bar stood two women, a plump, middle-aged woman with thinning, bright henna-red hair, alabaster skin, and the most beautiful face I'd ever seen, wearing a bright, flowered tent dress. The other woman was much younger, tall and lithe, with her long blonde hair dressed in Roman fashion falling in tresses, dressed in yellow chiffon. Her face was identical to the older woman's. She even wore the same makeup and bright red lipstick as her mother. Here in the Ruins, mother and daughter presided over a refuge for the preterit of West Berlin. I was now among them. *Die Ruine* was not only a bar but a hotel. A metal sign behind the bar advertised "*Zimmer frei*," a room available in the Ruins. Stepping around the green glass beer bottles and over a man dressed in the uniform of the German merchant marine, I made my way to the bar to order a beer. "*Warum biste so trauich, meen Kleener?*" asked the mother.[43]

---

43 "Why are you so sad my little one. . . . You're blubbering. OK, then, in High German, you're crying." Diary of Thomas Vonaechron, Diary Extract, 1983, trans. TV.

"Wieso trauig?"

"Du flennst ja."

"Flennst?"

"Na jut, dann auf Hochdeutsch, du weinst ja."

I didn't realize I was crying. I was frightened, scared, but not sad, not yet. I took a *Taschentuch* out of the inside pocket of my sport coat and wiped the tears from my face.

"Ein Bier bitte, 0.5."

"Junge, wat sollen det mit dem Bier? Am Ende," she turned to look at her daughter and then turned back to me, *"so wie du dir fühlst an diesem Ort, ist Durscht nicht schlimmer als Heimweh. Statt Bier, ruf ick dir lieba 'ne Taxe. Der Anruf kostet dir nüscht."*[44]

The barkeeper's beautiful daughter spoke softly to her mother, her blue eyes sparking, *"Vielleicht möchtet der Herr einen Tee um sich zu beruhigen, Maman? Er könnte dann die Nacht hier bei uns verbringen!"*[45] Her bright red lipstick highlighted her full, sensuous mouth. To fight the fear spreading from my chest through my arms, legs, and fingers, I watched her red lips form the words. Misunderstanding my attention, she smiled.

"Nee, nee, meene Liebste, der junge Mann muß die Ruine verlassen, er soll nach Hause. Wir wolln doch keene Missverständnis, wa'?" Before I could speak, she held the telephone receiver in her hand, *"Gleditschstraße 9."* She'd done this many times before. After hanging up, she turned to me, smiling benevolently in the same bright red lipstick as her daughter and said, *"Kannste draussen vor der Tür warten, Taxe kommt gleich. Jute Nacht und Alles Jute! Komma wieda meen Kleener, wenn Du nich so trauich bist!"*[46] Thanking them both, I walked back out through the door, carefully avoiding the sleeping sailor, the glasses and bottles scattered on the floor, and stood in the ruins facing the street. I could feel warm tears running down my cheeks. It was all too much, too much for me, too much for me to fix, to fix and develop, too many images. I was exhausted and no longer had the strength to hold everything together. The carefully constructed archival and architectural foundations of Berlin I, Berlin II, Berlin III, Berlin IV, Berlin V, and Berlin VI collapsed, along with my personal operational architecture, the points of reference, the lines of communications, my

44 "What do you want a beer for my boy? At the end, where you now find yourself, thirst is not worse than homesickness. Instead of the beer, I'll call you a taxi. It won't cost you anything." Diary of Thomas Vonaechron, Diary Extract, 1983, trans. TV.

45 "Perhaps a cup of tea would calm the gentleman down, Maman? He could then spend the night here with us." Diary of Thomas Vonaechron, Diary Extract, 1983, trans. TV.

46 "No, no, my dearest one, the young man must leave the Ruins, he must return home. We don't want a misunderstanding . . . you can wait outside, in front of the door, the taxi's coming. Good Night and the best of luck. Come again when you're not so sad." Diary of Thomas Vonaechron, Diary Extract, 1983, trans. TV.

entire communications zone. A big yellow Mercedes 200D taxi pulled up on the street in front of *Ruine*. Taxi? No illuminated advertisement for "(American Literature)"; it wasn't Rainer, what would've been the chances? Afraid to return to my one elegant Empire room alone, I gave the driver George's address on *Roseneck*. George was home and, fortunately, up late reading when I arrived.

"*Mein armer*, Thomas! What's the matter?" I tried to explain but was only able to sob. George held me in his arms for a long time and finally said, "Let me take you to the university hospital, Thomas. It's part of the *FU*. They'll be able to give you something to help you relax, to help you sleep." Once in George's car, I closed my eyes. After a short drive, we arrived at the *Klingsorstraße* entrance to the *Universitätsklinikum-Benjamin-Franklin*. "Thomas, we're here." I opened my eyes. George drove up the broad concrete entrance ramp leading to the modern building, parked the car out front, and walked with me through the metal and glass doors into the *Notaufnahme*—Emergency. He explained as best he could and, after I'd answered a few questions, helped me fill out the paperwork. "They have a bed for you, Thomas. It would be a good idea for you to rest here tonight and talk with a doctor in the morning. I'll come back later today, this afternoon." I agreed. A nurse joined us. The three of us walked together to a stainless steel elevator in the lobby, like the T-T Music Café but without windows. Before we entered it, George stopped. "Here's your shoulder bag, Thomas. I hope you're able to sleep well. I'm certain everything will work out fine." George smiled, hugged me, and stepped back. The nurse and I walked into the elevator together, then turned to face George. She pushed a button. George waved until the stainless steel elevator doors closed. The elevator took us up to the soothing silence of the seventh floor, to the *Psychiatrische Ambulanz*.

CHAPTER V:
Psychiatrische Ambulanz

*Cornegidouille! nous n'aurons point tout demoli si nous ne
démolissons même les ruines!
Or je n'y vois d'autre moyen que d'en équilibrer de beaux
édifices bien ordonnés.*[47]

—Alfred Jarry, *Ubu enchaîné*

Notaufnahme und Aufnahme
September 1983

OVEREXPOSED. Before the innumerable, unnumbered images could be
fixed, fixed and developed. Before the fixed and developed images could
be arranged, arranged and described. Before a finding-aid, *ein Findmittel*,
could be prepared and intellectual control over the images established,
an elementary exercise in archival science. Before the individual strata of
images could be identified and labeled "I" through "VI," an elementary
exercise in archeology. Innumerable, unnumbered, unfixed, undeveloped,
unarranged, intellectually uncontrolled images captured on color slides,
black-and-white contact prints, microfiche, in memory and imagination.
Sifting through the images spread out before me, I destroy their original
order and provenance while preserving intact the images themselves, the
faces and the facades of Berlin, fragments stored against *meine Ruine*.
Liberated from the Schliemannian schema, they become building blocks
for a new city, a fine, well-designed city constructed from repurposed
fragments, fantasy, and fraud to suit my fiction. Unreal HistoriCity.

When the stainless steel elevator doors opened out onto the seventh
floor, the nocturnal admissions nurse escorted me down a corridor to
the empty, dimly lit waiting room of *Psychiatrische Ambulanz*, politely
gesturing for me to take a seat. She handed my file to the nurse on duty at
the desk, walked back over to me, and after extending her hand and wishes
for a "*Gute Besserung*," took the elevator back down to the *Notaufnahme*, to

---

47 Silly horn. We will not have demolished everything, if we don't demolish the ruins! But I see
no other way to demolish the ruins than by using them to construct many beautiful, well-designed
buildings!'" trans. François Fontane.

Emergency Admissions—to the *Erdgeschoß*. Waiting in the empty waiting room, I could feel the fear beginning to rise again. Unable to contain it, I stood up, walked over to the duty nurse perusing my file, and asked if I could lie down. She nodded and escorted me to an adjacent examination room, furnished with a low, narrow, wheeled, white metal-frame bed, remarkably similar to the wheeled dollies I'd used to pull records in Vault Six, and a white metal chair. The fear receded somewhat as I lay down. A doctor joined us, under her right arm a folded copy of the biweekly Nadja wrote for occasionally, a daily catalog of the hundreds of events taking place in West Berlin. I'd used it to connect experience with coordinates on the *Falkplan* and construct my communications zone. Now my COMZ was in ruins, leaving in its place a residual fear so intense I had to walk or cry to exorcise it. *Civilement mort*. The doctor thanked the nurse, who returned to her desk in the waiting room. Leafing through my admissions paperwork, she said something I didn't understand. "*Wie bitte?*" I asked her.

"*Aufnahmefähig*," she repeated. "*Vielleicht sind Sie nicht mehr aufnahmefähig.*" She hesitated for a moment, smiled, and continued in English, "Perhaps you are no longer capable of absorbing, of taking in . . . experience." Standing next to the head of the wheeled white bed, she looked down at me. Neither young nor old, very attractive in an enameled *KPM* porcelain way. Her face, a study in professional interest and concern, was framed by a *bubi* haircut—thick, dishwater blonde hair, green eyes, no makeup. She understood I needed to be touched. Setting my paperwork and her magazine down on the white metal chair next to the bed, she leaned over me and took my hand in hers. Gently laying it palm down upon the bed, she began to massage my arms, then my shoulders in a detached, professional manner. Although she wore the long, bright white *Kittel* of her profession, it was unbuttoned. She'd been reading, and she had apparently slipped the coat on just before entering the examination room without buttoning it. I watched her breasts move rhythmically in the soft cups of her brassiere, visible beneath her black blouse. To mitigate my *Angst*, I tried to imagine making love to her on the wheeled bed. Although this practiced distraction didn't work, Pan yielded to the human touch. Standing behind the head of the bed, massaging my temples, she spoke to me in a soft, yet authoritative, professional voice. She was observing and evaluating, "I believe it would be . . . beneficial if you would consider staying here in the Ambulant Psychiatry for a few days. This would give us the time we need for an evaluation, and to help you." From her inverted perspective, my facial expression must have registered concern. From my inverted perspective, I could see she was smiling. "There's no need to be concerned, Mr. Vonaechron, this is not a closed ward, this is not a 'cuckoo's nest.' You would be free to come and go as you please." Placing myself under her care, I agreed to stay and removed myself, at least temporarily, from the world of self-imposed purpose, from history. *Psychiatrische Ambulanz* absorbed all the points of reference and my broken lines of communication, becoming for the next twenty-one days, my zone of communications. No longer *aufnahmefähig* and anchorless, I became anchorite.

During that three-week stay, I discovered the *Universitätsklinikum Benjamin Franklin (UKBF)* was a "teaching hospital." My on-site education continued. Part of the Free University, with facilities for instruction and research as well as patient care, the *UKBF* was additional, architectural proof of George's "*hier* in Berlin we have at least two of everything" hypothesis. The *Charité,* the oldest teaching hospital in Berlin, belonged to *Humboldt Universität* in East Berlin. As US occupation authorities had requisitioned the nearby hospital on *Unter der Eichen* that D3 and I recc'ed during our windshield tour of Little America, West Berlin's legendary Lord Mayor Willy Brandt went to Washington to request American funding for a new hospital. It was designed by the New Orleans-based firm Curtis and Davis, Architects, which also designed the US Embassy in Saigon and the James Forrestal Building for the Defense Department in Washington, DC. Curtis and Davis were assisted on site by Berlin architect Franz Mocken. When dedicated in 1968, the *Grauer Riese,* the "Gray Giant," as the *UKBF* was christened by *Berliner,* was the largest, most modern clinic in Europe. In keeping with current American thinking, all medical departments and educational facilities were consolidated under one roof. A gray giant of glass and steel. "*All architecture is what you do when you look upon it, (Did you think it was in the white or gray stone? or the lines of the arches and cornices?)*" During an in-house outpatient walk, I discovered a freestanding steel sculpture in the west entrance hall displaying the clinic's mission statement. Mounted beneath a geometric landscape of flat metal plates screwed to a stainless steel frame, not unlike the frames displaying the map of the Berlin transportation system in the *U-* and *S-Bahn* stations, it read, "The Benjamin Franklin Foundation erected this Medical Center in the spirit of German-American cooperation for the healing of the sick and advancement of education and research at the Free University of Berlin." For a student of the *FU* and walking casualty of *Deutsch Amerikanische Freundschaft,* the Gray Giant offered architectural refuge for psychological triage and recovery from an *Einsturz—in den Neubauten.*

Gigantomachy
September 1983

Stationary, no longer in movement, exhausted and *nicht mehr aufnahmefähig*. After I'd signed the additional admissions paperwork, the sympathetic psychiatrist in her long, white *Kittel* and black blouse offered me *Schlafmittel* from an ivory-colored plastic phial. I sat up on the bed, gratefully taking the tablet from the small plastic cup in her outstretched hand. After swallowing it with the glass of room-temperature sparkling mineral water she held in her other hand, I lay back down on my white wheeled dolly and closed my eyes, passing directly from her healing hands into the waiting arms of the fairies' midwife, Queen Mab.

I—there's the rub—found myself four-point harnessed into the shotgun seat of the Shield of Achilles with D3 at the wheel. We were both dressed in woodland pattern battle dress uniforms (BDUs), wearing Personnel Armor System for Ground Troops (PASGT) helmets. In spite of repeated denials by the Department of the Army, they looked very much like the German "coal-scuttle" helmets of both World Wars. This was no "off-pass" USMLM tour, no leisurely windshield tour of Little America—we were in hot pursuit of Clio, the muse of history, speeding down the *menschenleere Strasse des 17. Juni*. As we careened around the Chick-on-a-Stick at *Grosser Stern*, tires squealing and rubber burning, D3 put the Shield into a four-wheel drift. Moltke and Roon turned on their pedestals to look on in shock and awe as we drifted by. Accelerating out of the drift onto the far side of *Strasse des 17. Juni*, D3 drove on past the Soviet Memorial. Observing the Shield engaged in pursuit, former members of the Soviet Military Liaison Mission ran to their black Opel Kombi, parked on the street in front of the memorial. Turning to me with a broad grin spreading across his battle face, D3 said, "Let's go east, Thomas!" The Wall was down. We drove on. As we approached the center passageway of the Brandenburg Gate, *Eirēnē-cum-Viktoria-cum Eirēnē* wheeled her four-horsed chariot 180 degrees to face the Shield. Undaunted by the oncoming quadriga, D3 passed beneath the goddess into the former Soviet Sector of Berlin and *Hauptstadt der DDR*. As we slowed to circumnavigate *Pariser Platz,* I saw the American flag flying from the Embassy of the United States in the restored neoclassical *Blücher Palais* on our right. A tall, portly, white-haired gentleman wearing horn-rimmed glasses and standing on the balcony overlooking *Pariser Platz* observed our progress.

"Hey, D3, isn't that General Vernon Walters standing on the balcony of the embassy?"

"Sorry, Thomas," he answered. "No disrespect to the good general intended, but if we stop, we'll lose Clio," and accelerated down the deserted *Unter den Linden.* We passed by the Hotel Adlon on our right, where Colonel Arthur Conger, US Army, also watched from the balcony of his suite, and the artificially illuminated white Russian Embassy. The larger-than-life marble bust of Vladimir Ilych Ulyanov in the center of the forecourt had already been boxed for storage. What was to be done? We drove on, down *Unter den Linden.* As we passed *Humboldt Universität*, both Wilhelm and Alexander turned their heads to watch but remained seated. Enthroned in the center courtyard, Theodore Mommsen, white hair blown back by a storm blowing from paradise, attempted to struggle to his feet but was held down by the weight of the heavy marble history book open upon his lap. The roar of the Shield's high-performance ThunderJet engine startled Condé, Frederick the Great's mount atop the monument on the median. Rearing back on his hind legs, Condé knocked the four virtues, Fortitude, Justice, Prudence, and Temperance from their pedestal at Frederick's feet to the ground. Frederick held on tightly as Condé clambered down from the monument to join in pursuit. Looking in the Shield's rear view mirror, I watched as General George D. McKiernan, Army of the Republic, jumped his favorite mount, Kentuck, over the Prussian officers assembled at the base of the pedestal to the top, taking up the position vacated by Frederick the Great. Immanuel Kant, one of the few civilians, shook his walking stick at us categorically as we drove on. Standing on the balcony of the *Kronprinzenpalais* supported by four Corinthian columns, *Kaiser* Bill took the parade, though it was more of a *mêlée* at this point, as we passed in review. "Eyes right!" As he returned my salute, I wondered what my grandfather would think. Braking hard as we approached the *Zeughaus*, the former Prussian-arsenal-turned-German-historical-museum, D3 took a sharp left turn into *Am Zeughaus*. From under glass, I saw the *neue Alte Kommandantur* and noted with pleasure the monstrous, neo-Renaissance Prussian St. Peter's had been deconstructed, the neoclassical Schinkel *Dom* reconstructed in its place. I made a mental note to tell George. Crossing over *Bodestraße*, we continued straight ahead onto *Am Kupfergraben*. Slowing the Shield to pedestrian speed, D3 turned right, driving over the pedestrian bridge across the *Spreekanal* onto Museum Island, up the stairs leading to the main entrance of the Pergamon Museum. Our four-point harnesses held us firmly in place as the Shield jounced up the concrete stairs. "This is just the 'shakedown' these heavy-duty shocks and suspension needed," joked D3. As we reached the top of the stairs, I looked in the rearview mirror to see if the black SOXMIS/SMLM Opel Kombi and Frederick the Great mounted on Condé were still following us. In their stead, I saw an older, dignified stateswoman with reddish brown hair, wearing a red sport coat, observing us from the third-floor balcony of a four-story gray townhouse directly opposite the Pergamon. As she watched, she pressed the thumbs and forefingers of her hands together over her red sport coat, forming a heart—a good omen.

"Hang on, Thomas, here we go!" shouted D3. Taking my eyes from the rearview mirror, I looked straight ahead. On the facade of what appeared to be the seventh antiaircraft bunker built by the *GBI,* silver letters spelled out "PERGAMONMUSEUM." We drove on, through the glass portico and the massive front doors, the great doors of history, which Clio had left open, either intentionally or in haste, on through the entrance hall into the central exhibition room.

We approached the Pergamon Altar in the Shield of Achilles from the west on the fortress road, entering immediately into *Gigantomachia,* the war between the giants and the Olympians. We took up a position at the base of the white marble staircase leading up to the colonnade enclosing the altar for burnt offerings. D3 shook his helmeted head. "Even with the heavy-duty shocks, the Shield won't make it up those stairs, Thomas!" From under hardened glass, I could see Zeus, Pallas Athena and Hercules engaged in hand-to-hand combat with the giants Typhoeus, Enkeladus, Rhoetus, and Poryphyrius, the children of Ge and Uranus. The struggle had reached its culmination point; it was uncertain whether or not order and reason would prevail over chaos. At the height of the fighting, neither gods nor giants paid any attention to the idling of the Shield's ThunderJet engine. Turning to me, D3 said, "You know a lot, Thomas, but I bet you didn't know Pergamon was the first city in Asia Minor to embrace emperor worship, long before Berlin. Why, it's even mentioned in the Book of Revelation!" Taking out a pocketbook New Testament bound in an unfamiliar sand, gray, and green digital camouflage pattern from the blouse pocket of his BDUs, D3 smiled and said, "American Standard Version," then read aloud, "'And to the angel of the church in Pergamun write: The One who has the sharp two-edged sword says this: "I know where you dwell, where Satan's throne is;"'" Re-pocketing the New Testament, D3 backed the Shield slowly away from the stairs, turned to the right, and drove on, through the open doors, across the column-lined marketplace of Miletus. Phoenician philosopher Thales, who looked a lot like Dr. Schneider wearing a white linen *chiton,* suddenly stepped out in front of the Shield with hands cupped around his mouth, shouting *"symmachia."* D3 had to swerve sharply to avoid running him down.

"Phew, that was close! Can't stop, Thomas—thar she blows and thar she goes!" D3 said, following Clio through the Ishtar Gate into Babylon.

As we drove through the city walls, our woodland pattern BDUs pixelated into the desert sand, urban gray, and foliage green universal camouflage pattern (UCP) of the Army Combat Uniform (ACU), the same pattern as on the cover of D3's pocket-sized New Testament. The front seat divided into bucket seats, shifting as the Shield metamorphosed from a Ford Custom Police Interceptor into an M3 Bradley Calvary Fighting Vehicle (CFV*)*. The driver's seat, with D3 at the wheel, moved forward. My seat moved backward toward the center of the vehicle, then up into the gunner's position in the turret. An empty seat, the commander's seat, appeared beside me. Although I could no longer see D3, the digital readout on the display screen in front of me indicated he drove on at the Bradley's maximum speed, forty-one miles per hour. Scraping both sides of the lion-lined Processional Way, a Walled Street canyon, the Shield smashed the glazed-bricks and crushed the 2,600-year-old brick pavement, grinding the shards in the Bradley's treads. "*All architecture is what you do when you look upon it, (Did you think it was in the white or gray stone? or the lines of the arches and cornices?)*" After taking Clio into protective custody, we would be able to back the Shield up the Processional Way into the Pergamon Museum, turning back the continuous tracks of history, and reverse all collateral damage done. In Babylon, our German coal-scoop helmets metamorphosed into combat vehicle crewman helmets, upside-down colanders with built-in Bose noise-reduction headsets and boom microphones. I adjusted the boom microphone attached to my coarse-flared CVC helmet and switched on the intercom, "D3, perhaps we should have stopped and picked up Dr. Schneider back there, on the marketplace in Miletus. What was the word he shouted, '*Symmachia?*'"

"Roger that, Thomas! I was just wonderin' about that, too. *Symmachia* is an ancient Greek word for 'alliance,' for 'collective security.' Oh you know, Thomas . . . Dr. Schneider's a political theorist. When we drove into the house of the great gods, he would have probably quoted Saint Augustine, 'Behold with what companions I walked the streets of Babylon, and wallowed in the mire thereof, as if in a bed of spices and precious ointments.'"

"Roger that, D3!"

There was one more person in the Bradley than before, a third crewmember, sitting on my left in the commander's seat. When he turned to face me, nodding politely in the European fashion, I could read the nametape on his ACUs, Ziemßen. Centered on the front of his shirt, between the two, tilted chest pockets and the *litewka* collar, he wore a black-plated metal oak leaf, the subdued rank of lieutenant colonel. His gaunt, shadowy hollow cheeks beneath the deep-set, gentle eyes of the artist in the Frankfurt waiting lounge; warrior's beard; and full lips were thrown into eerie relief by the green light of the thermal viewer.

Lieutenant Colonel Ziemßen smiled at me, pointing to the hatch above my head. Popping the cover, I elevated my bucket seat and looked out from under the thick, bulletproof block glass. Under the glare of the midday sun and the vengeance-filled eyes of the Lion of Babylon, guarded by a US Marine apparently unaware of the prostrate human figure beneath, Coalition Camp Alpha was being constructed upon the ruins of Babylon. Sections of the ancient city had already been leveled to build a helicopter landing pad, hard stands for heavy vehicles and storage sites. A misinformation site had been established on top of the *Etemenanki ziggurat*. At its base, a billboard had been erected at great effort and expense by US Defense Department contractors, proudly proclaiming, "WE OWN THE OLD TESTAMENT!" Other contractors were busy constructing a cable car over the ancient city. Looking up at me, the friendly Marine guard called out, "Hey, Captain, here's a souvenir of Babylon for ya'," tossing me a brick he picked up from the ground at his feet.

Standing up in my seat to catch it, I called out, "Thanks, Gunny, keep your eye on the lion!" Sitting back down, I lowered my seat into the turret and handed the brick to LTC Ziemßen. There was an inscription, which, after adjusting the boom mike on his CVC helmet and switching on the vehicle intercom, he translated and read aloud to us, "This was built by Saddam Hussein, son of Nebuchadnezzar, to glorify Iraq." We did not dismount to wallow in the mire of Babylon but joined in the joint push north to Baghdad, in hot pursuit of Clio and the End of History. Over the intercom, D3 replied to LTC Ziemßen with a line from Book III of Aristotle's *Politics* that Dr. Schneider had cited during our Accidental *Polis* Seminar: "Peloponnesus itself surrounded with a wall, as Babylon was, and every other place, which rather encircles many nations than one city, and that they say was taken three days when some of the inhabitants knew nothing of it." The Shield was now lead vehicle of US Infantry Division Task Force *Weltgeist*, with war cars spread out in attack formation on Route 8. A road sign overhead indicated we were ninety kilometers south of Baghdad. After I'd secured the hatch above my head, LTC Ziemßen smiled, gave me a thumbs up, switched on the intercom, and said, "Baghdad's the center of gravity, and if the city is fallen, then all history is lost. I shall now recite *The Siege of Baghdad*:

An American Army austerely arrayed, adventured ahead against advice; Abrams advanced,

Bradleys bravely besieged Baghdad, Britain's Blair before Bush's bravado blanched;

CIA caught CURVEBALL, CENTCOM commands CFLCC, COBRA II—culmination,
Drones deployed, depleted destruction, dictator destabilized, desertion, death, domination;

Emissaries embedded, expeditionary excess ends empire exceptional,
Franks forays, firefights for Feith, for FREEDOM, for FIASCO finale!

Grim Gen'ral grudgingly Garner-ed; ghoulish guards garrote, gash guarded—gracious God!
HUMVs Hillah highway hold, Hooah! History harbors, hides Hussein's hideous hole;

Iraqi insurgency, IED insertion, intelligence interrogation, ISIS impregnation,
Joyriding journalists join Jarheads' jackhammer juggernaut—Joint jubilation!
Kinetic killing, kidnappings, Kamikazes, *Kleiö's Kulmination*!

Laconic leadership lacks legal limits—landings lag, LOC laid, liberation;
Misused military mops-up 'mid murderous mines, missing munitions—MRAPs.

Neither Nebechudneezer nor Napoleon, net-centric nonsense, new National nadir,
OSP, offensive operations ongoing, oily objectives—obstacles overcome, Oorah! occupation;

President perfidious, policies pernicious—petroleum, personal profit, poor promulgation.
Quai d'Orsay quandry, quagmire, Qatar, Qods, al-Qaedia, questionable quantification;

Rove rants, Rumsfeld rages, regime removed, RMA ruse revealed—reinforcements required,
Sectarian stupidity, Shia strike Sunni, Sunni strike Shia, Saddam sought, soldiers sequestered;

Termination turns turmoil to torture, tyranny to terrorist tragedy—
twaddle tops truth!
US, UK undercut UN, underestimated unknowns—unnecessary,
unsustainable, uncouth!
Vanity vanquish vengeance, violence, vitiate victory vainglorious—
Veep, Vulcans, vamoose!

Wisdom wails W's, Wolfowitz's wacky wartime weasel words—
WMDs, waterboarding, Xenophon? Xanthus? Xenophobia!

Yet yield your Yellowcake yarns, your youthful Yankee yammer!
Zone, Zulu, Zero, Ziggurat, zany zeal,

Advocate against arrogance, all ambitious aims and armed
adventurism!
Et cetera, et cetera, et cetera.

After LTC Ziemßen had ended his transmission with the standard
"Out here," we discovered someone else had been monitoring the Shield's
intercom system.
"What the fuck?! Over!"
"Heard, understood, acknowledged, HUA!" replied LTC Ziemßen.
"Out here!" Switching off the intercom, he took a self-recorded ORWO K
420-minute cassette tape from the tilted chest pocket of his ACUs, slipping
it smoothly into the *Laufwerk* of the Bradley's built-in *Blaupunkt Berlin
IQR-188*. Click! Dance tracks from the *Dschungel*, way back in West Berlin,
came over our Bose headsets as we headed up Route 8 into Baghdad for our
rendezvous with Clio in the ruins: "(We Don't Need This) Facist Groove
Thang" from Heaven 17, "History Repeating" from Propellerheads, *"ein
jahr (es geht voran)"* from Fehlfarben, "The Western World is such a bore"
from Mad Wolf and the City Indians, Iggy Pop's "The Passenger," and
"Concrete Dub" from Leningrad Sandwich. Over the background noise, I
didn't understand all the lyrics. Did she sing "lost" or "love?" I couldn't tell,
and there was no time to rewind the tape.
After seven hours of continuous replay, TF *Weltgeist* closed on Baghdad.
Turning to me, LTC Ziemßen said, "Captain Vonaechron, please take
the *Falkplan* from your shoulder bag, identify the coordinates of the
Republican Palace, and punch them into the GPS."
Unfolding the *Falkplan* on my lap, I replied, "The Palace is located
at Q-R/10, sir," simultaneously programming the coordinates into the
GPS. At Baghdad City Limits, a broken black anarchist arrow pointed

in the direction of City Center. Over the vehicle intercom system, LTC Ziemßen solemnly addressed us along with everyone else monitoring the Shield's intercom: "Gentlemen, your undivided attention please! All-source intelligence reporting has determined Clio is currently holed-up in the Republican Palace. The National Command Authority, the President of the United States and the Secretary of Defense have directed us to execute a Thunder Run to the *Schwerpunkt* of the HistoriCity, the Palace, and take Clio into protective custody. Vanward in Task Force *Weltgeist*, we have now become the vanguard of history. Major Durchschouer, Drive on!"

"Roger that, sir!"

Moved by LTC Ziemßen's words, I stepped on the floor switch activating the intercom and said, "Wow, D3, can you believe it? The Shield of Achilles has now become the 'Car of History,' just like the Franzoni sculpture in the National Statuary Hall of the Capital Building in Washington, DC!"

"Roger that, Thomas! I was thinking about DC, too, about President Eisenhower's 'farewell address.' We're driving 'down the long lane of history yet to be written.' But once you get on that road, you're on that road!"

Activating his mike, LTC Ziemßen said, "Captain Vonaechron, fire at my command!" Our Bradley was heavily armed, equipped with a 25-mm M242 chain gun and M919 armor-piercing fin stabilized discarding sabot (with) tracer—finned depleted uranium penetrators, a coaxially mounted 7.62-mm M240C machine gun, and externally mounted tube-launched optically tracked wire-to-command-link antitank guided missiles. His order to "fire and adjust" followed immediately.

"On the way!" I replied. Looking out through the integrated sight unit mounted directly in front of me, I fired smoke grenades instead of ordnance from the two four-barreled launchers, shielding the Shield from all adversaries foreign and domestic in a defensive smoke screen. We entered Baghdad on Highway 8, not a very good road, passing unseen beneath all three cloverleaf overpasses ID'd by Brigade as Objectives Curly, Larry, and Moe. Driving out onto the *4. Juli-Platz*, we drove past the VIP reviewing stand, then underneath the gigantic crossed swords of Ares and Pallas Athena. "Gee 3, with the monuments and all, it's kinda like bein' back on Pennsylvania Avenue in Washington, DC!" joked D3 over the intercom. There was a large crowd dancing wildly around a toppled bronze statute with an American flag wrapped around its head, illuminated by the light of a burning Bush. The Bush was blazing and it was consumed. "*Blutsau*" ran in red letters down the side of the empty marble pedestal where the statue had once stood. Turning east onto the *Ost-West-Achse*, we drove on our final objective, *Schloßplatz*, where an even larger crowd of soldiers, sailors, and civilians had gathered in front of *Portal IV* of the Palace. They were cheering an unshaven, short, dark-haired, middle-aged man, dressed in a white-collared dress shirt with a black, plastic bow tie, blue bib overalls, and worn out tennis shoes, haranguing them while suspended from the Palace balcony on bicycle tire tubes. Activating the Shield's external microphone, I could hear the crowd chanting "*Ebé Ubu, Ebé Ubu*" in unison as we drove by. D3 drove on through *Schloßportal Nummer* IV out onto the *Grosser Schloßhof*, where we took up position next to an equestrian statute of St. George with banner held high and sword uplifted to dispatch the bat-winged dragon, recoiling from the bronze hooves of his terrified mount, a *Freiheitsdenkmal*. Mission accomplished, we stood down momentarily awaiting further instructions.

It was growing dark. Over the intercom, LTC Ziemßen said, "Well done, Major Durchschouer, well done, Captain Vonaechron! If the dialectician's right, we can stay the night, because if we can stay the night, we can stay forever and the next day. If we're in the HistoriCity and we stay there, then history's over. Over."

"Roger that, sir," D3 and I replied in unison.

Though surrounded by the *Handwerk* of history, there was still no sign of its muse, of Clio. For a brief moment, I thought I'd made a positive ID, smiling down from the Baroque frieze decorating the outside of the Palace picture gallery, just below a large banner reading "Mission Accomplished." Suddenly, the entire outer court caught fire and was immediately engulfed in red flames. Framed by the flames in the picture gallery windows were silhouettes of the giants Typhoeus, Enkeladus, Rhoetus, and Poryphyrius, who had apparently broken free from the Pergamon Frieze. Chaos had prevailed over order. It suddenly occurred to me, the muses were also the children of Ge and Uranus and sisters of the giants. But would Clio have freed her brothers from the frieze to wreak havoc upon the HistoriCity? Looking up from the outer court, up to the Baroque frieze below the picture gallery, I saw a woman, arrayed with the weapons of war. With red flames reflected in her armor, she appeared to be covered in blood. But was it Clio or Enyò, "Waster of Cities," sister of Pallas Athena, mother of Atë, close companion of Ares, the god of War? She looked down at me, smiled, and vanished. Columns of thick black smoke woven with red flames rose overhead into the night sky, creating a later day *Lichtdom*, commemorating the sacking of the HistoriCity and the End of History.

Moved by the scene unfolding before us, D3 switched on the intercom and observed, "Back at Leavenworth, Winfried Wolf would quote Hegel following our discussion of a historical military operation, of a—to use your expression, Thomas—a 'reality opera,' '*Geschichte als Schlachtbank*'— 'History as a butcher block,' he would say. It became our military-historical mantra. That certainly seems to be the lesson we should have, once again, learned here!"

"Roger that, D3, whether *Schlachtbank* or *Schlachthof,* 'Human History is the History of War.'"

D3 respectfully requested LTC Ziemßen to switch positions with him. Nodding to me politely, LTC Ziemßen went forward, allowing D3 to take the commander's seat. Now seated on my left, as he had been when we first began our hot pursuit of Clio in the Shield, D3 took out a pocket edition JPS Tanakh bound in the familiar sand, gray, and green digital camouflage pattern from the other blouse pocket of his BDUs. Smiling at me, D3 said, "Yirmiyahu," and began to read aloud, 'And the man of wickedness shall stumble and fall, and he shall have no one to raise him up, and I will kindle fire in his cities, and it shall consume all those around him.' Repocketing the Tanakh, D3 sank back into his black bucket seat.

Live images from an MQ-1 Predator drone loitering overhead at twenty-five-thousand feet were displayed on the monitors in front of us. We could observe how the firestorm generated by the burning Republican Palace shot red embers across the Spree to the Potomac, showering Capitol Hill in Washington, DC, another city devoted to the making of history. One after another, the representational buildings lining *menschenleere* Constitution Avenue were consumed by the flames, the US Courthouse, the National Gallery of Art, the National Archives and Records Service (my former employer), the Justice Department, the National Museum of Natural History, the Department of Internal Revenue, the National Museum of American History, and the Commerce Department. The buildings on the parallel Independence Avenue, including the Rayburn and Forrestal Office Buildings, met the same fiery fate. "*All architecture is what you do when you look upon it, (Did you think it was in the white or gray stone? or the lines of the arches and cornices?)*" Below the Mall, now the Meadow of Atë, the Jefferson Memorial slowly titled forward and slid like the *Titanic* beneath the rising waters of the Tidal Basin. It was the End of History, and the last man was frantically treading water against the incoming tide. "Operator, zoom on target, please!" The target turned out to be Dr. Kens L. Suisse, former president of Mary & William University. Above the sound of the rushing waters closing in over the broken dome, I could hear his voice clearly over my Bose headset, "Peace and friendship with all mankind is our wisest policy, and I wish we may be permitted to pursue it." The firestorm spread down the Potomac, engulfing Olde Towne Alexandria, the torpedo factory, and Mount Vernon and its gift shop with the parchment copies of the Declaration of Independence and the Constitution.

"Operator, please task Search and Rescue at Fort McNair to drop an Inflatoplane on the target in the Tidal Basin ASAP! Over."

"Wilco, sir! Out here!" The Predator loitered overhead, gathering raw data as Berlin and Washington burned—burning, burning, burning, burning, the chaos of fire, the "red business" of the war. Someday, all of this will have to be fixed, fixed and developed into multidimensional data sets. It began to rain. Fire kindled the evening sky into a fiery glow over the HistoriCities, a scene both solemn and beautiful. Out on the frontier of freedom, at freedom's edge, at the edge and end of history, I sank back into the Bradley's black leather bucket seat and closed my eyes, imagining a field of poppies. Hypnos poured himself into the Shield in a soft, soothing slumber. At the end of the night, I awoke, though it was no true awakening, to find myself comfortably installed in a double room in *Psychiatrische Ambulanz,* the sun shining through the window and the hazy September morning air. The owl of Minerva had flown. Its place had been taken by an *Amsel,* perched on the railing outside my seventh floor window. "Poo-tee-weet?"

The Unbearable Heaviness of Seeing
September 1983

Together with my dream and the night, the sympathetic psychiatrist in black and white with the *bubi* haircut had vanished. After a late breakfast of *Aufschnitt* and *Brötchen* in the patient dining room, I was placed in the care of Dr. Tomáš Hanšan, a Czech psychiatrist in his midforties, tall and slender, also wearing a white *Kittel.* He wore his dark beard in the Freudian fashion, lacing his bedside manner with a dry, Central European humor which shone in his brown eyes. Within a few days, we discovered we shared more than first names. While posing a series of routine diagnostic questions, he casually asked if I'd noticed *Psychiatrische Ambulanz* was located on the seventh floor, the top floor of the *Universitätsklinikum,* while *Oncologie* was located on the ground floor, the *Erdgeschoß.* "This gives the *Universitätslinikum* a human symmetry, don't you think?" *Das Erdgeschoß*—the ground floor. The word brought to mind not only my own mortality but also *Fräulein* Asta Otto, the helpful *Palast der Republik Hostess* who first explained its meaning to me. "Under other circumstances, I'd be pleased to join you . . ." By the end of the first week, I felt as much Tomáš's friend as his patient. Dr. Hanšan had himself been a casualty, of the 1968 Prague Spring. Prohibited from practicing medicine, he earned a living writing Czech subtitles for American feature films. To make a point, he would often quote dialogue taken from an American film.

In addition to American movies, Tomáš also told me about his countryman Dr. Franz Kafka, who first visited Berlin during the winter of 1910. After meeting and corresponding with Felice Bauer, Kafka returned to Berlin in 1913 and again in 1914. In September 1923, sixty years ago, Kafka moved to Berlin, taking rooms with Dora Diamant, first in Steglitz and then in Zehlendorf. From November 1923 until February 1924, they lived together in a two-room apartment on the first floor of a small redbrick house at *Grunewaldstraße 13*, not far from the *Universitätsklinikum*. Kafka appreciated the proximity of the *Botanischer Garten*, walking there whenever possible. Taking a book from the floor-to-ceiling bookcase running the length of the wall behind his desk, Tomáš read aloud from a letter Franz Kafka wrote to his friend Felix Welch, *"An lauen Abenden ist ein so starker Duft, wie ich ihn von anderswo kaum kenne. Dann ist da noch der große botanische Garten, eine Viertelstunde von mir . . ."*[48] Although the short stories *"Eine kleine Frau"* and *"Der Bau"* survived, the archivist in me was inflamed to learn Dora Diamant had, at Franz Kafka's request, burned many of his letters, stories, and notes in that nearby apartment.

Tomáš listened closely, occasionally making notes, as I talked about my education, work at the National Archives, my fascination with Berlin—including the *Dörpfeld'sche* divisions developed for on-site research—and my decision to leave Washington, DC, to pursue a degree in history at the Free University Berlin. In addition to the contract work at the *Stadtstaatsarchiv Berlin* and graduate studies at the Clay Institute, I described my associated extracurricular activities in some detail, the points of reference, the lines of communication, and the establishment of my personal communications zone in West Berlin. When I'd finished, he smiled and said, "You know, Thomas, there might be some interesting coincidences, even parallels here. Sigmund Freud thought the mind, much like your Berlin, your HistoriCity as you call it, is also composed of layers. He used the architectural development of Rome to illustrate his point, coincidentally referring to remnants of walls, the Servian and Aurelian, still standing in today's Rome. As a consequence, the analyst becomes an archeologist on a very personal level, looking for fragments, not necessarily ruins mind you, of the analysand's past in her or his present, in particular for those fragments that might inform her or his behavior. Freud reputedly once said he owned more books on archaeology than psychology, so you're

---

48 "On warm evenings, there's a strong fragrance in the air, which I haven't experienced anywhere else. The large Botanical Gardens are a quarter of an hour from me." Diary of Thomas Vonaechron, Diary Extract, 1983, trans. Dr. Tomáš Hanšan.

in good company. Psychoanalysis is actually founded upon the principle that present problems are rooted in the past, so the past is, in a sense, always present. Please tell me about the circumstances that brought you here. Did you have any symptoms, anxiety or panic attacks, in days or weeks prior to your admission?" Recounting previous anxiety and paralyzing panic attacks, as well as my attempts at "self-medication" with alcohol, I assured him I had fortunately not yet awoken to discover I had metamorphosed into an "*ungeheures Ungeziefer.*"

He laughed, "That's very good to know, Thomas, though something is apparently bugging you! As you told me about all your varied activities over the past year, it occurred to me you simply might have been trying to do too much. There's an English idiom I like very much, you 'had too many irons in the fire.' One can almost see the red glow of the iron, the fire, and feel the heat. Your 'communications zone,' as you called it, might have been an attempt to structure and fill your new life in West Berlin with purposeful activity, with meaning. On the surface, or just below it, for the sake of archaeology and for that matter psychology, too, much of this activity had to do with examining remnants of Berlin's past in the light of the present, your present. As an unanticipated consequence, you coincidentally weighted yourself down, not only with the formidable burden of Berlin's history, but you also burdened yourself with your own experience—once again in the attempt to find, or perhaps even to create, meaning." Tomáš paused for a moment, smiled, and said, "Something interesting just occurred to me, Thomas. While still in Prague, I met a writer, who in the meantime also left and is now living in France. In an unfortunately yet-unpublished novel, he posits a personal dilemma diametrically opposed to yours—not the weight but the weightlessness, the lightness, of history. He recently sent me a copy of his manuscript along with a request for my assistance in finding a German publisher." Walking back over to the bookcase, he took it down from the shelf. While leafing through the well-worn typescript pages, he said, "I found one sentence in particular so thought-provoking, so disturbing actually, I marked it with a paperclip. "Here it is, let me try to translate it into English, 'History is as light as individual human life, unbearably light, light as a feather, as dust swirling into the air, as what will no longer exist tomorrow.' Who knows, perhaps I found this sentence in anticipation of your admission, Thomas?" Closing the manuscript, he placed it on his desk next to the copy of Kafka's letters. But let's allow the gravity of your situation to, at least temporarily, overcome any weightlessness of history. From what you've told me, at times you seemed to be driven, almost manic, moving from one thing to the next without taking the time necessary to digest, to develop your experiences. What could have been your motivation for doing so—*horror vacui*? Could a possible answer lie not only in the history of Berlin but within your personal history as well? Although it sounds like a cliché—and there's a nice German word for it, *klischeehaft*—please don't take it as one. Maybe you were, still are I should say, really trying to discover yourself here in West Berlin."

"Now that's an interesting, a very interesting, thought, Tomáš. Last semester, I took a seminar at the *FU* on West Berlin as an 'accidental *polis*.' While introducing the Athenian *polis* and Plato to the members of our seminar, Dr. Schneider, an exchange professor from Kent State University, told us Plato's intent behind *The Republic* was actually to examine and understand the individual. As a kind of citizen writ large, the *polis* offered a case study for examination employing the Socratic method. Perhaps, as you suggest, I have been looking for something more than just archives and architecture in Berlin. But now my search has brought me here, to *Psychiatrische Ambulanz* on the seventh floor of the *Graue Riese*. My COMZ has collapsed and I'm left contemplating my own ruins, along with exhaustion, anxiety, panic attacks, and depression. Am I 'clinically depressed?'"

"Well, although you are in a clinic and do indeed exhibit some classical symptoms of depression, I wouldn't call it 'clinical depression.' To be honest with you, Thomas, in many cases we're never completely certain what our patients are suffering from. We try to diagnose their problems to the best of our ability from what they tell us and from what we observe, then apply different therapies to ascertain whether or not anything actually helps. I believe you are exhausted and might be experiencing what our American colleagues refer to as 'nervous exhaustion' or 'neurasthenia.' It seems to be common among your countrymen. I've even heard nervous exhaustion referred to as 'Americanitis!' Another possibility might be disturbance of the *vegetative Nervensystem*, the autonomic nervous system. Given your symptoms, periods of elation and ecstasy followed by anxiety, panic attacks, fatigue, and depression, a third possibility suggests itself as well—a bipolar disorder."

"Manic depression?"

"Yes, that is another term for it, but once again, Thomas, please don't take it as a diagnosis. Lithium has proven to be an effective mood stabilizer in treating bipolar disorders. It just might be worth a try, to see if it helps you."

"Lithium? A metal?" Recalling "Li" from the alkali group of metals on the periodic table memorized for high school chemistry, I was relieved to remember it occurred in nature and not just in the laboratory. Light metal as a remedy for heavy metal, at least for the *Neue Deutsche Welle*.

"Yes, lithium has proven to be quite effective for a very long time. Even the Greek physician Galen of Pergamon . . ."

"'Of Pergamon' . . . as in the 'Pergamon Altar' in East Berlin?"

"Why yes, the very same! Have you visited the Pergamon Museum? Seen the altar, the marvelous Market Gate of Miletus, and the Ishtar Gate of Babylon?"

"Yes, nine, ten years ago now, during a seven-day study trip to Berlin from Basel, where, as I told you, I spent an academic year. I walked by it again last December during a day trip to East Berlin but didn't go in. But on the night I was admitted, I did go in, drove in—in a dream! The friezes on the Pergamon Altar unfroze, we drove over the Market of Miletus, past the Market Gate through the Ishtar Gate down the Processional Way into Babylon, and then on to Baghdad. I was pretty upset when my friend George brought me to the *UKBF*, so your colleague on duty that night kindly gave me a sleeping pill. The next thing I knew, I was dreaming of Berlin, Babylon, Baghdad, and Washington, DC."

"Now there's yet another unusual coincidence, Thomas. In addition to describing the benefits of bathing in and taking the waters of alkaline springs, Galen of Pergamon also discusses the diagnostic value of dreams. Would you be willing to tell me your dream about the unfrozen Pergamon Altar friezes and driving into Babylon?"

"Certainly, isn't the interpretation of dreams *de riguer* for psychoanalysis?"

"Sigmund Freud would certainly concur with Galen on that point!"

Tomáš listened attentively, once again jotting down a few notes as I recounted the pursuit of Clio, the muse of history, through a reunified Berlin with my fellow seminar student and US army major, Dwight David Durchschouer, at the wheel of a custom-built Ford sedan. Beginning with the race down the *Straße des 17. Junis* and *Unter den Linden*, I described entering the Pergamon Museum and joining in the Gigantomachy, driving across the Marketplace of Miletus and the triumphant entry into Babylon through the Ishtar Gate. Laughing, I said, "Oh no, Tomáš, there is a metamorphosis after all, our Ford changed into a Bradley Calvary Fighting Vehicle as we entered Babylon!"

"What's a Bradley Calvary Fighting Vehicle, Thomas?"

"An armored personal carrier, like a small tank."

"Ah, yes, I learned a lot about tanks in Prague."

I also told Tomáš about the eerie appearance of LTC Ziemßen, the drive of Infantry Division Task Force *Weltgeist* on Baghdad from Babylon, our history-making, if not history-ending thunder run to the conflated Republican Palace/*Stadtschloß*, and finally, the triumph of chaos and burning of Berlin and Washington, DC. He thought for a few moments, tapping his pen on his notebook, and said "*Geträumte Geschichte!* I don't know about prophecy, Thomas, but your dream would certainly make a great script for a sci-fi short film! Special effects might pose a problem, though! Sigmund Freud once described the interpretation of dreams as the 'royal road to knowledge of the unconscious activities of the mind.' You chose the 'Processional Way' instead of the 'royal road,' but you seemed to have arrived at the same destination. As you yourself have no doubt realized, the initial dream sequence seems to draw heavily on your experiences in both West and East Berlin for images, as well as upon your knowledge of historiography. What I find particularly interesting about the dream is the idea of following, or being 'led' by Clio, up to that point where you actually become an instrument of history, if not history itself. This metamorphosis, if you will permit, simultaneously triggers the release of chaos, leading to the destruction of order—political as well as architectural, and the end of history. In his discussion of dreams, Galen of Pergamon, whose own career in medicine may actually have been inspired by a dream his father had, also considers prophetic dreams. To be honest, your dream seems more likely to have been inspired by a muse rather than an oracle—maybe the sleeping pill had something to do with it, too. I wonder what my colleague gave you as a 'seda-give,' I mean a sedative of course. Do you remember Gene Wilder's charades scene in the Mel Brooks film *Young Frankenstein*? 'Seda-give!' A play on words always poses an enjoyable challenge for translation. In any case, I'll check her notes. Perhaps I might try it once myself if I haven't already! Together with many other students and citizens, I received 'hands-on' instruction in history in August 1968 in Prague, from tanks too, Russian tanks, and since that time, I've often wondered where history might be 'leading' us.

"Galen was born in Pergamon, some seventeen centuries before the altar friezes were unearthed and shipped here to Berlin from Bergama. His name might have been derived from the adjective for 'calm.' Apropos calm, as I mentioned, among the various therapies he recommends, including psychotherapy and the interpretation of dreams, are bathing in and drinking water from alkaline springs. Although I believe your primary problem to be exhaustion—*Americanitis*—perhaps lithium might help you. Although it will hopefully decrease your anxiety and depression, and minimize the panic attacks, it won't make you a braver man. With the help of Galen of Pergamon and Greek medicine, we'll see if we can't exchange your *Weltschmerz* for *eudaimonia*." There were, however, lithium limits. Tomáš explained that drinking too deeply, an overdose, could be fatal— hence the critical significance of the lithium *Spiegelbild*, a reflection of the lithium level in the bloodstream. My *Spiegelbild* would have to be carefully monitored and controlled before I could be discharged from *Psychiatrische*

Ambulanz. I would have to remain in *Psychiatrische Ambulanz* for two more weeks, for a total of twenty-one days.

For those twenty-one days, I lived in an intimate *Gesellschaft* (or was it actually a *Gemeinschaft?*) of seven patients, two women and five men, suffering from as many psychological maladies. Within *Psychiatrische Ambulanz,* every effort was made to restore and reinforce the familiar rituals of outside everyday life, *der Alltag,* in the hope of reintegrating patients into their former lives as quickly as possible. We took regular meals together in the patient dining room and were encouraged to wear street clothes instead of hospital clothing, as did the staff. Only the doctors were set apart from staff and patients by their white *Kittel.* It didn't seem to work. Once inside, even temporarily, the patient becomes apart. There is a world inside and a world outside, the latter belonging to both the known past and the uncertain future.

One of the two young female patients was deeply concerned that, once discharged from *Psychiatrische Ambulanz,* she would no longer be eligible for the *Krankengeld* she needed to buy a new Walkman. Instead of her street clothes, she chose to wear the *UKBF*-issued hospital gown during the day. She rolled her own cigarettes with fingers stained brown by tobacco, and chain smoked in the patient dining room, repeatedly telling anyone who'd listen why she believed she would likely lose the income linked to her illness. Although I knew her name, I thought of her as "Walkwoman." Walkwoman had fallen under the influence of Dr. Krankenschein, Dr. Caligari's state-subsidized successor in this latter-day, half-Hollstenwall.

Friends came to the *Klinikum* bringing concern, flowers, books, even food and drink. George von Garlitz came in the afternoon after my admission and every other day thereafter until my discharge. "I'm very grateful to you for bringing me here, George. I guess I'd reached, no, exceeded my limits."

"I'm very sorry I was unable to help you in any other way, Thomas. I felt responsible because I encouraged you to leave Washington and come here to West Berlin. You seem rested and more relaxed today. When you came to my house last night, and I'm very glad you did, you were *vollständig durchgedreht*—I don't know the English expression. Rest now and regain your strength. I do hope you're planning to resume your studies at the *FU,* not right away, of course, but when you're ready. I stopped by the *Lothringerstrasse* on the way here to pick up a few of your things," he said, placing my orange backpack next to my shoulder bag on the floor next to the nightstand. "Dr. Kahler asked me to pass along his very best wishes for a rapid recovery. If it's OK with you, he would like to come visit you, too. He has some gifts he'd like to bring you."

"That would be very kind."

After George left, I picked up my shoulder bag and opened it on my bed. In the side pocket, I found Lorelei's letter, Neal's poem, Govinda's calling card, the Alfred Jarry quotation written out for me by François Fontane, and the scrap of paper I found in the boxcar at *Anhalter Bahnhof* with "*Thos=Mann=Tick*" written on it. Yes, three weeks in the clinic should be just about right. Rainer brought a half-liter can of ice cold *Berliner Kindl* and a Turkish *Kebab* from Görlitzer *Bahnhof* in Kreuzberg, filling the antiseptic hallways with the aroma of roasted lamb and garlic. Dr. Kahler brought two books, the Penguin paperback edition of *Li Po and Tu Fu* he'd once leant to me, and the hardback first edition of Hermann Hesse's *Steppenwolf.* "These books from my library are gifts for you, *Herr* Vonaechron. I'm quite certain they will not only provide you with good company here in the clinic but also in the future. We two have a similar disposition, you know. I have had similar experiences."

Thanking him for the books, I repeated the warning he had given me about West Berlin, "A word of caution, Mr. Vonaechron, one must be very careful in West Berlin. There's simply too much going on. You can easily enjoy yourself into a state of exhaustion."

Smiling his tight, wolfish grin, he nodded his closely-cropped head while flipping through *Steppenwolf,* and read aloud in reply, '*Intensiv leben kann man nur auf Kosten des Ichs,*'[49] adding, "Although it may seem inappropriate to say so under the present circumstances, and please do not take offense at my observation, *Herr* Vonaechron, but perhaps this experience might have been necessary, a necessary part of your education outside the university." It's very important to know one's personal limits. In order to know them, it's necessary to exceed them once or twice. But please forgive me, *Herr* Vonaechron, it almost slipped my mind. This came for you with the post yesterday." Reaching into the pocket of his green velvet sport coat, he took out a postal card and handed it to me. It was a Superchrome aerial photograph of the Wentworth-by-the-Sea, a grand hotel on the Atlantic Coast at Newcastle, New Hampshire. Turning it over, I recognized the handwriting at once as Neal's. Although I had written to him from Berlin, thanking him for his poem, I hadn't heard from him since my departure. Unfortunately, the postal card had apparently been soaked in salt water, or, perhaps like the poem he gave me at The Republic, in beer, besmearing Neal's nearly illegible handwriting. It was a poem too, but other than the title, "Zero to the Bone," I could only read two sentences, "Sex and salt and large bodies of water—all these sunsets and mornings

---

49 One can live intensively only at the expense of the self (Hesse, 1927), Diary of Thomas Vonaechreon, Diary excerpt, 1983, trans. TV.

turning already to memory at the moment of desire—salt in the air, salt in the wound: I am refining all my loves. They are refining me to someone else as history, and lust alone lunges toward some bruised anonymous future." At our next appointment, I showed Tomáš the postal card and asked if a similar aerial shot of the *Universitätsklinikum* was available. Laughing, he said the *UKBF* was not usually considered a holiday destination by patients, or staff for that matter, but he would ask.

D3 stopped by *Psychiatrische Ambulanz* in civilian clothes with very best wishes for a speedy recovery and well-worn copies of Eisenhower's *Crusade in Europe* and *At Ease* in hand. "You might want to read *At Ease* first, Thomas, then go crusading in Europe with Ike! Yuck, yuck, yuck!" Although uncertain how he might react, I recounted the dream I had the night I was admitted. D3 listened thoughtfully, with a smile on his face, as I described our pursuit of Clio through Berlin, Babylon, Baghdad, and Washington, DC. Shaking his head, he laughed heartily, "I don't know, Thomas, I really don't know what to tell ya. I do like the part about the drive through downtown Berlin, from West to East through the center passageway of the Brandenburg Gate in the Shield, and then the part about the Shield morphing into a Bradley. You're a pretty perceptive guy. After all, you did ID that Russian Pershing II mock-up on the road to Magdeburg, information greatly appreciated by the higher-ups by the way. Anything's possible, I guess, but from the strategic standpoint, and I'm talking about grand strategy in the Clausewitzian sense, I just can't imagine under what possible circumstances the National Command Authority, POTUS, and SECDEF would direct the Commander-in-Chief, Central Command to invade Iraq. We studied British military operations in Iraq at the School for Advanced Military Studies in Leavenworth. The Brits actually invaded Iraq twice, the first time in 1917 and then again in 1941. Although both military campaigns were successful in establishing temporary control over Iraq, the governments the British installed there proved ineffective and ultimately unstable, the mounting costs of continued military occupation unaffordable. There's no reason to expect any other results than these. We don't know whether your dream came through the 'Gate of Horn' or the 'Gate of Ivory.' There just might be something to it, however. We'll just have Kuwait and see! Get it? 'Have Ku-wait and see!' Yuck, yuck, yuck! You're a bud of the Bard, Thomas—remember what Romeo's bud Mercutio said about dreams, 'children of an idle brain'? Maybe you shouldn't let your brain idle for too long. Get some much-needed R and R and then get to work on your dissertation! As you know, after Vietnam, I was out there in the perimeter where there are no constellations, I found research and writing—focused, purposeful activity—to be the best therapy! *Sans doute,* those two years I spent at Leavenworth, at Command and General Staff College and SAMS saved what little remained of my sanity after my special ops tour in Vietnam. Although I didn't want to load you down with *Vom Kriege* again today, Carl von Clausewitz does have something to say about intentional irrationality in human nature. I read it aloud graveside in Burg back in June, remember? You know, Thomas, I've read it so often I should be able to recite it from memory, *auswendig*, let's see . . .

Obgleich sich unser Verstand immer zur Klarheit und Gewißheit hingedrängt fühlt, so fühlt sich doch unser Geist oft von der Ungewißheit angezogen. Statt sich mit dem Verstande auf dem engen Pfade philosophischer Untersuchung und logischer Schlußfolgen durchzuwinden, um, seiner selbst sich kaum bewußt, in Räumen anzukommen, wo er sich fremd fühlt, und wo ihn alle bekannten Gegenstände zu verlassen scheinen, weilt er lieber mit der Einbildungskraft im Reiche der Zufälle und des Glücks. Statt jener dürftigen Notwendigkeit schwelgt er hier im Reichtum von Möglichkeiten; begeistert davon, beflügelt sich der Mut, und so wird Wagnis und Gefahr das Element, in welches er sich wirft wie der mutige Schwimmer in den Strom.[50]

Rest up and jump back in, Thomas. Be that brave swimmer, whether you choose to swim with or against the currents of history!" Just before leaving, D3 walked over to the window, taking time to take in the panorama below. "That's quite a view you have from up here on the seventh floor, Thomas! My, my, you do have the 'room with a view.' Turning back to face me he said, "Call me when you get back home and up on your feet again, my friend. We'll fire up the Shield and 'drive on' *beziehungsweise* 'out' to the Wannsee US Army Recreation Center. Who knows, maybe the Shield'll turn into a DUKW when we get out to the Wannsee—quack, quack, quack!"

There was another young female patient in the *Psychiatrische Ambulanz*. Tall, statuesque, with her thick blonde hair cut short, just below her ears. She wasn't concerned about receiving *Krankengeld*; there was something else was on her mind. During our daily group therapy sessions, which were

---

50 "Even though our mind always strives for clarity and certainty, our spirit is often attracted by uncertainty. Instead of following the intellect along the narrow path of philosophical inquiry and turning to logical conclusions, in order to, unknown even to itself, arrive at places, where it feels unfamiliar and everything familiar seems to be lost, spirit would rather spend time with fantasy in the realm of coincidence and chance. Instead of bare necessity, spirit revels in a richness of possibilities, inspiration giving wings to courage, so hazardous undertakings and danger become the element into which it dives, a brave swimmer in the current." trans. Captain Dwight D. Durchschouer, US Army, School for Advanced Military Studies, Fort Leavenworth, Kansas, *On War*, p. 14.

as quiet as Quaker meetings, she would occasionally become upset, jump up from her chair with her arms rigidly extended, and flee the room. Over lunch, Walkwoman told me she would hurry down the hallway to the bath, a large white-tiled closet with chrome fixtures, and bathe in the large white porcelain tub. This occurred not only during therapy but several times a day. She told Walkwoman the hot bath helped her to deal with her depression. Once, as she stood up during group therapy to leave, I asked her where she was going. Much to my surprise, and to the surprise of our therapist, she told me she was going to take a bath and asked me if I would like to join her. A beautiful Bonnard reclining in the big white porcelain tub, *un nu dans le bains*. When she stood up to allow me to bathe, droplets of water clung to her tightly-curled *Schamhaare* like morning dew. The sight of her shoulders, breasts, abdomen, thighs, and long legs did as much to restore my health as Lexotanil or lithium. I could sense an affirmation of life in desire, but any kind of sexual gratification, even fantasy, was out of the question. Through her charcoal sketches of nudes, my mother had given me a Blake-like appreciation for the essential beauty of the female body, "The nakedness of woman is the work of God." This aesthetic now came to my aid.

After bathing, we dressed and walked hand in hand through the corridors of the *Universitätsklinikum*, brother and sister, a habit we continued until she was discharged a few days before me. One day, we worked our way around the *Westhalle*, reading all the commemorative plaques set in the wall. Walking over to the freestanding, stainless steel sculpture bearing the mission statement of the *UKBF*, we discovered it also displayed an observation from Johann Wolfgang von Goethe: "Science and art belong to the whole world, and before them vanish the barriers of nationality." We checked the reverse side of the sculpture for Goethe's words. My blonde sister quietly read them aloud: "*Wissenschaft und Kunst gehören der Welt an, und vor ihnen verschwinden die Schranken der Nationalität.*" On the London-to-Frankfurt leg of Pan Am's "Round-the-World" flight, Govinda taught me nationality, *Nationalität*, was artifice. But weren't science and art artifice too? Weren't "capital S" Science and "capital A" Art, like "capital H" History, often bound and bordered, even weaponized by nationality? Behind the sculpture, I noticed a small gift shop I hadn't seen before. Hand in hand we walked inside. In addition to shelves of essentials such as toothbrushes, toothpaste, tissues, and sanitary napkins, there was also a black metal rack of cards. Next to colorful variations on the "get well" theme, running from humorous to humorless, there was one single postal card of the *Universitätsklinikum Benjamin Franklin*, the "Gray Giant." An aerial view, the focal point of the photograph was, coincidentally, the window of my seventh-floor room. I bought the card, and after returning to my room following our walk, drew an "X" on the photograph to ID my current location. Taking the card Dr. Kahler had delivered to me out of my backpack, I addressed the postal card to Neal in care of the Wentworth by-the-Sea in New Castle, New Hampshire. After rereading the fragments of his "Zero to the Bone," I replied "Sister and *lithium* and a large white porcelain tub full of warm water—all these seventh-floor sunsets and mornings turning already to memory at the moment of desire, lithium taken from the earth reflected in the blood: I am refining all my lusts. They are refining me to someone else as history, and love alone lunges toward some salubrious salvation."

I shared my large sunny room with an amicable depressive in his fifties, who each day would carefully dress and take breakfast, lunch, and dinner in the patient dining room, return to the room afterward, undress, and get back into bed, a practitioner of the horizontal. "*Es lebe das Bett,*" the nurses would say to him, and he would smile, nodding his head in agreement. The staff made every effort keep him vertical. Occasionally, I would return to the room to find him being fed intravenously. He occasionally spent a night at his home in distant Spandau, in the British Sector. One of the four walls of our room was glass, a private, single-sided Turn-Tower. From the seventh floor we looked out over a green not-sea, trees and parks with no hint of sector or zonal boundaries. There was, however, another kind of architecture to contend with. Rising from the green foliage nearby was the ultramodern *Zentralen Tierlaboratorien* (*ZTL*), laboratories for vivisection and experimentation, a postindustrial *Zootomie*. Although both the intended purpose and architecture were alarming, three-cornered windows with massive blue horizontal exhaust pipes looking like the Battleship Bismarck's "guns as big as steers," the nurses told us determined efforts of animal rights activists kept the *Mäusebunker,* as they referred to it, unoccupied by both academics and animals. It did, however, house a museum, displaying the mounted skeleton of Frederick the Great's great horse, Condé, in a glass case. To the northwest stood the tall domed white tower and twin radomes of the US Army Field Station Berlin atop the "T-berg," the *Teufelsberg*, the Devil's Mountain deep in the Grunewald. And at the foot of the *Teufelsberg*, the *Teufelssee*, the Devil's Sea, where Rainer, Silka, lunar goddess, and I had bathed together in the glacial waters, not so very long ago—though it seemed as if in another lifetime. From the seventh floor of the *UKBF*, my *Z-berg*, the distinctly phallic appearance of the *T-berg* was exposed for all to see, a white temple to Pan built upon a mountain of ruins above West Berlin. Although he must have seen it, D3 didn't mention Field Station Berlin when he'd looked out the window.

One night nurse was particularly merciful to us. Stocky, with sculptured calves and frosted blonde hair, she radiated good health—mental and physical, well-being and contentment. I admired her sensible, jargon-free, no-nonsense approach to anxiety and depression delivered in rapid-fire Berlin dialect. Rather than sanction our sadness, she would talk to us about life. Her blue eyes shone when she told us about her baby daughter. Late one night during my first week in *Psychiatrische Ambulanz,* the panic returned with such intensity, it tore me from a deep sleep, running through my veins like electricity. It felt as if a band was slowly being tightened around my head. Even though my roommate had returned to Spandau for the night, I was too embarrassed to cry out, deciding to force myself to cry in instead. Taking my pillow in both hands, I pressed it firmly over my mouth. First came the tears, then the sobs, from somewhere deep inside. I was crying but coincidentally watching myself cry, sobbing while at the same time listening to myself sob. After a few minutes, the merciful *Schwester* came into the room. She walked over to my bed and took my hand. The warmth of her hand forced the electric current from my arm. *"Wie trauig du bist,"*[51] she said. I lowered the pillow from my face. My eyes were filled and I could not speak. Although her presence comforted me greatly, the sobs continued to surface. I closed my eyes and continued watching.

After a few minutes, she let go of my hand. Terrified she might leave, I opened my eyes and was about to ask her to stay, when I saw that she had raised her sweater above her breasts and was unfastening her *Büstenhalter.* As I opened my mouth to speak, she gently placed the nipple of her right breast in my mouth. It was warm and erect. I instinctively began to lick and then suck. She was lactating; the warm milk began to flow into my mouth. With gentle pressure from her practiced forefinger on her breast, she helped me to drink. She ran her other hand through my hair and began to sigh softly. I took her left breast gently in my left hand and then moved my mouth to the nipple. She turned slightly to the side and took a deep breath. My right hand slipped across her stomach. She inhaled again abruptly as the tips of my fingers slipped under the waistband of her skirt into her panties. She gasped and, placing both hands on the waistband of her skirt, took a step back. Instead of reprimanding me for my impossible behavior, she unfastened then unzipped her skirt, gently lowering it and her panties to the floor. Lifting my *Bettdecke,* she lay down beside me, gracefully swinging one leg over mine and, suddenly, was sitting on top of me. I was inside of her. She began to rock slowly back and forth, both nipples brushing my tongue. The gentle swaying of her breasts was hypnotic. Gently, ever

---

51 "How sad you are." Diary of Thomas Vonaechron, Diary Extract, 1983, trans. TV.

so gently, she was pulling me back. Immediately after I came, I fell back into the deep sleep. When I awoke, she and the panic were gone. It never happened again, and although we talked as before, we never mentioned that night. As days became weeks in the clinic routine, I began to doubt my memory as, in the past, I'd used sexual fantasy to mitigate anxiety. Weeks later, after my discharge from the *Klinikum*, I saw her again, playing with her daughter in a park not far from my apartment. When our eyes met briefly over the silky blonde hair of her beautiful daughter, I knew it hadn't been a dream.

At the end of the second week, Tomáš went on vacation, leaving me in the very capable hands of his colleague, Dr. med. Sofia Abrassimow, a Russian psychiatrist in her late thirties with thick, curled, flaming henna-red hair, and the standard-issue white *Kittel*. Although buttoned up, her *Kittel* wasn't long enough to contain the brightly-colored flowered skirts she wore, often with a petticoat. She could not speak English, so we conversed in German, an initially inconvenient but ultimately enlightening experience due to her professional interest in *Psychoanalyse und Sexualphantasien*. Fortunately, for Russian-American *Verständigung*, Russian-German and English-German dictionaries were close at hand. Together with dreams, fantasies also form fragments useful to psycho-archeologists excavating the layered mind of the analysand. Dr. Abrassimov was preparing for a presentation on "Male Fantasies" at a Salzburg conference, coincidentally focusing on the use of sexual fantasy to mitigate anxiety and panic attacks. "*Ist es Ihnen, Herr von Aechron, auch schon aufgefallen, daß die Mehrzahl der Phantasien, die Sie mir im Gespräch erzählt, haben entweder mit Lehranstalten, wie Archiven und Bibliotheken, oder mit Heilanstalten, wie Krankenhäusern oder Kliniken zu tun haben? Ich finde die dadurch angedeutete Verbindung zwischen Angst und Wissen, in diesem Zusammenhang Wissen als eine Art Gegengewicht, nicht nur informativ, sondern geradezu aufschlußreich.*"[52] We would both have liked to continue with our analytic excavations, but my prescribed three-week stay in *Psychiatrische Ambulanz* was coming to an end. In preparation for my upcoming diurnal discharge, she encouraged me to leave *UKBJ* at least once a day for an hour or two, suggesting a *Spaziergang* in the adjacent *Schloßpark* or even in the nearby *Botanischer Garten*. From my earlier conversations with Tomáš, I remembered Franz Kafka used to walk in the Botanical Gardens. Hopefully, Kafka's "*so starker Duft*" would still be

---

52 "Has it ever occurred to you, *Herr* V., that most of the sexual fantasies you have discussed with me take place in archives, libraries, or clinics? I find the implied relationship between anxiety and knowledge, the latter as a balance to the former, not only informative but illuminating." Dr. med Sofia Abrassimov, "Seducing Clio at her Source: Sexual Arousal in Archives, Libraries, and Clinics," trans. Anne E. Maah, "Magnus Hirschfeld Lecture" given at the University Clinic for Psychiatry, Psychotherapy, and Psychosomatics, University of Salzburg, May 14, 1984.

in the air. A walk. *Per pedes Piglrimorum.* Although the *Falkplan* was in my shoulder bag with my notebook and camera, I hadn't taken it out since my fateful return trip to the T-T Music Café over two weeks ago. I was afraid to open it, afraid the very act of unfolding it might rerelease the *Falkplan* Furies and trigger a panic attack.

Pairidaeza
September 1983

The following afternoon, fortified by a buffet lunch of *Aufschnitt* and *Käse*, I returned to my room and, taking the map cautiously out of my shoulder bag, unfolded it on the bed. The *Universitätsklinikum Benjamin Franklin (UKBF)* was at coordinates M4. It was only a short, one letter, one digit walk to the *Botanischer Garten* (L5). I noted the route and carefully refolded the map, slipping it, together with a small blue bottle of the liquid tranquilizer Lexotanil, just in case, into my shoulder bag. Putting on my well-worn tweed sport coat, I walked down the hall to the elevator. During the descent from the seventh floor to the *Erdgeschoß*, I felt apprehensive but not afraid. When the stainless steel doors opened onto the *Erdgeschoß*, I thought again about Tomáš's observation on the human symmetry of the *UKBF*. Yet, death was waiting patiently for all the patients and, for that matter, all the doctors and staff members of the *UKBF*, regardless of the floor they currently occupied. Walking down the main corridor, I left the *Graue Riese* through the memorial tablet-lined West Hall of the clinic, out into a warm September afternoon. Crossing over an underground access road on a concrete walkway, I came to a pleasant park lined with maple trees. Midway between the clinic and the street bordering the park on the far side, surrounded by a grove of trees, stood a statue of Benjamin Franklin holding papers in one hand, his hat in the other. According to the memorial plaque mounted on the pedestal, it was an exact replica of a statue standing in San Francisco's Washington Square. But there was something unusual about this statue. Franklin sported a long Nietzsche-like mustache covering his upper lip. Instead of the standard issue three-cornered hat, he held an unblocked, broad-brimmed bowler. Perhaps people pictured Franklin differently in Frisco than in Philly. Running round the pedestal were four words which I assumed were addressed to the four-corners of the world, if not to the four sectors of Berlin, *WILKOMMEN* to the East, *WILKOMMEN* to the West, *WILKOMMEN* to the South, and *WILKOMMEN* to the North. A good omen.

I continued on my way to the Botanical Gardens. Strolling through the park, anticipating a panic attack that didn't come, I arrived at

Hindenburgdamm. Recalling D3's wordplay, "Damn Ludendorf," I laughed out loud. The *UKBF* must be just to the north of Little America. On my left stood another of the towered redbrick Gothic churches that had survived the war. Another good omen. I walked on. Crossing over the broad six-lane thoroughfare, I found *Moltkestraße*, which, according to the *Falkplan*, led directly to *Plantanenplatz* and, just behind it, the *Botanischer Garten*. It was a pleasant walk, past pre- and postwar houses and apartment houses, set back from the cobblestone street. Walking across a small market-square, which could have been brought back from the Alsace as a war trophy by the victorious field marshal, I stopped for a moment to read the sign posted in the center, "*Ludwig Beck Platz.*" Colonel General Beck was executed in the *Wehrmacht* Supreme Headquarters building on July 21, 1944, the day after Claus von Staffenberg. I thought again about the memorial plaque and the solitary bronze in the courtyard of the *Bendlerblock*. Continuing along *Moltkestraße*, I came to an ornamental iron gate. Standing open, it led through a pointed stone arch adorned with a high relief of Jesus into the walled *Friedhof Lichterfelde*. I stopped for a moment outside, looking at the stately trees lining the path leading deeper into the cemetery. But the Botanical Gardens were on today's agenda, not a graveyard. That would come later. On the far side of the cemetery, *Moltkestraße* was intersected by *Manteuffel-* and then by *Roonstraßen*, boulevards-in-arms. Crossing over *Gardeschützenweg*, I saw Roosevelt Barracks with its German-American *Kantine* on my left. Just beyond the boarded-up side entrance to the *S-Bahnhof Botanischer Garten*, a stately *Jugendstil* train station, *Moltkestraße* suddenly blossomed into *Mohnstraße*. The Botanical Gardens must be very close by. Skirting the edge of the adjacent *Plantanenplatz*, I saw a tall, older, white-haired man with horn-rimmed glasses walking a smooth dachshund under the spreading sycamore trees lining the center of the square. He wore a worn-out, faded pink polo shirt and shorts cut from a US Army desert battle dress uniform. Looking over at me, he smiled, waving pleasantly in recognition as if we knew each other. We did! It was the very same person who'd been drinking the off-the-menu *Riesling* at the bar of the T-T Music Café. "No Future," he'd said, lifting his empty glass as the stainless steel elevator doors shut. Now he answered my question before I could ask it. "The entrance to the *Botanischer Garten* is just up the street. Turn right on *Unter den Eichen*; it's on the left-hand side," he said, pointing in the general direction through the sycamore trees with his free hand.

"Thank you very much," I answered. He waved again cordially, smiled, and returned his attention to the dachshund, neither of us interested in pursuing a conversation. After crossing over the broad, tree-lined *Unter den Eichen*, I came to the high, black cast-iron fence surrounding the

Botanical Gardens. Following the directions given to me by the white-haired gentleman, I walked along the tall iron fence to the entrance. The gardens were immense. An entire HistoriCity block, a walled *pairidaeza* where an exhausted, exhaust-filled West Berlin could come to rest and recuperate, to breathe. Ornamental cast-iron flowers topped the fence posts flanking the redbrick gate. *Ante portas*, I was surprised to discover the *Botanischer Garten* was also part of the *Freie Universität Berlin*. The *Lucius-D.-Clay-Institut*, the *Hajo-Holborn-Institut, Universitätsklinikum Benjamin Franklin*, and now the *Botanischer Garten*—all part of my higher education in West Berlin. Taking the well-wiped student ID from my pocket, I was pleased to discover that although this iron gate also stood wide open, there was no one waiting in what had once been the ticket booth. Just like the Free University itself, paradise was free, open to the public. Coincidence took me by the hand, leading me down the wide, paved garden path, through the section dedicated to *Atlantisches Nordamerika*, trees and shrubbery identical to those lining the banks of the Potomac between Washington, DC, and Alexandria, Virginia. *Nemos.* A breeze came up; the branches swayed gently. Although I didn't see a single small bird, birdsong filled the air. One sang, "Poo-tee-weet? Poo-tee-weet?" from the branches of a sycamore tree. Leaving the main path, I took a narrow trail to the left, venturing into the dark woods of *Pazifisches Nordamerika.* Warmed by September sunlight, the vegetation filled the air with the dry, brittle fragrance of autumn, the breath of home. How beautiful it was! As I walked along, I closed my eyes for a few moments at a time. Just ahead, I heard the hum of human activity. Opening my eyes, I found myself surrounded by the foliage of Asia. With eyes closed, I'd walked across the Pacific from *Amerika* to *Asien.* The trees led me to a clearing, to a park. In the center of the park stood a Buddhist temple, the Buddha of the Botanical Garden, the Buddha of Berlin. Many other visitors had arrived before me, at least a hundred Asians and Europeans, young and old, boys and girls, women and men, families, talking, playing, dancing, eating in the park surrounding the temple. There were colorful canopies and sun umbrellas. Banners and kites danced gaily on the breeze. Many were dressed in colorful, light cotton clothing, well suited to this warm September afternoon. Food was being prepared on open grills and served all around. Exotic aromas and spices filled the air, as did the music of flutes and stringed instruments, guitar and sitar. One young woman sat with her back to me playing a paixiao, her long, shining black hair tied back. Sophia? It couldn't be. Another young woman, loosening her blue yukata at the shoulder, breastfed her baby. An aura of tranquility and peace, heightened by the dry yet sensuous incense of autumn, filled the park surrounding the temple. A slender young man standing off to one side of the temple saw me observing from the edge. Although I felt as if I had been caught, a voyeur, he smiled as if he knew me, waved, and motioned for me to join the celebration, for although casual, it had a ceremonial air about it. Smiling, waving both thanks and regrets in return, I continued along the edge of the park, past the temple, following the path toward what appeared to be a shining crystal palace rising above the green trees—a mirage? As I came closer, I realized it was a gigantic glass greenhouse, the largest I'd ever seen, its windows sparkling in the afternoon sunlight like facets of a gigantic diamond. First North America, then Asia, and now the Mediterranean, I entered the *Mittelmeerhaus*. Palm trees towered over my head. I walked underneath, below a glass ceiling, through vines, groves of giant bamboo, past goldfish ponds, sitting down on a wooden bench to rest and listen to the sound of water running from an unseen source, to inhale the humid tropical air, so different from the dry autumn air outside. A young woman wearing a summer hat and pleated dress, a sun umbrella folded on her lap, sat on the wooden bench directly across from me, gazing absently off into the palm trees above my head. Her bearded companion stood behind her, elegantly dressed in a black velvet sport coat and khaki slacks, gesturing with his left hand, attempting to make a point or win her attention. Frozen for a moment, framed in the lush beauty of the tropical greenhouse, they unknowingly joined the permanent collection of the *Neue Nationalgalerie*.

Temporarily freed of all responsibilities, anxieties, and the burdens of History, I sat on the bench, breathing, being. Time passed, the elegantly attired couple moved on. I decided to move on too, back to the *UKBJ* for dinner. Leaving the great glass pavilion, I discovered puddles on the paved path running in front of the *Mittelmeerhaus*. It had rained while I rested inside, and a rainbow now spanned the *Botanischer Garten*, bright and perfect, its colorful arc shimmering down into the thick, lustrous green trees. Rather than follow the rainbow back down toward the Buddhist temple, I took the paved path back to the entrance on *Unter den Eichen*, returning through the North American woodlands, wet leaves glistening in the light of the late afternoon sun, breathing in Franz Kafka's *"starker Duft."* Still hesitant to retrieve the *Falkplan* from my shoulder bag, I decided to retrace the route I'd taken earlier, across *Unter den Eichen*, down *Mohnstraße* to *Moltkestraße*, *Hindenburgdamm*, and *Schloßpark*. There was no sign of *Herr und Hund* as I walked under the cool shade of the sycamore trees on *Plantanenplatz* on my way back to the *UKBJ*. Dr. Abrassimov's recommended *Spaziergang* had proven therapeutic. Hopefully, I would be able to internalize the green peacefulness of this festive September afternoon and draw upon it after my discharge from *Psychiatrische Ambulanz*.

Toward the end of the third week, Dr. Abrassimov determined my *Spiegelbild* reflected the proper amount of lithium, so I could be released. The day before my discharge, D minus one, I asked to meet briefly with the *Chefarzt* of *Psychiatrische Ambulanz,* Professor Dr. Berghoff, an, according to my fellow patients, unusual request which was nonetheless instantly granted by his secretary. She made an appointment for the following day at 10:00, just after the morning staff meeting. When I walked into the outer office the next day, a few minutes before ten, the secretary smiled and waved me through. "*Guten Morgen Herr von Aechron, Herr Professor Berghoff erwartet Sie schon.*"[53]

Dressed in his immaculate, buttoned, white *Kittel,* Professor Dr. Berghoff was a slender man in his midfifties. Although I'd seen him occasionally in the hallway of *Psychiatrische Ambulanz,* I had not yet had the opportunity to speak with him. A strip of hair, cut short, ran around the sides and back of his head, placing white laurels of professional dignity on his baldness and bearing. He smiled warmly and stood up from behind his large wooden desk, walking over to meet me with his right hand extended. "Good morning, Mr. Vonaechron, I'm very pleased to have the opportunity to meet you. I understand you will be leaving us later today. Please do have a seat. May I offer you something, a cup of tea?"

"Good morning, Professor Berghoff. No, no, but thank you very much just the same. I'm very grateful to you for taking the time to meet with me this morning." I took a seat on the sofa next to the coffee table across from his desk, where an open copy of Gottfried Benn's *Trunkener Flut* lay on top of medical journals. Rather than returning to his desk, he sat down in the chair next to the sofa. "Yes, I understand I'll be discharged after lunch, but before leaving, I wanted to thank you personally for the care I have received over the past three weeks from your staff, from the doctors and the nurse, the nurses."

He smiled at my slip of the tongue—"the nurse." I wonder if my merciful night nurse had told him about our unusual nocturnal therapy session. "You're certainly welcome, Mr. Vonaechron. That's exactly why we're here, to provide our patients with the best possible care. To be honest with you, though, we don't often receive feedback from our patients. When we do, it tends to be negative rather than positive, so on behalf of myself and the doctors and nurses on my staff, thank you!"

"There is, however, one question which I would like to ask you before I leave, Professor. What is your diagnosis. What exactly was or is wrong with me?"

---

53 "Good morning, *Herr* von Aechron, *Herr Professor* Berghoff is waiting for you." Diary of Thomas Vonaechron, Diary Extract, 1983, trans. TV.

Professor Berghoff smiled, "To be honest with you, Mr. Vonaechron, we haven't really come to any definite conclusions. Basically, you are fine, but have been working, and perhaps playing, too hard over the past year—what is the American expression, 'burning the candle at both ends?' My colleague, the doctor on duty the night you were admitted, wrote in her report she felt you were no longer . . ."

"'*Aufnahmefähig!*' I won't ever forget that word! She was very kind and knew just what to do to help me in a difficult situation. Unfortunately, I haven't seen her in *Psychiatrische Ambulanz* since that evening."

"No, she completed her residency with us the night you were admitted. I was very sorry to lose her. Yes, *aufnahmefähig*. You'd simply absorbed or tried to absorb too much. There might also be another factor, a related factor, something you should be conscious of for your own personal and psychological well-being. You know, Mr. Vonaechron, there are many different kinds of people here in West Berlin, in the world for that matter, each with a unique personality. It's really quite miraculous when you think about it. Many people go through life without too many major doubts or difficulties, beyond those plaguing all of us. Others are more sensitive to their environment, to the people and things around them, the myriad details of their social and psychological environments. They tend to isolate and internalize these perceptions, occasionally absorbing—*aufnehmen*, hence *aufnahmefähig*—them into their sense of self, the bad along with the good, the painful along with the pleasant. This sensitivity, this eye for detail, is a *Janus-Kopf*. Do you understand what I mean? My colleagues and I feel you might be one of those people, Mr. Vonaechron. The same sensitivity that allows you to enjoy the aesthetic anarchism of life here in West Berlin also absorbs the tragedy, melancholy, fear, and anxiety of this remarkable city, which in turn accentuates and augments your own basic fears or *Ängste*—to use an overused German word. If you'll also forgive my use of an equally well-worn cliché, it is an existential anxiety, *Existenzangst*. Not in the sense of the fear of loss of the means of existence, such as income or housing, but the fear of existence itself, the fear of being. If, however, you are aware of this and can successfully incorporate it into your life, you shouldn't be too often troubled by similar problems in the future. This sensitivity is a gift, in both the English and German—"poison"—sense of the word. Understood and embraced, it will add depth and texture to your life. Joy as well as pain, and even panic too, occasionally. Your wish for a diagnosis is understandable. The attempt of an academically—let's say in your case, historically—trained mind, to provide an explanation. When you analyze a particular historical event, you attempt to discover the variables that explain it. When you analyze your own personal, individual history, it's understandable you'd want to apply the same methodology. Left uncontrolled, anxiety can lead to problems such as hypochondria, or fear of fatal disease, but it doesn't have to. Much depends upon the patient, upon you, Mr. Vonaechron. Although we have prescribed lithium for the time being, providing you with a supply for the next few weeks, it will very likely not be necessary for you to continue to take it. As we see it, your problem is primarily exhaustion. Once you've had the opportunity to rest and recuperate, you should be fine."

"Thank you, Professor—my own portable lithium spring, from which I can drink as necessary, in moderation of course."

He laughed. "Yes, indeed, that's correct, all things in moderation! It is, however, very important you consult a doctor and make the decision to go off lithium together. Unless you already have someone here in West Berlin, I'll have my secretary provide you with the name, address, and telephone number of a close colleague of mine with your discharge paperwork. Her *Praxis* is not too far from Friedenau, on *Duisbergerstraße* in Wilmersdorf. Prioritize, cut back on the number of activities, Mr. Vonaechron. Make certain you get regular and sufficient rest. From my colleagues, I understand you are preparing a dissertation in history at the Free University. While research and writing can be exhausting, they can also be therapeutic. Believe me, Mr. Vonaechron, and I know this from my own experience at the university, it's not at all unusual for medical students to suffer from emotional distress, particularly under the pressure of study, research, residency, and the required state examinations. You must learn how to relax, how to intentionally let go, *abzuschalten*. You might consider autogenic training or meditation. If you don't learn to relax in a rejuvenating manner, your mind will let go for you. While I don't recommend alcohol as a means of 'self-medication,' there is nothing wrong with occasionally sitting in a café with a '*Glässchen*' of wine, once again, in moderation of course."

"Thank you very much for your recommendations, Professor Berghoff. I'll do my best to 'swallow' them along with the lithium, though I'd prefer meditation to the medication. If you'll permit me one last, unrelated question, the copy of Gottfried Benn's *Trunkene Flut* on your coffee table. Several years ago, I attended a reading of poems from this same edition at the University of Virginia in Charlottesville. It made quite an impression on me at the time. Gottfried Benn was also a medical doctor, wasn't he?"

"Yes, yes, he was. Dr. med. Gottfried Benn, a fascinating figure— problematic, politically, artistically, somewhat like your Ezra Pound, though Benn wasn't an avowed anti-Semite. Initially, he embraced the National Socialist movement but quickly became disenchanted joining the *Wehrmacht* in 1935 as, how did he put it, 'the aristocratic form of immigration.' He'd actually already served as an army doctor prior to and during the First World War. He might even have worked in *Psychiatrie* at the *Charité* before the war. As you might know, because of his association with the *NSDAP*, he was not permitted to publish until 1948. In one of those ironies of history with which I'm certain you are well acquainted, the *NSDAP* had prohibited Benn from publishing his work from 1938 until the end of the war. Yet, I too find his poetry fascinating, deeply disturbing as well, particularly the poems written before the First World War—a poetry informed if not inspired by his chosen profession. His first book, *Morgue und andere Gedichte*, was published in 1912 while he was working as a pathologist. It caused quite a scandal at the time. Although *Trunkene Flut* was published much later, it contains poems written between 1912 and 1936. As a historian, you might be interested in Benn's observations on history. He felt that history has essentially no meaning. That there is no progress, only illusion and, at best, history can only provide us with textbook examples of the fragmentary.

"Textbook examples of the fragmentary?"

"Yes, Mr. Vonaechron. Benn's is an essentially existential position.

"Why, thank you, Professor Berghoff, that particular insight is very helpful!"

Leaning forward in his chair, he picked up the book from the coffee table, handed it to me, and said, "Here, let me give it to you, Mr. Vonaechron as a 'gift,'" Professor Berghoff laughed, paused for a moment and said, "a souvenir of your three-week stay with us. We're here, of course, if you should require our assistance again, but I don't believe you will."

"Thank you again, Professor Berghoff. My heartfelt thanks for taking the time to talk with me this morning, and thank you so very much for this book." Returning to my room, I found another gift waiting for me, a medium-sized package wrapped in what appeared to be a brown paper shopping bag with a Fourteenth Street return address on it, lying on my bed. Sitting down, I carefully unwrapped it. Inside, I found Laura's brown, cotton flower-print dress together with an oversize picture postcard of the Jefferson Memorial at night. Intentionally overexposed to capture the internal illumination, the memorial appeared to be burning, the reddish-orange light reflected in the clouds in the night sky over the Tidal Basin. On the back of the postcard, there was a note from Laura: "My Dearest Thomas, I send you our special dress as a present, not to wear of course, maybe you could use it as your pillowcase. I don't want to encourage *Sexueller Fetischismus*, but it's all I can think of, and hope it makes you feel better! I think of you often, especially when visiting libraries and art galleries! I'm enjoying Fourteenth Street life in 'Chocolate City,' though the inner city poverty is heartbreaking. Why didn't you warn me about the university? Courses are much more difficult at GW than they are at the *FU*! There are midterm examinations, final examinations, and research papers to write! Although I drop by DC Space for lunch once in a while, I've only made it up to the 9:30 Club twice. The second time I went, *Einstürzende Neubauten* was here from West Berlin! Sometimes I too wonder if I'm not moving in the wrong direction. Nadja's in New York this week, covering Max's Kansas City and CBGB/OMFUG with Clarence. She sends her heartfelt wishes for a *Gute Besserung*! Smooch, Laura." Only indirect mention of André. Rainer must have written her.

Over lunch, I said goodbye to the five patients remaining in *Psychiatrische Ambulanz*. None of the others, not even Walkwoman, knew the name of the blonde Bonnard bathing beauty, my sad sister, who'd been discharged a few days earlier. She did know she was engaged to be married, and her *Verlobter* had come to the *UKBF* to pick her up. Why hadn't I asked her name in the bath, or as we walked through the corridors of the *Klinikum* hand in hand? After lunch, I gathered up my seven things and placed them, together with the books, my new pillowcase, and picture postcard, into my burnt orange backpack. Taking leave of my roommate, I shook his hand and said "*Es lebe das Bett!*" He smiled, nodding his head in agreement. I looked at what had been *mein Bett* for the past three weeks, thinking once again of the sister of mercy and, for one last time, I savored the seventh-floor view from my room. After receiving my discharge paperwork, prescriptions, and Dr. Berghoff's referral from the nurse at the waiting room desk, it was time to descend from the seventh floor, time to return to the flatland. The nurse kindly offered to call a taxi.

When I saw the big yellow Mercedes taxi waiting like a human engine in the driveway in front of the *Universitätslinikum*, I hesitated for a moment, thinking it might be Rainer, but there wasn't an "(American Literature)" light on the roof. I hadn't told him, George, D3, or anyone else exactly when I would be discharged from the *UKBF*. I wanted to return to Friedenau and work my way deliberately into my new routine before calling on friends. Leaning over the shotgun seat, the driver asked if I'd ordered a taxi. I nodded, hesitating for a moment, before opening the back door and climbing in. It had been exactly three weeks since George drove me up this same concrete ramp to the *Notaufnahme*. As we drove back down, turning into *Klingsorstraße*, I looked up at the Gray Giant until it disappeared in the green trees. Taxiing back to Freidenau seemed to take longer. Steglitz seemed different, *entfremdet*, unfamiliar. Just as I was about to ask the driver where we were, he turned onto *Schloßstraße*, which became *Rheinstraße* and then *Hauptstraße*. When he turned into

Hedwigstraße across from the *Rathaus Friedenau*, I looked up from under the glass of the rear window at the stone angel. Looking down from her tower, she seemed to be smiling directly at me, offering her green frond in a gesture of peace. *Lothringerstrasse* was just around the corner.

Golgotha
September 1983

The heavy wooden front door was open, with the dead bolt extended to prevent it from closing. The *Hausmeister* must be at work in the *Treppenhaus*. I pushed it open with my shoulder, making my way quietly past Govinda's apartment to the staircase, without turning on the hallway light. Grasping the heavy wooden railing in my right hand, I placed one foot purposely in front of the other on the stairs, slowly pulling myself up the staircase. Unlocking top and bottom locks, I opened the door to the apartment and walked in, closing the door behind me. There was no one home. During his visit to the *Universitätsklinikum*, Dr. Kahler told me he would likely be vacationing in southern Switzerland with a friend when I returned to the apartment. The hallway seemed longer, darker, than on the afternoon I left to return to the Turn-Tower. Although I had only been gone for three weeks, it was as if three years had passed between the closing and opening of that dark wooden door. Afternoon light filtered through the windows of French doors leading into my room, inviting me to reenter. I opened the doors. The sun shone through windows opening onto *Lothringerstrasse*, reflecting off dust particles in the air, giving the familiar scene a pointillist quality. Although the one elegant Empire room hadn't changed—the posters on the wall, the red umbrella hanging from the ceiling, the abnormally heavy brass dolphin clock on the floor—I had. The flounder eyed me apprehensively from the far wall; its fear-filled, fishy facial expression remained unchanged. For a brief moment, I thought about taking the print down or turning the fish to face the wall but didn't. It wasn't the flounder's fault. It was my own—I hadn't headed the warning. Uneasy, I set backpack and shoulder bag down on the makeshift desk and sat down. Opening the side pocket of the shoulder bag, I spread the contents out on the desktop. Together, with the poem Neal prepared for my departure, Govinda's calling card, the *Zettel* found in the boxcar at *Anhalter Bahnhof*, the quotation from Alfred Jarry the actor François Fontane had given me at the *Saubühne*, and prescriptions from the *UKBF*, was the letter from my father's friend Lorelei Rhine. Lorelei's letter had proven prophetic after all. Cassandra. I chose to ignore her warning about the constellations found in combinations of the letters, B-E-R-L-I-N and paid the price. Perhaps, as Dr. Kahler suggested, it had been necessary. Perhaps. Putting the documents into one of the cardboard boxes that served as drawers under the desk, I resolved to keep the discordant forces contained in the constellation of B-E-R-L-I-N at bay, and myself under intellectual control.

Opening my backpack, I took out Laura's dress and, walking over to the bed, slipped the dress carefully over the down pillow, buttons down. The bottom button was missing. I took off my sport coat and shoes and stretched out. Light coming in through the large windows illuminated the intricate fin de siècle plaster of paris ceiling three meters over my head. Breathing in the scent of Laura's perfume, she'd washed and perfumed the dress before sending it to me. I rewound the events of the past twenty-one days and played them back in chronological order. Excess and *Einsturz*, George's kindness, my Czech and Russian psychiatrists, my sad blonde sister whose name I'd never know, and the merciful night nurse who'd nurtured me so lovingly with her breasts and her thighs. Well-rested, I decided to rest well for the rest of the day so the next day I could resume writing, just as I'd decided to do three weeks earlier. All the primary and secondary sources required for the time being, being in time, were already organized into piles arranged on the floor next to my desk—my own, in-house privy archive. There was much work to be done before the meeting with my *Doktormutter* in the *Café Wellenstein* scheduled for next month, the beginning of winter semester.

Though the taxi had returned me from the *Refugium* of the *Universitätsklinikum* to the flatland, to the well-walled reality of West Berlin, that reality was not yet absolute. I still had the sensation of being apart, *apart* in my room, *apart* in Dr. Kahler's apartment. A kind of reentry, a kind of reintegration into the city itself, was still necessary. Waking early the next morning to the *Quetschenfragen* posed musically by the birds outside my window, I took a long hot bath, thinking about nothing at all, then about bathing with my long blonde sister in *Psychiatrische Ambulanz*. Firmly committed to the routine of research and writing recommended to me by both D3 and Professor Berghoff, I decided to take one more day, this day, to reenter West Berlin. For the first time since my arrival over a year ago, I didn't know where to go. Outside of completing my degree, I no longer had any objectives to be taken, any points of reference to be exploited in the HistoriCity. *Ziellos*, afraid of nothing but the fear itself, I felt free. No longer driven, I decided to walk once again, *per pedes Pilgrimorum*, allowing the streets to carry me along. Just in case, I placed the small, blue glass bottle of Lexotanil, together with the *Falkplan*, into my shoulder bag. After drying off and dressing, I closed the French doors, locked the front door, and set out.

On this late morning in mid-September, the streets of Friedenau were inviting, lined with linden trees, filling the air with the warm, dry scent of immanent decay, reminding me Friedenau was, as George had explained to me en route from Tempelhof Central Airport, once a *Landhauskolonie*. Linden trees led me back to the intersection across from *Rathaus Friedenau*, where the taxi from the *Universitätslinikum* had turned into the *Hedwigstraße* the day before. Although Hedwig wasn't waiting for me today, the angel was, still smiling at me, though I was now standing on the far side of the broad *Rheinstraße*. Yet the angel, or perhaps the angle, was somehow different. Yesterday, from under the rear window of the taxi, she stood foreshortened, Persian wings supporting a benevolent face with palm leaf extended in a gesture of peace. From across the street, I could see she was much taller, lithe and very graceful. The folds of her gown emphasized the elegance of her stature, the length and beauty of her limbs. As I held her in my gaze, she seemed to turn and extend her right hand, indicating with the palm frond the direction I should take up *Rheinstraße*. Keeping the *Falkplan* securely stowed in my shoulder bag with the blue bottle, I turned the corner, following her direction without hesitation.

Although *Rheinstraße* was the main north-south thoroughfare running through southwest Berlin, the droning of the morning traffic seemed distant, enoesque, ambient, and almost agreeable, suggesting the Baltic Sea to the north. Led on by the linden trees, I walked back into the heart of West Berlin. Just beyond *Rathaus Freidenau*, where *Rheinstraße* metamorphosed into *Hauptstraße*, I saw the *LaBelle* disco on the far side of the street and thought again of Nadja, Laura, and Sophia in Washington, DC. At *Insbrücker Platz,* a single Doric column surmounted by a golden globe marked the miles to a center of an earlier Berlin without the Wall. Looking to the left while crossing *Dominicusstraße*, I could see the massive gray square tower of *Rathaus Schöneberg*. "Two thousand years ago, the proudest boast was *'civis Romanus sum.'* Today, in the world of freedom, the proudest boast is *'Ich bin ein Berliner.'*" Just ahead, the gray postwar concrete and plate glass facades parted on the left, revealing a small village, *Alt Schöneberg*. The green patina on the copper roof of the rose-colored church rose above the intersection. Crossing over to the far side of the *Hauptstraße*, I discovered a small marble monument enclosed in a black ornamental iron fence on the green traffic island. Indifferent to its weathered inscription, I continued over the street to the sidewalk on the far side. Climbing the stairway leading up from the sidewalk to the rose-colored church, my eyes met the thousand-yard stare of a weathered bronze, half-size statue of a First World War German soldier, standing solemnly at ease with *Stahlhelm* in his right hand, flowers in his left, sculptor Hermann

Hosaeus's preemptive reply to Pete Seeger's coming question about where all the flowers and soldiers have gone. At the top of the staircase was the entrance to the church graveyard. Another fly-specked angel, wounded by both the war and time, right arm upraised, a palm frond cradled in her shattered left, stood ready to receive me. A dirge coming from the side door of the church drew my attention, encouraging me to walk around the church, where I discovered a funeral already in progress. Only the six pallbearers, dressed in long black coats and top hats, and the pastor, in his long black *Talar* and white *Beffchen*, were present. I followed at a respectful distance as the dark wooden coffin was borne through the open side door, down a cobblestone path, leading past the massive mausoleums and monuments forming the outside wall of the cemetery. Stately temples in neoclassical and neo-Gothic styles, with family names carved on lintels or arches over iron entrance doors, set into stone for eternity. Following the cortege, I continued down the path, deeper into the cemetery. Black cast-iron sunflowers and buds crowing an ornamental iron fence identical to the one running around the Botanical Gardens caught my attention. Stopping, I turned to take a closer look. On the far side of the fence, purple rhododendron framed an engraved black marble tablet set into a red sandstone monument pockmarked by two large caliber shell holes. The war hadn't stopped at the cemetery gate. Flowering vines had been carved into the sandstone arch framing the tablet, held in place by three slender pillars on each side. Beneath a Celtic Cross, a haloed owl with wings spread crowned the flowered arch. The name framed in purple blossoms was Franz Heinrich Schwechten, his title and position inscribed in the black marble beneath his name: "*Geh. Baurat, Professor*"—a privy planning officer and professor, an architect. Schwechten. The name was familiar. Yes, the friendly bookseller in East Berlin told me Franz Schwechten designed the Anhalter Train Station, the Kaiser Wilhelm Memorial Church, and the New War Academy, the engraving bought with the last of my East German marks. An architect of religion and of war, reifications of love and hate. Two of his celebrated construction projects, the *Anhalter Bahnhof* and the *Kaiser-Wilhelm-Gedächtnis-Kirche*, were now celebrated as ruins in West Berlin. Leveled by the war, his *Neue Kriegsakademie* had been replaced by the Afghan Embassy. *Eirönïa.*

Looking back down the path, I discovered the cortege had disappeared around the corner of a large mausoleum on its way even deeper into the cemetery, and decided to retrace my steps. Walking back up the cobblestone path to the entrance, taking leave of the weathered angel and the sorrowful soldier, I returned to *Hauptstraße*. The *Gründerzeit* buildings just beyond the rose-colored *Dorfkirche* were painted off-white and pale yellow, completing an architectural ensemble standing in colorful contrast to the gray concrete facades framing it. One of the old buildings even presented passersby with a Prussian Porch of the Maiden, a single caryatid, deserted by her five sisters, holding up the heavy stone roof alone.

At *Kaiser-Wilhelm-Platz*, where a bent black metal sign, identical to the one on *Wittenbergplatz*, reminded passersby of the thirteen "*Ort des Schreckens die wir nie vergessen dürfen*," *Hauptstraße* metamorphosed into *Potsdamer Straße*. On the far side of the street, the same side I'd been walking on before I'd crossed over to the church, I saw Robert Jones leave the front door of the apartment building at 156 and walk into the *Café Anderes Ufer* next door at 157. He was wearing the same red checkered shirt he'd worn when we met at the *Arlecchino*. Although I'd often thought about our conversation, I hadn't been back to the *Arlecchino* since our chance meeting. I would have liked to continue our discussion, but not today. I walked alongside a massive building in the stripped-classicism style, with black, cast-iron lamps reminiscent of those lighting the *Ost-West-Achse* and the former Japanese Embassy in the Tiergarten. For a second time, the concrete and brick facades parted on the left, revealing two parallel, elegant, classical colonnades leading to a great neo-Baroque building set well back from the street in a large park. I recognized the building at once from the Office of Military Government—Berlin Sector records I'd reviewed in Washington and arranged in Berlin as the seat of the Allied Control Council for Germany, the once and future *Kammergericht*. A raised stone tablet, set like a tombstone on the grass between the colonnades, reminded passersby that here, in the *Volksgerichthof*, Roland Freisler staged the show trials following the aborted coup d'état of July 20, 1944. At the far end of the colonnades, a bronze angel bearing a small torch appeared to cast aside the heavy, cast-bronze books of history and walk toward me.

Walking on, past the Hotel Potsdam and the dive bars Rainer and I had occasionally visited in the early hours of the morning, before sunlight exposed the broken facades of the prewar buildings and the gray, poured-concrete facades of those erected in great haste after the war, I stood for a few minutes at the intersection with *Bülow Straße*. On the right stood the out-of-service *U-Bahnhof Bülowstraße*, a latter-day casualty of the Wall. The artfully constructed, aboveground *Art Nouveau* station now housed a Turkish bazaar and Berliner *Kneipe* in refurbished *U-bahn* coaches. But on this sunny September afternoon, neither artifacts nor alcohol could help me reenter West Berlin. As I crossed *Bülow Straße*, I could see the tall, slender bell tower of the American Church in Berlin on *Dennewitzplatz* beyond the *U-Bahnhof*, another restored redbrick survivor.

I continued on, up *Potsdamer Straße*, underneath blackened steel girders supporting the *U-Bahn* tracks and coaches overhead, on past the *Baan Vietnamienne*. At *Kurfürstenstraße*, I crossed from *Stadtbezirk Schöneberg* into Tiergarten. The linden trees lining *Potsdamer Straße* led on, until buildings on both sides of the street ended in the vast empty space created by the war. I had reached the banks of the *Landwehkanal*. On the far side of the canal stood the *Kulturforum*, the *Neue Nationalgalerie*, the *Staatsbibliothek*, and beyond, the *Philharmonie* and the Wall separating Tiergarten from *Mitte*. I remembered tracing the border between the two *Bezirke* from the heights of the Turn-Tower Music Café three weeks earlier. Rising above the flat roof of the *Neue Nationalgalerie* were the delicate redbrick towers of the *St.-Matthäus-Kirche*. The heavy, granulated *Berliner Luft* also revealed an augmented reality. Directly in front of me, the *Reichstag*, with its glass dome restored, and beyond, behind the *Philharmonie*, a new city of shimmering glass rising into the sky from the *intervallum* at *Potsdamer Platz*, the no-man's-land between West and East. Oz shimmering in the afternoon sunlight. As I strained to see more of the city, with its great tent and towers of glass, the mirage dissolved back into the hazy emptiness of the September sky. Rather than crossing over *Potsdamer Brücke* to investigate, I followed the last few remaining linden trees to the edge of the *Schöneberger Ufer*, lined with stately chestnut trees on both sides, and looked down into the water. On the far side, graffiti on the embankment at the base of the *Neue Nationalgalerie* still posed the same questions: "*Warum (nicht) Kunst?*" The answer to this question no longer seemed important—I was looking for another way to reenter West Berlin.

Schöneberger Ufer metamorphosed into *Tempelhofer Ufer* as I continued along the left bank of the *Landwehrkanal*, under spreading chestnut and weeping willow trees. In the distance, at the intersection with *Schönebergerstraße*, I could see the tower of another red *Backsteinkirche*, a good omen. I continued along the banks of the canal. From a Juliet balcony outside the window in the *Dachgeschoß* of an apartment building on the corner of *Tempelhofer Ufer* and *Großbeerenstraße*, another single caryatid watched over the intersection. I stopped for a moment. The pleasant, linden-lined *Großbeerenstraße* reminded me I should slowly begin to walk back in the direction of Freidenau and *Lothringerstrasse*. There was much work to be done the next day. Although the surviving facades of the apartment buildings lining *Großbeerenstraße* were gray and badly weathered, they still retained their nineteenth-century charm. At number 21, a young woman dressed in a Roman tunic, her long hair dressed in Roman fashion, falling in tresses, raised her right hand in greeting. Her sister on the other side of the doorway looked on with mild interest.

Looking left, crossing over *Hornstraße*, I saw another redbrick church tower of delicate, almost airy construction with an oxidized copper spire, and beyond it, rising through the trees on the median, yet another church tower. It was remarkable how many of these nineteenth-century churches had survived the war. Coming to the "T" at the end of *Großbeerenstraße*, I found myself directly across the street from a highland waterfall, cascading down a wooded hillside from a monument at the summit, a Teutonic trout stream. Instinctively reaching for the *Falkplan*, I caught myself and crossed the street to investigate. At the base of the hill, in the center of a large fishpond, were two bronze figures frozen in apprehension and passion. A bemused muscular fisherman contemplated the beautiful mermaid writhing in his net, holding her firmly across his loins. The octopus also caught in his net was of no interest. Curiously, the mermaid's tail formed just below her hips and delicately scaled thighs, serving up her *mons veneris* on the half-shell to *flâneur* and voyeur alike, a seductive invitation to visit *Viktoriapark*. The trees of West Berlin had carried me to the foot of the *Kreuzberg*. A wooden sign posted next to the paved path leading up to the summit advertised a *Freiheitsdenkmal*, and, to provide additional encouragement for those unmotivated by history, it also offered a *Rundblick vom Plateau über Berlin*. Although I wasn't interested in the "Liberation Monument," the promised panorama of Berlin won me over. Beyond the pond, the broad path branched out into several smaller paths, leading up through linden and maple trees, past stone benches, where tired wanderers could rest. I chose the middle way. Soothed by the sound of the falling water, I kept climbing, working my way up the slope, following the stream through trees and bushes, along winding paths and switchbacks. Accompanied only by the sound of the stream and the questions of birds unseen, I met no one either ascending or descending.

By the time I reached the summit, it was growing dark. A monumental stone staircase led up the front of a stone bastion to the *Freiheitsdenkmal*, an iron replica of a neo-Gothic cathedral tower enclosed by a cast-iron, eight-sided fence crowning the *Kreuzberg*. Twelve iron angels, two female and ten male, clad in historical armament, wings at parade rest behind their backs, guarded the octagonal base of the tower. Some brandished weapons; others crowned themselves with laurel victory wreaths. Each angel bore the name and dates of a battle beneath. *Freiheitsdenkmal*, a monument to liberation through the war. I wondered if D3 had made the pilgrimage up here yet and made a mental note to ask him. The need to identify the twelve battles, along with which war and particular stratum of Berlin the monument memorialized vanished three weeks ago in *die Ruine*. Although all twelve angels wore green patina, not one of them held out a palm frond.

At the very top of the tower, an Iron Cross was silhouetted against the darkening sky. These winged, cast-iron militant angels were not what I was looking for.

The panoramic view from the monument was well worth the climb, however, reminding me of my seventh-floor room with a view at the *Universitätsklinikum. Berlin leuchtet.* On the *Großer Stern*, the golden Chick-on-a-Stick glowed in her spotlights. Fewer and dimmer than those of West Berlin, the lights of East Berlin shone due north. To the southeast stood Tempelhof Central Airport, my point of arrival in West Berlin. Ernst Sagebiel's Central Hall, the great hall of stone and glass where time and history seemed to stand still, was oriented on the *Freiheitsdenkmal* where I now stood. Yet time had not stood still in West Berlin. Thirteen months had passed since my arrival. My chance meeting with Govinda on Pan Am's "Round-the-World" flight from London to Frankfurt and the terra-cotta Buddha sitting across the street from the *Clay-Institut* in the *Museum für Indische Kunst* came to mind. Both shared the same serene smile, radiating peace, joy, and gratitude.

After completing a circuit of the tower, the twelve stations of the *Kreuzberg*, while looking out over Berlin, I couldn't recall exactly which of the paths at the foot of the monument had led me to the summit. *Großbeerenstraße*, illuminated by parallel rows of streetlights in the night, was directly below me. Once again choosing the middle way, I set out into the darkness. Not far from the monument, a pentagonal sign heralded Golgotha, *Terrassen am Kreuzberg*, offering a place to sit and rest for a few minutes before the long walk back to Friedenau. Following the sign down a side path, I came upon a single-story redbrick building situated between a playground and a sports field. Golgotha turned out to be a *Biergarten*, with long wooden tables set up adjacent to and on top of the building. With the exception of the waitress seen through a window of the building à la Edward Hopper, the *Biergarten* was deserted. I climbed the stairs to the top of the building, taking a seat on a wooden bench at a table facing down the *Kreuzberg*. Illumination came from brightly colored lights running along the roof railing. Through the trees, light was also coming from the windows of the nineteenth-century apartment buildings lining *Viktoriapark*. I turned around on the bench to look back up toward the summit, through the trees in the direction of the neo-Gothic *Freiheitsdenkmal*, with its Iron Cross and twelve iron angels. It was no longer in my line of sight. When I turned back around, there was a young man sitting directly across from me at my table. I'd neither seen him when I sat down nor heard him sit down. Comfortably dressed in casual white linen clothing, a smock over shirt and pants, he had short, whitish-blonde hair and eyes the color of the Aegean Sea. Although the sun had set, his hair had a reddish halo from the colored lights running along the wall behind him. Smiling serenely as Govinda, he said, "Do not be afraid." I should have been startled by his sudden appearance but wasn't. It was as if we had made plans to meet at Golgotha. He spoke softly, in a casual, engaging manner, his presence radiating calmness and contentment. His gestures were graceful and natural. We drank the cold half-liter glasses of draft *Berliner Kindl* beer set out on the wooden table before us. Caught up in our conversation, I didn't remember the waitress coming upstairs to take our order. We spoke earnestly about *Gott und die Welt*, life in West Berlin, even my three weeks in the *Universitätsklinikum*. He listened closely with empathy and understanding. He seemed to know everything already, my activities, my anxieties, the *Einstürz* in the *Ruine*; he was even familiar with the medications I'd been prescribed in *Psychiatrische Ambulanz*. Assuring me all would be well, he finished his beer, smiled, raised his right hand in farewell, palm outward, said "Peace be with you, Thomas," and was gone, leaving me with two empty beer glasses and a sense of peace. Refreshed and rested, I thought about having some salad for dinner but decided to walk back down the stairs and continue my descent from the *Kreuzberg*. There were now a few customers sitting at the wooden tables adjacent to the building. One looked a lot like Laura, but it couldn't have been. I caught the waitress's attention, saying, "*Ich möchte gern zahlen, bitte!*" Smiling and shaking her head, she waved me off. Leaving the *Biergarten* through the lower exit leading down to the illuminated apartment buildings bordering *Viktoriapark*, I discovered the handwriting, in light green phosphorous letters, on the redbrick wall of Golgotha.

Dorthin mein Erdenpilger,
dort halte süße Rast,
dort wirft dem Sündentilger
zu Füßen deine Last!
Dann geh und rühme selig,
Wie wohl dir dort geschah,
der Weg zum Paradiese
geht über GOLGATHA![54]

Per pedes Pilgrimorum, I passed a brewery, walked through vineyards, and came to the cross in a clearing, over two meters tall, made of wood,

---

54 "There, my earthly pilgrim, there take sweet rest, there throw your burden at the feet of one who takes away sin! Then go, singing praises, of what really happened there, the way to paradise leads over Golgotha!" Diary of Thomas Vonaechron, Diary Extract, 1983, trans. TV.

stained dark brown, crowned with barbed wire. There was a sign, not at the head, but on a piece of broken marble below the metal mount at the foot, "17. Juni 1953." I looked back up the *Kreuzberg*, toward the invisible Iron Cross at the summit. Below, through the linden trees, I could still see lights in the windows of the buildings bordering *Viktoriapark*. Smaller streams and waterfalls led me through the trees, past stone staircases, back down to the foot of the *Kreuzberg* and to *Großbeerenstraße*. In the darkness, I could discern the outline of the fortunate fisherman and his unfortunate *Unusual Catch*. Retracing my route, I followed *Großbeerenstraße* back to the *Landwehrkanal* as far as the *U-Bahnhof Möckernbrücke*. Instead of walking home as planned, I decided to fall back on the *U-Bahn*, taking the *U-7* to *Berlinerstraße*, then changing to *U-9* to *Friedrich-Wilhelm-Platz*. Although much of my uneasiness and anxiety had dissolved in conversation and draught beer at Golgotha, I was not looking forward to returning to a rented room in an empty apartment. The front door was locked. Opening it quietly, I did not turn on the hallway light.

"Wall-Gazing"—*Pi-kuan*
September 1983

The soothing sounds of sitar and drum and a welcome mat of warm light came out from underneath Govinda Hemd's door. As I walked past and was about to climb the wooden staircase, the door opened. A soft light framed the person I assumed to be Govinda. From his silhouette, I could see he was slender, of medium height. "You're home at last," he said smiling. "I was hoping I might have the chance to finally meet you this evening." The sounds of the sitar and drum, and the scent of sandalwood incense came from the open door behind him. "If you have the time and would like to, please do come in for a few minutes." I followed him into his apartment, took off my shoes in the hallway, placing them on the wooden rack next to the door, and walked into what was once the parlor, the room directly below mine. It belonged to another building in another city. The walls were painted in soft, sandy colors—light brown, ochre, burnt orange, burnt sienna—*kiva* colors of the American Southwest. With the exception of several low tables made of teak, there was no furniture. The hardwood floor was completely covered with thick, woven wool rugs. White reindeer pranced around the edge of a thick, wine-colored carpet in the center of the room. Large, well-worn, silk-covered pillows with tassels were scattered about. Heavy embroidered curtains were drawn across the windows facing *Lothringerstrasse*. Light came from antique brass floor lamps, shaded in soft colors, and from candles, creating an ambiance of amity and serenity. I sat down in the center of the room on the wine-colored reindeer carpet, stretching out my legs.

"May I offer you something to drink, a cup of tea, a glass of fruit juice, or water?"

"Fruit juice, please. I've just returned from climbing the *Kreuzberg*." Govinda nodded and smiled at my reference to *Kreuzberg* and left the room for a few moments, returning with two glasses of juice on a small brass tray.

"It's *Granatapfel*, ah . . . pomegranate juice, I hope you like it, as I'm afraid it's all I have to offer you this evening."

"Thank you, I do like it very much." Govinda sat down across from me on the floor, instinctively folding his legs into the half-lotus position. Dressed in the loose-fitting cotton clothing popular with university students and *Hausbesetzer*, he wore his black hair long, combed back over his ears. His facial expression was kind and genuine.

"Could it be I saw you last week, walking in the *Botanischer Garten* near the Buddhist temple? As I hadn't noticed you coming and going over the past three weeks, I thought you might have moved away and was pleased to see you are still here in West Berlin."

"Yes, yes, I'm still living here in West Berlin. I apologize. I did see someone, it must have been you, waving at me, near the Buddhist temple. Unfortunately, because we hadn't yet met, I didn't recognize you. On that day, I wasn't in the best of spirits, so I declined your kind invitation to join in. Under other circumstances, I would have liked to. It was all so colorful, so peaceful, paradisiacal. But please forgive me! After over a year of living in this building, I haven't yet found the opportunity to introduce myself. My name is Thomas, Thomas Vonaechron," I said, extending my hand.

Taking my hand in his, he replied, "I'm very pleased to finally meet you. I'm Govinda, Govinda Hemd. I saw your name, taped onto Dr. Kahler's mailbox in the hallway. You know, Thomas, as my teacher would say, perhaps we simply were not supposed to meet until this evening. I have that feeling, too. Our community meets regularly at the Buddhist temple in the *Botanischer Garten*. For us, it truly is a garden of peace, so I'm pleased to hear you also experienced it. The plants and trees in the park surrounding the temple have been carefully placed according to principles of *feng shui*. Are you familiar with *feng shui*, Thomas? May I call you Thomas?"

"Yes, I've heard of *feng shui* and yes, please do call me Thomas. Forgive me Govinda, but I'm very curious about your first name. May I tell you why?" Govinda smiled and nodded in reply. "Just over a year ago, on the London-to-Frankfurt leg of Pan Am's "Round-the-World" flight, I met a professor of political science from the University of Hawaii named Govinda

Nayaka, We had a very interesting conversation about Mahatma Gandhi as a 'nation builder.' As a historian, I found his observations on 'nation building' very stimulating. Govinda also kindly put me in contact with his friend and former professor, Dr. Richard Schneider, an exchange professor at the Clay Institute of the Free University. I hadn't heard the name 'Govinda' before and because of the chance meeting, was quite surprised later that same day when my friend George von Garlitz and I came by to look at the room for rent in Dr. Kahler's apartment upstairs, and I saw the nameplate outside your door! I took it as a good omen. Govinda M. Nayaka was born in India. "M." stands for Mahatma. His father, a London-educated barrister, was a friend of Gandhi's. Govinda even attended his school at Wardha. Do you also have Indian roots, Govinda?"

Govinda laughed. "No, no, Thomas, I'm German but was given the name 'Govinda' by my teacher. It is of Sanskrit origin, meaning 'one who cares for the cattle,' possibly an Asian variation on the 'Good Shepherd' theme! In the Hindu religion, Govinda is often used in association with Krishna. Although very much interested in Hinduism—I even studied it for some time—I have been practicing Shin Buddhism since moving to West Berlin several years ago. The origins of Buddhism are also found in India. Some scholars see Buddhism as a branch of Hinduism. It doesn't really matter which is the tree and which is the branch as long as both grow together. My teacher says, 'Here in West Berlin, everyone finds a teacher.' Mahatma Gandhi was truly enlightened. Your friend Govinda Mahatma Nayaka was very fortunate to have found him."

"When I climb the staircase, late in the evening or very early in the morning, I often hear sitar and drum music, and smell the sandalwood incense coming from underneath your front door. I actually look forward to it on the way home. It's very soothing, calming. Over this past year, I've discovered many things here in West Berlin. Some are interesting, some disturbing, some disruptive, and some even destructive. You seem to have discovered or have created a kind of paradise here in West Berlin, Govinda, not just in the *Botanischer Garten*, but here in the *Lothringerstrasse*. This room radiates peace and well-being."

"Thank you for the compliment, Thomas! Among friends I refer to it as my 'Happy-*Bude*' and spend much time here in study and meditation. There are more islands of peace here in West Berlin. There has been a Buddhist temple in Frohnau since the mid-twenties. But please let me pose another question if I may. You seem to be often *unterwegs*. I've heard you depart late at night and heard your footsteps on the staircase in the early hours of the morning. Please do not misunderstand, it does not disturb me in the slightest and I am very pleased to learn the music and incense coming from my Happy-*Bude* helps you to relax. I came to West Berlin many years ago from West Germany, looking for an alternative way to live. Many do the same for many different reasons. One reason often heard among young German men is to escape the military service mandatory in the Federal Republic. But there are other reasons as well. Although it took time, as it was supposed to, I discovered I was looking for 'the middle way,' 'the middle path,' the way of enlightenment. May I ask you what you are looking for here in West Berlin, Thomas? Have you discovered it yet, or are you still in the process of learning what it might be?"

"When I moved here from Washington, DC, last year, it was to study history, the history of Berlin as preserved in archives and architecture. Some of the research work I was able to complete in Washington. So much of historic interest and influence seems to have happened in Berlin over the past one hundred years. My original intent was—is, I should say—is to complete the requirements for a doctorate in contemporary history. In spite of my good intentions, I found myself drawn out of the university into the history of the city itself, into the HistoriCity, as I called it. I have spent much time in contemplation too, Govinda, but on the ruins of Berlin past and present. There was and is so much going on here, apparently too much for me to work through, though. I'd have likely been better off if I'd stayed upstairs in my room, directly over this one, and contemplated the piles of documents stacked on my desk and on the floor!" I laughed. "Dr. Kahler tried to warn me about the dangers of West Berlin in advance, as did a prescient friend of my father's, even before I moved here. I should have heeded their warnings. When Dr. Kahler visited me at the *Klinikum Steglitz*, he said the experience might have been necessary for me. If, as your teacher says, 'Here in West Berlin, everyone finds a teacher,' Dr. Kahler is certainly one of the teachers I was supposed to find here."

"So, Thomas, you have been ill. That is why I haven't heard you on the stairs recently. The *Klinikum Steglitz* has a very good reputation. I hope the doctors and nurses there were able to help you."

"Yes, they were . . . both the doctors and the nurses. I stayed there, in *Psychiatrische Ambulanz*, for medical tests. My friend George von Garlitz, the colleague of Dr. Kahler who brought me here to look at the room, took me there three weeks ago. It was a kind of nervous exhaustion that had been building for some time. As I increased my activities, I felt an increasing sense of anxiety, leading to undefined *Angst* and, finally, panic. Instead of slowing down, I kept going, using alcohol as a form of self-medication, which of course only increased the anxiety, a cycle of sorts—an uphill bicycle race. Dr. Kahler suggested by exceeding my limits, I was able to discover them. Perhaps, the experience will prove useful, but it certainly wasn't pleasant. In any case, I've decided to reduce my activities and learn how to relax. A friend and classmate from the *FU* and the *Chefärzt* of *Psychiatrische Ambulanz* both recommended the self-discipline and deliberation required by academic work. The professor also suggested autogenous training or meditation."

"Please do forgive me for saying so, Thomas, but I can see the fear and anger in your eyes. You know, there is an interesting interrelationship between fear and anger, different sides of the same thing—how do you Americans put it? 'Two sides of the same coin?' Could it be that here in West Berlin you have been searching too hard, searching for too much? With all your activities, with all your searching, perhaps you simply didn't allow yourself the time necessary for finding. My teacher says, 'Searching requires that you search for something, a goal. To be able to find, you must dispense with goals. You must be open to experience and be free.' Your friend and your doctor have given you very good, practical advice, and I recommend you follow it. Return to your studies! You also said you would also like to learn how to relax. Your doctor recommended meditation. I can be of assistance to you there. You might have seen a Buddha, seated or standing, with right hand raised, palm outward. This raised right hand represents a shield. The left hand is extended outward or upturned, with palm in the lap, like this." Moving into the full-lotus, Govinda illustrated the position. "This position is called the 'protection Buddha,' signifying, among many other things, protection from fear. This is a posture you can learn, practice, and use to calm yourself. It is also a form of study, and like academic work, it also requires discipline."

"Yes, Govinda, I have seen a 'protection Buddha,' here in Berlin, in Dahlem at the *Museum für Indische Kunst*! The posture is exactly the same as yours, and the face, strangely enough, is that of Govinda Nayaka, the professor of political science from the University of Hawaii I met on the Pan Am "Round-the-World" flight, the other Govinda I referred to!"

"Now that's truly astonishing, Thomas! I'm quite familiar with the collection of the *Museum für Indische Kunst* but don't remember seeing a protection Buddha. I would be very grateful to you if you could show it to me sometime, at your convenience of course."

"Of course, whenever you like."

"We all experience *Angst*, Thomas. My 'Happy-*Bude*' and the protection Buddha posture help, but they do not always shield me completely. Fear is a common, a human, experience; it may be one of those essential things defining, even uniting us as human beings. I seek refuge from fear in *Amida Buddha* by repeating a mantra. If you choose to do so, you can too, though like the protection Buddha posture, it must be learned and then practiced, repeated. Repetition of a mantra can, in and of itself, be very calming, serving to focus the mind and then to empty it. My Catholic friends tell me saying the rosary serves the same function. The rosary beads help the supplicant to focus. Confronting and overcoming fear, and for that matter many other problems, is, according to my teacher, often a question of the ability to focus the mind and then empty it. You might see it as a two-step process, requiring self-discipline and practice. The advice given to you by your friend from the university and by your doctor would be the first step. Study is an exercise in focus and concentration. With concentration comes contradiction, however. Too much concentration, too much focus, can actually prevent one from seeing. It is therefore important you also learn how to empty your mind. That is the second step. There are different techniques you can use to do so. Taken together, these techniques, postures, mantras, meditations, and exercises build a raft, which can be used to cross over the stream. Once you've reached the other side, you might find you no longer have use for the raft and release it into the current."

"'Into the current!'" I laughed, "My friend from the university, D3, is a member of the 'Dead . . . is a student of the German officer and philosopher Carl von Clausewitz. When he came to visit me at the *Klinikum Steglitz*, he recommended I jump into the stream and swim with or against the current of history. Crossing over the stream on a raft and then letting go of it sounds like a much better idea than jumping into the stream to me!"

Govinda laughed in reply, "Let me be your ferryman, Thomas. The exercise in meditation and mind-emptying I practice is called '*Pi-kuan*' or 'wall-gazing.' In Chinese, '*pi*' is the word for 'wall,' '*kuan*' the word for observation. It is very useful for quieting the mind while coincidentally developing a 'mind-full,' or should I say out of respect to Bodhidharma, 'mind-less,' attitude? Don't try to make or force things to happen or read meaning into them when they do. Listen. Learn to observe everything with gentle indifference. Leave things as they are, appreciate them, enjoy being part of them, believe and be thankful. Ultimately, the Wall will prove as unnecessary as the raft. You might not only be richly rewarded with inner peace and insight but someday with the suddenness and the steepness of enlightenment! We are taught Bodhidharma, the 'blue-eyed barbarian,' patriarch of the Zen tradition, which incidentally shares much with Shin-Buddhism, 'gazed' at a wall in a cave for nine years. Japanese Soto Zennists still face a wall while practicing *zazen*. Consider practicing *pi-kuan* as a complement, the second stage of the concentration in addition to your academic studies, Thomas. I'd be very happy to help you to learn how to do so. Might I ask if you now follow a way, a path, a teaching, faith or religion—are you a member of any denomination?"

"Yes, Govinda. I was raised Methodist and still find value in the writings of John Wesley. But I've also considered the history, teachings, and most recently, the poetry of Zen Buddhism. Dr. Kahler introduced me to Li Po and Tu Fu. Although I've found many interesting, even startling parallels with Christianity, I don't yet consider myself a 'Zen-Methodist!'"

Govinda laughed and clapped his hands. "'Ha Ha, Zen-Methodist!' Now that's a good one, Thomas! I have a friend, also Methodist by the way, who lives in London. At Foundry Chapel, she learned John Wesley would often pray kneeling on a wooden prayer stool, facing the redbrick wall of the airshaft just outside his bedroom window. She even tried it several times herself. Could this be a 'Zen-Methodist' form of *pi-kuan*?"

"John Wesley a 'wall-gazer,'" I laughed, "well then there must be something to it! I would be very grateful to you, Govinda, if you would please teach me how to practice 'wall-gazing.' Last semester, I took a seminar at the Clay Institute of the Free University with Dr. Schneider, Govinda's dissertation advisor. His course, an examination of West Berlin as an 'accidental *polis*' was largely based upon *The Republic* of Plato. As you have explained it to me Govinda, *pi-kuan* reminds me of Plato's 'Allegory of the Cave.'

"Yes, it's true there are similarities, Thomas, but some important differences, too. In Plato's cave, the wall serves primarily as a screen onto which the shadows of the forms are projected, like sitting in a cinema, watching a movie."

"It's interesting you refer to the cinema. One of the other students in the seminar used that very idea for her presentation on postwar cinema in Berlin." Laura.

"It makes sense to me, too, Thomas. In order to obtain 'enlightenment,' however, one has to get up out of one's seat, stand up, turn one's back to the shadows on the wall, and walk out of the cave, out of the cinema, into the sunlight, into the state of being enlightened. What I find particularly appealing about Plato's allegory is the obligation of the enlightened to return to the cave and encourage others to do the same. Bodhidharma teaches, if we strive to abandon what is false and return to what is true through pure contemplation, through 'wall-gazing,' through *pi-kuan*, we will come to realize that there is neither self nor other, that there is a unity between governors and governed, and that what is holy and what is profane are essentially the same. If we can hold to this belief, we will not become slaves to any doctrine, as we will be enlightened directly by reason and freed from all discrimination, enjoying both serenity and spontaneity. As I understand Bodhidharma's teaching, the wall is not necessarily a wall in the concrete sense of the word, but rather a device which serves to focus and inform our meditation. Although our life in West Berlin is circumscribed by a Wall, we rarely meditate or reflect upon it, only when travelling to and from West Germany. While preserving the freedom of those living within it, the Wall poses an obstacle to freedom for those living without, in East Germany. Someday, the Wall might become their way to freedom."

"Do you carry a notebook with you, Thomas? I'd like to write something in it for you."

"Yes, I do." Reaching into my shoulder bag for the notebook, I remember I'd intentionally left it lying on my desk so I would not be tempted to take notes during my walk. In addition to the *Falkplan* and the small blue bottle of Lexotanil, I found one of the prescriptions Professor Berghoff had written and included with my discharge papers. It must have fallen out of the folder. I gave it to Govinda, who read it, smiled, turned it over, and wrote on the back, "1—suffering injustice, 2—adapting to conditions, 3—seeking nothing, 4—practicing the Dharma," and handed the annotated prescription back to me.

After reading it carefully, I put it back into my shoulder bag. "Thank you, Govinda, for your kindness, your insights, and especially for your kind offer to help me practice *pi-kuan*. I accept your offer with my heartfelt thanks! What might I give you in return?"

"Why, nothing, nothing at all, Thomas. But if you do have some old airplane tickets you no longer need, please give them to me. I collect them, and from time to time look at them and imagine flying to different destinations, back to London to see my Methodist friend, for example. And please don't forget our trip to the *Museum für Indische Kunst*, when you have time of course. I'd very much like to see the protection Buddha who reminds you of your friend and my namesake 'Govinda.' Such an interesting coincidence!"

"There's another coincidence too. The *Museum für Indische Kunst* is located directly across the street, the *Boxerstraße*, from the Clay Institute where I attended Dr. Schneider's seminar last semester. When Govinda and I parted at Tempelhof last year, he said he would be watching 'from across the street.' I though he meant to say 'from across the sea,' but now I'm not so sure." Thanking him again, I set my empty glass on the brass tray, stood up, walked out of his Happy-*Bude* into the hallway, put on my shoes, and opened the door. Hopefully, the peacefulness of the 'Happy-*Bude*' would rise upstairs to my room, directly overhead.

Shaking his hand, I said, "Good night, Govinda, thank you again for inviting me in. I'm very sorry we didn't have the opportunity to meet sooner, but your teacher just might be right. Perhaps we were not supposed to meet until this evening. Had we met when I first arrived, or before my three weeks in the *Klinikum Steglitz*, all my searching would more than likely have prevented me from finding what you now offer. The timing couldn't have been better. Sleep well!'

"Good night, Thomas, and peace be with you. Do not be afraid!" I pushed the red button, turning on the lights in the hallway, and, once again to the music of the sitar and drum, climbed the dark wooden staircase up to Dr. Kahler's apartment. Although it had taken over a year, perhaps our aprés *Spaziergang* meeting was—as Govinda's teacher suggested—meant to be. The apartment building no longer seemed empty and, to my surprise, I no longer had to pull myself up the stairs. Back in my room, I set my shoulder bag down on the desk and, taking off my shoes and sport coat, lay down on the bed, my head nested in my new brown cotton pillowcase, another kind of incense, sensuous and sweet. Tomorrow I would return to work as I had intended to do three weeks and one day ago, begin to draft the first two chapters of my dissertation for next month's meeting with my *Doktormutter* Duana Jordan. This day, the next day, had proven to be quite a day. My walk brought me back down to West Berlin, back down to the flatland. No longer apart, I would now work at becoming 'gently indifferent.' In addition to the medication and the good advice given by D3 and Professor Berghoff, there was revelation on the *Kreuzberg* and in-house meditation with Govinda. Just as the idea of the accidental *polis* captured my imagination when Govinda first mentioned it, I was now taken with Govinda's "wall-gazing," the one defined and illuminated by the other.

CHAPTER VI:
The Sublime City (Berlin VII)

*Und jetzt bin ich darin begriffen, in dem Ruin meiner
bisherigen Lebensansicht umherzuschaufeln, und an den
alten Fundamenten das noch einigermaßen, wenn auch
anderswie, brauchbar hervorzusuchen—freilich ob ich
allein damit zu Stande käme das weiß Gott, ja ich hätte
selbst schwerlich das Werk allein begonnen.*[55]

—Jacob Burckhardt,
Letter to Friedrich von Tschudi,
Berlin, December 1, 1839

*Man wird immer offener, immer ehrlicher werden müssen,
und auf den Trümmern der alten Staaten wird die Liebe
vielleicht eine Neues Reich gründen.*[56]

—Jacob Burckhardt,
Letter to Gottfried Kinkel,
Berlin, June 3, 1842

Managing Clio
September 1983

FOLLOWING THE twenty-one day *Aufenthalt* in *Psychiatrische Ambulanz*
and the one-day walk back into West Berlin, I began to implement the
new routine based upon the recommendations made by D3, Professor
Berghoff, and my downstairs/across-the-street neighbor, Govinda. One of
the prescribed benefits of being an in-house outpatient was the enforced
return to a regular routine of eating and sleeping. Sleep, *percocet* to dream,
but sleep that knits up the ravell'd sieve of fear nevertheless. The day after
settling back into my rented room in the *Lothringerstrasse*, I called George,

---

55 "And now I am occupied with shoveling through the ruins of the views I used to hold, the old
foundations, to discover whether or not they might be useful, in another way—if I can do it by myself
only God knows, I would have hardly begun the work on my own," Diary of Thomas Vonaechron,
Diary Extract, 1983, trans TV.
56 "One must become more open, more honest, and on top of the ruins of the old states, perhaps love
will found a new kingdom," Diary of Thomas Vonaechron, Diary Extract, 1983, trans TV.

Rainer, and D3 to let them know I was home at last and to thank them for their visits to the *Universitätsklinikum*. George stopped by later that afternoon. He seemed greatly relieved and was particularly pleased I'd decided to return to my dissertation. "I was afraid you might decide you'd had enough of West Berlin and return to Washington, Thomas."

"I've certainly had enough of the West Berlin scene for right now, George, but that's another good reason for me to stay right here in my room and work. Life may indeed be a cabaret but there may be some good to sitting all alone in my room after all!"

On the phone, Rainer told me, "I don't know, maybe I should follow your example, Thomas. I don't mean check into *Psychiatrische Ambulanz*, though I've thought about that, too, but to get back to work on my degree. You know, I still haven't revised my seminar paper for Dr. Schneider. I seem to be taxiing more and more around West Berlin and writing less and less. Of course, the money's nice, but I'd really like to finish up. At all the parties I've been at lately, I've noticed the girls are getting younger. I'm starting to worry about all tomorrow's parties."

D3 wished me success with my new routine, repeating his invitation for a drive out to the U.S. Army Wannsee Recreation Center. "There's a lot goin' on these days, Thomas. I'll bring you up to date when we get together. I'm very glad to hear the R and R did the trick and you're starting back to work on your diss. Dive in and drive on!" Rainer, D3, and I decided to meet again for lunch at *Luise* following my upcoming meeting with Professor Jourdan to discuss my dissertation.

Reading, writing and wall-gazing with Govinda became my new threefold mantra. On Tuesday and Thursday afternoons, we would meet downstairs in his Happy-*Bude* with other members of the Shin Buddhist Community, for *zazen*, sitting *Zen,* training and practice. Sitting on the tasseled, well-worn, silk-covered cushions, using smaller cushions placed under our *Po* to ensure proper upright Po-sture, we faced the wall, while up against the Wall surrounding the greater community of West Berlin. In order to control my wandering thoughts, Govinda recommended I stare at the wall as if "staring at an enemy." Immobile, sitting and breathing, we strove for *samadhi*, if not *kensho* and the elusive "sudden enlightenment." Govinda placed great emphasis on breathing in the practice of *zazen*, "Relaxing through deep breathing is very important. Remember on exhalation to draw the stomach up toward the spinal column, this empties the lungs." Consciously counting exhalations to control wandering thoughts, I was surprised to sense the relationship between body and mind. This experience deepened as I began following each breath mentally and, over time, began to meditate on nothing, the *koan Mu*. Once we were individually able to arrive at *samadhi*, Govinda taught us the benefit of taking that state of consciousness back, into the world of the routine, into our everyday existence, into the *Alltag*, like the enlightened theatergoer returning to the audience still watching the show in Plato's cave. After hours spent sitting at the makeshift wooden-door desk in the room directly overhead, *pi-kuan* proved to be a way, if not the Way, of emptying my mind, not only to relax, but to work without self-imposed stress, without being driven—just what the doctor ordered!

My landlord, Dr. Kahler, returned from Switzerland to find me working my way deliberately through stacks of documents, carefully arranged on the desk and floor of my room. I'd curtailed all evening activities, while he maintained his regular late-night forays. Every now and then, we would share a glass of *Trollinger*, as prescribed by Professor Berghoff in moderation, and conversation at the heavy wooden kitchen table. "I must say *Herr* Vonaechron, I'm genuinely pleased to see you so diligently at work. Now that you've discovered your limits, you should be able to work productively, and might I add, even enjoyably within them. Nevertheless, I'm quite certain all your experiences in Berlin, including the stay in the *Universitätsklinikum-Benjamin-Franklin*, will prove valuable, not only in limiting, but informing your future activities, whatever you choose to do, wherever you choose to live. As I told you before leaving for Montagnola, I was able to discover my own limits only by exceeding them, on several occasions, I might add." With his characteristic tight, lupine smile, he continued, "To be frank, I still find it necessary to walk out along those limits, testing them occasionally, just to make certain they're still there!"

"Yes, Dr. Kahler, I've certainly learned a lot about limits, *Spiegelbilder*, too! Now that I've cut back on pretty much all extra-curricular activity, I've been able to focus my attention upon my dissertation. As both D3 and Professor Berghoff suggested, writing is therapeutic and, as you suggest, enjoyable as well. Given what I've learned about Berlin, and about myself, over the past year, I'm actually enjoying the work." After our conversation ended, the metal twist-off cap twisted securely back on the green bottle of *Trollinger*, Dr. Kahler went out for the evening while I returned to my room.

"History-as-therapy" seemed to work well. Working my way, once again, backward from the paper prepared for Dr. Schneider's Accidental *Polis* Seminar on *Geschichtswissenschaft*, the "science of history" in West Berlin, I enlarged my focus to examine the teaching of history as a subject at Berlin's universities over the *longue durée*. George and Johannes Festzelt helped me assemble additional essential elements of information, not only on the subject of "capital H" History as taught at Berlin Universities during the Cold War but also on the historical programs and professors of the

Third Reich, the Weimar Republic, and the German Empire, as far back as the Kingdom of Prussia and the martial birth of the *Universität zu Berlin.*

As Johannes explained over lunch in the *Kantine* of the *Stadtstaatsarchiv*, the *Universität zu Berlin* was established in 1809 following the closure of the *Friedrichs-Universität zu Halle* on order of Napoleon Bonaparte. George explained how the decisive military defeat of the Prussian Army at the battles of Jena and Auerstädt, and the follow-on occupation of Berlin by *la Grande Armeé* in October 1806, shocked and awed the upper classes of Prussian society, catalyzing a reform movement. The lower echelons of Prussian society seemed curiously indifferent to the sudden appearance of *gens d'armes* in Berlin. The debacle of 1807 destabilized the position of the privileged, allowing enlightened elements to enact reforms long contemplated but vehemently opposed. Reeducation, a critical element of reform, was reified in the *Universität zu Berlin*, a *Reformsuniversität.* The midwife of the new university, Wilhelm von Humboldt, conceived it as a kindly *"Mutter aller modernen Universitäten."*[57] In spite of Prussia's overwhelming defeat, Humboldt held war to be a permanent feature of human society, with a positive, pedagogical part to play on the historical stage. Back from the battlefields of Jena and Auerstädt, Clio helped organize the new Prussian *avant-garde*, not only at the *Universität zu Berlin* but also at the *Preußische Kriegesakademie,* the Prussian Academy of War, established by Auerstädt veteran Gerhard Johann David von Scharnhorst in 1810, the same year the *Universität zu Berlin* opened its doors. At the Prussian War Academy, faculty members drawn from both universities instructed a select class of officers in the military campaigns employed by Frederick the Great to elevate Prussia to great power status, as well as those used by Napoleon Bonaparte to subjugate it. At the tomb of the former, the latter had reportedly told his *maréchaux*, "If he were alive I wouldn't be here." At the *Kriegsakademie,* a younger veteran of the Battle of Jena, Carl von Clausewitz, later of Dead Carl Club fame, working intimately with his gifted wife, *Gräfin* Marie Sophie von Brühl, would distill the operational essence of the campaigns of Frederick and Napoleon into *Vom Kriege.* In addition to lessons learned, *On War* offers insight into how the war affects the arts and the sciences, history included:

Der Krieg is also ein Akt der Gewalt, um den Gegner zur Erfüllung unseres Willens zwingen. Die Gewalt rüstet sich mit der Erfindungen der Künste und Wissenschaft aus, um der Gewalt zu begegnen.[58]

---

57 "Mother of all modern universities," cited in Thomas Vonaechron, *Clio Muse Militante: Geschichtswissenschaft an den Berliner Universitäten, 1806–1986, Dissertation,* Free University Berlin, 1988.
58 "War is therefore a violent act to force an opponent to do our will. Violence arms itself with the discoveries of the Arts and Science to counter violence," Ibid.

This insight proved critical in the development of my working hypothesis. There was also something of greater significance to be learned from *On War*, something introduced but not spelled out. In time, I would discover it. For now, I was grateful to D3 and an unknown Red Army officer for the opportunity to visit the Clausewitz grave during the aborted USMLM Flag Tour to Burg.

Although Clio had previously been courted in Berlin, reforms made in the wake of the catastrophic Prussian defeats changed the way she was celebrated by her suitors. While remaining an integral part of the *Philosophischer Fakultät*, history shifted focus, at least superficially, from the philosophical to the factual—" . . . *bloß sagen, wie es eigentlich gewesen* . . ."—just say how it actually was. History was to be painsgivingly reconstructed from original sources, "*Quellen*," through a directed line of questioning, "*Fragestellung*." Archives and libraries consequently assumed world historical significance. In 1810, the over five-hundred-year-old *Geheimes Staatarchiv*, the current employer of my landlord, Dr. Kahler, was placed directly under the Office of the Prussian State Chancellor. Twelve years after Napoleon Bonaparte rode into Berlin as a conqueror, George Wilhelm Friedrich Hegel followed his "*Weltseele zu Pferde*," taking the chair of philosophy formerly held by Johann Gottlieb Fichte. Johannes told us how, in 1813, Fichte had canceled his lectures so his students could take the field as soldiers in the Wars of Liberation against Napoleon. Taking a more pessimistic view of the situation, including the possibilities of imminent attack upon the city and impressment into Prussian military service, Fichte's student Arthur Schopenhauer fled Berlin for Weimar. Fichte apparently died of an infection contracted from his wife, Johanna Marie, who had volunteered as a nurse at a Berlin military hospital. An instance of romantic irony. In addition to Fichte's chair, Hegel also took over his "thesis-antithesis-synthesis" argument, creating a dynamic, dialectical theory of history. The idealized state, *der Staat*, became both the incarnation and vehicle of history, an instrument in the hands of 'world historical individuals' like Napoleon Bonaparte. Hegel's former student Arthur Schopenhauer completed his dissertation coincident with Napoleon's defeat, returning to the University of Berlin in 1820. He scheduled his lectures to compete with Hegel's. Low attendance would lead Schopenhauer to leave the university.

One of the primary missions of the new Berlin University was to train civil servants for the growing civil service state, the *Beamtenstaat*. In 1828, the university was expanded and rechristened *Friedrich-Wilhelms-Universität*, in honor of Prussian King Friedrich Wilhelm III. Although Karl Marx transferred to Berlin from Bonn five years after Hegel's death, he was initiated into the Hegelian "worldview," falling in with the young Hegelians who had adopted the Fichtian-Hegelian dialectic with more concrete implications. Skeptical of *der Staat* in its Prussian incarnation, in a critique of Hegel, Marx writes, *"Die Geschichte ist gründlich und macht viele Phasen durch, wenn sie eine ältere Gestalt zu Grabe trägt. Die letzte Phase einer weltgeschichtlichen Gestalt ist ihre Komödie."*[59] Karl Marx would later (in)famously stand Hegel on his head, eventually turning Europe and Asia upside down along with him. His handwriting was still on the wall of his alma mater, in golden letters above the red marble grand staircase in the magnificent entrance hall, *"Die Philosophen haben die Welt nur verschieden interpretiert, es kommt aber darauf an sie zu verändern."*[60]

Historians of note, together with students taking notes, frocked to the new university where Leopold von Ranke, one of the founders of the modern discipline of history, carried the torch for Clio for almost half a century, from 1824 to 1871. Under his tutelage, the watch and ward of historicism becoming became *Ad fontes*, to the sources. Only original sources could allow historians to, in Von Ranke's words, "just say, how it actually was." Through thorough examination of the sources, it was possible for the creative historian to discover the *"leitenden Ideen,"* the "leading ideas" that had been understood and instrumentalized by those in a position to do so. Over the coming years, the creative license given the historian would prove to be licentious. Embracing *der Staat* as the vehicle of history, even serving the Prussian State as its official historian, von Ranke distanced himself from the nationalism and patriotism propagated by the reigning House of Hohenzollern. Following Ranke's retirement, his former student Jacob Burckhardt, professor of history and art history at the University of Basel, was offered his chair. As a student, Burckhardt, like Henry Adams who would follow him to the Prussian capital eighteen years later, had not been not impressed by Berlin, *"Auch ist Berlin ein ganz widerwärtige Ort; eine langweilige, große Stadt in einer unabsehbaren, sadigen Ebene."*[61] Critical of great power ambitions, he opposed Bismarck's creation of a new German *Reich*. Loyal to his university and city-state, and unwilling to become the Prussian court historian, Professor Burckhardt decided not to return to Berlin. Fortunate for Basel, this decision proved disastrous for Berlin when Heinrich von Treitschke was appointed as von Ranke's successor. Writing about his decision in June 1872, Burckhardt observed, *"Für Treitschke ist es dagegen ein großer Lebenstriumph—Heil ihm."*[62] Less of an historian than

59 "History is thorough and goes through many phases when it lays a dead institution to rest. The final phase of a world-historical institution is its comedy." Ibid.
60 "Philosophers have interpreted the world in various ways, but the point is to change it." Ibid.
61 "Berlin is also a disgusting place; a boring, large city situated on an unending, sandy plain." Ibid.
62 "For Treitschke on the other hand it is a great achievement—Heil him!" Ibid.

publicist and politician, von Treitschke served in the *Reichstag* from 1871 to 1884. He turned from von Ranke's source-based "objective" history to a more politicized interpretation of national history, with emphasis upon Prussia. Clio was compromised and impressed into the service of the state. The approach of the new in-house historian found favor. Von Treitschke's nationalistic, racist interpretation of history, culminating in the "Berlin Anti-Semitism Controversy," attracted like-minded academics and students, fertilizing the ground for National Socialist sentiment after the First World War. Following his death in 1896, he was rewarded for his service to the *Staat* with a street in Steglitz, an honor yet to be revoked by Clio. Treitschke was succeeded by his colleague Hans Delbrück, a charter member of the Dead Carl Club. Also a member of the *Reichstag*, he rejected the nationalism and militarism propagated by his predecessor. Unfortunately, both -isms were already ingrained in the gray, grainy *Berliner Luft*.

During and following the First World War, the *Friedrich-Wilhelms-Universität* continued to expand, becoming a major intellectual center within Germany, though history and the humanities were increasingly clouded over by achievements in the natural sciences. Professor Fritz Haber, who not only developed mustard gas but oversaw its initial employment at the Second Battle of Ypres in 1915, was awarded the Nobel Prize in Chemistry for 1918 in 1919, for developing a process to synthesize ammonia from hydrogen and nitrogen gases. Towards the end of the Weimar Republic, many of the faculty members and students began to embrace National Socialism. The title page of *Der Stürmer*, a virulently anti-Semitic newspaper, even carried a quotation from Professor von Treitschke on its front page: "*Die Juden sind unser Unglück.*"[63] In March 1933, the *Rektor* of *Friedrich-Wilhelms-Universität*, Professor Dr. Eugen Fischer, signed the "*Bekenntnis der Professoren an den deutschen Universitäten und Hochschulen zu Adolf Hitler und dem nationalsozialistischen Staat,*"[64] published in the National Socialist house organ "*Völkischer Beobachter.*" Two months later, Professor Dr. Fischer joined the *Reichsminister für Volksaufklärung und Propaganda*, Josef Goebbels, on *Bebelplatz* for the burning of books pulled from the shelves of his university's library. Historian Walter Frank, president of the *Reichsinstitut für Geschichte des neuen Deutschlands*, argued history must become a "*kämpfende Wissenschaft,*" a "fighting science," a "*Kriegsdienst des Geistes,*" a "war service of the intellect." *Friedrich-Wilhelms-Universität* continued to turn out civil servants through the metastasis of the *Machtstaat* in 1933, which brought the war in 1939 and

63 "The Jews are our bad fortune." Ibid.
64 Declaration of German University and College Professors to Adof Hitler and the National-Socialist State, Ibid.

the destruction of the university in 1945. Following the demise of the National Socialist State came the abolition of Prussia by the victorious Allies in 1947. All that remained afterward was the *Stiftung Preussischer Kulturbesitz*, a rearguard action executed to preserve the ruins of Prussia's cultural heritage. *Zeitgeist* would unseat *Weltgeist* in the reconstructed ruins of the *Martin-Gropius-Bau*.

Following the unconditional surrender of Germany in May 1945, the three R's—reform, reorientation, and reeducation—once again became the orders of the day, this time issued by the victorious Allies, midwives to the birth of three Berlin universities in the Soviet (January 1946), British (April 1946) and American (December 1948) Sectors. *Geschichtswissenschaft*, the "science of history," topic of my Accidental *Polis* paper, was once again hoisted high up on the academic agenda. As the wartime relationship among the victorious Allies began to freeze over, Clio was once again recalled from the last battlefield, found "fit for duty," and pressed into service. Friedrich Meinecke, first *Rektor* of the *Freie Universität*, historian and eyewitness to the *Königreich Preußen, Kaiserreich, Weimar Republik*, and *Drittes Reich*, called the founding of the Free University Berlin in the American Sector, "a single point of the great battlefield of the world, in the great battle of the spirits and the real powers." Less than twenty years later, repercussions from another "point of the great battle of the world," Vietnam, would reverberate through the halls of all three Berlin universities. The "great battle of the spirits and the real powers" continued. Following the shooting of *FU* student Benno Ohnesorg at the *Deutsche Oper* in June 1967, an unsanctioned fourth university, the *Kritische Universität (KU)*, was founded in the *Auditorium Maximum* of the *FU*. The spirit of Karl Marx, together with the kindred spirits of the theorists and nation builders he inspired—Vladimir Lenin, Leon Trotsky, Joseph Stalin, Mao Tse-tung, Franklin Roosevelt's pen pal Fidel Castro, and Harry Truman's pen pal Ho Chi Minh—haunted the hallways of the *HU*, the *TU*, the *FU*, and the *KU*, inspiring Rudi Dutschke and others to believe *Geschichte ist machbar!*[65]

Looking back over the *longue durée*, it seemed the science of history, as taught at the various incarnations of Berlin universities in the decades between 1810 and 1980, had consistently provided, and continued to provide, justification for particular political philosophies, orientations, or ideologies—more *Willenschaft* than *Wissenschaft*. *Eureka!* Review of the *Quellen* on hand, together with those on the floor, had distilled a working hypothesis for my dissertation. At first, I didn't realize I was a fellow traveler, along for a right-seat ride with history on the road trip from historicism to

---

65 "History can be made!" Ibid.

historicity, on my way back to the HistoriCity. Although Clio, under the heady influence of the mid-to-late sixties, would only be addressed *bzw.* undressed in the later chapters of my dissertation, I decided to present my "Clio in the service of the State" *Hypothese,* along with the first two draft chapters of my dissertation, to my Doctor-Mother Professor Duana Jourdan over *mélange* in the garden of *Café Wellenstein.*

George graciously agreed to go over the two draft chapters with me before my meeting with Professor Jordan. After a lively, helpful discussion, including my Clio hypothesis, George asked me, "You do know what Arthur Schopenhauer writes about Clio don't you, Thomas? Not waiting for an answer he continued, '*die Geschichtsmuse Klio mit der Lüge so durch und durch infisiert ist, wie eine Gassenhure mit der Syphilis.*'"[66]

"Ouch, I hadn't heard that particular Schopenhauer-*Zitat* before, George. It's a pretty rough analogy for a philosopher to make. Do you think he might have been writing from experience instead of from the sources? But it does support my hypothesis!"

"He also offers us another, less graphic way of saying the same thing, which also supports your hypotheis, '*Was die Geschichte erzählt, ist in der That nur der lange, schwere und verworrene Traum der Menscheit.*'[67] I'm certain your Doctor-Mother knows her Schopenhauer, I'm ver-r-ry inter-r-rested to learn what she might have to say about his musings!"

Dr. Schneider's introduction had indeed proven fortunate. Prior to joining the *Holborn-Institut* in the late 'seventies, Dr. Jourdan had been *Professeur d'Histoire* at the *Université de Paris,* her alma mater. Through the *FU* faculty exchange program, she'd even spent a year teaching in the Department of History of Georgetown University in Washington, DC, the year before I enrolled and discovered the electric blue *FU* catalog waiting for me on the library shelf, another interesting coincidence. Perhaps, as Govinda's teacher suggested, we simply weren't supposed to meet until now.

Die Doktormutter
October 1983

The October day set for my in-progress review was sunny and unseasonably warm, ideal for the brick-walled garden behind the *Café Wellenstein.* We met in the elegant entrance hall stairway, leading to the café and the upstairs *DAAD* gallery. I hadn't heard from my former *Kommilitonen* Sophia Werner since we'd met here to discuss her dissertation research,

66 "The Muse of History Clio is as infected with lies as an alley whore is with syphilis," Ibid.
67 "What History actually teaches is the long, difficult, confusing dream of mankind," Ibid.

and I wondered if her application for a *DAAD* grant in Washington, DC, had been successful. The owner of the café, Professor Jourdan's Viennese friend, DDr. Anna Schmidt, had a table set up for us under the trellis, on the elevated platform against the back wall of the garden. She joined us as we walked through the high-ceilinged café, past bentwood chairs and café tables through the back door, down the stairs, and out into the fall garden. Fallen leaves were scattered throughout walled *Pairidaeza*, adorning the marble café tabletops.

After we'd finished breakfast, DDr. Schmidt left us "to go back to work" inside the villa, while Professor Jourdan and I began to work our way through the first two draft chapters of my dissertation. At our first meeting with Dr. Schneider, she had critiqued the draft proposal he sent to her on my behalf. After she kindly agreed to be my *Doktormutter*, I submitted the final proposal to the *Hajo-Holborn-Institut*. This was the first opportunity for her to react to what I'd written. I was nervous. She seemed satisfied with the obligatory introductory review of academic literature and, much to my relief, quite positive, almost enthusiastic, about my working hypothesis, a Berlin-based Clio in the service of the state.

"I find your hypothesis quite provocative, Mr. Vonaechron," she said, looking up from my draft over the frames of her reading glasses, "quite intriguing. It is actually strikingly similar to the conclusions I reached as a graduate student in Paris following the events of May 1968. Raised in a socialist household in the Midwest, I majored in history at the University of Nebraska, where I was also active in the Young People's Socialist League. At Lincoln, I took Edgar Johnson's two-year slash course on 'The History of Western Culture,' spending a semester abroad at the Sorbonne. The seminal part played by France in the genesis of the Western tradition fascinated me. After leaving Lincoln with a bachelor's degree and with no immediate job prospects, I returned to the Sorbonne for graduate study. Karl Marx seemed to hold the key to the past, the European socialists the key to the future. *Les existentialistes* were also of interest. True to my midwestern roots, I joined the socialist students from *Nantaerre* and the Sorbonne on the barricades in Paris on May 10, 1968, yes, *une soixante-huitarde* sits here repentant before you! To be quite honest, Mr. Vonaechron, and you know, of course, as historians, we must strive for honesty, I must confess to an academic interest as well. As you might recall from our meeting with Professor Schneider at the *Holborn-Institut*, I wrote my dissertation on the renovation of Paris under prefect of the Seine Georges Eugène Haussmann. In addition to the direction given by Napoleon III to '*aérer, unifier, et embellier Paris,*' Haussmann was also very interested in the architecture of crowd control, what we might call 'physical security' today. Let me give you an example. The *Boulevard Sébastopol,* a section of the north-south axis, was conceived for the, in Hausmann's words, 'gutting of old Paris, of the quarter of riots and barricades.' I was particularly interested in the social disruption in the *Quartier Latin* caused by the construction of the *Boulevard St.-Michel* between 1855 and 1859, and the *Boulevard Saint-Germain* between 1857 and 1877, as history would have it, the very same streets we would occupy in May 1968. *Vive la Commune!*"

"*Eirönïa!*"

Dr. Jourdan smiled. "Yes, Mr. Vonaechron, *eirönïa!*" A very attractive woman in her early forties, I could picture her fifteen years earlier as Marianne *das la rue* wearing a Phrygian cap, bearing the red standard on the barricades, baring her breasts *à la* Delacroix to the forces of reaction.

"A north-south axis running through Paris!" That reminds me of Albert Speer's planning for Berlin, '*Germania.*'"

Professor Jourdan laughed, "Yes, indeed, a north-south axis composed of the new *Boulevards Strasbourg* and *Sébastapol,* complemented by an east-west axis, composed of the *Rue de Rivoli* and the *Rue Saint-Antoine,* intersecting at the *grande croisée de Paris.* Adolf Hitler purportedly charged and challenged Albert Speer to become his Haussmann. That must have come as quite a compliment, as I understand *Herr* Speer held *M.* Haussmann to be the greatest city planner in history. I find it noteworthy, given his reputation, that Haussmann was not an architect but a bureaucrat. In any event, his planning for *l'utilisation militaire* did not serve the authorities well in 1968. Workers joined us, sparking a series of unsanctioned wildcat strikes, and the *Quatier Latin* fell to the insurgents. "*Marx, Mao, Marcuse!*" It seemed as if the vanguard, as we thought of ourselves at the time, and the proletariat had finally, historically, found common cause. Unfortunately, it didn't work out that way. *Mais oui,* superficially, there was solidarity, largely through a shared negative self-identification with the government of President Charles de Gaulle. The problem lay below the superstructure, with an infrastructure composed of diverse groups pursuing independent interests. Not just workers and students but within the student movement itself, as political organization splintered into variations upon the Marxist theme. Labeled a 'Trotskyist,' I was ostracized by the Leninist and Maoist factions at the university.

"The evaporation of the strike following the June elections caused me to painfully reexamine and revise my politics. '*Élections, piège à cons!*' After the students had returned to the universities, the workers to the factories, it seemed to me as if 'May 1968' had largely been political theater. Certainly, there were some changes in the social landscape. It also spawned a number of good films and songs, but sadly not much more. Pre-May Paris remained in place, intact with the Gaulist party even stronger than before. Spiritually broken, I decided to break with Marxism and my Midwest socialist roots. If things were going to change, Karl Marx would have to be stood on his head and G. W. F. Hegel put back on his feet again. The *Weltgeist* continued to move forward, though not through the class struggle but through the state, as Hegel originally envisioned. In this sense, I find Hegel much more realistic than Marx, *ein Realpolitiker*. Although no *bonapartiste*, I couldn't help but admire the ability of Napoleon III to change the face of Paris, not only physically but socially, let alone Napoleon I's ability to change the face of Europe. I was also intrigued by Leon Trotsky's establishment and employment of the Red Army as the 'People's Commissar of Military and Naval Affairs.'" Professor Jourdan thought for a moment, smiled, and laughed, "Perhaps there was something to that charge of 'Trotskyism' after all! Following the Second World War, the United States of America, not the Union of Soviet Socialist Republics, seemed to embody Hegel's *Weltgeist*. I began to understand the critical importance of the military as an instrument of progress, and the significance of warfare in the world historical process, particularly in the rise of the West, of capitalism, technology, and democracy. The West has the better story, *la meilleure historie*—what's the German phrase, '*die bessere Erzählung*?' Progress comes with the expansion of capitalism and liberal democracy, using the military instrument when necessary, to implement it. In Lenin's words, 'Sometimes—history needs a push!'"

"Lenin! What would Trotsky say, Professor Jourdan? Though I do like the idea of standing poor Hegel back on his feet again, I share Burckhardt's concern about the inherent vice of the state, the United States included. Take the French, the British, the Russian, the Austrian, and particularly, the Prussian-German examples. Each state, nation, or empire believed itself to be bearer of the *Weltgeist*, executing an historical mission for the betterment of mankind. The consequences have been catastrophic, not only for the individual nation-states and empires concerned but for the international order as well. What about Vietnam? I have a good friend here in Berlin, a major in the army, graduate of West Point, who deployed to Vietnam after most of the US forces had been withdrawn in 1973. It was a deeply traumatic experience for him, personally as well as politically, causing him to seriously consider resigning his commission. While working at the Archives, I found a letter from Ho Chi Minh to Harry S Truman, asking him to 'interfere for the immediate solution of the Vietnam issue' and help Vietnam achieve 'full independence.' Thousands of American and millions of Vietnamese lives could have been saved. The United States could have had a valuable ally in the Far

East, if only we had had the courage to live up to our own Declaration of Independence!"

"Yes, I agree and completely understand your friend's self-doubt, the gravity of his dilemma. After the debacle at Dien Bien Phu, I wouldn't have held the build-up of American ground forces in Vietnam for feasible. At the time I thought, 'How could the United States fail to recognize its own history in Vietnam's struggle to free itself from colonial rule?' You might recall Franklin Roosevelt made it quite clear he had no intention of restoring French Indochina after the Second World War. Yet French cooperation was essential here in postwar Germany, and the Truman administration had no such scruples, even providing financial support for French military operations under the 'Truman Doctrine.' Oftentimes a short-term solution sought in haste has unintentional, unfortunate second- and third-order long-term effects. American military intervention in Vietnam happened over time incrementally, without the necessary critical strategic reevaluation. I would argue the war was conducted as much for domestic as international reasons. It has now been ten years since direct American involvement ended, eight years since the fall of Saigon. With the benefit of hindsight, I see the Vietnam War as an unfortunate aberration in the larger and, on the whole, successful strategy of containment. Hopefully, the painful lessons dearly paid for in our national blood and treasure will mitigate future misuse of the military instrument by the National Command Authority. Nonetheless, prudent warfare remains an integral part of grand strategy, of history. In your draft, you observe no less than Wilhelm von Humboldt held war to be a permanent feature of human society, with a positive, pedagogical part to play on the historical stage."

"Forgive me, Professor Jourdan, but I'm not convinced. Leopold von Ranke and his student Jacob Burckhardt were opposed to broader, more general theories or philosophies of history, like Hegel's." The word "*Weltgeist*" came to mind and with it the dream of the "Thunder Run" into Baghdad. "Burckhardt was even more skeptical of the state in general, Bismarck's Prussia in particular. It's very difficult to understand what lessons, if any at all, are to be distilled from the study of history. What does Hajo Holborn write? 'History gives answers only to those who know how to ask the questions.'"

"Ah yes, Professor Holborn, our institute's namesake, continuation of the prewar German historical tradition, of which he himself was quite critical. Did you know he completed his doctorate at Humboldt University under Friedrich Meinecke, the future *Rektor* of the *FU*, in 1924? I, for one, would have preferred a cleaner break with the German tradition, a *Marc-Bloch-Institut*, though Bloch's avowedly Marxist approach would not have found favor when the Free University was founded in 1948. Twenty years later maybe, or at some point in the future when the Cold War itself is a subject of historical investigation. Our conversation has taken me back to the Sorbonne and once again to Trotsky, who argues that cause in history 'refracts itself through a natural selection of accidents.' A 'natural selection of accidents' that seems to be a 'synthesis' of some sort! Well, Mr. Vonaechron, I can see we have a host of topics for future breakfast meetings, but let's return our attention to your two draft chapters for the time being." DDr. Schmidt kindly brought us each another mélange as we moved from the first chapter into the second. On the whole, Professor Jourdan was pleased with my progress to date, and I was greatly relieved. We set a date early in the coming year for our next meeting. By that time, I planned to revise the first two chapters and have two more chapters in draft for her review. Walking up the stairs back into the café, Professor Jourdan turned to look back at the walled garden and said, "What a beautiful day, today, Mr. Vonaechron. Our next meeting will be inside the café. Not as much sunlight as out here in the garden, but on the other hand, the atmosphere is so authentically Viennese, it could be *Café Griensteidel*. May the critical spirit of Karl Kraus inspire us! If I remember correctly, there's a discussion between two historians in his *The Last Days of Mankind*. When Professor Jourdan stopped to talk with DDr. Schmidt, I thanked both of them and excused myself, leaving by the front door. Walking toward the *Kurfürstenstraße U-Bahn* station, I was approached by a beautiful young blonde girl in a white turtleneck sweater wearing a very short blue-jean skirt. Recalling what Sophia Werner had told me about the West Berliner *Babystrich*, I smiled at her and shook my head as she opened her mouth to ask.

Botschaften
October 1983

Returning home from the *Wellenstein*, I discovered the long-anticipated invitation from the Danish Embassy to Gabriel Kielerförde's exhibition in mid-November waiting for me. Although I hadn't attended a *vernissage* since *Galerie Buraq*, this would be the long-awaited exception to my new routine. At *Galerie Buraq*, Gabriel told Laura, André, and me he wanted to reach as many people as possible with his exhibition—artists, historians, educators, citizens, and, in particular, politicians. I was interested not only in the kinds and the arrangement of objects he'd found in the former Danish Legation in the *Tiergartenviertel* but also in the kinds of people who would find their way to the exhibition. When I first told George about the *vernissage*, the day I met Gabriel among the ruins, he'd expressed an interest in coming along and readily accepted the invitation to join me. His presence was more calming than the small blue bottle of Lexotanil in my shoulder bag.

It was a very large, diverse crowd, ranging from the affably diplomatic to the affectedly disaffected, the very essence of a West Berlin *vernissage*. As the former Danish Legation could no longer safely receive guests, the found objects and the photographs taken were displayed, together with archival photographs, in the Berlin Museum on *Lindenstraße* in Kreuzberg. Perhaps more than any other museum East or West, the reconstructed *Kammergericht*, where E. T. A. Hoffmann had once Bartleby-ed over his files, captured the essence of what Berlin had once been and what it had lost. The intimate *Alt-Berliner Weißbierstube* in the cellar was a popular place to drink the beer of the same name, so I was pleased to see the invitation indicated it would be open until 11:00 p.m. *Aprés* the *vernissage*, George and I could raise a glass of *Berliner Weiße*, the beer that first brought us together, to Mr. Henry's on Washington Circle. With so many guests, Gabriel did not have much time to talk with us. "Thank you both for coming! I'm very pleased to meet you, Georg. Thomas told me about your work and showed me the interesting book on Berlin published by the *Stadtstaatsarchiv* when we first met. Let me give you a copy of the exhibition catalog for the *Stadtstaatsarchiv Berlin*. And Thomas, here's one for you, too." Signing both copies with a flourish, Gabriel presented them to us before the other *vernissage* guests vying for his attention. "Don't forget, Thomas, someday you might write about me, the artist Gabriel Kielerförde!"

"I won't forget, Gabriel!" After thanking him for the catalogs and the invitation, George and I took time to carefully study each of the "then and now" black-and-white exterior and interior photographs running round the walls of the exhibition room. Afterward, we carefully examined the various found objects meticulously arranged by Gabriel in the center of the floor. The interplay between the images and the objects was unsettling, calling not only the apparent solidity of the former legation building into question but the activities and occupants of all the former "representative buildings" in West Berlin as well. Gabriel's exhibit documented the temporal nature of both architecture and human activity—in this particular case, diplomacy. Perhaps a few of the diplomats attending the *vernissage*, not just the melancholy Danes, would look at their embassies and offices differently once they'd returned from Berlin to Bonn, *Berlin Nebenstelle*.

Throughout the long, dark, wet West Berlin fall and winter, I regularly met Rainer and D3 for lunch under the eyes of Luise. D3 told us he'd received a copy of the article Nadja's friend Clarence had written for *Thumpasorus People* magazine on the music scene surrounding American military installations in West Germany, providing each of us with a copy. I laughed when I saw the header, "Printed at US Government Expense," at the top of each page. One day in late November, when Rainer was unable to join us, D3 mentioned he'd been quite busy. "You do remember the mock-up of the Pershing II you positively ID'd when we were on the road to Magdeburg, don't you, Thomas? Well, things are now moving rapidly, or should I say, 'deploying' rapidly in that direction. You no doubt followed the *'Heißer Herbst'* protest at Mutlangen this past September with Petra Kelly, Heinrich Böll, Philip Berrigan, and Daniel Ellsberg in attendance, and the 108-kilometer-long *Menschenkette* between Neu-Ulm and Stuttgart last month."

"Yes, D3, I did, and I had to think about that Magdeburg mock-up, too. To be honest, though, since moving to West Berlin, I haven't been following the SS-22/Pershing II-Tomahawk debate as closely as I did while living in DC. I've been so attuned to the past, I haven't paid as much attention as I should have to . . . what did we used to say in school . . . to 'current events.' D3 smiled. "Here in West Berlin and in *Restdeutschland*, it seems as if the NATO Pershing II deployment has given new life to the anti-war movement, which dissipated at the end of the Vietnam War."

"It certainly has, Thomas! Although I too subscribe to the long-term reduction goals, I submit to you NATO's deployment of Pershings and Tomahawks in response to the Warsaw Pact's deployment of the SS-20s does not, at least in my book, fall under the heading of aggression. Remember the 'Sun Tzu Soldier' standing guard at the bottom of the stairway in Building 1, the USCOB Headquarters Building? Sun Tzu says, position your military assets in such a way that your adversary understands war would only bring defeat. The war of no war. But in order for the Pershings and Tomahawks to be stationed in the Federal Republic, the *Bundestag* had to approve the NATO 'Double-Track' decision—that is, to go ahead with the approved NATO upgrades while continuing to negotiate for their withdrawal with the Warsaw Pact. Well, Thomas, as you might already know, the *Bundestag* gave 'thumbs-up' yesterday. Hmm, it just now occurs to me that yesterday was the twentieth anniversary of President Kennedy's assassination. So, the wheels, or should I say the rotors, have been set in motion. Don't be surprised if you should see pictures of real Pershing IIs in West Germany real soon!" That evening, a German government spokesman announced the arrival of the first missile components in the Federal Republic. Scheduled to be operational by the end of the year, according to press reporting, the Pershing IIs would be stationed near Mutlangen, home of the US Army's Fifty-Sixth Field Artillery Brigade, current location of the Pershing 1a's. One hundred-eight Pershing II missiles and ninety-six Tomahawk cruise missiles were to be stationed in West Germany by 1988. No wonder D3 had been busy. His other boss, the *Gruppa Sovetskix Voisk Germani*, no doubt had many questions for him.

At the beginning of December, I had an appointment with Professor Berghoff's colleague in Wilmersdorf. Her office was located on the third floor of a large, prewar apartment building just off the *Kurfürstendamm*. She had requested my file from the *Universitätsklinikum* in advance and was completely familiar with my case when I arrived. A sympathetic, solid woman of middle age and height, with short hair, large black-rimmed glasses, and an infectious smile, Dr. Ursula Schönbart listened closely as I recounted my activities since leaving *Psychiatrische Ambulanz*, the lifestyle changes I'd made based on the advice given by D3 and her colleague, Dr. Berghoff, including the progress to date on my dissertation. "Now that you know your limits, it is important for you to accept them, *Herr* Vonaechron. Over the past two months, it appears you have been quite successful in doing so." She asked about my dissertation and my interest in the history of Berlin. I told her about my archival work in Washington, DC, and Berlin. Dr. Schönbart told me she had lived through the bombardment of Berlin and "the last battle" as a teenager. In a soft, neutral, professional voice, she told me how she, together with a friend, struggled to escape the carnage, making their way on foot west through intense street fighting out to Spandau, then through the lines of the Red Army units encircling Berlin. Unfortunately, her friend died along the way. Her story was history.

Dr. Schönbart told me I could dispense with lithium. "The primary cause for your anxiety and panic attacks was very likely a state of nervous exhaustion, Mr. Vonaechron. Based upon what I've read in your file and on what you've told me today, I see no reason to continue the lithium therapy. Should the symptoms return however, please do contact me at once." She gave me a timetable for going off the lithium. A *Spiegelbild* was no longer necessary, and although I would no longer be sitting with Galen by the waters of Pergamon, it was reassuring to know I still had a safety net in West Berlin.

Rainer joined D3 and me under the portrait of Luise the next time we met, just before Christmas. He seemed to know as much, maybe more, about the stationing of the missiles in the Federal Republic as D3. Although sympathetic to the Pershing II protestors, he had decided not to join them. Like D3, he saw NATO's Dual Track decision as a response to the Warsaw Pact decision, going so far as to commend President Reagan on his offer to eliminate all midrange missiles in Europe. "I hate to admit it, but at *Schloss*

Charlottenburg, I had the feeling Reagan was sincerely trying to reach out to Brezhnev." I told them I was impressed by the open, honest approach taken by both the German government and the press to the deployment. Given all the ongoing activities surrounding the stationing and upcoming activation of the missiles, D3 and I decided to delay our trip out to the US Army Wannsee Recreation Center until the spring. This would allow us to make the most out of it.

The year 1983 became 1984. At our meeting in the *Café Wellenstein* just after the first of the year, Dr. Jourdan recommended I apply for a *Luftbrüken-Dank-Stipendium,* a fund originally established by the *FU* to provide financial resources for the surviving children of military personnel whose names were inscribed on the "Hunger Claw" at Tempelhof Central Airport. As there were no longer any eligible applicants, the funds were made available to American, British, and French doctoral candidates. Pleased with my drafts for chapters three and four, Dr. Jourdan recommended submitting all four chapters for consideration. I was very grateful to her for her recommendation, as the money I'd saved up for study in West Berlin was slowly running out.

In addition to meeting with Professor Jourdan, to prepare for my oral examinations, I attended seminars at the Hajo Holborn—referred to by some students as the *"HaHo"*—and Lucius D. Clay Institutes, making frequent use of the open-door policy practiced by Dr. Schneider's colleague, former American Ambassador Hubert Spero. He had agreed to be the "second reader" of my dissertation required for *Promotion*. In spite, or perhaps because of, the open-door policy, Ambassador Spero seemed unimpressed with the German *FU* students. He confided they were the laziest students he had encountered in his years of experience as a university teacher, sharing with me a presentation he'd prepared for Harvard University, his alma mater. "With very few but remarkable exceptions," he observed, "they attend irregularly, read minimally, show very little interest in the subject matter of the courses they choose voluntarily, and write papers, theses, dissertations, and *Habilitationschriften* that compare unfavorably with American high school themes, freshman essays, and senior honors theses."

Once again, good fortune intervened, bringing Professor Georg Iggers to the *HaHo* from the University at Buffalo, New York. A native of Hamburg, he fled Germany with his family in 1938, receiving his education and establishing his academic reputation in the United States. Like Professor Schneider, with whom he shared his thick, unruly white hair, he was a participant in the *FU* faculty exchange program. The seminars he offered on the development and demise of historicism in Germany were not only

Taylor-made for my dissertation topic but also spoke to me personally. In his introductory remarks, he told us, "History then becomes the only guide to a understanding of things human. There is no constant human nature; rather the character of each man reveals itself only in his development." He would return to this argument throughout the semester as we considered the successive German schools of history. Professor Iggers argued the legacy of historicism was historicity (*Geschichtlichkeit*) and temporality (*Zeitlichkeit*). The historicity of humanity leads to an "anarchy of values," discontinuity, rupture, and, finally, the abyss. In his final presentation, he seemed to speak directly to me, "But man has no stable nature; his nature is in constant growth and consists in his historicity." My nature, constant in growth, consists in my HistoriCity.

Winter became spring. Gray again grudgingly gave ground to green, though misty spring weather kept the grainy, indefinite quality in the *Berliner Luft, Luft, Luft.* As a consequence of the lunchtime seminars with D3 and Rainer at *Luise*, I began to pay more attention to current events unfolding around West Berlin in both Germanys, and throughout Europe, East and West. Following deployment and activation of the Pershing II and Tomahawk missiles, widespread popular support for disarmament within the Federal Republic continued to grow. On April 23, 1984, 600,000 people participated in an "Easter March for Disarmament and Peace."

Intelligence and Wisdom
May 1984

D3 called on May Day to let me know the US Army Wannsee Recreation Center had put the boats back in the water and would open early for business on the coming weekend. The weather report was good, so he'd reserved a small sailboat for us. "I made my *Segelschein* down in Bavaria on the *Chiemsee* with an interesting instructor, a Hungarian who works at Radio Free Europe in Munich. Should be smooth sailing out on the Wannsee this Saturday, Thomas. We'll just have to watch out for the American Sector border west of the *Pfaueninsel*—not a good place to 'Go West!' Should we accidentally sail into East Germany, though, I'm sure our Soviet Military Liaison Mission friends would get us off the hook, and hopefully get the sailboat back too! Be sure to wear layered clothing so we can layer up or down as needed. If it's warm enough, we can even have lunch out on the rec center terrace afterwards."

As promised, D3 came by *Lothringerstrasse* in the Shield to pick me up. It was a beautiful morning, the sun shining down through the linden leaves and the clear coat lacquer, illuminating Judith l'Angelos marvelous hood painting. I reflected on it for a few minutes too, before opening the passenger door, sitting down in the shotgun seat, and buckling on my four-point seat harness. D3 took *Hedwigstraße*, turning left onto *Hauptstraße* for the ride out to Wannsee. The angel on *Rathaus Friedenau* smiled down upon us as we made the turn, gracefully pointing south, toward Zehlendorf and Wannsee with her outstretched palm frond. After successfully riding a green wave of traffic lights carrying us as far as *Botanischer Garten*, we were caught by a red light at *Plantanenplatz*. While waiting for the light to change, I saw the tall, white-haired gentleman with the horn-rimmed glasses again, walking his smooth dachshund under the sycamore trees. Although he wore a dark blue nylon jacket, I could see the faded pink polo shirt underneath, and the same US Army desert battle dress uniform cut-off shorts he'd been wearing last autumn, when I'd left the clinic to take the walk in the Botanical Gardens suggested by Dr. Abrassimow. He waved at the Shield, turning to follow us as we drove on after the light turned green. We drove on down *Unter den Eichen*, past the US Army Hospital Berlin. "It's strange how I keep running into that white-haired guy, first at the T-T Music Café in Kreuzberg and now, for the second time here on *Plantanenplatz*."

"Maybe he lives around here somewhere," D3 answered, driving through Zehlendorf down the broad, six-lane, tree-lined *Potsdamer Chausee* toward Wannsee.

"He wears a pair of cut-offs made from desert BDUs."

"Chocolate chips? No wonder, there's probably quite a surplus. Woodland camouflage is where it's at, Thomas! Not much going on in the desert these days. He's probably retired military. West Berlin has a pretty large population of retired soldiers and DACs. After all, the army's been out here on the frontier of freedom since 1945. That's one year shy of forty, Thomas."

"DACs, D3?"

"Department of the Army Civilians." Just before the *Wannseebrücke*, we turned right off of *Potsdamer Chausee*, the road out to the US Army Golf Course and the *Brücke der Einheit*, the "Bridge of Unity," our entry point into Potsdam and the German Democratic Republic, onto *Kronprinzessenweg*. D3 said, "*Am Grossen Wannsee* runs along the far side. The 'Wannsee Conference' was held in a villa on that street on 20 January 1942." Mention of the Wannsee Conference reminded me of the tragedy documented by the file I'd reviewed back in Vault Six.

Just past *S-Bahnhof Wannsee*, we turned left onto *Am Sandwerder*. Opulent, extravagant villas were set back on both sides of the tree-lined street. "Some of the these villas, including our rec center, date back to the last century. As I might have told you during our tour of Little America, the rec center was originally built as the *Villa Oppenheim*. Bought by Franz Arnhold in 1935, it was taken over three years later by the National Socialist government. The minister for economic affairs, Walter Funk, lived there. As you probably know, Funk was tried at *Nürnberg* and sentenced to life imprisonment in Spandau. US forces originally requisitioned the villa in 1945 as an officers' club. In the early fifties, the Berlin *Senat* used it to house Eastern European refugees. In the late fifties, the German government purchased it for the US forces, and we've been here ever since. Lucky US!" Set back from *am Sandwerder* at the far end of a prewar, tree-lined oval drive and postwar parking lot, the villa now housed the *Hotel am Wannsee*, sharing an access drive with the white boathouse next door. We drove on, past the hotel and the boathouse, to take a brief look at the *Wannsee* guest residence further down *am Sandwerder*. "Quite an impressive hideaway, Thomas, *nicht wahr?* The house was built in 1935 for the 'zipper king' of Germany. Just like his product, his fortunes went up and down—yuck, yuck, yuck!"

"I've heard that one before, D3."

"Sorry, Thomas!"

Returning to the Wannsee Rec Center, we parked the Shield in the postwar parking lot, took our sailing gear from the trunk, and walked down to the boathouse, the first customers on the first day of the season. Our sailboat was in the water, ready to cast off. After D3 presented his ID and *Segelschein* for inspection, the friendly German facility manager gave us a briefing. In addition to going over the basic rules of sailing, he pointed to a large white metal sign mounted on the wall of the boathouse depicting the American Sector boundary running right through the river Havel. Red crosshatching drew our attention to the restricted areas. ACHTUNG SPERRGEBIET! "The border is marked with white buoys, but if you're close enough to read them in a sailboat, you're much too close to the border. The *Grenzschutz* will keep a close eye or two on you, and will come out in a patrol boat if they think you might violate their territorial waters. It's best to give them a wide berth. Although private sailboats have been seized, we haven't lost one yet." D3 rapped his knuckles on his head in reply.

"It's the closest thing made out of wood," he explained, laughing. As we cast off, I could see villas lining the far side, wondering which was the site of the Wannsee Conference. Directly across from the rec center was a smaller, elegant summerhouse with a large garden bordering on the Wannsee. An easel had been set up at the edge of the garden, facing the house. An elderly gentlemen dressed in white with a straw hat on his head and paintbrush in hand, waved to us as we came about and sailed north, toward *Strandbad Wannsee*, one of the largest inland beaches in Europe. "I don't think it's quite warm enough for *FKK* today, Thomas, but some of these Berlin women are pretty tough. Let's do a 'sail-by' just in case!" After we sailed by the *Strandbad* and architect Martin Wagner's sprawling *Neue Sachlichkeit* bathhouse, we entered the Havel River heading north, much to my relief away from the American Sector border. D3 took the tiller under his arm, leaned back against the stern, and said, "I've got an action item I'd like to discuss with you, Thomas, an offer you can refuse."

"Drive on, D3!"

"Last August, the United States Army Reserve Military Intelligence Group, Europe—'MIG,' now there's a good Cold War acronym for you—was activated at US Army, Europe and Seventh Army Headquarters in Heidelberg. MIG Detachment One was set up in Munich, just before the deployment of the Pershing II's and Tomahawks. With your professional background, you could guess its mission might be to study the so-called 'rear area threats' and make recommendations for countermeasures. This past January, the MIG established a second detachment here in West Berlin. As I understand it, the mission of Detachment Two might be to compile Intelligence Information Reports and analyze avenues of access to West Berlin for contingency planning. Information used to compile the 'IIRs' and analyze access will be primarily but not exclusively derived from open-source materials like host-nation publications. For the most part, it would be PIC, excuse me, Thomas, 'passive intelligence collection.'"

"Did you say 'PIC,' D3?"

"Yes, passive intelligence collection. You know, spying, but no operatives or collection operations, just observation, passive observation."

"What a fascinating acronym and a ver-r-ry inter-r-resting coincidence! Have you ever heard of *pi-kuan*, D3?

"I have, but to be honest, Thomas, I don't remember too much about it other than it's a kind of meditation. Most of the reading I did on Chinese subjects at Leavenworth was on Sun Tzu's *Art of War*. Sun Tzu says, 'Hence it is only the enlightened ruler and the wise general who will use the highest intelligence of the army for the purposes of spying, and thereby they achieve great results.' I also found Lao-Tzu's *Tao Te Ching* interesting, more philosophic than strategic, but with many valuable insights into the nature of warfare. His thoughts on the use of deadly force spoke directly to me as a professional soldier and combat veteran. Like Clausewitz, Lao-Tzu helped me to come to terms with Vietnam. Let me see now, it's been a while, but I memorized chapter 31.

Now arms, however beautiful, are instruments of evil omen, hateful, it may be said to all creatures. Therefore they who have the Tao do not like to employ them. . . . Those sharp weapons are instruments of evil omen, and not the instruments of the superior man—he uses them only on the compulsion of necessity. Calm and repose are what he considers prizes; victory (by force of arms) is to him undesirable. To consider this desirable would be to delight in the slaughter of men. . . . The second in command of the army has his place on the left; the general commanding in chief has his on the right—his place, that is, is assigned to him as in the rites of mourning. He who has killed multitudes of men should weep for them with the bitterest of grief.

Ya know, Thomas, Lao-Tzu was rumored to be a 'record-keeper,' an archivist, like you. Now it's your turn, record-keeper, tell me about *pi-kuan*!"

"I must say I'm quite impressed, D3, Lao-Tzu speaks to me too! *Pi-kuan* means 'wall gazing' or 'wall observation.' I've actually been practicing it with my downstairs neighbor, Govinda Hemd, a Shin-Buddhist. Remember Dr. Berghoff recommended mediation as a form of relaxation? By coincidence, I found an in-house teacher! It really does help, particularly now that I'm back at the books full-time. I'm just surprised by the the similarity, a coincidence, between 'observation' and 'passive intelligence collection.' 'PIC-*kuan*'—I like it!"

"Zat so, Thomas? Well then, Detachment Two, the 'Berlin Det,' just might be the thing for you! With your professional background and knowledge of German, it might not only be interesting, it'll certainly bring you up to date on what's going on in Germany and Europe, East and West, and help finance your studies. It shouldn't take too much time away from your work. You'd have weekend drill, Saturday and Sunday once a month here in Berlin, and every so often a temporary duty trip down to the MIG in Heidelberg, maybe even to Detachment One in Munich, hopefully during the *Oktoberfest*! There's always the possibility you could be called to active duty—unlikely, but it could happen. And oh, by the way, Thomas, while 'drilling,' you're authorized to shop at the commissary and PX on Truman Plaza, and, yes, even check books out from the post library! The same goes for Heidelberg, which boasts the best post library in the US Army, outside of Leavenworth, of course. When I was down at headquarters last month, I stopped by the US Army Reserve Europe Office to co-or-di-nate with the commander. We know each other from a former life. He believes as a so-called 'qualified civilian,' you would be eligible for direct commission as an intelligence officer in the United States Army Reserve, probably as a second lieutenant. Given your government service, your academic background, and, of course, my yet-to-be-written stellar letter of recommendation—the chief of mission said he'd write one for you too by the way—your package should be favorably reviewed by the selection board. Once selected, you'd be required to sign an oath and be sworn in by an officer. You'd also have to take the Basic Officer Leadership Course, 'BOLC,' in intelligence, your assigned area of concentration, probably at US Army Reserve Forces School on McGraw Barracks down in Munich, conveniently home to the Sixty-Sixth Military Intelligence Group.

"Second Lieutenant Vonaechron? Yikes, D3! That reminds me of the dream I had the night I was admitted to the clinic. Scary, scary!"

"To tell ya the truth, Thomas, I had to think about your dream too, but West Berlin is not Baghdad! Although you'd be assigned to the MIG in Heidelberg, because of the distance, you'd be OPCONed to Office of Deputy Chief of Staff, Intelligence, US Command Berlin, 'DCSI,' Dixie. To be brutally honest, Thomas, what makes you attractive to the MIG is not your archival skill, your academic ability, your skill as a cunning linguist, or your charming personality, but your TS clearance. It costs Uncle Sugar big bucks and much time to conduct the 'SBI,' the sensitive background investigation required for a top secret security clearance. We activated your clearance for your presentation on USMLM at the Mission a year ago, remember? It was still in the system, so you could be easily read back on. I checked on it again in Heidelberg, just to be certain. Should you decide to sign up, it shouldn't take too long to put you to work—one weekend a month that is. So, what d'ya think? Would you be interested in becoming an US Army Reserve Officer? I know you're working hard on your dissertation and honestly hesitate even to suggest it to you, but it's, like I said, a decision you can refuse!"

"OPCONed? You got me this time, D3!"

"Operational Control."

"Ah, I should have guessed! 'OPCONed' is the past tense of 'to OPCON!' 'OPCONed to Dixie!' Well, to tell you the truth, D3, I'm surprised and flattered by your suggestion. Do you think I'd still be eligible for intelligence work after my three-week vacation in the *Universitätsklinikum*?

"Yes, of course, Thomas, we're all crazy! I told you what I went through after Vietnam. I'm quite certain the United States Army, in its infinite wisdom and even greater indifference, will view your 'vacation' as a valuable 'lesson learned.'"

"It certainly sounds very interesting, D3. I'll need to give it some thought, though. You know, put a little PIC-*kuan* on it! After all the IRs and

INTSUMs I reviewed in Vault Six, the thought of preparing Intelligence Information Reports, IIRs, on Berlin for current operations and, of course, coincidentally for the historical record, certainly is tempting. If the reports are consolidated largely from open sources and 'passive intelligence collection,' there shouldn't be too many security classification issues. Who knows? Maybe someday the reports will be shipped back to WNRC from Berlin for declassification review in Vault Six! I can imagine an archivist twenty years from now, reviewing the reports, wondering what it was like to be stationed in West Berlin in the Year of George Orwell."

"WNRC? Now you've got me, Thomas!"

"The 'Washington National Records Center' in Suitland, Maryland."

"HUA! You've no doubt heard the curse often attributed to the Chinese, but more than likely of British origin: 'May you live in interesting times.' Well, Thomas, we're living in interesting times. Something's in the air. We're on the cusp of change. It's just a bit too early to tell what, but the tectonic, or should I say 'Teutonic,' plates, yuck, yuck, yuck, are beginning to shift. You could make a contribution, not only to Detachment Two and to the MIG but to the US Army, the United States of America, and of course to our seductress, Clio. End of citation!"

We came about across from Gatow, not too far from the Royal Air Force base of the same name, which, together with Tempelhof in the American sector and Tegel in the French Sector, played a critical part in the Berlin Airlift. According to Harry Dannington's report reviewed in Vault Six, the Royal Air Force landed giant Sunderland flying boats on the *Havelsee* to demonstrate its all-out effort. As it was the beginning of the season, there weren't many boats out. It was smooth sailing all the way, with trees lining the shore on both sides of the *Havel.* Sailing past Kladow, we continued down as far as the *Pfaueninsel.* Not only did D3 successfully evade the marked sector border below Peacock Island, though the East German border patrol boats did come out to shadow our sailboat, he brought us skillfully back into the Recreation Area boathouse. As we stowed the sail and gathered up our gear, I said, "I'm impressed, D3! I must confess, at first I was somewhat concerned when you, an officer in the United States Army, suggested sailing, but now I'm certain you would have breezed through the US Naval Academy, too!"

"I'll pretend to take that as a compliment, Thomas. C'mon, let's see if they'll serve us a late lunch and a beer outdoors on the hotel terrace next door!"

Intrigued by D3's suggestion, I decided to think about it for a while before making a decision. As he had anticipated, I was most concerned about the possible impact on my new routine, my work, and my state of mind. It had been over seven months since my three-week stay in

Psychiatrische Ambulanz. The combination of study and meditation with a regular routine of eating and sleeping was effective and, as Dr. Kahler suggested, enjoyable. Although I still allowed myself the occasional glass of wine or *Berliner Weiße*, I no longer needed Lexotanil or lithium. Things were going so well that I hesitated to take on any additional activities. Although my work at the National Archives had given me a pretty good idea about "army life," actually being in uniform, if only for one weekend a month, was something else. More than anything else, I was gratified by the friendship, confidence, and trust D3's suggestion implied. The army was, after all, his profession, his chosen career, and he thought I should be part of it. I called him on D-Day, June 6, to let him know I'd decided to apply for direct commissioning as an intelligence officer in the US Army Reserve.

"D-Day, why how appropriate, Thomas! I can't tell you just how pleased I am. As I thought you just might decide to do so, I took the liberty of requesting US Army Reserve Europe to forward the necessary application materials. When you have a moment, maybe even two, you can stop by the Mission and fill them out. Call ahead. If I'm not there, Sergeant Miller can help you put the package together. He's a 71-Lima and will no doubt in any case do a much better job than I would. I'll send it down to Heidelberg and see if my battle buddy can't grease the skids a little bit. The chief told me if you decided to join up, he'd be pleased to swear you in. I'd very much like to see you in BDUs before PCSing to Carlisle Barracks next summer. Oh yeah, I just found out I was picked up for the US Army War College resident program."

"You're leaving Berlin for the *Preussische*, I mean, of course, the *Amerikanische Kriegsakademie*? Congratulations, D3! Doesn't one usually have to be a lieutenant colonel to be selected for Army War College? "

"We'll see, Thomas, we'll see. Yes, yes, it's back to CONUS but only for a year or so, and not until next year. In any case, I'm planning on coming back to Berlin when I'm finished, maybe not right away but eventually. I'll have to see how things go at Carlisle and then work it through my branch assignments officer."

After hanging up, I remembered D-Day was also the first anniversary of my library date with Laura. I had sent her a longer letter, thanking her for her thoughtful gift, still serving as my pillowcase, and received a postcard with a picture of the National Archives on it in return. She hadn't mentioned returning to West Berlin. I wanted to ask Gabriel if he'd heard from André at the Berlin Museum, but I didn't have the chance to do so. At *Galerie Buraq*, André had mentioned the possibility of an exhibition in Berlin this autumn. Perhaps Laura would return for fall semester.

Two days later, "D+2," I stopped by the Mission. With Sergeant Miller's expert assistance, I filled out the paperwork, which he then professionally packaged for submission to US Army Reserve Europe Headquarters in Heidelberg. "The only thing missing is your physical, sir. Let me call MEDDAC to see if they can get you in next week."

"MEDDAC, Sergeant Miller?"

"Medical Activity, sir, the Berlin Army Hospital."

I waited while Sergeant Miller placed the call. "We're in luck, sir, they had a cancellation this morning. If you can get over there by thirteen hundred hours, they can get you in today. If our luck holds, they'll have your lab results by the end of the day, Monday morning at the latest. Once we have them, I can complete your package and send it off to Heidelberg. I'd run you over there myself, but I don't have a vehicle available. When you get there, ask for Specialist Karl O. Reinhardt. He'll be waiting for you, and he'll walk you through the wickets."

"Thanks very much, Sergeant Miller!" I left the Mission and walked back out to *Clay-Allee*, taking the first bus down to Zehlendorf, where I caught Bus 48 running up *Berliner Straße* and *Unter den Eichen* to the US Army Hospital. I was early. The friendly German Labor Service guard called the front desk and Specialist Reinhardt came out to meet me. He was tall, heavy-set, pink-and-blond-faced, and very personable as it turned out—a literate big man.

"Pleased to meet you, sir. Specialist Karl Reinhardt. It's a German name. Sergeant Miller said you'd be here by 13:00 and it's only 12:45. Are you that anxious to join the Army Reserves, sir? May I offer you some unsolicited personal advice?"

"Yes, please, Specialist Reinhardt!"

"Once you're in the reserves, try not to act too eager, you'll be branded as a 'spring-butt' and be given all kinds of fun things to do!"

After I filled out the medical forms, I had an interview with a doctor, an older gentleman with a kindly expression and a shock of thick white hair. After a thorough physical examination, he asked me to tell him more about my three-week stay in the *Universitätsklinikum*. After I'd finished recounting everything I could think of, with the exception of the after-hours therapy administered by the benevolent night nurse, he said, "It sounds to me like you've learned a valuable lesson, Mr. Vonaechron, and have been given some very good professional advice. I honestly don't see a problem here." Blood, urine, and X-rays taken, I rejoined SPC Reinhardt in the waiting area for the walk back the front gate. When he asked me how it went, I recounted my conversation with the doctor.

"Don't sweat it, sir, you're not the first person to go crazy in Berlin, you know! In its institutional indifference, the army can be infinitely understanding."

"Thank you for your kind assistance and for your good advice, Specialist Reinhardt." I took the 48 Bus up to Friedenau and walked back to *Lothringerstrasse*. Resuming my practiced routine, I used *pi-kuan* to put PIC out of mind for the time being.

After finishing my work for the day on July 24, I turned on the television in the *Berliner Zimmer* to learn the *Kunst und Kulturzentrum Kreuzberg*, the *KuKuCK*, had been emptied out, *geräumt*, by the Berlin Police. In the cardboard box containing old tickets, programs, and invitations on the floor under my desk, I found the fateful flyer advertising the *Deutsch Amerikanische Freundschaft* benefit concert for the *KuKuCK* at SO 36, with the telephone number of Nicole's *WG* written on the back. When I asked for her, I was told she was out. I left Dr. Kahler's phone number just in case she no longer had it. Hopefully, she hadn't been sitting on the overstuffed sofa in the INFO-RAUM when the *Polizei* went in. I didn't hear back from her, and when I called again, I was told she'd returned to *Restdeutschland*. She hadn't found the alternative life she was looking for in West Berlin after all.

In mid-August, almost two years to the day of my flight from Washington, DC, to West Berlin, D3 called to tell me the reserve officer selection board had acted favorably on my application and I could now sign the oath and be sworn in as a second lieutenant in the United States Army Reserve. Normally, the oath would have been administered by the Commander, US Army Reserve Europe in Heidelberg, but Colonel Patrick, Chief of the USMLM, had offered to administer the oath in Berlin, with D3 posting the orders. D3 also told me I'd also been scheduled for the condensed, three-week basic officer leadership course at McGraw *Kaserne* in Munich, two weeks at the 3747th US Army Reserve Forces School, followed by one week with the Sixty-Sixth Military Intelligence Group. "The course has been scheduled for the third week of September. Although it's coming up pretty quickly, you'll be able to get it out of the way before you start drilling. Should you pass, you'll be able celebrate at the *Oktoberfest*! Should you fail, you can drown your sorrows there, too! As a SME..."

"SME, D3?"

"As a 'subject matter expert,' as a historian, you're no doubt aware this will be the 150th *Oktoberfest*, not the 150th anniversary of the *Oktoberfest* but a good reason nevertheless to visit the *'Wiese'* even for those historians who don't drink beer. Are there any? Since you'll be new to the army, we thought it might be in your best interest if Sergeant Miller and I escort you down to Munich in the Shield, just to make certain you get off to a good start, and then pick you up again at the end of the course to make sure you come back!"

My *Doktormutter* was surprised, even pleased when I told her of my decision to join the US Army Reserve Europe unit in West Berlin. From our discussions at the *Café Wellenstein*, I knew her to be an advocate of the prudent use of the military instrument to defend and advance the Western agenda. With D3 and the chief's concurrence, I invited her, along with George and Rainer, to the short commissioning ceremony at the Harnack House Officers Club, former guesthouse of the *Kaiser-Wilhelm-Gesellschaft*, on Monday, September 4. The ceremony was held in the ballroom, the former lecture hall where Albert Speer presided over a meeting of German scientists in 1942 to determine the priority to be given to the development of atomic weapons. The American flag, the army flag, and the US Army, Europe flag, with General Eisenhower's flaming sword prominently displayed—no doubt D3's handwork—had been set up on a small, temporary wooden stage at the front of the once elegant lecture hall, where dance bands and DJs now held court on Friday and Saturday nights. After Colonel Patrick had welcomed the guests and made a few introductory remarks, he turned to me and in an official voice said, "Raise your right hand and repeat after me."

"I, Thomas Vonaechron, having been appointed an officer in the Army of the United States, as indicated above in the grade of second lieutenant, do solemnly swear that I will support and defend the Constitution of the United States against all enemies, foreign and domestic, that I will bear true faith and allegiance to the same; that I take this obligation freely, without any mental reservations or purpose of evasion; and that I will well and faithfully discharge the duties of the office upon which I am about to enter; so help me God."

Turning to face the few guests he said, "Lady and gentlemen, may I present Second Lieutenant Thomas Vonaechron, US Army Reserve. At this time, we will publish the orders designating him as a second lieutenant in the United States Army Reserve. Attention to orders! Major Durchschouer, please publish the orders." D3 read the orders and, once he'd finished, Colonel Patrick said, "This concludes the army commissioning ceremony." Prior to the ceremony, D3 instructed me in the basics of military courtesy. Although in civilian clothes, I was allowed to accept the traditional first salute, rendered to me by Sergeant Miller. I returned it as best I could, presenting him with a silver dollar, a tradition which D3 told me originated with British units stationed in the North American colonies prior to the

Revolutionary War. D3 also kindly provided me with an out-of-circulation Eisenhower silver dollar, an "Ike dollar" as he called it, for the occasion.

"Not too bad, Lieutenant. We'll work on it once we get you in BDUs!"

"Thank you, Sergeant Miller."

Laughing, George shook my hand. "When I first encouraged you to come to West Berlin, it was a Free University *Doktor der Philosophie*, not an US Army commission, I had in mind for you. But as you know from your work in Suitland and here in West Berlin, Thomas, the US Army has played, and continues to play, a very important part in the history of Berlin. Now you have become part of that history, as well as a student of it. My heartfelt congratulations *Herr Leutnant der Reserve*!"

Rainer reacted skeptically when I first told him about my decision to join the Army Reserves. Although he seemed to enjoy the atmosphere of the officers' club—"I must have driven past the Harnack House a hundred times but never thought I'd have the chance to come in"—he seemed preoccupied, distant, as he shook my hand.

D3 joined us. "Not only to 'come in' but to have a beer, maybe even two, on Lieutenant Vonaechron's tab. Let's adjourn downstairs to Fiddlers Green. Congratulations, 'Lt.!'"

"Thank you, sir," I replied, overanxious to display my recently acquired knowledge of military courtesy.

"As you were, Thomas, not in the club. It's just like *Luise* here. You can call Colonel Patrick here 'sir,' though, if you want to. It makes him feel like he's important." The Chief of Mission laughed and shook my hand. I thanked him for supporting my application and for hosting the ceremony at the Harnack House. As I followed the others to the stairs leading to Fiddlers Green on the ground floor, Professor Jourdan dropped back to talk with me. She was striking in her navy blue skirt-suit. At all our previous meetings, she'd been dressed much more informally. The suit suited her. She could have been a diplomat.

"I must say, Mr. Vonaechron—or should I now say Lieutenant Vonaechron?—I think you have made a very important decision. You know my thoughts on the significance of the military, the US military in particular. As Hannah Arendt might say, today you have crossed over from the *bios theoretikos* to the *bios politikos*, from the *vita contemplativa* to the *vita activa*. It's a big step and, to be quite honest, not without its dangers. Yet, I'm certain if you let the *bios theoretikos* inform the *bios politikos*, you'll not only do well but discover much. I'm hopeful that in the not too distant future, we'll also be able to add *Doktor der Philosophie* to your list of titles!"

"Thank you very much for coming today, Professor Jourdan. To be honest, I was hesitant to accept a reserve commission because of the impact it might have on my writing. It seems to be going well, but that's of course for you to decide. It's only one weekend a month, and D3 assures me the likelihood of being called to active duty is small, though it could happen. Thanks to you and our discussions at the *Wellenstein*, I've been able to better keep abreast, I mean better keep up with, what's going on in Germany and Europe. D3 feels there's an important change, a shift of some kind beginning to take place. If I understand correctly, I'll be preparing Intelligence Information Reports, IIRs, and intelligence summaries, 'INTSUMS,' based primarily on open sources, hopefully making a contribution to both current operations and, coincidentally, the historical record. As I reviewed those hundreds of IIRs and INTSUMs prepared in Berlin back at the Archives, little did I suspect I might someday be preparing them myself. What do they, what do we say in the army? 'Be careful what you wish for, you just might get it!'"

Professor Jourdan laughed, nodding her head in agreement. "You'll recall the words of Professor Holborn, namesake of our institute: "States must assert their particular nature, and wars, therefore, are inevitable." I do hope, however, you will not have the opportunity to test the Holborn hypothesis from the front line." We'd reached the ground floor, *das Erdgeschoß*, and followed the sounds of conversation coming from a farther room, from the Fiddlers Green bar. It was a large, dark, wood-paneled room, with a drop ceiling and a long, polished wooden bar. Although there were tables lining the walls, our small group took seats at the bar. Unlike the barstools in the *Palast der Republik*, they could be easily rearranged to facilitate conversation.

When D3 saw me walk into the bar with Professor Jourdan, he turned to the German bartender, dressed in a long-sleeve white shirt and slender black tie, his white hair pomaded back over his ears, pointed at me, and in a loud voice said, "His tab today, Heinz!" Hanging over our heads, on a wooden beam running the length of the entire bar, was a wooden rack of stone beer mugs, personalized with the names and units of the Fiddlers Green regulars. D3 walked over to me with a *Bierkrug* in each hand. He held up the one with "2LT Thomas Vonaechron, USAR" on one side and a reproduction of the white and red *ACHTUNG SPERRGEBIET* sign from the Wannsee on the other. "Congratulations, Thomas!" he said and, politely asking Professor Jourdan to step back, poured the mug out over my head. Before I could react, he laughed and said, "It's your 'wetting down,' Thomas! It's actually a navy tradition, but since you told me I'd make a good sailor, I thought I'd take advantage of it. Besides, the week after next we're off to Munich and you need to get in SHAPE. Get it? Get in SHAPE, Supreme Headquarters Allied Powers Europe, get it? Yuck, yuck, yuck! If I ever get promoted to lieutenant colonel, you'll be able to return the favor! Heinz, *Herr Leutnant* here needs a refill."

Dripping beer, I introduced D3 to Professor Jourdan. "My friend D3 is the major I mentioned about during our discussions at the *Café Wellenstein.*"

"I thought he might be, it's a great pleasure to finally meet you, Major Durchschouer! Mr. Vonaechron told me you were named after President Eisenhower. In addition to given names, do you, as a military historian, share his views on the nation and history? How did he put it in his first inaugural address? 'We know that we are not the helpless prisoners of history. We are free men.'"

D3 smiled and said, "*Je suis très heureux de vous rencontrer Professeur Jourdan.* Yes, on the surface it appears to be an argument for taking history into American hands, but in that same address, President Eisenhower pleads nine 'fixed principles' before what he calls the 'bar of history.' After my tour in Vietnam, I memorized the fourth one: 'Honoring the identity and the special heritage of each nation in the world, we shall never use our strength to try to impress upon another people our own cherished political and economic institutions.'"

"*Une excellente réponse, Major Durchschouer!* Mr. Vonaechron also told me you served in Vietnam and then studied at Fort Leavenworth. I would be very interested in how your experiences influenced your military education, your move from the *vita activa* to the *vita contemplativa.*" Always the officer and quite the gentleman, D3 delighted Professor Jourdan by continuing in French. Laughing, Heinz handed me another beer and a bar towel. I took a step back, dried myself off as best I could, and leaned back against the bar. I was in the army now, at least in the reserves, "living the dream." The small celebration broke up after the first beer—back to the Mission, back to the university, back to the *Stadtstaatsarchiv*, and, in Rainer's case, back to the streets of West Berlin. He left the club without saying anything, before I had the chance to thank him for coming and to say goodbye.

The next day, D3 took me to the provost marshal's office to pick up my official US Army Reserve ID and ration cards. We also stopped by Military Clothing Sales to pick up two sets of woodland camouflage BDUs and my TA-50 gear, my "army-issued individual equipment." After pulling all the equipment from the rows of metal shelving and stacking it neatly on the counter, the friendly local national asked me if I needed anything else. Just like the cooks in the Roosevelt Barracks *Kantine*, he seemed to have been doing this for a long time. I surprised myself when I asked him, "Do you have any desert BDUs in stock?"

"Desert BDUs! No, but they might have them down at Military Clothing Sales in Stuttgart at EUCOM, US European Command. I can order them for you. Are you going TDY, Lieutenant?"

"No, no, thanks very much, I was just curious. I've seen an older gentleman around town with a pair of shorts made out of them. I thought perhaps he'd picked them up while on active duty here in Berlin."

"Not likely, Lieutenant. There is a military surplus store behind the *Europa Center* on *Kurfürstenstraße*, but I doubt they have desert BDUs for sale."

D3 saved the best for last. He took me to the post library to meet Head Librarian Nancy Little and apply for a US Army, Europe library card. "As I've often told you Thomas, Nancy here can get you whatever you need, not only from in theater but from CONUS. Nancy, I told Thomas the most important reason for him to join the Army Reserves would be library privileges."

Nancy smiled. "D3's one of our library's very best customers, Thomas, here in Berlin and down in Heidelberg. He's probably told you about the US Army Library and Resource Center. They have books and a historic document collection. It's really a kind of a combination library and archives. Originally set up in Port-aux-Poules, Algeria, in 1943, the library moved along with the US Army through Italy, to Vittel, France, and then on to Heidelberg. D3 tells me you used to work at the National Archives, so I'm certain you would find it very interesting and useful. In any case, it's so nice to finally meet you, Thomas. D3 often talks about you and the seminar on West Berlin you took together at the Free University. I'd be very happy to help you any way I can. My husband, Klaus, works in the Personnel Office on post. He's a local national. We're planning to stay on in West Berlin until we both retire or the US forces depart the American Sector, whichever comes first!"

Just before leaving for temporary duty in Munich, I went to Marion, Nadja's hairdresser in Berlin, taking the British band Haircut 100's single "Favourite Shirts (Boy Meets Girl)" with me. There was an army barbershop on-post, but D3 found their "high and tight" haircuts a bit too severe and usually went off-post. His prematurely peppered hair looked long and thick even after it had been cut. "Helmet hair," he called it. "Can you make me look like him?" I asked, pointing to the picture of the lead singer on the record sleeve, neatly setting myself up for Marion's reply.

"I can make your hair look like his, Thomas, but I'm afraid there's nothing I can do to make you look like him," she replied, laughing.

"Please do your best, Marion."

"I received a postcard from Nadja. She's back in Paris. I think she's planning to return to Berlin this fall."

"Did she say anything about Laura and André? Are they coming back, too?"

"No, she didn't but, I'm sure she'll have more to say when she's here."

My first temporary duty assignment as a US Army Reserve officer went smoothly. D3 and Sergeant Miller drove me down to Munich in the Shield. When they picked me up at *Lothringerstrasse*, D3 looked at me and said, "So you decided to go to the barber on-post for a regulation haircut after all. Whad'ya think of 'LT' Vonaechron's haircut, Sergeant Miller?"

"Looks pretty 'high and tight' to me, sir. He'll knock 'em dead down in Munich!" The Commander of the United States Army Reserve, Europe, D3's friend "from another life," met us at the 3747th US Army Reserve Forces School to welcome the seven new BOLC students. After D3 introduced me to him, he said, "If you're as smart as D3 thinks you are, I can't understand how you let him talk you into joining the reserves, Lieutenant. Needless to say, USAR-E is very glad to have you!" At the Reserve Forces School, we received formal instruction in military courtesy and discipline, then worked our way through basic leadership skills and small unit tactics. At the end of the first two weeks, we were divided up into subgroups for branch-specific instruction. Two of us had been scheduled for the "Introduction Intelligence Course."

I was pleased to discover my "Intel 100" classmate was the only female member of our course, First Lieutenant Kyra O. "K. O." DeGetria, an intelligent, articulate young woman with an inquisitive, enticing manner and thick brown hair, regulation cut to her BDU blouse collar. Lieutenant DeGetria seemed vaguely familiar to me. There were certain similarities, the flashing eyes and sun-tanned skin of Bendis at The Republic on the Potomac and her *Doppelgängerin* in the Tiergarten Flea Market. The self-assured sensuality of the Pan Am stewardess aboard the *Spirit of Berlin*—something about a woman in uniform. The abundant dark brown hair and humor of *Fräulein* Asta Otto, my hostess at East Berlin's Palace of the Republic, another woman in uniform, "Under other circumstances, I'd be pleased to join you . . ." Although BDUs tend to be ill-fitting, Lieutenant DeGetria wore her uniform well, the brim of the woodland combat cap pulled down low over her brown eyes. New to Munich Det, K. O. told us she taught for the University of Maryland University College, also located on McGraw Kaserne.

Although familiar with the various sources and methods of intelligence from my work at the National Archives, it was interesting to look back at Washington, DC, from Munich, from the field. Due to the provisions of the Executive Order on the Classification and Declassification of National Security Information and Material, I'd only been able to review documents created between 1944 and 1954. I'd worked my way backward from 1944 at the Main Archives building but hadn't been able to work forward from 1954. As we listened to the lectures and classified briefings given by our instructors from the Sixty-Sixth Military Intelligence Group and guest speakers from the American Consulate General, and as we worked our way through the assigned readings, the intelligence picture of the past thirty years began to come into focus, at least from the American perspective. From my work in Vault Six, I knew there were other perspectives, alternative stories, alternative histories. In October 1984, Sixty-Sixth MIG seemed more focused on the deployment of the Pershing IIs and GLCMs in Western Europe than on developments in Eastern Europe, though the two were closely interrelated. Kyra and I completed our coursework and, together with our five classmates, were given oral and written examinations covering the entire three weeks of instruction. All seven of us passed. Together with our instructors from McGraw and Kyra's colleagues from Munich Det, we decided to celebrate at the *Oktoberfest.*

Fortunately, USAR-E had had the foresight to reserve a table, as there wasn't an open one to be seen among the hundreds of wooden tables and benches set up inside the huge festival tent on the *Theresienwiese*, a field and former racetrack in front of the old city gates. Making our way slowly through the celebrants, we finally reached our table, where D3 and Sergeant Miller patiently waited, large liters of beer in hand, preparing to escort me back to Berlin in the Shield the following day. The air inside the enormous canvas tent was heavy with the smell of cigarette, cigar, and pipe smoke, stale beer, perspiration, and urine. The tuba player of the traditional Bavarian oompah band, elevated on a wooden stage in the center of the tent, did his best to punctuate, to punch through, the deafening cacophony of voices—Bavarian, German, English, French, and Japanese. After we sat down at our table, D3 turned to me and said, "I wonder how our Alpha Jazz Band would do up there on stage, Thomas?"

"I'm not sure, D3, but it looks like there's a few saints here ready to march in, and not just those assembled here from the *Kaserne.*" D3 nodded, smiled thoughtfully, and set his heavy *Paulaner Maß* down hard on the wooden table.

"Why, Thomas, you've just given me an idea. Be right back! When he finally made it back through the crowd to the table, he smiled and said, "I made a request!"

"'When the Saints Go Marching In,' D3?"

"No, no, wait and see, I mean wait and hear, if you can!" After finishing the "*Im Himmel Gibt's Kein Bier*," the trumpeter stood up and played what sounded very much like *Zapfenstreich,* the military signal to return to barracks. He had the attention of the crowd. As he finished, the band began to play "*Lili Marlene.*" The noise level dropped measurably, many began to sing along. Not far from the bandstand, there were two tables occupied by elderly American veterans and their wives, identifiable by their dark green VFW uniform and Ladies Member caps. Some of them stood up and sang along, arm in arm, in broken German and English. Several of the old soldiers were sobbing as they sang. Surveying the other tables, I noticed several German men of the same age also crying as they sang. After the band had finished and the oompah music and the noise resumed, the bandleader leaned forward to talk with someone and pointed toward our table. A few minutes later, a solid Bavarian waitress, with her henna-red hair running in a thick braid down over her shoulder, across her breast, dressed in the traditional *Dirndl* over a white *Dirndlbluse*, stood at the head of our table. The waitress spoke to one of our instructors, who stood up when she addressed him, and politely escorted her to where D3 was sitting. "Major, she has something for you, from the band, it's on the house!" From a small dark wooden keg supported by a strap over her shoulder, she expertly poured out a thick, clear liquid into a *Schnapsglas.* Smiling, she took the *Schnapsglas* and, instead of placing it in D3's outstretched hand, secured it in her *Dekolleté.* Surprised and somewhat embarrassed, I turned to look at Kyra, who was sitting next to me on the wooden bench. She laughed, looked at the waitress, and said in a loud voice, "I'm jealous!" Although hesitant at first, his head between the practiced hands of the waitress, D3 removed his Ray Bans and bravely drank the shot of *Williams Christ Birnenbrand* from between her breasts.

After returning to Berlin, I resumed my routine of research, writing, meditation, and rest, now augmented by monthly weekend drills with the Berlin Det. There were only three us, the detachment commander, Captain Ralph Stivers; the non-comissioned-officer-in-charge, Sergeant First Class Bill Vogt; and myself. We were occasionally augmented by members of the Berlin Command Office of the deputy chief of staff, intelligence, "Dixie," and the local the 766th MI Detachment, who occasionally provided classified information for our intelligence reports. Ralph and Bill were Department of the Army Civilians, "DACs," stationed in Berlin. They were surprised to learn I was a student, but as a former government employee, I was immediately accepted as part of the team. With my new assignment came the opportunity to review, distill, and record the current events of which I had only vaguely been aware since beginning my excavation of the HistoriCity over two years ago. During our week with the Sixty-Sixth MIG in Munich, Kyra and I learned the Embassy of the Federal Republic in Prague had been temporarily closed due to the large number of refugees from the German Democratic Republic seeking political asylum. D3 was right, something was in the air.

There were new outdoor as well as indoor activities. As a reserve officer, I was expected to "demonstrate and maintain proficiency" with the "(Colt) Pistol, caliber .45, automatic M1911A1 (semi-automatic ACP .45 service pistol)." Although my pistol was secured in the arms room, I drew it out to go out to Rose Range in the *Düppel* Forest for target practice, usually with Colonel Patrick and D3. I'd enjoyed target shooting as a boy and now found myself in West Berlin preparing for "the balloon to go up." As I took aim at the full-size military silhouette targets at the far end of the pistol range, I thought about the Red Army soldiers I'd met at *Sans, Soucci.* and those buried in the Tiergarten who died taking the *Reichstag* on the last day of the last battle. My .45 in hand, I silently promised myself, if I could help it, I would never lift it, or any other weapon, against a member of the Red Army.

Although I hadn't talked with D3 about his Vietnam tour in detail, I wondered if he'd ever had to use deadly force. One afternoon at Rose Range, when Colonel Patrick was unable to join us, I decided to ask him. He looked at me for a moment, exhaled, and nodded sadly. The deep expression lines in his face added gravity and solemnity to his words. "Yes, Thomas, yes I have. I was attached to an ARVN, an Army of the Republic of Vietnam Ranger unit, as a military assistant training advisor, a 'MATA.' This was sometime after US ground forces had officially been withdrawn from South Vietnam. The Rangers were attempting to interdict PAVN— sorry, Thomas 'People's Army of Viet Nam'—and supporting Viet Cong operations northwest of Saigon. We set out from a firebase in two jeeps to demolish two bunkers, which intel indicated were being used by the Viet Cong. We located the bunkers in a field, not far apart from each other, parked our vehicles, dismounted, fanned out, and approached them cautiously on foot. I was carrying an M16 and wearing my .45. After the Rangers cleared the first bunker, removing the remains of dead Viet Cong soldiers, they blew it up. As we advanced cautiously toward the second bunker, someone yelled, "VC!" Before I could move, a grenade bounced across the ground and rolled to a stop at my feet. I looked at it for an eternity. It was an M26 fragmentation grenade, and it was a dud. Dropping to the ground, I rolled as far away as I could, losing my M16. I unholstered my .45 and chambered a round. A second grenade was thrown, also a dud. This time, I saw the arm and the hand that lobbed the grenade and was able to fix the location of the foxhole not far from my position. A third grenade flew through the air. Another dud. Fortunately, everyone had taken cover when the fourth grenade exploded. Suddenly, a soldier jumped out of the foxhole and began to run, firing an assault rifle, a Chinese Type 56 as it turned out. I fired my .45 several times, hitting him once in the forehead. He died instantly. After we made certain there were no other Viet Cong in the area, I walked over to his body. Dressed in a camouflage shirt, he was wearing shorts and the regulation rubber Ho Chi Minh sandals. After firing my .45, I could not let go of the grip and had to use my left hand to remove the pistol from my right. As I was going through his papers, looking for ID and any intel, I suddenly saw him, with alarming clarity I might add, going through my papers, through my wallet, looking at the picture of my parents I carried with me during my deployment. He could have been me, I could have been him. A terrifying, a clarifying moment. The ARVN Rangers blew up the second bunker, and we returned to our base, mission accomplished. My 'VC vision' haunted me until I left Vietnam shortly thereafter, and whenever I'm out on a firing range practicing with a pistol, I think about the man I killed, I think about myself."

I was also required to undergo Mission Oriented Protective Posture training with the special clothing designed for protection from a biological or chemical weapons attack, the living legacy of Nobel Prize-laureate Professor Fritz Haber. MOPP levels zero through five determined the type of protective clothing required. Levels three through five required wearing a protective mask, the most recent incarnation of the World War I gas mask. Sergeant First Class Vogt would sit beside me, stopwatch in hand, as I attempted to put my gas mask on properly within the time limit. "You're dead, sir!" he'd say, over and over again, "You're dead," until it became a Cold War mantra. When I asked him what protection the cumbersome MOPP equipment would give in the event of a nuclear weapons attack, he replied as nonchalantly as only an NCOIC can, "Why, none whatsoever, sir." Apparently my only hope was to fall back on the "duck and cover" training I'd received in elementary school.

On November 6, 1984, Ronald Reagan was reelected President of the United States. I remembered what Rainer, Nadya, and Laura had told Dr. Schneider's Accidental *Polis* Seminar about the events, violent and nonviolent, surrounding the president's short stay in Berlin back in June 1982. In spite of Rainer's dislike for him, President Reagan had been able to convince him of the sincerity of his efforts to reach some kind of understanding with Secretary General Brezhnev. Now that he'd been reelected, maybe he'd venture back out onto "freedom's edge" and try again with Secretary General Chernenko. I would like to be there if he did. Rainer might be able to help me get tickets. Although D3 and I continued to meet regularly at *Luise,* Rainer had not joined us since my commissioning ceremony. Although he said he was busy with work and his studies and would be there "next time," he never came. Something was bothering him; I was certain it was my decision to join the reserves.

Nadja called from Paris to tell me she would be in Berlin during the last week of November and would very much like to see me again. We set a date for *le week-end*. I told her I hadn't heard from Laura in quite a while, wondering if she might have already returned to Berlin. "No, Thomas, Laura 'as decided to remain in DC until next fall. She will return to Berlin for the winter semester next year . . . with André. I'm afraid I once again 'ave some bad news for you, Thomas. Laura and André are married. She wanted to write to you about 'er decision but couldn't find the words. Also, Rainer must 'ave written to Laura about your decision to join the army in Berlin. Rainer doesn't understand why you did it, and to be 'onest with you, Thomas, neither does Laura. She also wanted to write to you to ask about your decision too, but didn't. I'm sorry, Thomas. The only thing I can say is that I do understand your decision and do not think badly of you for it. I have learned a lot about the US Army in Germany from Clarence. I think it will be very interesting for you, and I sincerely 'ope you will let me know what you are doing. After all, Thomas, you are a 'special friend of Nadja's!'"

"So Laura's married André and I married the army! Nadja, I simply can't tell you how much I'm looking forward to seeing you again! Yes, of course, I'm very happy to be able to count myself as a 'special friend of Nadja's.' Perhaps you can help me, once again, dance my way out of my afflictions. At least I now have access to the on-post clubs!" The same happy coincidence that took me to Munich for BOLC during *Oktoberfest* brought Nadja back to Berlin for the "Dual Disco with DJ Spiderman and DJ Secret Weapon" at the Checkpoint NCO Club, the modern, single-story redbrick Building 88 across *Saargemünderstraße* from headquarters. We surprised DJ Secret Weapon with our request for "One Nation Under a Groove," one of his all-time Funkadelic favorites. As we had in the *Dschungel*, after sipping a champagne cocktail made this time with California champagne, we danced until our feet failed us. After closing out the Checkpoint, we caught a cab downtown for breakfast at the *Schwarzes Café* on *Kanstraße*, close to *Savignyplatz*. Although I hadn't been out this late *bzw.* early for over a year, after resting my feet in the back seat of the taxi, I didn't feel tired. Nadja and I discussed *Gott und die Welt* until the sun came up. She'd had a very productive trip, first to Washington, DC, with Laura and André, and then up to New York with Clarence. Clarence decided to expand the article he wrote for *Thumpasorus People* magazine, which had been very well received by both his editor and his readers, into a book on the history of the Black American music scene in West Germany and West Berlin, which

Nadja would coauthor. In addition to the book, their common interest in Black American music had led them to each other. Love. In turn, I told Nadja about the progress I'd made on my dissertation with the assistance of Professor Jourdan, on *pi-kuan* with Govinda, and my once a month weekend life as a second lieutenant in West Berlin.

"So much 'as 'appened since we first met in the Villa, Thomas. I would very much like to meet your *Doktormutter*," she laughed at the expression, "Professor Jourdan. You know she 'as a very controversial reputation at the Sorbonne. Perhaps the three of us could meet in Paris sometime. Did you know there's still a USO Club for the American soldiers in the 'otel *Georges V*. Maybe we could 'ave a champage cocktail together at *le Bar*! In spite of the loss of Laura, and to be 'onest, you can't really call it a loss, Thomas, because she was already lost to you before you met 'er, it sounds like you are fine. This makes me very 'appy. I do 'ope you 'ave the chance to talk with 'er again when she and André return to Berlin. 'Is exhibition is supposed to finally take place next fall. Eh ah, by the way, *tu connais*, I don't think Laura ever told 'im about the library."

"But Laura obviously told you about the library!"

"Yes, yes, of course she did, Thomas, but please don't forget, Laura is also my special friend. She also told me every time she walks into a library, any library, she thinks of you. As you might imagine, as an academic, she's walking into libraries quite often so . . ."

"Thank you, Nadja, that makes me feel much better, but I won't give back the brown dress! But now it's time to go. You're returning home to Paris later today. A wonderful evening on the dance floor with you, my special friend, has once again freed me from my afflictions! Please write down your contact information in my notebook, just to be certain I have it. Do you know when you might be coming back to Berlin? D3 wanted to meet us here tonight but couldn't. He sends you—what did he tell me to say?—his *salutations distinguées* and 'drive on!'"

Nadja laughed. "*Merci*, Thomas. Please give him *beaucoup de bisous* from me—don't worry, Thomas, French Army officers kiss each other all the time! I hope to come back to Berlin again next year maybe in October, for Andre's *vernissage*."

In early December, the Warsaw Pact Committee of the Ministers of Foreign Affairs met in East Berlin, shifting the focus of Berlin Det collection and reporting back to Eastern Europe, where it would remain for the rest of the month. Although the communiqué condemned the NATO deployment of intermediate-range nuclear weapons, justifying the Warsaw Pact predeployment as a legitimate response, it coincidentally called for both an end to the arms race and for disarmament. In mid-December, there was a hunger strike among the refugees from East Germany living in the West German Embassy in Prague.

In addition to up-to-date "situational awareness," my reserve assignment also provided a monthly paycheck. Together with the monthly allotment from the *Luftbrüken-Dank-Stipendium* I'd been awarded, it allowed me to restore my sorely depleted savings and to move into a small, one-bedroom apartment in Lichterfelde-West, near the *Botanischer Garten*, at the beginning of 1985. Although the elegant four-story, turn-of-the-century apartment building had survived the war intact, as had the three other buildings standing at the intersection of *Mohnstraße* and *Hortensienstraße,* its once spacious, representative apartments had been subdivided into smaller units to provide postwar West Berlin with urgently needed living space. When I told the *Hausmeister* I was studying history at the Free University, he told me the noted German naval historian *Konteradmiral* Brix von Seemann had lived in one of the apartments during the Weimar Republic. I took it as a good omen. The appropriately rose-tinted apartment building stood just down the street from *Plantanenplatz*, where I'd twice seen the white-haired gentleman with the cut-off desert BDU shorts walking his dachshund. Now that we were apparently neighbors, I hoped to finally have the chance to talk with him. George helped me move to the *Mohnstraße*, loading books, files, and the warmly wrapped frightened fish into the trunk of his car. I left the borrowed bed and makeshift wooden-door desk behind, along with the large, abnormally heavy dolphin clock on the floor next to the *Kachelofen*. My new apartment had steam heating, so I'd no longer have to regularly feed the tiled beast. Dr. Kahler walked us down the stairs to George's car. It was difficult for me to say goodbye to him. He was one of the teachers I was supposed to find in West Berlin. *Mohnstraße* wasn't too far from *Lothringerstrasse*, and as I continued to meet Govinda twice a week for instruction in *Pi-kuan*, I hoped to see Dr. Kahler occasionally, maybe even over a glass of *Trollinger* at his kitchen table.

Events in Eastern Europe and the Soviet Union remained the primary topics of the Intelligence Information Reports the Berlin Det prepared during our monthly drills in the basement of Building Three. In March 1985, Secretary General Konstantin Chernenko died after only thirteen months in office. The Politburo of the USSR Communist Party Central Committee elected Mikhail Sergeyevich Gorbachev as his successor. Once again, I hoped our recently reelected commander-in-chief might take the opportunity to address the new Soviet secretary general from "the edge of freedom."

Early Monday morning, March 25, Ralph Stivers, the Berlin Det Commander, called to tell me an army officer assigned to the USMLM had been shot and killed the day before by a Soviet soldier while photographing tank sheds near Ludwigslust, just under 200 klicks northwest of Berlin. He did not know who it was, but he did know it was not D3. Drill, scheduled for the coming weekend, was canceled and rescheduled for the following weekend. Although there had been British and French fatalities in the past, I didn't recall any previous American deaths documented in the USMLM Annual Unit Histories.   I thought about the "Dead Carl" tour with D3 and Sergeant Miller to Burg *bei* Magdeburg, and my "discovery" of the Pershing II mock-up. What had seemed an elaborate, enjoyable game at the time had become deadly serious. Though deeply concerned, I did not call D3 or Sergeant Miller, knowing the USMLM staff would be completely immersed in the investigations surrounding the incident. That evening, I attended the farewell ceremony for the fallen officer at Tempelhof Central Airport with the three other members of the Berlin Det. Following the Tempelhof ceremony, D3 joined the chief of mission and other members of the USMLM staff for the funeral at Arlington National Cemetery. The following Saturday, late in the evening after the other members of the Det had returned home, D3 came to our drilling space in the basement of Building Three. He related the death of his colleague in a very professional, matter-of-fact manner. There was apparently some confusion as to whether or not he had ignored a "Mission Restricted Sign," violating a "Permanently Restricted Area." "It's likely the Soviet sentry panicked and the chain of command simply froze." In spite of the heated exchange between the chief and the Soviet authorities on site, D3 did not believe the shooting was premeditated, either on the part of the sentry or D3's other boss, the CINCGSFG. On the other hand, he vehemently condemned the refusal of the Soviet authorities to allow emergency medical treatment, and then their lack of any remorse whatsoever for the shooting. As a consequence, USMLM tours were restricted to showing the flag, no collection operations until standard operating procedures for the military liaison missions could be reviewed, refined, and agreed upon. D3 hoped meaningful dialogue would follow from the tragedy. Before returning to the Mission, he asked me to please keep his remarks to myself, as they did not represent the official position of CINCUSAREUR. Although members of the USMLM were unarmed on tour, I thought again about the promise I'd made to myself never to lift a weapon against a soldier of the Red Army. Would I have been able to keep it under similar circumstances?

The shooting presented Secretary General Gorbachev with one of his first foreign policy challenges. In Washington, DC, the Soviet ambassador was summoned to Foggy Bottom for a meeting with the secretary of state. There were immediate, visible consequences. A Soviet diplomat was expelled, the United States canceled its participation in all Soviet-sponsored events commemorating the fortieth anniversary of the end of the Second World War. The unseen consequences were much more far-reaching and much more positive. Arrangements were made for a senior-level meeting between representatives of the commander-in-Chief U.S Army, Europe and Seventh Army, and the Commander-in-Chief of Group of Soviet Forces Germany to review regulations governing military liaison missions, and to establish procedures designed to prevent similar incidents in the future. The unfortunate, unnecessary death of a member of the USMLM served as the catalyst for renewed efforts by both the Soviet Union and the United States to find acceptable, workable solutions to disagreements, which, over the course of the next four years, would grow in significance from the tactical to the strategic and finally, the political.

President Reagan did return to Germany, in May, to commemorate the fortieth anniversary of the end of the war. He did not, however, venture from *Restdeutschland* back out onto freedom's edge to address the new secretary general. Instead, he joined *Bundeskanzler* Helmut Kohl for a controversial wreath-laying ceremony at the military cemetery at Bitburg-Kolmeshöhe in the Eifel, where forty-three members of the *Waffen-SS* had been buried. D3 confided to me that one of the president's trusted advisors, in a rush to get to Munich and order a new BMW, rejected alternative cemeteries proposed for the ceremony by the *Bundeswehr* and approved presidential participation in Bitburg. Leave it to Deaver. In reading through the Berlin press reports surrounding the controversy during our weekend drill, I found several pictures of German author Günter Grass. There was a remarkable resemblance to the distraught artist who'd given me the print of the frightened flounder rejected by Anna, shortly after my arrival in West Berlin, now hanging on the wall of the *Mohnstraße* apartment. Instead of accusing the *Bundeskanzler* of *Geschichtsklitterung*, of falsifying history, Günter Grass might have put his literary talents to better use describing the dilemma of the thirty-three members of the *Waffens-SS* between the ages of seventeen and nineteen who were buried at Bitburg. After all, he knew how to effectively use creative writing as a means history to reflect upon history from below.

Although I did not receive an invitation to attend the ceremony in Bitburg, I did receive an invitation to the *vernissage* of André's new *Fauve* group at the Pictures of Chairman Mao Gallery on *Lützowplatz* on October 18, as Nadja told me at the Checkpoint Club, the eightieth anniversary of the *Salon d'automne de 1905*. She called from Paris to tell me she was coming back to West Berlin and would meet me at the gallery. "*Pauvre* Thomas, please do not be too sad when you see your Laura again, and always remember, you are a 'special friend' of Nadja's."

Life not only not infrequently imitates French novels but British novels as well. In June, I observed the largest exchange of espionage agents since the end of the war. Although the US Air Force Office of Special Investigations (OSI) ran the operation on the *Glienicker Brücke*, army intelligence reps were invited to attend as observers. The husband of the first lady's former social secretary, the US ambassador to the Federal Republic of Germany, represented the United States, while Dr. Wolfgang Vogel and his breathtakingly beautiful wife, Helga, held high the flag of the German Democratic Republic. Although representatives of the Soviet Union were also requested to contribute compromised agents to the exchange, they diplomatically declined. Twenty-five Western agents held in East Germany and Poland were exchanged for four Eastern Europeans flown in from the United States to Tempelhof Central Airport, an exchange rate of over six to one. When two of the compromised Western agents decided not to join the others immediately, the rate fell somewhat, twenty-three to four, but was still over five to one. After the chartered Mercedes bus carrying the twenty-three Western agents successfully negotiated the labyrinth of physical security barriers in the center of the *Brücke der Einheit*, the border between Potsdam and the American Sector of Berlin, the four Eastern agents were returned. An aura of polite cordiality pervaded the entire operation, which took place at thirteen hundred hours on Tuesday, the eleventh of June, under cover of neither the night nor the fog of the Cold War.

The following month, D3 received official notification of his promotion to lieutenant colonel and his Permanent Change of Station orders for the Army War College at Carlisle Barracks, Pennsylvania. Although it conflicted with the parade, ceremony, and US Embassy reception, he scheduled his promotion ceremony for the early morning of July Fourth at the Mission. This time, I was the only guest. The mood at the Mission had been somber and subdued since the shooting. On my way to the *Föhrenweg*, I nevertheless stopped by Fiddler's Green, found Heinz, and asked him to please fill D3's stone *Bierkrug*, which I covered with clear plastic wrap and concealed in my shoulder bag. At the conclusion of the ceremony, while he was receiving the congratulations of members of the USMLM, I walked up behind him and, emptying his beer mug over his head, said, "Congratulations, Colonel!" Sergeant Miller had seen me coming with *Bierkrug* in hand, stifled a laugh and looked the other way.

"I knew you'd do that, Thomas! I guess I did ask for it, so just in case, I brought another set of BDUs along for the parade and reception this afternoon. Although I'm looking forward to the war college, I'm going to miss all of you! But as Douglas . . . ah . . ."

"MacArthur!"

"Why thank you, Thomas, I knew you'd remember, but as Douglas MacArthur once said, 'I shall return!'" We had lunch under Luise one last time before D3 departed at the end of the month. He was planning to spend some time with his family in Pennsylvania before reporting to the war college. We'd hoped Rainer might join us, but, once again, he couldn't make it.

"I'd be grateful if you could have copies of your Intelligence Information Reports sent to me so I can keep up-to-date on what's going on in Germany and Europe, Thomas. Please add the Army War College address to your distribution list and put the IIRs to my attention. The classified mailroom will notify when they come in. Once I find a place to stay in Carlisle, I'll send you my address. We should be able to talk on the DSN phone once in a while, too."

"It just won't be the same American Sector without you, D3. You've been a big part of my West Berlin over the past three years. I'm very grateful to you. I know you'll have fun at the war college. With your background at CGSC and SAMS, you'll make the most of it and find a fulfilling follow-on assignment. I really do hope you're able to work your way back to Berlin though. While in Carlisle, maybe you can make it over to Kent State University and walk the May 4, 1970, battlefield with Dr. Schneider. If you do, please give him my very best regards. You know he's a Quaker. Hopefully, he won't be disappointed with my decision to join the reserves, too."

"That's a very good suggestion, I'll try and do that, Thomas. I don't think you need worry about Dr. Schneider. Didn't he tell us a member of his Friends meeting was at the Battle of the Bulge? Why, Thomas, even Socrates served as a hoplite in the Peloponnesian War if memory serves, at the battles of Amphipolis, Delium, and Potidaea. You might remember in the *Symposium*, Alcibiades credits Socrates with saving his life at Potidaea. Besides, you're livin' the dream now! Out here on freedom's edge, riding the circuit wall of the accidental *polis*, a Sun Tzu soldier patiently holding the fort!"

Placing my hands firmly on his shoulders, I looked into his eyes and, doing my very best not to laugh said, "D3 . . . be all you can be!" Both Colonel Patrick and Sergeant Miller chuckled and, before I left the Mission, invited me to stop by. After D3 had PCS'd to Pennsylvania, I made another attempt to invite Rainer to lunch at *Luise*. Once again he was busy, so I asked him to call me whenever he had the chance. He said he would.

The eightieth anniversary of the *Salon d'automne de 1905* was at hand. Almost a year had gone by since George and I attended Gabriel Kielerförde's *vernissage*. Gabriel would likely be at André's exhibition. I thought about wearing my woodland camouflage BDUs in *homage á* the fallen German expressionist painter *Leutnant* Franz Marc but then thought better of it. Instead, I put on my old tweed sport coat with patched elbows, the one identical to André's *Audiocoat*. Bus 48 would take me from *Plantanenplatz* to *Lützowstraße,* a short walk from *Lützowplatz*. I took a front seat on the upper deck, so I would have the *Überblick* as we drove past *Botanischer Garten* and *Rathaus Steglitz*. The bus route ran right through the center of Friedenau, my old neighborhood. As we approached *Rathaus Friedenau,* I looked up to the angel on top of the tower, but to my surprise and dismay, she had flown. There was only an ornamental iron spire where she once stood proffering the palm of peace. A bad omen? Maybe George knew what had happened to her. Perhaps she'd been temporarily removed for restoration. Next door to the *Rathaus, LaBelle's* lights were on, customers standing outside under the red and white awning. Although close to my former *Lothringerstrasse* room, I'd only been there once, with Rainer, D3, Nadja, and Clarence. One of my "Dixie" contacts told me *LaBelle* housed more entertainment than just disco music. As we drove on, up *Hauptstraße,* the 48 Bus passed by the formerly occupied, turn-of-the-century apartment building on *Kaiser-Wilhelm-Platz,* where the red banners of the *Instandbesetzer* no longer proclaimed, "*Lieber Instand-Besetzen als Kaputt Besitzen!*" Although the American, British, French and Soviet flags had also been lowered, I could see the massive building housing the Allied Control Council just beyond *Kleistpark*. As we approached *Lützowstraße,* my thoughts turned to Laura and André. What should I say? Offer my congratulations of course. There would be no time for intimate conversation, let alone other intimacies, yuck, yuck, yuck! I decided to empty my mind and see what didn't happen. By happy coincidence, I arrived at Pictures of Chairman Mao at the same time as François Fontane. "Ah, Thomas, our 'kind of historian!' How good to see you again, it's been quite a while, has it not? I told Victorine you'd probably be here tonight. You seemed to have made some kind of impression on her. She'd like to see you again!"

"*Tiens!* François Fontane *au milieu des fauves!* To be honest, François, I'd like to see more of Victorine as well!"

"Well said, Thomas, very well said after the way she took her leave of you! Well, let's see what we can do. Would you please give me your telephone number? By the way, have you seen your beautiful blonde friend Laura this evening? I understand she and André are now married. *Tant pis pour toi,* Thomas. Perhaps an afternoon with *Mère* Ubu unbound would exorcise your heartbreak! But look, there stand our hostess and our host as we speak, talking with, if I'm not mistaken, that notable *Förderer* of found objects, Gabriel Kielerförde. Shall we join them?" François provided the perfect cover. Laura smiled. André spoke first. "Thomas, it's good to see you again! Thank you so much for coming tonight, Laura told me you were still in West Berlin. Unfortunately, the arrangements for our exhibition took much longer than planned, but I must say I'm fairly satisfied with the result. I'd be very grateful to you if you would give me your impressions, once you've had the chance to look around, of course. François, it's good to see you again, too. It's been quite a while. I'd of course be grateful for your impressions as well. Laura, may I introduce François Fontane? François's a member of the *Saubühne ensemble*."

Smiling broadly, Laura extended her hand, "Hallo, François!"

"*Enchantez*," he replied politely, turning his gaze from Laura to me, wordlessly inviting me into the conversation.

"Congratulations are in order, André, not only on your exhibition but also to you and to Laura on your marriage. Nadja told me when we last met here in Berlin. I wish you both much happiness."

"Thank you, Thomas. You'll receive an invitation to the reception. We had one immediately following the wedding in Washington in the Nest of the old Willard Hotel on Pennsylvania Avenue, but many of our friends in Paris and Berlin were unable to attend."

After he'd finished, Laura looked at me. "Dear Thomas, I don't know what to say. I'm so sorry I haven't written in so long. Thank you for your letter. I'm so pleased to know you are feeling better. I wanted to answer but so much has been going on." Laura lowered her eyes and leaned toward me as she spoke. I put my arms around her and kissed her gently on both cheeks.

"Dear Laura, it's so good to see you again! I wish you and André much happiness! Don't worry about not writing, I understand. So much has been going on here, too. Nadja told me you've both been very productive in Washington."

"*Tiens!*" As if on cue, Nadja walked through the gallery door and joined us. She also kissed Laura on both cheeks, accepting the same from André and me. She shook hands with Gabriel and François. "*Enchantez!* My congratulations, *cher* André, I'm so 'appy your ex'ibition 'as finally opened. Are these paintings from Berlin, 'ave you added some of your paintings from Washington? Laura tells me you both 'ave been very busy."

"Most of the paintings hung in the exhibition were done here in Berlin before we left. As you might remember, Nadja, mine have been finished for some time. After the exhibition closes here next month, we will take it to the Franz Bader Gallery on Pennsylvania Avenue in Washington. Perhaps I'll be able to add some of my more recent work." The evening passed painlessly in pleasant conversation and paintings, with background music once again provided by André's *Audiocoat*, prominently displayed under the portrait of Chairman Mao at the back of the gallery. As I stood listening to the music, a number of gallery-goers commented on the similarity between André's *Audiocoat* and my sport coat; one even asked me if I were part of the exhibition. I told her I wasn't certain but was beginning to think I might be. There was no farther room. Once again, I was enchanted by the simplicity, the childish playfulness of the new *Fauve*, free of both the serious intentions of the original Expressionists, and the anti-Abstract Expressionist strategy of the *Zeitgeist* exhibition in the *Martin-Gropius-Bau*. While a few of the paintings were very good, André's among them, the other appeared weak in subject matter and technique. I vondered vat Franz Bader vould haf to say. Although our eyes met several times in the course of the evening, neither Laura nor I was moved to words; there was really nothing more to be said. After an hour and a half, I decided to return to *Mohnstraße*. Before departing, I discussed my initial impressions, or should I say 'expressions,' of the exhibitions with André, who politely invited me to a late-night dinner party following the *vernissage*.

Doing my best to politely decline in return, I said, "I'm sure we'll have the chance to get together again before you leave West Berlin." Putting my arms lightly around Laura's waist, I kissed her on both cheeks and wished her a good night. She smiled, tilting her head to the right, tossing her long, uncombed blonde hair. Before leaving, I looked for François Fontane who, I discovered, had been watching us from the far side of the gallery.

"Bravo, Thomas, bravo, very well executed, you should have been an actor! Please forgive me for observing from a distance. I'll pass your regards and telephone number to Victorine. She'll be very unhappy she decided not to join me this evening. She just might call you—*Salut!*"

"*Salut*, François, or, considering several of the paintings hanging on the wall here tonight, should we not rather say "*Sau-loo*" *Père Ubu?*"

"*Mais trés bien, cher* Thomas. *Tu ést vraiment un Cabaretist!*"

In November, President Reagan and Secretary General Gorbachev finally did meet, at a summit conference, not out on freedom's edge in Berlin but at Karim Aga Kahn's *Maison de Saussure* in Geneva. Although there were no written agreements, they agreed "nuclear war cannot be won and must never be fought." I wondered if President Reagan had ever met a Russian, let alone a Russian Communist face-to-face before, and if this personal encounter might have mitigated his anti-Soviet stance. Two months later, the secretary general would surprise the president, along with the US Departments of State and Defense, with his proposal to abolish all nuclear weapons by the end of the century. November's detachment drill date coincidentally fell on the same day as Laura and André's West Berlin wedding reception in the ruins of the *Hotel Esplanade*. The *Kaisersaal*, where *Kaiser Wilhelm II* hosted his *Herrenabende*, had survived intact—not only the war, but the *GBI* as well. In 1941, Albert Speer announced the *Esplanade* had been slated for demolition. I probably could have slipped away for an hour or two but decided not to and, once again, politely declined the invitation.

In the basement of Building Three, Detachment Two compiled and analyzed the overwhelmingly favorable German reaction to the Soviet leader's initiative. As I drafted an Intelligence Information Report for Captain Stivers, the Berlin detachment commander, it occurred to me Detachment One was likely doing something similar down in Munich and decided to call my BOLC classmate Kyra DeGetria to find out. I'd enjoyed Kyra's company in Munich at McGraw Barracks and the *Oktoberfest*, and had been hoping for another opportunity to see this intelligent, intriguing female intelligence officer. I'd thought about calling her and now had "official cover." Sometimes, opportunity like history needs a push. Our DSN-FOR-OFFICIAL-USE-ONLY conversation ranged from the military to the academic, remaining professional while probing the personal. We decided to recommend that our respective detachment commanders propose a meeting in Heidelberg to the MIG commander to review what had been done to date and discuss how to better coordinate our efforts in the future.

A Woman and an Officer

December 1985

True to the not-so-long-established BOLC Class of '84 tradition, the MIG detachment commander set our three-day temporary duty assignment for the second week of December so the members of both detachments could take advantage of the Heidelberg Christmas Market. The *Weihnachtsmarkt*, a three-dimensional, life-sized Hallmark Christmas card, ran parallel to the *Neckar* River along *Hauptstraße*, through the snow-covered squares of the *Altstadt*, beneath the *Schloß*. The TDY also provided me with the long-awaited chance to spend time after the duty day in both the legendary US Army, Europe Library and Resource Center and the Heidelberg University Library. D3's friend from a former life, the Commander of US Army Reserve Europe, together with the Commander of the US Army Reserve Military Intelligence Group joined us to review MIG taskings, Detachment One and Two activities, and our production to date. While readily acknowledging the need for closer coordination, MIG headquarters seemed pleased with output coming from both Munich and Berlin.

Following the final "hot wash" session at MIG headquarters, Kyra asked if she could accompany me to the Heidelberg University Library in the *Altstadt*. After it closed, we made our way back down to *Hauptstraße*, walking through the darkened Christmas Market to the *Sonder Bar* on *Marktplatz,* a student café recommended by a MIG colleague. The *Sonder Bar* lived up to its name, an exception in "Old Heidelberg." The student prince stood outside, shivering in the snow while serious students and sympathetic faculty members discussed the changes sweeping across Europe. With our fingers wrapped securely around rims of steaming white bowls of *Milchkaffee,* Kyra told me about the undergraduate class on "Historical Methods" she taught for "U of M," University College at McGraw. Her students had just completed the introductory unit on "Philosophies of History" in preparation for the introduction of "Historical Methodologies" following the break. As her course coincidentally complemented my *Dissetation-im-werden*, I told Kyra about Clio in the service of the state and my *Doktormutter* Professor Jourdan. Planning to eventually enroll in the *Ludwigs-Maximilian-Universität München* to study for a doctorate in history, Kyra had signed up for evening German lessons at the *Goethe-Insitut* on *Sendlinger Tor*. She was pleased to hear how well the *Goethe-Insitut* Washington had prepared me for the two-day admission examination required by the *Freie Universität Berlin*. After taxiing out to our transient billets in the US Army guest house, just outside of town on Patrick Henry Village, we shook hands, wished each other a safe trip home and "*Aufwieder-bye-bye*" in the lobby, and returned to our rooms. After showering and putting on my well-worn blue and white light-cotton yukata with kanji characters identifying me as a "great fireman," I turned out lights and stretched out on my bed. Just before slipping into unconsciousness, there was a light knock at the door. Climbing out of bed, I turned on the reading light on the nightstand, unlocked, and opened the door to find Kyra, dressed in a long, white terry cloth bathrobe, standing in the hallway. "Kyra! Please come in, " I said, stepping aside to let her pass, gesturing to the chair next to the wooden desk. "Please sit down." I closed the door behind her.

"No, no, thank you, Thomas" she replied, standing curiously erect, almost at attention. "I won't stay long. You must be tired, too. I'm exhausted and really need to get some sleep before driving back to Munich early tomorrow morning. I just wanted to thank you again, to tell you how much I enjoyed the university library, our coffee, and conversation at the *Sonder Bar*. I just had a nightcap in my room and thought you might like one, too." Before I could answer, she gently placed her hands on the soft white terrycloth lapels of her bathrobe, pulling it gently open above her waist, revealing a nonregulation black bustier, with a *Schnapsglas* securely seated in her *Dekolleté*. "It's not *Williams Christ Birnenbrand* this time, Thomas, it's absinthe," she said gently taking my head in her hands, as the waitress in Munich had done with D3, allowing me to kiss the green fairy between her breasts. Once I'd finished drinking, she gently raised my head, closed her robe, and said "Goodnight, Thomas. Thank you again for a lovely evening in Heidelberg." She turned and opened the door to leave.

"No need to be jealous, Kyra," I said. She turned her head, her brown eyes flashing, tossed her bangs and laughed, gently closing the door behind her.

Immersed in my dissertation, "wall-gazing," and weekend detachment drills, I took little notice as the gray Berlin winter once again grudgingly gave ground to a green spring. At 02:30 hours on Saturday morning, April 5, 1986, the 766th MI Detachment operations NCO called to report there had been an explosion at the *LaBelle* disco. Emergency response vehicles, the *Polizei*, and the military police were on the scene. Rather than add to the confusion, I reported to USCOB headquarters. According to the preliminary reports made available to us by the deputy chief of staff, intelligence, there were approximately 500 people in *LaBelle* at 01:09, when the bomb exploded. Two people, a Turkish woman and an American soldier, had been killed outright, and approximately 230 people were injured, some of them critically. American casualties had been evacuated to the US Army Hospital, other civilian casualties to the *Augusta-Viktoria-Krankenhaus*. After leaving the headquarters compound, I walked back home and, later that evening, walked down *Unter den Eichen* along the perimeter of the *Botanischer Garten* into Steglitz. As I approached *Rathaus Friedenau*, I could see the area surrounding *Hauptstraße* 78 had been cordoned off. German and American police officers were arriving and departing the scene. I looked up at the top of the tower, hoping to see the peaceful angel, but saw only the spiked ornamental iron spire I'd seen on the way to André's *vernissage*. I'd forgotten to ask George the whereabouts of the angel. Although the former *Roxy Palast* appeared to be intact, the scene directly in front of *LaBelle* was one of destruction and desolation. The entrance was in ruins. Debris covered the sidewalk in front of the disco.

Ten days later, President Reagan authorized Operation El Dorado Canyon, simultaneous air strikes against five targets in Tripoli and Benghazi, Libya. The assistant chief of staff, operations, the G3, briefed the US Commander, Berlin and the US Army Berlin staff on the operation. Denied over-flight rights by France and Spain, Navy A-6 Intruders and Air Force F-111 Aardvark aircraft were forced to circumvent their airspace. In-flight refueling was required. Over 100 aircraft were launched in support of El Dorado Canyon. One aircraft, an F-111 Karma 52, was lost in the Mediterranean. As the other aircraft returned to carrier and base, President Reagan addressed America and the world, "the evidence is now conclusive that the terrorist bombing of the *LaBelle* club was planned and executed under the direct orders of the Libyan regime." The deputy chief of staff, intelligence explained how intercepted Telex messages to the Libyan Embassy in East Berlin linked Tripoli directly to the bombing. A message sent from the Libyan People's Bureau in East Berlin to Tripoli on April 4 predicted you "will be very happy when you see the headlines tomorrow," adding "happening now" the following day. Although DCSI didn't mention the source of the intercepts, I assumed it was US Army Field Station Berlin, high atop the T-berg. According to an after-action report received from the Defense Intelligence Agency, the *LaBelle* bombing might have been intended as a response to Operation Prairie Fire, an earlier clash between American and Libyan naval forces in the Gulf of Sidra which left thirty to fifty Libyan sailors dead. The overwhelming negative European response to El Dorado Canyon included a voice from East Berlin. Erich Honecker, general secretary of the Socialist Unity Party of the German Democratic Republic, condemned the "barbaric bombardment of peaceful Libyan cities." European outrage was overshadowed on April 26, 1986, by an explosion in Block Four of the nuclear power plant *Tschernobyl W. I. Lenin* near the Ukrainian city of Prypjat.

Nadja called in mid-May. She and Clarence were back in West Berlin. There had been speculation in the American press that *LaBelle* had been targeted precisely because of its popularity with African American service personnel. Interested in a possible story on the bombing, the editor of *Thumpasorus People* magazine sent had them back to Berlin to attempt to interview injured US Army personnel and a representative of the Libyan Embassy in East Berlin. I was surprised to learn they were able to make an appointment at the Libyan Embassy, where they had been courteously received by a political officer. He took them to a conference room, where he repeatedly assured them there was absolutely no basis to the claims of Libyan involvement in the *LaBelle* bombing made by the United States government. As a consequence of Operation El Dorado Canyon, thirty-seven people had been killed, including the adopted baby daughter of Libyan leader, Colonel Muammar el-Qaddafi, and ninety-three injured. The residence of the French and Japanese ambassadors had also been damaged. Nadja and Clarence now wanted to request permission to interview soldiers wounded in the attack. "I'd be happy to call the Public Affairs Office for you, Nadja. The PAO would be interested in your East Berlin visit as well, as no doubt would 'Dixie'—sorry, the deputy chief of staff, intelligence. Would you be willing to talk to both the PAO and Dixie?" Nadja spoke briefly with Clarence, and they agreed. I wrote down the telephone number of their hotel and, after hanging up, called PAO and Dixie and made appointments for the following Monday morning. I called Nadja back with the information, suggesting I meet them at the front gate of the John F. Kennedy Headquarters Compound on the *Clayallee* and escort them to the Public Affairs Office.

Monday morning at "oh dark thirty," I signed them in at the front gate and walked them to the PAO shop in Building Two, where I dropped them off. Before I left, I asked the PAO non-commissioned officer in charge if she would please have Dixie call me in the Detachment Two Office once they were finished, so I could pick them up in Building Three and escort them out. I brought along a draft chapter of my dissertation so I could work on it downstairs in the Berlin Det office while Nadja and Clarence were busy on post. As it turned out, they spent the entire day on the headquarters compound or at the army hospital. It was after 1800 hours when Dixie called for me to come upstairs to pick them up. They were visibly exhausted. We decided to walk across the street to the Checkpoint NCO Club for dinner. As an army veteran, Clarence was enraged by the attack and determined to do everything he could to help identify those responsible. The PAO had been very helpful with both background information and arranging for the interviews, which were wrenching for interviewees and interviewers. Dixie was very interested in the myriad details surrounding their fact-finding trip to the Libyan Embassy in East Berlin. Clarence said, "We're pretty much good to go now, Thomas. We're going to try to wrap up a few more interviews with friends and family members tomorrow and return to Nadja's place in Paris on Wednesday to work up a draft. We're flying back to New York on Sunday. If we don't make the June issue, then July for sure. Thanks so much for your help!"

Nadja added, "Thank you so very much again for 'elping us, Thomas, on such short notice. *Un trés grand Merci!* I 'onestly don't know when I'll be back in Berlin. I 'aven't seen Laura since the wedding reception last November. Please take this the right way—I think she was relieved you didn't come. She should finish here in Berlin at the end of summer semester, in July, *n'est ce pas?* Please do try to talk Professor Jourdan into coming back to Paris for a visit. I'm certain they serve champagne cocktails made with real champagne at *le Bar*."

"I'll try, Nadja. I was happy to help, and even happier to see you both again, though not under these unhappy circumstances! Have a safe trip back to Paris and to New York, and please send me a copy of your article. I'll include it in my monthly report. I know D3 would be interested, so please send him a copy, too. Let me give you his address in Carlisle."

"I have a suggestion," said Clarence, "let's all have a champagne cocktail made with California champagne and say good night."

Nadja and I answered at the same time, "Approved!"

The summit meeting in Geneva bore fruit, fruit which would have long-term consequences for the HistoriCity. At the end of May, President Reagan announced the United States would no longer be bound by provisions of the Strategic Arms Limitation Talks II but would make decisions based on the threat posed by Soviet strategic forces. Yet the Reagan administration, perhaps in response to pressure from European Allies and also because of certain strategic advantages for the United States, nonetheless continued to abide by SALT II.

Together with the two other members of Detachment Two, I attended the "Parade and Ceremony in Recognition of the 210th Year of the Independence of the United States of America on July 4th." I thought about the tour D3 and I took of Little America. He had invited me to attend a Fourth of July parade, but I never thought I'd do so in uniform. Late that night, D3 called from Carlisle to wish me a "Happy Fourth" and tell me he had been requested to remain at Carlisle for another year as a member of the faculty. At the end of the 1986–1987 academic year, he would report to the Defense Language Institute in Monterey, California, for a year of intensive Russian language training. Although he didn't "confirm or deny" on the phone, it sounded very much like a return to Europe was in the offing for 1988. In its infinite wisdom or indifference, the United States Army had something in mind for D3. I hoped it was Berlin.

In September, I received notification of my promotion to first lieutenant. My intention was to celebrate quietly with the new MIG commander from Heidelberg and the two other members of the Berlin Det at the Marine Bar, following a short ceremony in the Leibnitz *Bibliothek* of the Harnack House. Much to my surprise, we were joined in the library by the members of the Munich Det. Afterward, we retired to the "underwater" bar where, surrounded by fish painted on the walls, Kyra wetted me down with a beer from my *Krug*. Squared away in her woodland camouflage BDUs, I wondered if she might be wearing her nonregulation black bustier underneath for the occasion. Unfortunately, I was unable to find out before Det One returned to Munich via Frankfurt later that same evening on the Berlin duty train from the Rail Transportation Office at Lichterfelde-West. On the way to the RTO, I did have the chance to ask her if she'd now put my photo on her piano, "To Kyra, Best Wishes, Thomas."

Both Dets and MIG headquarters were hard-pressed to keep up with the rapidly unfolding current events. As a consequence of the Heidelberg meeting, the Munich Det continued to focus on potential "rear area threats" to NATO and the peace movement, while the Berlin Det analyzed German reaction to developments in the Soviet Union and Eastern Europe. In October, approximately 200,000 people, led by a Protestant pastor from the village of Bell in the Rhineland-Palatinate, peacefully demonstrated against the stationing of ninety-six BGM-109G Gryphon cruise missiles at nearby Wüschheim Air Station. The very next day, President Reagan and Secretary Gorbachev met once again, not in Berlin but in Reykjavik. Although no arms control agreements were reached, building upon the renewed efforts to improve communications following the shooting of the USMLM officer and the atmospheric change of the Geneva Summit, the Reykjavik Summit was a watershed in Soviet-American relations. Open-source material available to the Berlin Det for the analysis of German public opinion included surveys conducted by Allensbach and Forsa organizations, and the weekly newsmagazine *Der Spiegel.* All survey results reflected an increase in the credibility of Secretary General Gorbachev at the expense of President Reagan.

Since moving to Berlin in August of 1982, the highlight of the holiday season had been attending a performance of Johann Sebastian Bach's *Weinachtsoratorium.* Although performed throughout West Berlin in several different redbrick churches, for the past four years, I had been able to purchase tickets for performances of all six cantatas in the *Kaiser-Wilhelm-Gedächtnis-Kirche.* The incomparable, invisible architecture of Bach's music resonated throughout the sanctuary bathed in blue light, rising above the restored ruin with the promise of redemption—for the combined total of 148 minutes and six seconds, a precious gift of structure and harmony.

Jauchzet! Frohlocket! Auf! preiset die Tage,
Rühmet, was heute der Höchste getan,
Lasset das Zagen, verbannet die Klage,
Stimmet voll Jauchzen und Fröhlichkeit an:
Dienet dem Höchsten mit herrlichen Chören
Laßt uns den Namen des Höchsten verehren.[68]

The days between Christmas and the New Year, the time "between the years," *zwischen den Jahren*, is the traditional time to reflect on the old year and plan for the new. It had now been over four years since my move

---

68 "Rejoice! Be joyful! Glorify the days, praise what the Highest has done today, fear no more, forsake lamentation, be filled with rejoicing and happiness: serve the Highest with glorious choirs. Let us honor the name of the Highest!" Diary of Thomas Vonaechron, Diary Extract, 1986, trans. TV.

from Washington, DC, to Berlin. Much had happened, anticipated and unanticipated. Though I hoped to complete my dissertation and take the required oral examinations in the new year, I hadn't given much thought to what to do afterward—a return to government service, to the National Archives, to the Washington National Records Center, to Vault Six? In a way, though still a student, *ein Doktorand*, I was already back in government service, at least once a month, as a first lieutenant in Detachment Two of the Military Intelligence Group, United States Army Reserve, Europe. What would my former fellow NARSians say if they knew? In four years, I had moved from the past to the present, and I was now beginning to look ahead into the future. As D3 said when he first suggested I join the reserves, there something was in the grainy *Berliner Luft, Luft, Luft. Ja ja, ja ja, ja ja ja ja ja ja!* Change, historical change, of some kind was coming. I should have been more careful for what I wished for while reviewing records of postwar Berlin back in Vault Six. Now I was in Berlin, in West Berlin, in the American Sector, back underground in Building Three of the US Command Berlin, John F. Kennedy Headquarters Compound, writing up Intelligence Information Reports, records of current events. Once I signed off on them over my signature block, they became the past, they became sources, they became Leopold von Ranke's *Quellen*. It's one thing for a historian to identify and utilize sources in an archives, something else for a historian to create, to become the source. Although I did my best to integrate all information available when compiling the IIRs, there was still a subjective, even a creative selection process involved. So, *wie war es eigentlich*? Were the IIRs I prepared an honest attempt to *"bloß sagen, wie es eigentlich gewesen"* or were they simply a professionally trained, informed opinion? The thought was troubling. It could also be valid for documents prepared before, during, and after the war, as well as for the much older *Quellen* available to von Ranke. One day, the declassified Berlin Det IIRs might be used as primary sources by historians. Just because information is contained in a document considered historic, does that make it the truth? And what about the policy decisions driving the missions, the military operations? Many of the factors involved in major policy decisions are not to be found in documents, remaining hidden from historians. Improbability was inherent in both historicity and the HistoriCity.

In assessing Soviet military capabilities, one of the most important questions concerned the effectiveness of Soviet Air Defense. Prior to the shooting down of the U-2 piloted by Francis Gary Powers on May 1, 1960, Soviet surface-to-air missiles were thought ineffective at high altitudes. A healthy skepticism had prevailed ever since. Twenty-eight years and twenty-eight days later, Mathias Rust, an eighteen-year-old German sport pilot, made a much lower-level flight from Germany to the Soviet Union, following the train tracks from Leningrad to Moscow on his last leg. After circling the Kremlin several times, he landed his Cessna 172P on nearby Bolshoy Moskvoretsky Bridge, parking it adjacent to St. Basil's Cathedral. US Army, Europe RUMINT reported the US Air Forces in Europe briefly considered swapping out their General Dynamics F-16A Fighting Falcons F-16A's for Cessna 172P Skyhawks. An embarrassment for the Soviet Union, General Secretary Gorbachev skillfully used the incident as a pretext for replacing senior government officials opposed to his reform agenda.

Although I hadn't been monitoring the West Berlin art and music scene as closely as I had politico-military developments, exhibitions and concerts associated with the 750th anniversary of the first documented mention of Cölln (*Colonia*), sister-city of Berlin, assumed political as well as cultural importance. As part of the *ZEITGEIST* strategy to unseat Abstract Expressionism, the exhibition *BERLINART* opened at the Museum of Modern Art in New York on June 4. After closing on September 8, it "went west" to the San Francisco Museum of Modern Art, opening on October 22, 1987.

Coincident with the opening day of *BERLINART* in New York, the three-day "Concert for Berlin," sponsored by *RIAS2*, took place on the *Platz der Republik*, the former *Königsplatz*, directly in front of the *Porticus* of the *Reichstag, Schwerpunkt* of the HistoriCity. "*Dem Deutschen Volk.*" Former West Berliner David Bowie returned with his *Glass Spider* tour on Saturday, June 6, 1987. It was not a drilling weekend, so I joined the approximately 60,000 other attendees on the *Platz der Republik. RIAS 2*, reaching listeners in both West and East, received permission to broadcast the entire eighteen-hour show. A few of the concert producers apparently aimed some of the loudspeakers, like late twentieth-century shofar, in the direction of the Wall and East Berlin. At first, only a few hundred assembled on the far side of the Brandenburg Gate to listen. As hundreds grew into thousands, the state security presence increased. East Berliners listening to *John F. und die Gropiuslerchen* singing, "*Berlin, Berlin (dein Herz kennt keine Mauer)*"[69] on their *Sternrecorder R 4100* portable tape recorders joined the embedded recording of Willy Brandt in demanding "*die Mauer muss weg,*" called out "Gorbi, Gorbi," and sang the *Internationale.* Arrests were made and a riot broke out. David Bowie had visited East Berlin the day before. Convinced some of his fans there would be listening the next day, he decided to play for both Berlins. As he sang "Heroes," a video loop

---

69 "Berlin, Berlin (no Wall runs through your heart). . . the Wall must go!" trans. TV, citation is UNCLASSIFIED, US Army Reserve Military Intelligence Group (MIG) Europe. Detachment Two, Intelligence Information Report 6/87, Heidelberg, Germany, 1987.

documenting the tearful separation of *Berliner* by the Wall ran repeatedly on the screen behind the stage. In an interview, which I cited in the Intelligence Information Report for June 1987, Bowie referred to it as a double concert divided by the Wall. As Bowie descended, *deus ex machina*, seated in a chrome office chair at the opening of the concert, singing into a telephone, I was astonished by his uncanny resemblance to Robert Jones, my *Arlecchino Gesprächspartner*.

The same 750th anniversary celebration that deployed *BERLINART* to New York and San Francisco brought President Ronald Reagan back to Berlin on June 12. Although he did not meet with Secretary General Gorbachev, during his speech at the Brandenburg Gate, President Reagan did invite him to come to Berlin. DCSI organized tickets for the detachment. I thought again about calling Rainer but didn't. Even though we were seated well back from the presidential podium, we could see the presidential seal. We heard the president refer to the sea change taking place in Moscow and then make an unmistakable invitation, "There is one sign the Soviets can make that would be unmistakable. That would advance dramatically the cause of freedom and peace. General Secretary Gorbachev, if you seek peace, if you seek prosperity for the Soviet Union and Eastern Europe, if you seek liberalization come here to this gate. Mr. Gorbachev open this gate. Mr. Gorbachev, Mr. Gorbachev tear down this wall." We looked at each other in disbelief. President Reagan continued, referring to the widespread protests following the NATO counter-deployment decision, even mentioning the protests surrounding his last visit to West Berlin back in 1982. I hadn't heard from Rainer since I invited him to *Luise* and wondered if he were somewhere in the crowd today. What would he think about the president's invitation to the secretary general? The next day, approximately 100,000 people demonstrated peacefully on the *Hofgartenwiese* in *Berlin Nebenstelle*, Bonn, the German Capital, for the destruction of all atomic weapons. "*Atomwaffen verschrotten!*"

In August, I met Professor Jourdan within the walled *Pairidaeza* of the *Café Wellenstein* for our final working breakfast. The weather was perfect. After our arrival, DDr. Schmidt had two mélange, together with a bottle of cold Austrian *Qualitätsschaumwein*, served to our table. After reviewing my final chapter, Professor Jourdan approved the completed dissertation for submission to the *Holborn-Institut*. She would be my *Erstgutachter*. My *Zweitgutachter* would be retired US Ambassador Dr. Hubertus Spero, who, following the departure of Dr. Schneider, was the only remaining practitioner of the "open-door policy" at the *Lucius-D.-Clay-Institut*.

In mid-September, a USMLM team member was wounded in an incident near Neuruppin in the German Democratic Republic. Although the wound was not serious, the incident was, and once again, military liaison mission procedures were carefully rereviewed in renewed hope of preventing future incidents. In spite of the precautions, chance continued to play a critical part in the execution of these highly sensitive, essential missions.

After putting in cameo appearances in Geneva and Reykjavik, Clio, this time with historic document in hand, mused over the summit conference held between December 8 and 10, 1987, in Washington, DC, where the personal at last became political. Building upon the trust established at Geneva and enhanced at Reykjavik, Secretary General Gorbachev and President Reagan signed the Intermediate-Range Nuclear Forces (INF) Treaty, stipulating, "each Party shall eliminate its intermediate-range and shorter-range missiles." The INF Treaty signaled the scrapping of the SS-20s, the Ground-Launched Cruise Missiles, and the Pershing II missiles.

In January 1988, DCSI reported police in Lübeck, Germany, had taken a suspect in the *LaBelle* bombing into custody. She had ties to a Palestinian being held in connection with the bombing of the Arab-German Friendship Society in Berlin and his brother imprisoned in England. Although the press speculated on possible Syrian responsibility for the *LaBelle* bombing, communications intelligence had confirmed Libyan involvement. It would take her another two years, but Clio would eventually hand over the source documents.

After my dissertation on Clio, *Muse Militante: Geschichtswissenschaft an den Berliner Universitäten 1806–1986*, was accepted by the faculty of the *Holborn-Instutit*, I took oral examinations in my major field of contemporary history and my minor fields, North American studies and political science, receiving the degree *Doktor der Philosophie* on January 22nd. The following Sunday, the 274th birthday of Frederick the Great, I invited Professors Jourdan and Spero, George, Dr. Kahler, Johannes Festzelt, who had returned to the *Stadtstaatsarchiv, and Rainer* to join me at the large wooden table in the side room at *Luise* to celebrate. Only after passing my final oral late Friday afternoon did I call Kyra DeGetria to invite her to come up from Munich, realizing it very was short notice. There wasn't enough time for her to request Travel Orders and make a reservation on the Berlin Duty Train. She would have had to fly, and she had to be back in Munich early Monday morning to teach. She asked me for a rain check. I said, "of course!" and thought about asking her to bring her bottle of absinthe along but didn't. She would bring it along if she wanted to. Laura and André had returned to Washington with *les fauves*. Nadja was in Paris. Unfortunately, I'd lost touch with Sophia and Eddie from the Accidental *Polis* Seminar. Someone mentioned Sophia had received a DAAD scholarship. I wondered if she'd made it to Mr.

Henry's. Rainer, however, accepted my invitation, and I was very pleased to see him again. Almost four years had passed since we'd last seen each other. He apologized, confirming what I had suspected—my decision to join the reserves bothered him deeply. After we talked for a while, it seemed as if we'd last met at *Luise* only the week before. During the festivities, a soldier in civies arrived with an unclassified message from the Defense Language Institute for "Lieutenant Doktor Thomas Vonaechron, USAR." I wonder how D3 knew I'd passed my examinations on Friday and knew where we would celebrate on Sunday, but where else? D3's congratulatory message was in Russian, so I asked Rainer if he would translate it for me, which he did. Professor Jourdan, dressed once again in her elegant navy blue skirt-suit, told me she'd called Dr. Schneider Friday afternoon after receiving word I'd passed my final oral examination. He, too, sent his heartfelt congratulations on my *Promotion*, requesting a copy of my dissertation with *Widmung* once it had been printed. As a graduation gift, Professor Jourdan gave me a signed copy of her book, *Hausmanns Historicité*. "Although it's written in French, we've discussed Hausmann's Paris so often you should have little trouble understanding it, Dr. Vonaechron!"

Before congratulating me, Johannes turned to the portrait of Luise Auguste Wilhelmine Amalie presiding over the *Promotion* party and lifted his glass to her, and then, "To Thomas and to Frederick the Grape!" I was surprised to see he had unbuttoned the top button of his white dress shirt and loosened his thin black tie. In turn, I thanked Johannes for the original inspiration and his continuing unselfish assistance.

Turning to George I said, "George, my heartfelt thanks for your encouragement and assistance over these past years, in Washington and especially here in West Berlin. Without you, I'd probably still be sitting underground in Vault Six, wondering what it would be like to be in West Berlin. Let me see, we'd have been up to 1958 by now, yes, in 1958."

"An interesting year, Thomas, the Khrushchev Ultimatum of November 10 and the beginning of the first Berlin crisis!"

"Yes, but George, how much better it is to actually be in Berlin, to be here! I'll admit, a few years ago when I had my own personal 'Berlin Crisis,' I wasn't so sure, but with your many kindnesses and support, I made it through! Thank you again! That does remind me of something I've been meaning to ask you for some time, though. What happened to the beautiful angel on top of *Rathhaus Friedenau*? You know, the tall slender, silver blonde statue, with red halo, golden wings, and the palm frond in her hand that seemed to point in different directions, depending upon which side of the street you viewed it from. Is she being restored, regilded? When will the benevolent angel return to watch over spy-flecked West Berlin? I hope *Friedenau* intends to put her back where she belongs!"

"To the very best of my knowledge, Thomas, there's never been a statue of an angel on top of *Rathhaus Friedenau*. There is, however, an angel with a red halo and palm leaf displayed on Friedenau's, *Wappen*, ah . . . coat of arms, but not on top of the *Rathhaus*. I think there's only an iron *Blitzableiter* on top, what's the word, a 'lightning rod.'"

"Are you certain?"

"Yes, but I'd be happy to check for you. Better yet, now that you have more time, you could even come back to the *Stadtstaatsarchiv* and check yourself. Johannes will be working at the archives for another week or so, so you could join us again for lunch in the *Kantine*." Enrolled as a student at the Free University only until September, the end of *Sommersemester* 1988, it was time to make preparations for my postgraduate life, a possible return to Washington, DC, and the National Archives. Almost five years had passed since I entered the *FU* in *Sommersemester* 1983. By some happy historical coincidence, though my dissertation-related research and writing had now come to an end, there was an increase in Intelligence Information Report requirements. Holding fast to my now proven routine of sleep, mediation, and moderation, as additional training funds became available to US Army Reserve Europe, I spent an increasing amount of time sifting through sources and preparing IIRs and summaries in the basement of Building Three. Clio kept me busy. On February 8, 1988, Secretary General Gorbachev released a statement announcing the withdrawal of Soviet troops from Afghanistan beginning on May 15, 1988.

In March, as a consequence of the 1971–72 Quadripartite Agreement on Berlin, an exchange of land between West Berlin and East Germany redrew the jagged boundary separating East from West Berlin. The "*Lenné*-Triangle," a thorn in the western side of the Wall where Erich Mendelssohn's *Columbushaus* once stood, belonged to East Berlin. The government of the German Democratic Republic agreed to exchange it for three exclaves, an additional strip of land belonging to West Berlin, and a payment of 76 million marks. Before the date set for the exchange, the triangle was occupied by squatters who renamed it "Kubat-Triangle" and erected a tent city. Prevented from intervening before the agreement came into effect on July 1, West Berlin police cleared the tents under the watchful eyes of East German border guards. Many of the squatters climbed over the Wall into East Berlin, where they were given breakfast and returned to the West. Two months later in Kreuzberg and Neukölln in the American Sector, the *Autonomen* struck back in anger with the *Revolutionäre 1. Mai Demonstration*. One-hundred-thirty-four of the approximately 6,000 participants were arrested. One hundred people were injured; just over half were police officers.

President Reagan and Secretary General Gorbachev met again in Moscow for their fourth summit conference in late May 29 and early June 1988 to finalize the Intermediate Nuclear Forces Agreement, ratified in the meantime by the US Senate. They released a joint statement mapping out the progress made during the four previous summit meetings. "The President and the Secretary General underscored the historic importance of the meetings in Geneva, Reykjavik, Washington, and Moscow in laying the foundation for a realistic approach to the problems of strengthening stability and reducing the risk of conflict. They reaffirmed their conviction that a nuclear war cannot be won and must never be fought, their determination to prevent war between the United States and the Soviet Union, whether nuclear or conventional, and their disavowal of any intention to achieve military superiority." The unfortunate death of a member of the US Military Liaison Mission shortly after Secretary General Gorbachev assumed office had made an initial, critical contribution to "reducing the risk of conflict" at the highest levels.

Out Along the Watchtowers
June 1988

On Monday June 6, 1988, D-Day, D3 called to tell me he was returning to Berlin as chief of mission, US Military Liaison Mission. I hadn't heard from him in a while and had the feeling something was up. Although I expected he would be returning to Europe following his year of intensive Russian at the Defense Language Institute in Monterey, he caught me by surprise. "How'd ya like to get out of the basement of Building Three and move into the Mission, Thomas?"

"Aren't USMLM billets usually filled with regular army officers, D3?"

"Yes, but just because there haven't been any US Army reserve officers with USMLM in the past doesn't mean there can't be an exception. We have an opening for an 0-2, and there isn't a "FAO," a foreign area officer, available right now. On the way from Monterey—and by the way, Thomas, I couldn't just resist 'Kerouac-ing' it back from California to DC, rereading *On the Road* on the road, Rainer would've enjoyed it—I stopped by the Army Reserve Personnel Command in St. Louis to make myself smart. We could set up an IMA, an individual mobilization augmentee billet, within USMLM and, if you're interested, have you transferred into it from the MIG. This way, the MIG would retain the Berlin Detachment billet you occupy. Following your transfer, I'd request an active duty assignment for twelve months with an option to extend for twelve more. This would take you through to June 1990. To be honest, Thomas, if you weren't finished, I wouldn't even suggest it, but since you have, I thought you might enjoy a little active duty time before returning to the National Archives or whatever you decide to do next. One of your duties would of course be preparation of the annual 'Unit History, United States Military Liaison Mission to Commander in Chief, Group of Soviet Forces in Germany.' Why, USMLM is just makin' history every day, Thomas, and besides, we need keep those NARSians down in Vault Six busy! Just think of all the fun you could have twenty years from now, reviewing your own work back underground at, what was it again, at WNRC!"

D3's offer sounded good. Again, I was genuinely touched by all the effort he'd gone to. Although I'd sent out preliminary inquiries to the National Archives, Library of Congress, and even to the Smithsonian about available positions, I hadn't made any definitive plans, and summer semester, along with my student status, would be over in three months. Without taking time to meditate on it, I answered, "Approved!" In July, I received orders for my transfer from the United States Army Reserve Military Intelligence Group, Europe, to the United States Military Liaison Mission Berlin, and the following month, notification of my twelve-month deployment. Once again, D3 had greased the skids. With the transfer came an exchange of shoulder sleeve insignia, Seventh Army Reserve Command for USMLM Potsdam, a variation on the US Army, Europe SSI, a shield with the American flag covering the flaming sword under the rainbow, identifying me as a member of the "United States Military Liaison Mission Potsdam."

As a member of Detachment Two, US Army Reserve Military Intelligence Group Europe, West Berlin had been the coign of vantage from which I'd observed and analyzed current events in Germany and Central Europe. As a member of the US Military Liaison Mission, I'd be observing those events from the other side of the Wall in the German Democratic Republic. West Berlin still remained my personal *Schwerpunkt*, but my professional activities would now take place outside of the accidental *polis* instead of within it, extramural vice intramural, a different perspective on "wall-gazing." Perhaps wisdom would come with passive intelligence collection as we toured East Germany. Although the Shield was coincidentally equipped with the same *Blaupunkt* radio and cassette player as Rainer's taxi, we rarely made use of it as Rainer and I had within well-walled West Berlin. Without well-walled West Berlin, we listened closely to the natural sounds of the surrounding countryside and the unnatural sounds emanating from the tree-lined Red Army training areas.

D3 found my concept of 'PIC-*kuan*' amusing and intriguing, and wanted to learn more about *pi-kuan*. One Tuesday evening after work, we stopped by Govinda's "Happy-*Bude*." After wall-gazing, D3 and Govinda entered into a lively discussion of classical Chinese thinking on military operations, strategy, and the use of intelligence. Govinda was surprised and pleased to hear D3 recite from chapter 31 of Lao-Tzu's *Tao Te Ching* from memory: "Now arms, however beautiful, are instruments of evil omen, hateful, it may be said to all creatures. Therefore they who have the Tao do not like to employ them. . . . Those sharp weapons are instruments of evil omen, and not the instruments of the superior man—he uses them only on the compulsion of necessity."

In response to Govinda's question about the purpose of the USMLM, D3 provided a brief, albeit unclassified overview of the history and activities of the Mission, including our tours through the German Democratic Republic. Using D3 as my straight man, I told Govinda about my substitution of "PIC-kuan" for *pi-kuan*. "Ha ha! There is wisdom in your wordplay, Thomas. Not bad for a Zen-Methodist!" Turning to D3 he said, "It sounds very much to me D3, that as you carry the Shield of Achilles, you also carry Bodhidharma's Sword of Wisdom." It was now D3's turn to be surprised, as Govinda was equally well versed in *The Art of War*. "Sun Tzu teaches, 'In an intense strategy, where one may face the other for a long time without engaging and without retreating, careful observations are essential.'" Smiling and nodding in agreement, D3 said, "Now I understand why Thomas always looks forward to 'wall-gazing' with you on Tuesdays and Thursdays, Govinda."

"But you two guys are wall-gazing, too, D3, from the other side, from the far side, from the outside. Here in the Happy-*Bude* we practice *zazen*, sitting Zen. You and Thomas are practicing 'driving Zen,' ha ha! As you both know, it is a very privileged position and may lead to enlightenment. Bodhidharma teaches, if we strive to abandon what is false and return to what is true through pure contemplation, through 'wall-gazing,' through *pi-kuan*, we will come to realize that there is neither self nor other, that there is a unity between the governors and governed, and that what is holy and what is profane are essentially the same. If we can hold to this belief, we will not become slaves to any doctrine, as we will be enlightened directly by reason and freed from all conceptual discrimination, enjoying both serenity and spontaneity. As I understand Bodhidharma's teaching, the wall is not necessarily a wall in the concrete sense of the word, but rather a device which serves to focus and inform our meditation. Although our life in West

Berlin is circumscribed by a Wall, we rarely meditate or reflect upon it, only when travelling to and from West Germany. While preserving the freedom of those living within it, the Wall poses an obstacle to freedom for those living without, in East Germany. Someday, the Wall might become a way, perhaps the Way to freedom. As a student of Sun Tzu and Lao-Tzu, you're heartily welcome to join us here in the Happy-*Bude*, or at the Buddhist temple in the Botanical Gardens, anytime you like, D3!"

In July, D3 and I joined observers from nineteen other member states of the Organization for Security and Cooperation in Europe, OSCE, to observe a combined exercise of the Group of Soviet Forces in Germany and the National People's Army of the German Democratic Republic. As the *Übung* was held at a training area just outside of Potsdam, we didn't have far to go. After returning to the Mission, D3 handed me a classified (*Streng geheim!*) translation of General Defense Plan 33001, prepared and distributed by the *Ministerium für Staatssicherheit*, the *Stasi*. The (SECRET/NATO SECRET) operational plan set out in meticulous detail the mission and functions of the US V Army Corps, guardian of the Fulda Gap, in the event of hostilities. "Surprised, Thomas? Well, we're certain the Warsaw Pact has copies of pretty much all NATO OPLANS. Our American boss, the Commander-in-chief US Army, Europe, and his boss the Commander-in-Chief, U.S. European Command, who as you know is also 'dual-hatted' as the Supreme Allied Commander Europe, want it that way. If they tell their Soviet counterparts our OPLANS are purely defensive, the Soviets won't believe them. But if the very same information comes from Soviet or East German intelligence sources, they do. So you see in this way, spies often serve a useful, if unintended function. You'll be interested to know over the past few years, the Group of Soviet Forces in East Germany has been incrementally mirroring our defensive posture in the West Germany, a pretty effective means of making certain NATO understands the defensive nature of Warsaw Pact planning.

On September 1, the forty-ninth anniversary of the German invasion of Poland, D3 and I drove down to *Waldheide* near Heilbronn in the Shield to observe the first removal of Pershing-IIs from West Germany. In addition to the commanding officer, staff and soldiers of the Third Battalion, Eighty-Fourth Field Artillery Regiment, German policemen, and reporters, there was a Soviet contingent verifying that all provisions of the Intermediate Nuclear Forces agreement were rigidly adhered to, assisted by our counterparts from the Soviet Military Liaison Mission. After exchanging pleasantries in Russian, D3 turned to me and said, "It's truly an historic occasion, Thomas, a victory for all the Sun Tzu soldiers, East and West!

On the forty-seventh anniversary of the Japanese attack on Pearl Harbor, President and Secretary General Mikhail Gorbachev surprised the US Military Liaison Mission in Potsdam along with the United Nations General Assembly in New York.

Today I can inform you of the following: The Soviet Union has made a decision on reducing its armed forces. In the next two years, their numerical strength will be reduced by 500,000 persons and the volume of conventional arms will also be cut considerably. These reductions will be made on a unilateral basis, unconnected with negotiations on the mandate for the Vienna meeting. By agreement with our allies in the Warsaw Pact, we have made the decision to withdraw six tank divisions from the GDR, Czechoslovakia, and Hungary and disband them by 1991. Assault landing formations and units, and a number of others, including assault river-crossing forces, with their armaments and combat equipment, will also be withdrawn from the groups of Soviet forces situated in those countries. The Soviet forces situated in those countries will be cut by 50,000 persons, and their arms by 5,000 tanks. All remaining Soviet divisions on the territory of our allies will be reorganized. They will be given a different structure from today's which will become unambiguously defensive, after the removal of a large number of their tanks.

Later that afternoon, he met with President Reagan and President-elect George H. W. Bush, the vice president, on nearby Governor's Island for their final summit. President Gorbachev had hoped to use the momentum generated by his speech to make further progress in arms reduction and to establish the necessary personal relationship with the incoming president. Rather than discuss any new initiatives however, President Reagan used the meeting to commemorate the achievements of their previous summits, while the vice-president-cum-president-elect said he would need "a little time" to review the issues.

D3 and I watched President Gorbachev's speech on C-SPAN at the Mission. "Unbelievable, D3, that was simply unbelievable! Secretary General Gorbachev just put the 'UN' in both unilateral troop reductions and the UN. It looks like we might be out of a job in the not-too-distant future. There won't be much of a Soviet Group of Forces to liaise with after the withdrawal."

"It's working, Thomas, it's working! For almost forty years now, our forces have been trained and ready, but they remained committed to defense IAW, the original North Atlantic Council instructions to establish, how does it go again, I should know, I've briefed it enough times, an 'integrated force under a centralized command, adequate to deter aggression and ensure the defense of Western Europe.' Defense is the key word here. Our forces are trained and ready to defend Western Europe, not to invade Eastern Europe and the Soviet Union."

❦

Clio Reopens the Great Doors of History
January 1989

Enraged by Franklin Delano Roosevelt's election to a fourth term in November 1944, the Republican-controlled Eightieth Congress passed the Twenty-Second Amendment to the Constitution of the United States, limiting the president to two terms. As a consequence, President Reagan's vice president was elected in his stead and sworn in as president of the United States on January 20, 1989. The new president did not embrace the changes taking place in the international security environment as readily as his predecessor had. Although his overcautious advisors and conservative supporters may have slowed the march of history somewhat, they could not put the *Weltgeist* back in the bottle. Fortunately, Clio was operating outside of their span of control. Together with the Luddites in his administration, the new president began "Withering into History."

Resistance to the changes taking place in the Soviet Union was perhaps nowhere more apparent in the Warsaw Pact nations than in the USMLM area of responsibility, East Germany, the German Democratic Republic. The day before the inauguration of the new president of the United States, Erich Honecker, general secretary of the Socialist Unity Party, defended the Wall, predicting it would *"in 50 und auch noch in 100 Jahren bestehen bleiben, wenn die dazu vorhandenden Gründe noch nicht beseitigt sind."*[70] Although USMLM did not see it coming, the Wall and Erich Honecker would both be *beseitigt*, be set aside by the end of 1989. In the meantime, it continued to pose a deadly threat to those disenchanted *DDR* citizens determined to defect. During the night of February 5, twenty-year-old Chris Gueffroy successfully surmounted the Wall but was shot and killed while trying to breach the metal security fence on the far side. Between 1961 and 1989, at least 140 lives were taken at the Wall.

The last Soviet troops departed Afghanistan in mid-February; the following month, conventional force reduction talks began in Vienna.

---

70 "in fifty and even in one hundred years remain standing, if the reasons for its construction have not been set aside." trans. TV, citation is UNCLASSIFIED, US Military Liaison Mission Situation Report (SITREP), 20 January 1989, Heidelberg, Germany.

401

❦

While compiling daily situation reports with the British and French liaison missions, and monthly Intelligence Information Reports, based upon our ground, air, naval, and technical collection activities, I was also, per D3's tasking, preparing the 1988 unit history for submission to the Commander-in-Chief, U.S. Army, Europe in April. "Don't worry about drafting up an introduction for my signature," he told me, smiling, "given the historical, no given the 'world historical' significance of last year's events, I just can't resist writing it myself." After tasking, compiling, correcting, and formatting the unit history, I sat at my desk in the *Föhrenweg* looking at the cover, which carried the colorful USMLM Potsdam shoulder sleeve insignia.

UNIT HISTORY (U)
UNITED STATES MILITARY LIAISON MISSION
TO THE COMMANDER IN CHIEF
GROUP OF SOVIET FORCES IN GERMANY
1988

I smiled, thinking again about the USMLM unit histories covering the years 1947 to 1954 I'd reviewed for declassification in Vault Six ten years ago—a decade. If the current declassification guidelines remained in place, this report could be reviewed for declassification in 2008. Who would review it? Would she or he also wish to be in Berlin, in the HistoriCity? Well, in accordance with conventional army wisdom, I got my wish. When I hand-carried the history *sans* introduction into D3's office, he said, "Do you have a few minutes, Thomas? Please sit down." He reached into his desk drawer and pulled out a document. As he handed it to me, I could see it was the introduction. "Now read through it carefully and tell me what you think. Remember when we first met in Dr. Schneider's Accidental *Polis* Seminar, we were *Komillitonen*, so I'm relying upon you for straight feedback. Would you like a cup of coffee to go with it? It might make my prose easier to swallow, yuck, yuck, yuck!" Taking one of the intentionally unwashed coffee cups from the shelf behind his desk, D3 went to the mess to get coffee while I read his introduction.

1988 was one of those remarkable years in which, if you were to listen closely, you could hear the great doors of history creaking upon their hinges. Listen:
As we thought, as we hoped change would be coming, we began to prepare for a time when liaison would again be a regular part of our mission, as well as part of our name. There were indications

in Moscow and in Washington, the cities from which change had to come from. In Moscow, Soviet periodicals published evidence George Kennan had been right. In the July 1947 issue of *Foreign Affairs*, the same year USMLM was established, Kennan wrote, "the main element of any United States policy toward the Soviet Union must be that of a long-term, patient but firm and vigilant containment of Russian expansive tendencies." Contained, or perhaps simply exhausted by fruitless expansion, the Soviet Union underwent accelerated change. In Washington, personnel departures and consequent attitude shifts brought the hope that when the other side finally quit fighting the Cold War, we just might quit, too.

Here in Potsdam, the great doors of history creaked twice. On 14 June, the Soviet Defense Minister apologized to the US Secretary of Defense for the March 1985 shooting death of our colleague, catching both USAREUR and GSFG totally unprepared. The very pregnant pause made us wonder if anyone knew what to do after so much blind, accusatory confrontation. Then came the 6 July meeting between Marshal Sergei Akhromeyev, Chief of the Soviet General Staff and Admiral William Crowe, Chairman of the Joint Chiefs of Staff in the Pentagon. The very first action item on their list of a two-year military exchange program was a meeting between the Commander-in-Chief, US Army, Europe and Seventh Army, and the Commander-in-Chief, Group of Soviet Forces Germany. Suddenly, USMLM was back in the liaison business again, cooperating with our Soviet counterparts to make things happen for a change instead of attacking or defending what had already happened. The second creak, perhaps even a crack, came on 7 December, when Secretary General Gorbachev stunned the UN, the US, the USMLM, and, apparently most of all, HQ GSFG with his announcement of withdrawal and reorganization. We searched for our *raison d'être* here too, finding it as Dutch uncle, elicitor, friend of the court, and honest broker, if not as an invited witness to the historical event.

The great doors, slammed shut in December 1979 by the invasion of Afghanistan and bolted in 1985 by the major's tragic death, suddenly opened again. We renewed broader contacts with the Soviets. After years of driving by his garrisons, we invited the Potsdam Artillery Division commander for Thanksgiving dinner. For good measure, we also invited the Russian Orthodox priest from the Church of St. Alexander Nevsky in Potsdam to say grace together with the Berlin Catholic chaplain. The renovated Torgau Room in Potsdam House, previously used as a portrait studio for US guests to have their pictures taken in front of the crossed American and Soviet flags, saw the chiefs of staff of USAREUR and GSFG sit down together at the round marble-top table. Liaison officers who usually only spoke with Soviets while being detained, interpreted between US and Soviet guests. Potsdam House, looking after extensive restoration like Sleeping Beauty's enchanted palace, was kissed by Clio and suddenly awakened. Liaison was once again alive, exciting, and interesting.

In the meantime, the other mission of the Mission continued. The stories of the ground, air, naval, and technical collection activities are all told in this history. They did their job well. The Director of Central Intelligence visited us, presenting USMLM with an "Outstanding Collector's Award" for 1987. Early in 1989, we were told we had earned it once again in 1988. It was a team effort. No one person or division made a spectacular diving catch in center field, like the one made back in 1983. It might be worth noting here the individual who made that catch is now a member of our team. The 1988 award was for smart targeting, aggressive collection, painstaking processing, and timely reporting, all backed up by dedicated if oftentimes unsung support. So while we had some star players, 1988 was a team year.

And through the crack in the great doors of history, we might have seen something of our own future in ongoing, expanded liaison opportunities—seeds sown during the CINC visit and Thanksgiving in 1988 are already sprouting in mid-1989. When the Conventional Arms Control teams do deploy to Europe, USMLM expertise will likely be called upon to develop and refine verification procedures. In any event, until all forces have departed, the headquarters of those forces will remain, and the remaining headquarters must communicate with one another. They must see each other as clearly as possible, without misperceptions. Consequently, I'm convinced there will be a continuing role for all the military liaison missions until the last handshake of the last commanding generals.

To have been Chief of Mission with the men and women of USLM during this year of fundamental, historical change and proven professional achievement was a privilege, a pleasure, and a most kind gift of Providence.

DWIGHT DAVID DURCHSCHOUER
COLONEL, GENERAL STAFF
CHIEF OF MISSION

"I like it Colonel …"

"D3, please."

"I like it, D3, I like it very much! Many thanks for the coffee by the way. 'The great doors of history creaking upon their hinges … through the crack in the great doors of history!' You've done a particularly good job of describing the effect the larger sea change taking place between Moscow and Washington has had upon USMLM, as well as highlighting the joint successes of our collection missions. You offer constructive criticism of the past and a positive way ahead for the future, which will hopefully be well taken by headquarters. Furthermore, you've done all of this in your own voice. Maybe that's what I like most about the introduction, it's you, D3! 'Kissed by Clio' is great, and I'm personally grateful to you for the honorable mention. I'll have to take a look at that '83 unit history again. You know, D3, I'd be happy to change 'happy' to 'glad' for you if you want me to, but I honestly don't think it's necessary. Oh, and here's the smooth draft of the rest of the unit history." I handed the introduction back to D3, along with my draft. He slipped the introduction neatly underneath the cover, placing the history carefully into the inbox on his desk.

"Thanks, Thomas. I'll read it through when we've finished, sign off on it, and send it off to Heidelberg in the morning in time for the April suspense date. Hopefully, the 1988 unit history will eventually make its way from Heidelberg all the way across the Atlantic to the National Archives, to WNRC. Our contribution to the historical record."

"You know, D3, while compiling the daily situation reports, the monthly Intelligence Information Reports and the unit history, it often occurs to me these documents reflect things as we saw them, based upon the sources available to us. Writing is also a selection process, and creativity is called for. Von Ranke writes about the creativity required to distill the *'leitende Ideen,'* the 'leading ideas' from the sources available. Let's imagine our USMLM reports do make it back to WNRC, and that in 20 years they will be reviewed, declassified, and made available for research. They will be considered 'primary sources,' *Quellen* as von Ranke understood them. But does the fact the information is contained in a historical document make it 'the Truth' or truthful, or is it just well-informed opinion? Gee D3, maybe Mr. Peabody was right after all. Any explanation found in recorded, in written History is questionable and oftentimes 'improbable!'"

Laughing, D3 pushed his chair back from his desk and, leaning back against the wall, said, "Don't be so dog-matic, General Sherman! Whether or not Mr. Peabody's right, and I do tend to agree with him, Clio must be pursued. But let's take it even a step further. If someone were so inclined to do so, she or he could insert an 'invisible hand' into history, where none actually existed, intentionally turning away from '*wie es eigentlich gewesen*' by creatively selecting sources, or even falsifying sources, to support decisions taken at a particular point in time. And from fake sources, historians write either intentionally or unintentionally, fake history! But given our professional training, the breadth and depth of the sources available to us, both classified and unclassified, I'd say overall we've done a pretty fair job."

"OK, D3. For the record, let's say we've done as best as we can. In the army, we often talk about a 'lesson learned' when referring to past military operations and the operational use of history. What did we learn from the First and Second World Wars? The importance of collective security? What are we learning from the Cold War? Does Private Love, your 'Sun Tzu Soldier' in the Headquarters Building, offer a useful lesson on deterrence? Waybac, when we began our Accidental *Polis* Seminar at the Clay Institute, Johannes Festzelt—remember Johannes from the *Stadtstaatsarchiv*?—he recommended I read Hegel's *Lectures on the Philosophy of History*. Before discussing the histories of China, Greece, Rome, and Europe, Hegel offers a disturbing conclusion, "What experience and History teach is, that nations and governments have never acted upon the lessons learned from experience and History!""

D3 nodded and said, "Out at the School for Advanced Military Studies in Leavenworth, we came to the conclusion that our army usually fights the last war. But at least from the standpoint of military history, I would submit to you that an effort is being made to learn—for example, from our involvement in Vietnam. Hmm, maybe that's just wishful thinking on my part. But whether those lessons are acted upon, well that's up to the policy makers, not to the military. We're just one tool in their toolbox. In any case, it certainly is a sobering thought, Thomas, and I guess we'll just have to wait and see while hoping for the best."

Looking up at the ceiling, D3 paused for a moment, then said, "As you know, for some time now, I've had the feeling something's in the air, I just didn't realize the historical magnitude of it. It truly is a sea change, into something 'rich and strange.' That's precisely why I wanted to come back to Berlin, back to the Mission and to Potsdam House. USMLM is the perfect place to watch it happen. You know, the USAREUR liaison officer at the embassy in Bonn, Colonel Schumann, told me our new ambassador to the Federal Republic, General Vernon Walters, told his deputy chief of mission it was a good time to be in Germany as the Wall was going to come down this year! The DCM thinks the new ambassador is crazy, and I must admit, it does sound somewhat far-fetched, but still there's something to it. General Walters has been around for a long time; he's seen a lot. He served as an interpreter for Presidents Truman and Eisenhower and, as you might remember, he was the one who told Vice President Nixon the protestors in Caracas were throwing rocks waybac in 1958! Walters seems to have an uncanny feeling, not just for flying rocks in Venezuela, but for the larger tectonic shifts in the international security environment, which, more often than not, political appointees plucked from positions law firms and industry do not."

In early May, Hungary shut down and began to dismantle the electric fence running along the 240-kilometer-long border with Austria. Although the number of Hungarian border patrols was consequently increased, the stage was being set for the deconstruction of the German Democratic Republic. Walls were coming down while we gazed, PIC-*kuan*! Within the GDR itself, popular protest was catalyzed by the revelation of election fraud in local elections. At the end of the month, D3 dropped a copy of a report on my desk. "I think you'll find this report 'ver-r-ry inter-r-resting,' Thomas—courtesy of our Soviet colleagues, by the way. You might want to consider appending it to the 1989 unit history. It's going to be quite a history by the way—how 'bout *Cold War and Peace* for a title? As you suggested after Gorbachev's UN speech, one of these days, USMLM is going to be history, and we want to make certain the historical record is complete!" The seven-page report entitled, "*Politische-operative Situation im Objekt der US-Militärverbindungsmission—Monate März / April 1989*" was dated May 22, 1989—not even a week old! It had been prepared in Potsdam by *Hauptabteilung VIII, Abteilung 5, Referat 5*, and it contained a circumstantial account of the comings and goings in Potsdam House, from the Ministry of State Security perspective, courtesy of the Local National and USMLM personnel!

In addition to monitoring events in Central Europe, we closely followed the student-led demonstrations on Tiananmen Square in Beijing, where the Statue of Liberty briefly lifted her lamp over the People's Republic of China. On June 4, less than a week after the protest on the *Platz des Himmlischen Friedens* was brutally suppressed by military force, the People's Chamber of the German Democratic Republic expressed its solidarity with the government of the People's Republic of China, reaffirming the right of the government "*Ordnung und Sicherheit unter Einsatz bewaffneter Kräfte wiederherzustellen.*"[71] This official pronouncement hinted at the frightening possibility of a "Chinese Solution" under similar circumstances in the German Democratic Republic, inspiring the "*Keine Gewalt,*" "No Violence," mantra of the East German opposition.

---

71 "to restore order and security through the use of armed force." trans. TV., citation is UNCLASSIFIED, US Military Liaison Mission Situation Report (SITREP), June 4, 1989, Heidelberg, Germany.

President Gorbachev was enthusiastically received when he arrived for his first state visit in the German Capital, *Berlin Nebenstelle*, in mid-June. He reacted positively to President Bush's proposal to reduce conventional forces stationed in Europe. He also replied to the statement Erich Honecker made about the Wall at the beginning of the year, "*Die Mauer kann wieder verschwinden, wenn die Voraussetzungen entfallen, die sie hervorgebracht haben.*"[72] Apparently, we weren't the only ones "wall-gazing."

Although registered as a political demonstration, West Berlin's first "Love Parade" was something else. On the first of July, a Saturday, I was sitting under an umbrella in a light rain on the terrace of the Kant Café in Charlottenburg, British Sector, rereading Wolfgang Borchert's reflections on returning from the war, *Im Mai, im Mai schrie der Kuckuk*: "*...das ist die neue, die großartige Stadt, in der sich alle hören und sehen und in der alle verstehen: mon coeur, the night, your heart, the day, der Tag, die Nacht, das Herz.*"[73] Hearing a cacophony of joyous, sensuous voices close by, I looked up from Borchert to see a group of exotically, erotically dressed women and men walking down *Schlüterstraße* in the direction of the *Kufürstendamm*. My waitress, *draußen vor der Tür* of the café, was standing next to my table under the umbrella watching. I paid my bill, placed Borchert carefully back into my backpack, and joined the parade. On the *Ku'damm*, cordoned off by the police for the event, officially a peace demonstration, we joined a larger parade of partygoers coming from the direction of *Wittenbergplatz*. It was fascinating to see a subset of *West Berliner* who only came out at night, dancing ecstatically in the daylight to techno music coming from large speakers mounted on Volkswagen buses and rented trucks, united by the rallying cry of "*Teknoidz*" under the peaceful banner of "*Friede, Freude, Eierkuchen—Peace, Joy, Pancakes.*" One float used stacked speakers to display the German flag. Following the parade, I decided not to dry out at the afterparty at the UFO (Acid House) but returned to *Mohnstraße* to reread Borchert. Perhaps it was just another one of those happy West Berlin coincidences, but somehow the Love Parade seemed to herald Borchert's vision of "the new city, the sublime city, where everyone listens and everyone sees, where everyone understands: my heart, the night, your heart, the day, the night, the heart." I wished he'd lived to see it.

This spirit of peace and festivity seemed to spread throughout Central Europe. After the foreign ministers of Hungary and Austria officially

72 "The Wall can disappear when the conditions which brought it about also disappear." trans. TV., citation is UNCLASSIFIED, US Military Liaison Mission Situation Report (SITREP), 15 June 1989, Heidelberg, Germany.
73 *In May, in May, the Cuckoo Cried*: "That is the new, the sublime city, where everyone listens, where everyone sees, where everyone understands: my heart, the night, your heart, the day, the night, the heart." Diary of Thomas Vonaechron, Diary Extract, 1989, trans. TV.

cut through the barbed wire border separating their two countries, Otto von Habsburg, His Imperial and Royal Highness, the Crown Prince of Austria, Hungary, Bohemia, and Croatia, helped sponsor a *Paneuropäissches Picknick* near Sopron in August, perhaps privately hoping for a spontaneous restoration of the Austro-Hungarian Empire. To mark the historic occasion, authorities in Hungary and Austria opened their common border for three hours. USMLM learned the picnic had been conceived not only symbolically but also politically, as a test to determine Soviet reaction to the opening of the border. The picnic had been widely advertised throughout Central Europe and during those three hours of free movement, seven hundred citizens of the GDR took the opportunity to pass through Hungary to Austria and on to the Federal Republic, the largest escape since the Wall was constructed in 1961.

Other citizens of the German Democratic Republic sought refuge in the embassies of the Federal Republic of Germany in Budapest, Prague, and Warsaw, which were forced to close down. Between September 10 and 11, Hungary once again opened its borders, this time on behalf of the citizens of East Germany. Thirty thousand took the opportunity to immigrate to West Germany. At the end of September, West German Foreign Minister Genschmann obtained permission for those citizens of the German Democratic Republic taking refuge in the embassies of the Federal Republic to leave. Based upon German sources, USMLM estimated approximately 7,000 people left the West German Embassy in Prague for West Germany.

Those who chose to remain in East Germany continued to agitate for change. The first Monday Demonstration, followed by a *Friedensgebet* in the *Nikolaikirche*, was held in Leipzig on September 4, 1989. Two weeks later, on September 25, USMLM reported approximately 5,000 protestors, on October 2, 20,000, and on October 9, 70,000. Recalling the statement of solidarity given by the government of the GDR to the government of the PRC sanctioning the use of military force, USMLM watched demonstrators shouting, "*Wir sind das Volk*—We are the People," calling for "*keine Gewalt—No Violence*," with *grenzenlose* admiration and growing apprehension. Three days earlier, President Gorbachev had arrived in East Berlin to commemorate the fortieth anniversary of the German Democratic Republic with a warning for the East German leadership: "*Wer zu spät kommt, den bestraft das Leben.*"[74] On Monday, October 16, USMLM reported approximately 120,000 demonstrators in the streets of Leipzig. Two days later, during the ninth meeting of the Central Committee of the

---

74 "Life will punish those who come too late," trans. TV, citation is UNCLASSIFIED, US Military Liaison Mission Situation Report (SITREP), 7 October 1989, Heidelberg, Germany.

Socialist Unity Party, Erich Honecker was relieved of all his offices and usurped by his deputy, Egon Krenz, as General Secretary of the Central Committee of the Socialist Unity Party. General Secretary Krenz also assumed Honecker's position as Chairman of the Council of State and Chairman of the National Defense Council. "*Et tu, Brute!*" On Saturday, November 4, USMLM estimated between 500,000 and one million protestors met on *Alexanderplatz* in East Berlin, the largest protest since the 1953 uprising, demonstrating for democratic reform and against the Socialist Unity Party. Photographs accompanying the reports of USMLM tours to Leipzig and Berlin were no longer black-and-white exposures of Soviet military vehicles and installations but color pictures of "*Das Volk.*" As I wrote up the intelligence summaries and Intelligence Information Reports, I made duplicate copies, packaging them for classified shipment to the National Archives in Washington, DC. At the tenth meeting of the Central Committee, the government and *Politbüro* of the German Democratic Republic resigned, though Egon Krenz remained Secretary General. The Socialist Unity Party also recognized the legality of *Neues Forum*, an independent political movement.

Things were happening so quickly, it was a challenge for us to monitor and prioritize events. USMLM's immediate concern was the effect the widespread peaceful protest might have on Soviet forces stationed throughout the German Democratic Republic. As a "Wall-gazer," *intra murum* and *extra murum*, my primary focus remained the Wall. On Thursday, November 9, D3 and I were watching television at the Mission, where we'd been following the sea change sweeping across Eastern and Central Europe. At 18:57, in response to a reporter's question about when citizens of the GDR would be allowed to travel legally to the FRG and West Berlin, *Politbüro* spokesman Günter Schabowski offered an improvisation that proved as consequential for Clio and for German history as Phillip Scheidemann's in 1918, "*Das trifft nach meiner Kenntnis . . . ist das sofort . . . unverzüglich.*"[75] Vaulting forward out of his chair, D3 ran to the Operations Center and ordered a USMLM tour to East Berlin to observe the border crossing points from the far side. "C'mon Thomas, let's take the Shield up to Checkpoint Charlie and see what's going on." It was quiet when we arrived. We waited inside the shack with the MPs for an hour or so, then drove over to the Allied Control Council Building at Kleist Park. D3 wanted to check in with the US element chief of the Berlin Air Safety Center, an Air Force colonel. "As you know better than I, Thomas, BASC has been in continuous

75 "To the best of my knowledge . . . it is effective at once . . . immediately," trans. TV, citation is UNCLASSIFIED, US Military Liaison Mission Situation Report (SITREP), 9 October 1989, Heidelberg, Germany.

operation since the end of the war, throughout the Berlin Airlift. In spite of the Cold War, there's quite a relaxed working atmosphere, and BASC occasionally serves as an informal channel of communication among the former wartime Allies. Let's ask the good colonel if he's heard anything." Welcoming us to the BASC operations room, Colonel Bill Branum told us shortly after the announcement was made, the Soviet major on duty walked over to his American counterpart, saluted, which was "quite unusual" given the casual working environment, and said, "Please tell the Supreme Allied Commander we will stay in our barracks." BASC immediately passed this information to US Command Berlin, who expedited it up the chain of command through Headquarters, US Army, Europe in Heidelberg, to Headquarters, US European Command, in Stuttgart-Vaihingen. From Stuttgart, the Soviet major's critical communication was relayed to the Supreme Headquarters, Allied Powers Europe in Mons, Belgium, and immediately passed to the Supreme Allied commander Europe, at his residence, "the *Chalet*." Without Soviet support, a "Chinese Solution" for the widespread protest in the German Democratic Republic would not be possible. Greatly relieved, satisfied all necessary notifications had been made by BASC, we returned to Checkpoint Charlie. The MPs on duty informed us the USMLM tour to East Berlin had already passed through. Although the situation had remained quiet while we were gone, unusual things were beginning to happen. At 20:00, several waiters from the Café Adler, carrying trays of coffee and *Sekt,* walked, together with some of their more courageous customers, over to the East German border guards, offering refreshment, which was politely refused. West Berliners and television teams began to gather at Checkpoint Charlie, while official traffic was processed as normal. A few observers from the West ventured hesitantly onto the territory of the GDR, but obligingly returned when requested to do so by West Berlin police officers. The number of observers increased on both sides of the Wall disproportionately, several thousand in the West, several hundred in the East. Many of those in the West called out, "Let us in!" while those in the East responded with, "Let us out!" Although the border had been sealed on the Eastern side to all but official traffic and enhanced with physical security measures, around midnight, it suddenly opened, and East Berliners began to *flâner* down *Friedrichstraße* through Checkpoint Charlie into the West. As they passed by the Allied guard shack on both sides, D3 nodded to the poster hanging on the wall behind the counter, his eyes filling with tears, and said, "Well, soldiers, it looks like we won't have to fight like hell for a free Berlin after all." Instead of fighting, we cried warm tears for Berliners East and West. Taking out a pocketbook New Testament bound in the familiar woodland green camouflage pattern from the blouse pocket of his BDUs, D3 smiled and said, "ASV," then read aloud, "For he is our peace, who made both groups one, and broke down the middle wall of partition." After D3 repocketed the New Testament, one of the MPs turned away to turn on the television. The border crossing points at nearby *Prinzenstraße,* as well as *Bornholmer Straße, Heinrich-Heine-Straße,* and *Sonnenallee* were all open. West Berliners had climbed up onto the Wall behind the Brandenburg Gate. George later told me he was among them. East Berliners walked out through the gate, past the guards and security barriers to join them. The graffiti handwriting on the Wall had proven prophetic: "Jump Over and Join the Party." Wiping the tears from his eyes, D3 turned to me and said, "Today might be an appropriate time to show the flag, whad'ya think, Thomas?"

At staff call later that morning, the US Commander, Berlin, Major General Raymond Haddock, told us he'd just returned to the John F. Kennedy Headquarters Building from a long walk in uniform, alone, through the streets of East Berlin. He too was briefly overcome as he related how many people had shaken his hand or even embraced him, saying, "Thank you, thank you!" Later that afternoon, a provisional border crossing was opened on the *Brücke der Einheit,* the Bridge of Unity cum Unification, by East German authorities. On the road in the Shield, we stopped at the Soviet checkpoint to exchange greetings and formalities, watching while hundreds of pedestrians coming from Potsdam simply walked across the *Glienicke Brücke* into West Berlin. D3 smiled and shook his head, "Well, I'll be, Thomas, it worked this time just like Sun Tzu said it would. This was the war of no war, and we're here to witness its end!" I thought about the exchange of intelligence agents I'd observed here as a member of the Berlin Detachment of the Military Intelligence Group, Europe four years earlier. Only the politically privileged could pass over the bridge back then. Although still the border between East Germany and West Berlin, it was now open, and I savored the *eirönïa* of waiting with D3 in the Shield for our papers to be processed while the Potsdam parade passed us by.

That evening, the former Chancellor of West Germany and Governing Mayor of West Berlin, Willy Brandt, returned with the current hancellor, Helmut Kohl, and Governing mayor of West Berlin, Walter Momper, to speak to *Berliner* gathered before *Rathhaus Schöneberg.* After the Wall was erected, Brandt had proclaimed, "*Meine Damen und Herrn, Die Mauer muß weg!*"[76]—the sentence dubbed into the pop song "Berlin, Berlin, Dein Herz kennt keine Mauer" and into the chants of protestors in East Berlin two years ago during the *RIAS*-sponsored Concert for Berlin. It had taken

---

76 "Ladies and Gentlemen, the Wall has to go!" Ibid.

twenty-eight years, but the Wall was coming down. I spent a sleepless weekend coordinating with the other three military liaison missions, the British Commanders'-in-Chief Mission to the Soviet Forces in Germany (BRIXMIS), *la Mission Militaire Française de Liaison* (MMFL), and the Soviet Forces (SOXMIS/SMLM), and preparing situation reports for submission to Heidelberg. After returning home Sunday evening, I called Kyra to ask her if she'd like to jump on the US Army duty train and join the party. She had to teach on Monday but told me she'd come up to Berlin as soon as she could.

Exhausted, I slept most of the following Monday and on Tuesday and took the 48 Bus to Friedenau for "wall-gazing" with Govinda in the *Lothringerstrasse*. Now that the Wall was open, I wondered what Govinda would say. He too, had been deeply moved by the events of the past few days. He also feared the protest might catalyze a violent response and was thankful for the celebration of peace. "You know, Thomas, when we received the news last Thursday, we were wall-gazing here in the Happy *Bude*—I wondered why you hadn't joined us, but now I know. You were Wall-gazing, too! Your 'PIC-kuan' might no longer be necessary, but I hope you will still continue to practice *pi-kuan*!"

"Yes, yes, Govinda, even without the Wall, I will continue with wall-gazing! It might help me to understand what I have seen and, in a small way, been a part of. Maybe not enlightenment, not yet anyway, but perhaps insight or wisdom. Is there wisdom to be found in the fall of the Wall?"

"Our friend, D3, spoke words of wisdom when speaking of Sun Tzu, do you remember? Sublime victory is the one in which there is no actual physical conflict. We also spoke about the Wall as a way to freedom. You gazed at the Wall from within and without, from the West and the East. It once was an obstacle to freedom for those living without. Although still standing, it is porous, the purpose for which it was originally constructed is gone. There are other walls still standing in our world; perhaps some are necessary, some are not. We have often recited Bodhidharma's teaching. Walls focus and inform our meditation. It will be very interesting to observe how those for whom the Wall defined their lives for so long will now adjust to its absence."

November was a busy month for the US Military Liaison Mission. When the systematic deconstruction of the inner-German border, the border between the Federal Republic of Germany and the German Democratic Republic, began, USMLM conducted regular tours to observe, document, and report progress. At the end of the month, in a speech before the *Bundestag*, Chancellor Helmut Kohl proposed a Ten Point Plan for the reunification of Germany, reaffirming, "*Die Wiedervereinigung, das heißt die*

Wiedervereinigung der staatlichen Einheit Deutschlands, bleibt das politische Ziel der Bundesregierung."[77] Speaking for the United States, Ambassador Vernon Walters, who had anticipated the "Fall of the Wall," gave the only response possible in his very personal German, *"Wir sind damit sehr bequem*—we're very comfortable with that." I received a long letter from Dr. Schneider reacting to the dramatic events of November 9. He had been thinking about them in the context of our Clay Institute seminar on Berlin as an accidental *polis*. "With the loss of purpose and its 'sacred center,' the *polis*, accidental or intentional, will begin to deconstruct, to dis-integrate. The carefully crafted theology of West Berlin we discussed will disappear, along with its status as 'the relevant area.'" Reunited with East Berlin, it would become the capitol of a reunified Germany. Bonn's days as *Berlin Nebenstelle* were numbered.

Heralded by some as the end of the Cold War, the "Seasick Summit" between President G. H. W. Bush and Secretary General Gorbachev, held on rough seas off the island of Malta in early December, was unfortunately unable to maintain the momentum in arms control generated by the earlier Gorbachev/Reagan summits. Apparently, President Reagan's successor still hadn't taken the "little time" necessary to review the issues since he last met with the general secretary at the summit on Governor's Island in New York. D3 and many other observers of Soviet-American relations saw, in what almost appeared calculated reluctance, a lost opportunity. Early December also saw the resignation of Erich Honecker's usurper, Egon Krenz, along with the *Politbüro* and the Central Committee of the Socialist Unity Party in East Berlin. Krenz was succeeded by Manfred Gerlach, head of the Liberal Democratic Party, one of the so-called "bloc parties" under the Socialist Unity Party's National Front of the German Democratic Republic.

Before Christmas shopping at *KadeWe*, *Wertheim*, and the other big West Berlin department stores, I decided to return to the *Flohmarkt* in the Tiergarten. With the Wall open for business, Berlin's flea markets were flooded with articles and artifacts from East Berlin and Eastern Europe. As I left the train at *S-Bahnhof Tiergarten* and crossed over *Stygian Straße*, I thought about my visit seven years ago and decided to look for the stand selling militaria. Maybe I could find a Red Army souvenir for D3. The *Flohmarket* was much larger and, in spite of the drab December weather, overflowing with Eastern Europeans looking for hard currency and West Berliners and tourists looking for a *Schnäppchen*. It took a while, but I finally found the booth, the table now draped in the bright, colorful flags

---

77 "The reunification, the reunification of Germany, remains the political goal of the Federal Republic," trans. TV, citation is UNCLASSIFIED, US Military Liaison Mission Situation Report (SITREP), November 28, 1989, Heidelberg, Germany.

of the German Democratic Republic and the Soviet Union. Prominently displayed in the center of the table was a stack of six mint-condition Russian *Ssh 68* helmets. The vendor walked over to me. She was wearing an open Red Army greatcoat and a *Ssh 68* helmet, flat green with "ВЕРДИН VII" stenciled in white letters on the front. She pushed the helmet back on her forehead, temporarily like Pallas Athena, smiled, and said, "Ah, I've been expecting you, I knew you would return to me. I saved this particular helmet just for you; it is the very first one I received." She was the very same lithe young woman with short dark hair and bright eyes I'd spoken with seven years ago. She wore the same single golden earring but instead of German, she now spoke English with a light Southern European accent. She definitely reminded me of someone, but whom—Pallas Athena, Clio? Bendis in Alexandria, Virginia, who unsuccessfully tried to prevent Neal and me from leaving The Republic on the afternoon of my departure for West Berlin? "Do you remember me? I told you to come back in seven years and I might be able to help you."

"Yes, yes, you did, and I do remember you. I thought I saw the helmet then but couldn't find it. How did you know?"

Smiling, she gently took the helmet from her head and handed it to me. "Maybe you did see the helmet. Here, it's for you, a gift. You can buy them everywhere in West Berlin now for twenty marks. Not just Russian helmets are for sale in West Berlin but complete uniforms, military equipment, night-vision goggles, even weapons and vehicles. But you chose to return here, to me. That kind of devotion must be rewarded."

"Why, thank you, thank you very much! I like your stand, this flea market. It's kind of a large, unarranged, outdoor museum of German history, all of it for sale. History for sale!" Feeling as I had seven years before—somewhat dizzy, dazed, disoriented in place and time, but this time not unpleasantly so—I took the helmet from her hands and placed it upon my head. It fit perfectly!

She laughed and, clapping her hands once, exclaimed, "Why it's you! But let me put it in a bag so you won't have to wear it home!" I took the helmet from my head and handed it back to her. She placed it in a bright red heavy plastic bag with "*Deutsch-Russisches Museum Berlin-Karlshorst*" printed in black block letters on both sides and handed it back to me.

"Thank you, again, very much, this so very kind of you! This helmet will have a place of honor on top of my bookshelf, right next to my helmet."

"So, you are a soldier after all, I thought you might be a historian."

"Well, actually I am a historian too, a historian and a soldier, an army reservist on active duty."

"Ah, you are a scholar and a soldier. May this helmet shield not only your head but your thoughts as well! As a soldier in the service of history, you're going to be quite busy for the next few years. You must be prudent and careful, too. The British Army has an old maxim, no pun intended, about the difficulty of being a hero with a cracked helmet. Eyes flashing, she laughed again, and speaking in lightly accented German said, "*Auf Wiedersehen und Alles Gute!*" Taking my leave from her, I turned around and, rather than return to the *S-Bahnhof,* reentered the river of shoppers, allowing it to carry me past lace and pottery from Poland, crystal from Czechoslovakia, stopping occasionally to purchase presents, carefully placing them in the red plastic bag with my helmet. My *Wiedersehen* with Bendis at the flea market in West Berlin brought *Fräulein* Otto and the *Palast der Republik* in East Berlin back to mind. "Under other circumstances, I'd be pleased to join you . . ." Although it had taken seven years, "other circumstances" were now at hand. Concerned about possible confiscation of my helmet at the border, I decided not to carry it back into East Berlin where it undoubtedly had come from, and return to the *Palast der Republik* in the "Capital of the German Democratic Republic" the next day. After returning to my apartment, I placed the *Ssh 68* helmet, a gift of the goddess with the flashing gray eyes, on top of the bookcase in my study/ living room next to my well-worn PASGT helmet. With black Magic Marker, I'd written "BORN TO WRITE" on my woodland camouflage helmet cover, a "soldier in the service of history."

Return to East Berlin
December 1989

Up early the next morning, I put the *Falkplan,* notebook, and pen in my shoulder bag, put on my trench coat without rank insignia over my old sport coat and olive drab wool scarf, and took the 48 Bus from *Plantanenplatz.* The 48 took me past the *Botanischen Garten* and through *Friedenau,* past the Allied Control Council Headquarters, across the *Landwehrkanal,* past the *Nationalgalerie* to the last stop on the line, the *Phlilharmonie* in the *Kulturform* at the edge of the Tiergarten. Proceeding *per Pedes Pilgrimorum,* I followed *Bellevuestraße* to the Wall, breached but still standing, following it south, then east to Checkpoint Charlie. One of the MPs who had been on duty the night of November 9 recognized me, saluted, and then, placing his left hand on my shoulder, shook my hand warmly. "I'll never forget that night as long as I live, Lieutenant!" After a cursory examination of my passport, the East German Border Police waved me through. There was no required currency exchange today.

Although the German Democratic Republic continued to exist, it was disintegrating. I walked up *Friedrichstraße* to *Unter den Linden*, turned to look in the direction of the Brandenburg Gate, and began to *flâner* with intent down *Unter den Linden* to the *Palast der Republik*. Although, with the bright white exception of the Embassy of the Union of Soviet Socialist Republics, the buildings were uniformly gray, the broad avenue was once again filled with *Fußgänger*, filled with life. With *Fräulein* Otto on my mind, it was difficult to focus upon what was happening around me as I retraced the route Georg and I had taken seven years earlier. By the time I crossed the Marx-Engels Bridge, I was walking double-time. Reaching the main entrance of the *Palast der Republik*, I Rocky-ed up the marble stairs, hoping against hope to find *Fräulein* Asta Otto in the lobby under the Glass Tree. She wasn't there. Recalling the information desk on the first floor, I took the escalator. There were several hostesses at the information desk, all dressed in the same zippered, mustard yellow jumpers *Fräulein* Otto wore when we met back in December 1982. I could still see the nameplate above her breast, *Frl. Asta Otto, Hostess*. None of the helpful hostesses knew her or knew of anyone who might know her, smiling sympathetically when I told them of our meeting seven years ago. Disappointed, I thanked them and walked over to the *Espressobar* for a *Mokka*. What did I expect after so long? Perhaps I should have come last year, during a USMLM tour to East Berlin, but that would have been difficult. Taking a seat on one of the bolted down barstools, I turned to the mosaic of *Meissener Porzellan* for solace, socialist sensuality in brown, yellow, and blue, and wished *Fräulein Asta Otto, Hostess* well, wherever she might be. After finishing my *Mokka*, I left the *Espressobar*, taking the escalator back down to the entrance hall. Walking once again beneath the translucent branches of the "Glass Tree," I left the *Palast der Republik*.

Still wondering about the whereabouts of *Fräulein Asta Otto, Hostess*, I wandered right onto *Karl-Liebknecht-Straße* rather than turning left in the direction of *Unter den Linden* and *Friedrichstraße*. Only after crossing over the Spree did I realize my mistake. Rather than retrace my steps, I decided to walk down to the river and *flâner* along the iron railing paralleling the paved riverbank. Sweet Spree run softly 'til my history is done. Sweet Spree run softly whether I've lost or won. The promenade along the eastern side of the river led to the *Nikolaiviertel*, the "Nicholas Quarter," built where the birthplace of Berlin had been laid waste by the war in 1944. Incorporating specially designed *Plattenbau* elements, city planner Dr. Günter Stahn had reimagined and reconstructed an ensemble of historical houses and narrow streets for the 750th anniversary of Berlin in 1987. Walking along the river, reflecting on reunification and this reification of a reimagined history, harbinger of a future *Deutsches Disneyland*, I was startled by a monumental equestrian bronze, a horror-stricken horse, rearing back upon powerful hind legs. The regal rider was neither King Frederick II of Prussia nor General David D. McClellan, Army of the Republic, but a member of the Praetorian Guard of Roman Emperor Diocletian, George of Lydda. With holy banner held high in his left hand and sword uplifted in his right, St. George was about to slay the horned, bat-winged dragon recoiling beneath the heavy bronze hooves of his mount. Although the Spree-side setting was unfamiliar, the monument was not. It was the very same sculpture featured in my drug-inspired dream, standing in the Great Courtyard of the Imperial Palace where D3 parked the Shield following our Thunder run into Baghdad/Berlin. After slowly circumventing the statue on its red marble base, I continued on to the Nicholas Church, chosen by Dr. Stahn as the namesake of his "historical" quarter. George told me it was, or had been, the oldest church in Berlin, standing from its construction in the early thirteenth century, until its destruction the mid-twentieth. Though the redbrick double spire, walls, and vaults had been meticulously reconstructed, the massive stone foundation appeared original. Alert following my unexpected encounter with St. George, I was nevertheless totally unprepared for my *Wiedersehen* with the muse of history on *Nikolaikirchplatz*, the small square next to the *Nikolai-Kirche*. Clio was breath-givingly beautiful, a bay laurel wreath wound into her braided bronze hair, fine facial features, arms bent at the elbows, raised upward in graceful gesture, as if appealing to something greater. Although she appeared to be dancing, her left knee rested firmly on a cuirass and stylized Roman helmet. Draped openly over her left shoulder, passing beneath her bared-breasts, her *himation* highlighted the lines of her full thighs. Eyes averted from passersby, Clio's gaze was inwardly directed. There was no marble pedestal, no open book, no spray graffiti. Through poise and gesture alone, the muse of history seemed to point to something else, to something of greater beauty. Was this something to be found in, or as her gesture and the stowed implements of war seemed to suggest, outside of history? I walked slowly around the small square several times, marveling at her beauty, trying to understand this unforeseen, unusual manifestation of the muse. Reluctantly taking my leave, I passed by the reconstructed house where Gotthold Ephraim Lessing did not finish writing his play *Minna von Barnhelm, or, The Soldiers' Happiness* in 1765, through a *Plattenbau* onto the broad *Spandauer Straße*, turning back in the direction of *Karl-Liebknecht-Straße*.

When I later asked George about the statue of Clio, he told me she'd actually been one of six figures gracing the base of an equestrian monument to Friedrich Wilhelm III, namesake of the Berlin University, which once stood in the *Lustgarten* in front of the Old Museum. With the exception of Clio, *Die Muse der Geschichtsschreibung* (*The Muse of Historical Writing*), and *Die Allegorie der Wissenschaft* (*The Allegory of Science*), the equestrian monument had been melted down for munitions during the war at the German Weapons and Munitions Factory in Wittenau, the same complex now housing the Berlin City-State Archives. Clio certainly knew when and how to separate herself from world-historical figures. Although pockmarked by small arms fire, the other surviving sculpture, *The Allegory of Science*, sitting on the far side of the *Nikolai-Kirche*, still balanced the world on one thigh, an open book on the other. Closer inspection revealed his book to be a *tabula rasa*, with no hint of "what to come." My dissertation research on Clio, *Muse Militante*, taught me, however, that together with "historical writing," "the allegory of science" would continue to play their parts after the Cold War, and in all likelihood, continue to do so during all the wars yet to come.

At *Karl-Liebknecht-Straße*, I once again opted for streets still unseen leading in the general direction of West Berlin, following *Spandauer Straße* as it curved underneath an *S-Bahn* bridge. Crossing over *Hackischer Markt* while watching carefully for streetcars, I continued on *Rosenthaler Straße*, coming to the intersection with *Sophienstraße*. In spite of decades of neglect and the gray patina of pollution, which made the old buildings practically indistinguishable from one another—"*All architecture is what you do when you look upon it, (Did you think it was in the white or gray stone? or the lines of the arches and cornices?)*"—the *Sophienstraße* retained its early eighteenth-century charm. Ahead on the left, a Baroque church steeple beckoned, and although it would take me away from *Unter den Linden*, I decided to have a closer look. Walking down the narrow street filled with small repair and workshops, I came to a gate in the low, black iron fence surrounding the churchyard. It stood open, and upon entering, I found myself in a graveyard. Making my way slowly through the heavily weathered tombstones, around the church, looking for the entrance, my attention was caught by a large white marble memorial, mounted on the redbrick wall bordering the far side of the churchyard. In the center, beneath a tympanum framed by faux pillars, was the high relief of a smartly attired gentleman, his long hair combed back, smiling at me benevolently, an invitation. Walking carefully over to what appeared to be a family plot, I read,

> *Hier ruhen in Gott*
> *Leopold von Ranke*
> *geb 21. Dez 1795*
> *gest. 25. Mai 1886*

Clarissa von Ranke geb Graves
geb 8. April 1808
gest 10. Juli 1850
Und deren jungsten Sohn
August Edwin Albrecht
geb 15. Nov 1849
gest 10. Juli 1850
Sie ruhen in Frieden und das
Ewige Licht leuchte ihnen[78]

The grave of Leopold von Ranke, subject and source of much of my research into Clio's activities in Berlin! *Ad fontes! Ad finem!* Berlin essayist and fellow *flâneur* Walter Benjamin referred to von Ranke's writings as "the strongest narcotic" of the previous century. *Historicism* seemed to have retained its narcotic quality throughout the twentieth century as well. What would be "the strongest narcotic" of the coming century, the End of History? Leopold von Ranke lived for ninety-one years. Reading though his diary while researching my dissertation, I found an entry from January 1877 of more than just academic interest and carefully copied it into my notebook. I took it from my shoulder bag, found the entry, and reread it at his grave.

But a historian must be old, not only because of the unmeasurable size of his field of study, but also because of the insight into the historical process, which a long life gives, particularly under changing conditions. It would hardly be bearable for him to experience only a short period. For his personal development, it is necessary that he observe great events come to completion, that others collapse, and that new forms be undertaken.

As I was pondering von Ranke's observations on long life, great events, collapse, and new forms, I sensed someone standing next to me and turned to look. An older woman, dressed for work outdoors on this dark December day, held a large ring of heavy metal keys. Smiling, she said, *"Niemand hat so viel Besuch wie Ranke. Viele Kinder besuchen ihn jeden Tag!"*[79] Noting my puzzled expression, she said, *"Hier ist nämlich ein Kinderspielplatz!"* The

---

78 "Here rests in God, Leopold von Ranke, born Dec. 21, 1795, died May 25, 1886; Clarissa von Ranke born Graves, born April 8, 1808, died July 10, 1850, and their youngest son August Edwin Albrecht, born Nov. 15, 1849, died July 10, 1850; They rest in Peace, illuminated by Light Eternal." Diary of Thomas Vonaechron, Diary Extract 1989, trans. TV.
79 "No one has as many visitors as Ranke. Many children visit him every day." Diary of Thomas Vonaechron, Diary Extract 1989, trans. TV.

fenced-in church graveyard served as a playground for the children of the neighborhood. Perhaps that was why von Ranke was smiling. "*Wenn Sie sich für Ranke interessiern, dann sollten Sie auch das Grab von Hegel besuchen. Er liegt nicht weit von hier begraben, auf dem Dorotheenstadt Friedhof.*"[80] The final resting places of von Ranke and Hegel. Clio had left them behind. Attempting to follow in their footsteps, I realized how important it was to see where those footsteps stopped. The kindly caretaker gave me directions to the cemetery on *Chauseestraße.* Turning to leave, I faced the bullet-scarred marble facade of the *Sophiengemeinde, ERBAUT 1901.* Over the entrance door, from underneath another tympanum, the owl of Minerva looked out over the churchyard. Without stopping to visit the *Gemeindehaus* or the *Sophienkirche*—it had, after all, been the Baroque tower which led me to von Ranke—I left the churchyard thorough the main entrance onto *Grosse Hamburgerstraße.* Bullet and shell holes also scarred the buildings on both sides of the narrow entranceway. *Sophienkirche* had apparently been the site of a small unit action, intense hand-to-hand combat during the last hours of last battle. A large metal frame had been mounted on one of the walls, framing the bullet-scarred masonry as both warning and obligation to passersby. The engraving at the top read "PAX," *Frieden,* Peace. Turning to the right, I walked to the intersection with *Wilhelm-Pieck-Straße,* which led me on to *Friedrichstraße.* I knew where I was without unfolding my *Falkplan* or asking a friendly guide. Instead of turning south toward the *Bahnhof,* I turned north onto *Chauseestraße.* As I walked, it occurred to me I should have tipped the helpful *Sophienkirche* caretaker. I found the gate to the high-walled cemetery at 126. It stood open. At the top of the path ascending gradually to the cemetery stood the caretaker's brick cottage. The caretaker was standing outside, looking down the path toward the gate. Could she have been waiting for me? As if in answer to my question, she smiled and walked me through the peaceful garden of stately maple, chestnut, and sycamore trees, bullet-scarred mausolea and tombstones, to Hegel's grave. No smiling high relief beckoned, just a stone slab mounted on a plinth.

GEORG
WILHELM FRIEDRICH
HEGEL.
GEB. D. XXVII AUGUST
MDCCLXX
GEST. D. XIV NOVEMBER
MDCCCXXXI

---

80 "If you're interested in Ranke, then you should also visit Hegel's grave. He's buried not far from here in the Dorotheen-City Cemetery." Diary of Thomas Vonaechron, Diary Extract 1989, trans. TV.

Buried beside him, his wife.

Marie Hegel geb. von Tucher
geb. zu Nürnberg d. 17 März 1791
gest. zu Berlin d. 6 Juli 1855

Beside the Hegels, I was surprised and pleased to discover the grave of Hegel's predecessor in the chair of philosophy at the *Universität zu Berlin*, its original occupant and proponent of the "thesis-antithesis-synthesis" argument.

Johann Gottlieb
FICHTE
Zur Seite ihres Gatten ruht
Johanna Marie Fichte
Geb. Rahn.

During a lunchtime discussion on the founding of the Berlin University, Johannes Festzelt told George and me that Johanna Marie Fichte, nee Rahn, "resting at the side of her husband," had volunteered her services as a nurse in a Berlin military hospital during the wars fought to free Prussia from France. Apparently, she contracted an infection and inadvertently passed it to her husband with fatal consequence.

The caretaker politely but firmly refused to take the five-*Mark* coin I offered her when she turned to return to her cottage. After standing before the four graves for some time, I walked slowly back to the entrance gate, discovering the graves of Carl Friedrich Schinkel, Christian Daniel Rauch, and Albert Dietrich Schadow along the path. In addition to historians, the *Dorothenstadt Friedhof* was the graveyard of architects and sculptors of Berlin. Leaving the cemetery, I followed *Chauseestraße* back down to *Friedrichstraße* and *Bahnhof Friedrichstraße*, taking the *S-Bahn* directly back to *Bahnhof Botanischer Garten*. Although the border-crossing formalities were still in place, they were largely *pro forma*, performed in an air of unreality. I no longer felt like "one of them." Although I hadn't found *Frl. Asta Otto, Hostess* under other circumstances, the memory of our meeting seven years ago led me back to East Berlin, to chance encounters with Clio, three of her disciples, and, perhaps even more significantly, with their wives. As a consequence, I began to think about love, not just as found in the archives and library but in history. Clausewitz, von Ranke, Hegel, and Fichte found their final rest with their wives: "*Zur Seite Ihres*

Gatten." Although the importance of marital intimacy is apparent in the martial "Foreword" Marie von Clausewitz wrote for *On War*, I had little idea what significance love might have held for these other historians and philosophers of history. Hegel's thoughts on love and lovers "alike in power" are found among his early writings in the fragment on love: "Love is stronger than fear." Identifying love as a determinant of human nature—"In love only is life:—without it is death and annihilation"— Fichte coincidentally fears love could also be a "mockery," a "phantom of the brain." I hadn't considered "love" as a variable in history—had they? After all, Aphrodite was a goddess, Clio only a muse. Yet, Clio was also the child of Ge and Uranus, a sister of the giants defeated by the Olympians. Perhaps love was what Clio was pointing to on *Nikolaikirchplatz*. Still, if love was a factor in the private lives of these historians and philosophers of history, as it appeared to be, what part did it play in their grand designs, in history? Niccolò Francesco Haym made use of Caesar's desire for Cleopatra to explain the Roman conquest of Egypt in Händel's opera, but was it history or rather his story? Does love, like long life, also confer insight into the historical process or does it serve to mitigate its absurdity? Could love offer a way to look at history, a way to move against history, or even a way out of history? Is it possible to be caught up in something larger, the dialectic, *im Weltgeist*, the staging of a country, the war, and still retain the ability to love and to be loved?

Europa déchaînée
December 1989

At the request of the Soviet Union, a meeting of the Allied ambassadors was held at Allied Control Council Headquarters at Kleist Park on December 11 to address issues concerning the future of the two German states and Allied rights and privileges in Germany. Once again, the four flags of the victorious Allies flew from the facade of the former *Kammergericht*. Excluded from the proceedings, German federal government officials fumed. They would, however, soon have their say, their day, and their way in the "Two Plus Four" negotiations, leading to the reunification of Germany.

The reunification of Berlin, the metamorphosis of Berlin V and Berlin VI into Berlin VII, began on the night of November 9. Deconstruction of the Wall precipitated other politico-architectural events, such as the reopening of the *Brandenburger Tor*, the Propylaea entrance to "Athens on the Spree," two days before Christmas. The reopening of the gate after thirty years had larger implications for Germany as well as for Berlin. Former

President of the Federal Republic of Germany, Richard von Weizäcker, once observed that as long as the Brandenburg Gate remained closed, the German Question remained open. Would the reopening of the gate close the German Question, or rather rephrase it? The Prime Minister of the German Democratic Republic, Hans Modrow, argued, "It must be a gate of peace," returning to architect Johann Gottfried Schadow's original, two-hundred-year-old intent. Eirēnē relieved Nike at the reins of the quadriga. As Dr. Schneider had suggested in his long letter, the opening of the gate into accidental *polis* fore-Schadowed its end.

The *Brandenburger Tor* became the backdrop for the celebration of New Year 1990. Although I knew *Pariser Platz* would be jammed with hundreds, thousands of celebrants, I decided to join them, taking the *S-Bahn* to *Bahnhof Friedrerichstraße*. Trains and stations were filled to overcapacity with people, traveling from West to East and from East to West. In spite of the enormous crowds, people moved cautiously and joyously, without the characteristic *Berliner Drängen*. *Bahnhof Friedrerichstraße* had been repurposed as a transit *Bahnhof* for visitors to East Berlin. All doors stood open in the labyrinth of passageways beneath the train station, reification of the Byzantine bureaucratic procedures previously required to enter *Ostberlin*. The minotaur had fled. Crowds from East and West Berlin flowed through the dark-tiled passageways like the Alpheus and Peneus Rivers cleansing the Augean stables. Adjacent to *Bahnhof Friedrichstraße* stood the "Palace of Tears," the *Tränenpalast*, where so many had parted or been reunited with families and friends. Turning right onto *Friedrichstraße*, I walked down to *Unter den Linden*, continuing on in the direction of the *Brandenburger Tor*, one of the thousands peacefully making their way to the celebration. Television and radio stations had set up studios along both sides of the grand boulevard. A cautious joy was in the gray *Berliner Luft, Luft, Luft, ja ja, ja ja, ja ja ja ja ja ja*, almost an unwillingness to believe.

A large Christmas tree had been set up in front of the *Brandenburger Tor*, close to the empty site of the Max Liebermann house. It was protected on three sides by a metal fence, offering a niche from which I could observe the celebration without being carried away. I stepped into the niche, climbing up onto the cinder blocks holding the fence in place, letting the river of people pass me by. From my elevated vantage point, I could see celebrants flowing through the *Brandenburger Tor* in both directions, and the quadriga on top facing *Unter den Linden* with Eirēnē back at the reigns. As midnight approached, partygoers continued to fill *Pariser Platz*.

Looking down, I saw a striking young woman making her way slowly through the crowd toward the niche, tall with long dark hair. When she reached the fence, she looked up and smiled at me, extended her arms, and began to climb the fence. I watched as the toes of her black suede boots moved higher. When she reached the top, she turned carefully toward the *Brandenburger Tor*, opening her arms to grasp the railing running along the top of the fence behind her with gloved hands. She wore a remarkable black velvet jacket cut to the waist. The names of capital cities of Europe were embroidered in a random pattern on her black jacket in heavy golden thread. At midnight, the fireworks exploding over the *Brandenburger Tor* illuminated the cities: Paris, London, Athens, Knossos, Prague, Rome, Moscow, Warsaw, and Berlin. From the top of the fence, she looked down and saw me looking up at her. Smiling in return, she closed her eyes and began to sway gently.

USMLM continued to conduct tours throughout Berlin and the German Democratic Republic in the New Year. Returning from a trip to Cottbus-Sachsendorf to photograph former *Wehrmacht Kasernen* recently vacated by the Red Army, we stopped for dinner at a hotel in Burg, not Burg *bei* Magdeburg, where Marie von Bruehl and her husband Carl von Clausewitz had been reburied, but Burg in the *Spreewald*. The hotel retained a pre-World War I ambiance. The dark, wood-paneled dining room was lighted by a wagon wheel lamp suspended from the ceiling. In the center of the lamp, presiding over the dining room, was a large, carved wooden owl. The owner, who seemed quite surprised but genuinely pleased to have German-speaking uniformed American guests, told us the owl had been there since the hotel was built in 1910. After dinner, D3 stood up to look closely at the owl. After a few minutes, he sat back down at the long wooden table and said, "You know, Thomas, this old owl has seen quite a bit over the past eighty years: Monarchy, Democracy, National Socialism, the war, Soviet occupation, Socialism, and now Democracy again. That just might qualify her to be the owl of Athena!"

"Now that's a very interesting thought, D3. This wise old owl has certainly seen and heard a lot over the past eighty years, in German, in Russian, and now in English! I'd certainly be interested in what she might have to tell Athena. And what about our seductress, Clio, what does she have to tell us? Is there wisdom to be found in warfare, in history, or do we have to go through it all over again? Remember the discussion you had with Govinda about Sun Tzu? He found wisdom in your words about the 'Sun Tzu' soldier. Will prudence be applied in the future as it was here in Germany? *Wie wird es eigentlich sein?* Had there been a 'hot' instead of a Cold War in Central Europe, it's highly unlikely the owl, the hotel, Burg, or Berlin for that matter would still be here. I reviewed the war plans back in Vault Six."

As a consequence of the withdrawal and reorganization of Soviet forces, President Gorbachev announced at the United Nations, our other headquarters, the Group of Soviet Forces in Germany became the Western Group of Forces. On February 9, 1990, the US Secretary of State met with his Soviet counterpart and President Gorbachev at the Kremlin in Moscow. He assured both that, "If we maintain a presence in Germany that is a part of NATO, there would be no extension of NATO's jurisdiction for forces of NATO one inch to the east."[81] He prepared a written briefing for German Chancellor Helmut Kohl. The day after the visit of the US secretary of state, Chancellor Kohl and the German foreign minister met with President Gorbachev in Moscow, underlining statements made by the US secretary of state: "we believe NATO should not expand the sphere of its activity."[82] Led to believe NATO would not expand its membership into Eastern Europe, President Gorbachev agreed there were no further impediments to reunification. This agreement was the basis for the NATO/Warsaw Pact Meeting in Ottawa a few days later, which further reduced stationed forces and set the stage for the "Two Plus Four." Two Germanys plus four Allies equals one Germany, German reunification.

In the meantime, there were ongoing developments within both East and West Germany. USMLM reported approximately 50,000 people had taken part in the final Monday Demonstration in Leipzig on March 14. The following month, US forces began the removal of the ground-launched cruise missiles from Germany. D3 and I drove down to Wüschheim Air Station in the Shield to take part in the festivities. Together with the hundred or so other onlookers, we cheered as the mammoth C-5 Galaxy military transport loaded with GLCMs taxied out to the runway for departure. Little did we realize that soon we, too would have the opportunity to fly on a Galaxy. D3 suggested we have lunch at the Cruise Inn, the small, wood-paneled restaurant in the on-station officers' club before returning to Berlin. Over *Kaffee* and the *Kuchen* of the day he said, "Maybe we should drive through Magdeburg on our way back to Berlin to see if that mock-up is still out on Route 1. After all, one could say, even though nonoperable, it did launch your career as a US Army reservist, yuck, yuck, yuck! Let's see, Thomas, it's been five, almost six years now since you ID'd that Pershing II mock-up on the road to Magdeburg and screwed up our Clausewitz tour. To celebrate that significant event and today's historic occasion, I'm pleased to be able to inform you, you have been selected for promotion to the rank of captain in the US Army Reserve!"

81 Memorandum of conversation between Secretary Baker, President Gorbachev, and Eduard Shevardnadze, Kremlin, February 9, 1990, DECLASSIFIED, December 20, 2002, 19950-4567 TV
82 Memorandum of "One-on-One Conversation of M. S. Gorbachev with H. Kohl," February 10, 1990, citation is UNCLASSIFIED, trans. TV. US Military Liaison Mission Situation Report (SITREP), February 11, 1990, Heidelberg, Germany

D3 had once again reserved the ballroom of the Harnack House so faculty and friends could be invited to my promotion ceremony. George, Rainer, and Professors Jourdan and Spero were all able to attend. Members of both the Berlin Det and the USMLM also joined us. Unfortunately, Johannes Festzelt had already returned to *Restdeutschland*. Much to my delight, D3 had been able to track down Sophia Sweelin Werner, who had returned to West Berlin from Washington, DC, received her doctorate in law from the *FU*, and followed her father into the German Foreign Service. She and D3 seemed to get along very well. I suspected all the effort he had invested in finding her wasn't only on my behalf. After the ceremony, she told us she'd been to Mr. Henry's, not only on Washington Circle but up on Capitol Hill and in Georgetown as well. Although she didn't particularly care for *Berliner Weiße*, she'd nonetheless raised a glass at each location to the success of my academic endeavor as I'd ask her to do. Reminiscing on Professor Schneider's seminar seven years ago and Sophia's lead presentation on the legal framework of West Berlin, we toasted the happy end of our "Accidental *Polis*." D3 said, "If I remember correctly, Sophia, you concluded your briefing with something along the lines of, 'The occupation of West Berlin by the Western Allies will only come to an end when all four former Allies agree upon German reunification. At that point in time, whether in seven years or seventy, the 'accidental *polis*' will cease to exist.' In retrospect, seven years was a pretty good estimate!"

This time, I'd called my Basic Officer Leadership Course classmate Kyra DeGetria well in advance, asking her if she would care to redeem her rain check for Berlin. Having exchanged our private *Bundespost* phone numbers, we no longer had to rely upon the Defense Service Network to communicate. Although we spoke frequently, we hadn't seen each other since my transfer from Berlin Det to USMLM. Physically separated, we grew closer through conversation. Kyra continued to drill with Munich Det at McGraw *Kaserne*. In the meantime, she'd been promoted to first lieutenant, teaching undergraduate history as part of the two-year program offered by University of Maryland University College. Kyra stepped off the duty train at the Berlin Rail Transportation Office in Lichterfelde West shortly after 06:00 on a morning in late April, dressed in a long, dark green *Trachtenmantel*, very becoming to her figure. She wore her coordinated, green-felt, feathered Tyrolean hat like her army patrol cap pulled down, her dark brown eyes flashing out from beneath the brim. "Welcome back to the American Sector," I said, and without thinking, I added, "I hope you brought your *Dirndl*, along with your hat and coat!"

Sensing my immediate embarrassment, she looked at me and laughed. "I'll bet you do, Thomas . . . and the absinthe, too," she replied. "Although

I was able get a berth on the duty train, there's unfortunately nothing available at the Visiting Officers' Quarters tonight. So I guess I'll just have to remain overnight at your quarters, if that's all right with you, of course," she said, handing me her woodland camouflage helmet bag, which complemented her fashionable forester's outfit.

"Of course, Kyra, it would be a pleasure!" We took the *S-Bahn* one stop to *Bahnhof Botanischer Garten* and walked to my apartment, knocking at the back door of the *Bäckerei* downstairs to pick up freshly baked *Brötchen* for breakfast.

"What a lovely apartment you have, Thomas."

"Why thank you, Kyra. I'm happy you approve of your temporary duty accommodations. Actually, it's only half of an apartment, subdivided due to the postwar housing shortage in the American Sector, but I like it very much. Although it's only half the size, and half the rent I might add, the ceilings are still high. Let me take your hat and coat. Make yourself at home. The bathroom is here on the right." I took off my shoes and, walking into the bathroom, took a washcloth and towel from the wooden IKEA shelf and handed them to her. "Just in case you'd like to freshen up after ten hours on the duty train. I'll get breakfast ready."

"Thank you, Thomas. I decided against the 'coffee, tea, or apple cake' on the train this morning, hoping we might be able to breakfast together!"

After breakfast Kyra said, "You know, Thomas, I'm bushed. I didn't sleep too well last night on the train, and you must be tired too, getting up so early this morning to meet me at the RTO. Let's take a short *siesta* before your ceremony, shall we? I'll bet the bedroom's in here." Before I could answer, she walked down the hall into the bedroom and stretched out, fully dressed on the bed. "Don't be so shy, Thomas. We're BOLC classmates, come and lie down next to me." She smiled, turned away toward the wall and fell asleep. I set the alarm clock, fell asleep inhaling her perfume, and didn't awake until it rang. After I'd changed into BDUs, we walked to the Harnack House for the short ceremony and the considerably longer wetting down in the Marine Bar afterwards. Damp from the pint of beer D3 poured over my head, I was about to ask Heinz to call a taxi to take us back to *Mohnstraße*, when I felt a friendly hand on my shoulder. It was Rainer.

"Thomas, please let me take you and Kyra back to your apartment. I have to work tonight. That's why I could unfortunately only have one beer, and we wouldn't want our freshly-baked *Hauptmann* to catch cold now, would we? Reveling in the happy hours spent with friends and colleagues in the intimate atmosphere of the Marine Bar, I'd had more than one beer and was very grateful for Rainer's kind offer. He had a new cab, a creamy yellow

Opel *Rekord* 2,3 Diesel, with no offer of academic instruction bolted to the roof. He did, however, have a superior Clarion sound system installed inside. Michael Hoenig's "Departure from the Northern Wasteland" set the scene for a serene drive through the sylvan suburbs back to *Mohnstraße*. Following Kyra up the stairs to the first floor, it suddenly occurred to me I'd left the apartment a first lieutenant and returned a captain, the same rank LTC Ziemßen addressed me by in my drug-inspired dream on the night I was admitted to *Pyschiatrische Ambulanz*. After helping Kyra take off her coat, she pointed to the bathroom saying, "After you, Captain."

"As you were, Ma'am!" In the bathroom, I took off my uniform and rinsed off under the shower. Taking my "a great fireman" *yukata* from the hook on the back of the door, I put it on and walked back out into the hallway, calling out, "Next please!"

Replying from the bedroom, Kyra answered, "I'm in here." She was waiting for me, standing in the indirect light coming from the hallway, with a nightcap prepared in the *Oktoberfest* fashion. She'd brought along both her black bustier and her bottle of absinthe. After I'd kissed the green fairy between her breasts, she removed the glass, set it down on the nightstand, and, putting her arms around my neck, said, "Now, if you'd like to, this time you can kiss me too, Captain Vonaechron." I kissed her gently on her open mouth, soft and wet, licking her licorice-flavored lips. Drawing Cupid's bow gently with my teeth, I began to pull her upper lip gently and then kissed her on the mouth again. Placing my arms round her waist, I unhooked the eyelets on the back of her bustier. As it fell to the floor, her breasts relaxed. Cupping them in my hands, I kissed her nipples, taking them gently in my mouth as they became erect. As she bent forward over me, I could feel her thick hair on the back of my neck. Kissing the gentle curve of her stomach, I realized she wasn't wearing anything else. The dark "V" I took for black string bikini panties, was thick, dark, electric fur. Kneeling in front of her, I placed my hands on the outside of her thighs and traced the perimeter of the "V" with my lips and tongue, across her stomach, down the inside of her thighs. Taking my arms in her hands, she raised me to my feet, untied and took off my *yukata*, and led me to bed. After dying our little deaths, individually, then together, after our cummings and groanings, Kyra fell asleep, once again facing the wall, but this time I was inside of her. Just before falling asleep, wandering thoughts wandered back to erotic encounters in the clinic, the institute library, and the underground archives, sexual acts driven by overwhelming fear, desire, and opportunity. Then there was the aesthetic encounter in the bath with my beautiful, sad, nameless sister. Making love with Kyra incorporated all these elements, but there was something more, something unifying, incorporating, something . . . scattered thoughts dissolved into sleep as Hypnos poured himself into the bedroom while his son Morpheus tenderly wrapped his arms around us.

Kyra and I spent the next day repurposing my apartment as our personal space. Making love, talking and not talking. It felt good. Eating light meals, thankful for the warmth of the bakery oven beneath us, enjoying each other's company. Taking time within this personal space to enter into the vulnerability and uncertainty offered by grace of our bodies, creating an intimate history, a historicity of love. By extending this story, our story, into the past, we began to lay a foundation for the future. She told me her grandfather had served as a captain in the US Army with the American Expeditionary Force in France during the First World War. His stories, his war stories, sparked her interest in history as a girl and, as a woman, inspired her to a career as in the US Army Reserve. "Maybe it was your captain's bars that got to me last night," she said, laughing, her dark eyes flashing, tossing back her thick brown hair. She laughed again when I told her my grandfather had also served in France, not as an officer but as a private first class. His stories had also inspired my interest in history, in Germany, and Europe, maybe even the in army, too, though I hadn't really thought about it until Kyra mentioned it.

"I joined the Reserve Officer's Training Corps as an undergraduate in 1970, when it was first opened up to women. I was the only woman in my class, and at first, it was not, I repeat 'not,' a pleasant experience. Fortunately, our battalion commander, LTC Hans Ziemßen, was very supportive of women in the military and quickly put a stop to all hazing. As the granddaughter of an army captain, I was self-confident and, to be honest, Thomas, assertive, maybe even overly aggressive, in my one-woman campaign to defend the place of women in the US Army. As, much to LTC Ziemßen's amusement, I verbally 'KOed' a few of my ROTC classmates who thought otherwise, he unofficially awarded me the nickname "KO."

"You know 'KO' can be interpreted in another way, KO."

"I do, Thomas, and, coming from you, I'll take that as a compliment, but I'd be very grateful if you didn't use my nickname, thank you!"

"'Roger that,' as D3 would say, but please excuse me Kyra, did you say LTC Hans Ziemßen?"

"Yes, he's second-generation American. His parents immigrated to Baltimore from Lübeck following the First World War. Together with military science, he also passed along his passionate interest in German language and literature and European history. Without intending to do so, he inspired me to move to Munich, learn German, and study history. Don't tell me you know him, Thomas?"

"No, no, well no, not exactly, but I've seen the name. I'll explain later. But please continue!"

"Unfortunately, not all army reserve unit commanders were as supportive of women in the army as LTC Ziemßen. Women were admitted to the special branches, as nurses, even as doctors. Female doctors, just imagine that! There were, however, very limited opportunities in the other officer branch specialties. So although there were drilling army reserve units near College Park, I remained in the Individual Ready Reserve while working on an MA in history with George Kent at Maryland, slowing down my promotion to captain. In retrospect, it's probably just as well. Only after I'd made the move to Munich to teach for University of Maryland University College did I find out about the US Army Reserve Military Group Europe and Detachment One. It seemed almost too good to be true, almost as if it were meant to be."

Nodding my head in agreement, I said, "When D3 and I first met at the Free University, it also seemed more than just coincidental to me. We even joked Clio had seduced us individually, then brought us to Berlin to meet. That was seven years ago. Since then, our friendship has deepened, opening the door to a career in the Army Reserve I'd never considered before. A career which has taken me even deeper into history, into the "making of history," whatever that means. But more importantly to me Kyra, the US Army brought us together, and I couldn't be more grateful. Maybe that was meant to be, too!"

When the time came for Kyra to report to the RTO for the obligatory predeparture briefing, I felt a bit like Robert Ryan in *Berlin Express*. I was grateful, thankful, for the close, intimate friendship of this woman with whom I shared much. If not out, love did seem to offer a way apart from history. "Well, Thomas, I've used up my rain check for Berlin, so now it's your turn to come back down to Munich. Please do come down soon. I have the unhappy feeling I'm going to miss you." I carried her helmet bag back to the RTO and waited with her until the mandatory briefing was finished. The noncommissioned officer in charge matter-of-factly reminded all duty train passengers, "Shirt and shoes must be worn outside your compartments at all times. As "and pants" was assumed to be understood, mischievous passengers occasionally interpreted the omission as an invitation. After the briefing, we left the station, walking out along the platform behind it, underneath the white globe lights hanging from the roof to her assigned coach. We kissed just before she boarded. I stood outside her compartment window, waving and walking along as the US Army duty train pulled out of Lichterfelde-West for the overnight run to Frankfurt. Life not unfrequently imitates the French cinematographers.

At the beginning of May, the first 'Two Plus Four' Meeting was held in Bonn, *Berlin Nebenstelle*. At the end of the month, Presidents Bush and Gorbachev met again, this time on dry land for a three-day summit in Washington, DC, and at Camp David, Maryland. Once again, President Gorbachev sadly discovered, "The West hasn't done much thinking."

In May, D3 called me into his office. "Thomas, with everything going on and a little unofficial assistance from USAREUR, I've been able to get a second twelve-month extension for you. This will cover you until June 1991. Barring some kind of operational necessity, it's highly unlikely I'll be able to extend it beyond that point, so you might want to give some thought to your next career move. If you do decide to return to Washington, to the National Archives for example, you could retain your reserve commission and perhaps apply for assignment to a Military History Detachment at the Army Center for Military History. I understand most of the active duty detachments will be put into the reserves and activated on an 'as needed' basis. As Germany has officially asked the United States to keep its stationed forces in Berlin until the Soviet departure in 1994, the current plan is for me to be extended—that could of course change. In any case, I'll be looking for another job too, in the not-too-distant."

"Again, my thanks for all your efforts on my behalf, D3! I've been giving it some thought. Maybe I could remain in Germany and teach for the University of Maryland University College or one of the other universities. On the other hand, I would like to go back to the National Archives, or maybe even to the Library of Congress. I'll start putting out feelers."

"Please do that, Thomas, and while you're at it, put out a few feelers for me, too!"

Although we were tracking the larger events happening throughout Germany and Europe, my gaze remained fixed on the Wall. Not content with the additional crossing points, *Berliner* and visitors began to break it down with the tools at hand. Some enterprising individuals even rented out chisels and mallets by the hour to "*Mauerspechte*." In mid-June, the systematic dismantling of the Wall separating Wedding from Mitte, West Berlin from East Berlin, began at *Ackerstraße*. When off-duty, I began to retrace the Wall walks I'd taken as a student, following the *Ruinen-im-werden* from Wedding through Tiergarten, Kreuzberg, and Neukölln. Given the pace and extent of the deconstruction, it seemed unlikely there would be ruins remaining to serve as a "bridge of tradition" to the past or to the future. I walked past the empty *KuKuK* awaiting renovation, and the towering Excelsior House. Although tempted, I decided not to take the elevator back up to the T-T Music Café. The music of the metal hammers ringing on concrete, filling the grainy *Berliner Luft, Luft, Luft* was all I needed, ja ja, ja ja, ja ja ja ja ja ja!

The second round of the "Two Plus Four" meetings began in the later part of June. On the first of July, the *Deutsch Mark* was introduced into East Germany. Economic unification preceded political reunification. Four days later, Bob Dylan brought his "Never Ending Tour" to the International Congress Centrum, a monstrous silver-plated mausoleum astride the *Avus Autobahn* in Charlottenburg, British Sector. *"All architecture is what you do when you look upon it, (Did you think it was in the white or gray stone? or the lines of the arches and cornices?)."* He came on stage wearing a Soviet *ushanka*-hat, telling his faithful followers it was "… a pleasure to play in this part of the world where Elvis spent so much time." Not quite this far East, Bob! With The Wall and its watchtowers coming down as he sang, his performance of "All Along the Watchtower" took on an unintended significance. As I left the ICC in the good company of thousands of other concert goers, I heard my name. "Thomas, Thomas!" Looking around, I couldn't see anyone I knew, or anyone waving to me. Curiously, the voice calling my name seemed to be coming from above, out the gray, granulated *Berliner Luft!* I stopped, facing Jean-Robert Ipousteguy's large, bronze figurative sculpture, *Ecbatana.* Instead of the City of Ecbatana, surrounded by its seven concentric walls of different colors, Alexander the Great contemplated the City of Berlin before him, surrounded but no longer bound by one wall, the Wall. Although seated, the helmeted Alexander seemed to be reaching out, reaching out for … well, for Rainer, perched out on what appeared to be a metallic forecastle! "Thomas, I was hoping to catch you after the concert! That's why I climbed up here. How was it? Wait, let me come down." Rainer wasn't actually interested in either Bob the Great or Alexander Dylan; he had something he wanted to show me.

Dodging the yellow taxicabs and double-decker buses of absolute reality on *Neue Kantsraße*, we walked over the *Autobahnbrücke*, turning left on *Wundtsraße*, which we followed to the *Lietzensee*. "Well, what do you think, Thomas?" Parked next to the small lake was what appeared to be a new Soviet UAZ 469 off-road light military utility vehicle, flat green with the red star and *Советская Армия*, "Soviet Army" still displayed on both the doors. How often I'd seen that insignia on Soviet vehicles during USMLM tours of the German Democratic Republic. "I bought it, insurance included, from a Russian *Oberstleutnant* this afternoon at the used car lot on *Luisienplatz* in Potsdam. He seemed very depressed about returning to Russia. Let's go for a drive! 'Let's go West!'" Rainer turned left onto *Kaiserserdamm*, which became *Heerstraße*. On the road again but this time without background music. We drove west, on through the deserted border crossing point in Spandau to the Wall. Rainer left the road, turning left onto the paved patrol road in the *intervallum*, in the direction of the old Fort Hahneberg. "Let's see just how 'off-road' this UAZ 469 is. Uh oh, Thomas!" Ahead, our headlights illuminated a patrol of armed East German border guards walking along the patrol road in our direction. Rainer slowed but did not stop the UAZ 469. As we approached, they politely stepped off to the side to let us pass by. As we did, I saluted smartly, just as Sergeant Miller had so patiently taught me to do. Fortunately, because of the ever-present chance of rain in Berlin, which fell on West and East alike, I had decided to wear my army-issue trench coat without rank insignia to the Dylan concert. The border guards came to attention and returned my salute. They watched us closely, laughing as we drove on. Observing them closely in the rearview mirror, I watched as they walked through a breech in the Wall into Spandau, into West Berlin, where they were apparently going for a beer at a *Kneipe* facing the Wall. Rainer drove on along the patrol road, until we came to a watchtower, parking the UAZ 469 in a reserved space next to it. We sat quietly for a moment. There were no lights in the watchtower, no sounds. The steel door at the base of the concrete tower stood open. We got out of the vehicle and climbed the stairs to the observation platform at the top of the watchtower to look back out over the Wall into Spandau.

In mid-July, Chancellor Kohl and President Gorbachev met again, this time in the Caucasus, both agreeing a unified, sovereign Germany should be able to choose its Alliance partners, to choose NATO. Cultural developments followed hard on the political the following week, when former band member Roger Waters brought Pink Floyd's *The Wall* to Berlin. Standing on a formerly restricted zone between *Brandenburger Tor* and *Potsdamer Platz*, I was one of a half a million. Images of the Wall coming down were projected onto a cardboard wall, which fell as the masses repeated the mantra echoing President Reagan's appeal to Secretary General Gorbachev three years earlier, "Tear down this wall!" *Wahrheit und Dichtung.*

But Clio, muse of history, was not only active on the Berlin Front. The thunderbolt struck again, this time not in Central Europe, but Southwest Asia. On August 2, 1990, at 02:00 local time, four Iraqi Divisions invaded neighboring Kuwait. The next day, the United Nations Security Council condemned the invasion, demanding the immediate withdrawal of all Iraqi forces. Rather than withdraw, Iraq consolidated its control over Kuwait. On August 7, President Bush ordered the deployment of US combat forces to Saudi Arabia, initiating Operation Desert Shield. At their

September summit meeting in Helsinki, Presidents Bush and Gorbachev turned their attention from the impending reunification of Germany to the Iraqi invasion, issuing a joint statement on the crisis in the Persian Gulf. Although we closely followed the developing crisis in the Gulf with great concern, neither D3 nor I realized repercussions would reach Berlin. Although the thunderbolt refocused the summit, it did not impede the momentum of German reunification. On September 12, 1990, the Two Plus Four Agreement was signed in Moscow.

The End of the Accidental *Polis*
October 1990

Following the August decision of the freely elected *Volkskammer*, the German Democratic Republic joined the Federal Republic of Germany under the provisions of Article 23 of the Basic Law, *das Grundgesetz*, on October 3, 1990. The day before, at the final meeting of the *Kommandatura*, the British commandant officially ended the military occupation of West Berlin. Berlins three- *bzw.* four-power occupation status, which had been expertly explained to the Accidental *Polis* Seminar by Sophia Sweelin Werner, now seven years ago, would end at midnight. Together with the commandants and a host of politicians, East and West, members of the USMLM watched as the white guard shack at Allied Checkpoint Charlie was hoisted into the air by crane, an artifact for a museum of the Cold War. The accidental *polis* no longer existed; its end had been both intentional and peaceful. Together with Checkpoint Charlie, the theology of Berlin became the stuff of another chapter in Cold War history. With the loss of its sacred purpose as the frontier of freedom and delimitation of its circuit wall, *teikhos*, deconstruction of the purified city, the Armed Camp was complete.

Technically, US Military Mission Potsdam deactivated with the termination of occupation status. As the Red Army prepared to withdraw from a reunited Germany, liaison with US forces became as critical as at any time in USMLM's history. Consequently, USMLM would be retained under Headquarters, US Army, Europe until the scheduled withdrawal of Soviet forces in the fall of 1994. Most of the USMLM members attended the farewell ceremony for triple-hatted Commandant, US Commander Berlin, and Commander, US Army Berlin at US Army, Europe Headquarters in Heidelberg on October 2. I hoped to be able to return to Berlin on October 3 for the ceremony in front of the *Reichstag*—according to my early on-site research, the fault zone, the *Schwerpunkt* of the HistoriCity. Although D3 and I tried all the tricks at our disposal, we were unable to arrange for air transportation, so following the reception for General Haddock, we took a train from Heidelberg to Frankfurt, where we boarded the US Army duty train for Berlin. When the train departed the Frankfurt *Hauptbahnhof* on the early evening of October 2, there were two Germanys: the Federal Republic and the German Democratic Republic, West Germany and East Germany. At midnight, while we were in transit through the GDR, it ceased to exist. The duty train arrived early in the morning of October 3 at the US Army Rail Transportation Office in a reunited Berlin, designated capital of a reunited Germany. Although I'd missed the ceremony at the *Reichstag*, *Schwerpunkt* of the HistoriCity, perhaps on board the Berlin duty train en route to the reunited city was a more appropriate place for a captain in the US Army Reserves to be.

As D3 had written in the introduction to the 1988 Annual Historical Report, the mission of the USMLM continued, becoming even more interesting with unification, as long as Soviet forces remained in Germany. The Mission closely monitored and documented the dramatic departure of Red Army units from Germany. In addition to liaison matters, D3 devoted part of the USMLM daily brief to developments in reunified Germany. Businesses in the former German Democratic Republic scrambled to retool production from a socialist to a capitalist model. In most instances, this proved difficult if not impossible. One enterprising entrepreneur in Dresden marketed tea imported from the People's Republic of China under the label "Red Zwinger." With his battle face in place, D3 informed us a city renamed by the East German government had decided to retake its historic name: "I'm pleased to be able to report *Karl-Marx-Stadt* has once again become *Groucho-Marx-Stadt!*"

One of the noncommissioned officers who knew the chief of mission was checking to see if we were paying attention to his "current events" lesson, spoke up at once. "Excuse me, sir, I don't mean to contradict you, but I believe the previous name of *Karl-Marx-Stadt* was Chemnitz."

"Roger that, First Sergeant, and thank you very much for the correction, I must have once again been misinformed by Captain Vonaechron!"

On an unusually sunny day in late October, D3 and I drove out to Rose Range for target practice. While drawing our handguns from the weapons room, D3 asked, "Hey, Thomas, how'd ja like to swap out your old, 'Pistol, Caliber .45, Automatic, M1911A1' for the new, 'Pistol, Semiautomatic, 9 mm, M9 (9mm Beretta M9)?'"

"No thanks, D3, do I have to? I like my old .45. I know it's heavier, but it's also historic, if you know what I mean. Hopefully, I'll never have to aim it at anything but a paper target." D3 looked at me thoughtfully, nodding his head in agreement. We were both thinking about the Viet Cong soldier he had killed in close combat, and the American army major lost at Ludwigslust in 1985.

During the ramp-up to reunification, the Berlin Station of the Central Intelligence Agency obtained select files of State Security Service, the *Stasi*, from a well-placed source in the front office of the *Normanenstraße* headquarters, prior to its peaceful occupation by 2,000 demonstrators on January 15. Among the documents marked *GEHEIM* and *STRENG GEHEIM*, there were files pertaining to the *LaBelle* disco bombing, incriminating five suspects, one employed by the Libyan Embassy in East Berlin. Perhaps it was the political officer Nadja and Clarence had spoken to. Touting my archival background and knowledge of the agency's history, D3 arranged for me to review the records in the basement of Building Six at the John F. Kennedy Headquarters Compound. It was much like being back in Vault Six, with one significant exception. Although authorized to review the documents, I was not authorized to release them.

Focused on the drawdown of the Soviet Western Group of Forces, we coincidentally monitored developments in the Middle East, where momentum continued to build. In early November, President Bush deployed the VII Corps from Germany to Saudi Arabia, providing a "coalition of the willing" with the forces necessary to conduct a ground offensive. Although it was one of the two US corps stationed in the Federal Republic of Germany since 1950 to deter Soviet aggression, the United States government forgot to notify the German government of the deployment in advance. The Cold War was truly over. This fact was underlined later that month in "Parisfrance," as my grandfather used to say, at a summit meeting where Presidents Bush and Gorbachev signed the Treaty on Conventional Armed Forces in Europe, and the Organization for Security and Cooperation in Europe produced the Charter of Paris for a New Europe, ending the division of Europe into East and West.

At the end of November, the United Nations Security Council issued Resolution 678, authorizing "Member States co-operating with the Government of Kuwait, unless Iraq on or before 15 January 1991 fully implements . . . the above mentioned resolutions, to use all necessary means to uphold and implement resolution 660 (1990) and all subsequent resolutions and to restore international peace and security in the area." After D3 finished reading the resolution out loud, I replied, "Well, D3, it seems the US Army is unfortunately going to have the opportunity to examine our war as 'reality opera' hypothesis. Remember our discussions at *Luise* and the *Deutsche Oper* with Professor Schneider? By the way, I also remember your unfortunate remarks about 'getting a head' in the army during the opera!"

D3 smiled, "Of course I do, Thomas. Now let's see, how does 'Norman Schwarzkopf in Kuwait' play as the title for an opera based upon current operations. Doesn't quite have the same aesthetic appeal as 'Julius Caesar in Egypt' does it, though John Adams got away with 'Nixon in China' a few years ago. Surely the name 'Schwarzkopf' would appeal to German opera fans. Maybe just 'Schwarfkopf in Kuwait?' Let's see now, Saddam Hussein is our Tolomeo, but who could be our Cleopatra?"

"You mean our Clio-patra don't you, D3!"

"Ouch, Thomas, that's almost as bad as . . ."

"I know, I know, 'Friedrich the Grape!'"

"Actually, I was going to say, 'One should never take history for granite!'"

Two days after the deadline established by the United Nations Security Council Resolution passed, coalition forces initiated Operation Desert Storm. The ground assault phase followed the air campaign on February 24. It lasted eighty-nine hours. Kuwait was liberated in accordance with the United Nations Security Council Resolution. Although Clio appeared to have abandoned D3 and me in Berlin when her focus shifted from Central Europe to Southwest Asia, after the storm in the desert had subsided at 0800 hours on Thursday, February 28, 1991, the muse of history reached out once again for her two suitors, still stationed in the HistoriCity.

CHAPTER VII:
The City Which is to Come

"For here we have no lasting city, but we are seekers after the city which is to come."

—Hebrews 13:14

"*. . . das ist die neue, die großartige Stadt, in der sich alle hören und sehen und in der alle verstehen: mon coeur, the night, your heart, the day, der Tag, die Nacht, das Herz.*"[83]

—Wolfgang Borchert,
Im Mai, im Mai schrie der Kuckuk

Sudden Enlightenment
February 1991

KYRA CALLED from Munich to remind me that spring recess for the University of Maryland University College fell between March 18 and 23. Making maximum use of the duty train, we'd been able to meet regularly in Munich and Berlin, though usually for not longer than two or three days at a time. A whole week together would qualify as a vacation. Her break coincidentally coincided with the ceremony marking the official departure of VII US Corps from Stuttgart. The storm in the desert had now passed, and VII Corps was scheduled to return to the continental United States for deactivation after forty-one years in the Federal Republic of Germany. The departure marked the end of the Cold War, but not of history. As the USMLM Chief of Mission, D3 received an official invitation to the festivities, but was unable to attend. Something was brewing in Berlin in the wake of Desert Storm. Designating me as his official representative, he generously approved my request for a week's leave to coincide with Kyra's time off. All available quarters at Kelley, Patch, and Robinson Barracks in and around Stuttgart had been booked for VIP guests coming from within the European Theater and CONUS. With the help of the travel office at Truman Plaza, I finally found a double room at the *Hotel Helm*

---

83 ". . . that is the new, the sublime city, where everyone listens, where everyone sees, where everyone understands: my heart, the night, your heart, the day, the night, the heart," Diary of Thomas Vonaechron, Diary Extract, 1989, trans. TV.

on *Holzmarkt* in Tübingen, the old university town forty-four kilometers south of Stuttgart. Arriving at the Frankfurt *Hauptbahnhof* from the Berlin Rail Transportation Office early on the morning of March 16, I continued on to Tübingen by train. Kyra would arrive there from Munich the next day. By the time I'd checked in to the *Helm*, a front-gabled, half-timbered hotel on the old *Holzmarkt*, it was already early afternoon. Before *flâner*-ing through the narrow medieval streets, up the hill to castle *Hohentübingen*, then back down through the old city and across the River Neckar, I decided to have lunch. Walking into the hotel restaurant, I was delighted to see my mentor and former landlord, Dr. Karl Kahler, sitting at a small wooden table next to the window, looking out onto the *Holzmarkt*. I should have been surprised by this chance meeting, but wasn't.

"*Salve*, Dr. Kahler, well met!"

Standing up to shake my hand, he replied, "Why, Dr. Vonaechron, or should I say 'Captain Dr. Vonaechron,' what an unexpected pleasure it is to see you here! Herr von Garlitz did mention to me that you would be coming down from Berlin to attend the ceremony in Stuttgart, but little did I expect to find you at the *Helm* in Tübingen!" Nodding to the newspaper open on the table he said, "I've just been reading about it in the *Schwäbisches Tageblatt*. Quite an historical event, your countrymen leaving Stuttgart after, what does it say here,' looking down through his wire-rimmed glasses, he read, "forty-one years! *Herr* von Garlitz also told me the Western Allies, our *Alliierte Schutzmächte*, are also planning to leave Berlin, but in 1994. The German government asked them to remain in Berlin until the Red Army has departed Germany." He smiled. "These are indeed remarkable times, and I must add quite an interesting time to be an archivist, historian, and, in your case, also an officer!"

"Will you also attend the ceremony on Monday afternoon, Dr. Kahler?"

"No, no, I won't. To be honest, I'm not as interested in military matters as I once was or perhaps should be. I'm returning to Berlin early tomorrow morning. I've been staying here with an old friend, now a *Professor der Germanistik* at the university. Many years ago, when he was a student, I worked as an apprentice at the *Antiquariat*, the second-hand bookstore across the *Holzmarkt*, *J. J. Heckenhauer*. Just over there, do you see it? It's worth a visit if you have the time. Whenever I return to Tübingen, I always come back to the *Helm*, sit here at this table with a glass of *Trollinger*, and watch the customers, mostly students, going in and out of the bookstore. Would you care to join me for a *Viertele*? It's been quite some time since we raised a glass together!" I ordered a glass of *Trollinger* at the bar, joining Dr. Kahler at the small wooden table by the window. "*Herr* von Garlitz speaks about you frequently. If I understood him correctly, now that you have completed your studies, you have accepted a full-time position with the US Army in Berlin."

"Yes, yes, I have. My friend, D3, you remember, the American who, how did you put it, 'sounds a little bit like a *Bundeswehroffizier* on the telephone,' the one who recommended I apply for a commission in the Army Reserve. When I first moved to *Mohnstraße*, I had a part-time position, one weekend a month and a few temporary duty trips down to Munich and to Heidelberg. After my *Promotion*, I accepted a full-time position with the US Military Liaison Mission Potsdam. Full-time, but temporary, only through this June. D3, who's also now my chief, has already extended me twice. It's unlikely he'll be able to do it again. Although my dissertation and examinations are finished, I'm still writing history, preparing reports on 'current events,' which ironically become 'the past' just as soon as I've signed them. Hopefully, those reports will eventually make their way to the National Archives in Washington, DC, and then maybe one day back from the National Archives to the *Stadtstaatsarchiv Berlin!*"

"Much can happen between now and June, Dr. Vonaechron! But tell me, please, have you considered returning to Washington, DC, to the National Archives, to make certain the reports you've written in Berlin arrive and that, once they've been—what was the term?—'reviewed,' copies are sent back to Berlin? I don't think *Herr* von Garlitz would mind returning to Washington to help you! Your doctoral degree and professional experience at the *Stadtstaatsarchiv* should open up a few more opportunities when you return."

"Yes, I have, Dr. Kahler. In fact, it's interesting you should raise that particular question. After learning D3 was able to extend me for another year, I sent a copy of my resume to the personnel office of the National Archives, together with a cover letter requesting consideration for any positions opening up over the next year. Apparently, there will be an opening for a supervisory archivist in the Modern Military Branch next year. Given my previous training, degree, and military experience, it would be a perfect fit. My *Promotion* just might help me get a promotion! But, there is also a young woman here in Germany, Kyra DeGetria, also an American. We met several years ago in Munich, where she lives and teaches. I honestly don't know if I could, or if, for that matter, if I should even try, to talk her into returning to Washington with me. She will join me here tomorrow morning. I'm very sorry you won't be here, I would have liked to introduce you to her. There were no rooms available at any of the army installations in and around Stuttgart, so I booked a room here at the *Helm*. During a temporary duty trip to Heidelberg, which we suggested to our superiors, we became better acquainted, working together at the university library, walking through the *Weinachtsmarkt*, spending hours discussing *Gott und die Welt* in the Sonder Bar on *Marktplatz*.

"The Sonder Bar on *Marktplatz*, I know it well, Dr. Vonaechron. It's a very good place to discuss *Gott und die Welt* with a young woman!"

"As you well know Dr. Kahler, Tübingen is also an old German college town. Like Heidelberg, it's picturesque, a place where we'll hopefully be able to relax for a few days and talk about life in Munich, Berlin, and maybe in Washington. Now that I'm here, I'm happy no rooms were available for us in Stuttgart. The *Helm* is more romantic than most visiting officers' quarters, though we did have an interesting interlude at the Heidelberg VOQ!"

"Why, Dr. Vonaechron, you sound quite serious!"

"Yes, yes, I believe am, Dr. Kahler. Kyra's also an historian, and an army officer, too! As we've come to know each over the years, we seem . . . what would be the right word, 'complementary.' Yes, complementary. We're different, but our differences dovetail nicely. It might sound odd, but when we're together, we seem to be two parts of one person. Just like Aristophanes muses in Plato's *Symposium*." Even though the accidental *polis* no longer existed, Dr. Schneider's insights into the "lovers of the city" remained with me.

"It doesn't sound odd at all, Dr. Vonaechron. You know, you're actually in the very best of company! *Animus* and *Anima*, that is how the Swiss psychiatrist Carl Jung described it, the female part of the male, the male part of the female. No doubt you've spoken with *Herrn* Hemd about the *yin* and the *yang*. Even our august predecessor in that all-too-wide field of history Georg Wilhelm Friedrich Hegel himself, writing on 'love' as a young man, and perhaps his youth had something to do with it, addresses the pair of lovers as paradox, '*In der Liebe ist das Getrennte noch, aber nicht mehr als Getrenntes—als Einiges und das Lebendige fühlt das Lebendige.*' Hmmm, let me try that in English, 'In love separateness remains, but no longer as something separate, rather as something united, living beings sensing one another.'" At Dr. Kahler's mention of Hegel, I remembered standing at the foot of his . . . standing at the foot of their—Marie and G. F.'s—grave in the *Dorotheenstadt Friedhof* in East Berlin. Love as a variable in history.

"Erich Fromm reaches a conclusion similar to Hegel's, looking at love as a union in which the lovers retain their individuality. Two become one, yet remain two. If you both find you 'complement,' to use your word, or 'complete,' to use Aristophanes's, each other, then I heartily encourage you to pursue love together, as one. Love is the most important thing. At the very worst, it could only be—how did a friend of mine once define it?—'. . . a kind of noble selectivity of sexuality.' Are you acquainted with the writings of the German Romantic poet Novalis, Georg Philipp Friedrich *Freiherr* von Hardenberg? Novalis believed love to be the final purpose of world history, the 'Amen of the Universe.' What did you say your young lady's given name is, again, please?"

"Kyra."

"Kyra. Perhaps from the Greek, likely of Hindi and/or Sanskrit origin. 'Beam of light.' In Russian, Kyra is understood as 'mistress' or 'ruler.' Hmmm, very interesting, Dr. Vonaechron. And her surname once more please was . . ."

"DeGetria, I believe it's Italian, but I'm not certain. I've been meaning to ask her and will do so tomorrow!"

"Italian, or it could once again be from the Greek, from *Hodegetria*, 'she who shows the way.' You know, now that you are a *Doktor der Philosophie*, no longer a student, and have reentered the professional world, if not yet as an archivist then as an army officer, I propose we drink *Brüderschaft*." Dr. Kahler leaned forward in his chair, reminding me once again of *The Past* sculpture guarding the Pennsylvania Avenue entrance to the Main Archives building in Washington, DC. Raising our glasses in our right hands, we intertwined arms and drank deeply from our *Viertele* of Trollinger.

"Karl."

"Thomas."

Finishing his *Viertele*, Karl set his glass gently down on the wooden table, smiled, and said, "Thomas, please forgive me for leaving you alone once again, but I must rejoin my friend for his lecture in less than half an hour in the *Aula*. Let's meet again in Berlin for a *Viertele*, perhaps the next time you come to meet with *Herrn* Hemd. What a happy coincidence to meet you in Tübingen today, I'm certain it was meant to be! When you take a walk through—what did you call it?—the 'old college town,' be sure to stop into the *Stiftskirche St. Georg* here on *Holzmarkt*. There's a lovely young blonde woman lying there in state among the *Wüttembürger*. She has such a beautiful bright red mouth I'm always tempted to kiss her, but, fortunately, there always seems to be someone standing nearby. I wouldn't want to provoke an incident!"

"Farewell, Karl, and thank you so much! Thank you, once again, for being my landlord, thank you for being my teacher—I look forward to our next symposium at your big wooden table in the *Lothringerstrasse*!"

When Kyra arrived at the *Bahnhof* the next morning, she was pleased and preoccupied. Stepping down from the *InterCity* coach onto the platform, she kissed me while handing me her helmet bag, our standard operating procedure. Dressed in her *Trachtenmantel* and feathered Tyrolean hat, she was lovely. Sensing her unease, I decided not to ask about her 'Dirndl.'

"Let's walk to our hotel," I suggested, "it's not far, and a little 'physical training' after three hours on the train might be invigorating. Besides, Kyra, I want to show you the remarkable view of old Tübingen from the bridge, just like a painting, perhaps not quite as much of a Hallmark as the *Heidelberger Weinachtsmarkt* but close!"

Kyra laughed and smiled, "Yes, yes, that's a good idea! Let's do, let's walk, Thomas. I need to talk with you. I need your input on a career decision." As we started to walk across the old bridge over the *Neckar*, she began to talk, "Not long ago, we learned University of Maryland University College will be moving from Munich to Reese *Kaserne* in Augsburg this coming May. McGraw *Kaserne* is scheduled to begin closing down operations the first of next year for return to the German government, another one of those painful payoffs of the post-Cold War 'peace-dividend.' Just like VII Corps in Stuttgart, U of M's been in Munich for forty-one years. As a consequence of the move and of the projected drop in student enrollment, the faculty will be cut in half. It doesn't appear there will be a job for me in Augsburg. As you know, U of M is a two-year program, and there simply won't be enough students. Furthermore, there's no on-campus housing available for the faculty members who do have the option to relocate. After taking the *Goethe-Institut* exams, I'd planned to start working on my doctorate at *Ludwigs-Maximilian-Universität*, but that no longer makes sense. To study in Munich, I need a job in Munich. You probably haven't heard, both Munich Det and Berlin Det will be deactivated. The 'peace-dividend' strikes again! So, I'd have to drill at Military Intelligence Group Headquarters in Heidelberg. I'm thinking about relocating to Heidelberg and studying at the *Universität Heidelberg* as a fallback. I had to think about our TDY trip there, the *Weinachtsmarkt*, the university library and, of course, the Sonder Bar, where I fell in love with you. Perhaps I could get a part-time teaching position with Schiller College. But another, a better option has just come up . . . at the University of Maryland in College Park, where I've informally, and please don't say anything about it to anyone at this point, not even to D3 please, tentatively been offered a teaching assistantship for the coming fall semester. The dean in Munich came from Main Campus and has excellent connections. It all sounds good, but . . . it's just that, well . . . College Park is so far away, so far away from Berlin, so far away from you, Thomas. 'Space Available' travel on MILAIR out of Dover Air Base to Ramstein Air Base is a bit more difficult than taking the duty train to and from Frankfurt. What do you think I should do, Thomas? Please tell me. I have to think for both of us, for all of us! I'm so sorry to ambush you on arrival like this, but I've been turning it over and over and need your input to decide. I wanted to call when I first heard about the College Park billet, but decided to wait until we could have some face time, until I could see you." Taking my arm, she stopped, looked into my eyes, pushed her green feathered felt hat back on her forehead, and kissed me gently.

Putting my right arm gently around her waist, I stepped over to the railing in the middle of the bridge to let the Sunday pedestrians pass us by. "All right, I will. But first, Kyra, please look, just for a moment!" The *Neckar* flowed slowly past the pale yellow Hölderlin Tower, past the pastel, half-timbered, gabled buildings fronting the tree-lined banks, passing under the bridge at our feet. A few pedestrians *flâner*-ed along the *Zwingel*, the narrow walkway leading to the tower. Someone was slipping a long wooden boat, *einen Stocherkahn,* into the river. Along with the room reservation, the travel office had provided me with a list of "Things to do in Tübingen." A ride in a *Stocherkahne,* used to punt, to pole passengers around the narrow, long island lined with stately sycamore trees in the middle of the river, was first on the list. The ferryman was familiar—Govinda, no, it was Karl, but it couldn't be! He'd told me yesterday he was planning to depart early this morning. Karl might have left, but his words remained behind: "Pursue love together, as one." My eyes were filling, but finding I could still speak, I said, "College Park's not that far from Washington, Kyra, just a few miles to the northeast, if I remember correctly."

Gently placing her hand on my shoulder, Kyra turned from the river to face me and said, "What do you mean, Thomas, 'College Park's not that far from Washington?'"

"Well, I might have a 'better option' too, Kyra! A position for a supervisory archivist in the Modern Military Branch of the National Archives will open up sometime next year, not underground in Suitland but aboveground, in downtown DC on Constitution Avenue at the Main Archives building. No guarantees, of course, but with my NARS background, 'advanced degree,' and army experience, I should have a pretty good shot at it. What's the name of that other 'Park' north of Washington, west of College Park . . . Takoma Park! I'm certain there's a place in Takoma Park with enough room for us and all our books and papers! Kyra, will you marry me?"

Looking directly into my eyes, her brown eyes flashing, she said, "Yes, Thomas, yes, yes, I will. I will marry you," and she asked in return, "Thomas, will you marry me?"

I answered, "Yes, Kyra, yes, yes, I will. I will marry you."

After exchanging our vows on the bridge over the *Neckar,* lover's lips to the ears of both the yielding bride and bridegroom alike, we walked up

Neckargaße to the *Helm* on *Holzmarkt* to celebrate our marriage. A more formal, follow-on ceremony would follow later, at Memorial Chapel in Fort Leavenworth, Kansas, with D3 serving as our best man.

Early the next morning, we took the train from Tübingen to the Stuttgart *Hauptbahnhof,* strolling hand-in-hand down the *Königstraße* to the *Neues Schloß,* formally dressed for the occasion in our class-A uniforms. Now a pedestrian zone—*eine Fußgängerzone*—the broad shopping street had been rapidly reconstructed after the war. A sense of loss remained, however, giving the postwar buildings a temporary, provisional quality. A reviewing stand with covered seating for invited guests had been set up on the *Schloßplatz,* in front of the reconstructed eighteenth-century Baroque palace. At least the war had left the facade standing.

Along with D3's invitation came two reserved seats. Many had come, invited guests and interested spectators alike, on this mild, sunny March day to watch. Some celebrated, others were saddened by the departure of the VII US Corps, which, over four decades, had become part of the city. Addressing soldiers, civilians, and their family members on behalf of all citizens of Stuttgart, Lord Mayor Manfred Rommel, in his wise and matter-of-fact manner, said, "I did not want you to leave us, but it cannot be denied that the Iron Curtain which had cut Europe in two has been lifted." I was sorry D3 missed the exchange between the VII Corps commander and the commander-in-chief, US Army, Europe and Seventh Army, a verbal validation of his "Sun-Tsu Soldier" theory.

"Sir: a final report. In November 1951, the VII Corps' mission was to maintain combat readiness and to defend and secure the borders of West Germany. Today, mission accomplished. Jayhawk 6, out."

"Well done! Take your soldiers home."

Along with the covered seats, our invitations also opened the doors of the New Palace to the lavish reception following the ceremony. After glasses of *Wüttemburger Wein* and heavy hors d'oeuvres, we were invited out onto the balcony overlooking *Schloßplatz* to view the *Großer Zapfenstreich* given by the *Bundeswehr* in honor of VII Corps. Darkness had fallen; the *Schloßplatz* was now illuminated by flickering torches held by German airmen, sailors, and soldiers, silently standing at parade rest, waiting for the ceremony to begin. Although Kyra and I both knew the *Großer Zapfenstreich* long predated its misuse by the National Socialists, the atmosphere was ominous. Just before the joyous fife and drum music heralding the beginning of the ceremony broke the spell, Kyra turned to me, the torchlight from below dancing in her eyes, and softly said, "Scary, scary."

Orders
March 1991

In the wake of Desert Storm and the decimation of Iraqi forces deployed to Kuwait, there were insurrections against the weakened central government in Baghdad, first in southern and then in northern Iraq. Shi'ites, encouraged by the United States during the war, revolted in the south, as did Kurds living in the north, close to the border with Turkey, after the war. Kurds who had been drafted into the Iraqi Army and Army Reserves joined the uprising in the north, taking control of several cities and towns close to the Turkish border. After suppressing the Shi'ite uprising in the south, Republic Guard units, their loyalty to Baghdad unshaken, moved north. The use of helicopters to deploy forces and helicopter gunships to brutally stem the Kurdish revolt was not challenged by the Desert Storm Coalition. The violence catalyzed an exodus of over half a million people from northwest Iraq across the mountains into neighboring Turkey. Fearing for their lives, the Kurdish populations of Dohuk, the provincial capital, and Zakho abandoned their cities for the uncertain security of the mountains. Driving as far as their vehicles could take them, they continued on foot through the mountain passes across the border into Turkey, where those not refused entry by Turkish soldiers were channeled into makeshift mountain camps. The government of Turkey estimated over 200,000 Kurdish refugees had crossed the border. Largely city-dwellers from Northern Iraq, without shelter, the refugees suffered enormous hardship in the barren mountains. Turkey's Red Crescent Society, the International Red Cross and nongovernmental organizations provided initial emergency relief but were quickly overwhelmed by the demand. Unsanitary conditions in the makeshift refugee camps fostered the spread of measles, cholera, typhus, and dysentery. International relief agencies estimated over one thousand persons were dying daily. Doctors without Borders described the situation as a "medical apocalypse."

In early April, US European Command established Joint Task Force Provide Comfort, which, as coalition partners joined the humanitarian assistance effort, evolved into a combined task force. The mission of CTF Provide Comfort was threefold: to stop the dying and suffering in the mountains, to resettle the refugees into temporary camps in Northern Iraq, and, finally, to return the refugees to their homes. US Special Operations Command, Europe organized immediate airdrops of relief supplies and prepared ground forces to assist refugees in the temporary camps. The Commander of Operation Provide Comfort, Lieutenant General John Shalikashvili, was ordered to establish a security zone, a safe haven, in Northern Iraq for repatriation of the refugees. He met with Lieutenant General Fariq Saber and Brigadier General Nashwan Thanoon, representing the Iraqi General Staff, at the Khabur Bridge Customs House on the border between Turkey and Iraq near Zakho on April 19, 1991. General Shalikashvili informed the Iraqi generals coalition forces were going to enter Iraq the following day to establish the temporary security zone, politely but vigorously issuing a demarche for withdrawal of all Iraqi units from Zakho, the designated location of Joint Task Force Bravo Headquarters. To mitigate misunderstandings and prevent conflict between coalition and Iraqi Forces, General Shalikashvili also proposed the establishment of a "Military Coordination Center." Brigadier General Nashwan Dahnoun became the senior Iraqi MCC representative.

When I returned to the Mission for duty on Monday of the last week in March following the *Flitterwoche* with Kyra in Tübingen, D3 called me into his office. USMLM Potsdam had received "prepare to deploy" instructions from US European Command, outlining the mission of a "Military Coordination Center" at a yet-to-be determined location. Supported by Mesopotamian Arabic and Kurdish linguists, the MCC would provide a twenty-four-hour-a-day-seven-days-a-week interface with Iraqi military and civilian authorities during the projected return and resettlement of the refugees from the mountains. After reading the message aloud, he looked up at me and said, "Kurdish refugees living in makeshift camps in the mountains passes and on the mountainsides are at great risk, particularly the very young and the very old. The challenge is to stabilize the situation and then to bring them back down from the mountains, back to the flatland, then back to their homes in Iraq. Most of the hundreds of thousands of refugees fleeing their homes in the cities were totally unprepared. Sickness and death are increasing, requiring humanitarian assistance and humanitarian intervention. The US Military Liaison Mission offers European Command a ready-made Military Coordination Center, with forty-six years of experience in the delicate art of adversarial negotiation. And since we have, and I quote, 'little work to do' right now," D3 looked at the ceiling, shaking his helmet-haired head and continued, "USMLM is being given an 'opportunity to excel!' Although we'll have to work with and through translators, though I'm hoping some of the senior Iraqi officers and officials speak Russian, there are significant similarities with what we're doing now. In dealing with the Iraqis, as with the Russians, it's critical we remain open, consistent, and predictable." He paused for a moment and looked directly at me. I knew what was coming. "Wanna come along, Thomas? You're not obliged to, you know. Your extension is up in two months and in spite of what Heidelberg thinks, there's a lot for you to do here. But, if you did want to come, I'm confident I could get an 'operational necessity' exception for the duration of the mission, with hazardous duty pay thrown in for good measure. Now I know you and Kyra have plans for the fall, but we should be able to wrap up the MCC mission before the end of the year, though as you well know, there are no guarantees. I'm assuming the Iraqis will want us out just as soon as possible and will reluctantly support return of the refugees. You know, Thomas, this deployment might be just the thing for you before returning to the National Archives. Just think of it, the Cold War's over, VII Corps's gone home, but USMLM is still out there on the border, a different border but a border nonetheless, makin' history. Why, who better to lead the staff of the Modern Military Branch of the National Archives back into the past than Captain Dr. Thomas Vonaechron, US Army Reserve? Yuck, yuck, yuck! And, if for some reason it doesn't work out at the Archives, both the Archives and the army are subject to the whims of the US government, then you could apply for an active duty assignment as commander of the Military History Detachment attached to the US Army Center for Military History. I can't imagine you'd ever have the chance to go back to Iraq with an MHD, so Provide Comfort will likely be your only opportunity in the unforeseeable future."

"I wouldn't miss it, D3, but please let me call Kyra. I want to discuss it with her before I accept. If I can catch her at her quarters, she could stop by 66th MI and use the secure phone to call us here."

Reaching for two unwashed coffee mugs on the shelf behind his desk, D3 said, "I'll go for coffee."

Fortunately, Kyra picked up and called back on the secure phone half an hour later. After I told her about the 'prepare to deploy' order, she didn't say anything for a moment and then laughed. "Well, Thomas, it seems I'm not only an officer in the US Army, but since we crossed that bridge together in Tübingen, an army wife too, the absolute worst of both worlds! Under other circumstances, I'd be pleased to join you . . . but I guess I'll just have to suck it up while you ruck it up for the next few months! I'll be teaching the introductory history course at College Park this fall, so I'll have my hold baggage shipped to the graduate dorm and put my household goods in storage until we have an idea when you might be coming back. When you do get back, we'll find that house in Takoma Park and arrange our lives along with our books and papers. In the meantime, I'll come up to Berlin ASAP for face time. I want you to remember the girl's behind you left behind! Tell D3 you're good to go!"

Immediately following the mid-April meeting between Generals Shalikashvili and Thanoon, orders came from US European Command in Stuttgart, through US Army, Europe in Heidelberg, directing seven members of the USMLM to deploy at once and establish the Military Coordination Center in Zahko, Iraq. "In Iraq, oh no, D3! This brings back the dream that came to me in *Psychiatrische Ambulanz* seven, eight, almost nine years ago. Yikes! Where is that dream taking us?"

D3 laughed, "I must confess, Thomas, I was fairly certain our temporary duty station would be in Iraq all along. You'll agree it does make sense, but I had to think about your dream, too. At least part of it seems to have come through the ivory gate after all. Coalition forces have already deployed to Iraq but only temporarily, and they will remain there only until the refugees have been safely returned to their homes. Joint Task Force Bravo has been set up by JTF Provide Comfort to administer and control the security zone. Under JTF Bravo, the Twenty-Fourth Marine Expeditionary Unit and the Forty-Five Commando Royal Marines have secured the area around Zakho. The MCC will be collocated with Headquarters, JTF Bravo in Zakho. For your information, in spite of the demarche, there are still Iraqi forces, military and civilian, remaining in and around Zakho. As I understand it, the military control the high ground overlooking the city, and police are present in the city as well. Hopefully, we won't have to 'fight like hell' when we get there! Are you certain you don't want to change out your old Colt .45 for a new Beretta? But seriously, remember. After defeating Iraqi forces in Kuwait, the coalition did not invade Iraq, though some of our senior policy makers strongly recommended we do so. The UN Security Council Resolution only authorized removal of Iraqi forces from Kuwait, not the invasion of Iraq. Maybe your dream was a 'worst possible case scenario,' a nightmare." D3 laughed. "Maybe, just maybe, we might be on the 'right side of history' again this time, Thomas!"

"Roger that, D3, but if memory serves, you did say, 'We'll just have Kuwait and see.' Well, now we've got Kuwait!"

"Ouch, did I say that? Why, Thomas, that's almost as bad as . . ."

"Yes, yes, I know, "Frederick the Grape!'"

"I still think 'one should never take history for granite' is worse! But apropos Frederick the Grape, *Unter den Linden* and your HistoriCity. It's 'Goodbye to Berlin,' at least for a while anyway. The *Schwerpunkt* of history seems to be shifting eastward, from Central Europe to Southwest Asia, toward Halford Mackinder's 'Geographical Pivot of History.' Iraq is already 'Rimland.' How does that old War College Mackinder litany go? 'Who rules East Europe commands the Heartland; Who rules the Heartland commands the World-Island; Who rules the World-Island commands the world.' I wonder what the muse of history has in mind for us, what Clio has in mind for the US?"

"That's just what concerns me, D3. Berlin was capital of the twentieth century, it may be that a new city, or even an ancient city, will become the capital of the twenty-first."

"Carry on, Clio!"

Breakfast
April 1991

When the alarm went off on the morning of my departure, I was already awake, lying on the big futon bed, fingers locked behind my head, listening to a cacophony of questions coming from birds talking in the linden trees just outside the large windows on the street-side of the bedroom. "Poo-tee-weet?" they asked, over and over again. Sunlight was beginning to filter in. Turning on my side, gently brushing away the hair from the back of her neck, I kissed Kyra softly, quietly got out of bed, slipped on my yukata, and, walking over to the door leading out onto the small tiled balcony facing *Mohnstraße*, opened it as quietly as I could. The view from the balcony captured the three-story *fin de siècle* apartment buildings across the street at the intersection of *Mohnstraße* and *Hortensienstraße* and off to the right, the stately sycamore trees lining *Plantanenplatz*. It was as if I had walked out through the door of Adolf von Menzel's painting *Balcony Room* into an earlier Berlin at a more peaceful time, in the days before the Great War, a Realist scene pointillised by morning light and filtered through the granular *Berliner Luft, Luft, Luft*. Steam rose from the damp street, steeping the leafing linden leaves, filling the air with their fragrance. In gratitude, I sang softly to myself, "*Wie lieblich ist der Lindenduft.*"[84] Looking at the birds perched among the leafing branches, I softly replied to their questioning with a question of my own, "*Tschlip-tschlip?*"[85] Looking down at the street, I was surprised to see a US government-issue green Ford Galaxy 500 'Custom Police Interceptor' parked directly beneath the balcony. The Shield of Achilles! The silver pinstriping running round the edges of the hood shone brightly in the morning sunlight. Looking more closely, I could make out some of the details of Judith l'Angelos's remarkable airbrush painting, cities of war and peace, the never-ending human dialectic. D3 had apparently arrived early and was no doubt having breakfast in the *Bäckerei* beneath our bedroom. Turning around, I stepped back inside the balcony door, surveying the high-ceilinged white room,

---

84 "How lovely is the lime fragrance" (Gustav Mahler/Friedrich Rückert). Diary of Thomas Vonaechron, Diary Extract, 1991, trans. TV.
85 "Poo-tee-weet," trans. Gregor Hens.

looking down at the big futon bed. Propped up on her elbows, her bright-red University of Maryland sleep shirt pulled up around her waist, Kyra was looking at me curiously. Tossing back her thick brown hair she asked, "*Tschlip-tschlip?*" Laughing, she stood up, pulled down her sleep shirt and said, "I'll make breakfast today. It'll be your turn when you get back!" She walked over to the balcony door, kissed me, and walked out of the bedroom into the hallway. After a few minutes, I followed her inside, performed the obligatory three S's, put on my BDUs, and then finished packing my TA-50 gear in the woodland camouflage rucksack that replaced the burnt-orange backpack given to me by my fellow NARsians nine years ago. EUCOM Military Clothing Sales in Stuttgart had not been able to provide us with US Army desert battle dress uniforms after all, so we were deploying to Iraq wearing our well-worn BDUs and the "army-issued individual equipment" we'd been issued in Berlin. Woodland camouflage had served the US Army well during D3's "War of no War" in Cold War Germany—why shouldn't it serve us equally well in the mountains of southeastern Turkey and out on the steppes of northwestern Iraq?

Kyra came back into the bedroom and put the yukata over her sleep shirt. "Mmmm, it smells like you, Thomas. Breakfast is served."

"Thank you, 'great firewoman!'" The Shield is parked out front. D3 came early and is probably breakfasting just below us."

"Well, that's just the perfect place for D3 to breakfast this morning! Thomas, once again, please don't be sad if I don't get dressed and walk downstairs with you. I'll watch the ceremonial USMLM Potsdam departure from the balcony, just like we did in Stuttgart."

I walked through the double doors into the next room, my study—the once and future living room, which also fronted on *Mohnstraße*. The birds perched in the Linden trees just outside the window continued their unrelenting questioning. Opening the drawer of the old wooden writing table Kyra and I discovered at *Antik Medina* on *Bergmannstraße* in Kreuzberg in the former American Sector, I took out the copies of my travel orders, my official passport—red to distinguish it from tourists and diplomats—my wallet, and keys. I also picked up Nadja's new paperback novel, *La fin d'une distraction de danse*, she'd sent me from Paris the week before. I left the letter from Lorelei Rhine, the poem Neal had prepared for my departure from Washington, Govinda Nayaka's calling card, the weathered slip of paper with "*Thos=Mann=Tick*" written on it I'd found in the boxcar at *Anhalter* Bahnhof, and the Alfred Jarry quotation written out for me by François Fontane in the drawer. The instructions from Govinda Hemd, carefully written on the back of the prescription I received when I left the clinic, were carefully folded in my wallet. Looking up from the desk, my eyes met the eyes of the *Bothidae* flounder, its fear-filled fishy expression unchanged. For some reason, with the end of the Cold War and the accidental *polis*, I'd expected some relaxation. If anything, the fish seemed even more frightened than when I'd first unwrapped Anna's unwanted gift in my temporary office at the *Stadtstaatsarchiv Berlin* nine years ago.

"Thomas, breakfast! Soon it will be time to meet D3 and, uh . . . meet D3 downstairs!

Having exchanged our good-byes all through the night until first light, after breakfast, I picked up my gear and walked down the dark wooden staircase. I shouldered the heavy wooden door open onto a beautiful April morning—sunshine, forsythia, budding linden and chestnut trees, "*ein so starker Duft*," the *Berliner Luft, Luft, Luft*. April is the coolest month. As I walked over to the Shield, the door of the *Bäckerei* opened. Out walked D3 with cup of coffee in each hand, together with George and Rainer. "Howdy, Thomas! Nice day to deploy, *nicht wahr?*"

"Why, if this isn't nice, I don't know what is!" Setting my gear down on the sidewalk, my eyes filling with warm tears, I embraced George and Rainer.

"We just couldn't leave it with the farewell luncheon at *Lusie*, we had to see you two off." From the balcony, I hadn't noticed Rainer's Opel taxi parked behind the Shield. Picking up my backpack, duffel bag, and shoulder bag, I stashed them next to D3's gear in the Shield's open trunk. The camera D3 used to capture the Pershing II mock-up so long ago on the road to Magdeburg was still stowed neatly inside. There was something else, too. "That's an Atari STBOOK, portable computer, Thomas. I thought we could use it to capture significant events as they occur during our deployment. That way, you'll have everything you need to prepare the 'After Action Report,' the final chapter of the 1991 Unit History of the USMLM-cum-MCC, when we return to Berlin!"

"How thoughtful of you, D3. A portable computer to carry along! Just think, if the US Army continues to automate at this rate, someday we may no longer have paper documents at all. All records will be 'machine readable.' You know machine readable's only a small branch of the National Archives now, much smaller than the modern military branch, but it could hold the future, as well as the past. Just imagine possible second- and third-order effects for future historians. No 'hard copies,' no records, no '*Quellen*' in the von Rankean sense of the word, no archives but data banks instead. History reduced to cliometrics, historians to cliometricians. Ay, there's the rub! Data can be altered or deleted, manipulated much easier than the written word. Word processing just might make it more difficult to actually discover *bloß wie es eigentlich gewesen* was. Or even worse than that, history could become anything anyone might want it to be, for whatever purpose, as easily rewritten as written. What did Günter Grass accuse Chancellor Kohl of again: '*Geschichtsklitterung?*' Historians will again become mythologists, maybe even novelists! From *ad fontes* to *ad absurdum*!"

"No documents, no archives, no history! *Ach, du leichte Muse*, I think I'll have to retire from the *Stadtstaatsarchiv* long before that happens," lamented George, smiling thoughtfully.

"And I'd better hurry up and finish my *Hausarbeiten*, too," laughed Rainer.

"Nothing left to throw into the 'wastebasket of the nation?' What will become of all the NARsians?" I added, shaking my head.

"You can worry about them when you get back there, Thomas, sorry, it's time to go!" said D3.

"Drive on D3," said Rainer. "George and I are looking forward to your 'After Action Report' at *Luise* when you return, hopefully later this year."

Before climbing into the shotgun seat of the Shield, I turned to look up at Kyra, standing out on the balcony dressed in the yukata and the morning light. From the expression on her face, it was evident she'd been in on the surprise. With her eyes flashing out from beneath her brown bangs, smiling a subdued smile halfway between that of an army officer and an army wife, Kyra called out, "Be all you can be, boyz, but be sure to keep your heads down while doing so!"

"OK, KO! *Aufwiedersehen* and thanks for letting us borrow Thomas. We'll take very good care of him and get him back to you just as soon as possible. Good luck with your students and your studies at the University of Maryland. Maybe they'll even let you teach the reserve officer training corps cadets there, too, yuck, yuck, yuck!"

Kyra laughed, saying, "Thanks a lot! I know you will, D3, you can't be best man without a bridegroom! *Tschüß*, George! *Tschüß*, Rainer! Please do try to make it down to Munich before I PCS in June," she said, turning and walking back into the apartment as we drove away. I waved at George and Rainer until they were out of sight.

As we drove on, down *Mohnstraße*, past the tree-lined *Plantanenplatz* on our way to Tempelhof Central Airport, I saw the white-haired gentleman with the blue nylon jacket, faded pink polo shirt, and chocolate chip shorts walking his smooth dachshund under the sycamores again.

"Now that's really strange, D3, I haven't seen that guy once since moving to *Mohnstraße* from *Lothringerstrasse* over six years ago, and there he is again. I thought he'd moved away!" The man with the dachshund followed the Shield with his eyes, waving as we turned right on *Unter den Eichen*. As I turned and waved back through my window, I could see tears running down his cheeks.

We passed by the well-walled *Botanischer Garten*. Before too long, Govinda and other members of Berlin's Shin Buddhist community would be meeting at the Buddhist temple. The week before, Govinda and I finally made it to the *Museum für Indische Kunst* in Dahlem, across *Boxerstraße* from the Lucius D. Clay Institute. Much to my mortification, I was unable to find the protection Buddha in the glass case Dr. Schneider had shown me. When I asked for assistance, the museum guide didn't seem to know what I was talking about. Govinda just smiled the protection Buddha smile and asked me, "How long did you 'wall gaze' in West Berlin, Thomas? Could it have been nine years? Ha Ha! You will be leaving us very soon. Before you return, you and our friend, D3, will likely see much pain, suffering, and misery. Your desire to help is sincere, and you will show great compassion. When one sees human beings without protection or sanctuary, it awakens great compassion which is prerequisite for perfect enlightenment. But please remember, Thomas, you must also find peace of mind and happiness within too. In this way, in spite of pain, misery, and other difficulties, you will have always the inner strength and confidence required to withstand them." Hopefully, D3 and I would return from Iraq in time to join Govinda and the others in their garden of peace later in the year.

The early morning traffic flowed smoothly in both directions down the broad avenue. The Shield was a pleasure to ride in, the hum of the powerful ThunderJet V8 engine, the smooth shifting of the heavy duty C6 automatic transmission in the even flow of the traffic, everything as it should be. As we passed *Rathaus Steglitz,* I looked left down *Grunewaldstraße*, where Franz Kafka had lived with Dora Diamant in the early twenties. Kafka had certainly been right about the quality of the air surrounding the Botanical Gardens, *"ein so starker Duft, wie ich ihn von anderswo kaum kennen."* I was very grateful to my Czech doctor, Tomáš Hanšan, for telling me about Kafka's life in Berlin and for so many other things. *Unter den Eichen* metamorphosed into *Rheinstraße*. No sign of Hedwig patrolling the *Hedwigstraße* intersection this morning. Just down the street, to the left, was *Lothringerstrasse*. Karl Kahler and I had had the chance to have a last glass of *Trollinger* together. He was very pleased to learn Kyra and I had decided "to pursue love together, as one." At *Rathaus Friedenau*, I looked up out of habit, as the Shield passed beneath the eyes of the invisible angel. If mine eyes had not been holden, I'm certain I would have seen the palm frond again pointing in the direction of Tempelhof. Next door to the *Rathhaus*, there was no indication *LaBelle* disco had once been housed in the former *Roxy Palast*, a horizontal temple to the old New Objectivity. Space once occupied by a cinema, then a disco, now served as a bargain carpet warehouse.

"D3, thanks again for setting up the appointment with the Agency for me to review the *LaBelle* bombing files. Nadja sent me a copy of the novel she just published on the bombing. She and Clarence did quite a bit of research for the article they published in *Thumpasorus People* on *LaBelle*, so she decided to use it for a novel. It's in French, so I might call upon your assistance. You might want to read it too!"

"*Mais qui*, Thomas! I sincerely hope *LaBelle* will remain an unfortunate, isolated incident, not the harbinger of things to come. Apropos harbinger, I received a rather cryptic message from W2, Winfried, last Sunday evening. As you know he's now up on the *Hardthöhe*, at the Ministry of Defense in Bonn. Hmm, I wonder how long it will take until MOD moves closer to the flagpole in Berlin? Back to the *Bendlerblock*. Anyway, it was a citation from *Faust*, which I had to look up at the post library. Reaching for an envelope under the sun visor, D3 handed it to me and said, "I brought it along for you to read."

Taking the unsealed shotgun distribution envelope from D3's hand, I took the document from it and read aloud:

> *Nichts besseres weiß ich mir an Sonn-und Feiertagen*
> *Als ein Gespräch von Krieg und Kriegsgeschrei,*
> *wenn hinten, weit in der Türkei,*
> *die Völker aufeinander schlagen.*
> *Man steht am Fenster, trinkt sein Gläschen aus*
> *Und segnet den Fluß hinab die bunten Schiffe gleiten,*
> *Dann kehrt man abends froh nach Haus*
> *Und segnet Fried und Friedenszeiten.*[86]

"The fact that it evokes the current situation makes it even more thought provoking. How fortunate we have been for so long, so far." Folding the paper and placing it back into the envelope, I handed it back to D3. *Rheinstraße* metamorphosed into *Hauptstraße*. After crossing *Innsbrucker Platz*, I looked left, down *Dominicusstraße*, catching a brief glimpse of *Rathaus Schöneberg*, "Two thousand years ago . . ." No time to reread President Kennedy's bronzed words this morning. Also on the left, we

---

86 "I know of nothing better on Sundays and holidays than a discussion of war and the screaming coming across the sky when, far away in Turkey, people attack one another. You stand by the window, drink your glass of wine, bless the colorful boats making their way down river, and then in the evening return home happy, blessing peace and peaceful times." Trans. TV, Diary of Thomas Vonaechron, Diary Extract, 1991, trans. TV.

passed by the pastel *Dorfkirche* in *Alt Schöneberg.* The half-size statue of the First World War German soldier standing guard at the cemetery entrance with *Stahlhelm* in one hand and flowers in the other had been doused with purple paint. When we reached *Kaiser-Wilhelm-Platz,* the bent black metal sign reminding us of the thirteen *"Orte des Schreckens, die wir nie vergessen dürfen,"* D3 turned right onto *Kolonnen Straße.* At that moment, it occurred to me we were retracing in reverse, the very route George and I had taken seven, eight, now nine years ago, from Tempelhof Central Airport to *Friedenau. Kolonnen Straße* metamorphosed into *Dudenstraße,* passing just south of *Viktoria Park,* where the iron angels of the Freedom Monument stood watch over the reunited HistoriCity while tired pilgrims refreshed themselves at Golgotha.

Rather than enter the semicircular driveway beneath the gaze of the stern stone eagles separating *FLUGHAFEN TEMPELHOF* from the parking lot, D3 took the parallel access road to the military entrance, passing underneath the massive building itself. Parked out in front of the Army Aviation Detachment, Berlin Brigade hanger, a UH-60 Blackhawk Helicopter was waiting to take us, along with five other members of the USMLM, to Ramstein Air Base for the flight to Incirlik Air Base in Turkey. Painted in high-gloss green lacquer and hand-polished to perfection, the Blackhawk, with "Freedom City" lettered in bright yellow over the open cargo cabin door, gleamed in the morning sunlight. Although Berlin was no longer the capital of the Cold War, it was still reassuring to see US ARMY AVIATION painted in large white block letters on the hangar doors behind it. Artifacts of the US forces, along with artifacts of British, French, and Russians in Berlin would become tell in another layer of the HistoriCity in just over three years' time. Perhaps the white block letters would be preserved, or at least permitted to naturally weather away—runes of the Armed Camp Berlin VI, holy hieroglyphs for future historians to decipher.

We parked the Shield in a space reserved for "Official Vehicles Only" underneath the overhang outside the hanger. "Someone from the Mission will come by and pick it up later today," said D3 as we collected our gear from the trunk.

"What will happen to the Shield of Achilles after US forces depart Berlin, D3?"

"The Shield will be shipped back to CONUS, along with a Mercedes *Geländewagen* 2.81 V-6 'Four-by-Four' and a coach from the Berlin duty train, artifacts for a yet-to-be-funded 'Museum of the United States Army.' It should be built out at Fort Leavenworth, Kansas, but, for the sake of the tourists, and the recruiters I might add, big army's planning to build it at Ft. Belvoir, Virginia, close to Mt. Vernon and George Washington, who helped start it all. You know, Thomas, I often wonder if George Washington had received the commission as a full colonel in the British Army he so desperately wanted, perhaps he wouldn't have joined the rebellion. Why, there'd be no Washington, DC!" We walked into the Army Aviation Detachment, Berlin Brigade hanger to wait for the other members of the USMLM deploying with us to Iraq. "Perhaps we should have ridden on the bus with the others, but somehow, I thought it would be appropriate for the two of us to take the Shield of Achilles on a farewell tour of West Berlin this morning!"

"You're either on the bus or off the bus, D3!"

"Roger that, Thomas!"

We met the bus when it arrived, and after our colleagues had checked in, we left the hanger and walked to the marshalling area.

The Tragic Mountains (Die Trauerberge)
April 1991

After the crew chief helped load our gear into *Freedom City* for the flight to Rhein-Main Air Base near Frankfurt, we buckled ourselves into our forward-facing seats with four-point safety harnesses, just like those in the Shield. I'd never flown in a helicopter before, and although looking forward to the flight, I was also quite nervous. Better looking forward to the flight than looking backward through the flight—the other seats faced the rear. Unknown to me, I would have the chance to look backward on the flight to Turkey later that same day. Sitting next to me, D3, who'd had numerous adventures with helicopters in Vietnam, did his best to reassure me. "Did you know, Thomas, that from an aerodynamic standpoint, helicopters aren't supposed to fly at all? Don't worry about the intense vibration, it doesn't necessarily mean the 'Jesus nut's' come unscrewed!"

"Say again, D3, the what's come unscrewed?

"The Jesus nut! The nut that holds the rotors on!" Smiling, he said, "Here, take these earplugs, they might help with the noise."

"Thanks, D3! But do you mean the noise made by the Blackhawk or all the noise you're making before takeoff?"

D3 laughed. "Acknowledged, Thomas!" After inserting the earplugs, I looked through my window. What did I see as we taxied out for take-off, but a restored Junkers Ju-52/3m, the legendary Tante Ju, an elegant aircraft with corrugated silver skin similar to the old Ford Trimotor. I couldn't help but think of the opening sequence of Leni Riefenstahl's *Triumph des Willens*, *Immelmann II*, Adolf Hitler's personal Ju-52, descending through the clouds into Nürnberg. I'd noted *Frau* Riefenstahl's signature several times while leafing through the guest book of the *Berghof*, Adolf Hitler's Obersalzberg retreat near Berchtergarten, in Vault Six among the exhibits of the Nuremberg War Crimes Trials. As we lifted off from the tarmac, rising above the terminal, I could see the Hunger Claw stretching out in front of Ernst Sagebiel's gigantic stone eagle. George told me a complementary "claw" had been constructed at Rhein-Main in 1985. Unfortunately, we didn't have the chance to see it before our connecting flight to Incirlik Air Base in Turkey. In spite of D3's numerous attempts to scare me, the *Blackhawk* flight was smooth. After landing at Rhein-Main, "Gateway to Europe," we collected our gear, thanked the crew, and walked over to the passenger terminal to check on the flight to Incirlik. This was also my first flight on a C-5 Galaxy, the largest aircraft I'd ever seen. Designed for "strategic airlift," D3 told me the vast cargo compartment was large enough to carry two Abrams M1A1 tanks or five M3 Bradley Calvary Fighting Vehicles.

"We'll need more than five Bradleys for our 'Thunder Run' into Baghdad, D3!"

D3 laughed, "Dream on, Thomas!" Troop compartments had been built into the front and rear of the upper deck. When required, another windowless passenger compartment could be inserted into the rear of the enormous cargo compartment. As there were only seven of us, we were fortunately seated in the forward passenger compartment. Though facing backward, we did have a few windows for orientation. It would have been even more disconcerting to be seated in the rear deck or in the cargo compartment for almost four hours where there were none. We reached our seats by climbing up a ladder from the cargo compartment. Once inside, it was much like a civilian airliner, with the seats facing in the wrong direction. After a loud, long, lumbering take-off, a crewmember came into our compartment, politely inviting us to visit the flight deck, one or two at a time. It was an airborne office, complete with sleeping quarters for the pilot, copilot and flight engineer.

When I told the friendly loadmaster who'd invited us to come forward that it was my first flight on a C5, he asked me, "Well, what do you think of FRED, sir?"

"FRED?"

Laughing, he replied, "That's what some people call the Galaxy, sir, FRED—'Fucking Ridiculous Environmental Disaster!'"

Walking back to my seat, I noticed a white plastic bag from the Stars and Stripes Bookstore lying on the floor of the compartment Bent. Inside was a new, quality paperback copy of *Ocean Steamships*. It must have been forgotten by a previous passenger. I leafed through it then, laying it down on my lap, closed my eyes, and thought about Kyra. D3 woke me during our descent into Incirlik. "Here we go again, Thomas!" Unlike Rhein-Main, there was no civilian side to Incirlik Air Base, a Turkish Air Force base not far from the Mediterranean. Incirlik had served as a base for American combat operations during Operation Desert Storm and the high operations tempo, OPTEMPO, continued on into Operation Provide Comfort. After reporting to the passenger terminal, we were driven out to a waiting Hercules C-130 for the flight to Diyarbakir Airport in southeastern Turkey, where another army Blackhawk was standing by to fly us forward to Zakho, to Iraq. As a result of the high priority given by European Command to the establishment of the Military Coordination Center, there was little or no waiting time. Unlike the Galaxy's comfortable airline seating, the Hercules, a four-engine turboprop military transport plane, was well-benched with webbed seats running the length of the sidewall. Before the Hercules taxied out to the runway for takeoff, D3 told us we were expected to hit the ground running in Zakho, setting up the MCC within twenty-four hours of our arrival for a meeting between the Commander of Joint Task Force Provide Comfort and senior Iraqi officials. Space had been set aside for the Military Coordination Center in a former Iraqi military installation. "Given the priority of our mission, I'm hopeful a communications suite has already been set up for us, but we can't assume so. And why not, troops?"

"Because," we answered in unison, "assume makes an ass out of 'u' and me."

"Roger that!" answered D3. Once we began to move down the taxiway for the runway, conversation became difficult due to the noise. I put the earplugs D3 had given me to good use during the hour flight to Diyarbakir City Airport.

Outwardly similar to *Freedom City*, which had ferried us from Tempelhof to Rhein-Main, the Blackhawk waiting for us on the runway at Diyarbakir was painted in a flat tan and earth desert camouflage pattern and configured for combat. A gunner sat behind the pilot, in the right seat next to the crew chief. An M-60 GP 7.62 mm machine gun was mounted aft of the flight deck, on the right side of the airframe. Prior to taking off, we were given a thorough briefing on emergency procedures, exits, and equipment. Repeated rapping on top of the helmet signified a crash landing. After she'd finished, the crew chief directed us to put on our body armor and helmets. When I reached into my helmet bag, I discovered I'd packed the wrong helmet the night before. Instead of my Army-issue PASGT helmet with the woodland camouflage cover with "Born to Write" handwritten on the side in black Magic Marker, I held the flat green Russian *Ssh* 68 helmet with "ВЕРДИН VII" stenciled in white letters in my hand, a gift from the goddess in the Tiergarten flea market. I put "BERLIN VII" on, hoping it would protect my head and my thoughts as the goddess had intended. D3 laughed. "Maybe it's a good omen, Thomas. In any case, I'm sure you'll be a big hit with the Iraqis!"

Blackhawk up! Flying roughly parallel with the Syrian border, not far from Aleppo, we flew over the mountains toward the border with Iraq and the Zakho corridor. From above, the landscape, steppes, and mountains revealed a barren beauty, *eine karge Schönheit.* As we flew low over the mountains, D3 shouted, "Look closely, Thomas!" Through the scattered clouds we could see the human cost of the war beneath us, refugees lost in a biblical wilderness of pain, suffering, and death. Turbulence on the ground and in the air. The conditions on the ground must have been insufferable. D3 shook his helmeted head in disbelief and compassion. We crossed over the Khabur River, the border between Turkey and Iraq, flowing into Iraq and the Tigris. Obscured by clouds, we caught glimpses of the open steppes and rolling farmland on the far side of the mountains, wheat fields lying fallow, upheaval, and the ruins of towns decimated by Iraqi forces during the Kurdish uprising—*polémopaysages*, war landscapes bearing the marks of history. It is the flatlands, it is the aftermath of the war. Zakho came into view. From our privileged aerial perspective, visible on the ground only as a moving shadow, it appeared forsaken, a ghost town. Excerptss from the *Dschungel* soundtrack loop began to play in my head: "History Repeating" from Propellerheads, *"ein jahr (es geht voran)"* from Fehlfarben, Iggy Pop's "The Passenger," and "Concrete Dub" from Leningrad Sandwich. A creaking came across the sky. Could it be the great doors of history opening again? "What was that, D3?" He said something I couldn't understand. "Say again, D3. What was that sound so high in the air? Where are we? Where has the dream brought us?"

"To Iraq, Thomas."

"What is that city over the mountains?"

"Zakho. The Military Coordination Center is collocated with Headquarters, Joint Task Force Bravo in the abandoned compound of the Iraqi Forty-Fourth Infantry Division. Not as comfortable quarters as the Mission, I'm afraid. You know it's been eighteen long years since I left the war in Vietnam, but it's certainly been a short flight back, look out the window!" Looking out from under glass as we flew over the ruins of the abandoned Iraqi Army headquarters, I saw it too had been laid to waste, most of the buildings raised or gutted, rubble and twisted vehicles everywhere. In the seven hours it took to fly from Berlin to Zakho, we'd flown from the temporal security of a Germany reuniting to the terrible insecurity of an Iraq disintegrating, from peace to the war. Turning my gaze back to my fellow travelers inside the Blackhawk, I saw that we all, with the exception of the flight crew, wore the subdued USMLM Potsdam shoulder sleeve insignia sewn on our BDUs. There hadn't been time to design an SSI for the Military Coordination Center. As our pilot set the Blackhawk down gently on the landing pad in what appeared to once have been a wheat field, I could see a reception committee waiting for us. "Time to go, Thomas, make sure you've got everything. The Blackhawk's headed right back to Diyarbakir after dropping us off. Tighten your chinstrap товарищ, and keep your head down once we exit the aircraft. Walk directly to the edge of the helispot from the door—do not, I repeat do not, walk around the front of the aircraft!"

"Say again, D3!"

Shaking his helmeted head, D3 laughed and said, "You can take your earplugs out now, Thomas! You know, while we were flying over the mountains, over the makeshift refugee camps, the conclusion of President Eisenhower's 'Farewell Address' kept running through my mind like a loop tape: 'in the goodness of time, all people will come together in a peace guaranteed by the binding force of mutual respect and love.' The binding force of mutual respect and love. Could it be possible, Thomas, someday, 'in the goodness of time?'" D3 sat silently for a moment, then said matter-of-factly, "Better get ready to disembark." We collected our gear, waiting until the crew chief opened the doors.

"Good luck!" she said as we jumped down from the Blackhawk.

"And to you, too, Chief," I shouted back in reply. "Thanks for the ride! Have a safe flight back to Diyarbakir. Hey, Chief, for the historical record, does your Blackhawk have a name?" She smiled at me, shaking her head as she shut the cargo cabin door. I was relieved to be back on the ground. Although not in hours, it had been a long trip from Berlin to Zakho. Exhausted, exalted, exhilarated by the odyssey, I did my best to "hit the ground running" in accordance with D3's instructions. Head down, weighed down with my equipment and the new Atari portable computer, clods of earth clinging to my boots, not on a bootless inquisition but a muddy boots pilgrimage to the *Quelle*, to the source of history. Struggling to keep up with D3 and the other MCC team members, double-timing it toward the soldiers coming to meet us, I sang softly to myself in dazed, thoughtless excitement. Once we reached the perimeter of the landing pad, the engine began to whine and the rotors to whirl.

Head lowered in enforced humility, face framed by the visor and chinstrap of his helmet, Thomas, bending under the burden of history, now disappears from our sight in the pillar of dust raised by the whirling rotor blades of the departing *Blackhawk*. We're leaving. With fingertips, we gently rub the dust and the mold from our eyes. Farewell, Thomas! You will live and redeploy to reunited Berlin, if only to return shortly thereafter to Washington, DC, where your story began nine years ago. Seven days, seven months, seven years did not suffice. It took nine! "*Das Schauspiel dauerte sehr lange.*" But your story is now over, a story neither short on boredom nor long on diversion, a history hermetic if not Hermannetic. Told to its end for the sake of the story itself, not for Thomas's sake. But nevertheless, it was his story. His story is over. Farewell, Thomas, the terrible *Totentanz* fueled by the blood and treasure of many nations, your own prominent among them, is just beginning, and will last many a fiscal year. Your sense of self, your *Selbstbewußtsein*, refined by your years in the HistoriCity, allows you to better understand what you one day will not survive. After all, we do have it on the very best of authority that "none of us here are getting out alive." There were, however, and will be times yet to come, conceived in overwhelming fear, born in all-consuming passion, when you loved and were loved. There were times when you dreamt and there will be times when you dream again. Where is that dream taking us? Could it be that the city, the self, you sought among the runes and ruins of the HistoriCity might yet be discovered in this later city, or in the city which is to come? Could the city which is to come be the city of yesterday? *Eirönïa! Erastai, Eirēnē, PAX, Frieden*, Peace. Out Here. Over!

THE END OF HIS STORY

Lichterfelde-West (former American Sector), Berlin
Cuyahoga Falls (former Western Reserve of Connecticut), Ohio

[This Page Intentionally Left Blank]

APPENDIX A:
ACRONYMS AND ABBREVIATIONS

AAR	After Action Report
ACU	Army Combat Uniform
Antifa	Anti-Fascist Movement
ASV	American Standard Version
BASC	Berlin Air Safety Center
BDU	Battle Dress Unit
BIGOT	Security classification compartment derived from "To Gibraltar"
BOLC	Basic Officer Leadership Course
BRIXMIS	British Commanders'-in-Chief Mission to the Soviet Forces in Germany
CFV	Cavalry Fighting Vehicle, a Bradley M3
CGSC	US Army Command and General Staff College, Fort Leavenworth, Kansas
CIA	Central Intelligence Agency
CIG	Central Intelligence Group, precursor to the CIA
CO	Conscientious Objector
COL	Colonel
COMINT	Communications Intelligence
COMZ	Communications Zone
CTF	Combined Task Force
DAC	Department of the Army Civilian

DCSI	Deputy Chief of Staff, Intelligence—pronounced "Dixie"
DDR	*Deutsche Demokratische Republic*, German Democratic Republic (GDR), East Germany
DIA	Defense Intelligence Agency, Department of Defense
DLI	Defense Language Institute, Presidio of Monterey, California
DR	*Deutsche Reichsbahn*, the German Railway
DSN	Defense Service Network (telephone)
DUKW	1942, utility (amphibious), all-wheel drive, two-powered rear axles
EEI	Essential Elements of Information
FAO	Foreign Area Officer
FHA	Federal Highway Administration
FKK	*Freikörperkultur*, nudism
FU	*Freie Universität Berlin*, the Free University Berlin
GBI	The *Generalbauinspektor für die Reichshauptstadt*, the senior building inspector for the Capital of the Reich, Albert Speer
GDR	German Democratic Republic, *Deutsche Demokratische Republik (DDR)*, East Germany
GI	Government Issue
GMDS	German Military Documents Section, National Archives and Records Service
GSA	General Services Administration, US government
HEMTT	Heavy Expanded Mobility Tactical Truck

HHI	*Hajo-Holborn-Institut*, Contemporary History Department of the Free University Berlin ("*HaHo*")
HU	*Humboldt Universität*, Humboldt University in Berlin
HUA	Heard, Understood, Acknowledged
HUMINT	Human Intelligence
IIR	Intelligence Information Report
IR	Intelligence Report
ISUM	Intelligence Summary
JAEDIA	John-Allen-Eleanor-Dulles International Airport, Willard, Virginia
JTF	Joint Task Force
KPM	*Königliche Porzellan-Manufaktur*, Royal Porcelain Factory
KuKuCK	*Kunst und Kultur Zentrum Kreuzberg*, the Kreuzberg Art and Cultural Center
LDCI	*Lucius-D.-Clay-Institute*, American Studies Institute of the Free University Berlin
LOC	Lines of Communication
LTC	Lieutenant Colonel
MACV	Military Assistance Command Vietnam
MCC	Military Coordination Center
MHD	Military History Detachment
MIG	Military Intelligence Group
MILAIR	Military Air Transportation
MMFL	*La Mission Militaire Française de Liaison*, the French Military Liaison Mission

MOD	Ministry of Defense
NARS	National Archives and Records Service
NCB	National Census Bureau
NCO	Noncommissioned Officer
NRL	US Naval Research Laboratory
NSA	National Security Agency, Department of Defense
OMGBS	Office of Military Government, Berlin Sector
OMGUS	Office of Military Government, United States
ONI	Office of Naval Intelligence, Department of the Navy
OPCON	Operational Control
OSCE	Organization for Security and Cooperation in Europe
OSI	US Air Force Office of Special Investigations
OSS	Office of Strategic Services
PAO	Public Affairs Office
PIC	Passive Intelligence Collection
POLAD	US Political Advisor, Office of Military Government, United States
POTUS	President of the United States of America
RIAS	Radio in the American Sector of Berlin
ROTC	Reserve Officers Training Corps
RTO	US Army Rail Transportation Office
RUMINT	Rumors Intelligence
SAR	Search and Rescue

S-Bahn	*Stadt-Bahn*, City-Train
SBI	Sensitive Background Investigation
SD	*Sicherheitsdienst*, Security Service of the *Schutzstaffel*, the Protection Staff of the National Socialist Party
SECDEF	Secretary of Defense
SIS	US Army Signals Intelligence Service
SITREP	Situation Report
SMLM	Soviet Military Liaison Mission, also SOXMIS
SOFA	Status of Forces Agreement
SOP	Standard Operation Procedure
SOXMIS	Soviet Military Liaison Mission, also SMLM
SS	*Schutzstaffel* the Protection Staff of the National Socialist Party
SSS	Shit, Shave, and Shower
SSU	Strategic Services Unit, successor to the Office of Strategic Services
TA-50	Table of Allowances-50, Army-issued individual equipment
TAGO	The Office of the Adjutant General, US Army
TCA	Tempelhof Central Airport
TDY	Temporary Duty (Official Travel)
TF	Task Force
TS	Top Secret security clearance
TU	*Technische Universität*, the Technical University in Berlin

TUWAT	"Do Something!"
U-Bahn	*Untergrund-Bahn*, the subway
UCP	Universal Camouflage Pattern
UKBF	*Universitätsklinikum Bejamin Franklin*, University Clinic Benjamin Franklin
USAR-E	US Army Reserve Europe
USCOB	US Commander, Berlin; Commandant; Commander, US Army, Berlin
USMLM	US Military Liaison Mission
Vopos	*Volkspolizei*, the People's Police
WACS	Washington Air Corridor Service
WASt	*Wehrmachtsauskunftstelle für Kriegsverluste und Kriegsgefangene*, the Wehrmacht Information Office for War Casualties and Prisoners of War
WG	*Wohngemeinschaft*, a group apartment or house
WILCO	Will comply (with request)
WJC	World Jewish Congress
WNRC	Washington National Records Center, National Archives and Records Service

APPENDIX B:
We Practice His German, French, Latin, and Greek: Words, Phrases and Vulgarisms

Abwehr	Wartime German Military Intelligence Service
Achtung!	Attention! Look Out!
Aktentasche	Briefcase
Alltag	Everyday, as in everyday life
Ami	Berlin slang for an American or for a cigarette
Anarcho	Anarchist
Anmeldung	Registration
Anstrengend	Arduous
Archiv	Archives
Arschlöcher	Assholes
Asbest	Asbestos
auf	Open
Aufguß	Infusion
Aufmerksamkeit	Attention, as in to "pay attention"
Aufnahme	Absorption
Aufnahmefähig	The ability to absorb and process
Aufschnitt	Cold cuts
Ausgang	Exit

Auslander, Ausländer	Foreigner, foreigners
Autowerkstatt	Automobile repair garage
Backsteinkirchen	(Red)brick churches
Balkonzimmer	A room with a balcony
Beamtenstaat	Civil service state
beseitigen	To clear away
Besucher	Visitors
Betriebsausflug	Office excursion (during duty hours)
Bezirk	District
Blick	Gaze, view
Blutsau	Literally "blood pig"
Braunkohl	Brown coal
Brötchen	White bread rolls
Brücke	Bridge
Bundesbürger	Citizens of the Federal Republic of Germany
Bundeswehr	The Army of the Federal Republic of Germany
bzw.	*beziehungsweise*, "as the case may be"
Doktormutter	Dissertation advisor (literally "Doctor-Mother")
Drängen	Pushing and shoving
Einheimische	Locals
Einstürz	Collapse

Eirēnē	Peace
Eirönïa	Irony
Eisdiele	Ice cream stand
Empörer	Insurgent
Erastai	Lovers of the city
Erdgeschoß	Ground floor
Fachbereich	Department (university)
Fachwerk	Half-timbered
flanieren	Walk slowly with indefinite intent
Flanuer	A self-invited, soulful loafer
Flitterwoche	Honeymoon
Flohmarkt	Flea market
Flugzeugtraum	Airplane dream
Förderer	Patron
Freiheitsdenkmal	Liberation (literally "Freedom") monument
Frieden	Peace
Friedensgebet	Prayer for peace
Freiherr	Baron
Freundeskreis	Circle of friends
Geheim	Secret, German security classification

Geheime Reichssache	Secret Reich matter, German Security classification compartment
Geheime Staatspoliziei	*Gestapo*, Secret State Police
Geisterbahnhöfe	literally "Ghost Stations," deserted stations on *U-* and *S-Bahn* lines in and under East Berlin
Generalbauinspektor	Senior construction supervisor (Albert Speer)
Generaldirektion	General administration
Geschichte	History
Geschichtswissenschaft	Department of History (university)
Gesprächstoff	Topic of conversation
Gipsformerei	Plaster casting workshop
gleichgeschaltet	Removal of opposition
Graf	Count
grenzenlos	Unlimited
Hakenkreuz	Swastika
Hardthöhe	District of Bonn, location of the Ministry of Defense
Hauptstaatsarchiv	Main State Archives
Hausarbeiten	Research papers
Heim	Home
Heldenfriedhof	Military cemetery, literally "Hero's Cemetery"
heruntergekommen	Run-down

Hochbunker	Aboveground bunker
im-werden	Becoming, as in "*Historiker-im-werden*"
instandsetzen	Repair, restore
Kälte	Cold
Karteileiche	Literally "a card-index file corpse," a student enrolled for too many semesters without examination
Klingelschild	Doorbell nameplate
Kommilitone	Fellow student
Kriegesakademie	Literally "war academy," military academy
Kriegsgeschichte	The history of warfare
Kuchen	Cake, pastry
Kugellagerfabrik	A munitions factory, also *Waffen- und Munitionsfabrik*, weapons and munitions factory
Künstler	Artist
Landwehrkanal	A canal originally constructed under the direction of Prussian landscape architect Peter Joseph Lenné to lighten the traffic load on Berlin's River Spree
Leitmotiv	Theme
Lesesaal	Reading room
Mäusebunker	"Mice bunker"
Magazinarbeiter	A worker in the stacks of an archives

Majestätsbeleidigung	*lèse-majesté*
Mannung	A warning (*Mahnung*) from Thomas Mann
Marine	Navy
Mauerspechte	Wall- (vice wood-)peckers
Menschengeschichte	Human history
Menschenkette	Human chain
menschenleere	Empty of people
Musterbeispiel	Pedagogical example
Naßkalt	Wet cold
Nationalgalerie	National gallery
Nebenstelle	Branch office
Neubauten	New construction (buildings)
Neugestaltungsplannung	Reconstruction planning
Notaufnahme	Emergency admissions, hospital
Oberkommando	Supreme Command (Headquarters)
Öde und Leer	Desolate and empty
Palituch	Palestinian headscarf worn as a scarf
Pißort	Urinal
Plattenbau	Prefabricated concrete slab construction
Po	Bottom/ Buttocks

Promotionsordnungen	Requirements for the Doctor of Philosophy degree
Psychiatrische Ambulanz	Ambulatory psychiatry
Quellen	Historical sources
Räumung	Eviction
Rathaus	City Hall
Rechnung	The tab
Reichshauptstadt	Capital of the *Reich*; although it also applies to Berlin II and III, it is used exclusively by Thomas Vonaechron to denote Berlin IV 1933 to 1945—see SECTIONS: Layers of the HistoriCity-Historische (Ge)Schichten
Restdeutschland	West Germany, not including West Berlin
Richtig	Correct
Rundblick	Panoramic view
Schade	Shame, as in "What a . . ."
Schamhaare	Pubic hair
Schaufenster	Display window
Scheine	Bills, currency, or certificates
Schlachtbank	Butcher block
Schlachthof	Slaughterhouse
Schlafmittel	Sleeping tablets
Schnäppchen	Bargain

Schutzstaffel	Protection staff
Schwerpunkt	Center of gravity
Selbstbewußtsein	Self-awareness, self-knowledge
Sicherheitsdienst	Security Service
Siegesaüle	Victory Column, the "chick-on-a-stick"
Soixante-huitard	Sixty-eighter
Sperrgebeit	Restricted area
Sprechgesang	Recitative
Staat	State
Staatsbibliothek	State Library
Stadtarchiv	City Archives
Stadtbahn or *S-Bahn*	City-train
Stadtstaat	City-State
Stadtstaatsarchiv Berlin	City-State Archives Berlin
Städtische Irrenanstalt	State-sponsored asylum for the mentally ill
Stahlhelm(Steel)	Helmet
Stechschritt	Goose-step
Straße	Street
Strassenschlachten	Street clashes
Streng Geheim	Top Secret, German security classification
Stuckwerk	Stucco

Suum cuique	"To each his own," motto of the Order of the Black Eagle, Kingdom of Prussia
Tchüß	Bye!
Totentanz	Dance of death
Trachtenmantel	Traditionally styled Austrian or Bavarian coat
Transparente	Banners
Treppenhaus	Stairwell
Trinkgeld	Tip
Trödelladen	Second-hand store
Trotz	In spite of
tun	To do
Übungen	Exercises, academic and military
ungeheures Ungeziefer	Monstrous vermin (e.g., a cockroach)
ungefähr	Approximately
Untergrundbahn or *U-Bahn*	Underground, subway
Unterhaltung	Conversation and/or entertainment
unterwegs	On the road
vergänglich	Transitory
verlassen	Deserted
verloren	Lost
vertraulich	Confidential, German security classification

verzettelt	Rendered into small pieces à la Arno Schmidt
Vorlesungen	Lectures
vraiment	Truly
Waffen- und Munitionsfabrik	Weapons and munitions factory
Wahnsinn	Madness
Wartesaal	Waiting room
Wasserwerfer	Pumper truck used to disperse crowds
Wehrmacht	The German Army from 1935 until 1946
Weltanschauung	Worldview
im Werden	Becoming
WG	*Wohngemeinschaft*, shared apartment
Widmung	Dedication
Wortspiel	Wordplay
Zentralflughafen	Central airport
Zerstörung	Destruction
ziellos	Aimless
Zulassung	Admission (e.g., university)
Zündstoff	Fuel

ACKNOWLEDGEMENTS

My heartfelt thanks to the Cuyahoga Falls, Ohio public school teachers who opened so much more than classroom doors so many years ago: Leanne Corbi, Gary Dye, Evalee Hart, Gerald Hupp, Louise Kittell, Linda McClain, Jimmie McKain, Joan Reinbolt, and Peter Ulrich. Heartfelt thanks to my Swiss "stepparents," Antoinette and Justus Gelzer, as well, for the gift of a *Weltanschauung*, Elsbeth, Paul, and Uwe Hohl for the gift of West Berlin, and especially to my dear friend, and "the Reader" of many years, Bonnie Hawk.

QUELLEN (SOURCES):
Notes on *HistoriCity*

To the majority of the artists and authors below, I am deeply indebted for their inspiration and gratefully acknowledge their influence. Not all are cited, but nonetheless are recognized for their contributions to the unique *Milljöh* that was Berlin between 1982 and 1991. There are, however, a handful of exceptions whose work should be considered in spite or even because of what they advocate. Thomas Vonaechron is *durchsichtig*, transparent by intent, inviting the reader to examine with and through him the *Quellen* informing his story. If *HistoriCity or Fragments of Berlin* should occasion the reader to follow Thomas and Leopold von Ranke *ad Fontes*, then my mission will have been accomplished.

ABC, "Poison Arrow" from *The Lexicon of Love*, ABC, 1982.

Henry Adams, *The Education of Henry Adams* (Boston, 1918; Project
   Gutenberg, December 15, 2011 [EBook #2044]), www.gutenberg.org.

Aeschylus, "Agamemnon," *The Dramas of Aeschylus*, trans. Anna Swanwick
   (London, 1886; Wikisource), en.m.wikisource.org.

Michael Anderson, dir., *The Quiller Memorandum*, 20th Century Fox,
   1966, 105 minutes.

Hannah Arendt, *The Human Condition*, Chicago, 1958.

Aristotle, *The Politics of Aristotle*, trans. Benjamin Jowett (Oxford, 1885; Wikisource), en.m.wikisource.org.

Augustine, *The Confessions of St. Augustine*, Trans. E.B. Pusey (1876; Project Gutenberg), March 19, 2001, www.gutenberg.org.

Johan Sebastian Bach, "Weinachts-Oratorium," BMV 248 (Leipzig, 1734; Wikimedia Commons), commons.m.wikimedia.org/wiki/File:BMV_248_Liebretto.JPG.

Gottfried Benn, *Der Trunkene Flut*, Limes *Verlag*, Wiesbaden, 1949.

Gottfried Benn, *Gesammlte Werke in viert Bänden*, hg. D. Wellershof, Wiesbaden, 1960-65.

Thomas Berger, *Crazy in Berlin*, Ballantine Books, New York, 1978.

Berlin in Geschichte und Gegenwart: Jarbuch des Landesarchivs Berlin, Siedler Verlag, Berlin, 1981, 1982, 1983, 1984, 1985, 1986, 1987, 1988, 1989, 1990, 1991, 1992.

Josef Beuys, *Jeder Mensch ein Künstler. Gespräch auf der documenta 5/1972*, 1988.

Stephan Beyer, *The Buddhist Experience; Sources and Interpretations*, Wadsworth Publishing Company, Belmott, California, 1974.

Bible (American Standard), (1901; Wikisource), en.m.wikisource.org/wiki/Bible_(American_Standard).

William Blake, "Proverbs of Hell" from *The Marriage of Heaven and Hell* (1790: The William Blake Archives) blakearchiv.com.

Carla Bley, "*Musique Mecanique*," Watt Works, 1979 and "Reactionary Tango (In Three Parts)," *Social Studies*, ECM, 1981.

Bohidharma, "The Twofold Entrance to the Tao," trans. John C. H. Wu, *The Golden Age of Zen*, World Wisdom, 1967.

Wolfgang Borchert, *Im Mai, im Mai schried der Kuckuk* (1947; Projekt-Gutenberg), projekt-gutenberg.org.

Tinto Brass, dir., *Salon Kitty*, 20th Century Fox, 1976, 130 minutes.

Richard Brautigan, *Trout Fishing in America*, Delta, New York, 1967.

Richard Brautigan, *Forellenfischen in Amerika, Verlag Volk und Welt*, Berlin, 1986.

Pam Bricker, Wayne Wilentz, and Jim West, *U-topia*, 1981.

Mel Brooks, dir., *Young Frankenstein*, 20th Century Fox, 1974, 105 minutes.

Jacob Burckhardt, *Briefe, Erster Band, Jugend und Schulzeit, erste Reisen nach Italien, Studium in Neuenburg, Basel, Berlin und Bonn, 1818 bis Mai 1843*, ed. Max Burckhardt, Insel-Verlag, Basel, 1949.

Jacob Burckhardt, *Briefe, Fünfter Band, Scheitelpunkt der historischen Professur, Entstehungszeit der "Weltgeschichtlichen Betrachtungen" und der "Griechischen Culturgeschichte," Wiederaufnahme kunstgeschichtlicher Vorlesungen, 1868 bis März 1875*, ed. Max Burckhardt, Insel-Verlag, Basel/Stuttgart, 1963.

Cabaret, Original Soundtrack Recording, ABC Records, 1972.

Dean Chamberlin, excerpts from poems by permission of the author.

The Clash, *Combat Rock*, CBS, 1982.

Carl von Clausewitz, *Vom Kriege*, Carl Höckner, *Königl. Hofbuchhändler*, Dresden, 1891.

Leonard Cohen, *The Future*, Columbia, 1992.

E.E. Cummings, *Collected Poems*, "96," Harcourt, Brace and Company, New York, 1938.

W. Gordon Cunliffe, "Cousin Joachim's Steel Helmet: *Der Zauberberg* and the War," *Monatshelfte für deutechen Unterricht, deutsche Sprache und Literatur*, Volume LXVII, Number 4, Winter 1976, 409–417.

Michael Curtiz, dir., *Casablanca*, Warner Bros., 1943, 102 minutes.

Philippe De Broca, dir., *King of Hearts*, Metro Goldwyn Mayer, 1967, 102 minutes.

Defunkt, *Thermonuclear Sweat*, Hannibal Records, 1982.

Deutsche Amerikanische Freudschaft, DAF, Alles ist gut, Virgin, 1981.

Tamara Domentat, *Coca Cola, Jazz und AFN: Berlin und die Amerikaner,* Schwarzkopf & Schwarzkopf, Berlin 1995.

Tamara Domentat, *Ende eines Tanzvergnügungs*, Hamburg, 1995.

Ian Dury, "Sex & Drugs & Rock & Roll," Stiff Records, 1977.

Ian Dury, *Do it Yourself,* CBS Inc. 1979.

Rudi Dutschke, *Geschichte Ist Machbar,* Wagenbach, Berlin, 1980.

Bob Dylan, *John Wesley Harding*, Columbia, 1967.

Bob Dylan, The Band, *Music from Big Pink*, Capitol, 1968.

Inaugural Address of Dwight D. Eisenhower, President of the United States, Delivered at the Capitol, Washington, DC, January 20, 1953, United States Government Printing Office, Washington, 1953.

Text of the Address by President Eisenhower, Broadcast and Televised from his Office in the White House, Tuesday Evening, January 17, 1961, 8:30 to 9:00 p.m. EST.

Thomas S. Eliot, "The Waste Land" in "The Criterion: A Quarterly Review," Vol. I, No. I, R. Cobden-Sanderson, London, October 1922.

Thomas S. Eliot, "The Love Song of J. Alfred Prufrock" (1977; Wikisource), en.m.wikisource.org.

Friedrich Engels, cited in Maritta Adam-Tkalec, "*Schrank, Esstische, Ansichte: Das steckt hinter dem legendären 'Berliner Zimmer,"* Berliner Zeitung, April 18, 2017.

Fehlfarben, Monarchie und Alltag, EMI Electrola, 1980.

Joschka Fischer in Hans Wilderotter, *Herausgeber, Das Haus am Werderschen Markt- Von der Reichsbank zum Auswärtigen Amt,* JOVIS *Verlag,* Berlin, 2000. Used by permission.

Theodor Fontane. "Das Trauerspiel von Afghanistan" (Stuttgart und Berlin, 1905; Wikisource), de.m.wikisource.org/wiki/Das_Trauerspiel_von_Afghanistan(Fontane).

Freie Universität Berlin, Nicolai, Berlin, 1998.

Funkadelic, *One Nation Under a Groove,* Warner Brothers, 1978.

Allen Ginsberg, *Howl and Other Poems,* City Lights Books, San Francisco, 1956.

Johann Wolfgang von Goethe, Faust: Eine Tragödie [erster Teil] (Tübingen, 1808; Project Gutenberg, April 6, 2007 [EBook #2100]), gutenberg.org.

Jutta Götzmann and Anna Havemann, *Die Wilden 80er in der Deutsch-Deutschen Malerei,* Michael Imhof *Verlag,* 2017.

Donald G. Goff, "Operation Provide Comfort," Personal Experience Monograph, US Army War College, Carlisle Barracks, Pennsylvania, May 1992.

Gregory G. Govan, "Introduction," Unit History (U), United States Military Liaison Mission Potsdam, UNITED STATES MILITARY LIAISON MISSION TO THE COMMANDER IN CHIEF GROUP OF SOVIET FORCES IN GERMANY, 1988.

Günter Grass, *Ein weites Feld, Hörbuch, Steidl Verlag,* 2006.

Günter Grass, Invitation to the exhibition "Günter Grass etchings," Franz Bader Gallery, August 24-September 10, 1977, Washington DC.

Christopher Grau, "Love and History," *Southern Journal of Philosophy,* 48(3): 246–271 (2010).

Robert P. Grathwol and Donita M. Moorhus, *American Forces in Berlin 1945-1994: Cold War Outpost*, US Government Printing Office, Washington, DC, 1994.

Grauzone, *Grauzone*, Off Course Records, 1981.

Thomas Gray, Chicago "Elegy Written in a Country Chuchyard," London, 1751.

Bernard Gwertzmann, "US Releases 4 and East Bloc 25 in Spy Exchange on Berlin Bridge," *New York Times*, June 12, 1985.

Haircut 100, "Favorite Shirts (Boy Meets Girl)," Arista Records, 1981.

Guy Hamilton, dir., *Funeral in Berlin*, Paramount, 1966, 102 minutes.

Heaven 17, *Penthouse and Pavement*, Virgin Records Limited, 1981.

Georg Frederich Wilhelm Hegel, "*Die Liebe*," in Herman Nohl, ed., *Hegels theologische Jugendschriften*, Tübingen, 1907.

Georg Frederich Wilhelm Hegel, *Vorlesungen über die Philosophie der Geschichte*, Reclam Verlag, Leipzig, 1924.

Heinrich Heine, *Almansor*, Vers 243f, 1823.

Rudolf Herz, *Fotographie und Revolution: München 1918/19*, Nishen, Berlin, 1988.

Hermann Hese, *Der Steppenwolf*, S. Fischer Verlag, Berlin, 1927. Used by permission.

Hermann Hesse, *Steppenwolf*, trans. Basil Creighton, Henry Holt, New York, 1929.

Stefan Heym, Zitat March 18, 1990," *Es wird keine DDR mehr geben. Sie wird nichts als eine Fußnote in der Weltgeschichte.*"

Adolf Hitler, *Mein Kampf, Verlag Franz Eher Nachfolger, München*, 1930.

Michael Hoenig, *Departure from the Northern Wasteland*, Warner Brothers, 1978.

Hajo Holborn, *A History of Modern Germany: 1648–1840*, Alfred A. Knopf, New York, 1964.

Hajo Holborn, *A History of Modern Germany: 1840–1945*, Alfred A. Knopf, New York, 1969.

Hajo Holborn, "History and the Humanities," *Journal of the History of Ideas*, Vol. 9, No. 1, ppg. 65-69, University of Pennsylvania Press. Used by permission.

Homer, *The Iliad*, trans. Alexander Pope (1899; Project Gutenberg, November 17, 2002 [EBook # 6131]), gutenberg.org/files/6130/6130-h/6130-h.htm.

Thomas Hoover, *Zen Culture*, Random House, New York, 1977. Project Gutenberg, Ebook-no. 34324, Nov. 14, 2010, Creative Commons Attribution 3.0 Unported License.

Anthony Hopkins (attributed to), "None of us here are getting out of here alive …," n.d.

Georg G. Iggers, *The German Conception of History: The National Tradition of Historical Thought from Herder to the Present*, Wesleyan University, 1984. Two excerpts used by permission.

Christopher Isherwood, *The Berlin Stories*, New Directions, New York, 1963.

Christopher Isherwood, *Christopher and His Kind*, Farrar, Straus, and Giroux, 1976.

Alfred Jarry, "Ubu Enchained," *The Ubu Plays*, ed. and trans. Simon Watson Taylor, Grove Press, Inc., New York, 1969.

John F. und die Gropiuslerchen, "Berlin, Berlin (…dein Herz kennt keine Mauern)," *Vielklang Musikproduktion*, 1987.

John F. Kennedy, "*Rede des amerikanischen Präsidenten in der Freien Universität Berlin*," "26. Juni 1963: John F. Kennedy in Berlin," TELDEC, no date.

Kesten, Hermann, *Dichter im Cafe*, 1959.

Hans-Gerd Koch, *Kafka in Berlin*, Berlin-Wilmersdorf, 2008.

Kömische Oper, "Julius Caesar in Ägypten Oper von Georg Friedrich Händel," flyer, Berlin, no date.

Milan Kundera, *The Unbearable Lightness of Being*, Harper & Row, New York, 1984. Used by permission.

Lothar Lambert, dir. *"Die Alptraum Frau,"* Lothar Lambert Film Production, 1981, 86 minutes.

Laozi, *The Tao Teh King*, trans. James Legge (Project Gutenberg, February 1, 1995 [EBook #216]), gutenberg.org.

Hartmut Lehmann and Kenneth F. Ledford, ed., *An Interrupted Past: German-Speaking Refugee Historians in the United States After 1933*, Cambridge University Press, 1991.

Leningrad Sandwich, "*concrete*" from *Bandsalat*, Good Noise, 1982.

Tony Le Tissier, "The Battle for the Reichstag" Terrain Walk, 21st Theater Army Area Command Staff Ride, April 1989.

Lili Berlin, *Süss und Erbarmungslos*, Roctopus, 1982.

Paul Lincke, *"Die Berliner Luft"* from *Frau Luna*, 1889.

Gabriel Loire in Martin Germer, *"Grandioses Wagnis: Die blauen Glaswände der Kaiser-Wilhelm-Gedächtnis-Kirche in Berlin—das spannungsvolle Gemeinschaftwerk von Egon Eiermann und Gabriel Loire*, 2016.

Halford Mackinder, "Democratic Ideals and Reality," National Defense University Press, Washington, DC, 1996.

Mad Wolf & the City Indians, "The Western World (Is Going Down)" from *Bandsalat*, Good Noise, 1982.

Thomas Mann, *Joseph and his Brothers*, trans. John E. Woods, Everyman's Library, 2005. Used by permission.

Thomas Mann, *The Magic Mountain*, trans. H. T. Lowe-Porter, Alfred A. Knopf, New York, 1944.

Thomas Mann, "The Making of the Magic Mountain," *The Atlantic Monthly*, January 1953, 41–45, used by permission. Copyright S. Fischer *Verlag GmbH*, Frankfurt am Main, All rights reserved by S. Fischer V*erlag GmbH*.

Thomas Mann, *The Magic Mountain*, trans. John E. Woods, Alfred A. Knopf, New York, 1995.

Karl Marx, "The Eleventh Thesis on Feuerbach," 1888.

Aram Mattioli, *Jacob Burckhardt und die Grenzen der Humanität*, *Bibliothek der Provinz Verlag*, Munich, 2001.

Rory McCarthy and Maev Kennedy, "Babylon wrecked by war," *The Guardian*, January 15, 2005.

Friedrich Meinicke, "*Die Stimme des Gewissen*," Dokument 70, Address broadcast in Berlin, December 4, 1948, https://web.fu-berlin.de.

Henry Miller, *Tropic of Cancer*, Obelisk Press, 1934.

John Cameron Mitchell and Stephen Trask, *Hedwig and the Angry Inch*, Overlook Books, 1998.

Michel de Montaigne, *The Essays of Montaigne*, trans. Charles Cotton, ed. William Carew Hazlitt (Kensington, 1877; Project Gutenberg, Septmber 17, 2006 [EBook #3600]), www.gutenberg.org.

Heiner Müller, *Germania Tod in Berlin*, Berlin, 1977.

Lewis Mumford, *The City in History: Its Origins, its Transformations and its Prospects*, New York, 1961. Excerpts used by permission (Robert Wojtowicz, June 27, 2022).

Nationalgalerie: Verzeichnis der vereinigten Kunstsammlungen Nationalgalerie (Pressischer Kulturbesitz) Galerie des 20. Jahrhunderts (Land Berlin), Staatliche Museen Preussischer Kulturbesitz, Berlin 1968.

Nico, *The Velvet Underground & Nico*, Verve, 1967.

Parliament, "Chocolate City," Casablanca Records, 1975.

Joseph R. Passonneau, *Washington Through Two Centuries: A History in Maps and Images*, The Monacelli Press, New York, 2004.

Red Pine, *The Zen Teaching of Bodhidharma*, North Point Press, 1989.

Plato, *The Laws*, trans. Benjamin Jowett (Project Guteneberg, October 29, 2008 [EBook #1750]), https://www.gutenberg.org.

Plato, *The Republic of Plato*, trans. Benjamin Jowett (London, 1888; Project Guteneberg, July 26, 2017 [EBook #55201]), gutenberg.org.

Plato, *The Symposium*, trans. Benjamin Jowett (Project Guteneberg, November 7, 2008 [EBook #1600]), https://www.gutenberg.org.

Iggy Pop (James Osterberg), *Lust for Life*, Virgin Records America, 1990.

Propellerheads, featuring Shirley Bassey, "History Repeating," Wall of Sound, 1997.

Thomas Pynchon, *Gravity's Rainbow*, Viking Press, 1973.

Thomas Pynchon, *V.*, J. B. Lippincott & Co., 1963.

Leopold von Ranke, "Betrachtung," Januar 1877, *Zur eigenen Lebensgeschicht*, Leipzig, 1890, p. 613.

Hans J. Reichardt *und* Wolfgang Schäche, *Von Berlin Nach Germania: Über die Zerstörung der "Reichshauptstadt" durch Albert Speers Neugestaltungsplannungen,* Transit, 1998.

Raffael Rheinsberg, *Botschaften: Archäologie eines Krieges*, Frölich &
Kaufmann, Berlin, 1982.

Michael E. Ruane, "Jefferson Memorial's Signs of Sinking Raise Fresh
Alarms," *Washington, Post*, June 16, 2007, A1, A9.

Friedrich Rückert, "Ich atmet' einen linden Duft!," Wiener
Philharminischer Verlag, n.d.

Gordon W. Rudd, *Humanitarian Intervention: Assisting the Irai Kurds in
Operation PROVIDE COMFORT, 1991*, Department of the Army,
CMH Pub 70-78-1, Washington, DC.

Cornelius Ryan, *The Last Battle*, Simon and Schuster, New York, 1966.

Svetlana Savaranskaya and Tom Blanton, National Security Archive,
"NATO Expansion: What Gorbachev Heard, Briefing Book #613,
December 12, 2017.

Karl Scheffler, *Berlin—ein Stadtschicksal*, Reiss, Berlin, 1910.

Arthur Schopenhauer, *Parerga und Paralipomena: Kleine philosophische
Schriften*, Friedrich Arnold Brockhaus, Leipzig, 1891.

George Seaton, dir. *The Big Lift*, 20th Century Fox, 1950, 120 minutes.

Katsuki Sekida, *Zen Training: Methods and Philosophy*, ed. A. V. Grimstone,
New York and Tokyo, 1975.

Sex Pistols, *Never Mind the Bollocks, Here's the Sexpistols*, Virgin, 1977.

Roger W. Shattuck, *The Banquet Years: The Origins of the Avant-Garde in
France, 1885 to World War 1*, Faber & Faber, 1955.

Soft Cell, "Tainted Love" from *Non-Stop Erotic Cabaret*, Vertigo, 1981.

Albert Speer, *Erinnerungen*, Ludwisburg, 1970.

Oswald Spengler, *Jahre der Entscheidung. Deutschland und die
Weltgeschectliche Entwicklungen, München*, 1933.

Herbert J. Spiro, "The Incompetence of the Germans," a lecture prepared for delivery at the Center for International Affairs, Harvard University, April 3, 1985.

Steely Dan, *Aja*, ABC Records, 1977.

Leo Strauss, *The City and Man*, Chicago, 1964.

Sun Tzu, Sun Tzu on the Art of War, trans. Lionel Giles, London, 1910.

Talking Heads, *Speaking in Tongues*, Sire Records, 1983.

James F. Tent, *Freie Universität Berlin 1948-1988: Eine deutsche Hochschule im Zeitgeschehen*, trans. Karl Heinz Siber, Colloquium Verlag Berlin, 1988.

William Irwin Thompson, *At the Edge of History*, Harper & Row, New York, 1972.

Barbara W. Tuchman, *Practicing History*, Alfred A. Knopf, New York, 1981.

Milan Vego, *Operational Warfare*, the United States Naval War College, NWC 1004, Newport Rhode Island, 2000.

Bernward Vesper, *Die Reise - Romanessay*, März *bei* Zweitausendeins, Jossa, 1979.

Kurt Vonnegut, *Slaughterhouse-Five, or The Children's Crusade*, Delacorte Press, New York, 1969. "Poo-tee-weet" used by permission of Penguin Random House.

Kurt Vonnegut, *Schlachthof 5 oder der Kinderkreuzzug*, trans. Gregor Hens, Hoffmann *und* Campe, 2016.

"Washington: Symbol and City," National Building Museum, Washington, DC, 2004.

Walt Whitman, "A Song for Occupations," *Leaves of Grass*, 1892.

Alaric Alexander Watts (1797-1864), "The Siege of Belgrade," 1828.

wpclipart, "Berlin skyline silhouette, WPClipart > buildings > city > skyline.wpclipart.com

Kurt Weil/Ogden Nash, "I'm a Stranger Here Myself," *One Touch of Venus,* 1943.

Jürgen Wetzel, *"'Jetzt ist Ruhe die erste Bürgerpflicht,' Die Französische Besatzung Berlins 1806 bis 1808,"* in *"Berliner Gescichte, Ausgabe 7,* Berlin, 2016.

Jürgen Wetzel, "Winning the Peace," in *Fünf Monate in Berlin: Briefe von Edgar N. Johnson aus dem Jahre 1946*, Oldenbourg, Munich 2014.

Wikipedia: The Free Encyclopedia, Wikimedia Foundation, Inc.

Billy Wilder, dir., *A Foreign Affair*, Paramount Pictures, 1948, 116 minutes.

Rowan Williams, "The Body's Grace," 1989.

Thomas Wolfe, *You Can't Go Home Again*, Harper & Row, New York, London, 1940.

Zeitgeist, International Art Exhibition Berlin 1982, Martin-Gropius-Bau, George Braziller, Inc., New York, printed in Berlin (West), 1983.

AFTERWORD

Some Young Foreigner

"For the thought of acting as my own historian I find a
little confusing; and, you know, there are few impartial
historians anyway."

—Thomas Mann, "The Making of the Magic Mountain"

"To be here is truly to stand on freedom's edge . . ."

The author, sitting "on freedom's edge" (truly) in the chair reserved
for the German foreign minister on the speakers' platform in the Baroque
garden of Charlottenburg Palace, British Sector, on June 11, 1982,
following the speech of the 40th President of the United States of America,
Ronald Wilson Reagan.

Photograph by Gerhard Wohlfart, 1982